Disney
real life #2

#Oh No!
My Parents!

CHAPTER 19

A complicated MEETING

London International High School
Marylebone
08:25 AM

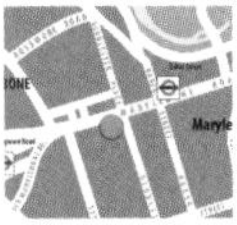

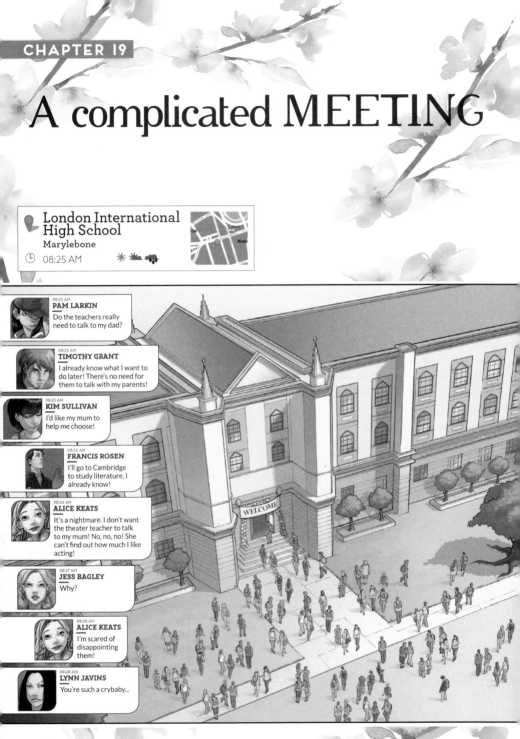

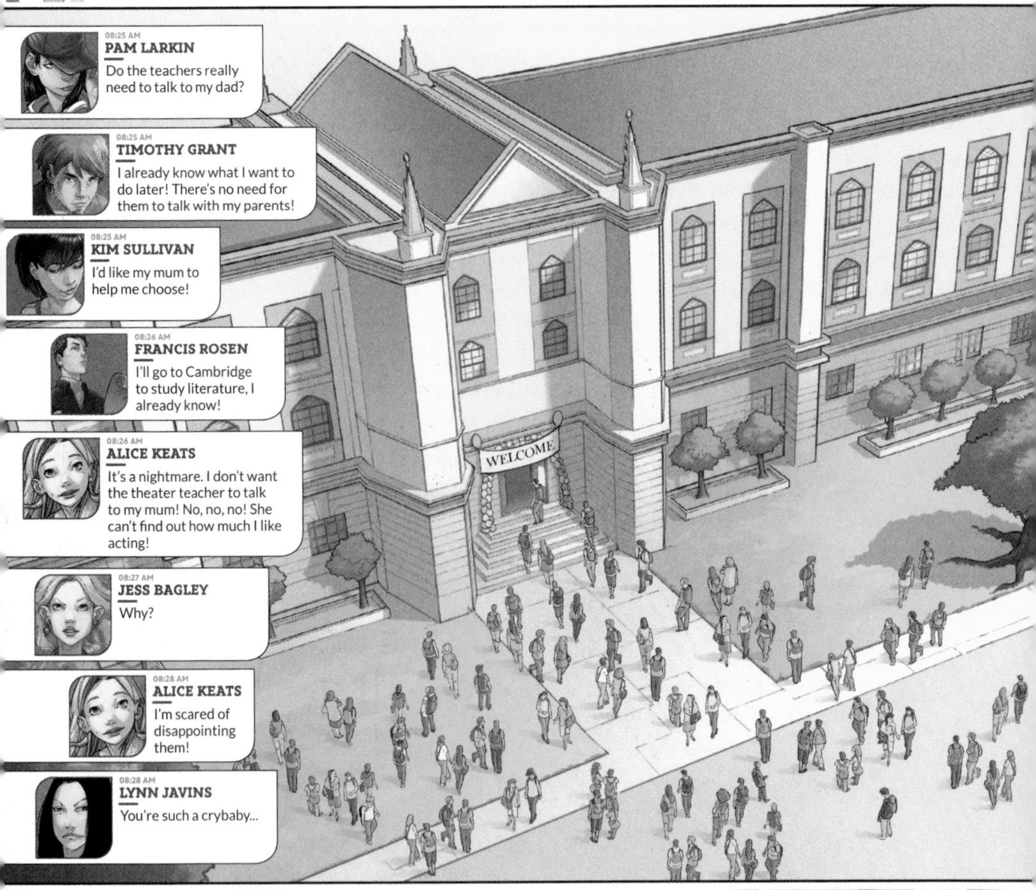
08:25 AM
PAM LARKIN
Do the teachers really need to talk to my dad?
08:25 AM
TIMOTHY GRANT
I already know what I want to do later! There's no need for them to talk with my parents!
08:25 AM
KIM SULLIVAN
I'd like my mum to help me choose!
08:26 AM
FRANCIS ROSEN
I'll go to Cambridge to study literature, I already know!
08:26 AM
ALICE KEATS
It's a nightmare. I don't want the theater teacher to talk to my mum! No, no, no! She can't find out how much I like acting!
08:27 AM
JESS BAGLEY
Why?
08:28 AM
ALICE KEATS
I'm scared of disappointing them!
08:28 AM
LYNN JAVINS
You're such a crybaby...
WELCOME

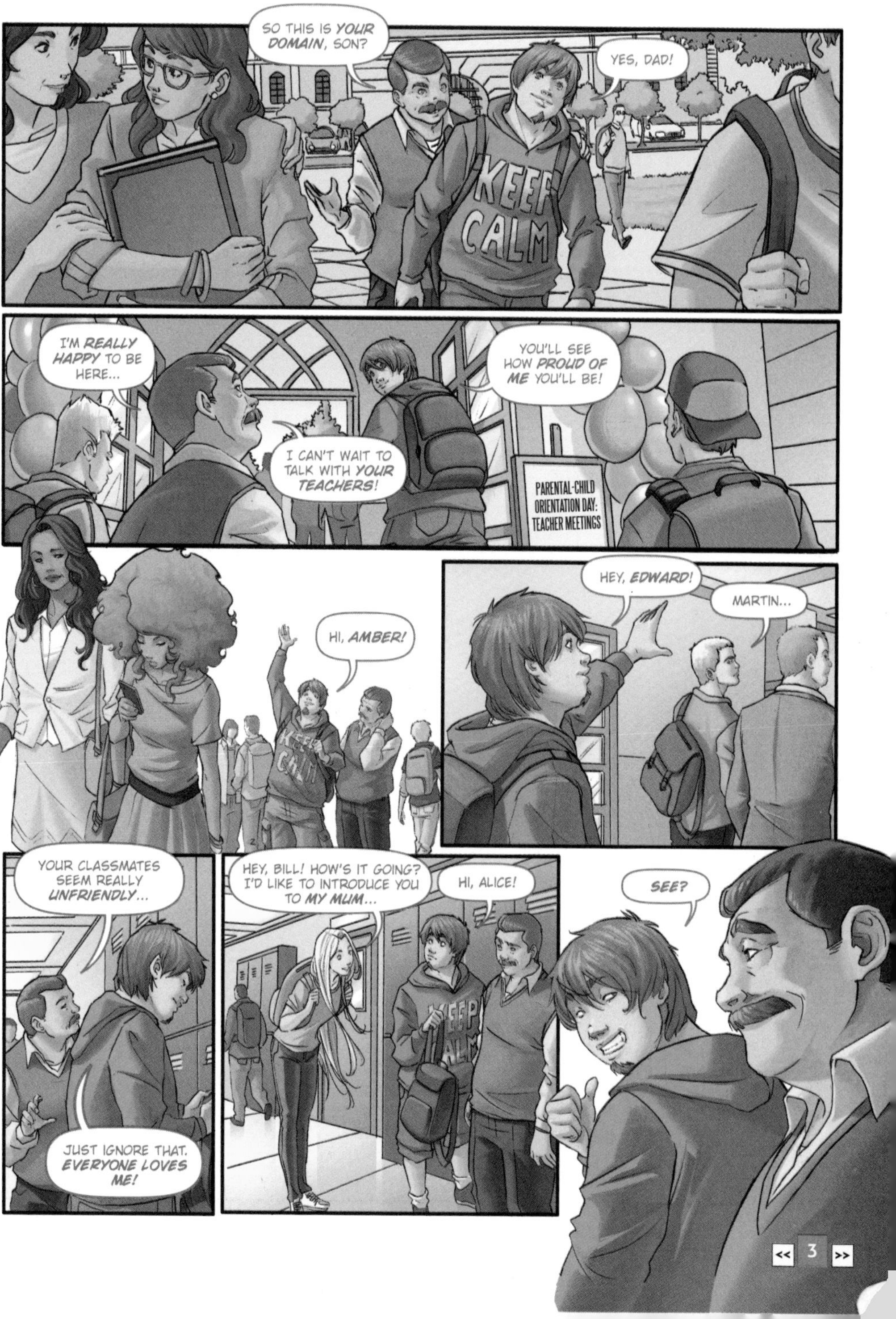

SO THIS IS YOUR DOMAIN, SON?
YES, DAD!
I'M REALLY HAPPY TO BE HERE...
I CAN'T WAIT TO TALK WITH YOUR TEACHERS!
YOU'LL SEE HOW PROUD OF ME YOU'LL BE!
PARENTAL-CHILD ORIENTATION DAY: TEACHER MEETINGS
HI, AMBER!
HEY, EDWARD!
MARTIN...
YOUR CLASSMATES SEEM REALLY UNFRIENDLY...
JUST IGNORE THAT. EVERYONE LOVES ME!
HEY, BILL! HOW'S IT GOING? I'D LIKE TO INTRODUCE YOU TO MY MUM...
HI, ALICE!
SEE?

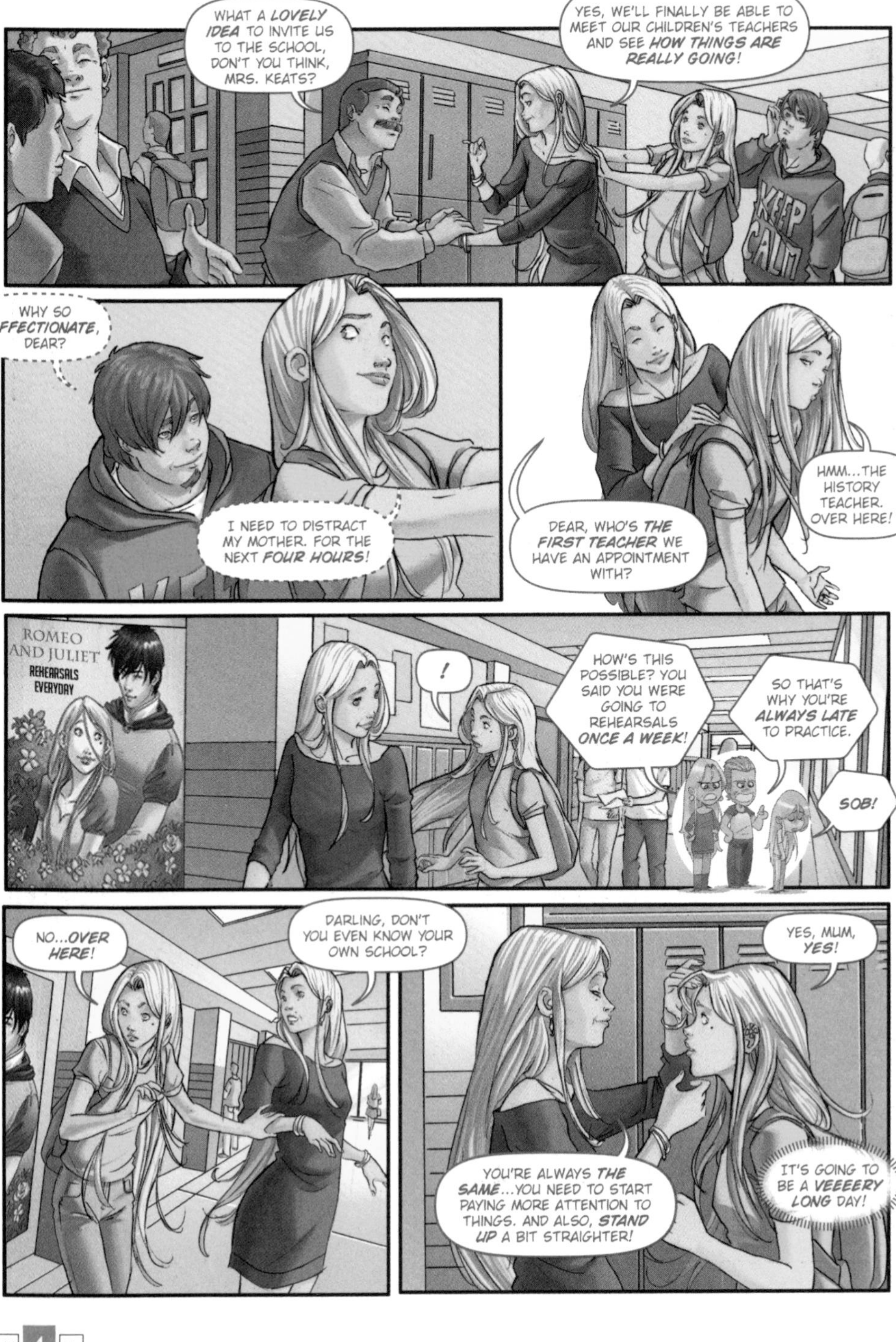
WHAT A LOVELY IDEA TO INVITE US TO THE SCHOOL, DON'T YOU THINK, MRS. KEATS?
YES, WE'LL FINALLY BE ABLE TO MEET OUR CHILDREN'S TEACHERS AND SEE HOW THINGS ARE REALLY GOING!
KEEP CALM
WHY SO AFFECTIONATE, DEAR?
I NEED TO DISTRACT MY MOTHER. FOR THE NEXT FOUR HOURS!
DEAR, WHO'S THE FIRST TEACHER WE HAVE AN APPOINTMENT WITH?
HMM...THE HISTORY TEACHER. OVER HERE!
ROMEO AND JULIET
REHEARSALS EVERYDAY
!
HOW'S THIS POSSIBLE? YOU SAID YOU WERE GOING TO REHEARSALS ONCE A WEEK!
SO THAT'S WHY YOU'RE ALWAYS LATE TO PRACTICE.
SOB!
NO...OVER HERE!
DARLING, DON'T YOU EVEN KNOW YOUR OWN SCHOOL?
YES, MUM, YES!
YOU'RE ALWAYS THE SAME...YOU NEED TO START PAYING MORE ATTENTION TO THINGS. AND ALSO, STAND UP A BIT STRAIGHTER!
IT'S GOING TO BE A VEEEERY LONG DAY!

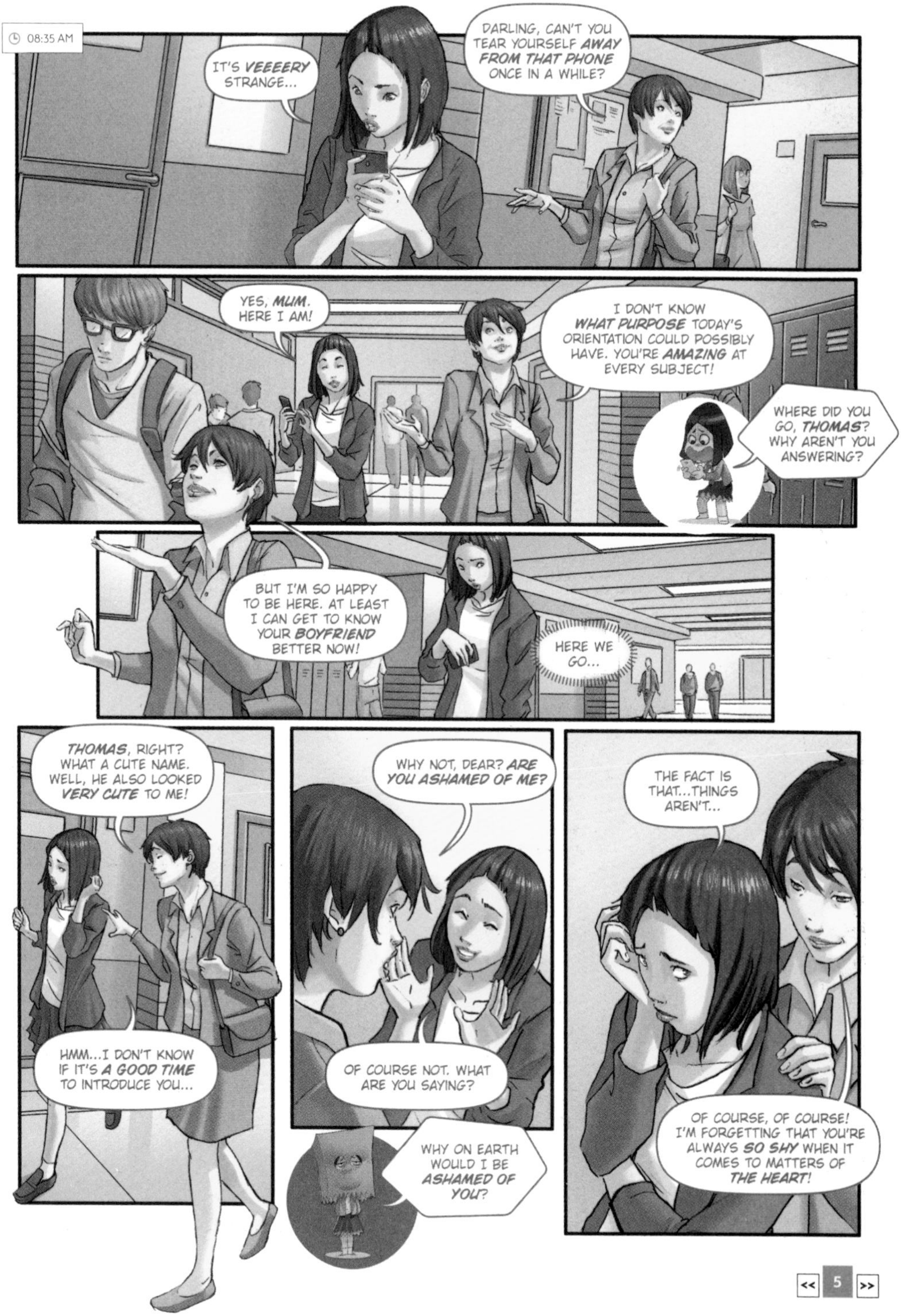

08:35 AM
IT'S VEEEERY STRANGE...
DARLING, CAN'T YOU TEAR YOURSELF AWAY FROM THAT PHONE ONCE IN A WHILE?
YES, MUM. HERE I AM!
I DON'T KNOW WHAT PURPOSE TODAY'S ORIENTATION COULD POSSIBLY HAVE. YOU'RE AMAZING AT EVERY SUBJECT!
WHERE DID YOU GO, THOMAS? WHY AREN'T YOU ANSWERING?
BUT I'M SO HAPPY TO BE HERE. AT LEAST I CAN GET TO KNOW YOUR BOYFRIEND BETTER NOW!
HERE WE GO...
THOMAS, RIGHT? WHAT A CUTE NAME. WELL, HE ALSO LOOKED VERY CUTE TO ME!
HMM...I DON'T KNOW IF IT'S A GOOD TIME TO INTRODUCE YOU...
WHY NOT, DEAR? ARE YOU ASHAMED OF ME?
OF COURSE NOT. WHAT ARE YOU SAYING?
WHY ON EARTH WOULD I BE ASHAMED OF YOU?
THE FACT IS THAT...THINGS AREN'T...
OF COURSE, OF COURSE! I'M FORGETTING THAT YOU'RE ALWAYS SO SHY WHEN IT COMES TO MATTERS OF THE HEART!

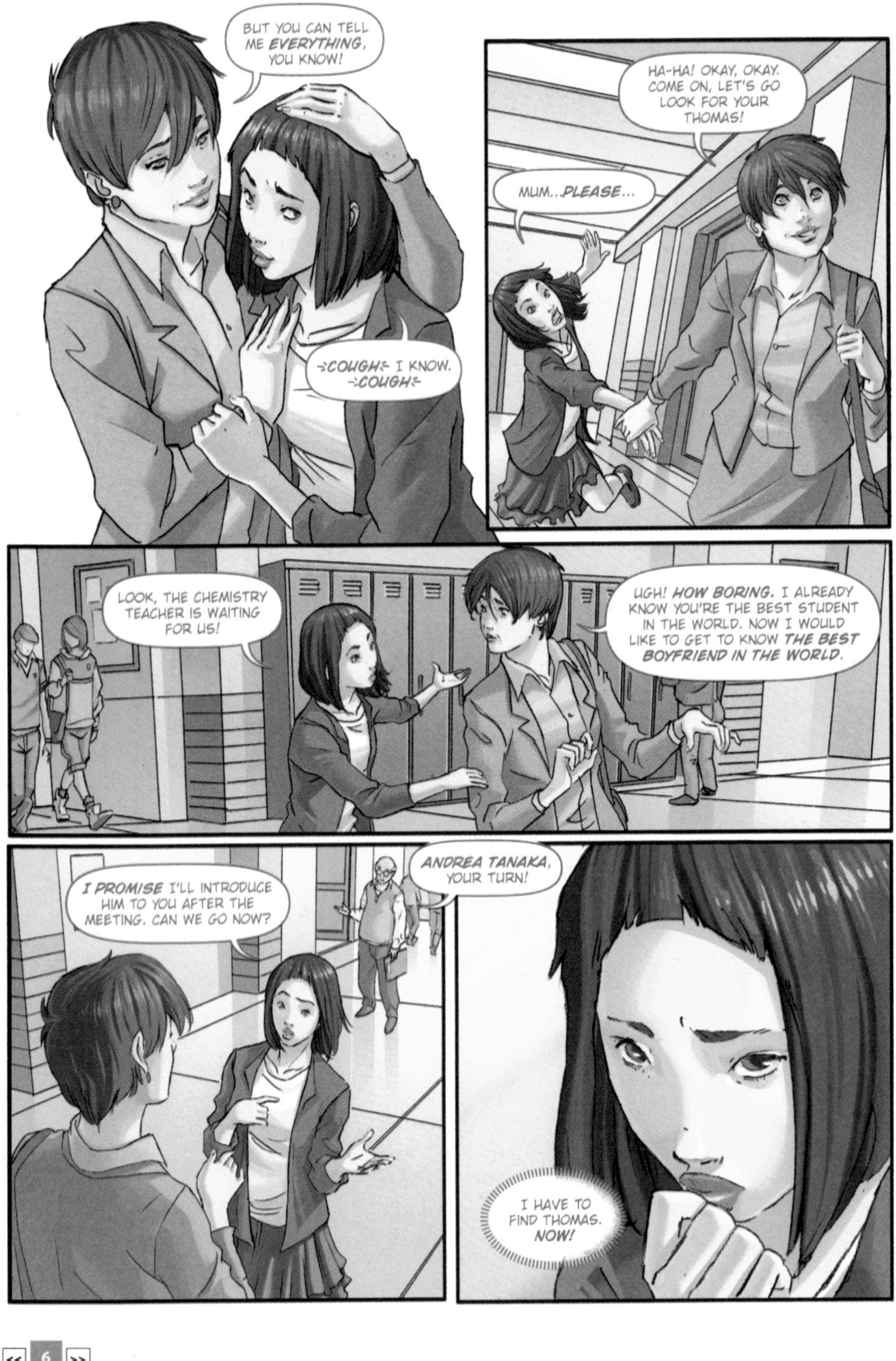
BUT YOU CAN TELL ME ***EVERYTHING***, YOU KNOW!
COUGH I KNOW. *COUGH*
HA-HA! OKAY, OKAY. COME ON, LET'S GO LOOK FOR YOUR THOMAS!
MUM... ***PLEASE***...
LOOK, THE CHEMISTRY TEACHER IS WAITING FOR US!
UGH! ***HOW BORING.*** I ALREADY KNOW YOU'RE THE BEST STUDENT IN THE WORLD. NOW I WOULD LIKE TO GET TO KNOW ***THE BEST BOYFRIEND IN THE WORLD.***
I PROMISE I'LL INTRODUCE HIM TO YOU AFTER THE MEETING. CAN WE GO NOW?
ANDREA TANAKA, YOUR TURN!
I HAVE TO FIND THOMAS. ***NOW!***

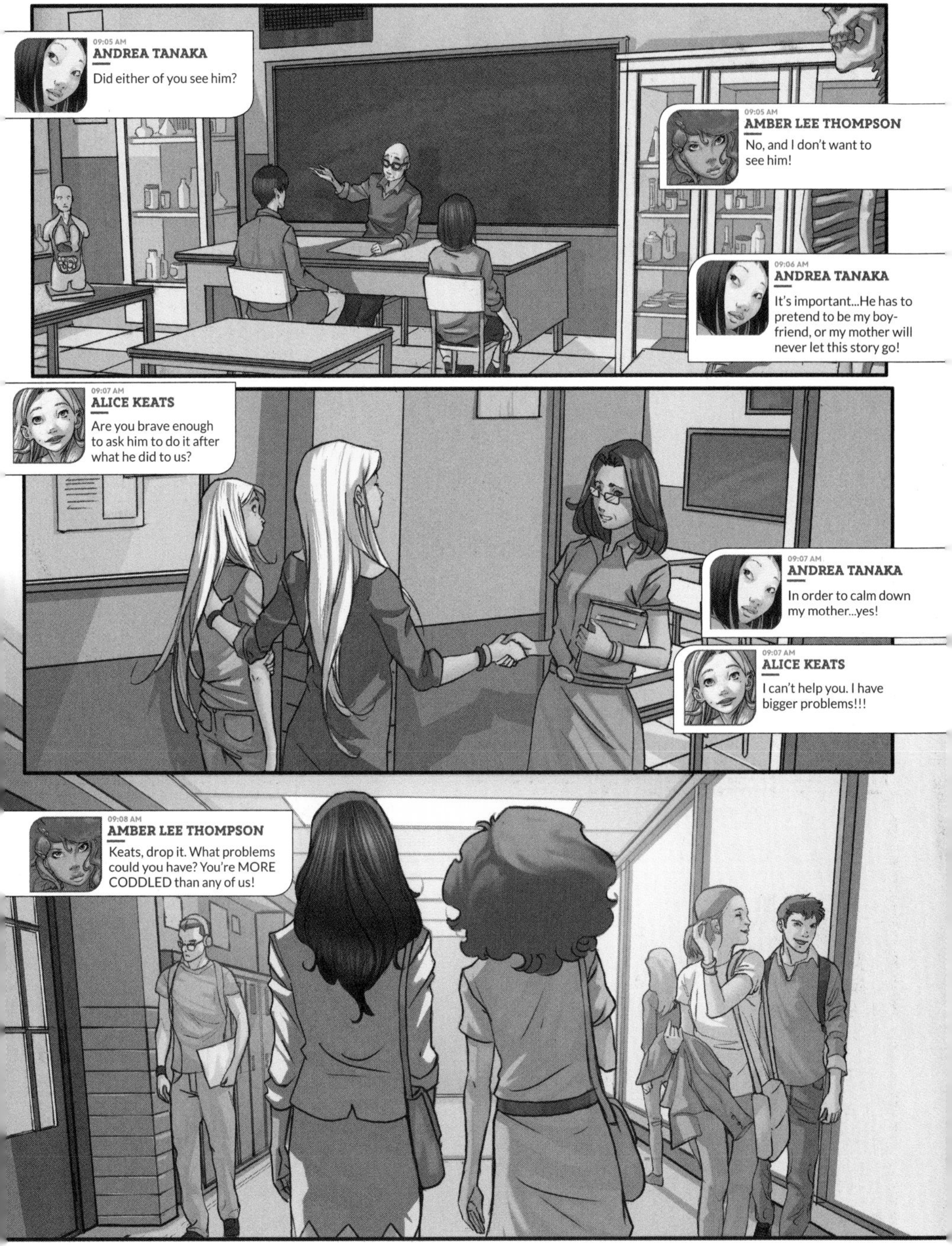
09:05 AM
ANDREA TANAKA
Did either of you see him?
09:05 AM
AMBER LEE THOMPSON
No, and I don't want to see him!
09:06 AM
ANDREA TANAKA
It's important...He has to pretend to be my boy-friend, or my mother will never let this story go!
09:07 AM
ALICE KEATS
Are you brave enough to ask him to do it after what he did to us?
09:07 AM
ANDREA TANAKA
In order to calm down my mother...yes!
09:07 AM
ALICE KEATS
I can't help you. I have bigger problems!!!
09:08 AM
AMBER LEE THOMPSON
Keats, drop it. What problems could you have? You're MORE CODDLED than any of us!

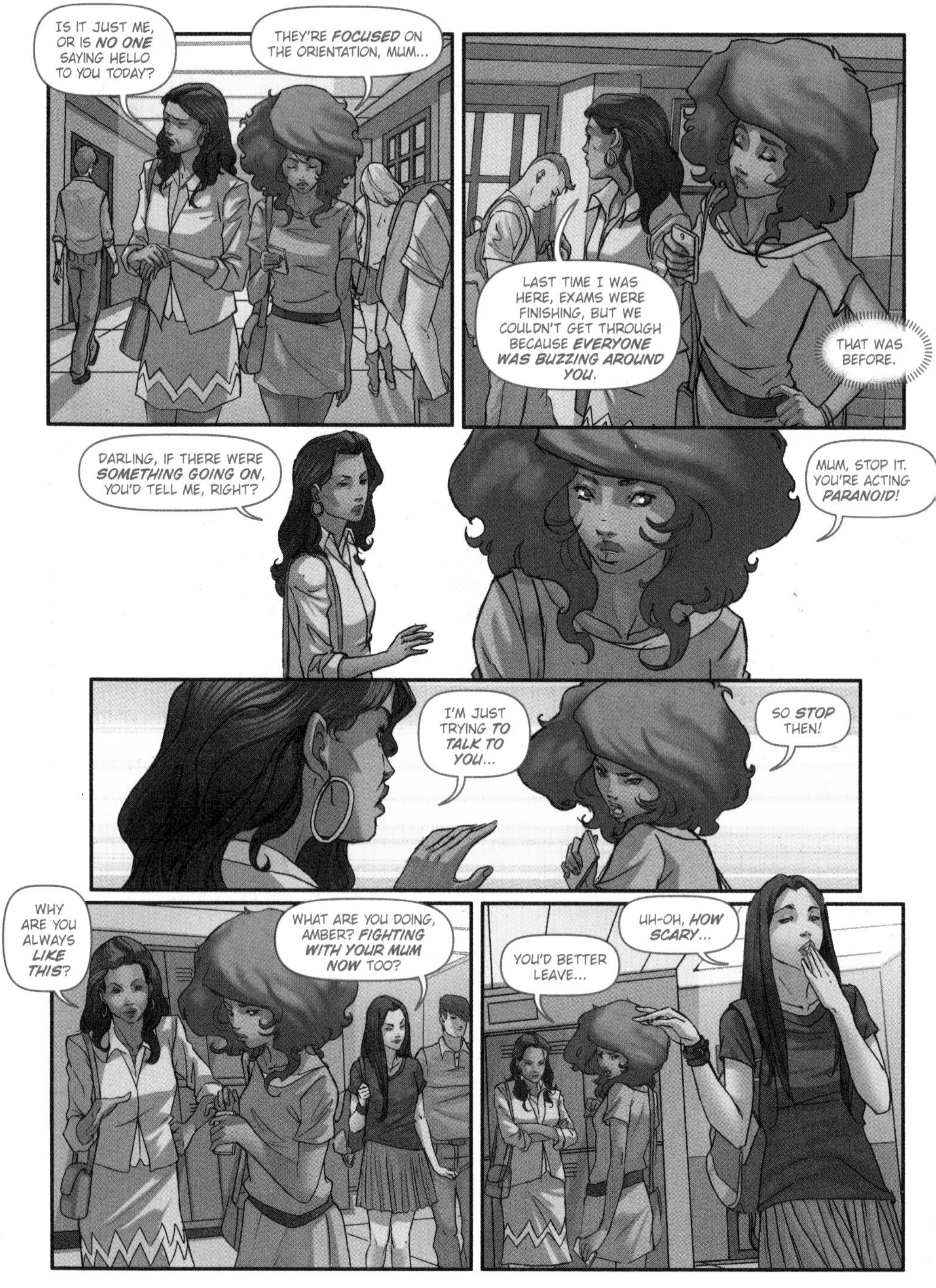
IS IT JUST ME, OR IS NO ONE SAYING HELLO TO YOU TODAY?
THEY'RE FOCUSED ON THE ORIENTATION, MUM...
LAST TIME I WAS HERE, EXAMS WERE FINISHING, BUT WE COULDN'T GET THROUGH BECAUSE EVERYONE WAS BUZZING AROUND YOU.
THAT WAS BEFORE.
DARLING, IF THERE WERE SOMETHING GOING ON, YOU'D TELL ME, RIGHT?
MUM, STOP IT. YOU'RE ACTING PARANOID!
I'M JUST TRYING TO TALK TO YOU...
SO STOP THEN!
WHY ARE YOU ALWAYS LIKE THIS?
WHAT ARE YOU DOING, AMBER? FIGHTING WITH YOUR MUM NOW TOO?
UH-OH, HOW SCARY...
YOU'D BETTER LEAVE...

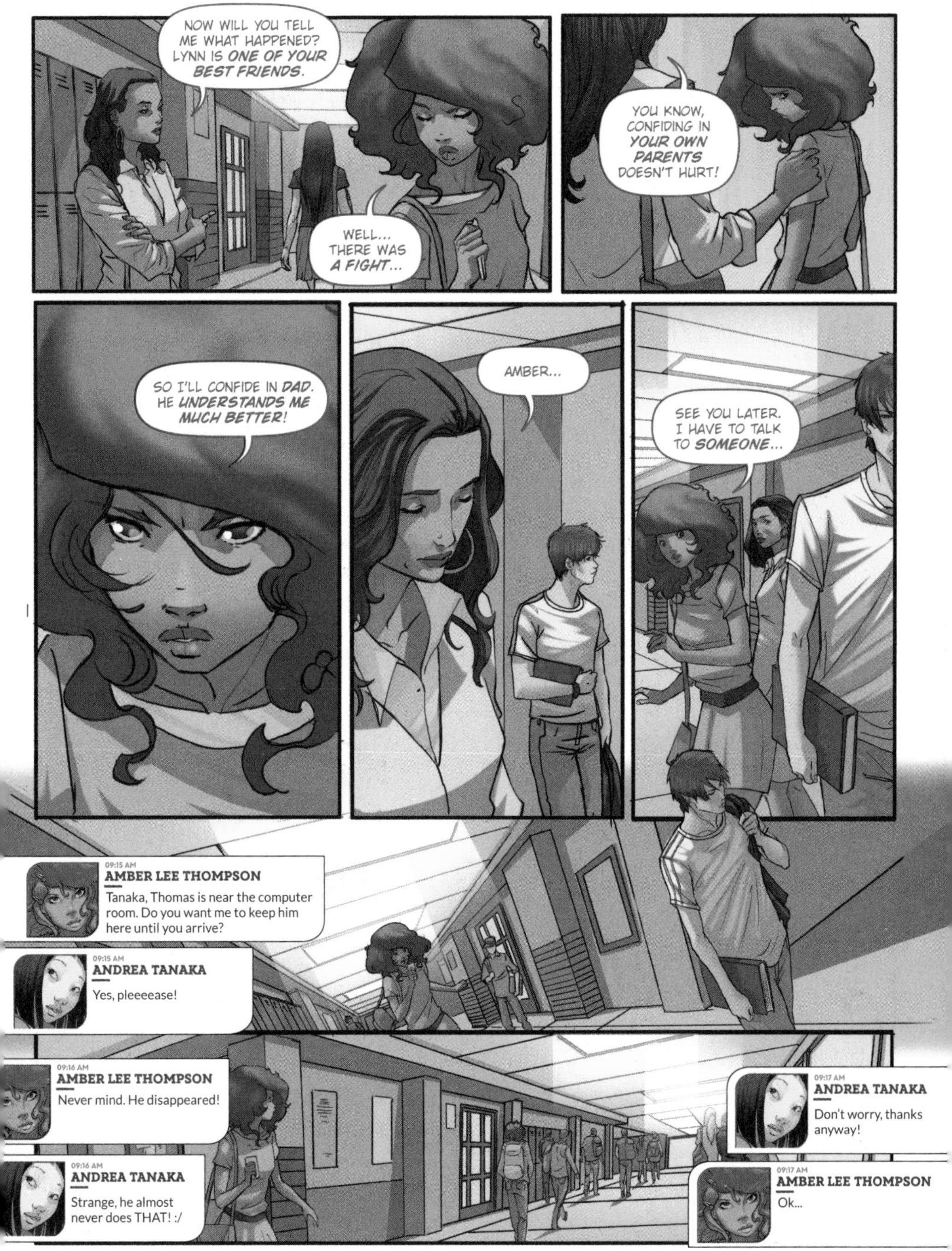

NOW WILL YOU TELL ME WHAT HAPPENED? LYNN IS ONE OF YOUR BEST FRIENDS.
WELL... THERE WAS A FIGHT...
YOU KNOW, CONFIDING IN YOUR OWN PARENTS DOESN'T HURT!
SO I'LL CONFIDE IN DAD. HE UNDERSTANDS ME MUCH BETTER!
AMBER...
SEE YOU LATER. I HAVE TO TALK TO SOMEONE...
09:15 AM
AMBER LEE THOMPSON
Tanaka, Thomas is near the computer room. Do you want me to keep him here until you arrive?
09:15 AM
ANDREA TANAKA
Yes, pleeeease!
09:16 AM
AMBER LEE THOMPSON
Never mind. He disappeared!
09:16 AM
ANDREA TANAKA
Strange, he almost never does THAT! :/
09:17 AM
ANDREA TANAKA
Don't worry, thanks anyway!
09:17 AM
AMBER LEE THOMPSON
Ok...

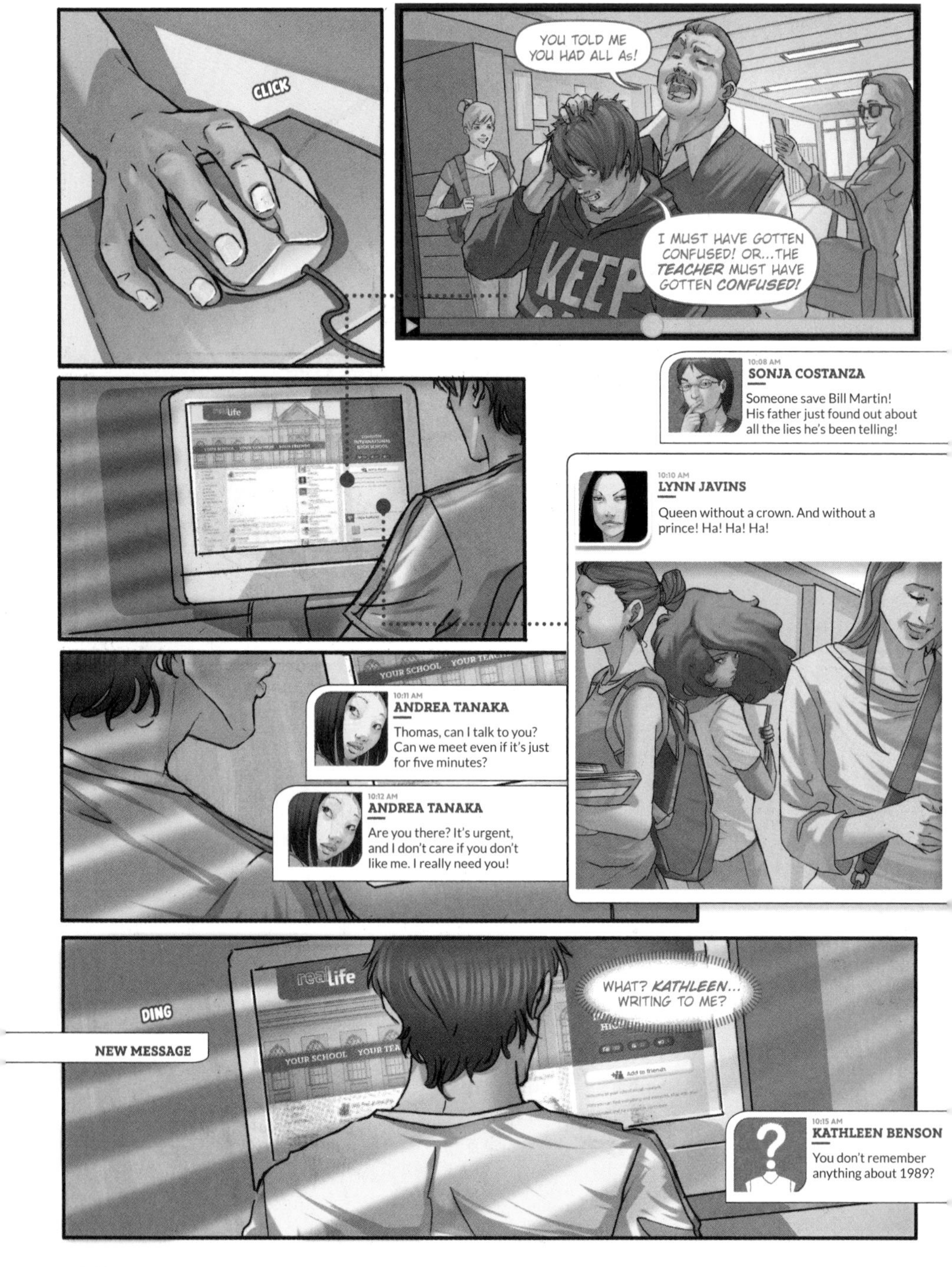
CLICK
YOU TOLD ME YOU HAD ALL As!
I MUST HAVE GOTTEN CONFUSED! OR...THE TEACHER MUST HAVE GOTTEN CONFUSED!
KEEP
10:08 AM
SONJA COSTANZA
Someone save Bill Martin! His father just found out about all the lies he's been telling!
10:10 AM
LYNN JAVINS
Queen without a crown. And without a prince! Ha! Ha! Ha!
YOUR SCHOOL YOUR TEACH
10:11 AM
ANDREA TANAKA
Thomas, can I talk to you? Can we meet even if it's just for five minutes?
10:12 AM
ANDREA TANAKA
Are you there? It's urgent, and I don't care if you don't like me. I really need you!
real life
DING
NEW MESSAGE
WHAT? KATHLEEN... WRITING TO ME?
YOUR SCHOOL YOUR TEA
Add to friends
10:15 AM
KATHLEEN BENSON
You don't remember anything about 1989?

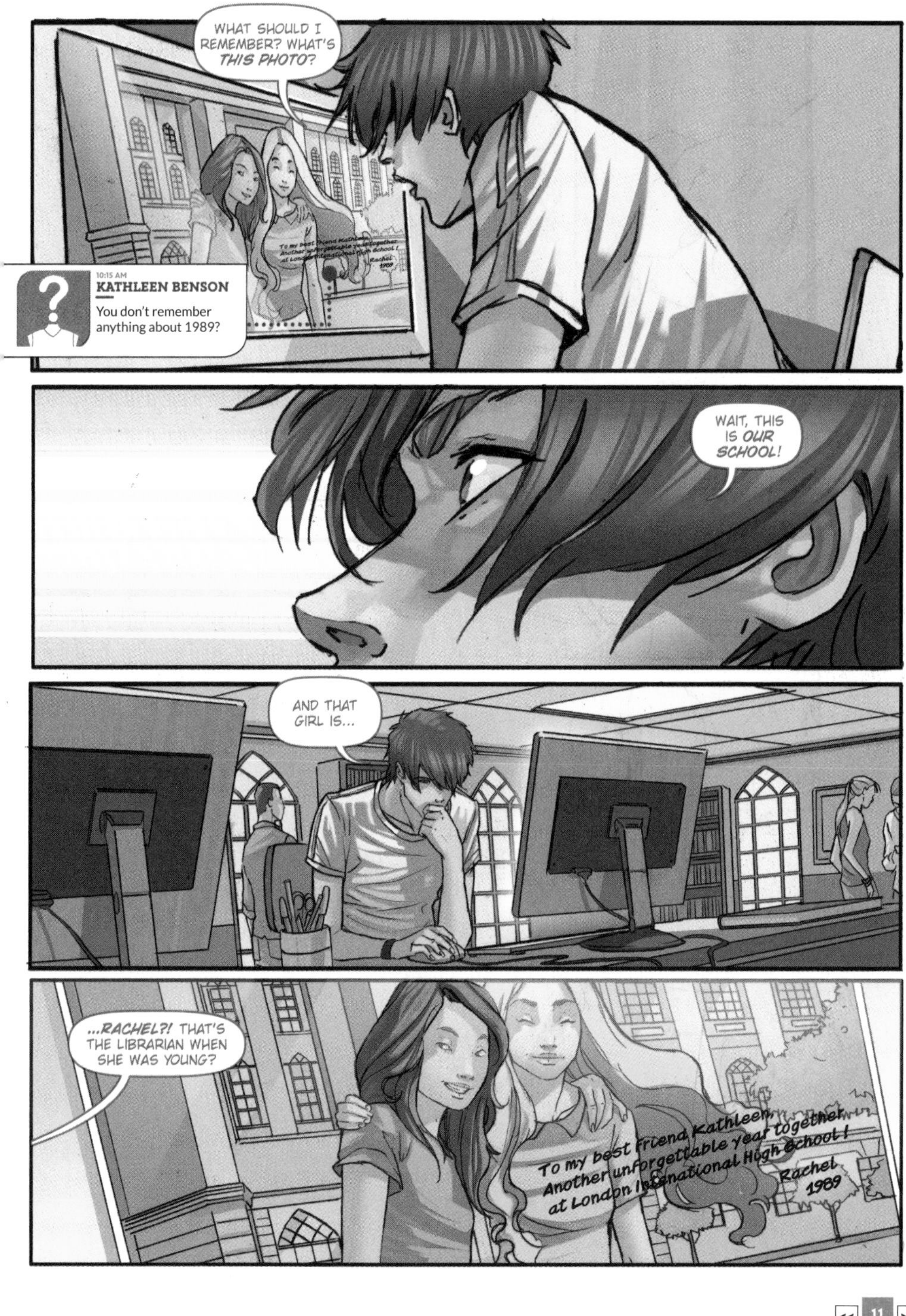
WHAT SHOULD I REMEMBER? WHAT'S *THIS PHOTO*?
10:15 AM
KATHLEEN BENSON
You don't remember anything about 1989?
WAIT, THIS IS *OUR SCHOOL*!
AND THAT GIRL IS...
...RACHEL?! THAT'S THE LIBRARIAN WHEN SHE WAS YOUNG?
To my best friend Kathleen,
Another unforgettable year together
at London International High School !
Rachel
1989

AND THE OTHER GIRL IS *KATHLEEN!* THAT *CRAZY WOMAN* WHO CAME TO WARN ME ABOUT WHO KNOWS WHAT TWO DAYS AGO...

To my best friend Kathleen, Another unforgettable year together at London Intenational High School!

Rachel 1989

THE THREE GIRLS, THOMAS. IT'S HAPPENING THE WAY IT DID *THE OTHER TIME.*

SO...THEY KNOW EACH OTHER?

I DON'T UNDERSTAND. WHAT DO I HAVE TO DO WITH YOU TWO?

WHAT DO I HAVE TO DO WITH *1989?*

y best frien er unforgettable year togethe at London Intenational High School!

Rachel 1989

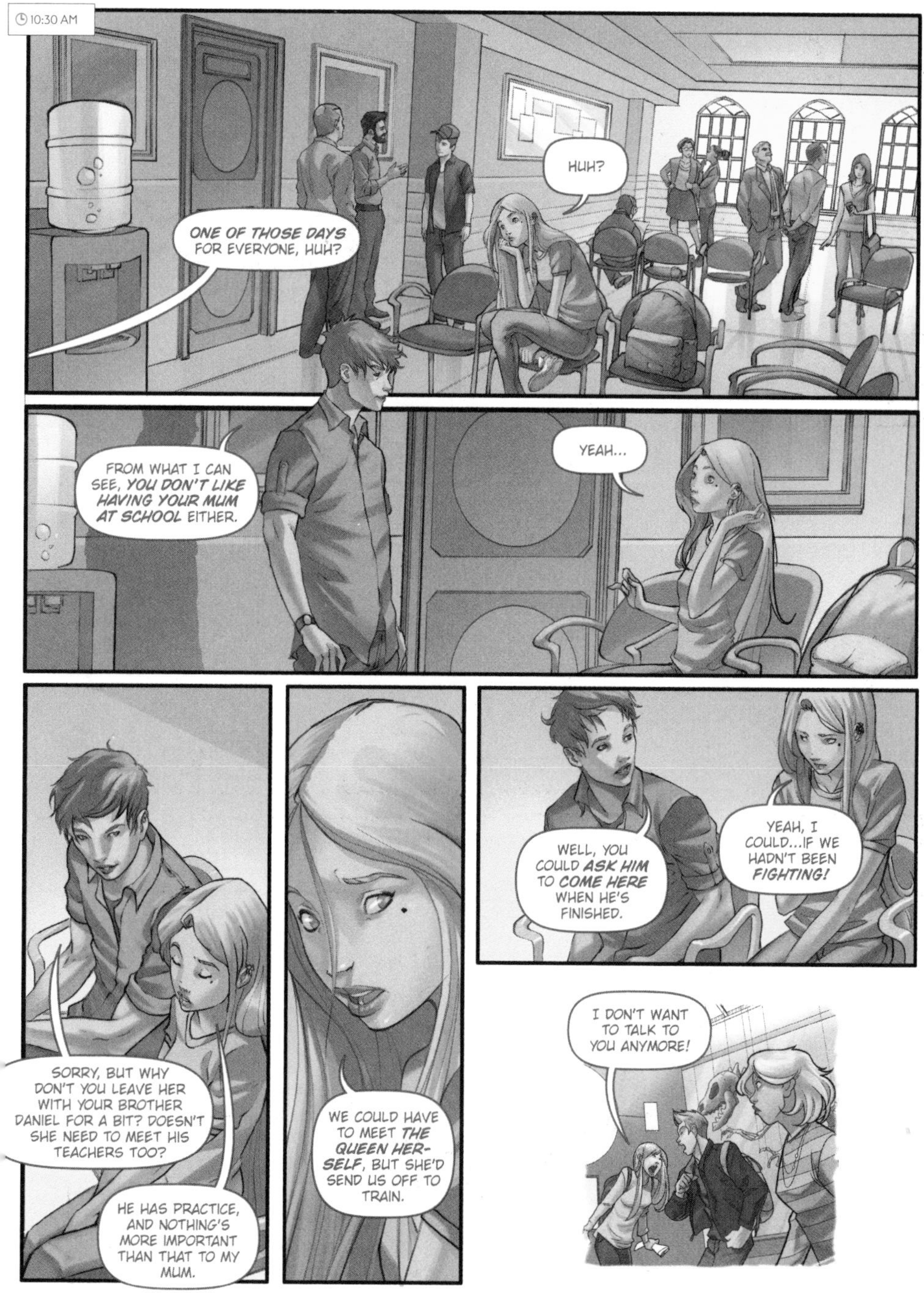
10:30 AM
HUH?
ONE OF THOSE DAYS FOR EVERYONE, HUH?
FROM WHAT I CAN SEE, YOU DON'T LIKE HAVING YOUR MUM AT SCHOOL EITHER.
YEAH...
SORRY, BUT WHY DON'T YOU LEAVE HER WITH YOUR BROTHER DANIEL FOR A BIT? DOESN'T SHE NEED TO MEET HIS TEACHERS TOO?
HE HAS PRACTICE, AND NOTHING'S MORE IMPORTANT THAN THAT TO MY MUM.
WE COULD HAVE TO MEET THE QUEEN HER-SELF, BUT SHE'D SEND US OFF TO TRAIN.
WELL, YOU COULD ASK HIM TO COME HERE WHEN HE'S FINISHED.
YEAH, I COULD...IF WE HADN'T BEEN FIGHTING!
I DON'T WANT TO TALK TO YOU ANYMORE!

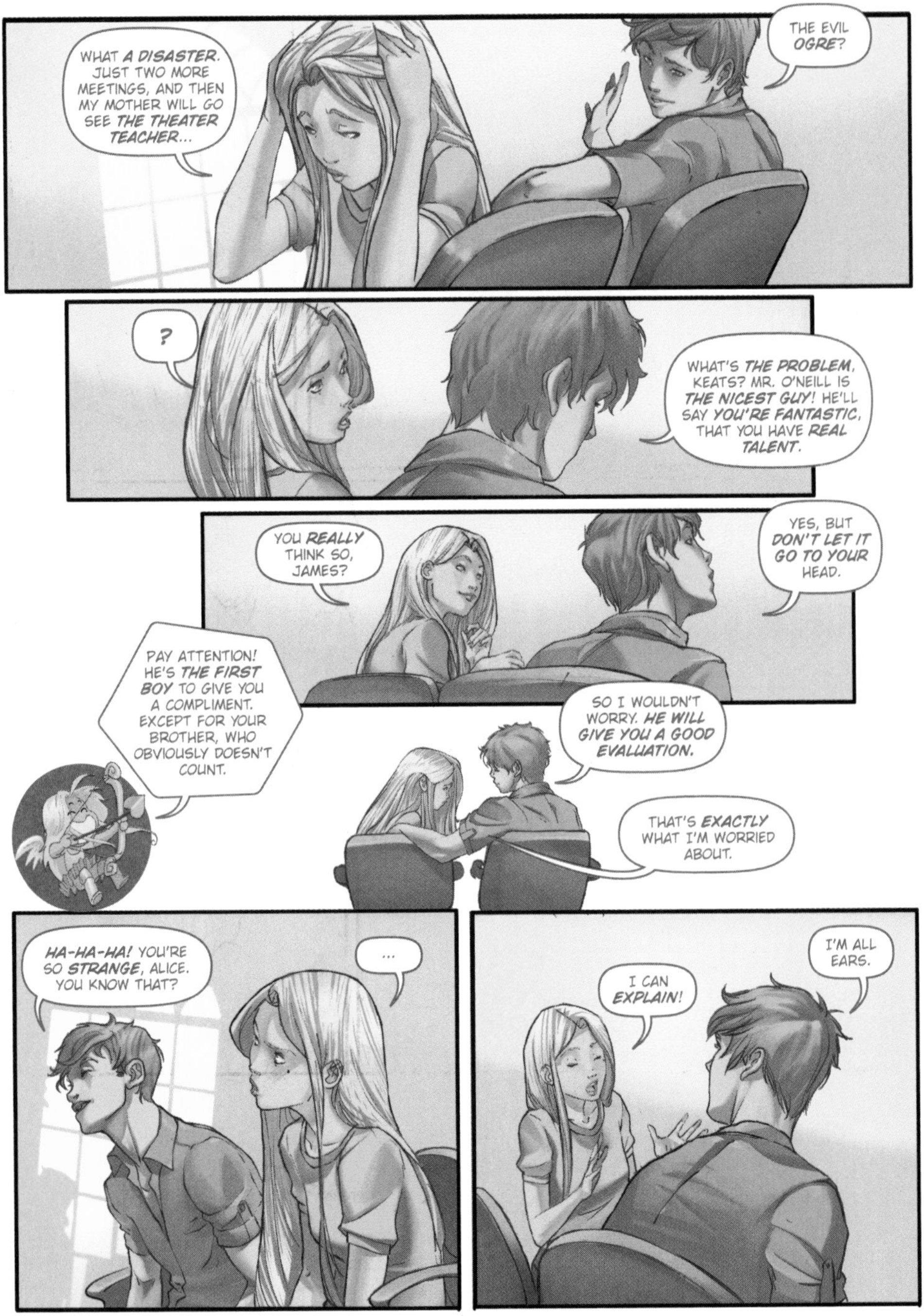
WHAT A DISASTER. JUST TWO MORE MEETINGS, AND THEN MY MOTHER WILL GO SEE THE THEATER TEACHER...
THE EVIL OGRE?
?
WHAT'S THE PROBLEM, KEATS? MR. O'NEILL IS THE NICEST GUY! HE'LL SAY YOU'RE FANTASTIC, THAT YOU HAVE REAL TALENT.
YOU REALLY THINK SO, JAMES?
YES, BUT DON'T LET IT GO TO YOUR HEAD.
PAY ATTENTION! HE'S THE FIRST BOY TO GIVE YOU A COMPLIMENT. EXCEPT FOR YOUR BROTHER, WHO OBVIOUSLY DOESN'T COUNT.
SO I WOULDN'T WORRY. HE WILL GIVE YOU A GOOD EVALUATION.
THAT'S EXACTLY WHAT I'M WORRIED ABOUT.
HA-HA-HA! YOU'RE SO STRANGE, ALICE. YOU KNOW THAT?
...
I CAN EXPLAIN!
I'M ALL EARS.

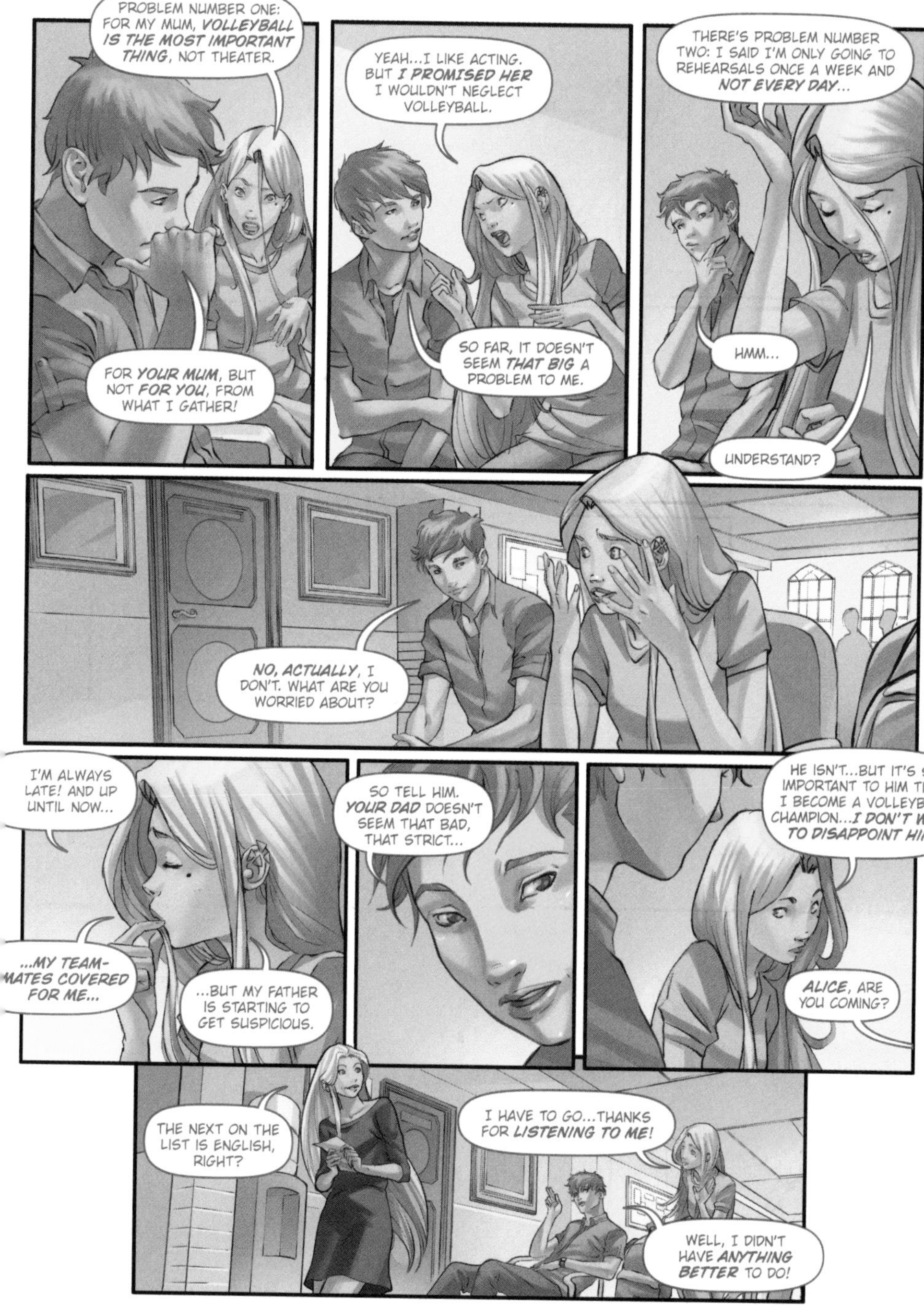
PROBLEM NUMBER ONE: FOR MY MUM, VOLLEYBALL IS THE MOST IMPORTANT THING, NOT THEATER.
FOR YOUR MUM, BUT NOT FOR YOU, FROM WHAT I GATHER!
YEAH...I LIKE ACTING. BUT I PROMISED HER I WOULDN'T NEGLECT VOLLEYBALL.
SO FAR, IT DOESN'T SEEM THAT BIG A PROBLEM TO ME.
THERE'S PROBLEM NUMBER TWO: I SAID I'M ONLY GOING TO REHEARSALS ONCE A WEEK AND NOT EVERY DAY...
HMM...
UNDERSTAND?
NO, ACTUALLY, I DON'T. WHAT ARE YOU WORRIED ABOUT?
I'M ALWAYS LATE! AND UP UNTIL NOW...
...MY TEAM-MATES COVERED FOR ME...
...BUT MY FATHER IS STARTING TO GET SUSPICIOUS.
SO TELL HIM. YOUR DAD DOESN'T SEEM THAT BAD, THAT STRICT...
HE ISN'T...BUT IT'S SO IMPORTANT TO HIM THAT I BECOME A VOLLEYBALL CHAMPION...I DON'T WANT TO DISAPPOINT HIM!
ALICE, ARE YOU COMING?
THE NEXT ON THE LIST IS ENGLISH, RIGHT?
I HAVE TO GO...THANKS FOR LISTENING TO ME!
WELL, I DIDN'T HAVE ANYTHING BETTER TO DO!

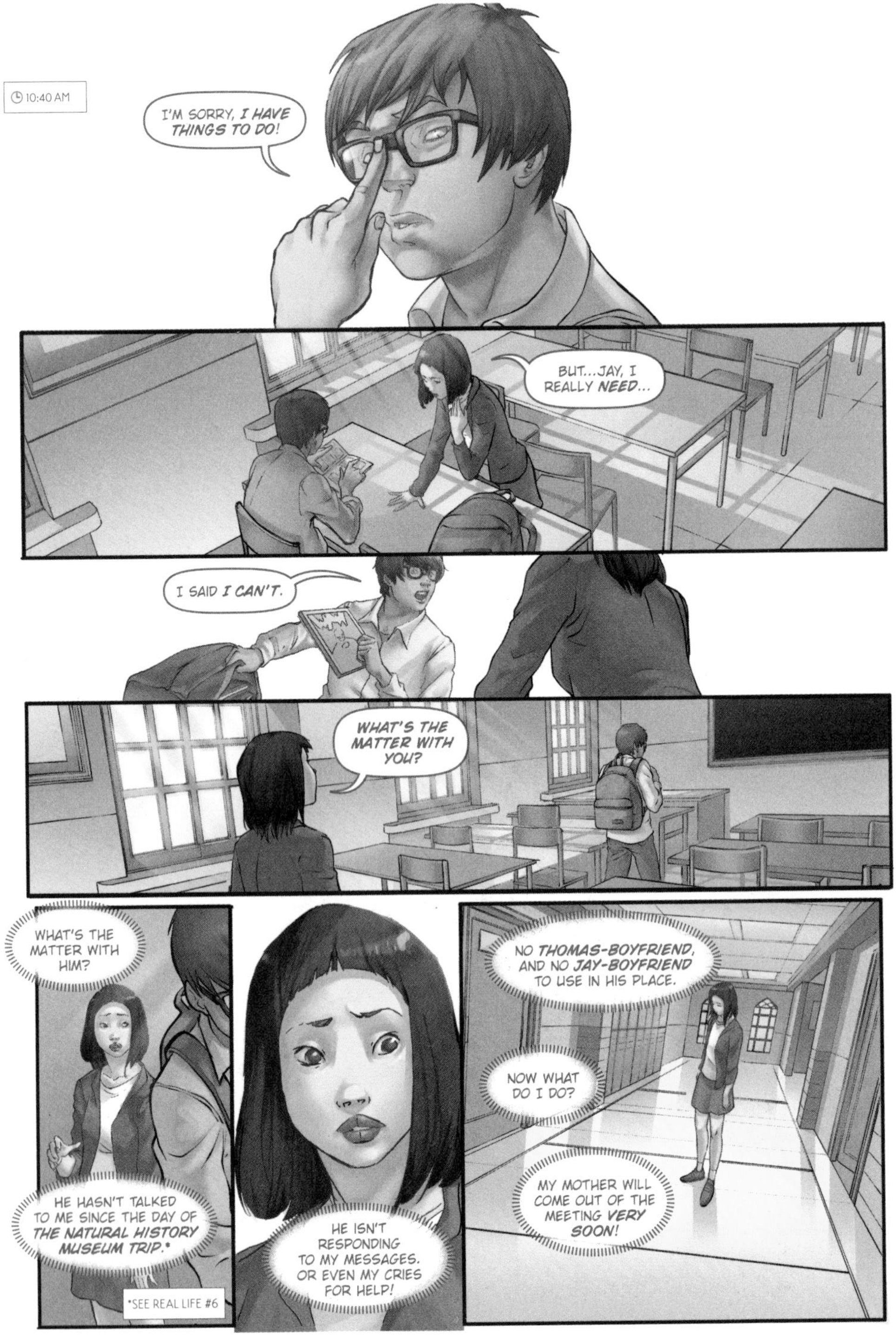
10:40 AM
I'M SORRY, I HAVE THINGS TO DO!
BUT...JAY, I REALLY NEED...
I SAID I CAN'T.
WHAT'S THE MATTER WITH YOU?
WHAT'S THE MATTER WITH HIM?
HE HASN'T TALKED TO ME SINCE THE DAY OF THE NATURAL HISTORY MUSEUM TRIP.*
*SEE REAL LIFE #6
HE ISN'T RESPONDING TO MY MESSAGES. OR EVEN MY CRIES FOR HELP!
NO THOMAS-BOYFRIEND, AND NO JAY-BOYFRIEND TO USE IN HIS PLACE.
NOW WHAT DO I DO?
MY MOTHER WILL COME OUT OF THE MEETING VERY SOON!

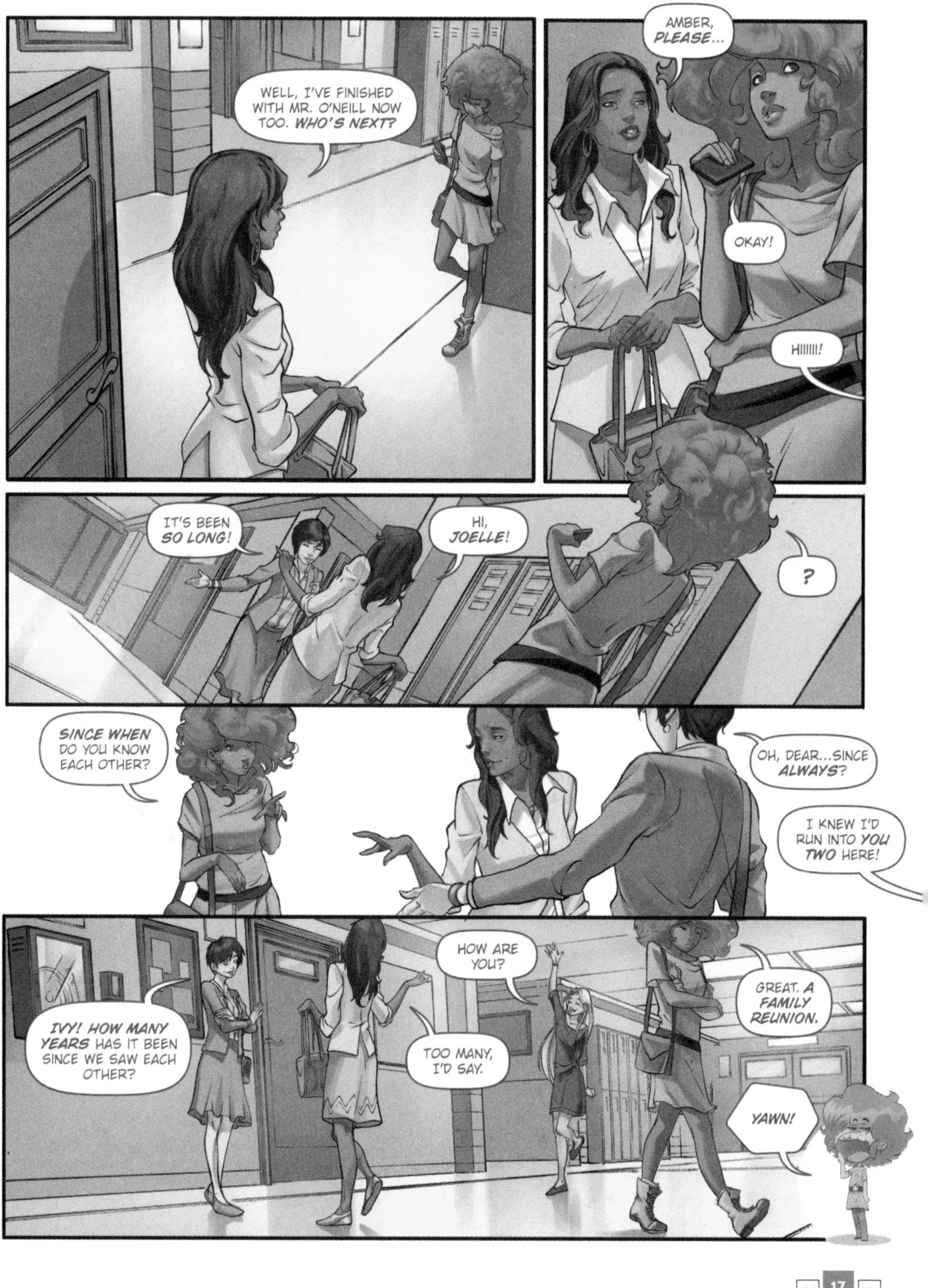
WELL, I'VE FINISHED WITH MR. O'NEILL NOW TOO. WHO'S NEXT?
AMBER, PLEASE...
OKAY!
HIIIII!
IT'S BEEN SO LONG!
HI, JOELLE!
?
SINCE WHEN DO YOU KNOW EACH OTHER?
OH, DEAR...SINCE ALWAYS?
I KNEW I'D RUN INTO YOU TWO HERE!
IVY! HOW MANY YEARS HAS IT BEEN SINCE WE SAW EACH OTHER?
HOW ARE YOU?
TOO MANY, I'D SAY.
GREAT. A FAMILY REUNION.
YAWN!

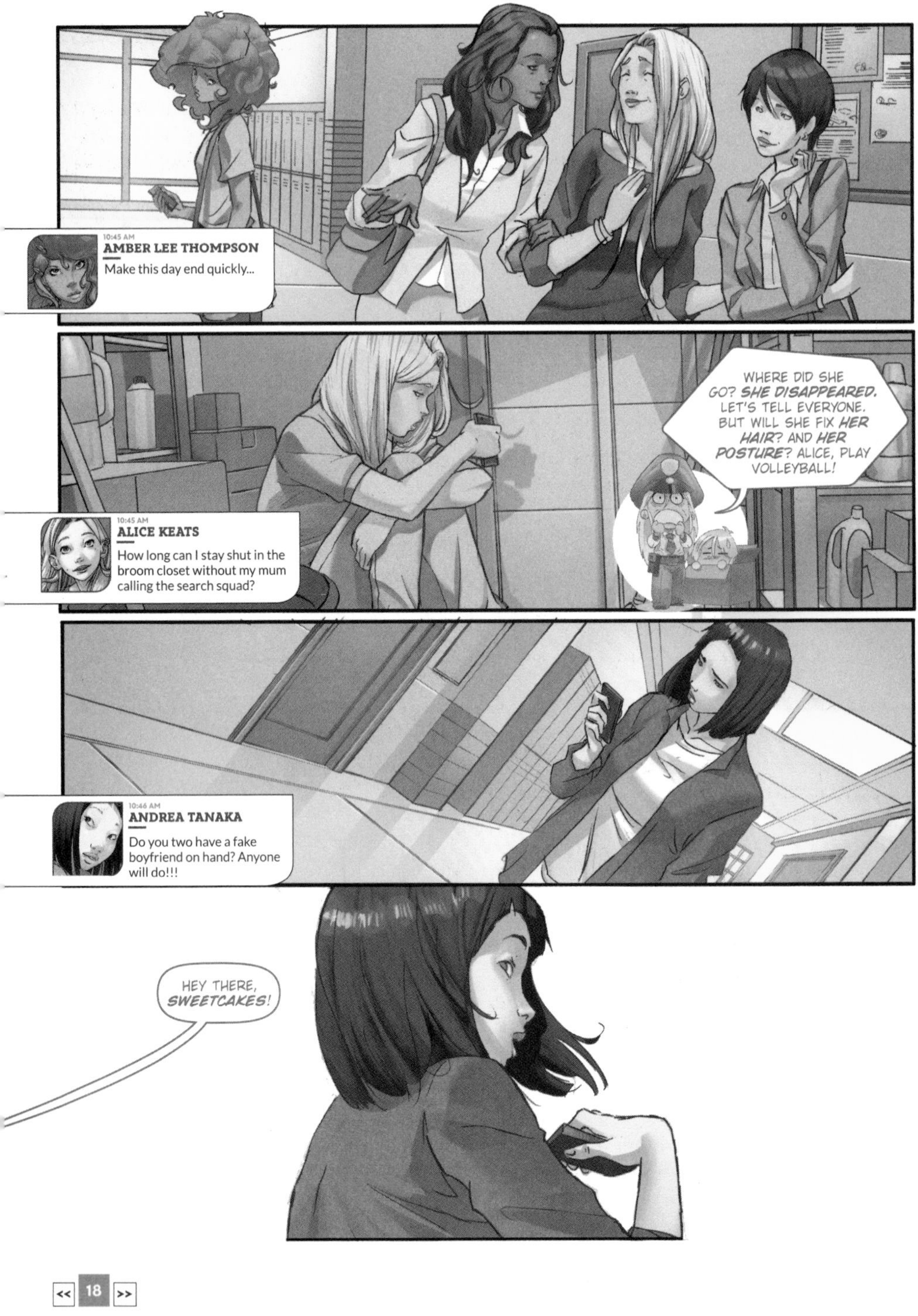
10:45 AM
AMBER LEE THOMPSON
Make this day end quickly...
10:45 AM
ALICE KEATS
How long can I stay shut in the broom closet without my mum calling the search squad?
WHERE DID SHE GO? SHE DISAPPEARED. LET'S TELL EVERYONE. BUT WILL SHE FIX HER HAIR? AND HER POSTURE? ALICE, PLAY VOLLEYBALL!
10:46 AM
ANDREA TANAKA
Do you two have a fake boyfriend on hand? Anyone will do!!!
HEY THERE, SWEETCAKES!

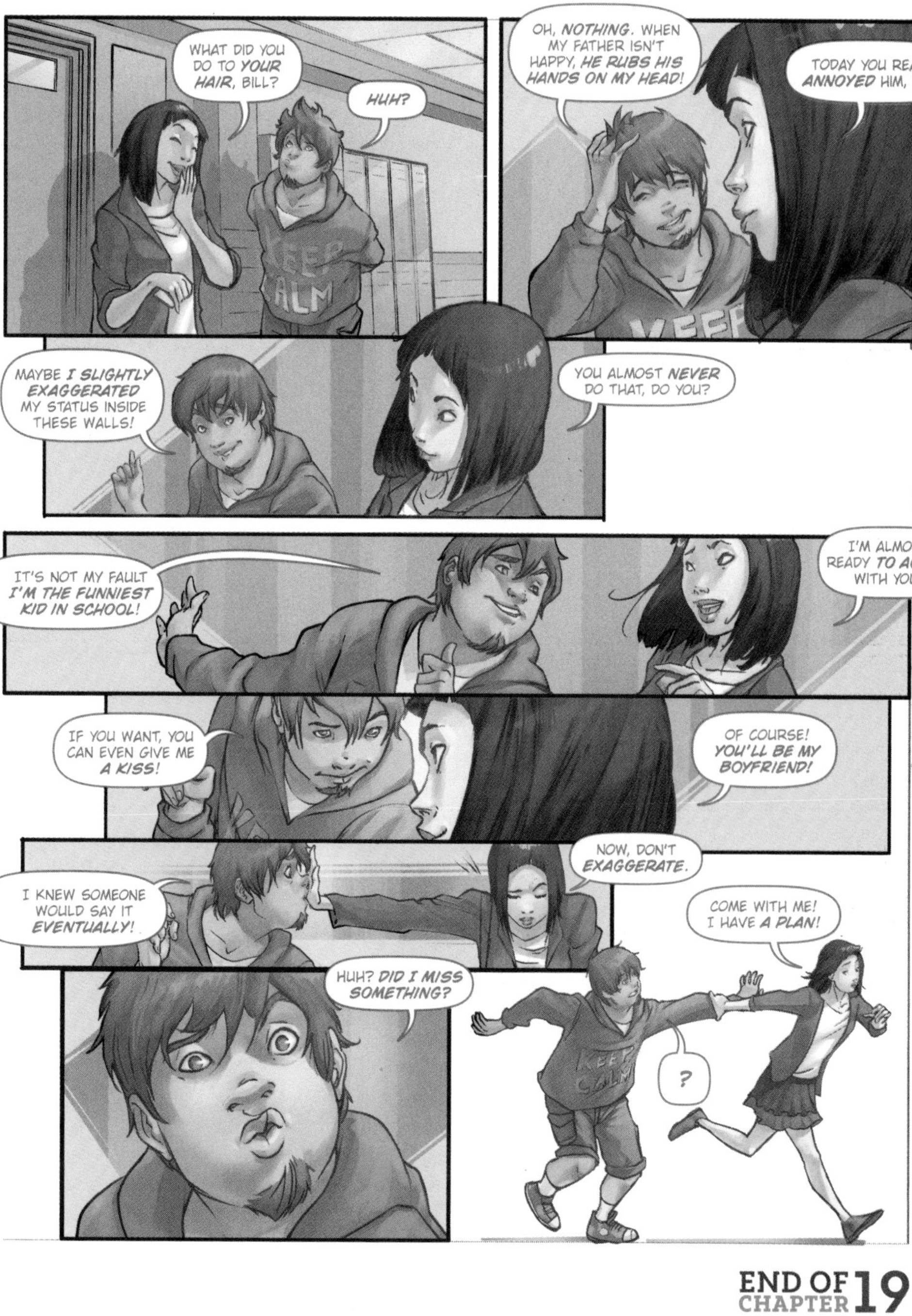
WHAT DID YOU DO TO YOUR HAIR, BILL?
HUH?
OH, NOTHING. WHEN MY FATHER ISN'T HAPPY, HE RUBS HIS HANDS ON MY HEAD!
TODAY YOU REALLY ANNOYED HIM, HUH?
MAYBE I SLIGHTLY EXAGGERATED MY STATUS INSIDE THESE WALLS!
YOU ALMOST NEVER DO THAT, DO YOU?
IT'S NOT MY FAULT I'M THE FUNNIEST KID IN SCHOOL!
I'M ALMOST READY TO AGREE WITH YOU!
IF YOU WANT, YOU CAN EVEN GIVE ME A KISS!
OF COURSE! YOU'LL BE MY BOYFRIEND!
I KNEW SOMEONE WOULD SAY IT EVENTUALLY!
NOW, DON'T EXAGGERATE.
HUH? DID I MISS SOMETHING?
COME WITH ME! I HAVE A PLAN!
?

END OF CHAPTER 19

CHAPTER 20

The QUEEN is BACK in TOWN

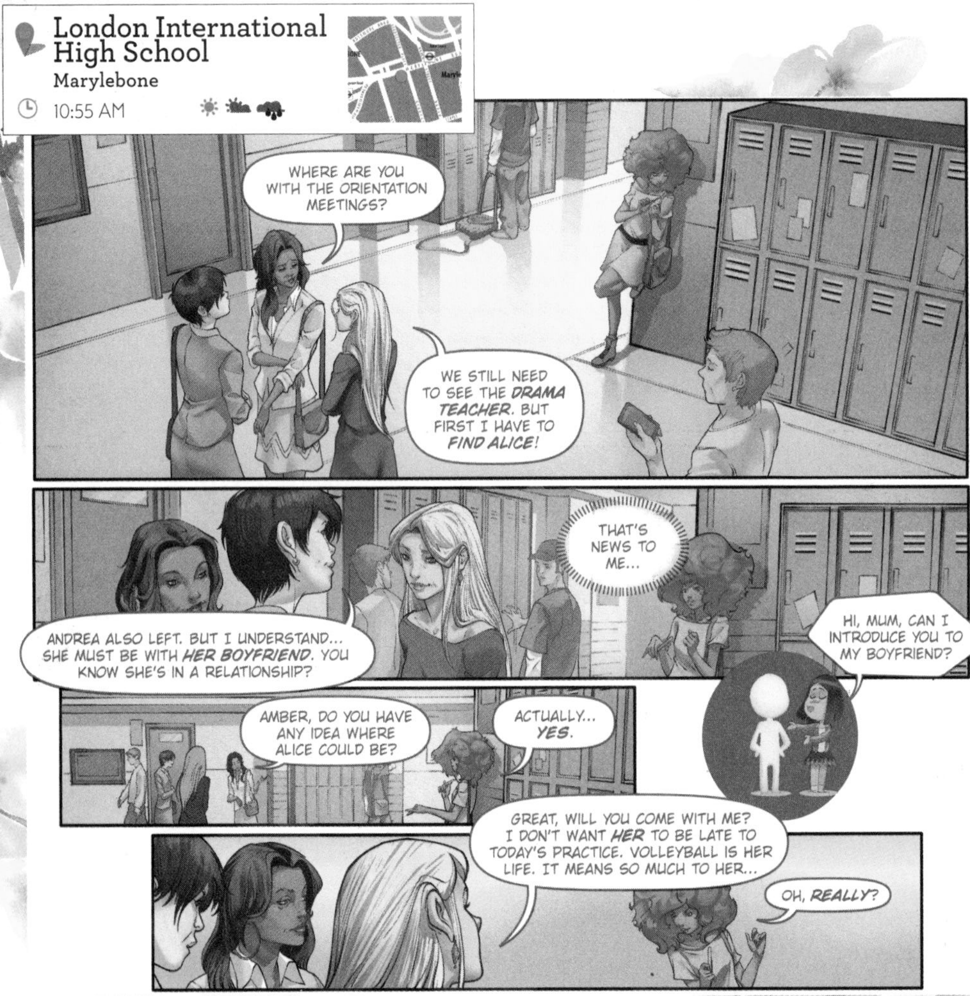
London International High School
Marylebone
10:55 AM
WHERE ARE YOU WITH THE ORIENTATION MEETINGS?
WE STILL NEED TO SEE THE DRAMA TEACHER. BUT FIRST I HAVE TO FIND ALICE!
ANDREA ALSO LEFT. BUT I UNDERSTAND... SHE MUST BE WITH HER BOYFRIEND. YOU KNOW SHE'S IN A RELATIONSHIP?
THAT'S NEWS TO ME...
HI, MUM, CAN I INTRODUCE YOU TO MY BOYFRIEND?
AMBER, DO YOU HAVE ANY IDEA WHERE ALICE COULD BE?
ACTUALLY... YES.
GREAT, WILL YOU COME WITH ME? I DON'T WANT HER TO BE LATE TO TODAY'S PRACTICE. VOLLEYBALL IS HER LIFE. IT MEANS SO MUCH TO HER...
OH, REALLY?

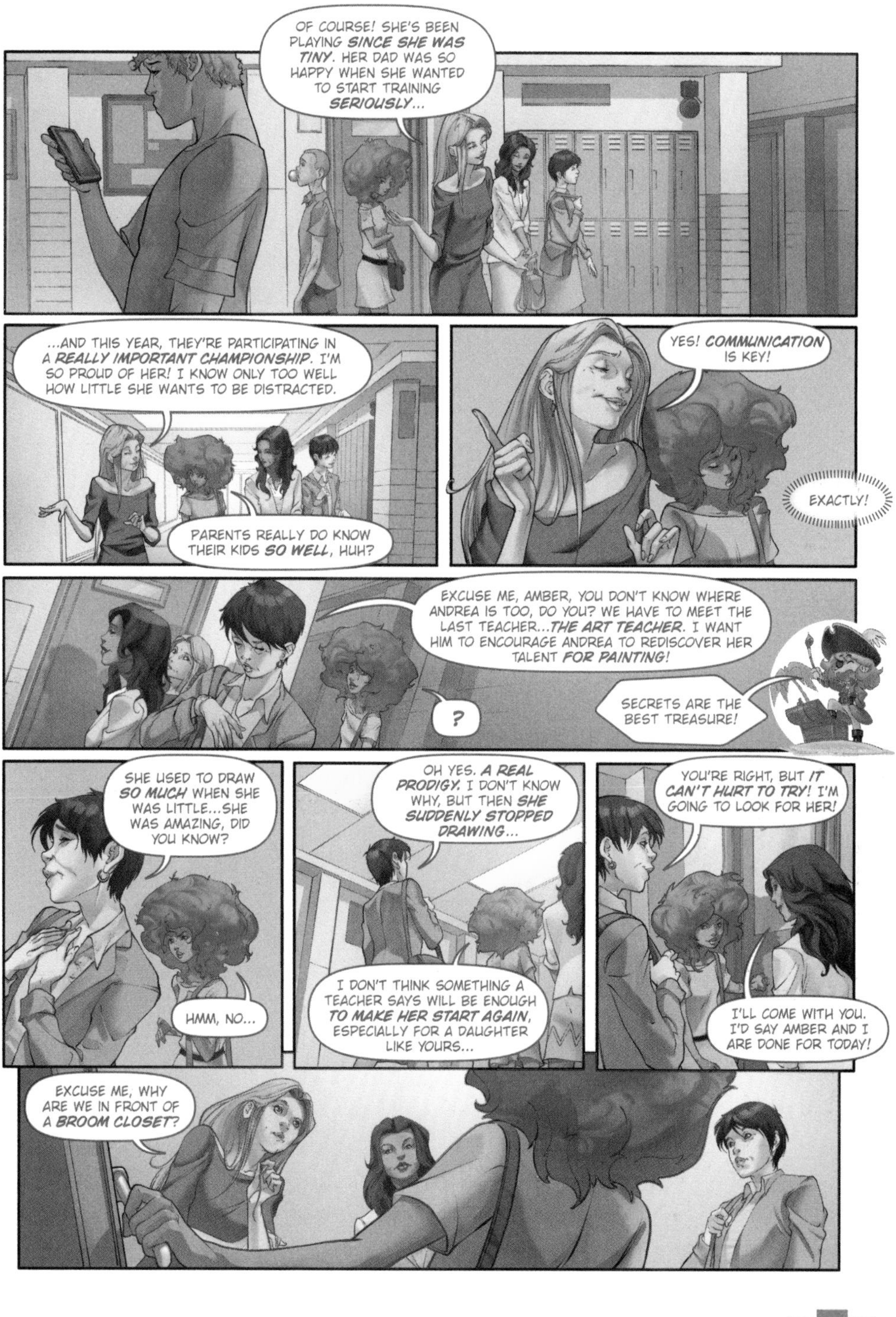
OF COURSE! SHE'S BEEN PLAYING SINCE SHE WAS TINY. HER DAD WAS SO HAPPY WHEN SHE WANTED TO START TRAINING SERIOUSLY...
...AND THIS YEAR, THEY'RE PARTICIPATING IN A REALLY IMPORTANT CHAMPIONSHIP. I'M SO PROUD OF HER! I KNOW ONLY TOO WELL HOW LITTLE SHE WANTS TO BE DISTRACTED.
PARENTS REALLY DO KNOW THEIR KIDS SO WELL, HUH?
YES! COMMUNICATION IS KEY!
EXACTLY!
EXCUSE ME, AMBER, YOU DON'T KNOW WHERE ANDREA IS TOO, DO YOU? WE HAVE TO MEET THE LAST TEACHER...THE ART TEACHER. I WANT HIM TO ENCOURAGE ANDREA TO REDISCOVER HER TALENT FOR PAINTING!
?
SECRETS ARE THE BEST TREASURE!
SHE USED TO DRAW SO MUCH WHEN SHE WAS LITTLE...SHE WAS AMAZING, DID YOU KNOW?
HMM, NO...
OH YES. A REAL PRODIGY. I DON'T KNOW WHY, BUT THEN SHE SUDDENLY STOPPED DRAWING...
I DON'T THINK SOMETHING A TEACHER SAYS WILL BE ENOUGH TO MAKE HER START AGAIN, ESPECIALLY FOR A DAUGHTER LIKE YOURS...
YOU'RE RIGHT, BUT IT CAN'T HURT TO TRY! I'M GOING TO LOOK FOR HER!
I'LL COME WITH YOU. I'D SAY AMBER AND I ARE DONE FOR TODAY!
EXCUSE ME, WHY ARE WE IN FRONT OF A BROOM CLOSET?

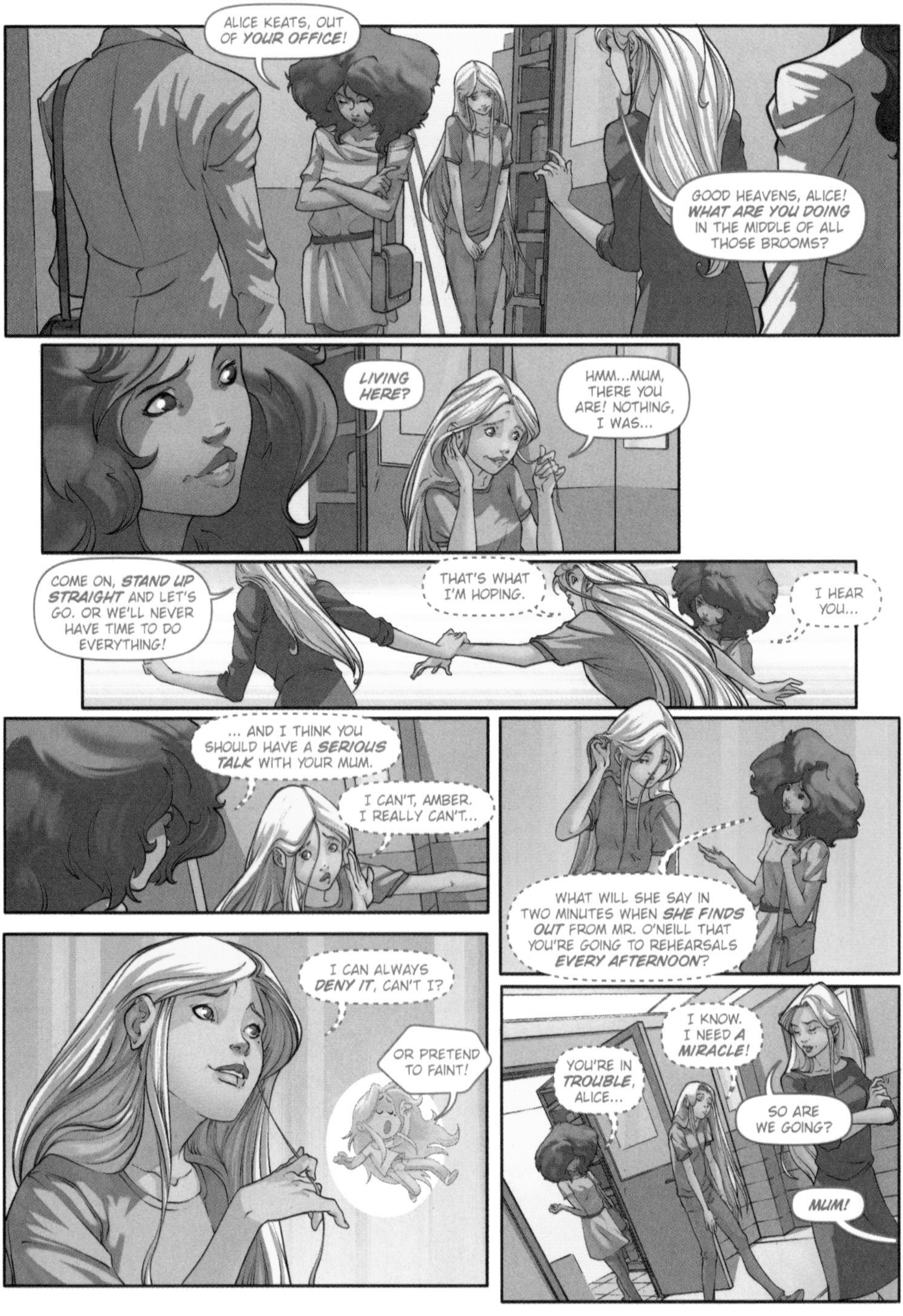
ALICE KEATS, OUT OF YOUR OFFICE!
GOOD HEAVENS, ALICE! WHAT ARE YOU DOING IN THE MIDDLE OF ALL THOSE BROOMS?
LIVING HERE?
HMM...MUM, THERE YOU ARE! NOTHING, I WAS...
COME ON, STAND UP STRAIGHT AND LET'S GO. OR WE'LL NEVER HAVE TIME TO DO EVERYTHING!
THAT'S WHAT I'M HOPING.
I HEAR YOU...
... AND I THINK YOU SHOULD HAVE A SERIOUS TALK WITH YOUR MUM.
I CAN'T, AMBER. I REALLY CAN'T...
WHAT WILL SHE SAY IN TWO MINUTES WHEN SHE FINDS OUT FROM MR. O'NEILL THAT YOU'RE GOING TO REHEARSALS EVERY AFTERNOON?
I CAN ALWAYS DENY IT, CAN'T I?
OR PRETEND TO FAINT!
YOU'RE IN TROUBLE, ALICE...
I KNOW. I NEED A MIRACLE!
SO ARE WE GOING?
MUM!

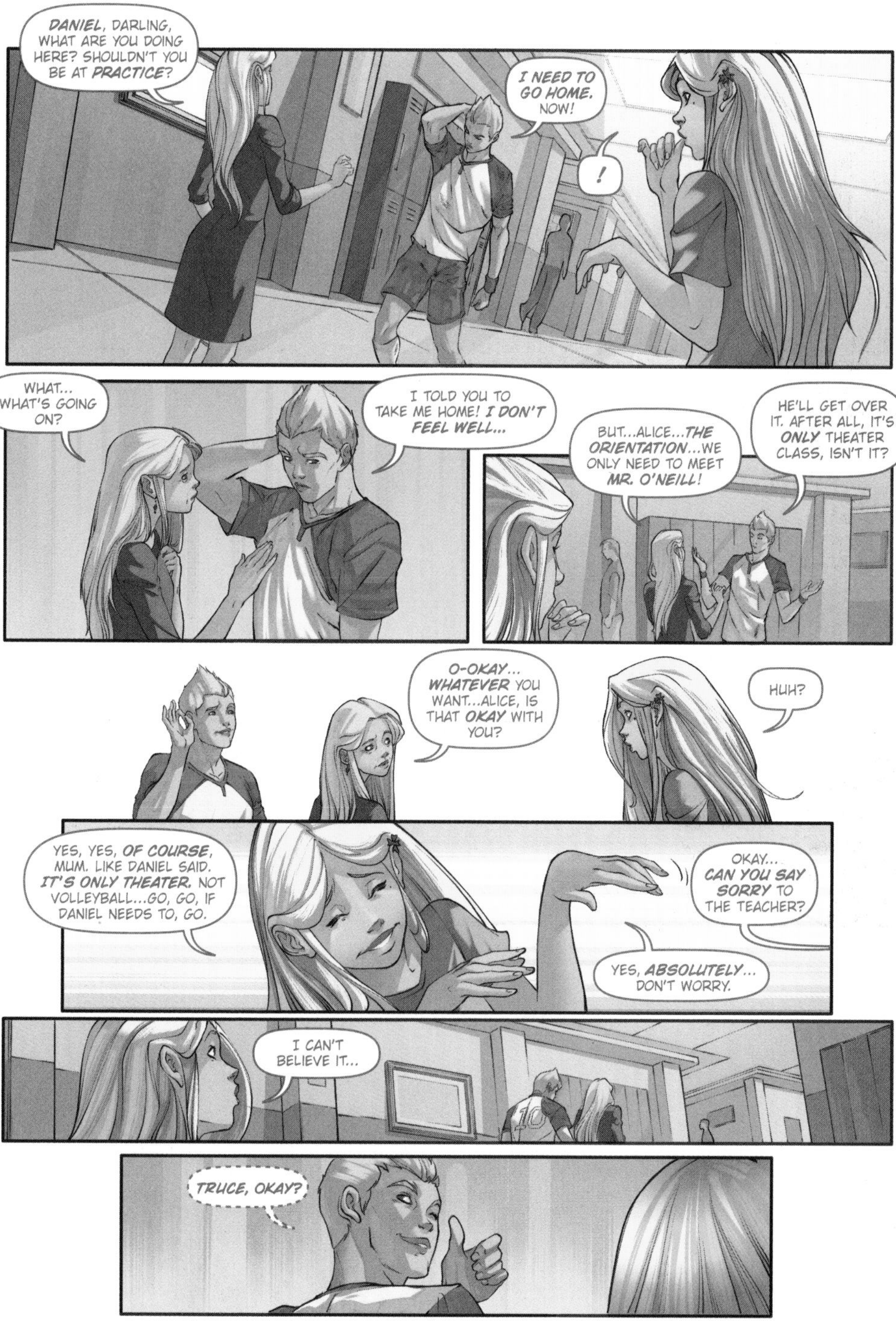
DANIEL, DARLING, WHAT ARE YOU DOING HERE? SHOULDN'T YOU BE AT PRACTICE?
I NEED TO GO HOME. NOW!
!
WHAT... WHAT'S GOING ON?
I TOLD YOU TO TAKE ME HOME! I DON'T FEEL WELL...
BUT...ALICE...THE ORIENTATION...WE ONLY NEED TO MEET MR. O'NEILL!
HE'LL GET OVER IT. AFTER ALL, IT'S ONLY THEATER CLASS, ISN'T IT?
O-OKAY... WHATEVER YOU WANT...ALICE, IS THAT OKAY WITH YOU?
HUH?
YES, YES, OF COURSE, MUM. LIKE DANIEL SAID. IT'S ONLY THEATER. NOT VOLLEYBALL...GO, GO, IF DANIEL NEEDS TO, GO.
OKAY... CAN YOU SAY SORRY TO THE TEACHER?
YES, ABSOLUTELY... DON'T WORRY.
I CAN'T BELIEVE IT...
TRUCE, OKAY?

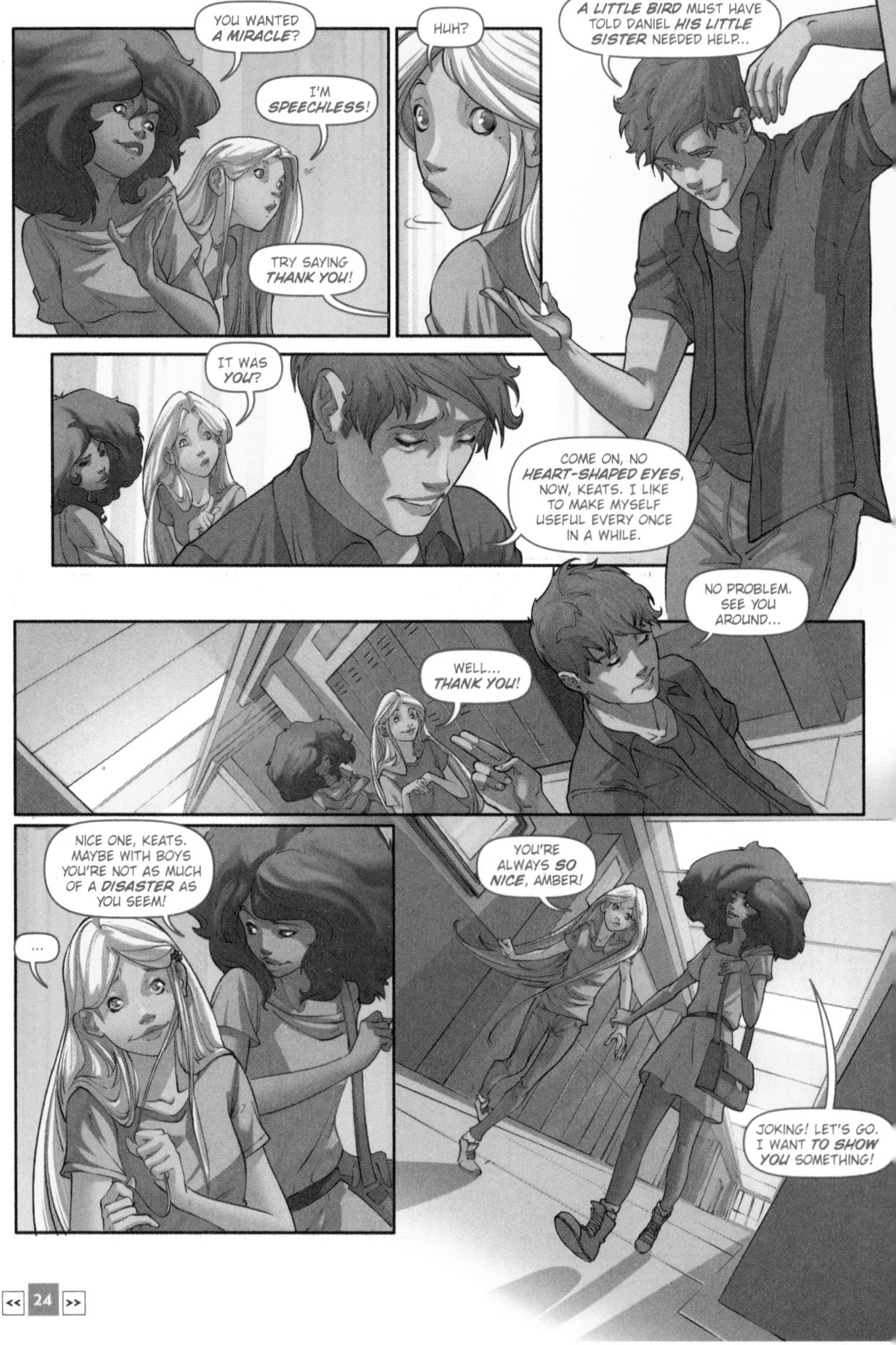

YOU WANTED A MIRACLE?
I'M SPEECHLESS!
TRY SAYING THANK YOU!
HUH?
A LITTLE BIRD MUST HAVE TOLD DANIEL HIS LITTLE SISTER NEEDED HELP...
IT WAS YOU?
COME ON, NO HEART-SHAPED EYES, NOW, KEATS. I LIKE TO MAKE MYSELF USEFUL EVERY ONCE IN A WHILE.
NO PROBLEM. SEE YOU AROUND...
WELL... THANK YOU!
NICE ONE, KEATS. MAYBE WITH BOYS YOU'RE NOT AS MUCH OF A DISASTER AS YOU SEEM!
...
YOU'RE ALWAYS SO NICE, AMBER!
JOKING! LET'S GO. I WANT TO SHOW YOU SOMETHING!

London International High School, Theater
11:15 AM

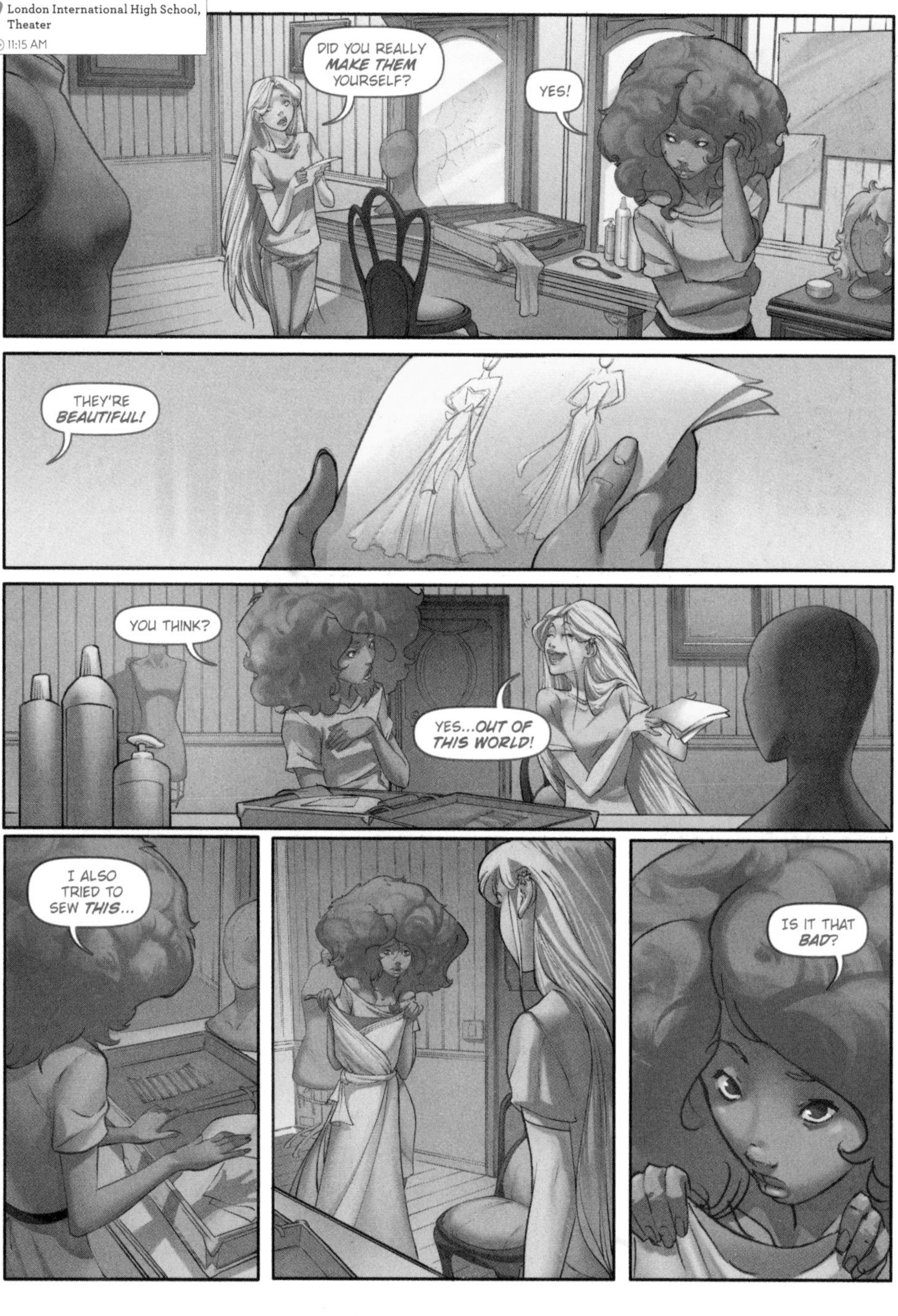

DID YOU REALLY *MAKE THEM* YOURSELF?
YES!
THEY'RE *BEAUTIFUL!*
YOU THINK?
YES...*OUT OF THIS WORLD!*
I ALSO TRIED TO SEW *THIS*...
IS IT THAT *BAD?*

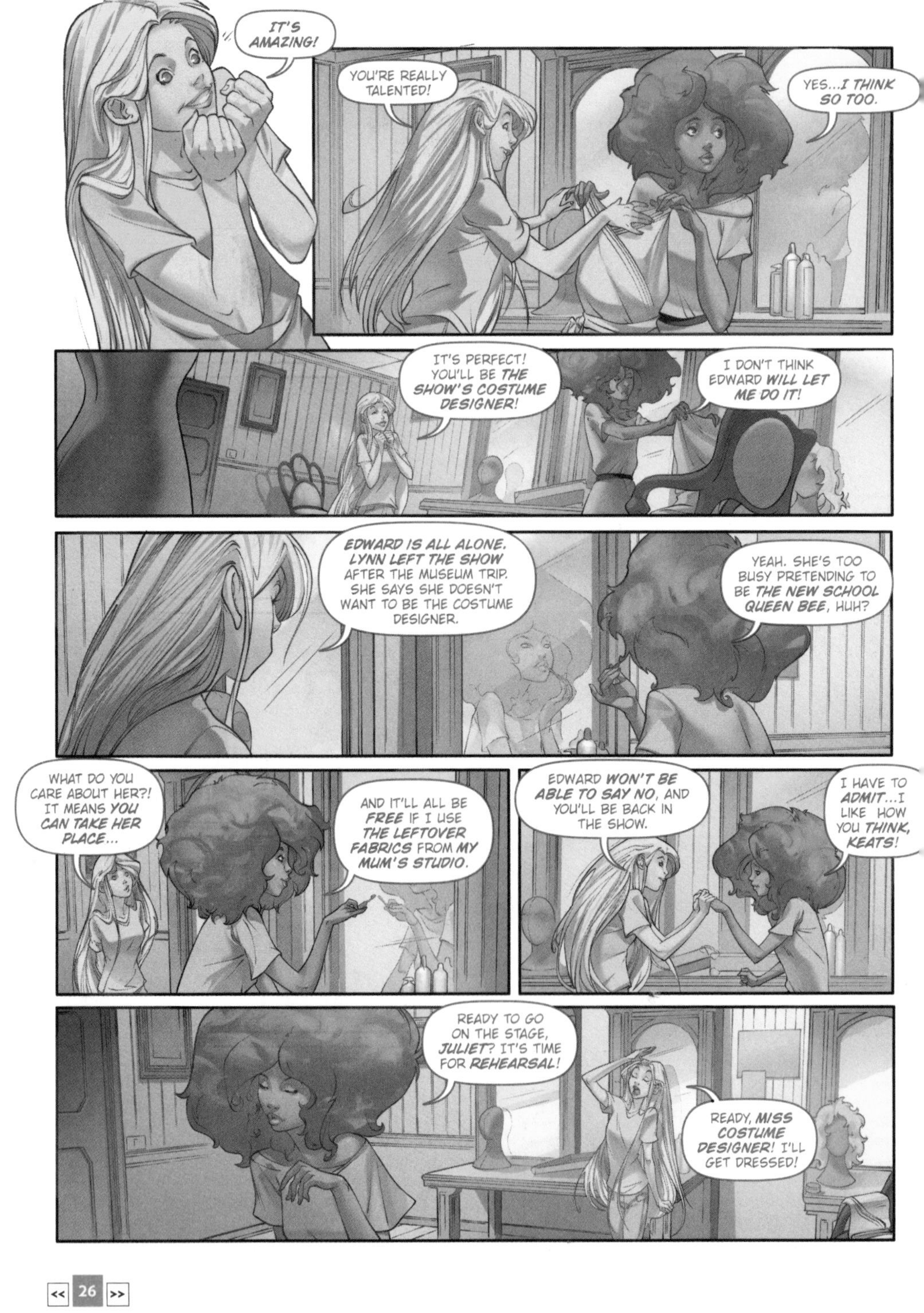
IT'S AMAZING!
YOU'RE REALLY TALENTED!
YES...I THINK SO TOO.
IT'S PERFECT! YOU'LL BE THE SHOW'S COSTUME DESIGNER!
I DON'T THINK EDWARD WILL LET ME DO IT!
EDWARD IS ALL ALONE. LYNN LEFT THE SHOW AFTER THE MUSEUM TRIP. SHE SAYS SHE DOESN'T WANT TO BE THE COSTUME DESIGNER.
YEAH. SHE'S TOO BUSY PRETENDING TO BE THE NEW SCHOOL QUEEN BEE, HUH?
WHAT DO YOU CARE ABOUT HER?! IT MEANS YOU CAN TAKE HER PLACE...
AND IT'LL ALL BE FREE IF I USE THE LEFTOVER FABRICS FROM MY MUM'S STUDIO.
EDWARD WON'T BE ABLE TO SAY NO, AND YOU'LL BE BACK IN THE SHOW.
I HAVE TO ADMIT...I LIKE HOW YOU THINK, KEATS!
READY TO GO ON THE STAGE, JULIET? IT'S TIME FOR REHEARSAL!
READY, MISS COSTUME DESIGNER! I'LL GET DRESSED!

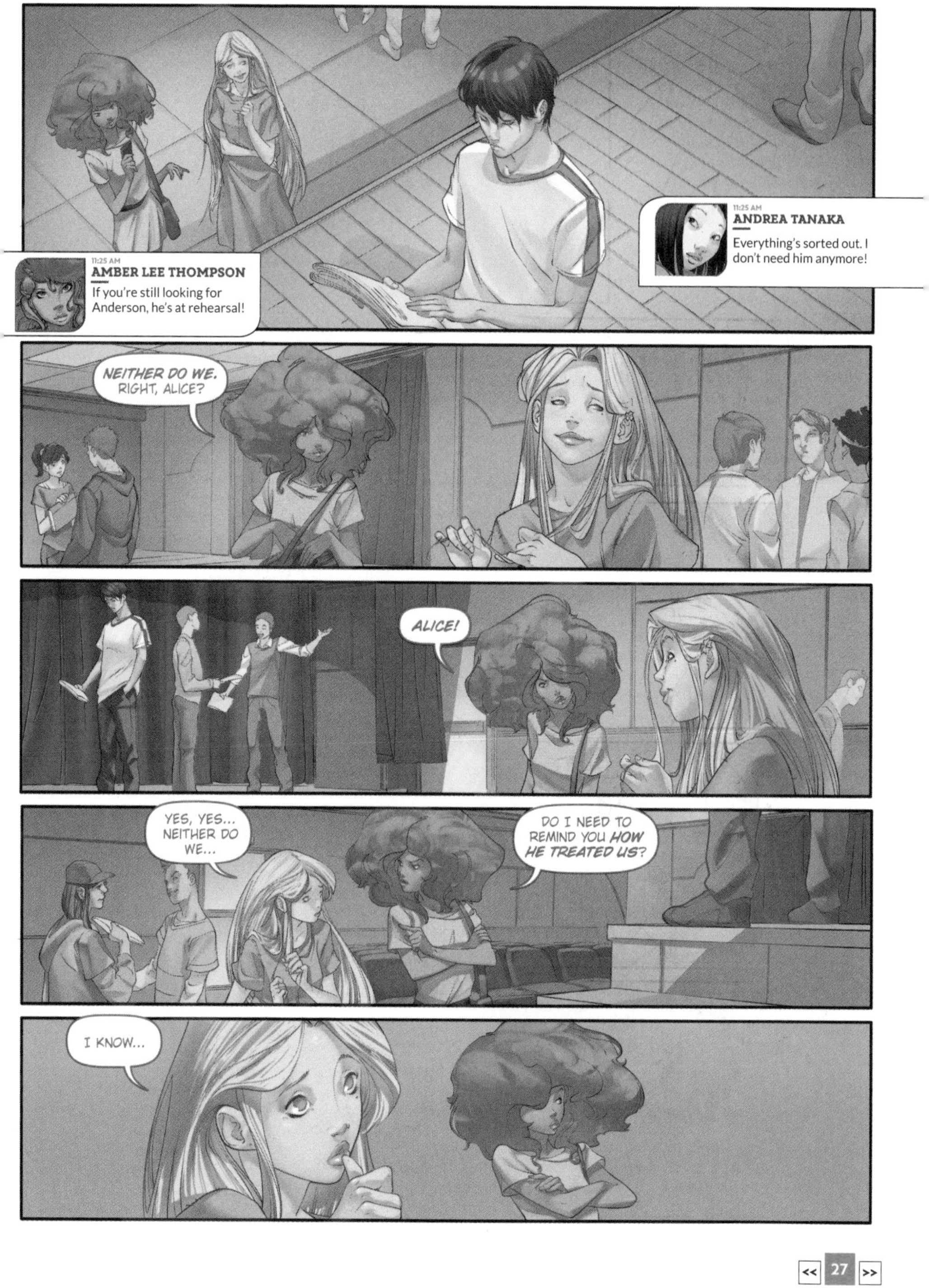
11:25 AM
AMBER LEE THOMPSON
If you're still looking for Anderson, he's at rehearsal!
11:25 AM
ANDREA TANAKA
Everything's sorted out. I don't need him anymore!
NEITHER DO WE. RIGHT, ALICE?
ALICE!
YES, YES... NEITHER DO WE...
DO I NEED TO REMIND YOU HOW HE TREATED US?
I KNOW...

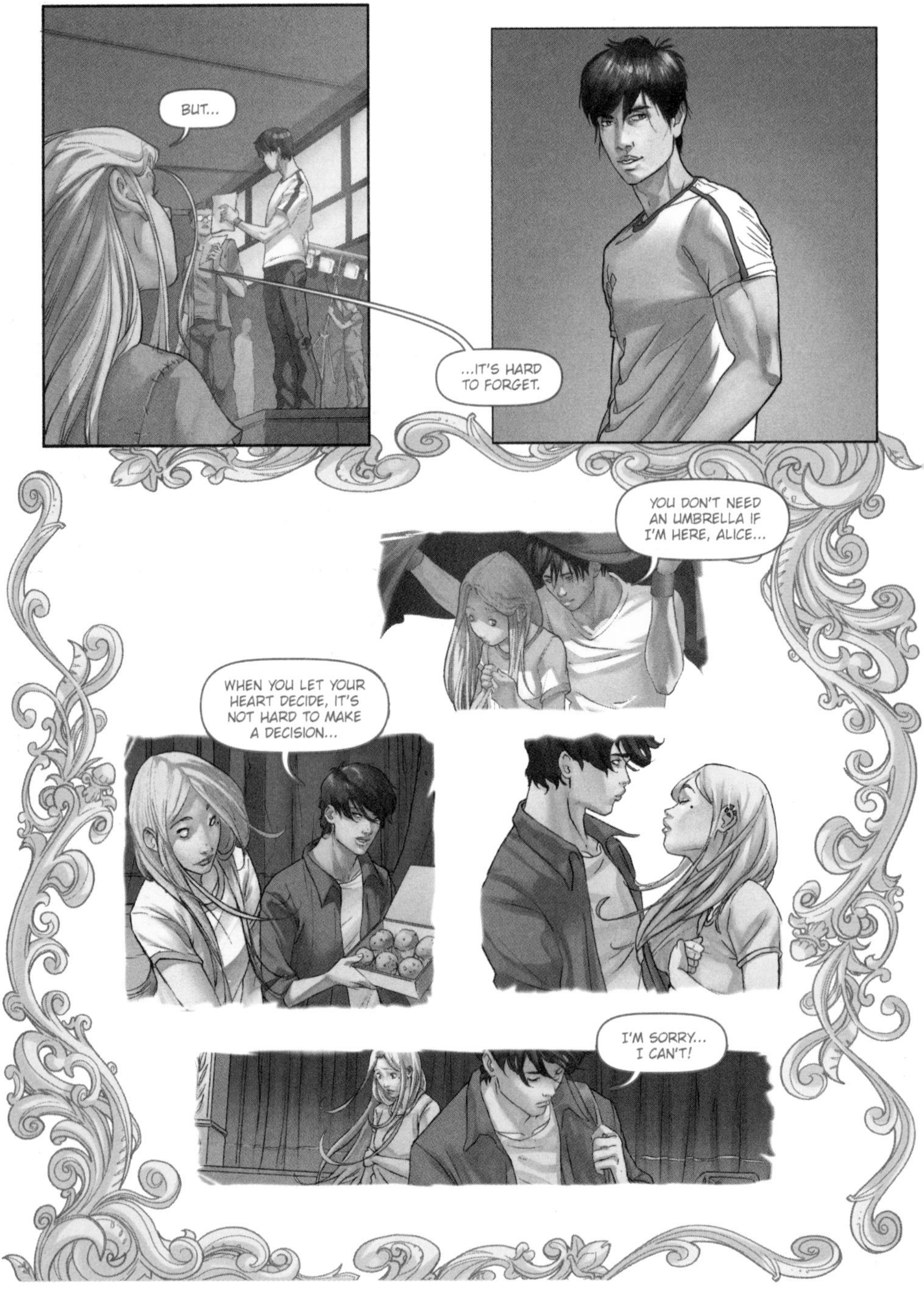
BUT...
...IT'S HARD TO FORGET.
YOU DON'T NEED AN UMBRELLA IF I'M HERE, ALICE...
WHEN YOU LET YOUR HEART DECIDE, IT'S NOT HARD TO MAKE A DECISION...
I'M SORRY... I CAN'T!

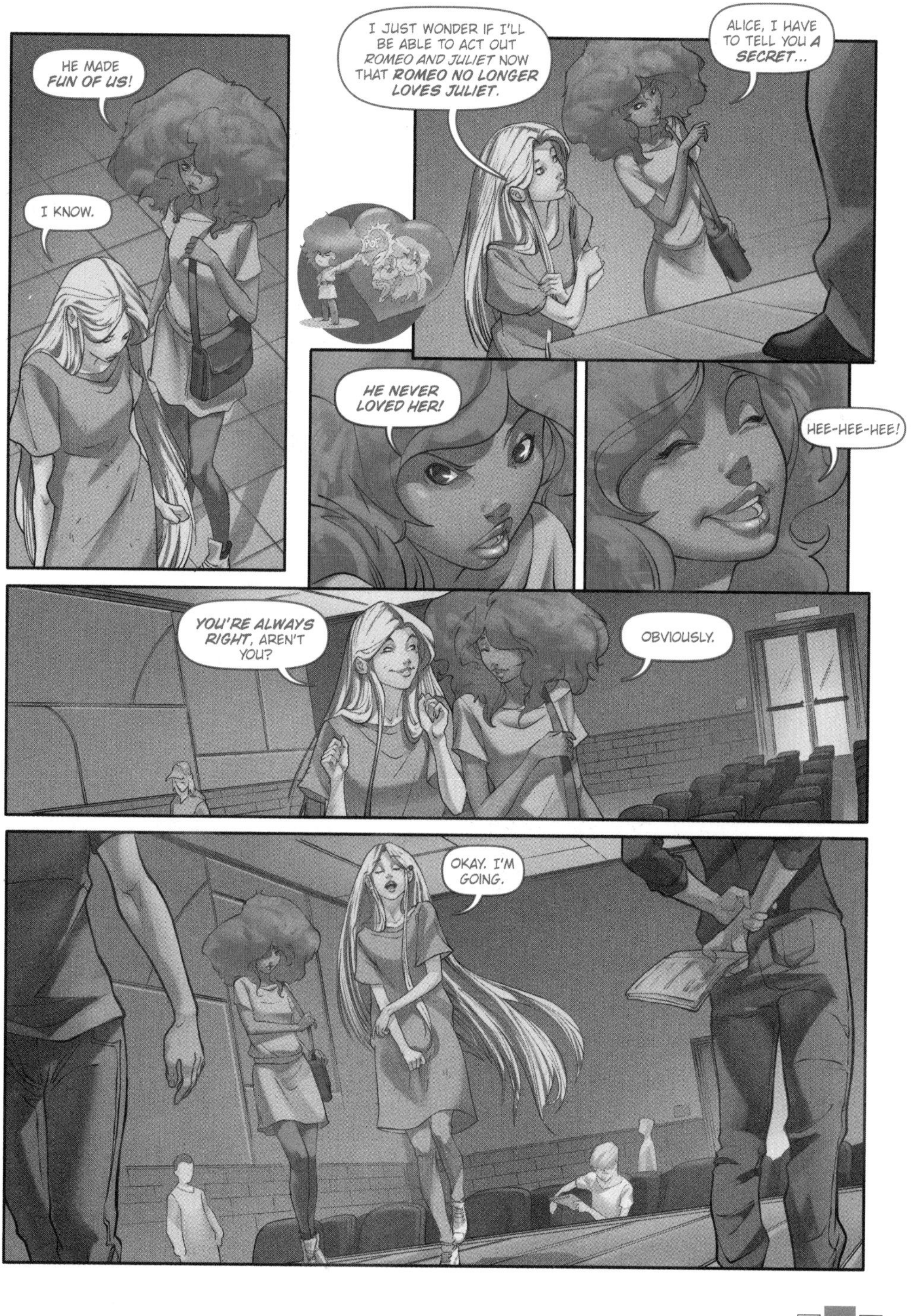
HE MADE FUN OF US!
I KNOW.
I JUST WONDER IF I'LL BE ABLE TO ACT OUT ROMEO AND JULIET NOW THAT ROMEO NO LONGER LOVES JULIET.
POP
ALICE, I HAVE TO TELL YOU A SECRET...
HE NEVER LOVED HER!
HEE-HEE-HEE!
YOU'RE ALWAYS RIGHT, AREN'T YOU?
OBVIOUSLY.
OKAY. I'M GOING.

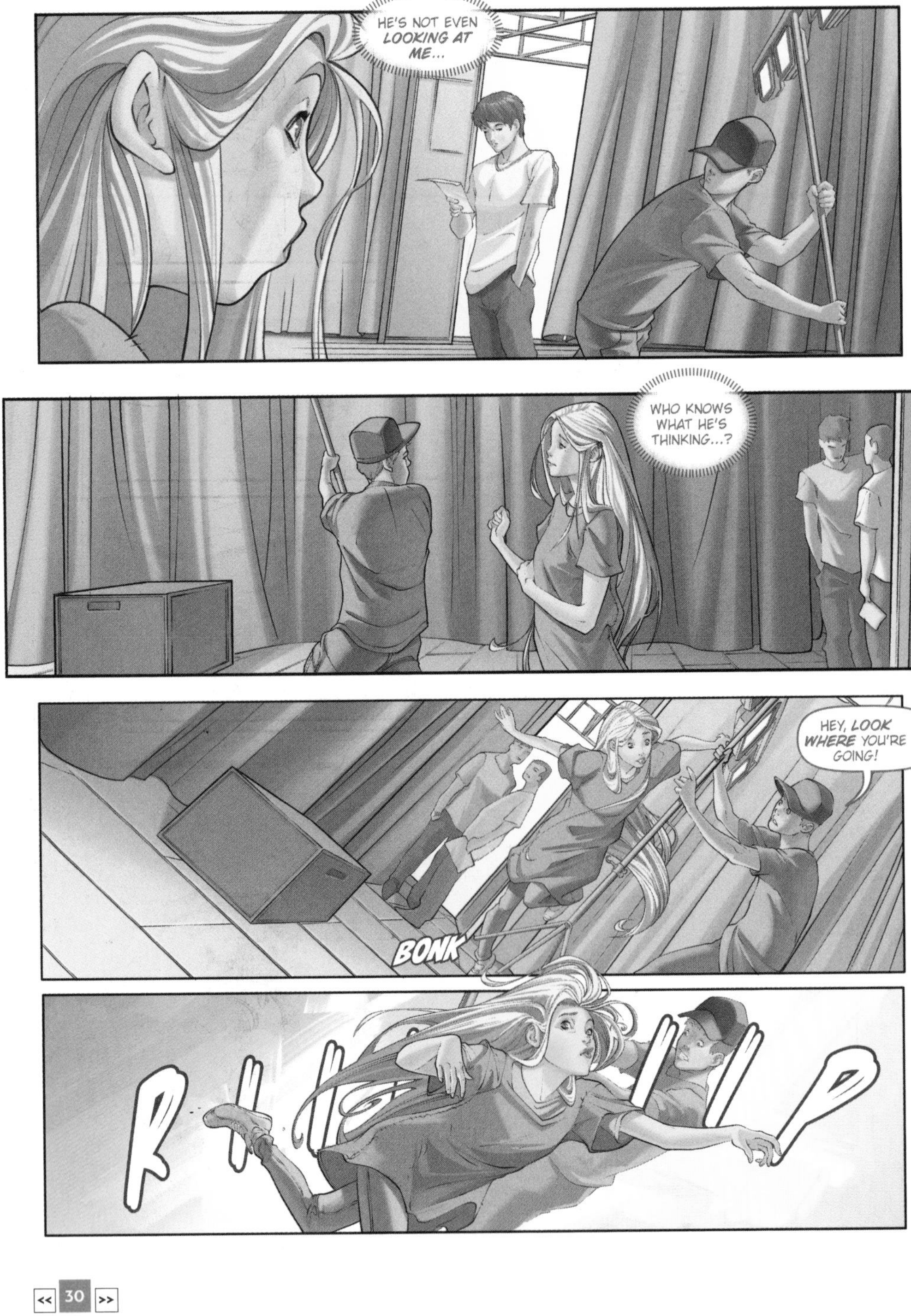
HE'S NOT EVEN LOOKING AT ME...
WHO KNOWS WHAT HE'S THINKING...?
BONK
HEY, LOOK WHERE YOU'RE GOING!
RIIP

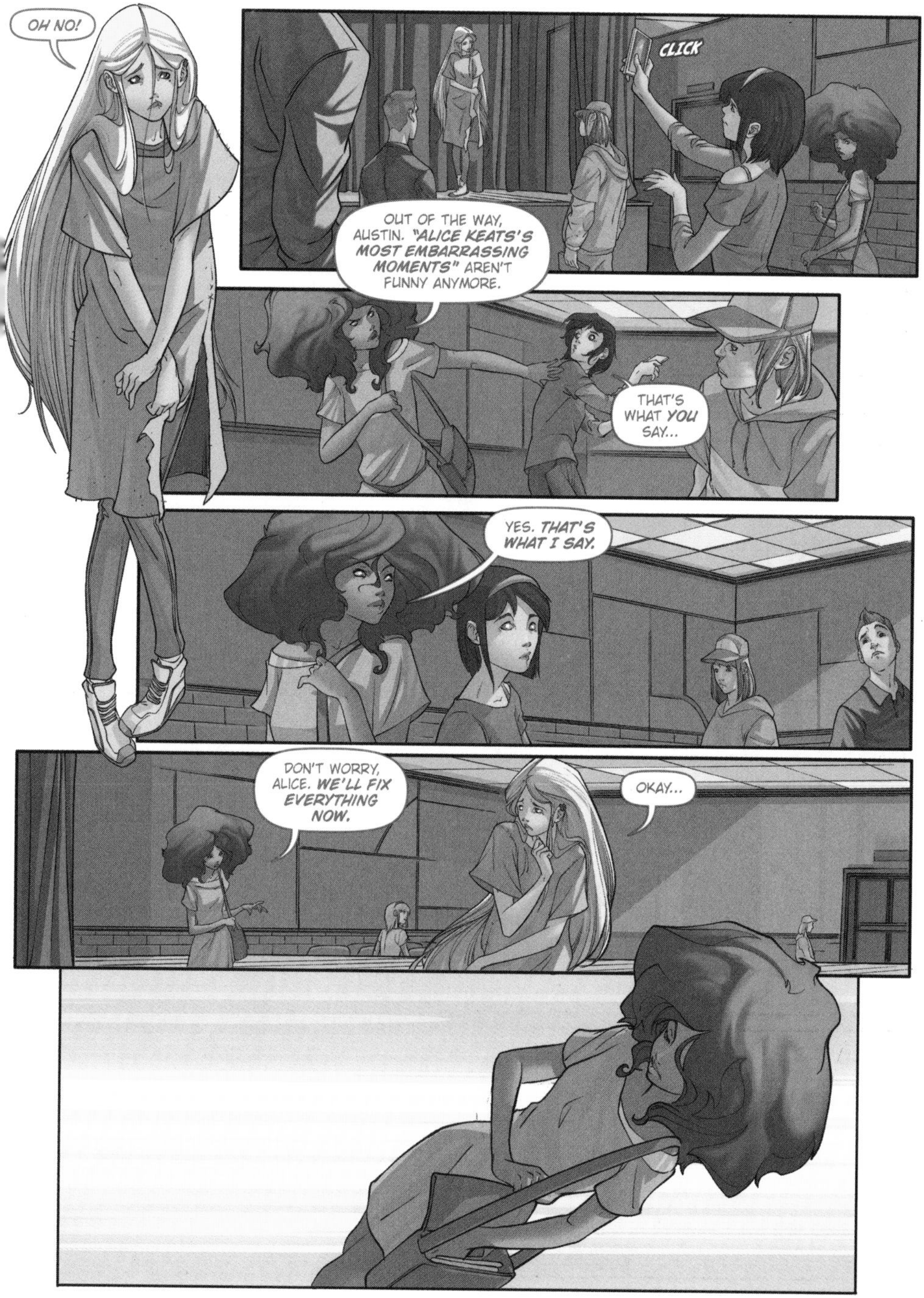
OH NO!
CLICK
OUT OF THE WAY, AUSTIN. "ALICE KEATS'S MOST EMBARRASSING MOMENTS" AREN'T FUNNY ANYMORE.
THAT'S WHAT YOU SAY...
YES. THAT'S WHAT I SAY.
DON'T WORRY, ALICE. WE'LL FIX EVERYTHING NOW.
OKAY...

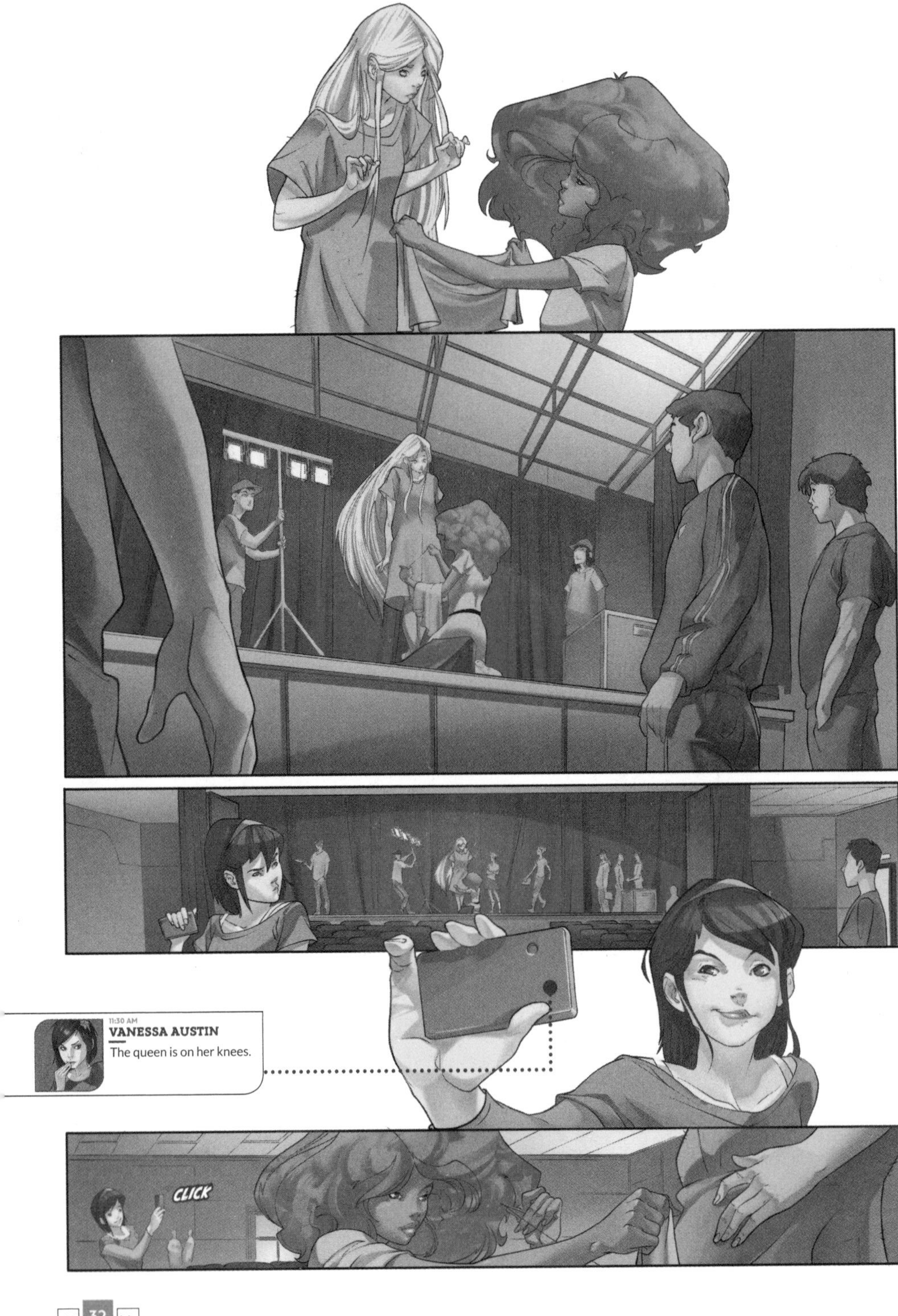
11:30 AM
VANESSA AUSTIN
The queen is on her knees.
CLICK

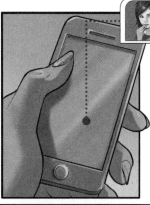

11:50 AM
VANESSA AUSTIN
The queen is on her knees.

11:32 AM
MAY RODRIGUEZ
So even Thompson knows what friendship is!

11:32 AM
LYNN JAVINS
Don't be followed...

11:33 AM
KIM SULLIVAN
Don't be jealous, Lynn. She's the queen.

11:33 AM
LYNN JAVINS
But she humiliated herself. And with someone like Keats...

11:33 AM
PAM LARKIN
That's not called humiliation. It's called FRIENDSHIP.

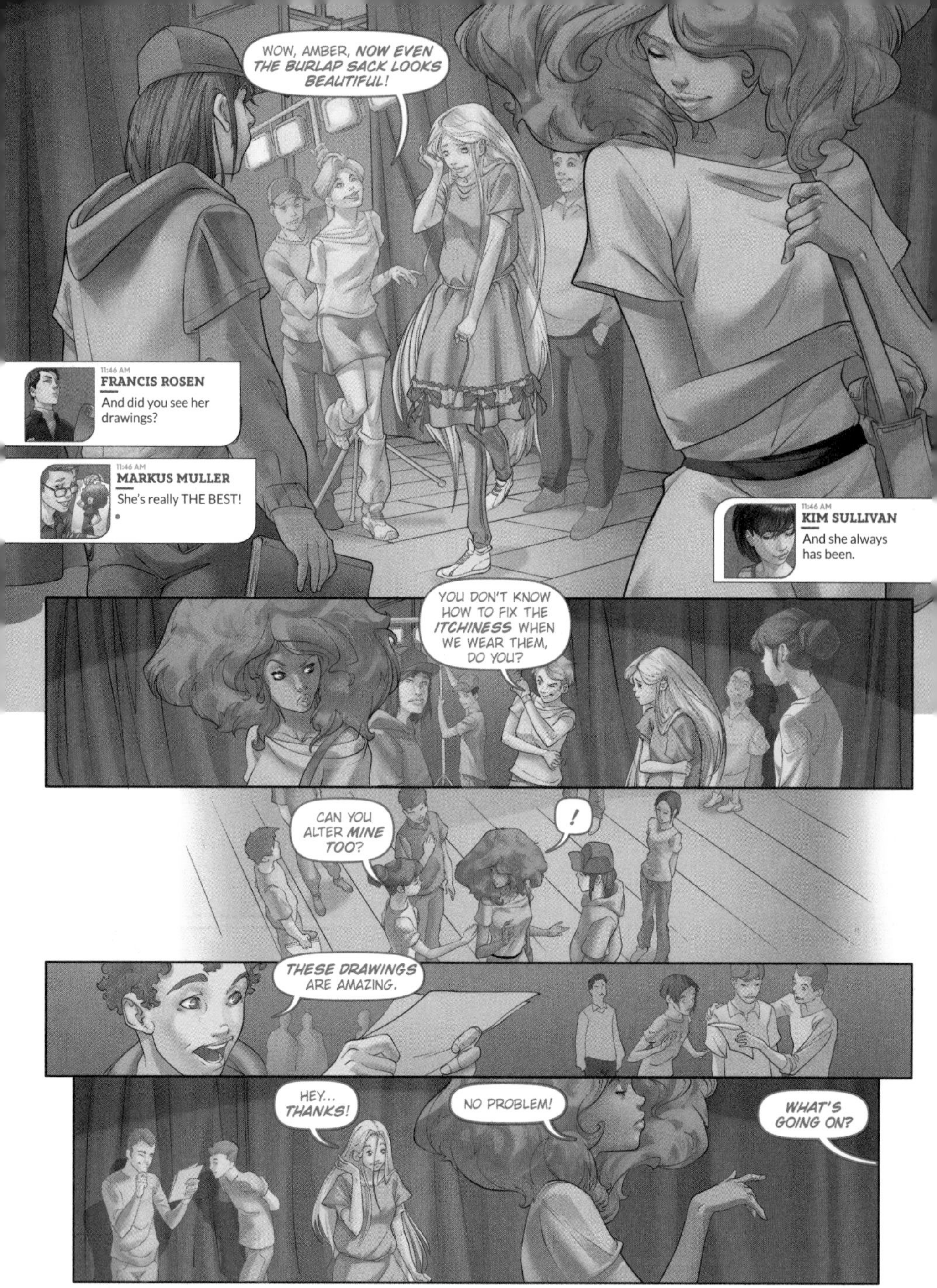
WOW, AMBER, NOW EVEN THE BURLAP SACK LOOKS BEAUTIFUL!
11:46 AM
FRANCIS ROSEN
And did you see her drawings?
11:46 AM
MARKUS MULLER
She's really THE BEST!
11:46 AM
KIM SULLIVAN
And she always has been.
YOU DON'T KNOW HOW TO FIX THE ITCHINESS WHEN WE WEAR THEM, DO YOU?
CAN YOU ALTER MINE TOO?
!
THESE DRAWINGS ARE AMAZING.
HEY... THANKS!
NO PROBLEM!
WHAT'S GOING ON?

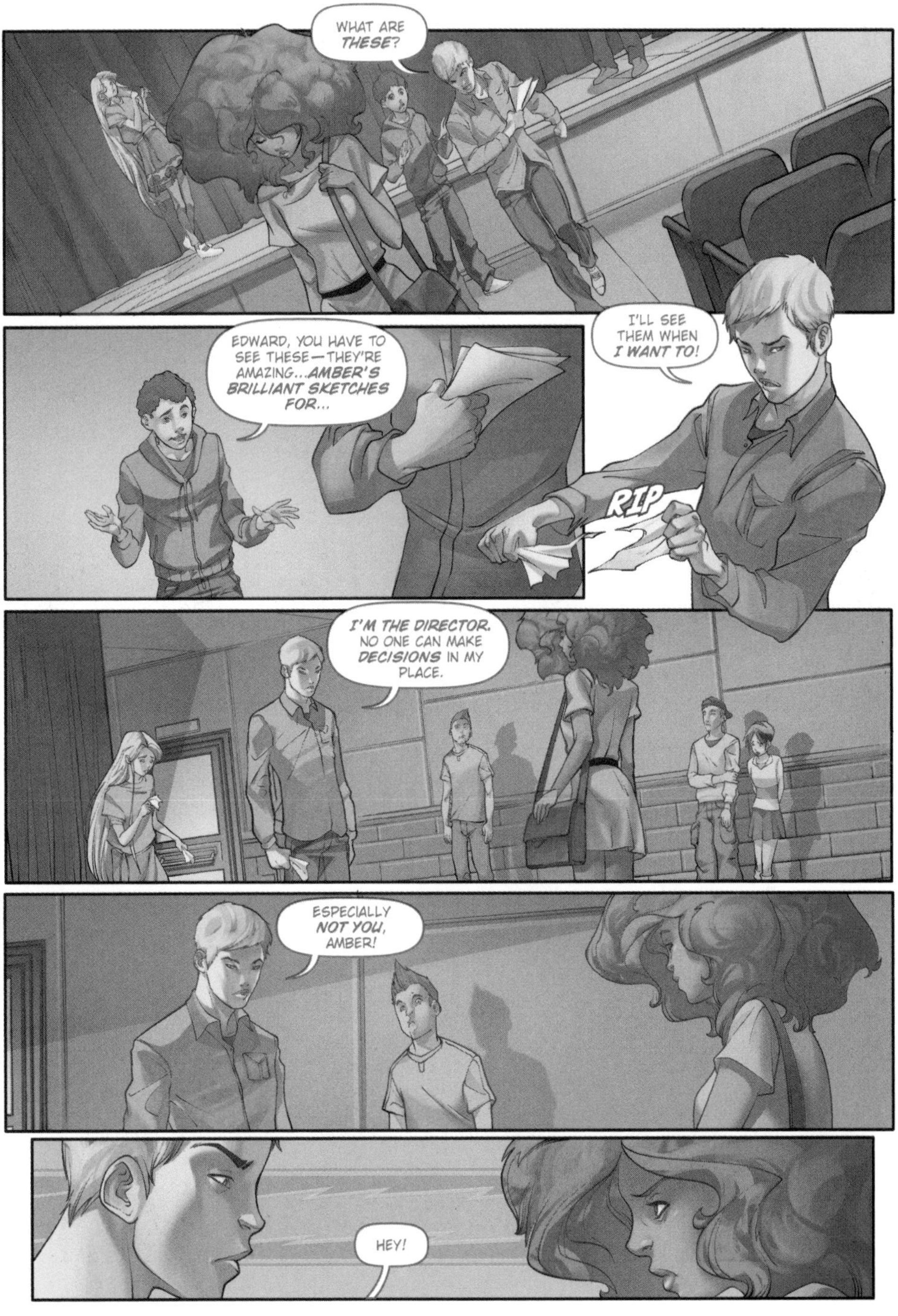
WHAT ARE THESE?
EDWARD, YOU HAVE TO SEE THESE—THEY'RE AMAZING...AMBER'S BRILLIANT SKETCHES FOR...
I'LL SEE THEM WHEN I WANT TO!
RIP
I'M THE DIRECTOR. NO ONE CAN MAKE DECISIONS IN MY PLACE.
ESPECIALLY NOT YOU, AMBER!
HEY!

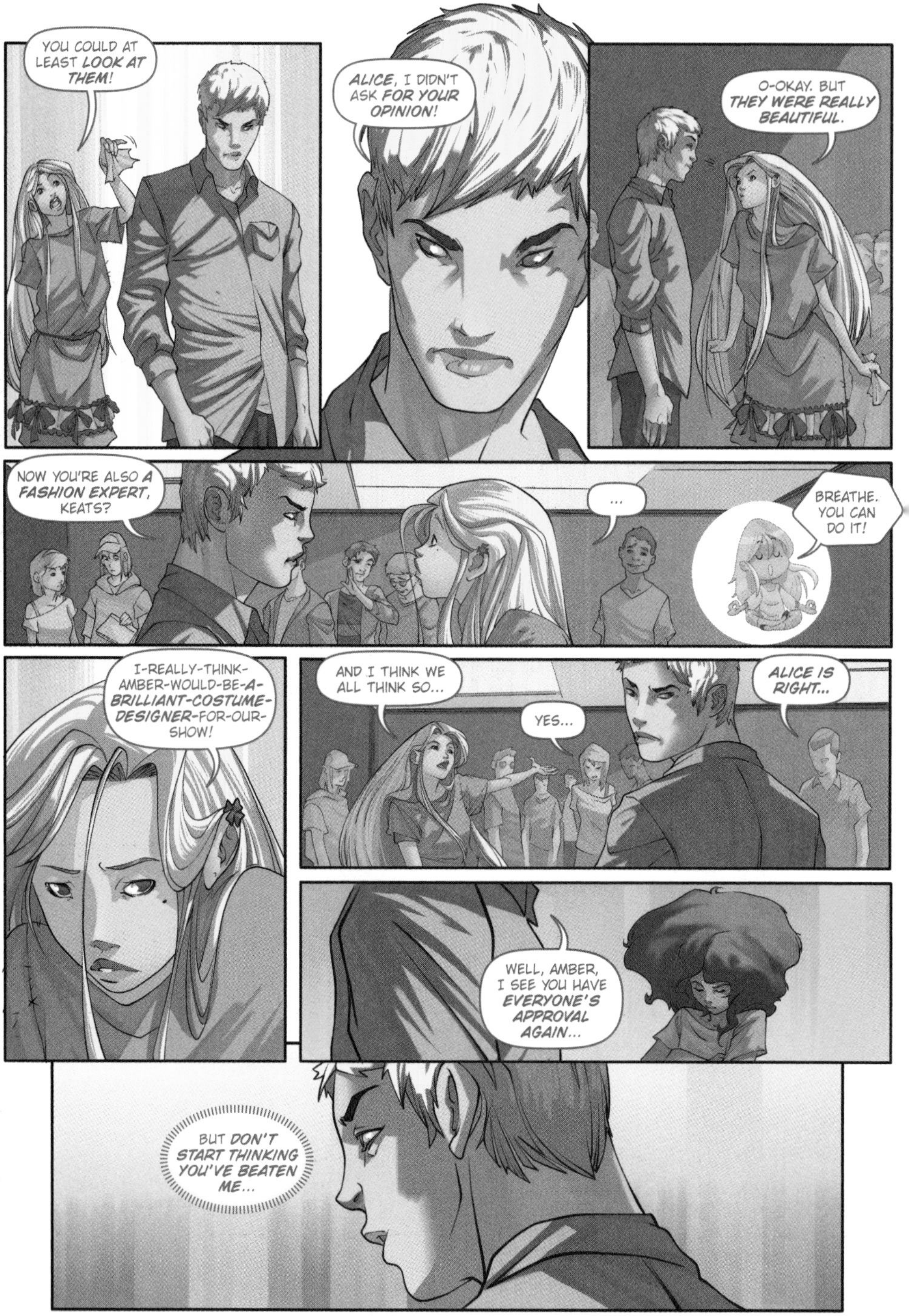
YOU COULD AT LEAST LOOK AT THEM!
ALICE, I DIDN'T ASK FOR YOUR OPINION!
O-OKAY. BUT THEY WERE REALLY BEAUTIFUL.
NOW YOU'RE ALSO A FASHION EXPERT, KEATS?
...
BREATHE. YOU CAN DO IT!
I-REALLY-THINK-AMBER-WOULD-BE-A-BRILLIANT-COSTUME-DESIGNER-FOR-OUR-SHOW!
AND I THINK WE ALL THINK SO...
YES...
ALICE IS RIGHT...
WELL, AMBER, I SEE YOU HAVE EVERYONE'S APPROVAL AGAIN...
BUT DON'T START THINKING YOU'VE BEATEN ME...

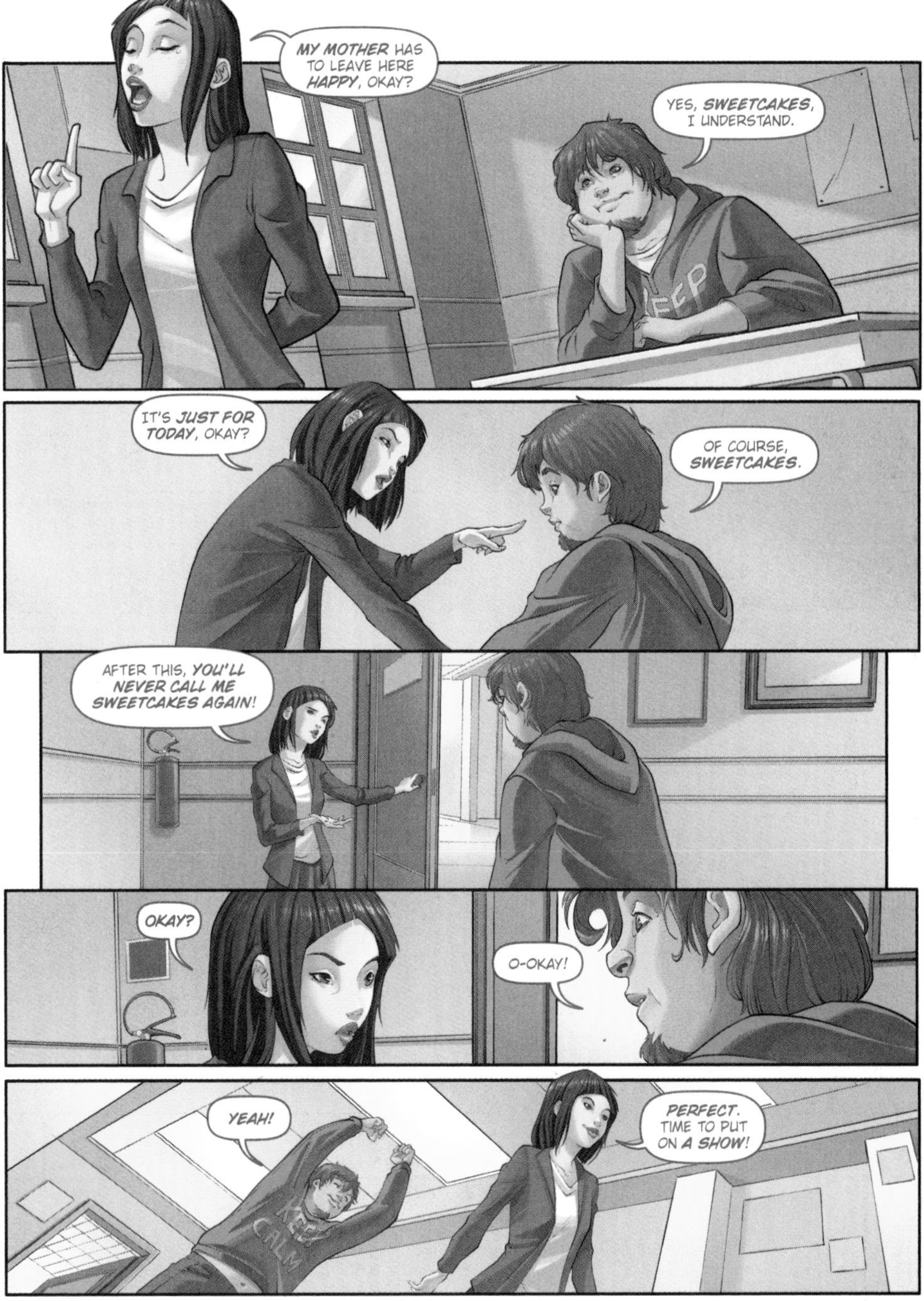
MY MOTHER HAS TO LEAVE HERE HAPPY, OKAY?
YES, SWEETCAKES, I UNDERSTAND.
IT'S JUST FOR TODAY, OKAY?
OF COURSE, SWEETCAKES.
AFTER THIS, YOU'LL NEVER CALL ME SWEETCAKES AGAIN!
OKAY?
O-OKAY!
YEAH!
PERFECT. TIME TO PUT ON A SHOW!

END OF CHAPTER 20

CHAPTER 21

I'll be THERE for YOU

London International High School
Marylebone
11:50 AM

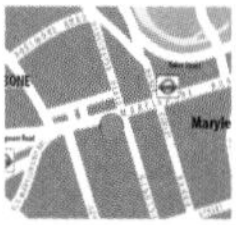

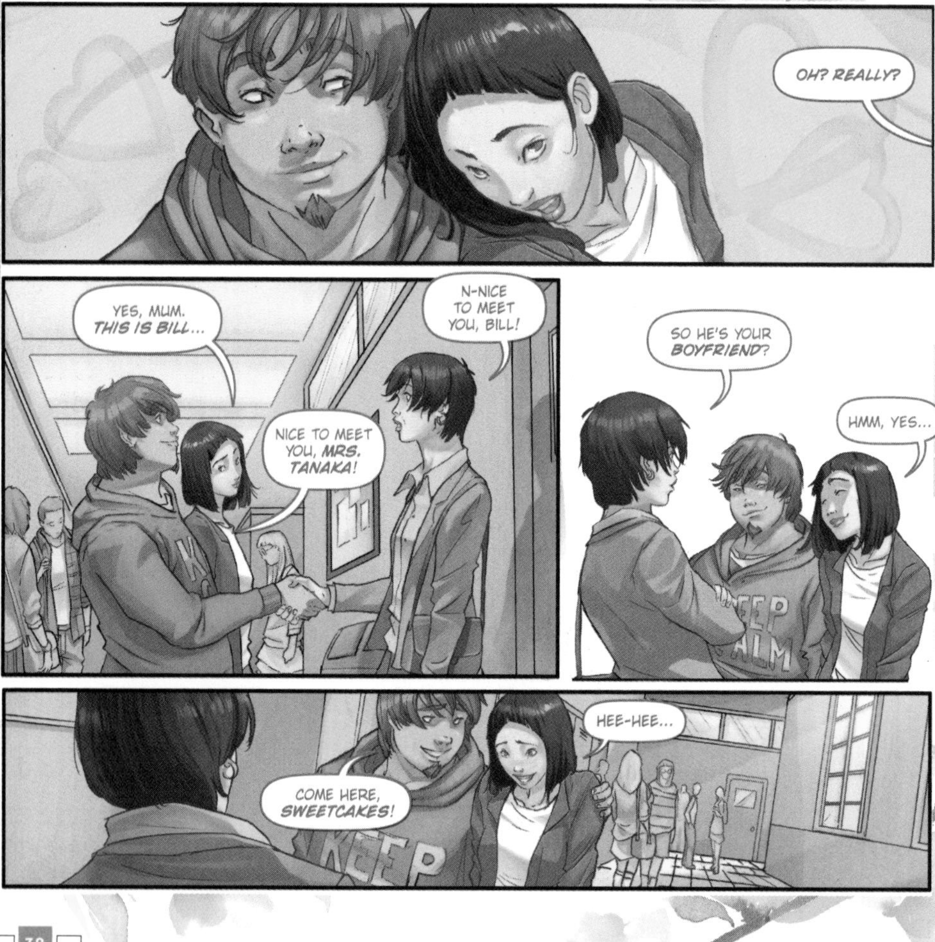
OH? REALLY?
YES, MUM. *THIS IS BILL...*
N-NICE TO MEET YOU, BILL!
NICE TO MEET YOU, *MRS. TANAKA!*
SO HE'S YOUR *BOYFRIEND?*
HMM, YES...
HEE-HEE...
COME HERE, *SWEETCAKES!*
KEEP CALM

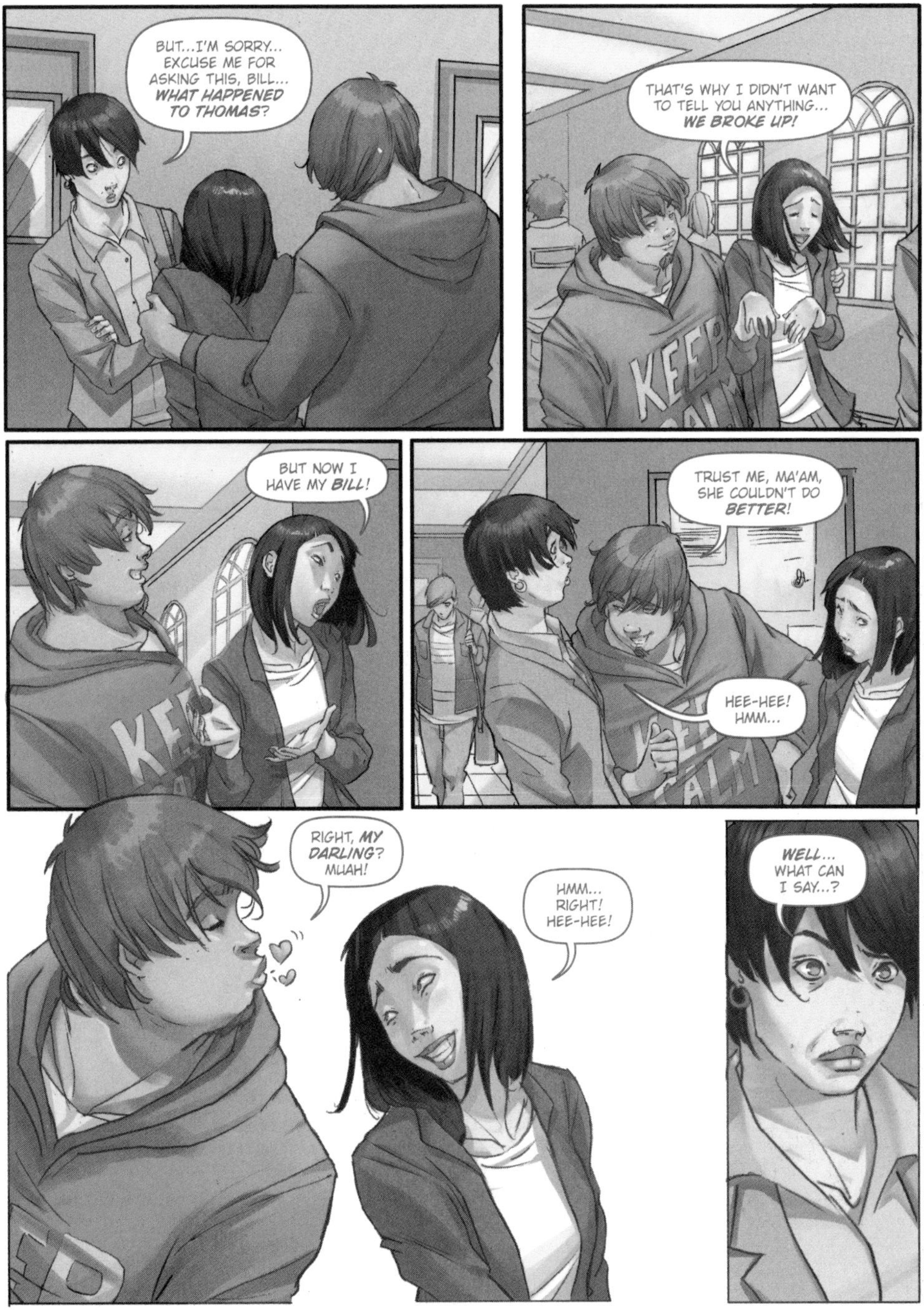
BUT...I'M SORRY... EXCUSE ME FOR ASKING THIS, BILL... *WHAT HAPPENED TO THOMAS*?
THAT'S WHY I DIDN'T WANT TO TELL YOU ANYTHING... *WE BROKE UP!*
KEEP
BUT NOW I HAVE MY *BILL*!
TRUST ME, MA'AM, SHE COULDN'T DO *BETTER*!
HEE-HEE! HMM...
KEEP CALM
RIGHT, *MY DARLING*? MUAH!
HMM... RIGHT! HEE-HEE!
WELL... WHAT CAN I SAY...?

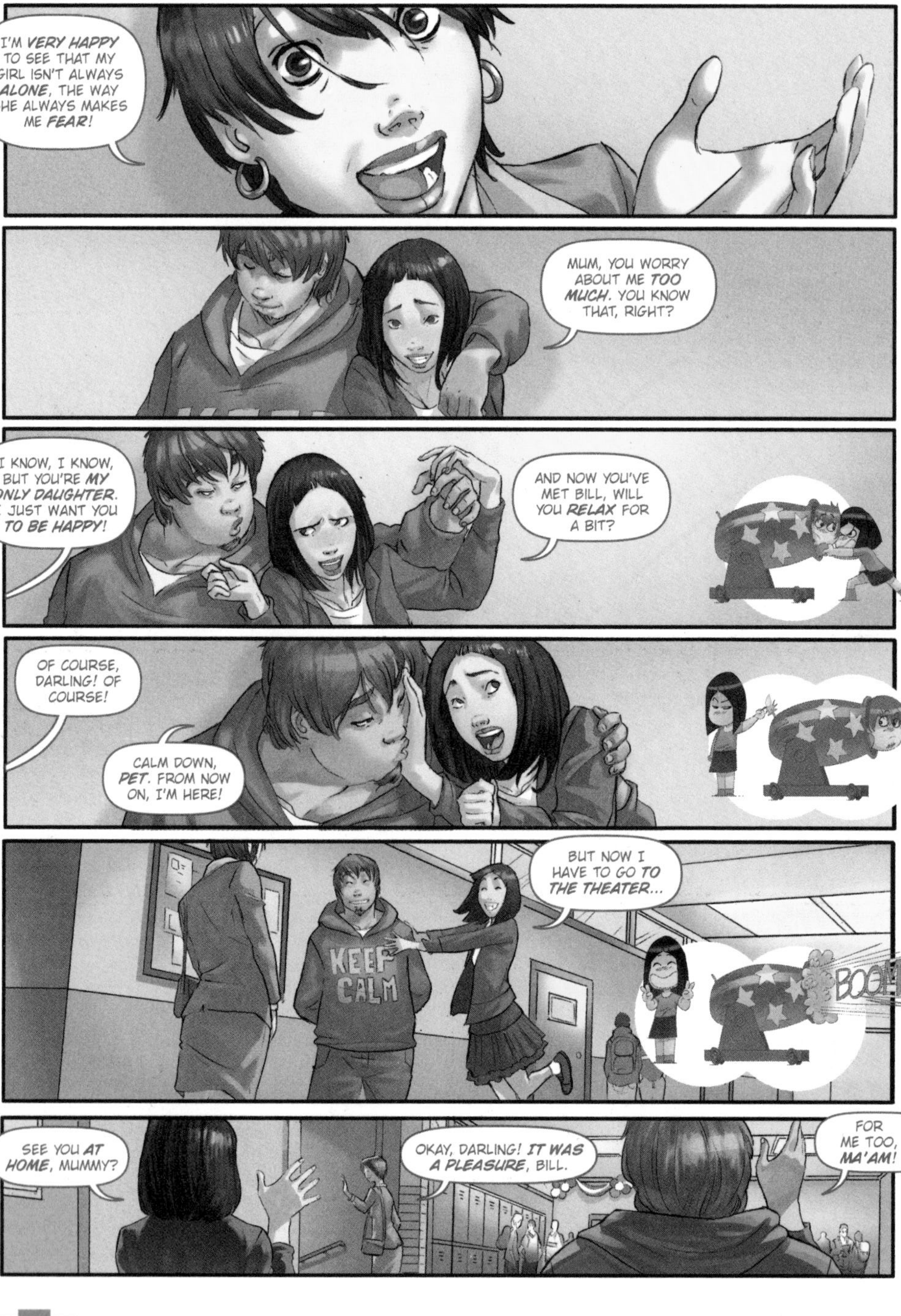
I'M VERY HAPPY TO SEE THAT MY GIRL ISN'T ALWAYS ALONE, THE WAY SHE ALWAYS MAKES ME FEAR!
MUM, YOU WORRY ABOUT ME TOO MUCH. YOU KNOW THAT, RIGHT?
I KNOW, I KNOW, BUT YOU'RE MY ONLY DAUGHTER. I JUST WANT YOU TO BE HAPPY!
AND NOW YOU'VE MET BILL, WILL YOU RELAX FOR A BIT?
OF COURSE, DARLING! OF COURSE!
CALM DOWN, PET. FROM NOW ON, I'M HERE!
BUT NOW I HAVE TO GO TO THE THEATER...
KEEP CALM
BOOM
SEE YOU AT HOME, MUMMY?
OKAY, DARLING! IT WAS A PLEASURE, BILL.
FOR ME TOO, MA'AM!

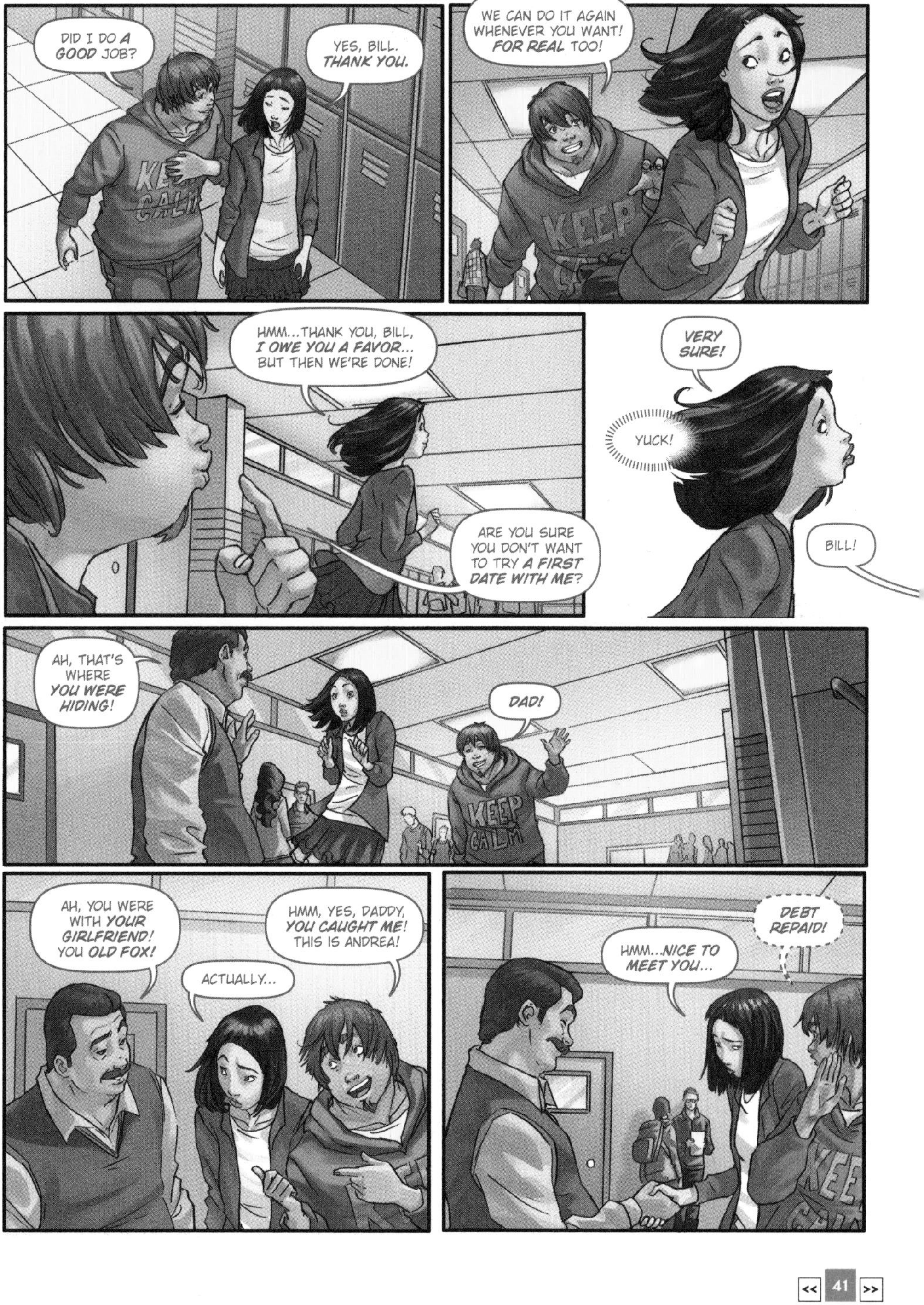
DID I DO A GOOD JOB?
YES, BILL. THANK YOU.
WE CAN DO IT AGAIN WHENEVER YOU WANT! FOR REAL TOO!
KEEP CALM
HMM...THANK YOU, BILL, I OWE YOU A FAVOR... BUT THEN WE'RE DONE!
ARE YOU SURE YOU DON'T WANT TO TRY A FIRST DATE WITH ME?
VERY SURE!
YUCK!
BILL!
AH, THAT'S WHERE YOU WERE HIDING!
DAD!
KEEP CALM
AH, YOU WERE WITH YOUR GIRLFRIEND! YOU OLD FOX!
ACTUALLY...
HMM, YES, DADDY, YOU CAUGHT ME! THIS IS ANDREA!
HMM...NICE TO MEET YOU...
DEBT REPAID!

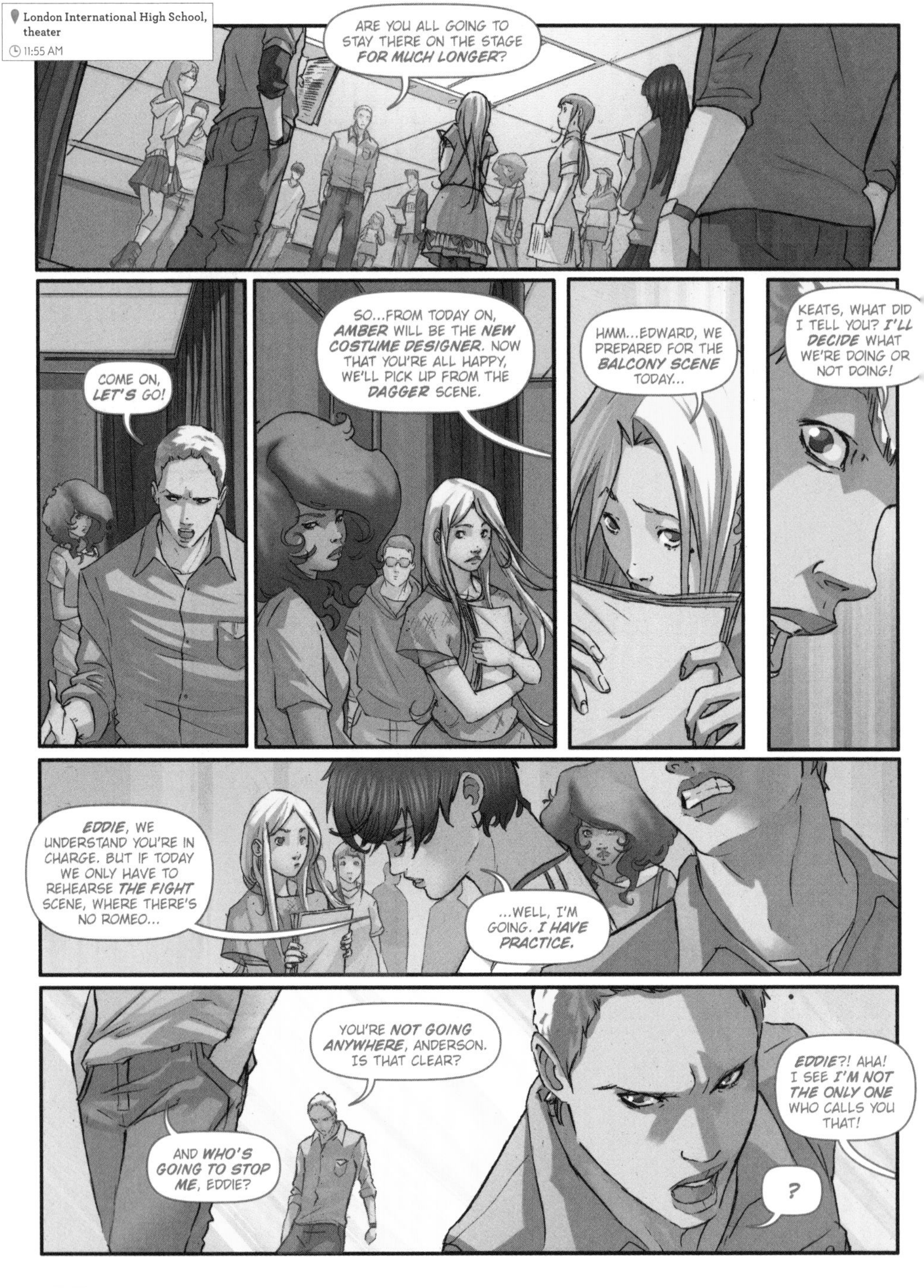
London International High School, theater
11:55 AM
ARE YOU ALL GOING TO STAY THERE ON THE STAGE FOR MUCH LONGER?
COME ON, LET'S GO!
SO...FROM TODAY ON, AMBER WILL BE THE NEW COSTUME DESIGNER. NOW THAT YOU'RE ALL HAPPY, WE'LL PICK UP FROM THE DAGGER SCENE.
HMM...EDWARD, WE PREPARED FOR THE BALCONY SCENE TODAY...
KEATS, WHAT DID I TELL YOU? I'LL DECIDE WHAT WE'RE DOING OR NOT DOING!
EDDIE, WE UNDERSTAND YOU'RE IN CHARGE. BUT IF TODAY WE ONLY HAVE TO REHEARSE THE FIGHT SCENE, WHERE THERE'S NO ROMEO...
...WELL, I'M GOING. I HAVE PRACTICE.
YOU'RE NOT GOING ANYWHERE, ANDERSON. IS THAT CLEAR?
AND WHO'S GOING TO STOP ME, EDDIE?
EDDIE?! AHA! I SEE I'M NOT THE ONLY ONE WHO CALLS YOU THAT!
?

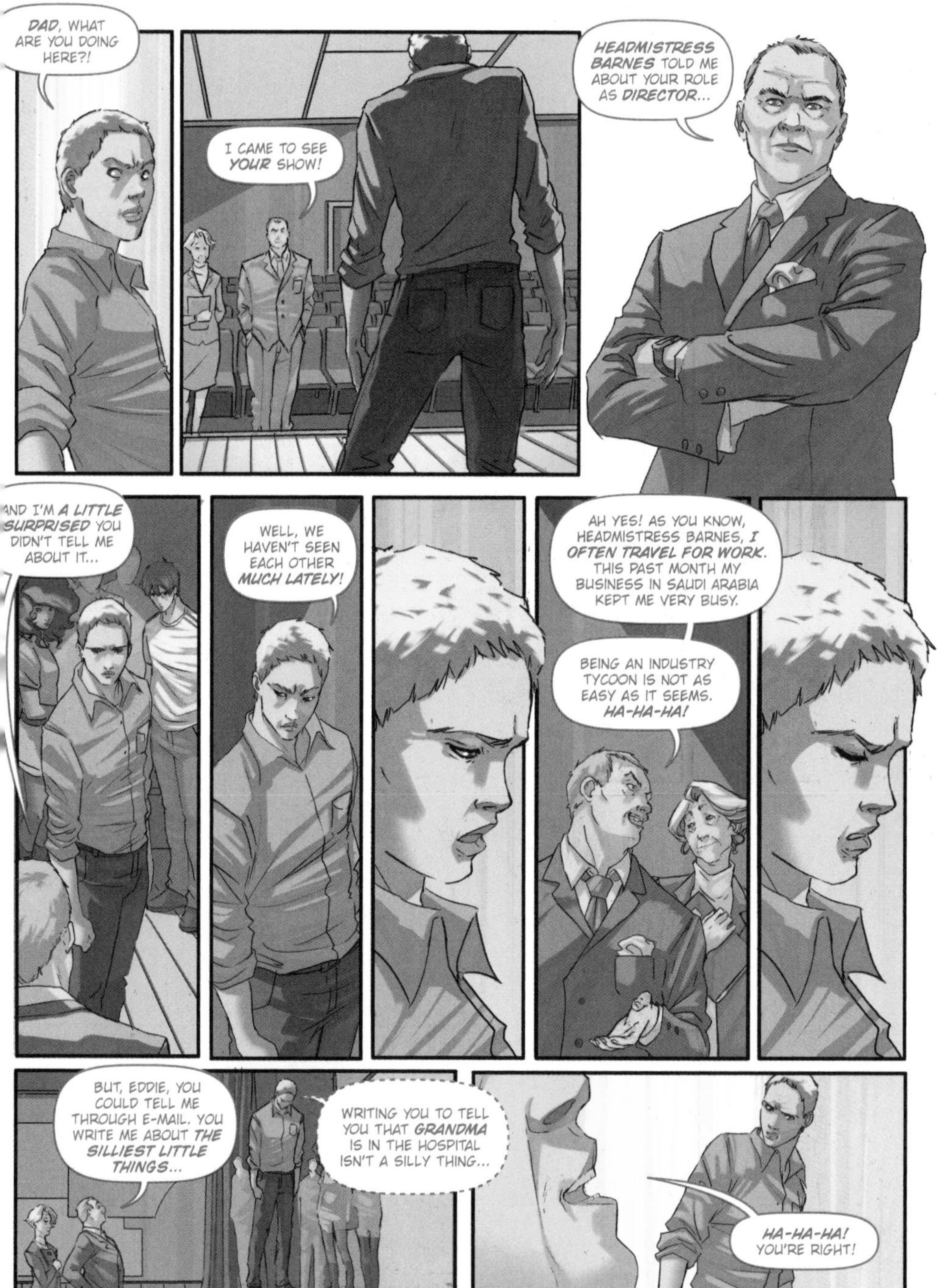
DAD, WHAT ARE YOU DOING HERE?!
I CAME TO SEE YOUR SHOW!
HEADMISTRESS BARNES TOLD ME ABOUT YOUR ROLE AS DIRECTOR...
AND I'M A LITTLE SURPRISED YOU DIDN'T TELL ME ABOUT IT...
WELL, WE HAVEN'T SEEN EACH OTHER MUCH LATELY!
AH YES! AS YOU KNOW, HEADMISTRESS BARNES, I OFTEN TRAVEL FOR WORK. THIS PAST MONTH MY BUSINESS IN SAUDI ARABIA KEPT ME VERY BUSY.
BEING AN INDUSTRY TYCOON IS NOT AS EASY AS IT SEEMS. HA-HA-HA!
BUT, EDDIE, YOU COULD TELL ME THROUGH E-MAIL. YOU WRITE ME ABOUT THE SILLIEST LITTLE THINGS...
WRITING YOU TO TELL YOU THAT GRANDMA IS IN THE HOSPITAL ISN'T A SILLY THING...
HA-HA-HA! YOU'RE RIGHT!

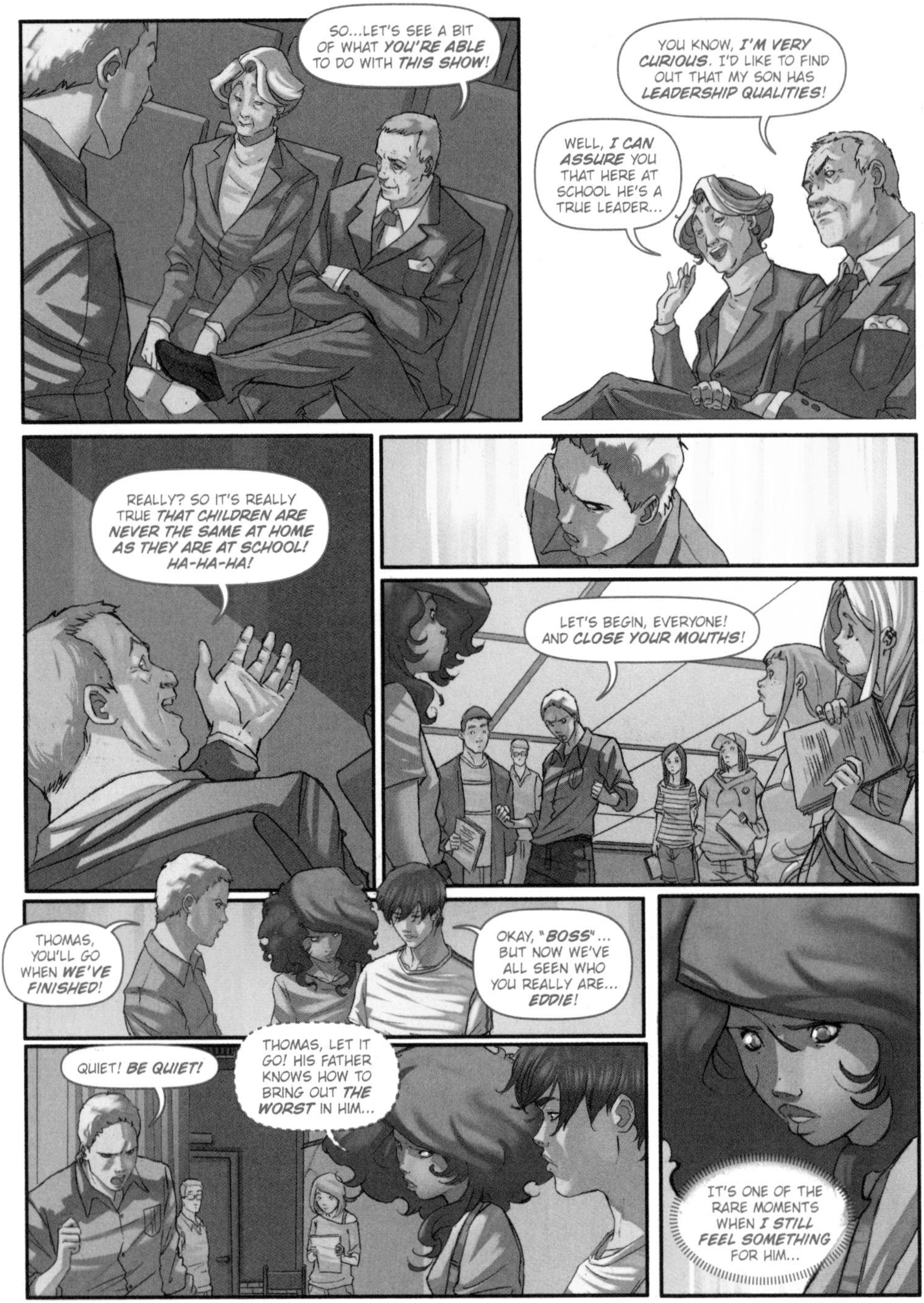

SO...LET'S SEE A BIT OF WHAT YOU'RE ABLE TO DO WITH THIS SHOW!
YOU KNOW, I'M VERY CURIOUS. I'D LIKE TO FIND OUT THAT MY SON HAS LEADERSHIP QUALITIES!
WELL, I CAN ASSURE YOU THAT HERE AT SCHOOL HE'S A TRUE LEADER...
REALLY? SO IT'S REALLY TRUE THAT CHILDREN ARE NEVER THE SAME AT HOME AS THEY ARE AT SCHOOL! HA-HA-HA!
LET'S BEGIN, EVERYONE! AND CLOSE YOUR MOUTHS!
THOMAS, YOU'LL GO WHEN WE'VE FINISHED!
OKAY, "BOSS"... BUT NOW WE'VE ALL SEEN WHO YOU REALLY ARE... EDDIE!
QUIET! BE QUIET!
THOMAS, LET IT GO! HIS FATHER KNOWS HOW TO BRING OUT THE WORST IN HIM...
IT'S ONE OF THE RARE MOMENTS WHEN I STILL FEEL SOMETHING FOR HIM...

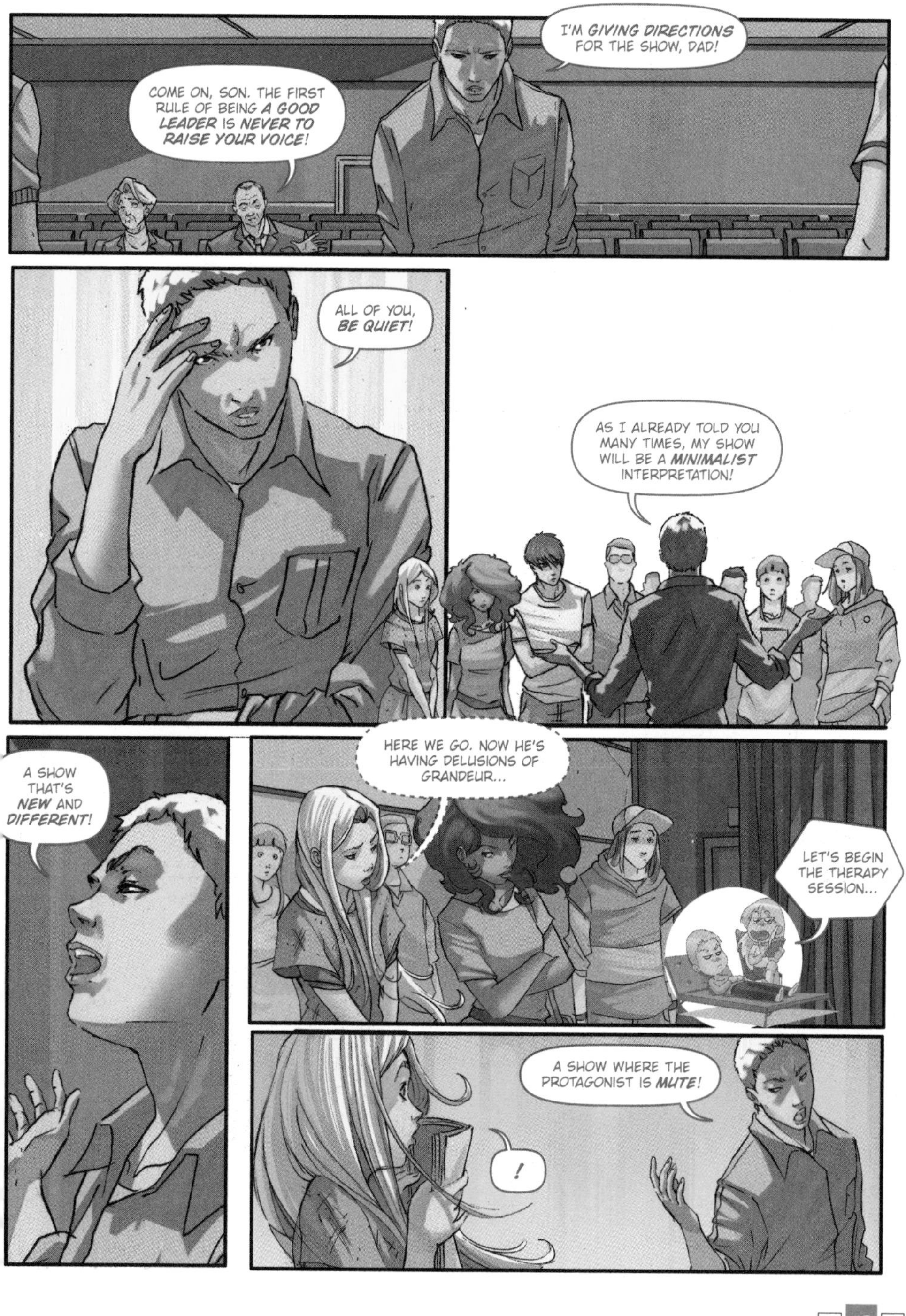
I'M GIVING DIRECTIONS FOR THE SHOW, DAD!
COME ON, SON. THE FIRST RULE OF BEING A GOOD LEADER IS NEVER TO RAISE YOUR VOICE!
ALL OF YOU, BE QUIET!
AS I ALREADY TOLD YOU MANY TIMES, MY SHOW WILL BE A MINIMALIST INTERPRETATION!
A SHOW THAT'S NEW AND DIFFERENT!
HERE WE GO. NOW HE'S HAVING DELUSIONS OF GRANDEUR...
LET'S BEGIN THE THERAPY SESSION...
A SHOW WHERE THE PROTAGONIST IS MUTE!
!

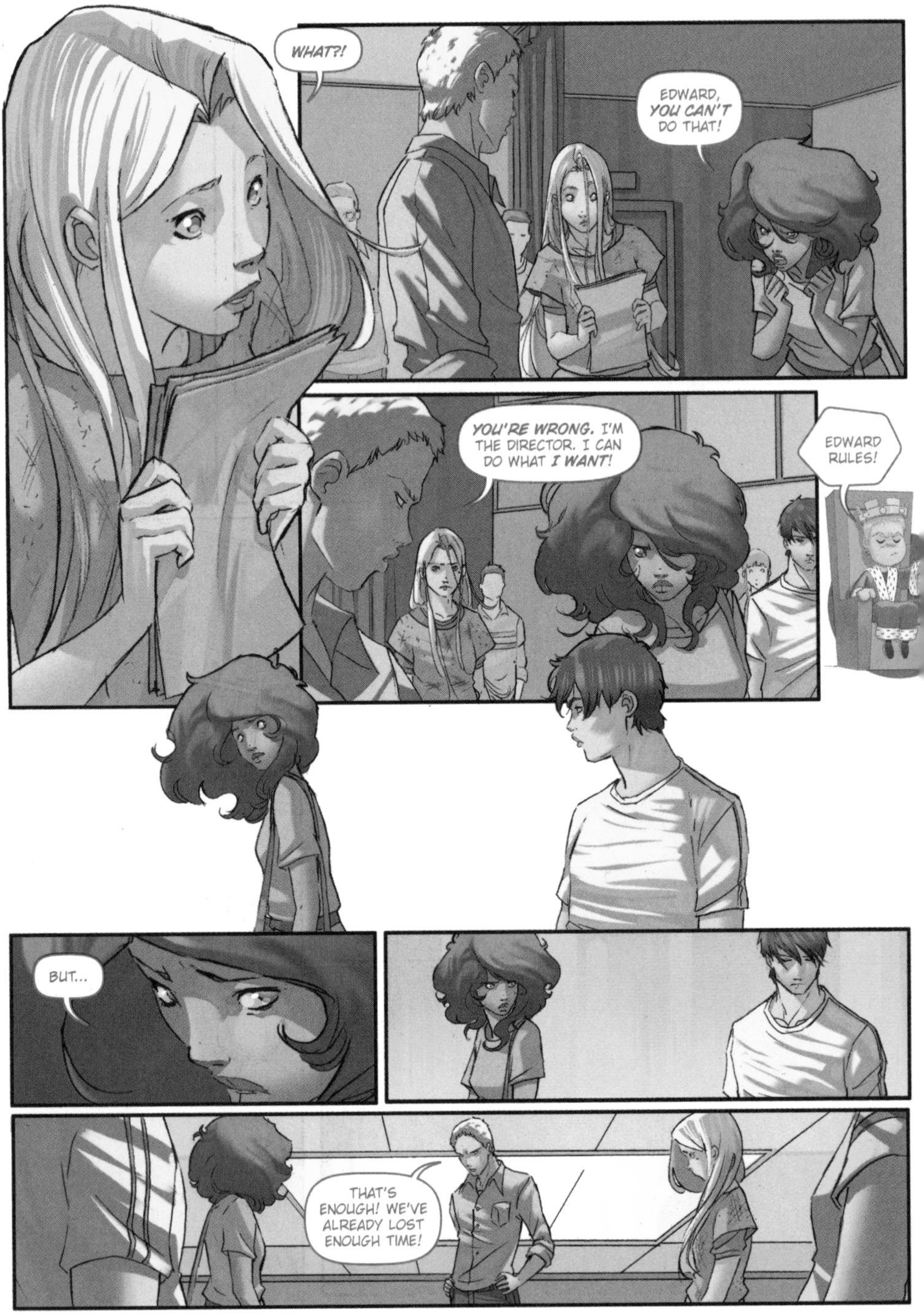
WHAT?!
EDWARD, YOU CAN'T DO THAT!
YOU'RE WRONG. I'M THE DIRECTOR. I CAN DO WHAT I WANT!
EDWARD RULES!
BUT...
THAT'S ENOUGH! WE'VE ALREADY LOST ENOUGH TIME!

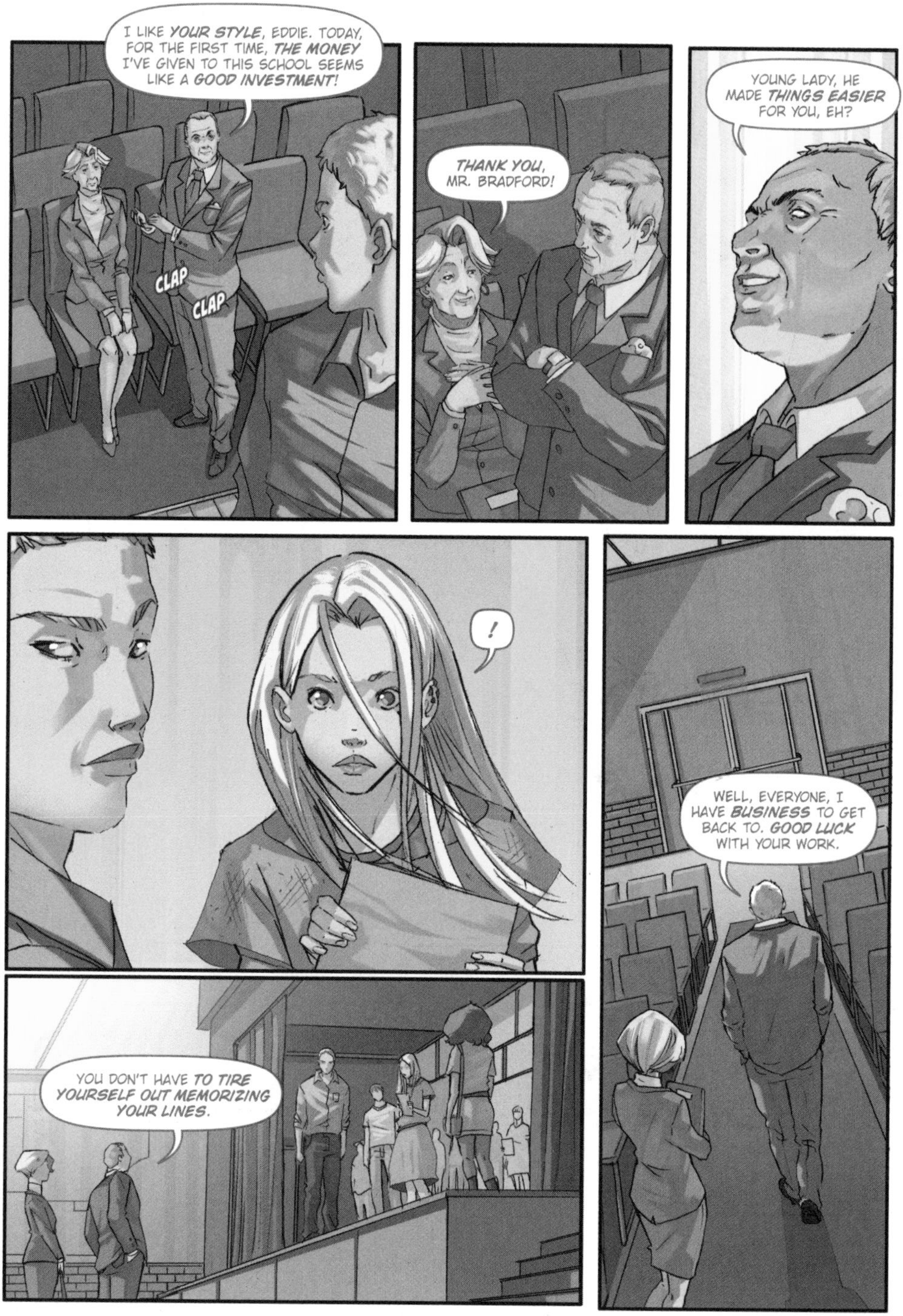
I LIKE YOUR STYLE, EDDIE. TODAY, FOR THE FIRST TIME, THE MONEY I'VE GIVEN TO THIS SCHOOL SEEMS LIKE A GOOD INVESTMENT!
CLAP
CLAP
THANK YOU, MR. BRADFORD!
YOUNG LADY, HE MADE THINGS EASIER FOR YOU, EH?
!
YOU DON'T HAVE TO TIRE YOURSELF OUT MEMORIZING YOUR LINES.
WELL, EVERYONE, I HAVE BUSINESS TO GET BACK TO. GOOD LUCK WITH YOUR WORK.

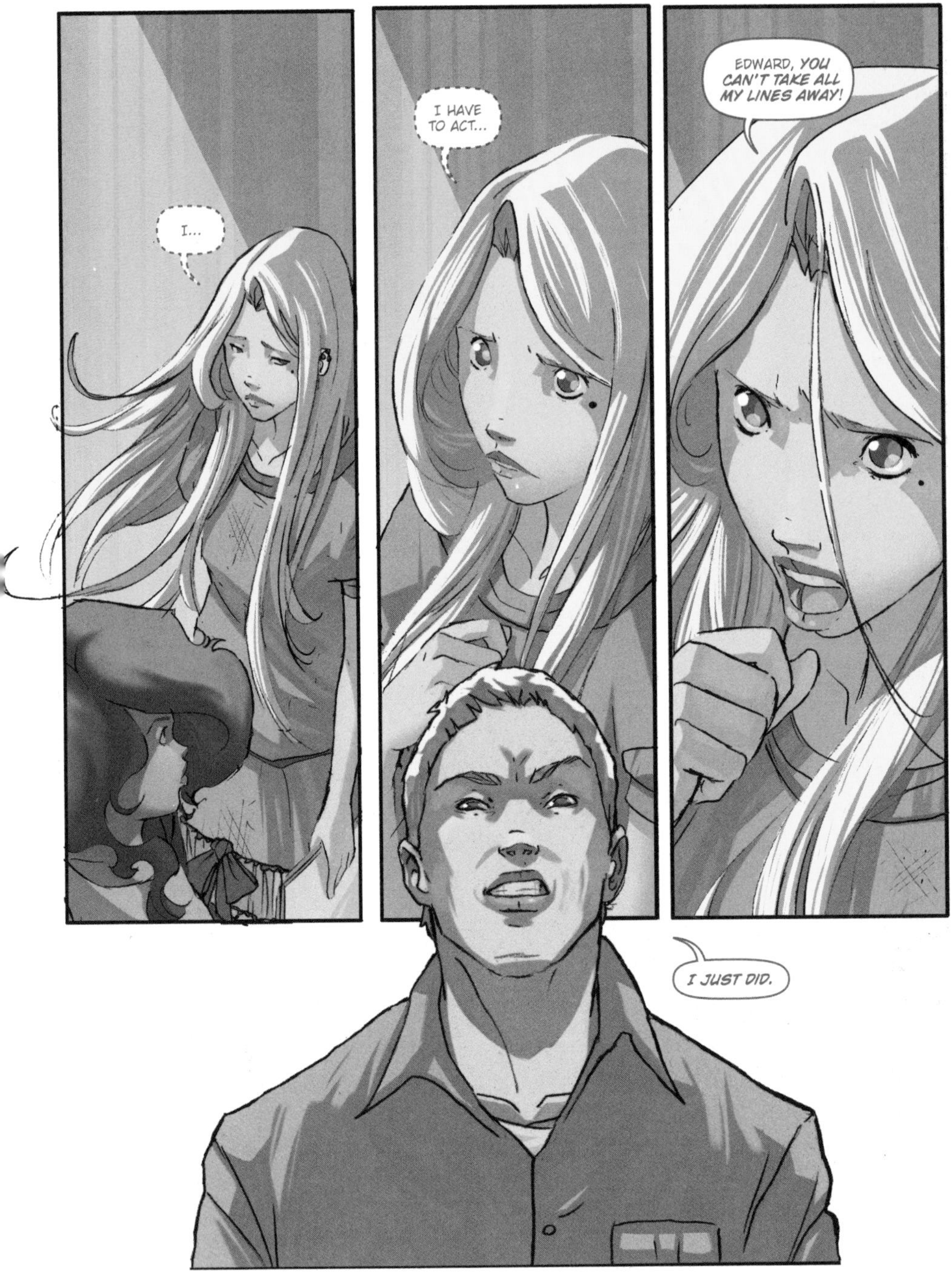
I...
I HAVE TO ACT...
EDWARD, YOU CAN'T TAKE ALL MY LINES AWAY!
I JUST DID.

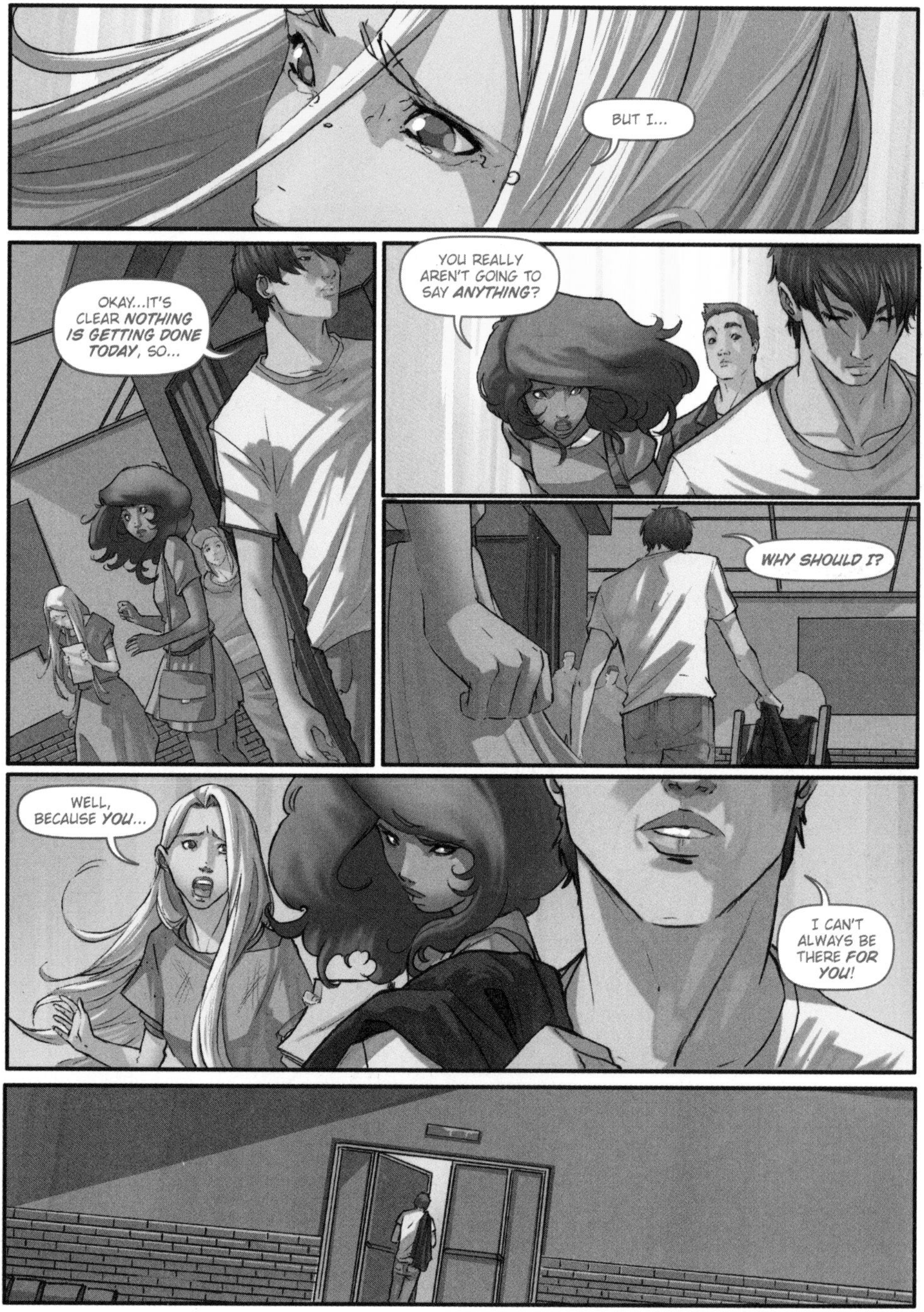
BUT I...
OKAY...IT'S CLEAR NOTHING IS GETTING DONE TODAY, SO...
YOU REALLY AREN'T GOING TO SAY ANYTHING?
WHY SHOULD I?
WELL, BECAUSE YOU...
I CAN'T ALWAYS BE THERE FOR YOU!

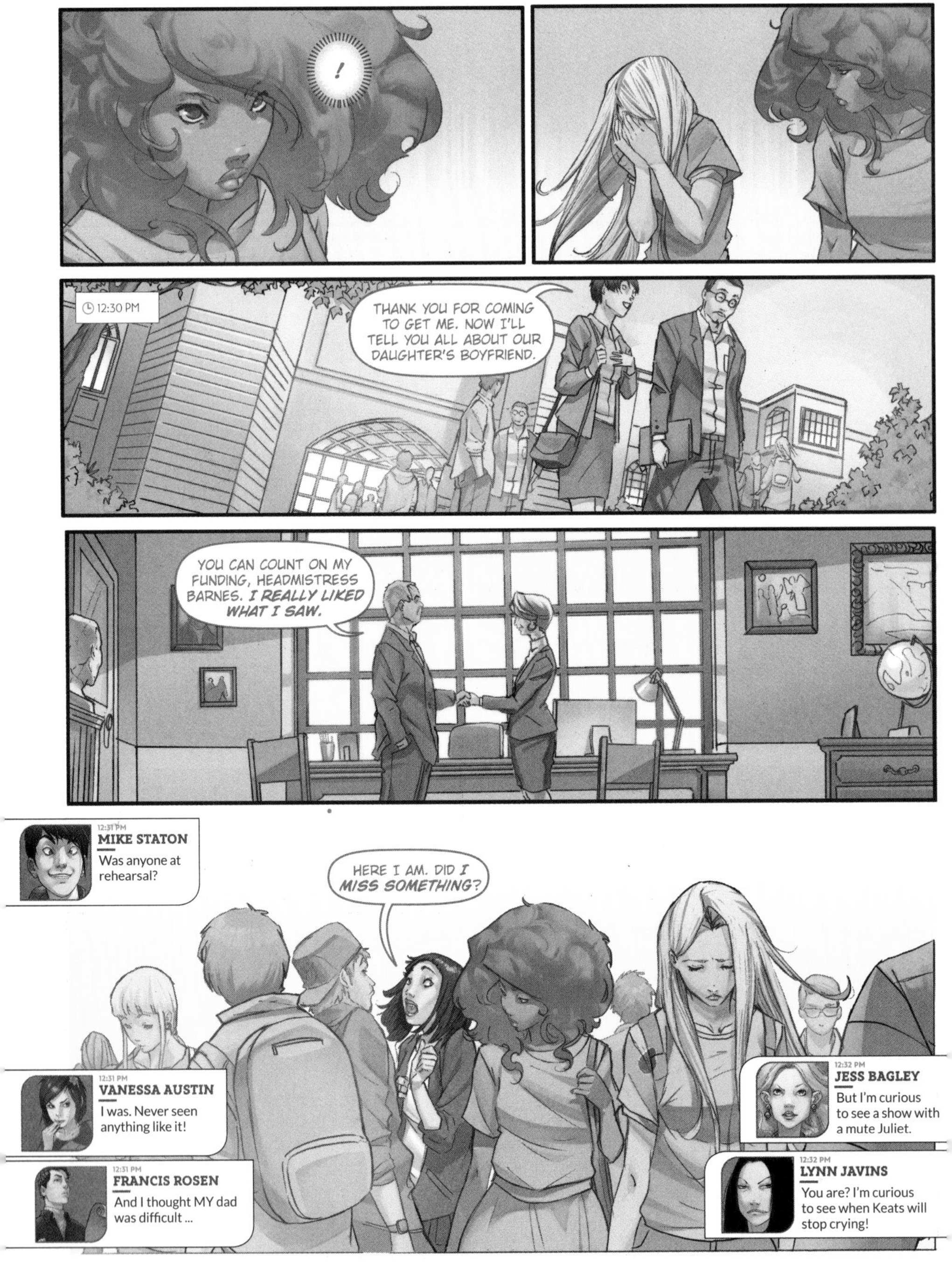
!
12:30 PM
THANK YOU FOR COMING TO GET ME. NOW I'LL TELL YOU ALL ABOUT OUR DAUGHTER'S BOYFRIEND.
YOU CAN COUNT ON MY FUNDING, HEADMISTRESS BARNES. *I REALLY LIKED WHAT I SAW.*
12:31 PM
MIKE STATON
Was anyone at rehearsal?
HERE I AM. DID *I MISS SOMETHING*?
12:31 PM
VANESSA AUSTIN
I was. Never seen anything like it!
12:31 PM
FRANCIS ROSEN
And I thought MY dad was difficult ...
12:32 PM
JESS BAGLEY
But I'm curious to see a show with a mute Juliet.
12:32 PM
LYNN JAVINS
You are? I'm curious to see when Keats will stop crying!

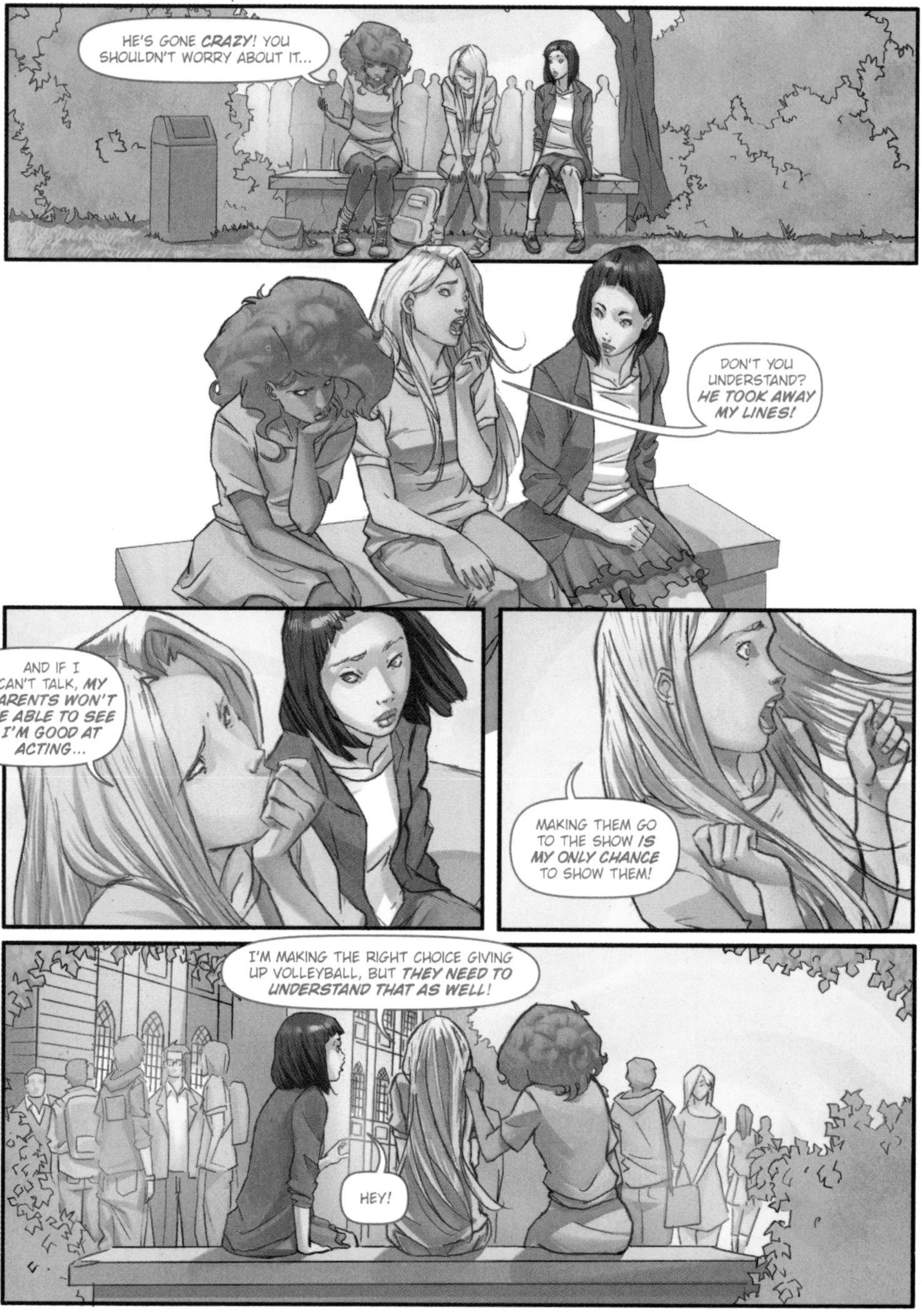
HE'S GONE **CRAZY**! YOU SHOULDN'T WORRY ABOUT IT...
DON'T YOU UNDERSTAND? **HE TOOK AWAY MY LINES!**
AND IF I CAN'T TALK, **MY PARENTS WON'T BE ABLE TO SEE I'M GOOD AT ACTING...**
MAKING THEM GO TO THE SHOW **IS MY ONLY CHANCE** TO SHOW THEM!
I'M MAKING THE RIGHT CHOICE GIVING UP VOLLEYBALL, BUT **THEY NEED TO UNDERSTAND THAT AS WELL**!
HEY!

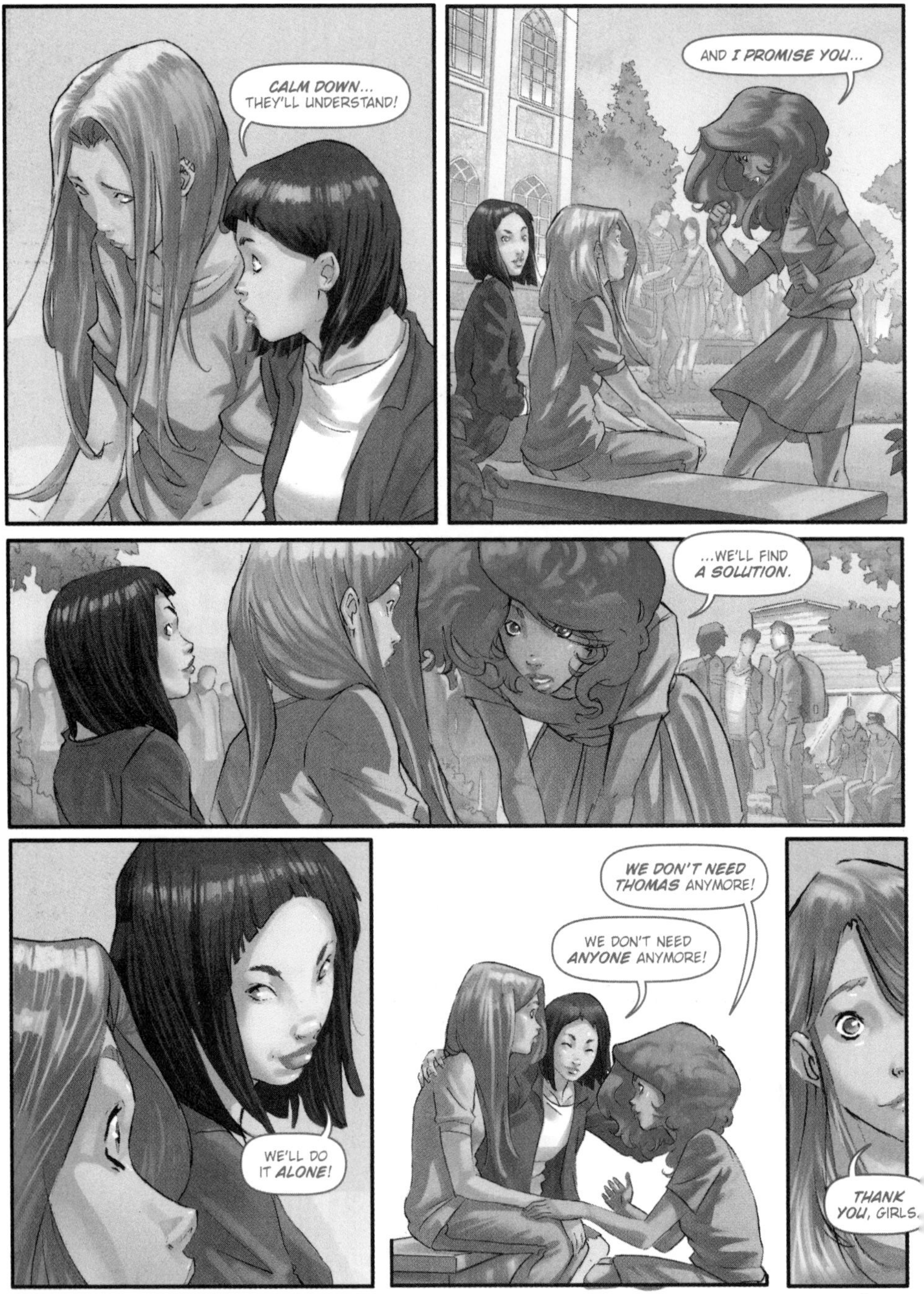
CALM DOWN... THEY'LL UNDERSTAND!
AND I PROMISE YOU...
...WE'LL FIND A SOLUTION.
WE'LL DO IT ALONE!
WE DON'T NEED THOMAS ANYMORE!
WE DON'T NEED ANYONE ANYMORE!
THANK YOU, GIRLS.

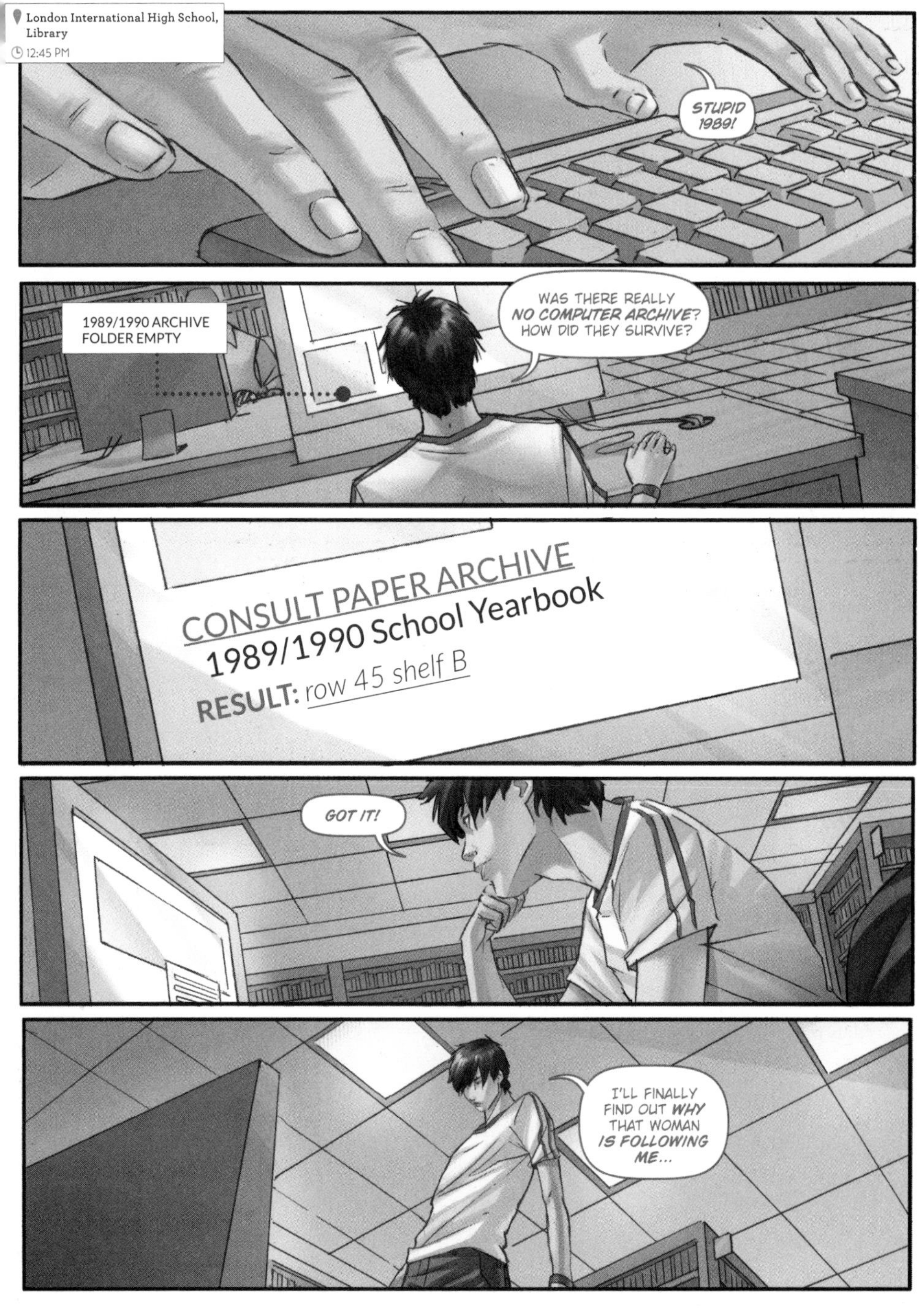
London International High School, Library
12:45 PM
STUPID 1989!
1989/1990 ARCHIVE FOLDER EMPTY
WAS THERE REALLY NO COMPUTER ARCHIVE? HOW DID THEY SURVIVE?
CONSULT PAPER ARCHIVE
1989/1990 School Yearbook
RESULT: row 45 shelf B
GOT IT!
I'LL FINALLY FIND OUT WHY THAT WOMAN IS FOLLOWING ME...

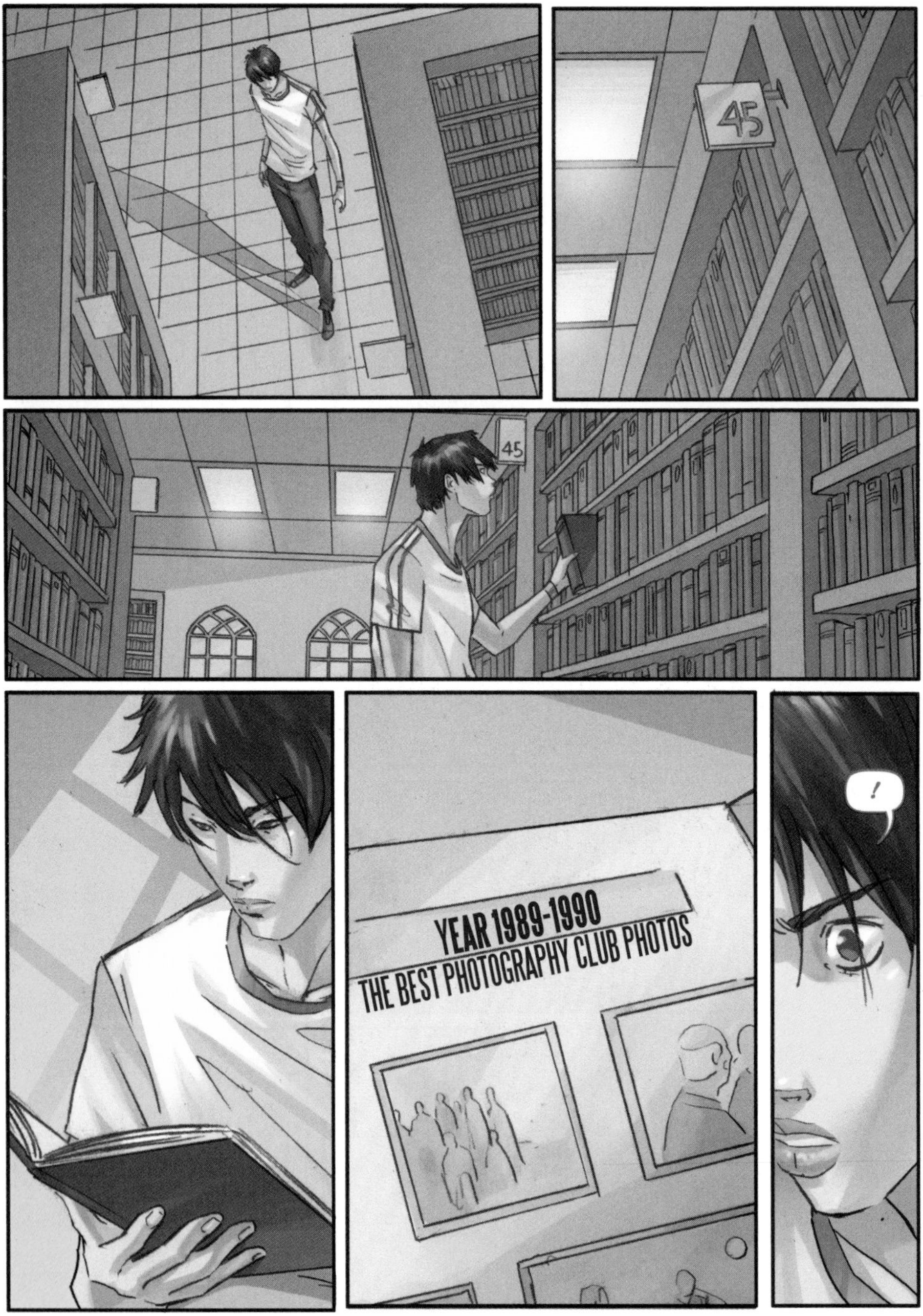
45
45
YEAR 1989-1990
THE BEST PHOTOGRAPHY CLUB PHOTOS
!

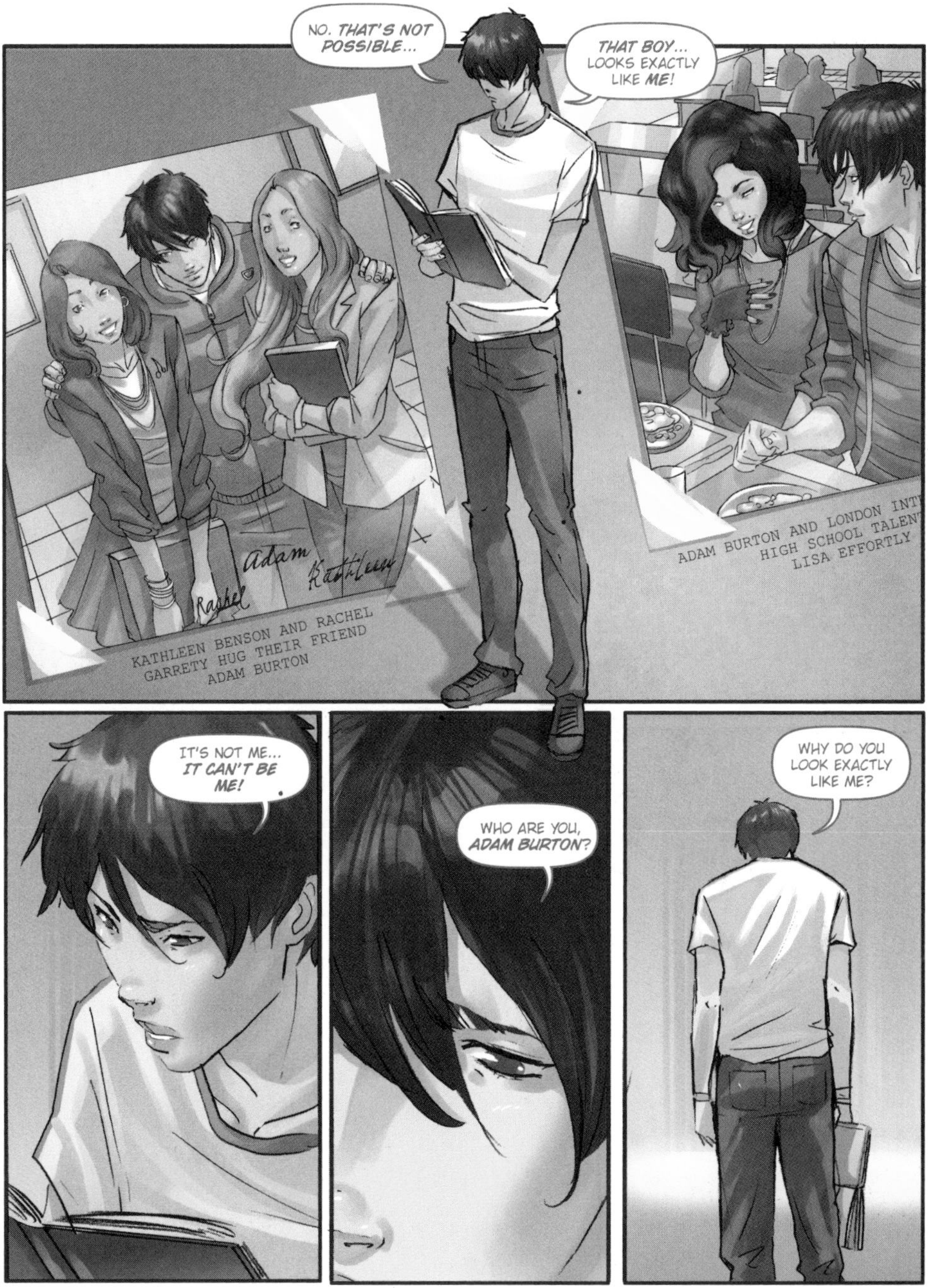
NO. THAT'S NOT POSSIBLE...
THAT BOY... LOOKS EXACTLY LIKE ME!
Adam
Kathleen
Rachel
KATHLEEN BENSON AND RACHEL GARRETY HUG THEIR FRIEND ADAM BURTON
ADAM BURTON AND LONDON
HIGH SCHOOL
LISA
IT'S NOT ME... IT CAN'T BE ME!
WHO ARE YOU, ADAM BURTON?
WHY DO YOU LOOK EXACTLY LIKE ME?

END OF CHAPTER 21

Disney
real life #7

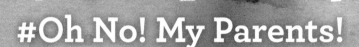

#Oh No! My Parents!

Plot: Alessandro Ferrari
Script: Silvia Gianatti
Layout: Simone Buonfantino, Alberto Zanon
Cleanup: Simone Buonfantino, Alberto Zanon
Emotidolls: Andrea Scoppetta
Color: Massimo Rocca, Pierluigi Casolino, Andrea Scoppetta, Mario Perrotta, Slava Panarin, Giuseppe Fontana, Gianluca Barone, Andrea Cagol
Watercolor backgrounds: Valeria Turati
Translation: Edizioni BD and Erin Brady
Lettering and Infographic: Edizioni BD

COVER
Layout and cleanup: Marco Ghiglione, Simone Buonfantino
Color: Massimo Rocca

CONTRIBUTORS
Tomatofarm

Original project developed by Disney Publishing with the contribution of Barbara Baraldi, Paola Barbato, Micol Beltramini and Diana Tomatozombie

#8

#RockSpeare

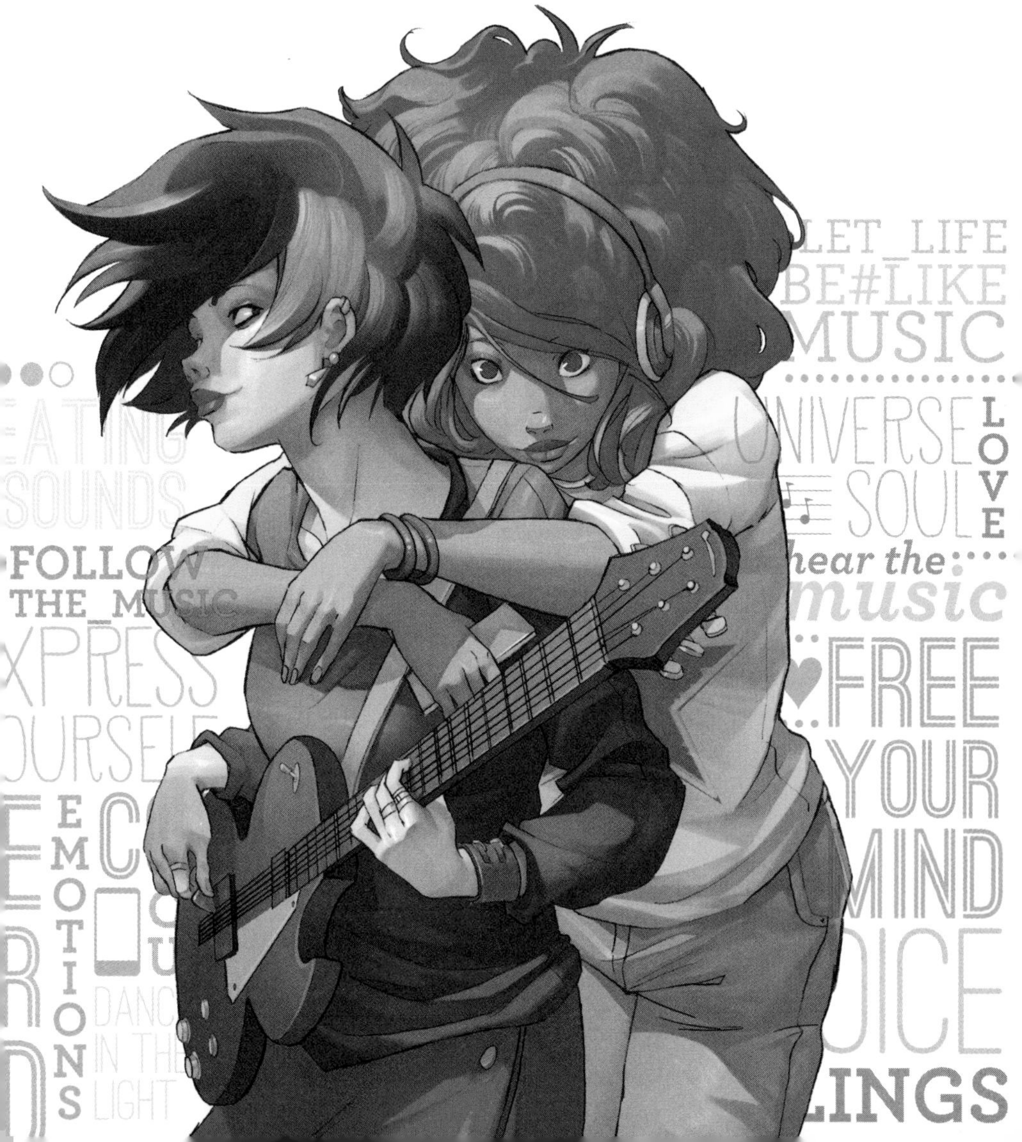
LET_LIFE BE#LIKE MUSIC
UNIVERSE
SOUL
LOVE
SOUNDS
FOLLOW THE_MUSIC
hear the music
FREE YOUR MIND
EMOTIONS
IN THE LIGHT

CHAPTER 22

a BRAVE PLAN

Ivy's Atelier
Bank
08:45 AM

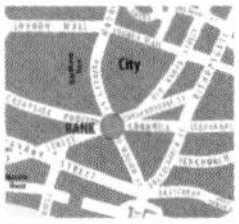

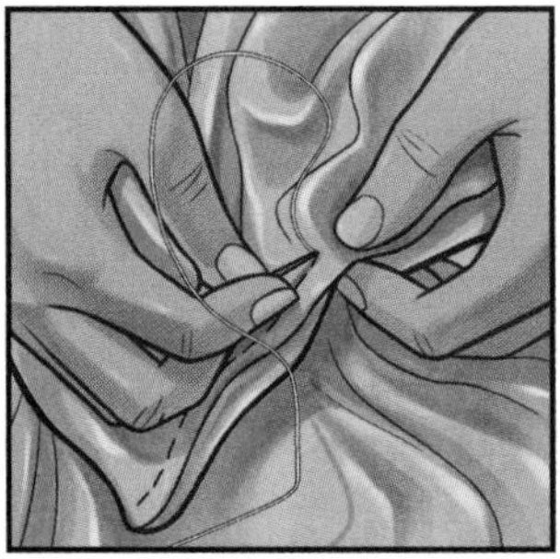

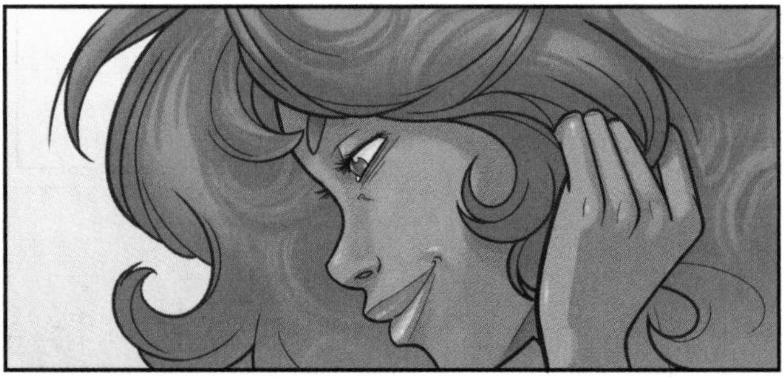

08:46 AM
AMBER LEE THOMPSON
Do not disturb. I'm working!

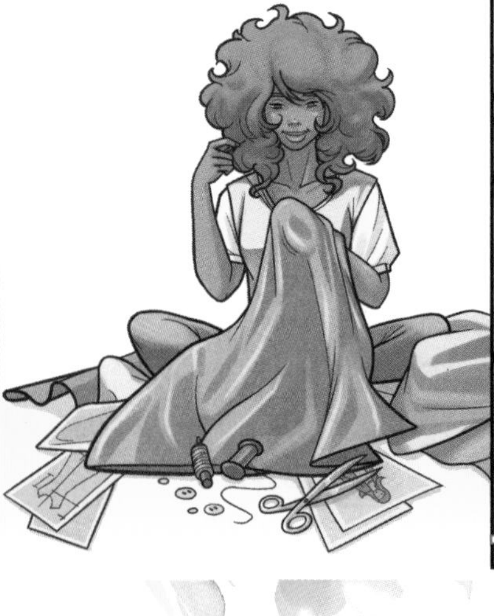

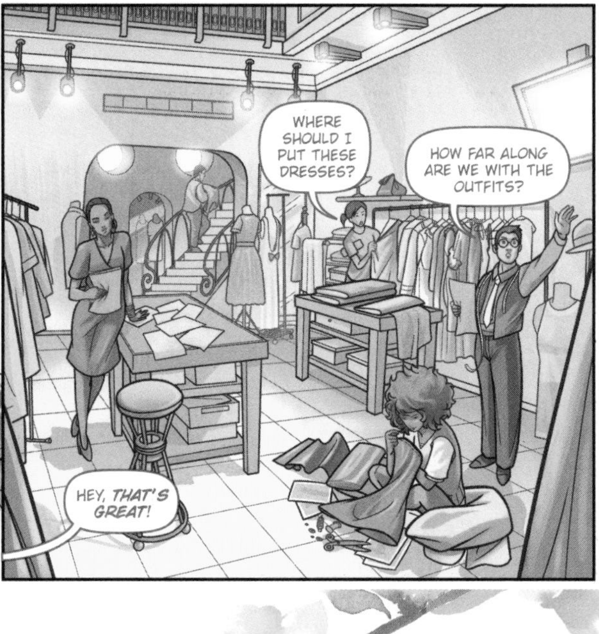
WHERE SHOULD I PUT THESE DRESSES?
HOW FAR ALONG ARE WE WITH THE OUTFITS?
HEY, THAT'S GREAT!

I DIDN'T KNOW YOU KNEW *HOW TO SEW*...

OH, YES. I LEARNED WHEN I WAS LITTLE, WITH MUM...

SHE MUST BE *VERY PROUD* OF YOU...

I DON'T KNOW...ANYWAY, I'M JUST GLAD SHE SAID I COULD STAY HERE SEWING DRESSES FOR THE *SCHOOL SHOW!*

ARE YOU THE *COSTUME DESIGNER?*

WELL, LET'S SAY SO...I JUST HAVE TO CONVINCE THE DIRECTOR! HEE-HEE!

A *WONDERFUL* COSTUME DESIGNER!

YOU MUST BE JOKING. I'LL NEVER PUT THAT ON!

IT'LL *RUIN MY IMAGE!* I REFUSE TO MODEL LIKE THIS!

IS THIS ONE OF YOUR DESIGNS, MUM?

NO, IT'S A SKETCH FROM THE CLIENT...*I HAD TO* MAKE IT.

BUT DON'T WORRY. WE'LL DO WHAT I DID WITH THE *GREEN ELEPHANT!*

WHAT?

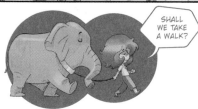

SHALL WE TAKE A WALK?

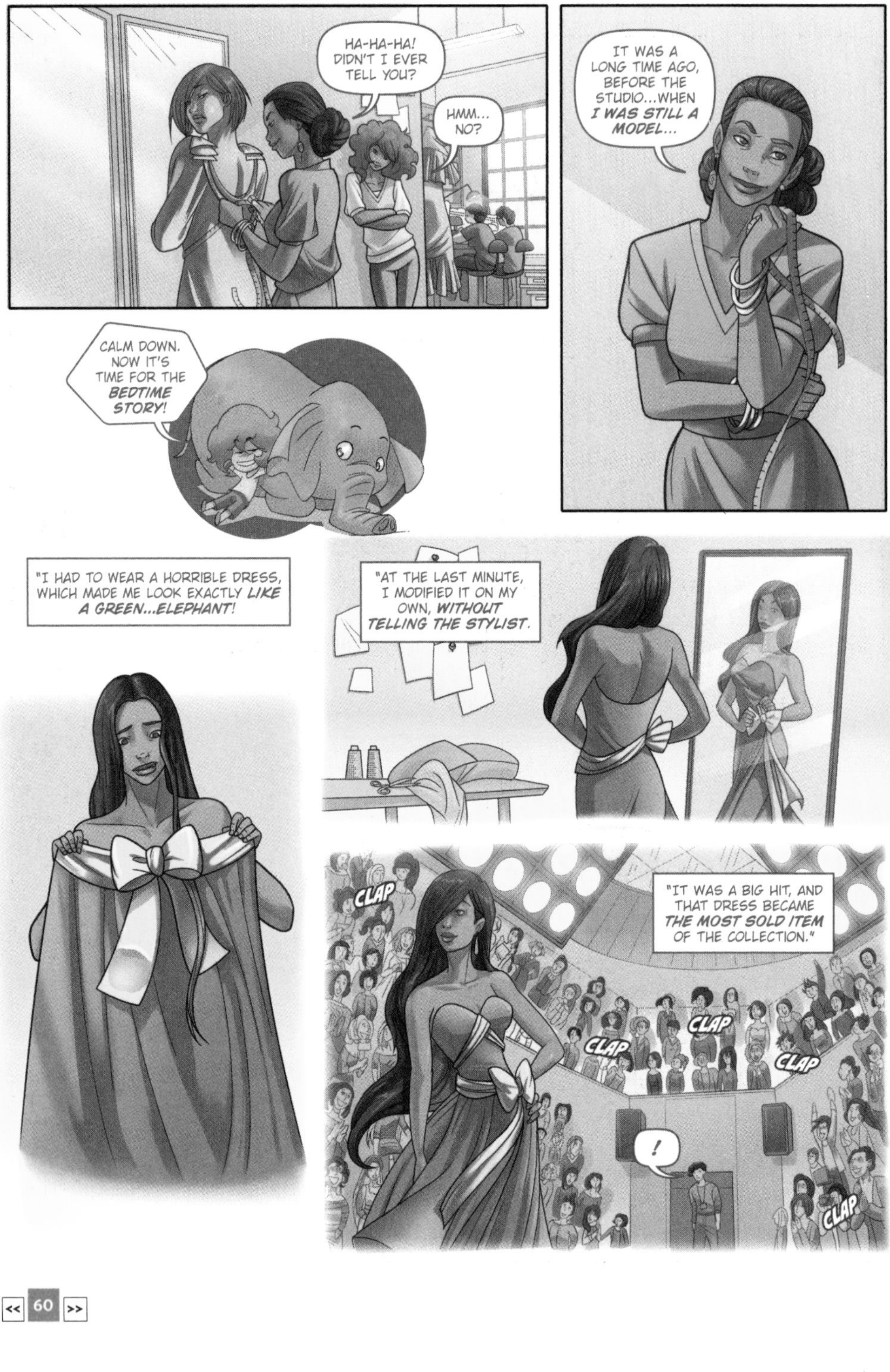
HA-HA-HA! DIDN'T I EVER TELL YOU?
HMM... NO?
IT WAS A LONG TIME AGO, BEFORE THE STUDIO...WHEN I WAS STILL A MODEL...
CALM DOWN. NOW IT'S TIME FOR THE BEDTIME STORY!
"I HAD TO WEAR A HORRIBLE DRESS, WHICH MADE ME LOOK EXACTLY LIKE A GREEN...ELEPHANT!
"AT THE LAST MINUTE, I MODIFIED IT ON MY OWN, WITHOUT TELLING THE STYLIST.
CLAP
"IT WAS A BIG HIT, AND THAT DRESS BECAME THE MOST SOLD ITEM OF THE COLLECTION."
CLAP
CLAP
CLAP
!
CLAP

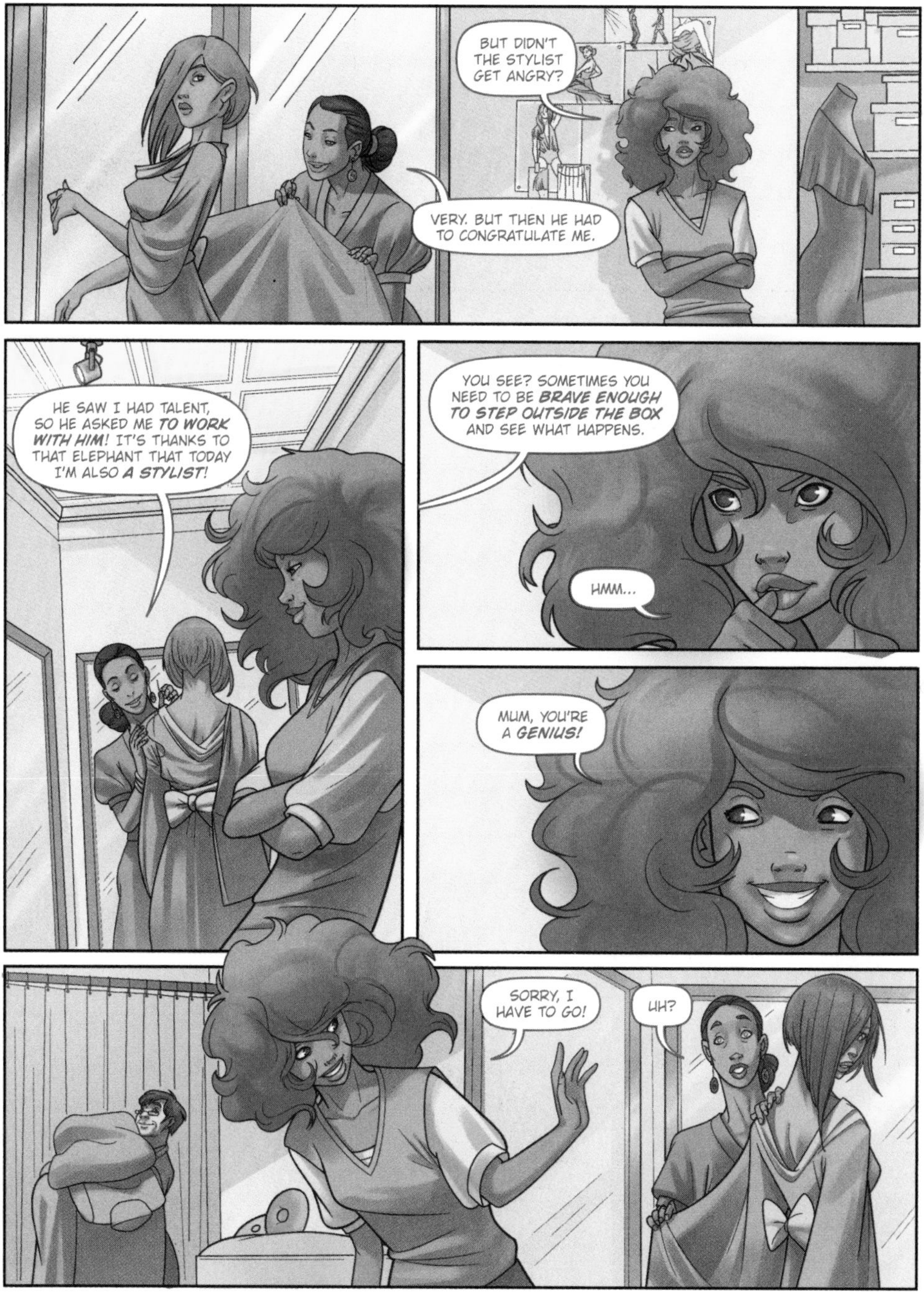
BUT DIDN'T THE STYLIST GET ANGRY?
VERY. BUT THEN HE HAD TO CONGRATULATE ME.
HE SAW I HAD TALENT, SO HE ASKED ME **TO WORK WITH HIM!** IT'S THANKS TO THAT ELEPHANT THAT TODAY I'M ALSO **A STYLIST!**
YOU SEE? SOMETIMES YOU NEED TO BE **BRAVE ENOUGH TO STEP OUTSIDE THE BOX** AND SEE WHAT HAPPENS.
HMM...
MUM, YOU'RE A **GENIUS!**
SORRY, I HAVE TO GO!
UH?

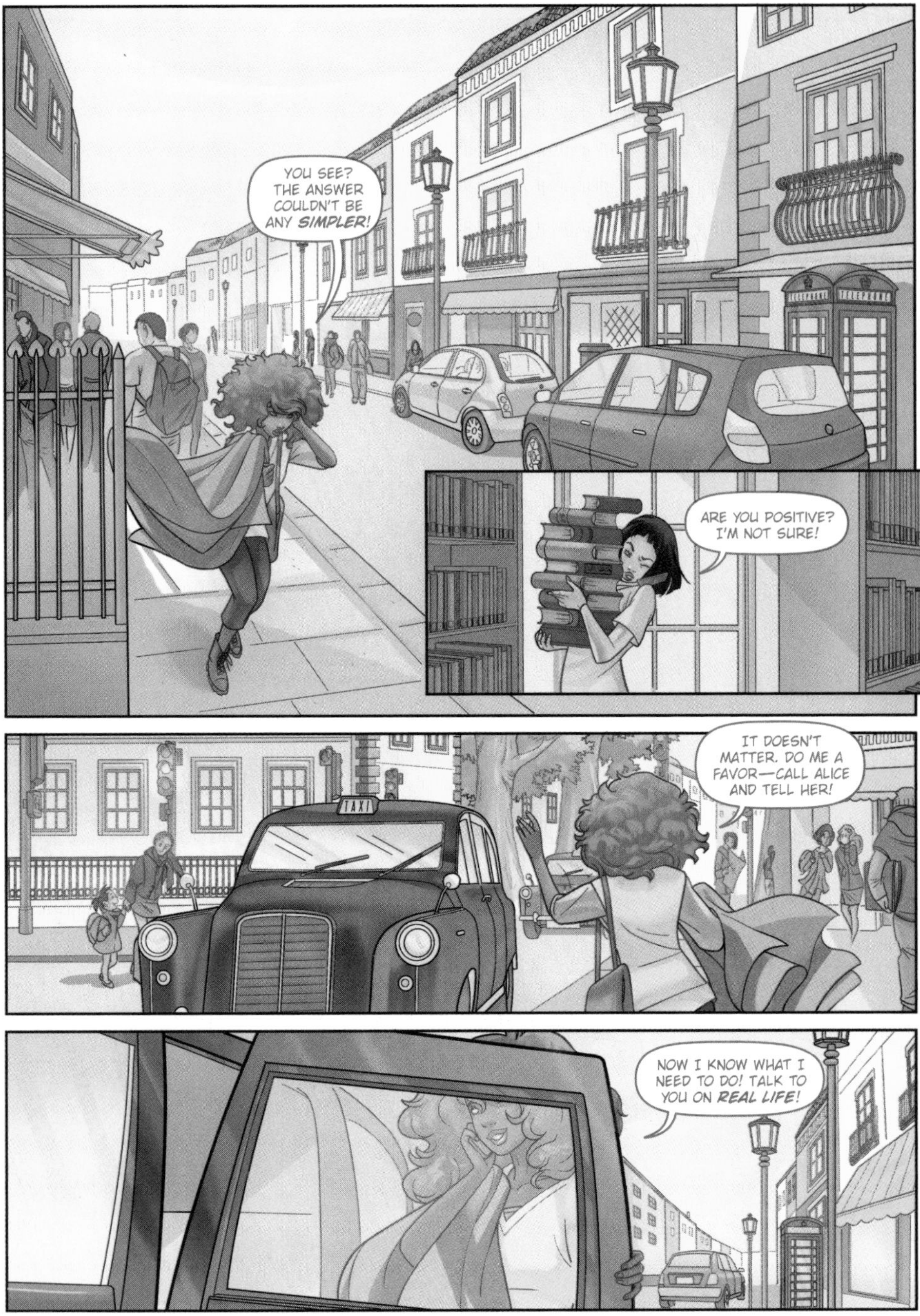
YOU SEE? THE ANSWER COULDN'T BE ANY SIMPLER!
ARE YOU POSITIVE? I'M NOT SURE!
TAXI
IT DOESN'T MATTER. DO ME A FAVOR—CALL ALICE AND TELL HER!
NOW I KNOW WHAT I NEED TO DO! TALK TO YOU ON REAL LIFE!

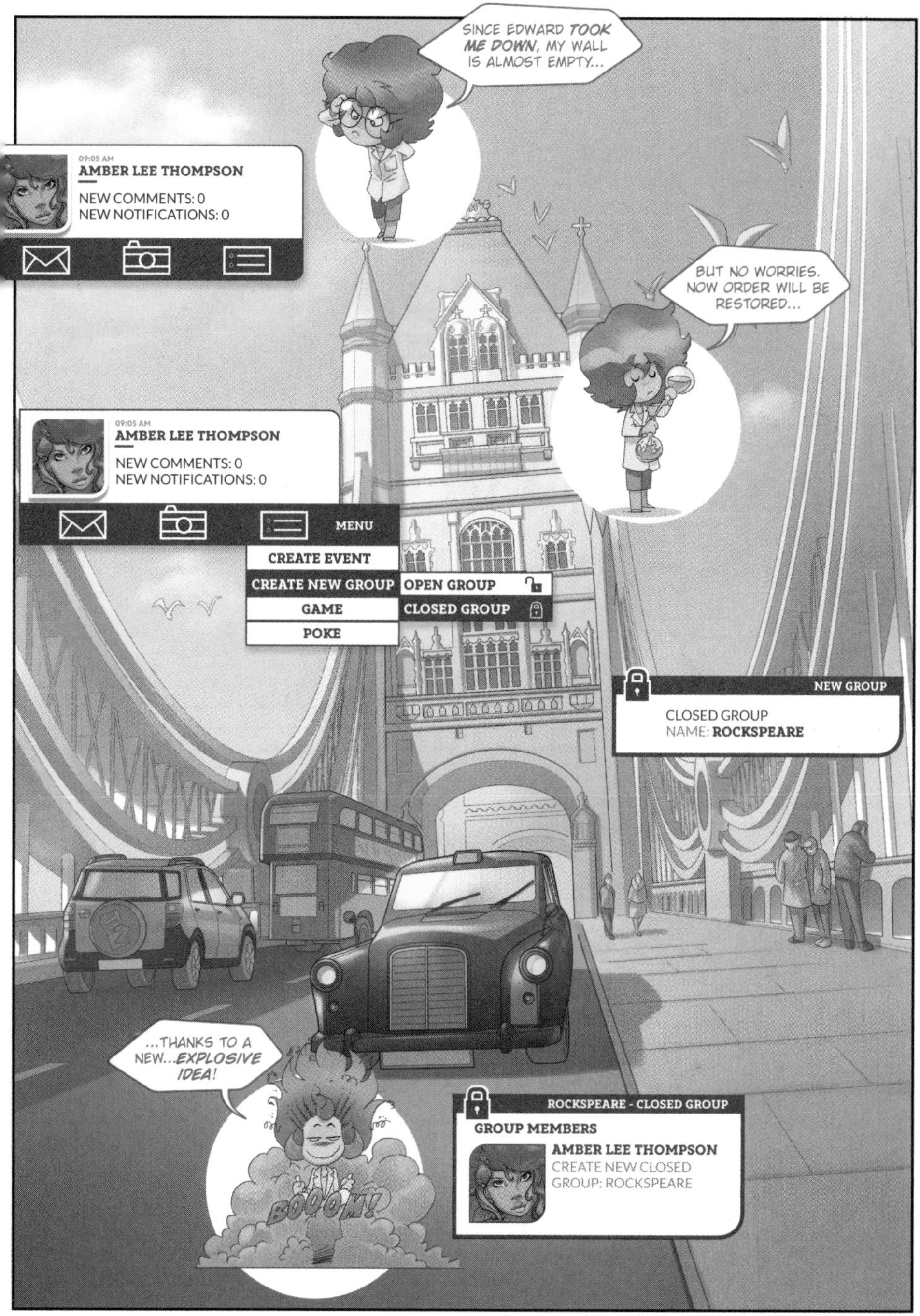

SINCE EDWARD *TOOK ME DOWN*, MY WALL IS ALMOST EMPTY...
09:05 AM
AMBER LEE THOMPSON
NEW COMMENTS: 0
NEW NOTIFICATIONS: 0
BUT NO WORRIES. NOW ORDER WILL BE RESTORED...
09:05 AM
AMBER LEE THOMPSON
NEW COMMENTS: 0
NEW NOTIFICATIONS: 0
MENU
CREATE EVENT
CREATE NEW GROUP
OPEN GROUP
CLOSED GROUP
GAME
POKE
NEW GROUP
CLOSED GROUP
NAME: **ROCKSPEARE**
...THANKS TO A NEW...*EXPLOSIVE IDEA!*
BOOOM!
ROCKSPEARE - CLOSED GROUP
GROUP MEMBERS
AMBER LEE THOMPSON
CREATE NEW CLOSED GROUP: ROCKSPEARE

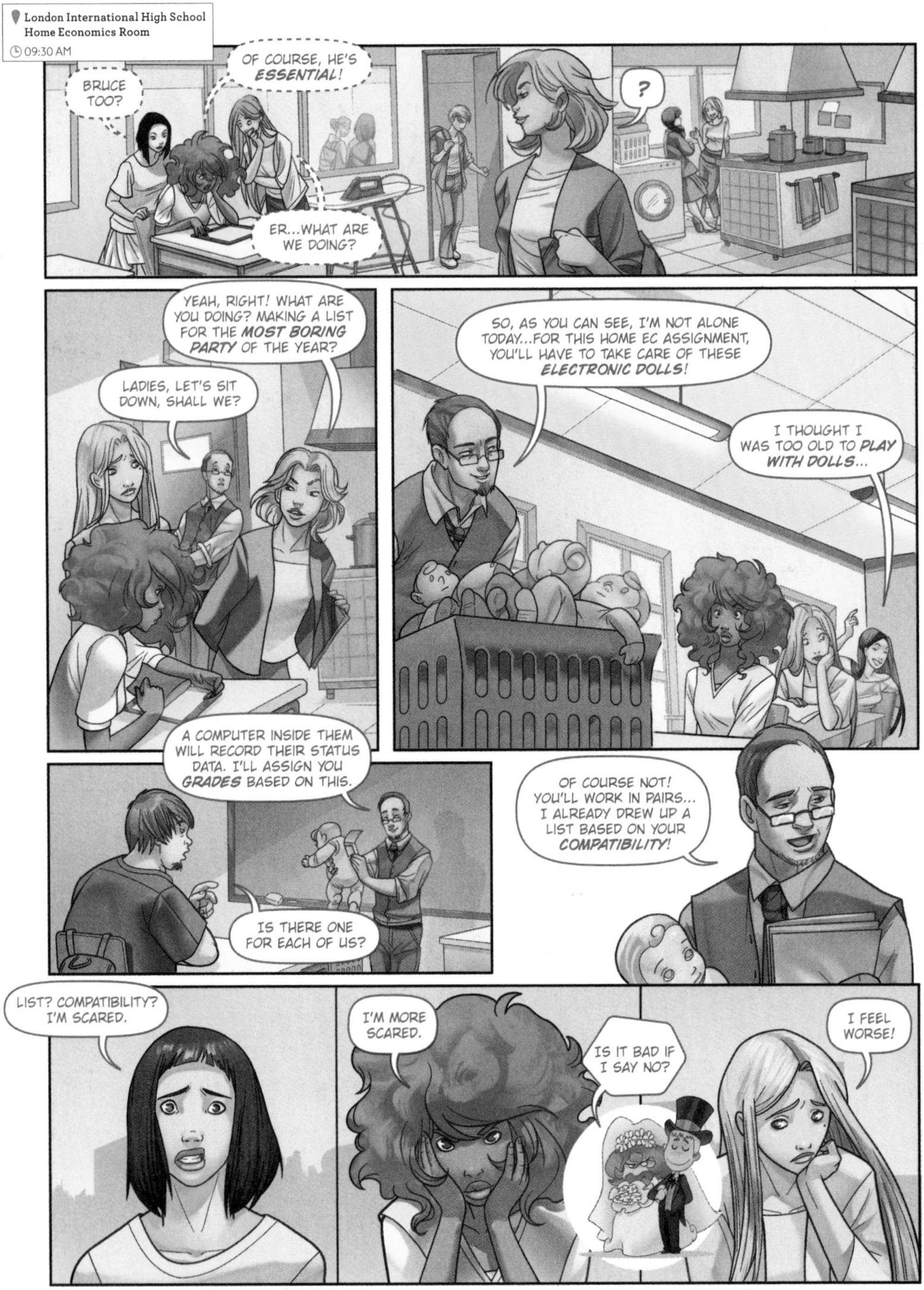
London International High School
Home Economics Room
09:30 AM
BRUCE TOO?
OF COURSE, HE'S ESSENTIAL!
ER...WHAT ARE WE DOING?
?
YEAH, RIGHT! WHAT ARE YOU DOING? MAKING A LIST FOR THE MOST BORING PARTY OF THE YEAR?
LADIES, LET'S SIT DOWN, SHALL WE?
SO, AS YOU CAN SEE, I'M NOT ALONE TODAY...FOR THIS HOME EC ASSIGNMENT, YOU'LL HAVE TO TAKE CARE OF THESE ELECTRONIC DOLLS!
I THOUGHT I WAS TOO OLD TO PLAY WITH DOLLS...
A COMPUTER INSIDE THEM WILL RECORD THEIR STATUS DATA. I'LL ASSIGN YOU GRADES BASED ON THIS.
IS THERE ONE FOR EACH OF US?
OF COURSE NOT! YOU'LL WORK IN PAIRS... I ALREADY DREW UP A LIST BASED ON YOUR COMPATIBILITY!
LIST? COMPATIBILITY? I'M SCARED.
I'M MORE SCARED.
IS IT BAD IF I SAY NO?
I FEEL WORSE!

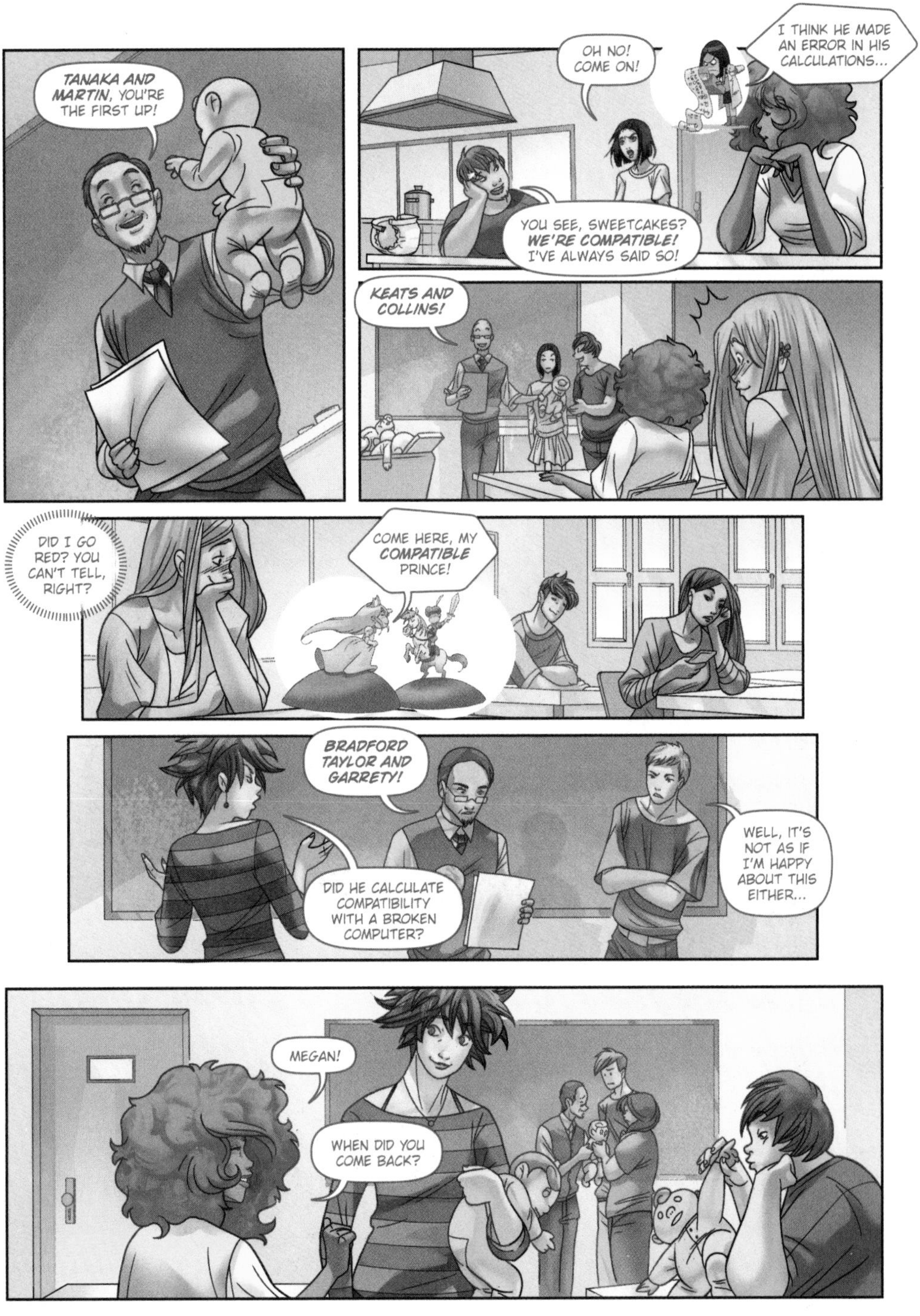
TANAKA AND MARTIN, YOU'RE THE FIRST UP!
OH NO! COME ON!
I THINK HE MADE AN ERROR IN HIS CALCULATIONS...
YOU SEE, SWEETCAKES? WE'RE COMPATIBLE! I'VE ALWAYS SAID SO!
KEATS AND COLLINS!
DID I GO RED? YOU CAN'T TELL, RIGHT?
COME HERE, MY COMPATIBLE PRINCE!
BRADFORD TAYLOR AND GARRETY!
DID HE CALCULATE COMPATIBILITY WITH A BROKEN COMPUTER?
WELL, IT'S NOT AS IF I'M HAPPY ABOUT THIS EITHER...
MEGAN!
WHEN DID YOU COME BACK?

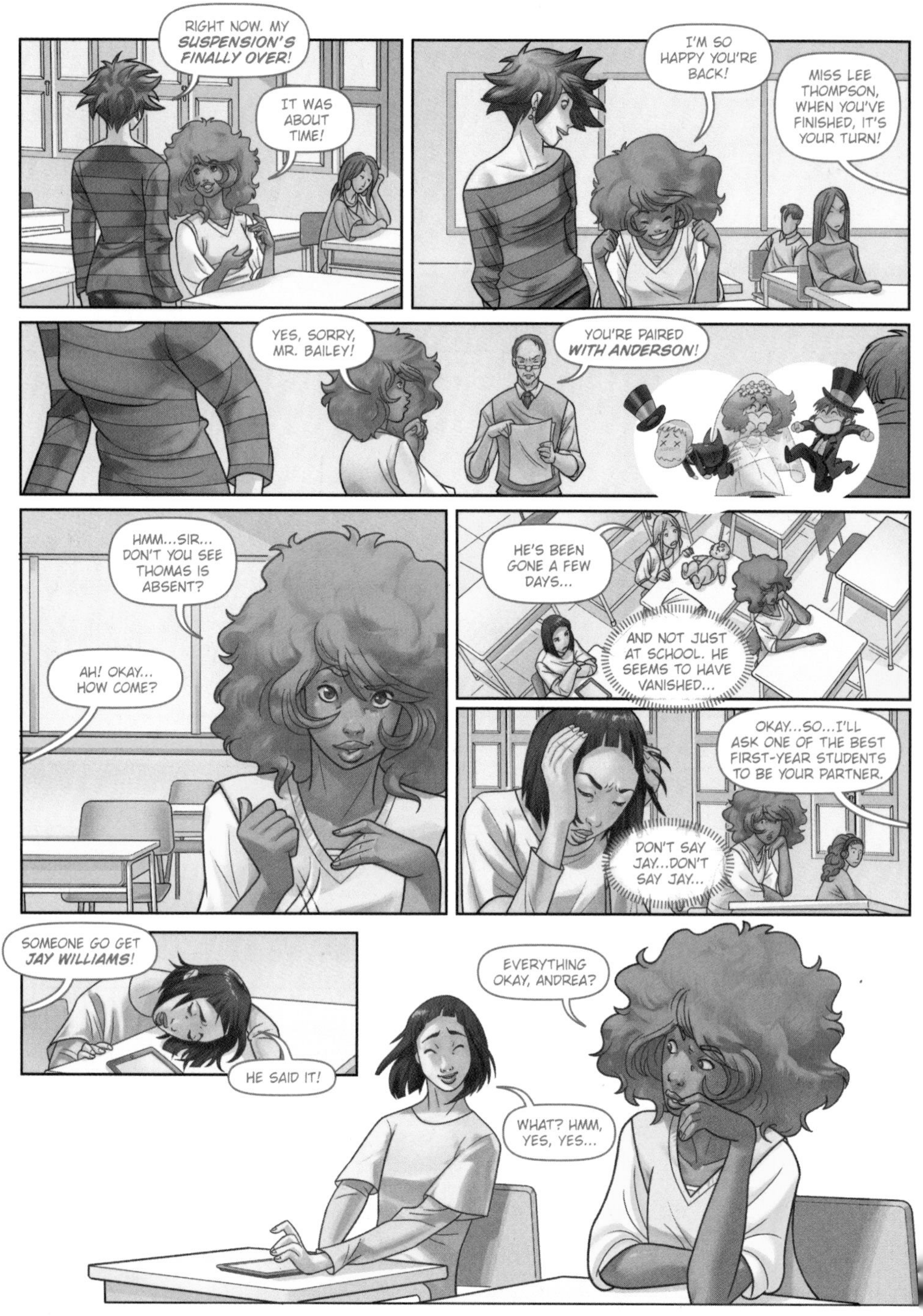
RIGHT NOW. MY SUSPENSION'S FINALLY OVER!
IT WAS ABOUT TIME!
I'M SO HAPPY YOU'RE BACK!
MISS LEE THOMPSON, WHEN YOU'VE FINISHED, IT'S YOUR TURN!
YES, SORRY, MR. BAILEY!
YOU'RE PAIRED WITH ANDERSON!
HMM...SIR... DON'T YOU SEE THOMAS IS ABSENT?
AH! OKAY... HOW COME?
HE'S BEEN GONE A FEW DAYS...
AND NOT JUST AT SCHOOL. HE SEEMS TO HAVE VANISHED...
OKAY...SO...I'LL ASK ONE OF THE BEST FIRST-YEAR STUDENTS TO BE YOUR PARTNER.
DON'T SAY JAY...DON'T SAY JAY...
SOMEONE GO GET JAY WILLIAMS!
HE SAID IT!
EVERYTHING OKAY, ANDREA?
WHAT? HMM, YES, YES...

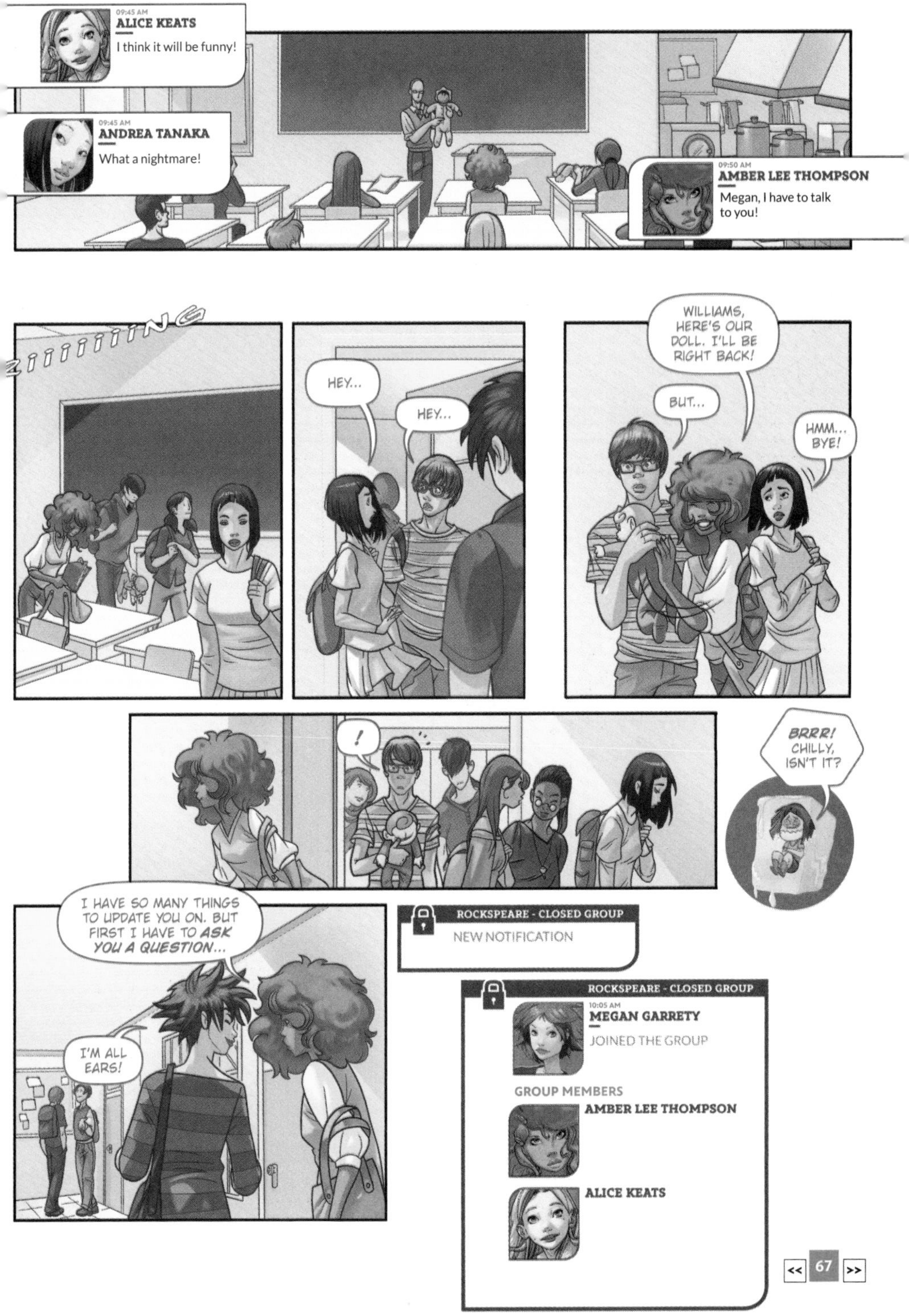
09:45 AM
ALICE KEATS
I think it will be funny!
09:45 AM
ANDREA TANAKA
What a nightmare!
09:50 AM
AMBER LEE THOMPSON
Megan, I have to talk to you!
ZIIIIIIIING
HEY...
HEY...
WILLIAMS, HERE'S OUR DOLL. I'LL BE RIGHT BACK!
BUT...
HMM... BYE!
!
BRRR! CHILLY, ISN'T IT?
I HAVE SO MANY THINGS TO UPDATE YOU ON. BUT FIRST I HAVE TO ASK YOU A QUESTION...
I'M ALL EARS!
ROCKSPEARE - CLOSED GROUP
NEW NOTIFICATION
ROCKSPEARE - CLOSED GROUP
10:05 AM
MEGAN GARRETY
JOINED THE GROUP
GROUP MEMBERS
AMBER LEE THOMPSON
ALICE KEATS

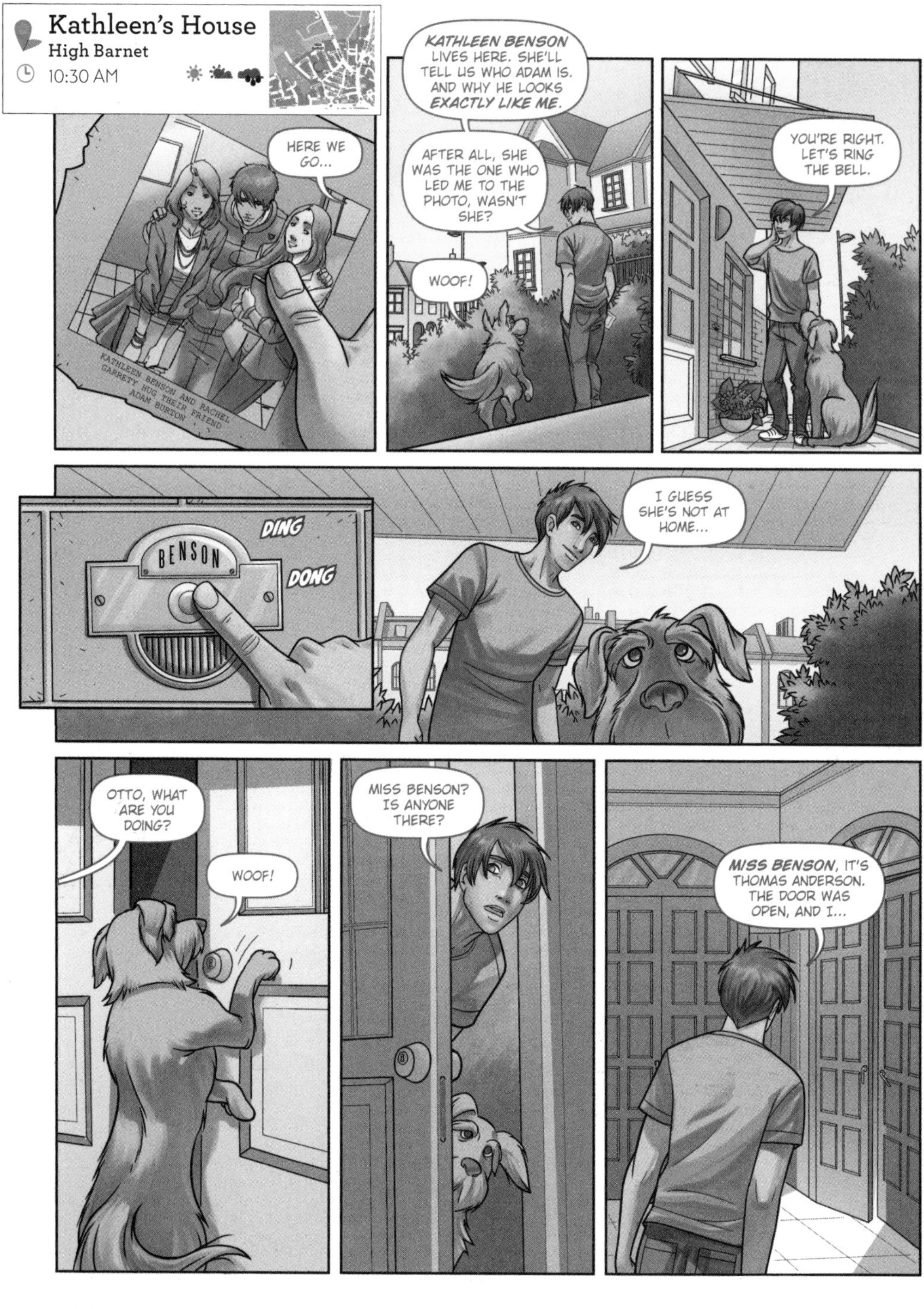
Kathleen's House
High Barnet
10:30 AM
HERE WE GO...
KATHLEEN BENSON AND RACHEL GARRETY HUG THEIR FRIEND ADAM BURTON
KATHLEEN BENSON LIVES HERE. SHE'LL TELL US WHO ADAM IS. AND WHY HE LOOKS EXACTLY LIKE ME.
AFTER ALL, SHE WAS THE ONE WHO LED ME TO THE PHOTO, WASN'T SHE?
WOOF!
YOU'RE RIGHT. LET'S RING THE BELL.
BENSON
DING
DONG
I GUESS SHE'S NOT AT HOME...
OTTO, WHAT ARE YOU DOING?
WOOF!
MISS BENSON? IS ANYONE THERE?
MISS BENSON, IT'S THOMAS ANDERSON. THE DOOR WAS OPEN, AND I...

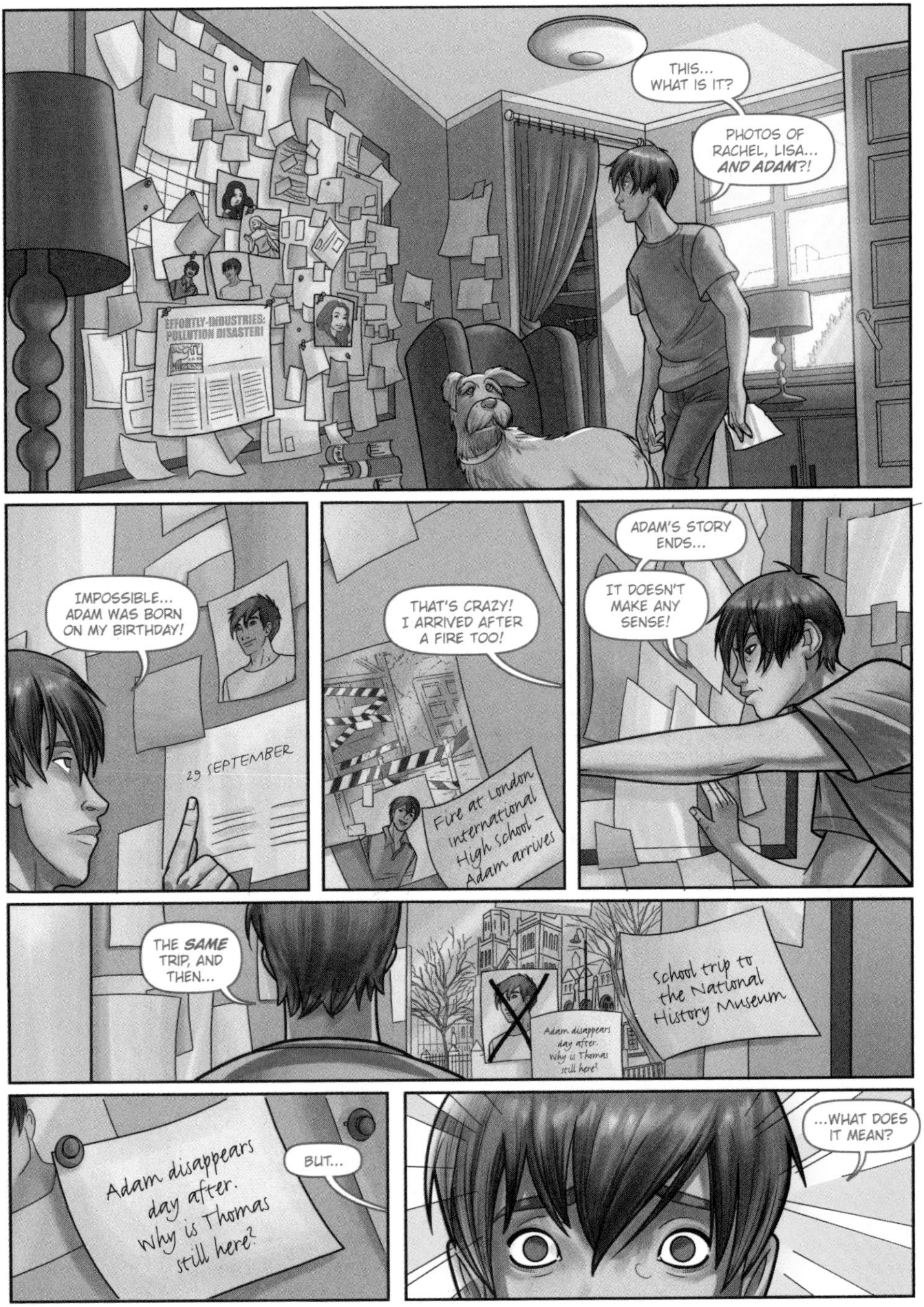

EFFORTLY-INDUSTRIES: POLLUTION DISASTER!
THIS... WHAT IS IT?
PHOTOS OF RACHEL, LISA... AND ADAM?!
IMPOSSIBLE... ADAM WAS BORN ON MY BIRTHDAY!
29 SEPTEMBER
THAT'S CRAZY! I ARRIVED AFTER A FIRE TOO!
Fire at London International High School – Adam arrives
ADAM'S STORY ENDS...
IT DOESN'T MAKE ANY SENSE!
THE SAME TRIP, AND THEN...
School trip to the National History Museum
Adam disappears day after. Why is Thomas still here?
Adam disappears day after. Why is Thomas still here?
BUT...
...WHAT DOES IT MEAN?

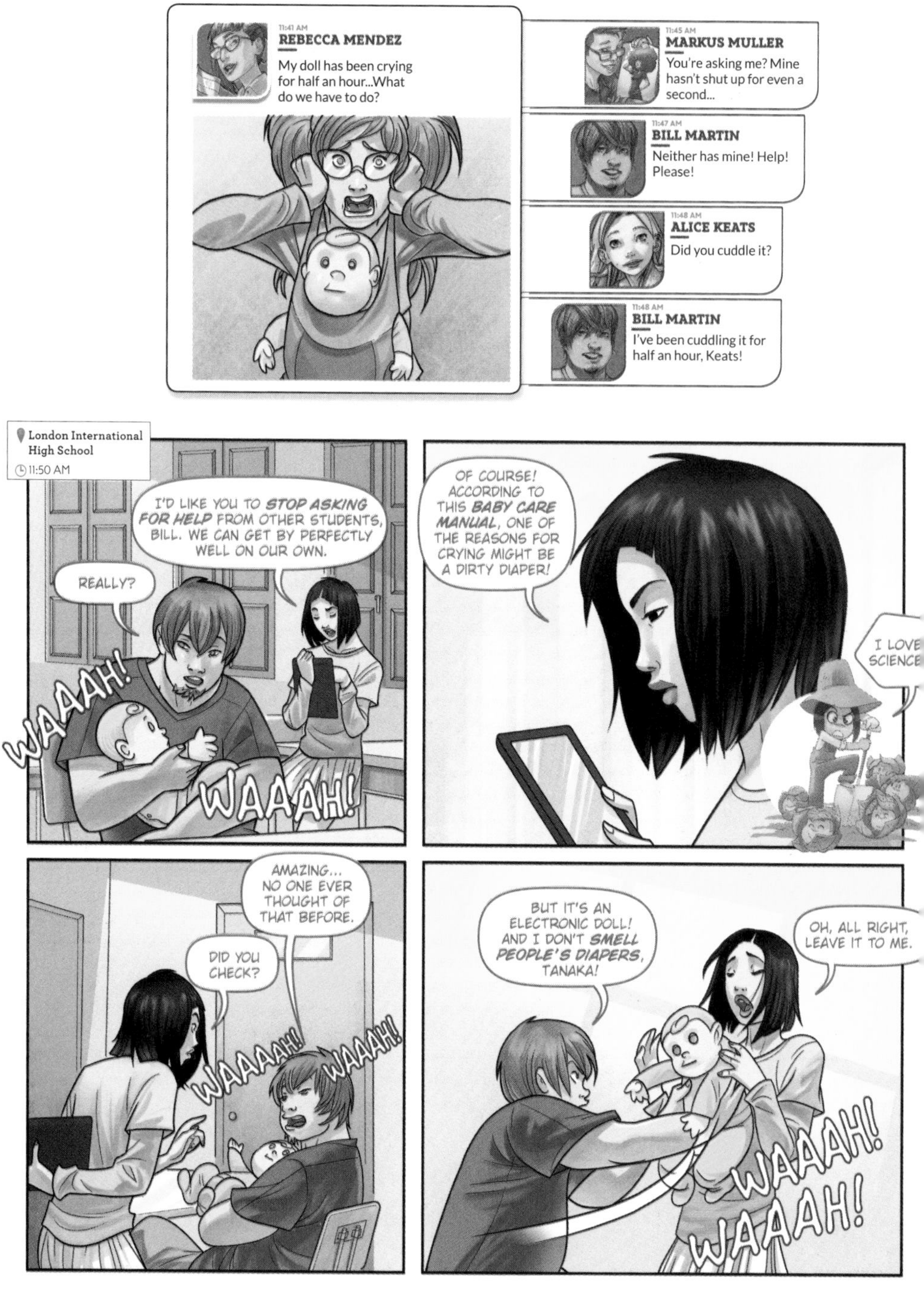

11:41 AM
REBECCA MENDEZ
My doll has been crying for half an hour...What do we have to do?
11:45 AM
MARKUS MULLER
You're asking me? Mine hasn't shut up for even a second...
11:47 AM
BILL MARTIN
Neither has mine! Help! Please!
11:48 AM
ALICE KEATS
Did you cuddle it?
11:48 AM
BILL MARTIN
I've been cuddling it for half an hour, Keats!
London International High School
11:50 AM
I'D LIKE YOU TO STOP ASKING FOR HELP FROM OTHER STUDENTS, BILL. WE CAN GET BY PERFECTLY WELL ON OUR OWN.
REALLY?
WAAAH!
WAAAH!
OF COURSE! ACCORDING TO THIS BABY CARE MANUAL, ONE OF THE REASONS FOR CRYING MIGHT BE A DIRTY DIAPER!
I LOVE SCIENCE
AMAZING... NO ONE EVER THOUGHT OF THAT BEFORE.
DID YOU CHECK?
WAAAAH!
WAAAH!
BUT IT'S AN ELECTRONIC DOLL! AND I DON'T SMELL PEOPLE'S DIAPERS, TANAKA!
OH, ALL RIGHT, LEAVE IT TO ME.
WAAAAH!
WAAAH!

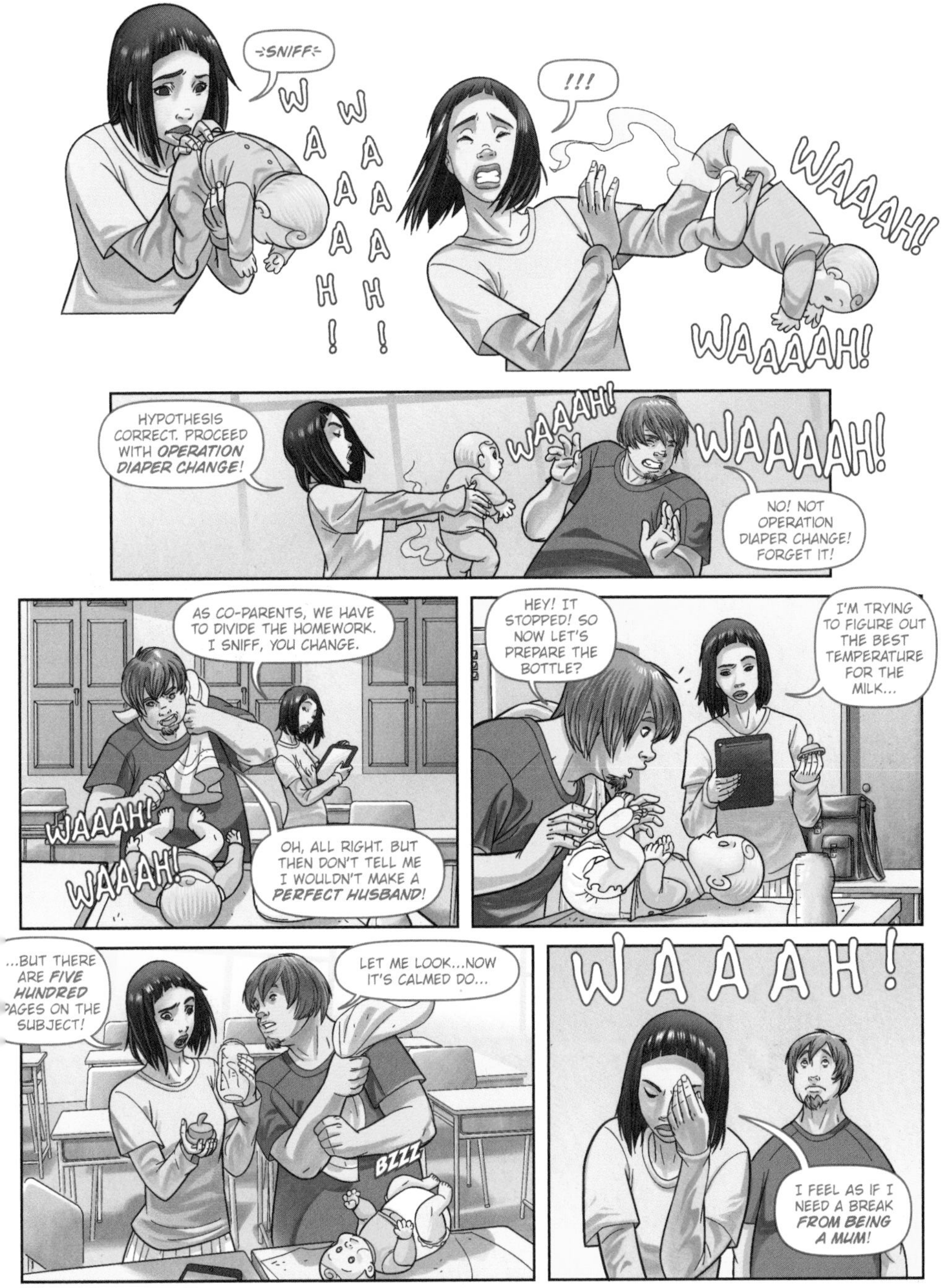

SNIFF
WAAAAH!
WAAAAH!
!!!
WAAAAH!
WAAAAAH!
HYPOTHESIS CORRECT. PROCEED WITH OPERATION DIAPER CHANGE!
WAAAAH!
WAAAAAH!
NO! NOT OPERATION DIAPER CHANGE! FORGET IT!
AS CO-PARENTS, WE HAVE TO DIVIDE THE HOMEWORK. I SNIFF, YOU CHANGE.
WAAAH!
WAAAH!
OH, ALL RIGHT. BUT THEN DON'T TELL ME I WOULDN'T MAKE A PERFECT HUSBAND!
HEY! IT STOPPED! SO NOW LET'S PREPARE THE BOTTLE?
I'M TRYING TO FIGURE OUT THE BEST TEMPERATURE FOR THE MILK...
...BUT THERE ARE FIVE HUNDRED PAGES ON THE SUBJECT!
LET ME LOOK...NOW IT'S CALMED DO...
BZZZ
WAAAH!
I FEEL AS IF I NEED A BREAK FROM BEING A MUM!

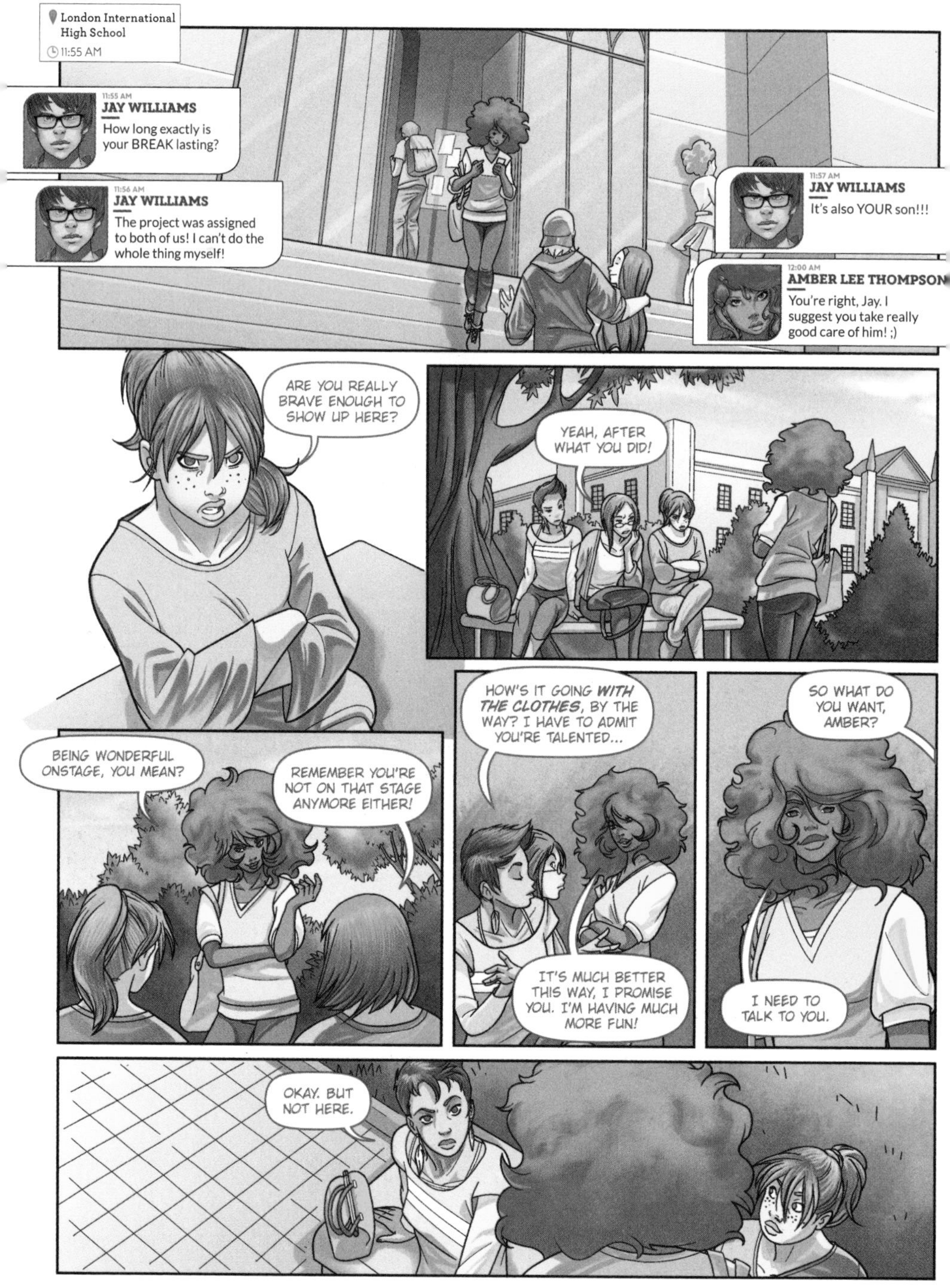

London International High School
11:55 AM
11:55 AM
JAY WILLIAMS
How long exactly is your BREAK lasting?
11:56 AM
JAY WILLIAMS
The project was assigned to both of us! I can't do the whole thing myself!
11:57 AM
JAY WILLIAMS
It's also YOUR son!!!
12:00 AM
AMBER LEE THOMPSON
You're right, Jay. I suggest you take really good care of him! ;)
ARE YOU REALLY BRAVE ENOUGH TO SHOW UP HERE?
YEAH, AFTER WHAT YOU DID!
BEING WONDERFUL ONSTAGE, YOU MEAN?
REMEMBER YOU'RE NOT ON THAT STAGE ANYMORE EITHER!
HOW'S IT GOING WITH THE CLOTHES, BY THE WAY? I HAVE TO ADMIT YOU'RE TALENTED...
IT'S MUCH BETTER THIS WAY, I PROMISE YOU. I'M HAVING MUCH MORE FUN!
SO WHAT DO YOU WANT, AMBER?
I NEED TO TALK TO YOU.
OKAY. BUT NOT HERE.

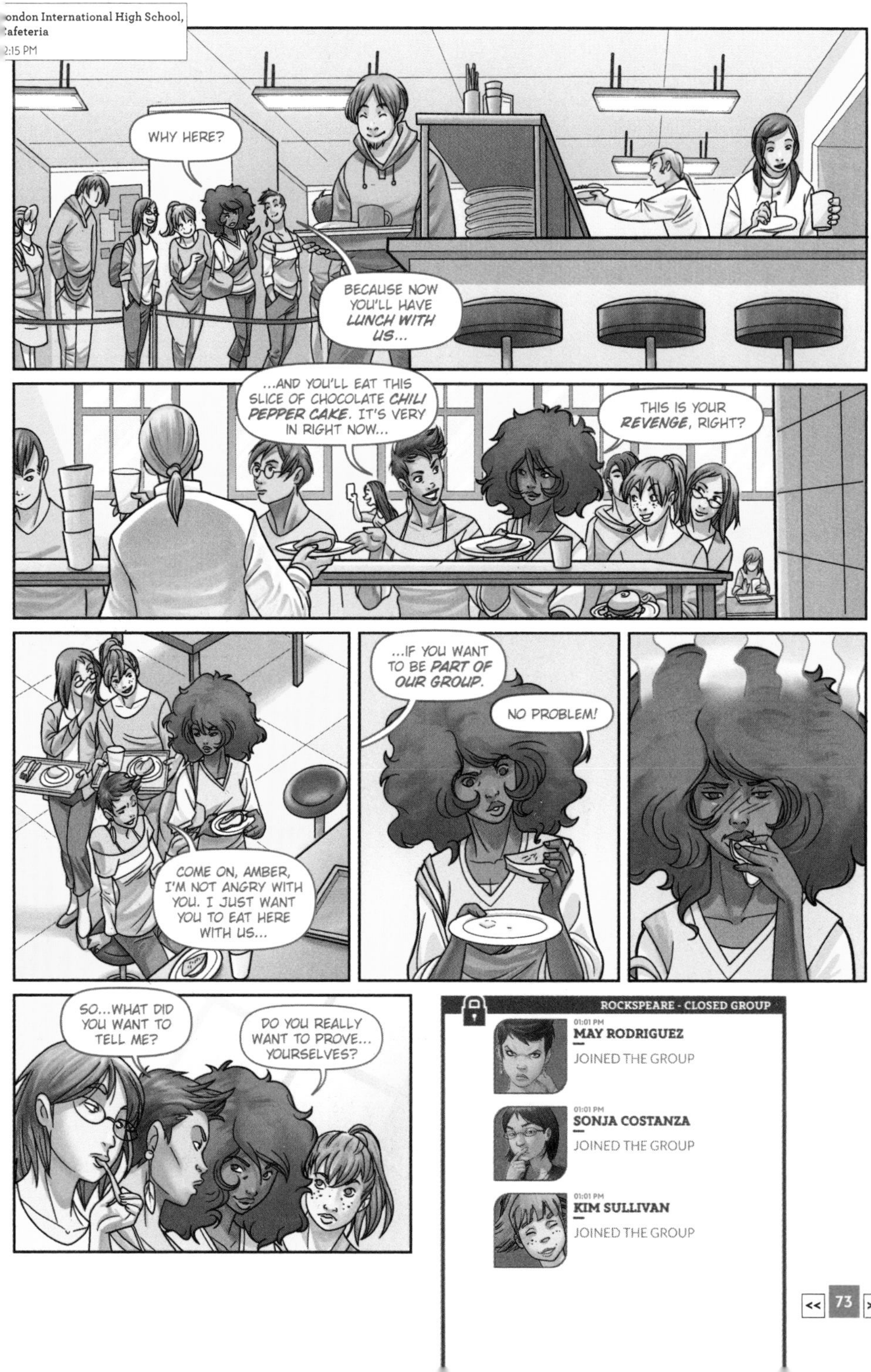
ondon International High School,
afeteria
2:15 PM
WHY HERE?
BECAUSE NOW YOU'LL HAVE LUNCH WITH US...
...AND YOU'LL EAT THIS SLICE OF CHOCOLATE CHILI PEPPER CAKE. IT'S VERY IN RIGHT NOW...
THIS IS YOUR REVENGE, RIGHT?
COME ON, AMBER, I'M NOT ANGRY WITH YOU. I JUST WANT YOU TO EAT HERE WITH US...
...IF YOU WANT TO BE PART OF OUR GROUP.
NO PROBLEM!
SO...WHAT DID YOU WANT TO TELL ME?
DO YOU REALLY WANT TO PROVE... YOURSELVES?
ROCKSPEARE - CLOSED GROUP
01:01 PM
MAY RODRIGUEZ
JOINED THE GROUP
01:01 PM
SONJA COSTANZA
JOINED THE GROUP
01:01 PM
KIM SULLIVAN
JOINED THE GROUP

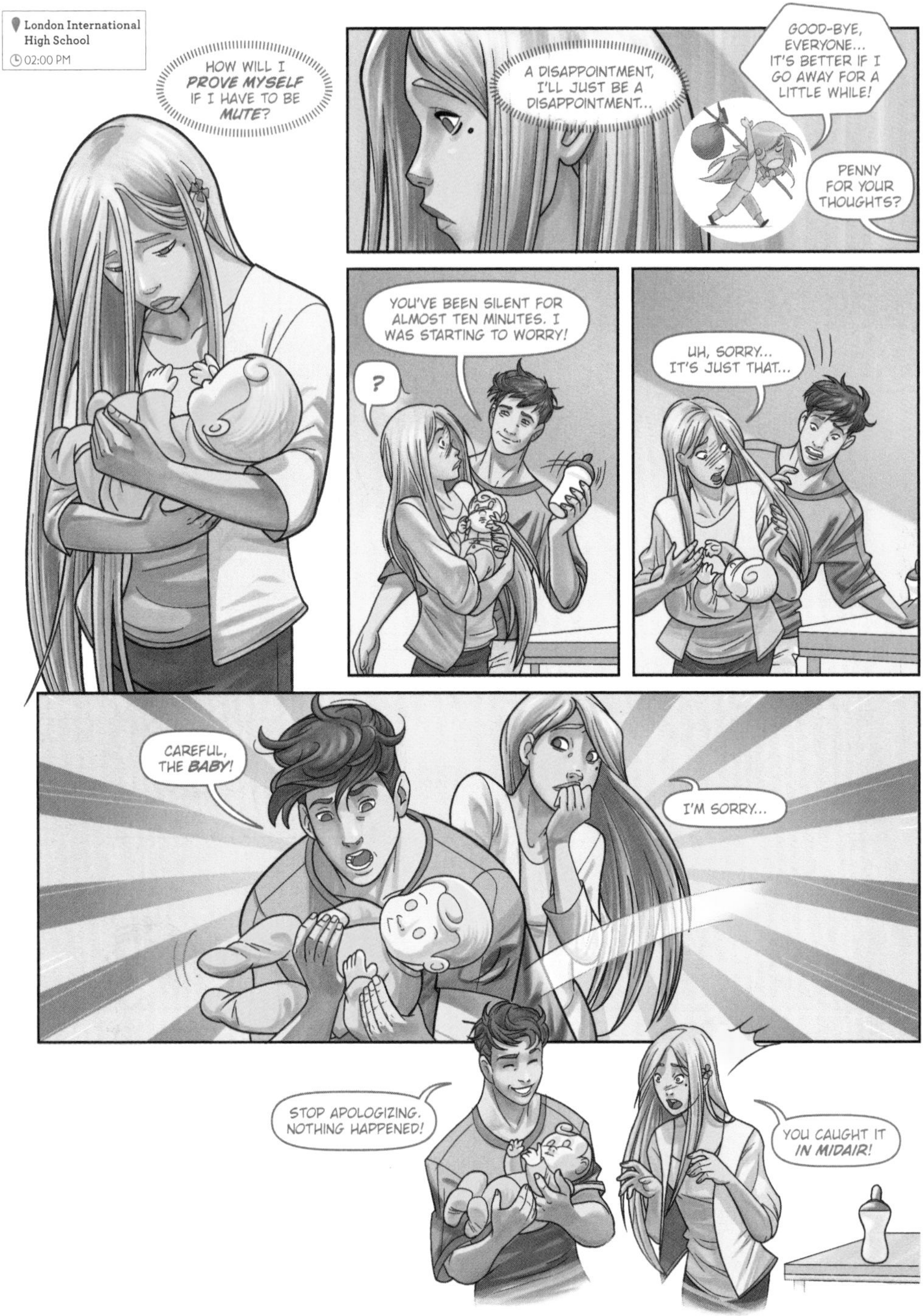
London International High School
02:00 PM
HOW WILL I PROVE MYSELF IF I HAVE TO BE MUTE?
A DISAPPOINTMENT, I'LL JUST BE A DISAPPOINTMENT...
GOOD-BYE, EVERYONE... IT'S BETTER IF I GO AWAY FOR A LITTLE WHILE!
PENNY FOR YOUR THOUGHTS?
YOU'VE BEEN SILENT FOR ALMOST TEN MINUTES. I WAS STARTING TO WORRY!
?
UH, SORRY... IT'S JUST THAT...
CAREFUL, THE BABY!
I'M SORRY...
STOP APOLOGIZING. NOTHING HAPPENED!
YOU CAUGHT IT IN MIDAIR!

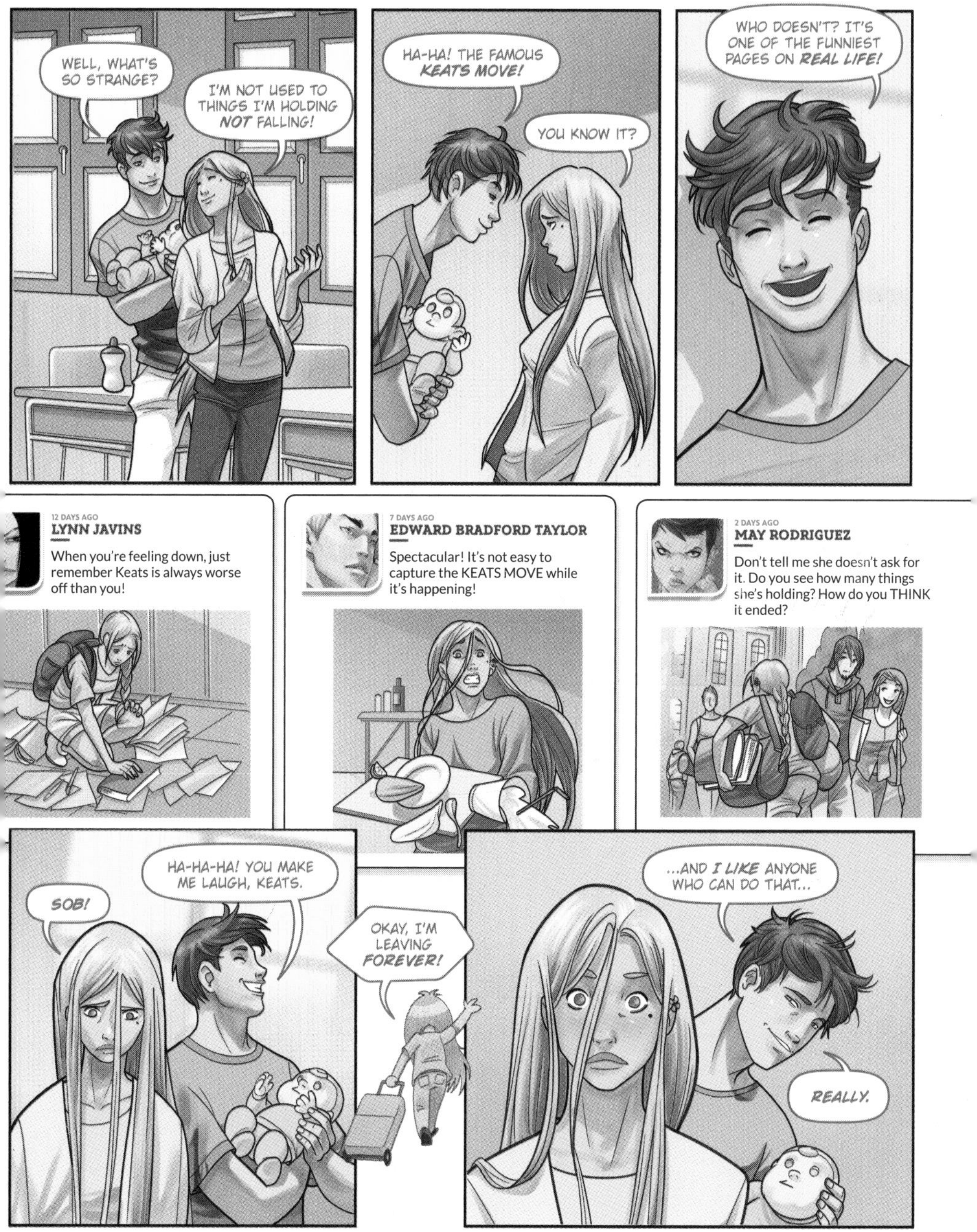
WELL, WHAT'S SO STRANGE?
I'M NOT USED TO THINGS I'M HOLDING NOT FALLING!
HA-HA! THE FAMOUS KEATS MOVE!
YOU KNOW IT?
WHO DOESN'T? IT'S ONE OF THE FUNNIEST PAGES ON REAL LIFE!
12 DAYS AGO
LYNN JAVINS
When you're feeling down, just remember Keats is always worse off than you!
7 DAYS AGO
EDWARD BRADFORD TAYLOR
Spectacular! It's not easy to capture the KEATS MOVE while it's happening!
2 DAYS AGO
MAY RODRIGUEZ
Don't tell me she doesn't ask for it. Do you see how many things she's holding? How do you THINK it ended?
SOB!
HA-HA-HA! YOU MAKE ME LAUGH, KEATS.
OKAY, I'M LEAVING FOREVER!
...AND I LIKE ANYONE WHO CAN DO THAT...
REALLY.

END OF CHAPTER 22

CHAPTER 23

UNEXPECTED MOVES

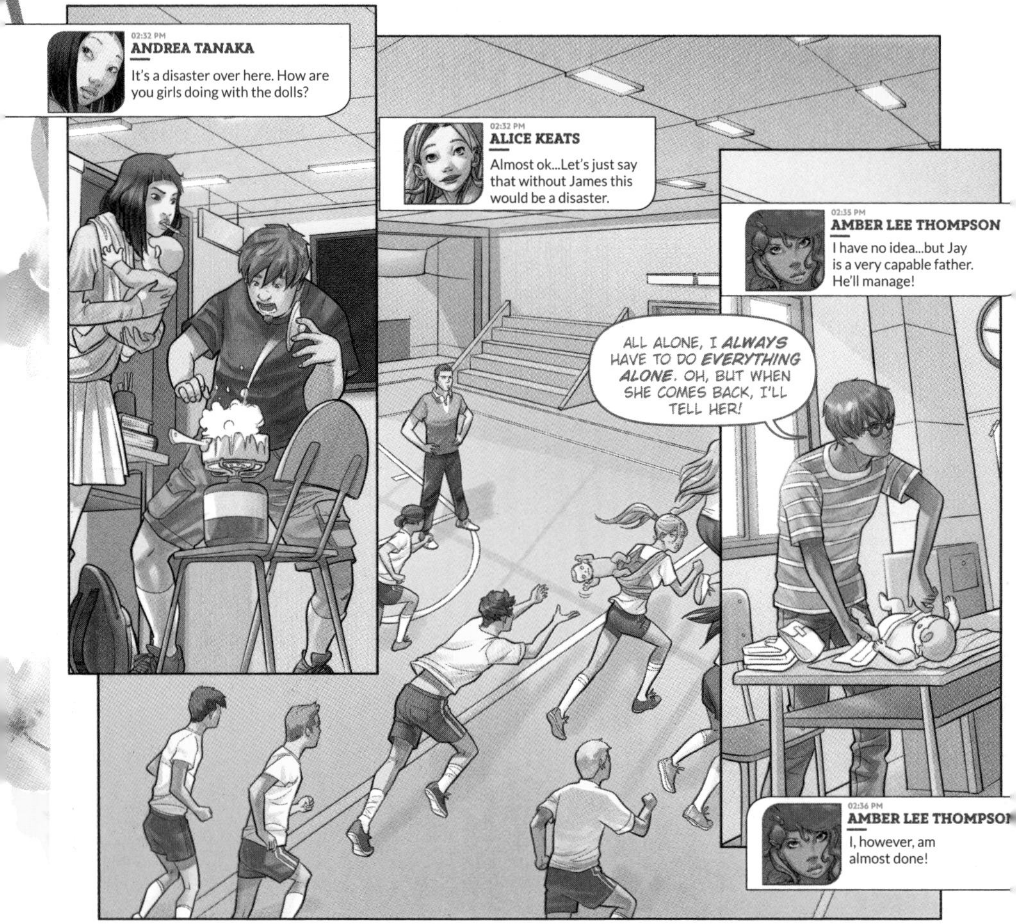
02:32 PM
ANDREA TANAKA
It's a disaster over here. How are you girls doing with the dolls?
02:32 PM
ALICE KEATS
Almost ok...Let's just say that without James this would be a disaster.
02:35 PM
AMBER LEE THOMPSON
I have no idea...but Jay is a very capable father. He'll manage!
ALL ALONE, I ALWAYS HAVE TO DO EVERYTHING ALONE. OH, BUT WHEN SHE COMES BACK, I'LL TELL HER!
02:36 PM
AMBER LEE THOMPSON
I, however, am almost done!

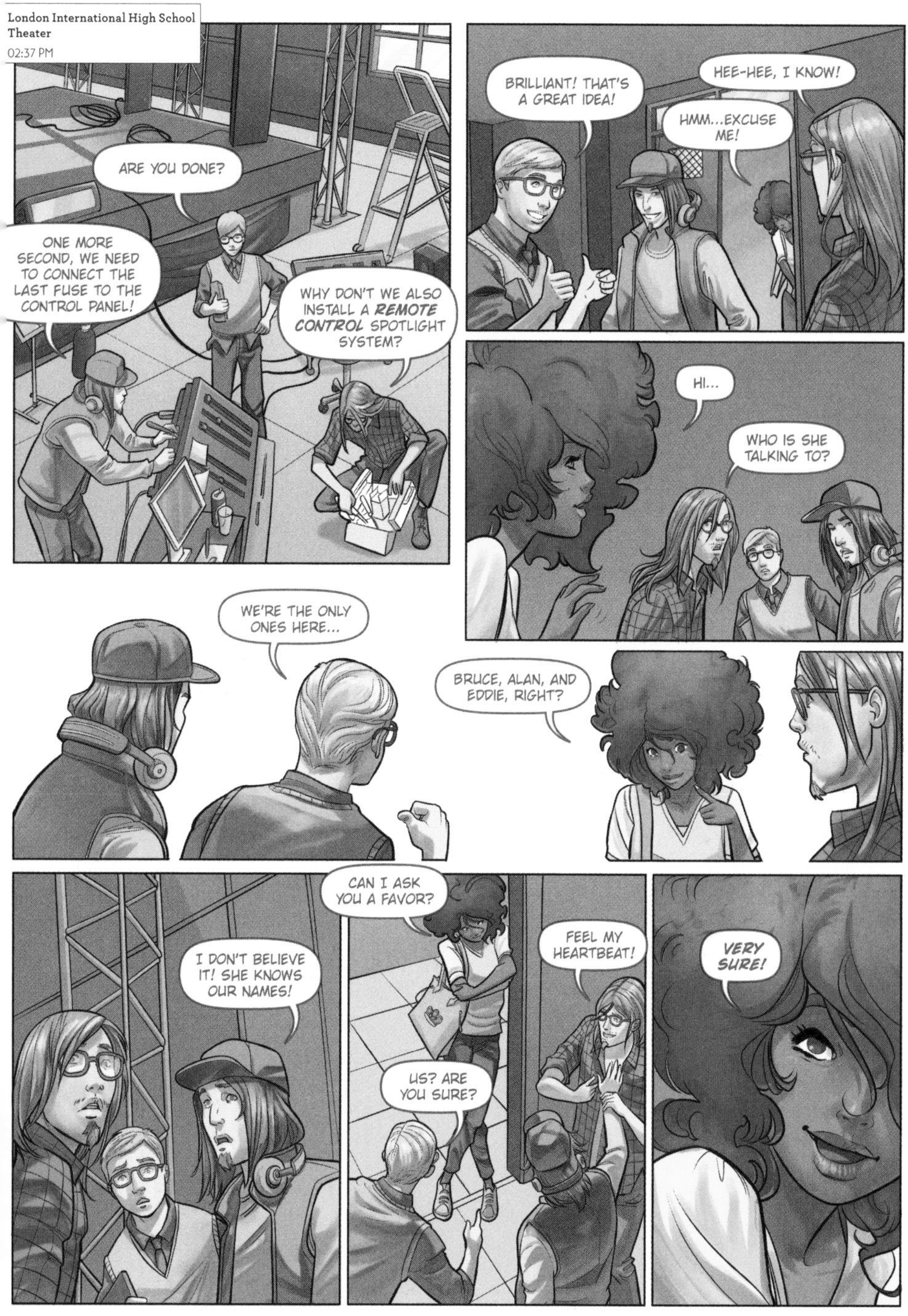
London International High School Theater
02:37 PM
ARE YOU DONE?
ONE MORE SECOND, WE NEED TO CONNECT THE LAST FUSE TO THE CONTROL PANEL!
WHY DON'T WE ALSO INSTALL A **REMOTE CONTROL** SPOTLIGHT SYSTEM?
BRILLIANT! THAT'S A GREAT IDEA!
HEE-HEE, I KNOW!
HMM...EXCUSE ME!
HI...
WHO IS SHE TALKING TO?
WE'RE THE ONLY ONES HERE...
BRUCE, ALAN, AND EDDIE, RIGHT?
I DON'T BELIEVE IT! SHE KNOWS OUR NAMES!
CAN I ASK YOU A FAVOR?
US? ARE YOU SURE?
FEEL MY HEARTBEAT!
VERY SURE!

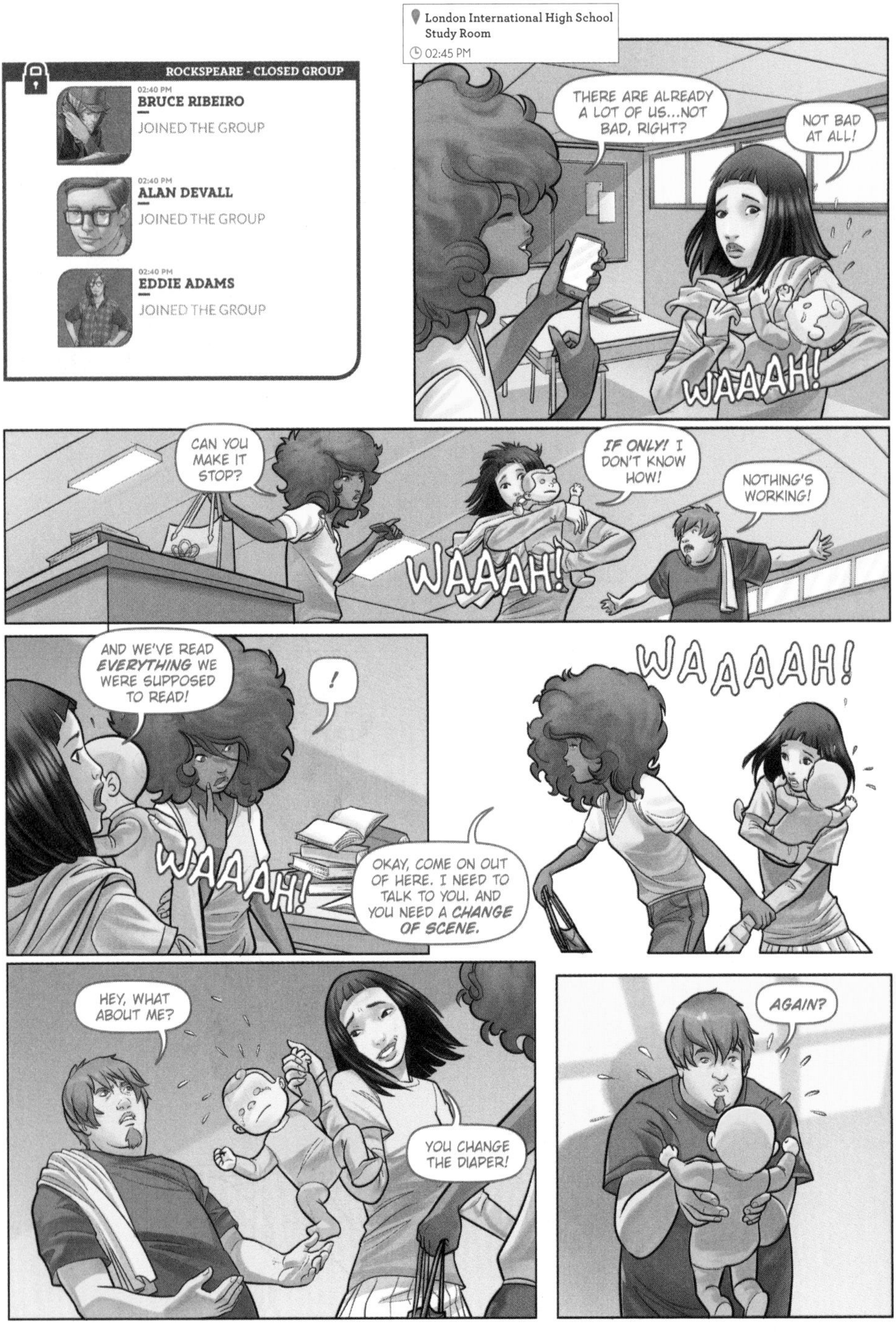
ROCKSPEARE - CLOSED GROUP
02:40 PM
BRUCE RIBEIRO
JOINED THE GROUP
02:40 PM
ALAN DEVALL
JOINED THE GROUP
02:40 PM
EDDIE ADAMS
JOINED THE GROUP
London International High School
Study Room
02:45 PM
THERE ARE ALREADY A LOT OF US...NOT BAD, RIGHT?
NOT BAD AT ALL!
WAAAAH!
CAN YOU MAKE IT STOP?
IF ONLY! I DON'T KNOW HOW!
NOTHING'S WORKING!
WAAAAH!
AND WE'VE READ EVERYTHING WE WERE SUPPOSED TO READ!
!
WAAAAH!
OKAY, COME ON OUT OF HERE. I NEED TO TALK TO YOU. AND YOU NEED A CHANGE OF SCENE.
WAAAAH!
HEY, WHAT ABOUT ME?
YOU CHANGE THE DIAPER!
AGAIN?

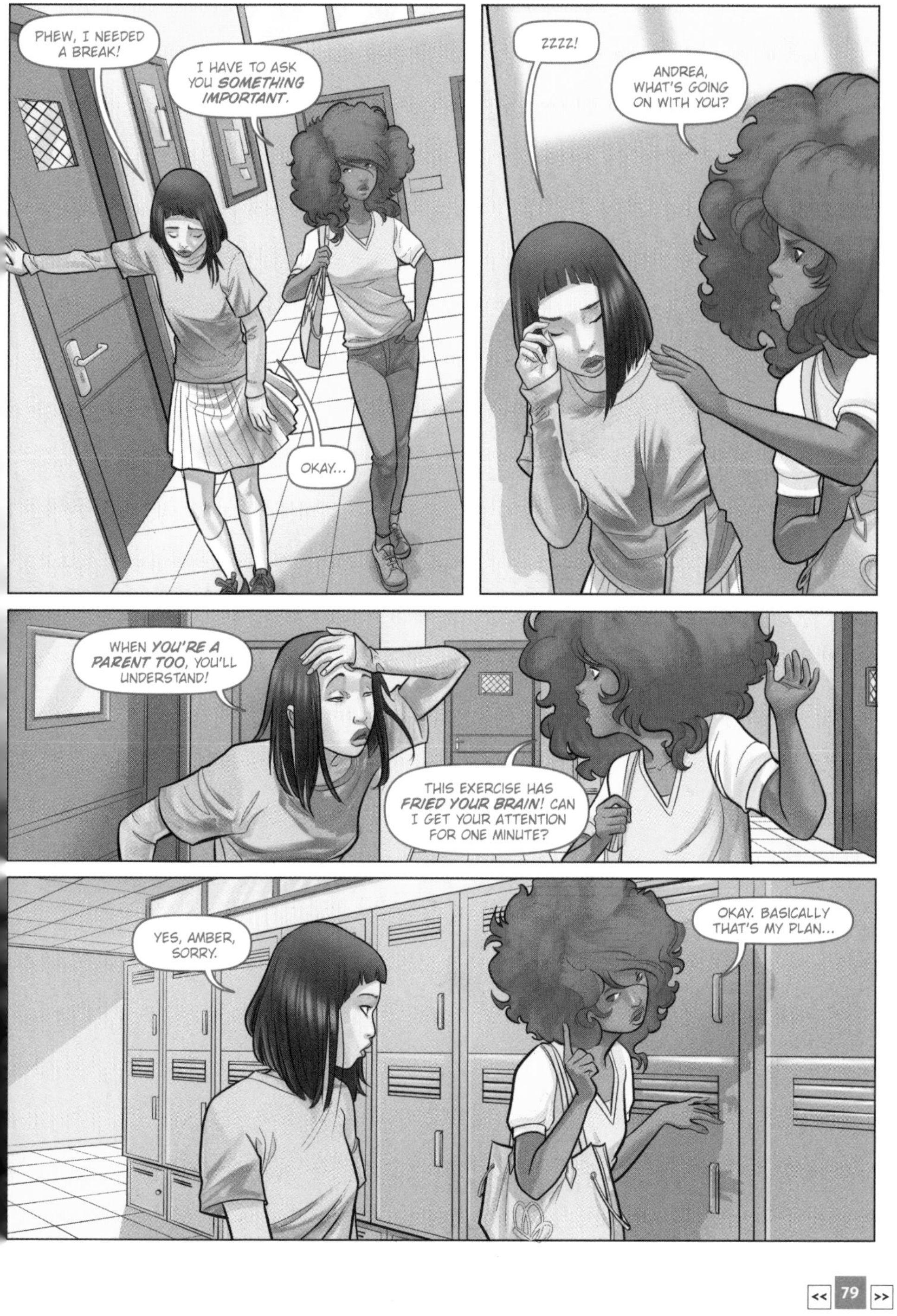
PHEW, I NEEDED A BREAK!
I HAVE TO ASK YOU **SOMETHING IMPORTANT**.
OKAY...
ZZZZ!
ANDREA, WHAT'S GOING ON WITH YOU?
WHEN **YOU'RE A PARENT TOO**, YOU'LL UNDERSTAND!
THIS EXERCISE HAS **FRIED YOUR BRAIN**! CAN I GET YOUR ATTENTION FOR ONE MINUTE?
YES, AMBER, SORRY.
OKAY. BASICALLY THAT'S MY PLAN...

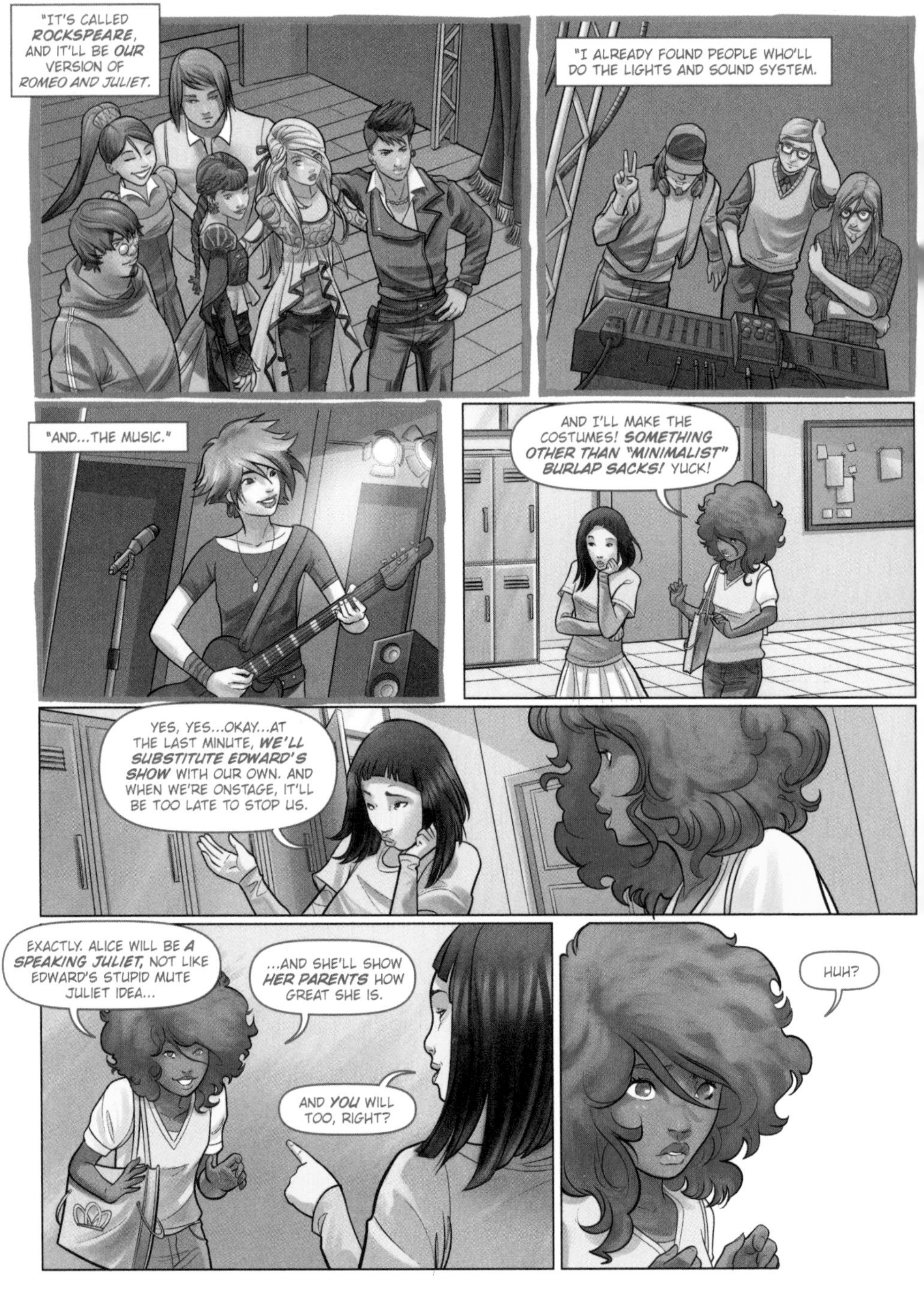
"IT'S CALLED ROCKSPEARE, AND IT'LL BE OUR VERSION OF ROMEO AND JULIET.
"I ALREADY FOUND PEOPLE WHO'LL DO THE LIGHTS AND SOUND SYSTEM.
"AND...THE MUSIC."
AND I'LL MAKE THE COSTUMES! SOMETHING OTHER THAN "MINIMALIST" BURLAP SACKS! YUCK!
YES, YES...OKAY...AT THE LAST MINUTE, WE'LL SUBSTITUTE EDWARD'S SHOW WITH OUR OWN. AND WHEN WE'RE ONSTAGE, IT'LL BE TOO LATE TO STOP US.
EXACTLY. ALICE WILL BE A SPEAKING JULIET, NOT LIKE EDWARD'S STUPID MUTE JULIET IDEA...
...AND SHE'LL SHOW HER PARENTS HOW GREAT SHE IS.
AND YOU WILL TOO, RIGHT?
HUH?

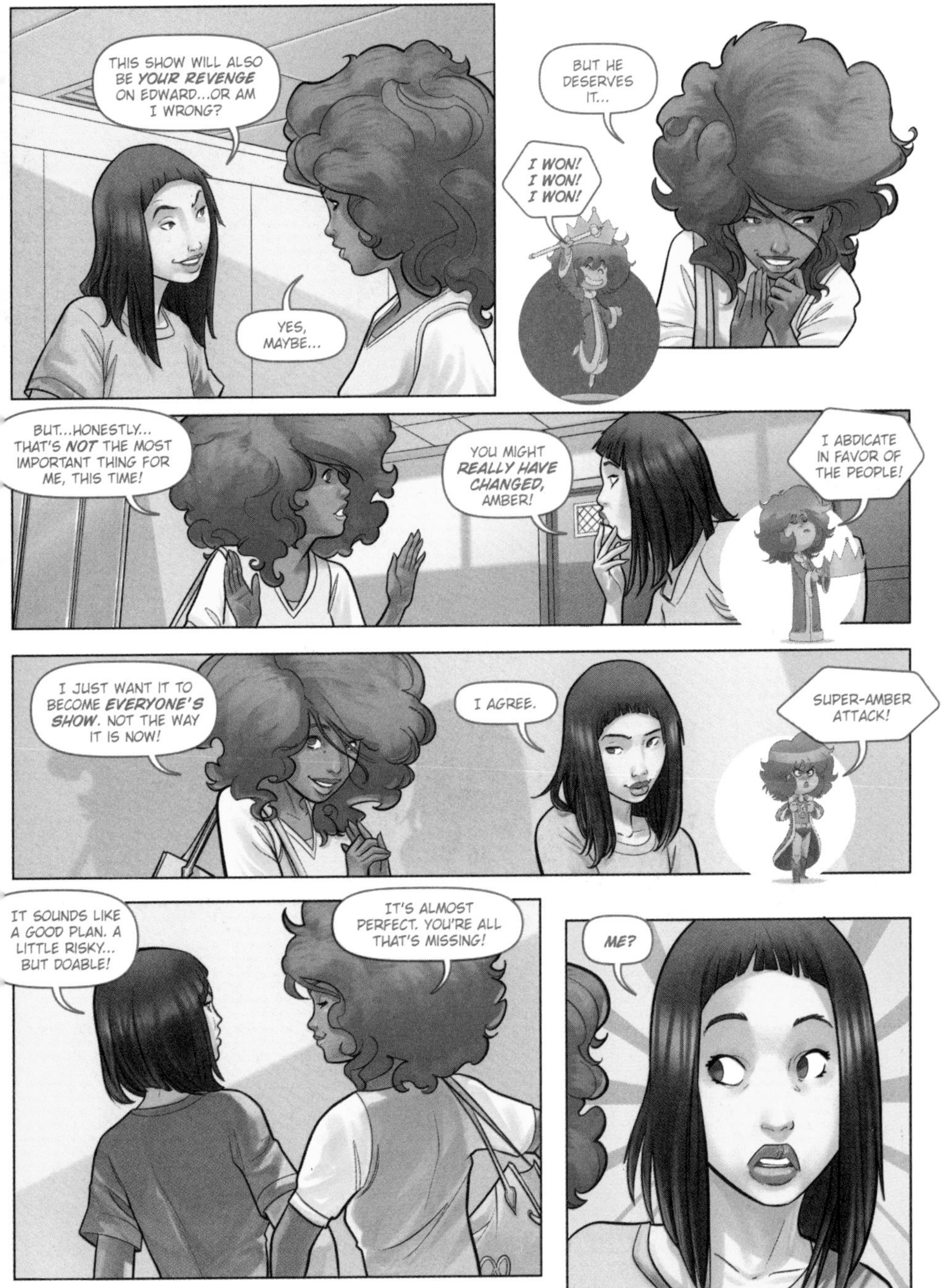
THIS SHOW WILL ALSO BE YOUR REVENGE ON EDWARD...OR AM I WRONG?
YES, MAYBE...
BUT HE DESERVES IT...
I WON! I WON! I WON!
BUT...HONESTLY... THAT'S NOT THE MOST IMPORTANT THING FOR ME, THIS TIME!
YOU MIGHT REALLY HAVE CHANGED, AMBER!
I ABDICATE IN FAVOR OF THE PEOPLE!
I JUST WANT IT TO BECOME EVERYONE'S SHOW. NOT THE WAY IT IS NOW!
I AGREE.
SUPER-AMBER ATTACK!
IT SOUNDS LIKE A GOOD PLAN. A LITTLE RISKY... BUT DOABLE!
IT'S ALMOST PERFECT. YOU'RE ALL THAT'S MISSING!
ME?

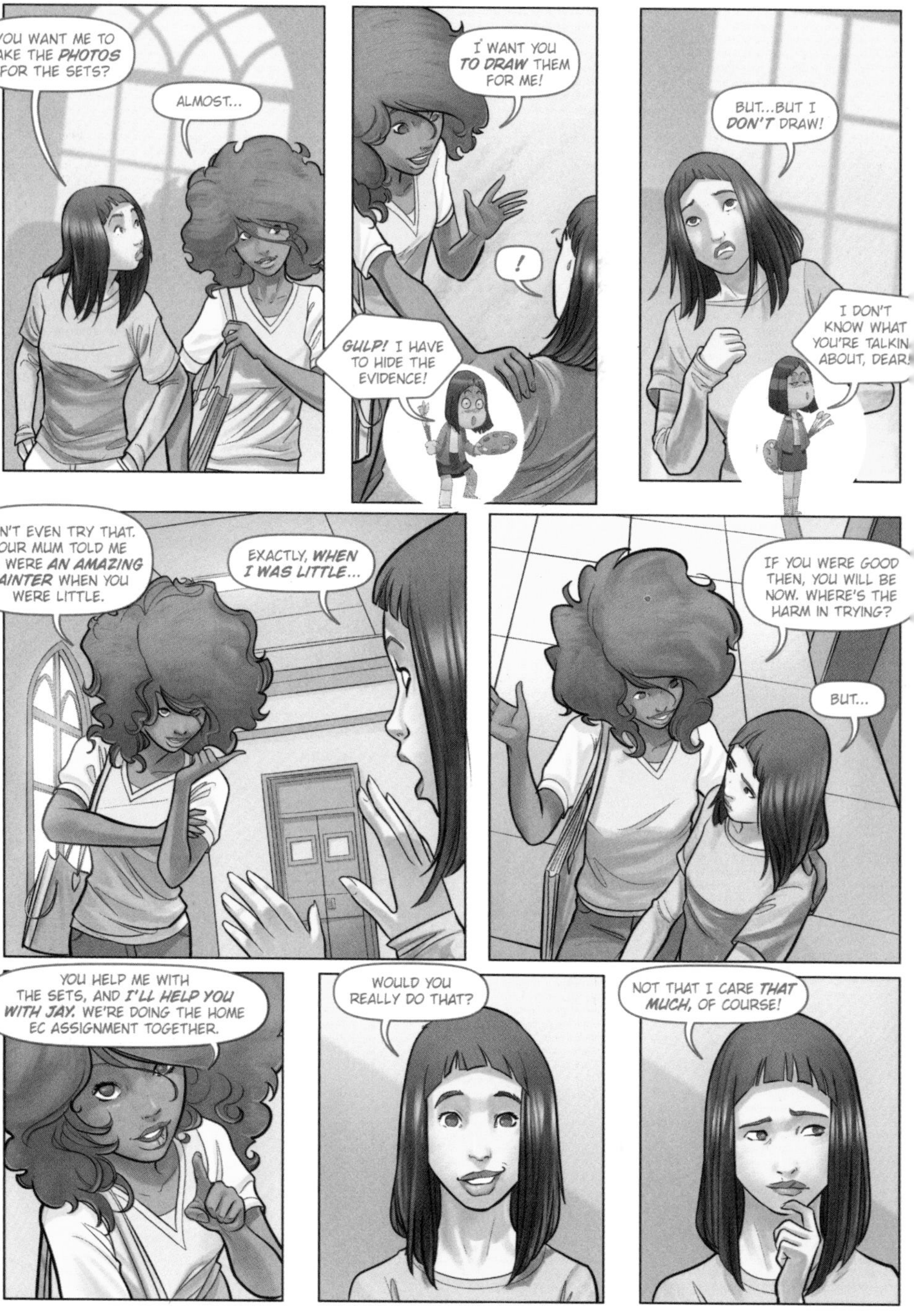

YOU WANT ME TO TAKE THE PHOTOS FOR THE SETS?
ALMOST...
I WANT YOU TO DRAW THEM FOR ME!
!
GULP! I HAVE TO HIDE THE EVIDENCE!
BUT...BUT I DON'T DRAW!
I DON'T KNOW WHAT YOU'RE TALKIN ABOUT, DEAR!
DON'T EVEN TRY THAT. YOUR MUM TOLD ME YOU WERE AN AMAZING PAINTER WHEN YOU WERE LITTLE.
EXACTLY, WHEN I WAS LITTLE...
IF YOU WERE GOOD THEN, YOU WILL BE NOW. WHERE'S THE HARM IN TRYING?
BUT...
YOU HELP ME WITH THE SETS, AND I'LL HELP YOU WITH JAY. WE'RE DOING THE HOME EC ASSIGNMENT TOGETHER.
WOULD YOU REALLY DO THAT?
NOT THAT I CARE THAT MUCH, OF COURSE!

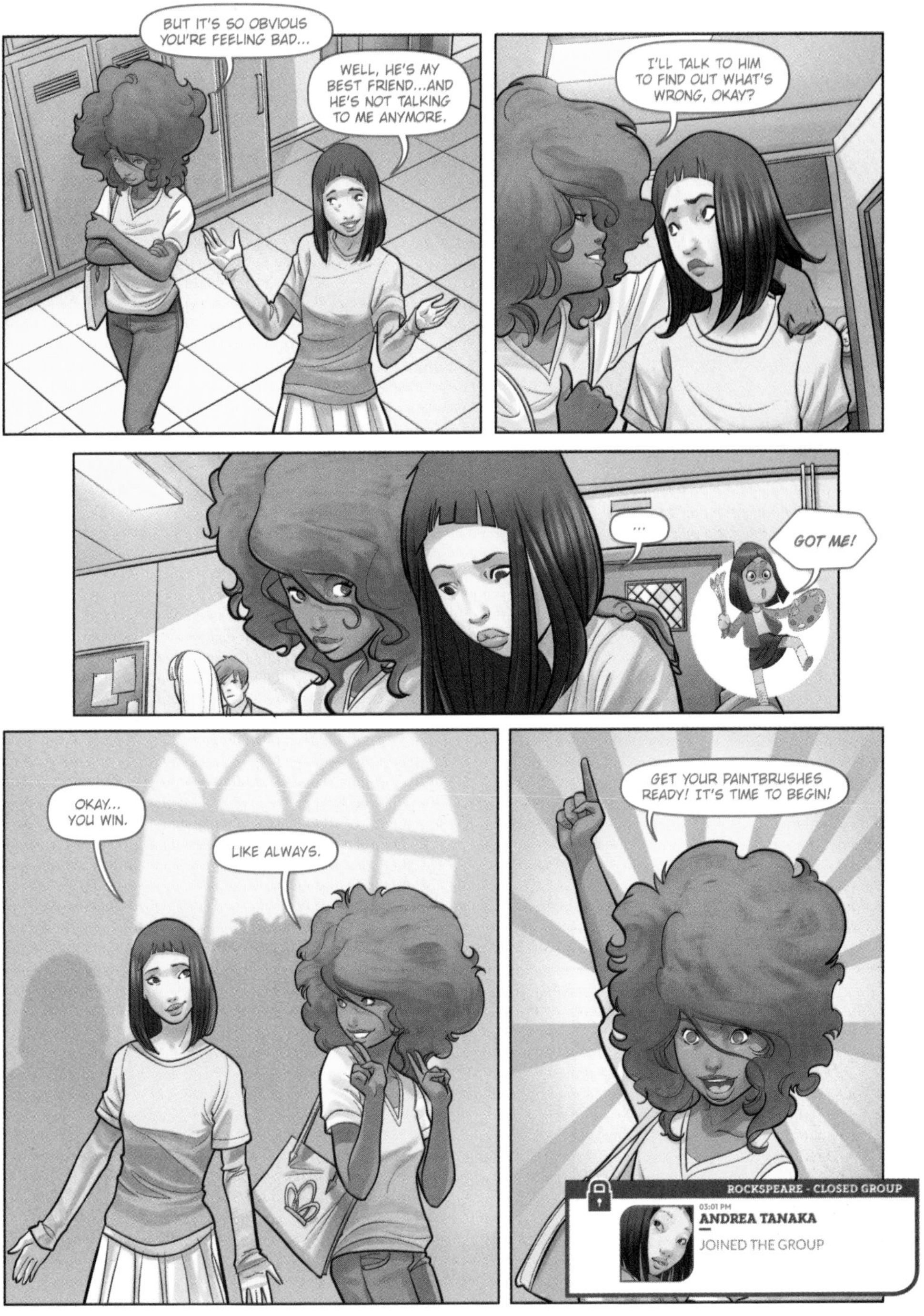
BUT IT'S SO OBVIOUS YOU'RE FEELING BAD...
WELL, HE'S MY BEST FRIEND...AND HE'S NOT TALKING TO ME ANYMORE.
I'LL TALK TO HIM TO FIND OUT WHAT'S WRONG, OKAY?
...
GOT ME!
OKAY... YOU WIN.
LIKE ALWAYS.
GET YOUR PAINTBRUSHES READY! IT'S TIME TO BEGIN!
ROCKSPEARE - CLOSED GROUP
03:01 PM
ANDREA TANAKA
JOINED THE GROUP

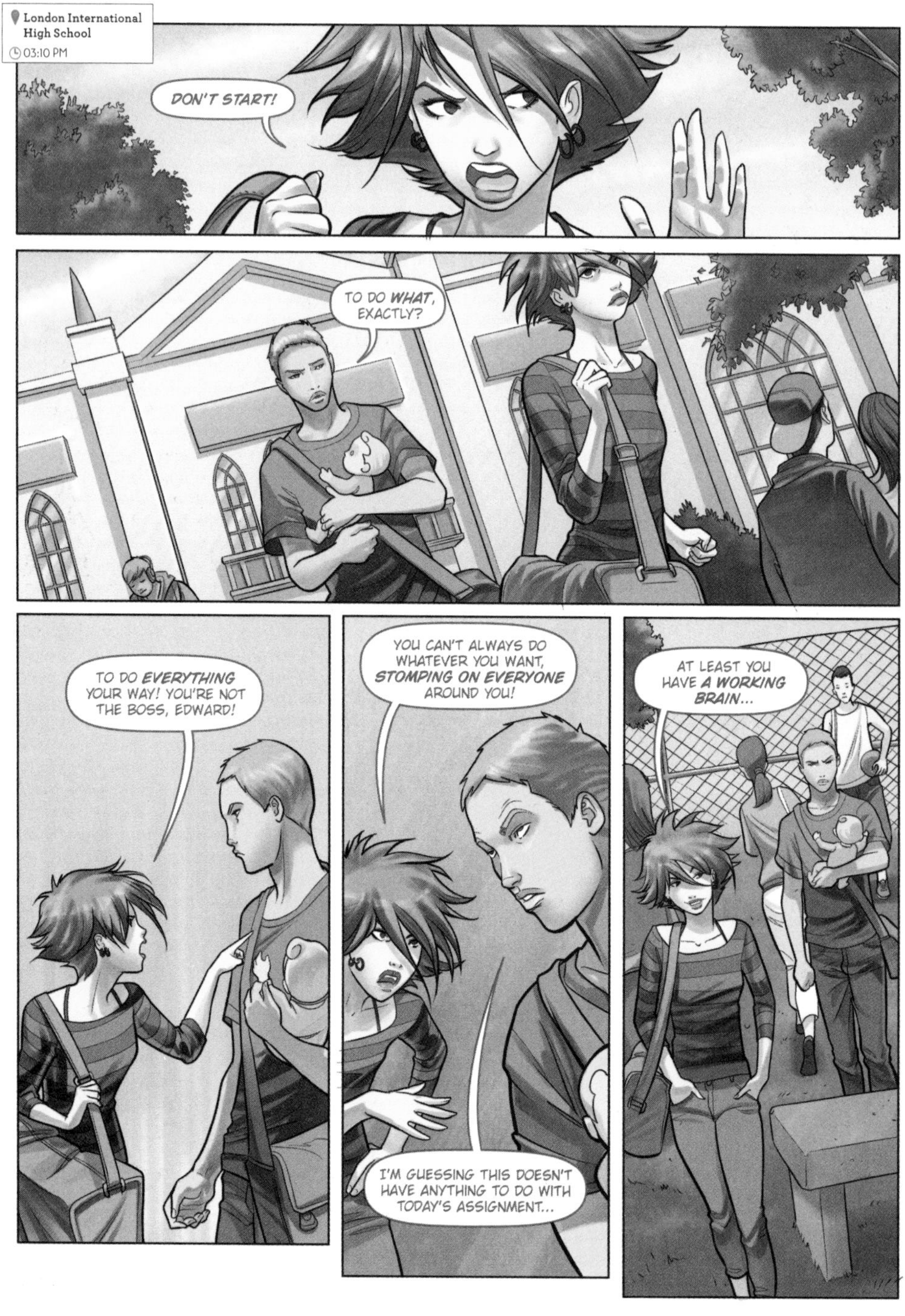
London International High School
03:10 PM
DON'T START!
TO DO WHAT, EXACTLY?
TO DO EVERYTHING YOUR WAY! YOU'RE NOT THE BOSS, EDWARD!
YOU CAN'T ALWAYS DO WHATEVER YOU WANT, STOMPING ON EVERYONE AROUND YOU!
I'M GUESSING THIS DOESN'T HAVE ANYTHING TO DO WITH TODAY'S ASSIGNMENT...
AT LEAST YOU HAVE A WORKING BRAIN...

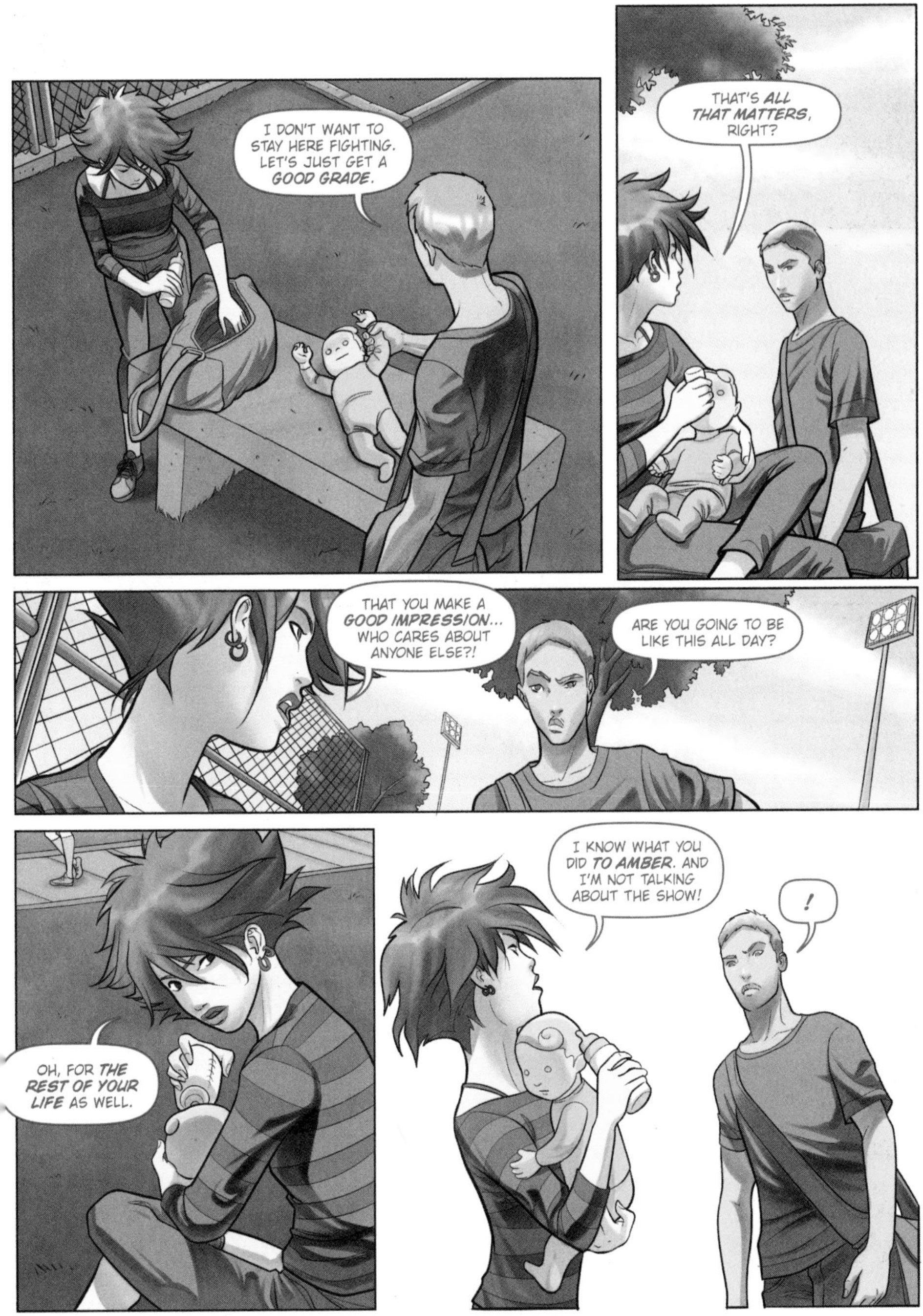
I DON'T WANT TO STAY HERE FIGHTING. LET'S JUST GET A GOOD GRADE.
THAT'S ALL THAT MATTERS, RIGHT?
THAT YOU MAKE A GOOD IMPRESSION... WHO CARES ABOUT ANYONE ELSE?!
ARE YOU GOING TO BE LIKE THIS ALL DAY?
OH, FOR THE REST OF YOUR LIFE AS WELL.
I KNOW WHAT YOU DID TO AMBER. AND I'M NOT TALKING ABOUT THE SHOW!
!

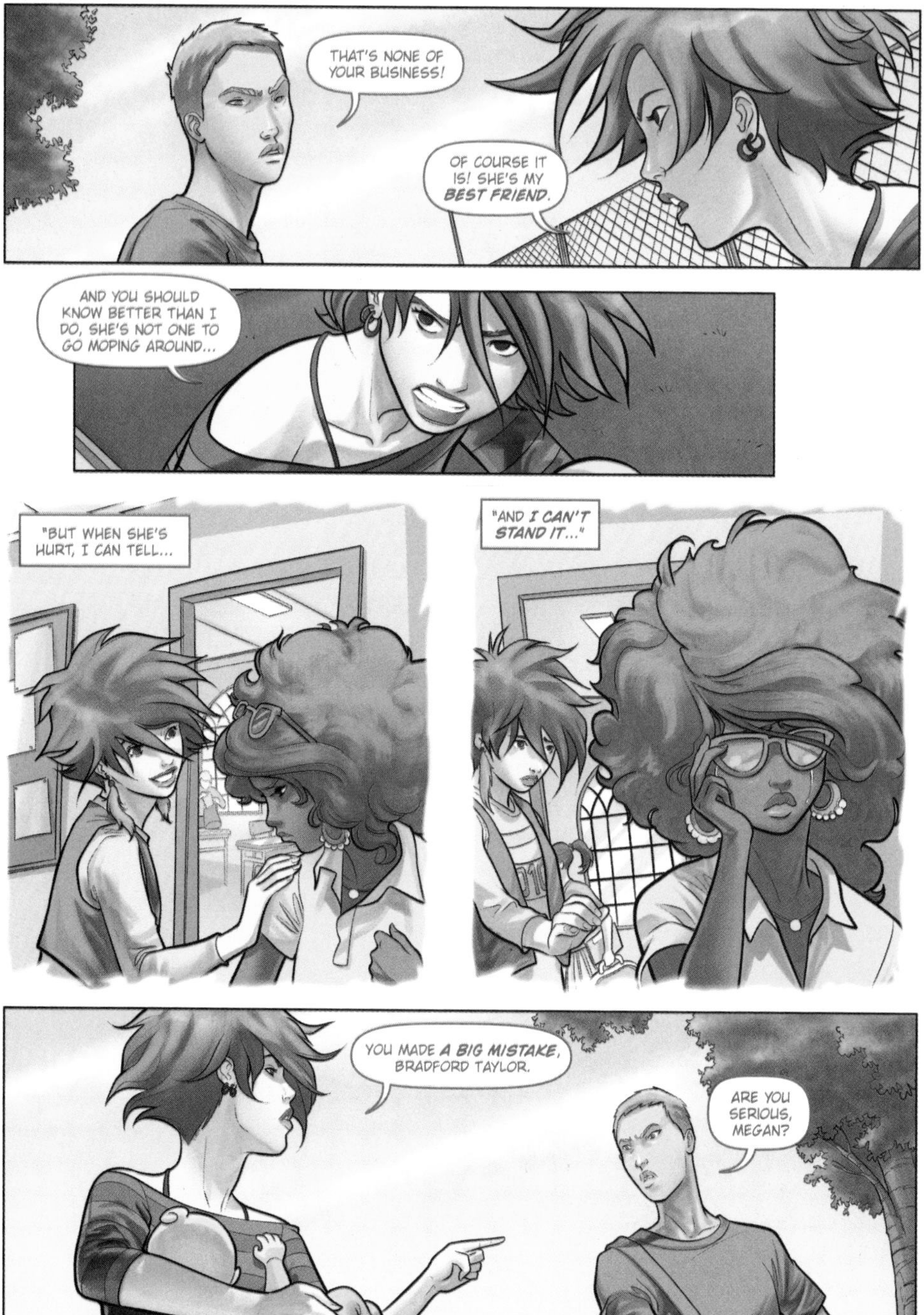
THAT'S NONE OF YOUR BUSINESS!
OF COURSE IT IS! SHE'S MY **BEST FRIEND**.
AND YOU SHOULD KNOW BETTER THAN I DO, SHE'S NOT ONE TO GO MOPING AROUND...
"BUT WHEN SHE'S HURT, I CAN TELL...
"AND ***I CAN'T STAND IT***..."
YOU MADE ***A BIG MISTAKE***, BRADFORD TAYLOR.
ARE YOU SERIOUS, MEGAN?

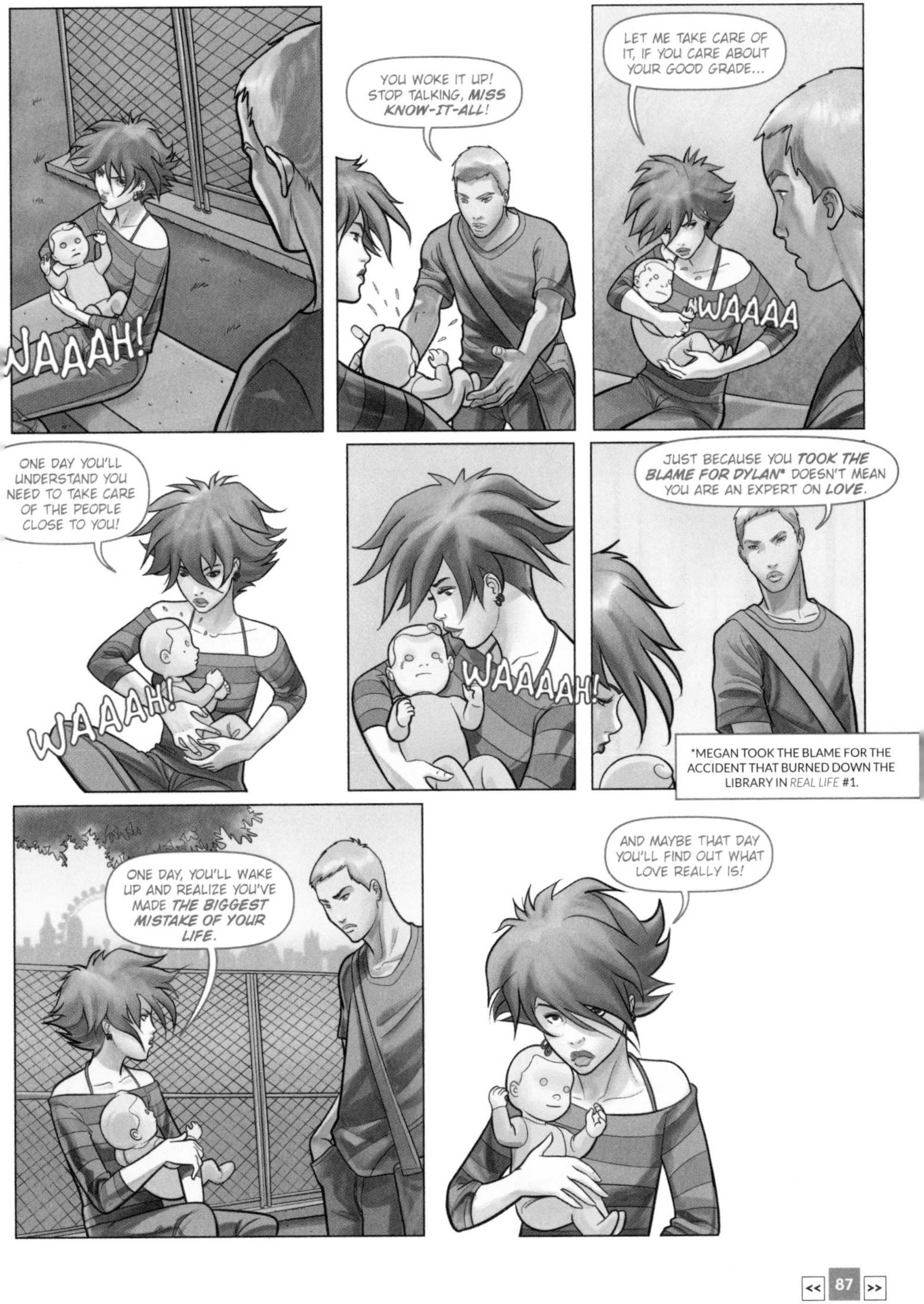
WAAAH!
YOU WOKE IT UP! STOP TALKING, MISS KNOW-IT-ALL!
LET ME TAKE CARE OF IT, IF YOU CARE ABOUT YOUR GOOD GRADE...
WAAAA
ONE DAY YOU'LL UNDERSTAND YOU NEED TO TAKE CARE OF THE PEOPLE CLOSE TO YOU!
WAAAAH!
WAAAAAH!
JUST BECAUSE YOU TOOK THE BLAME FOR DYLAN* DOESN'T MEAN YOU ARE AN EXPERT ON LOVE.
*MEGAN TOOK THE BLAME FOR THE ACCIDENT THAT BURNED DOWN THE LIBRARY IN REAL LIFE #1.
ONE DAY, YOU'LL WAKE UP AND REALIZE YOU'VE MADE THE BIGGEST MISTAKE OF YOUR LIFE.
AND MAYBE THAT DAY YOU'LL FIND OUT WHAT LOVE REALLY IS!

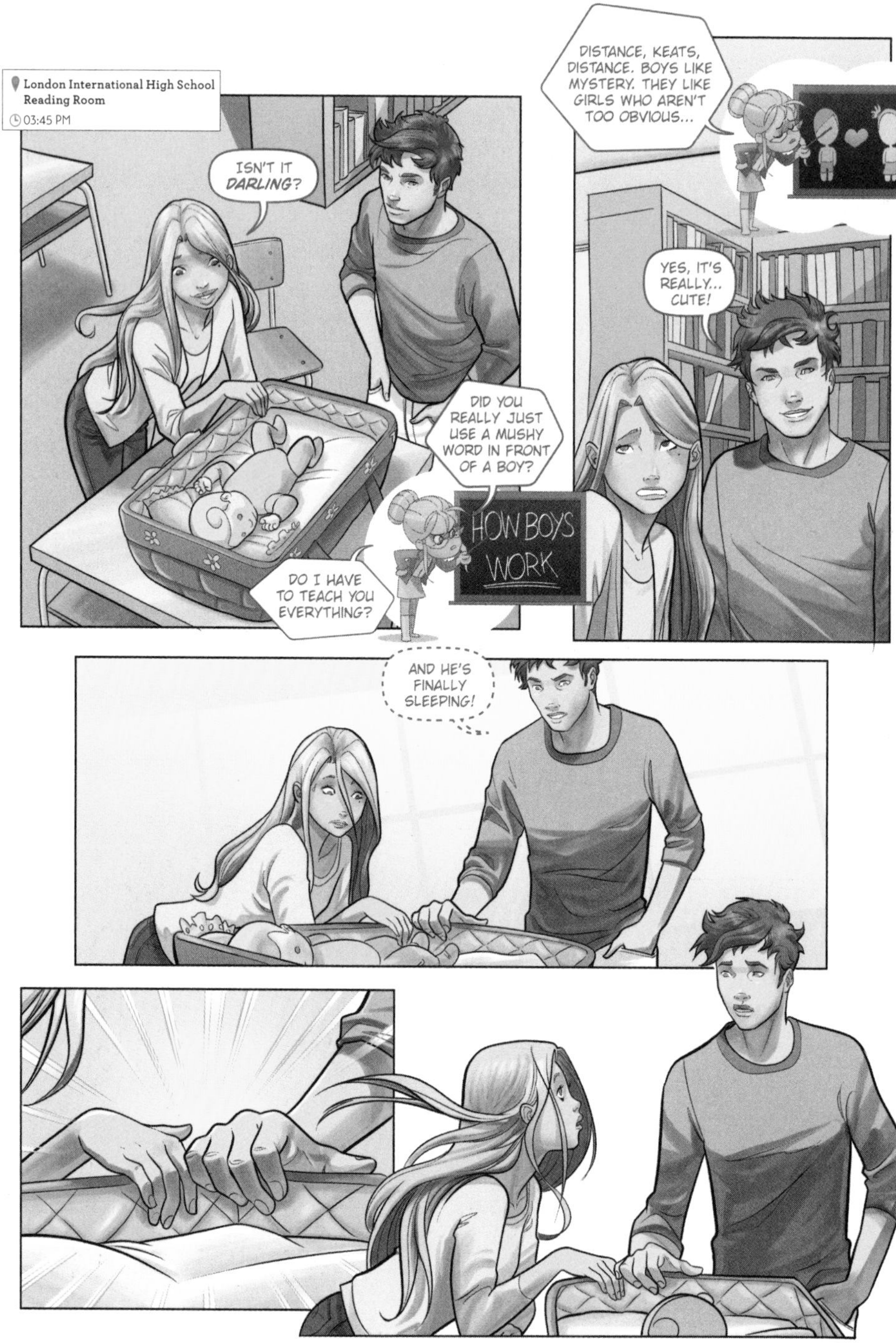
London International High School
Reading Room
03:45 PM
ISN'T IT DARLING?
DID YOU REALLY JUST USE A MUSHY WORD IN FRONT OF A BOY?
HOW BOYS WORK
DO I HAVE TO TEACH YOU EVERYTHING?
DISTANCE, KEATS, DISTANCE. BOYS LIKE MYSTERY. THEY LIKE GIRLS WHO AREN'T TOO OBVIOUS...
YES, IT'S REALLY... CUTE!
AND HE'S FINALLY SLEEPING!

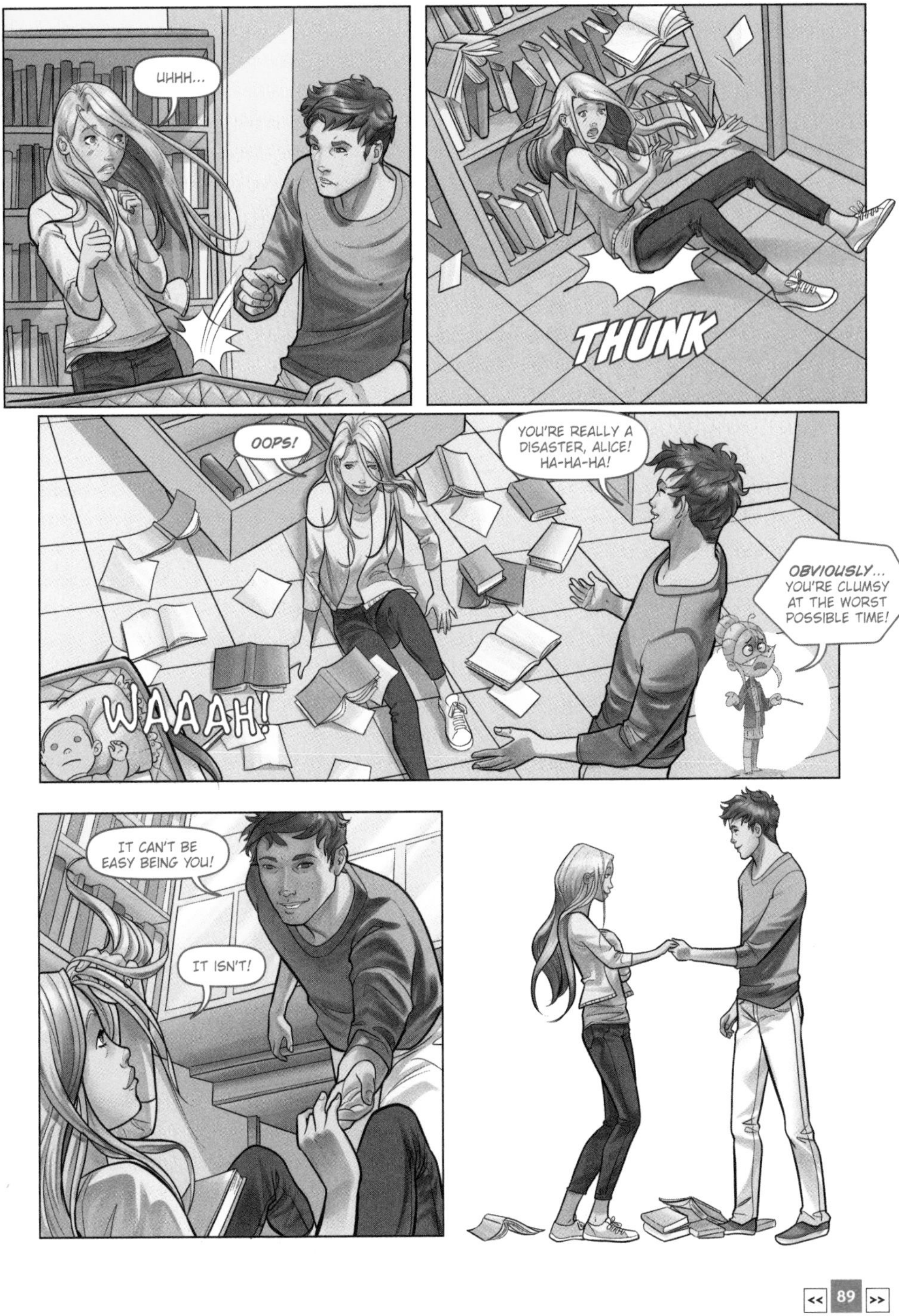
UHHH...
THUNK
OOPS!
YOU'RE REALLY A DISASTER, ALICE! HA-HA-HA!
WAAAAH!
OBVIOUSLY... YOU'RE CLUMSY AT THE WORST POSSIBLE TIME!
IT CAN'T BE EASY BEING YOU!
IT ISN'T!

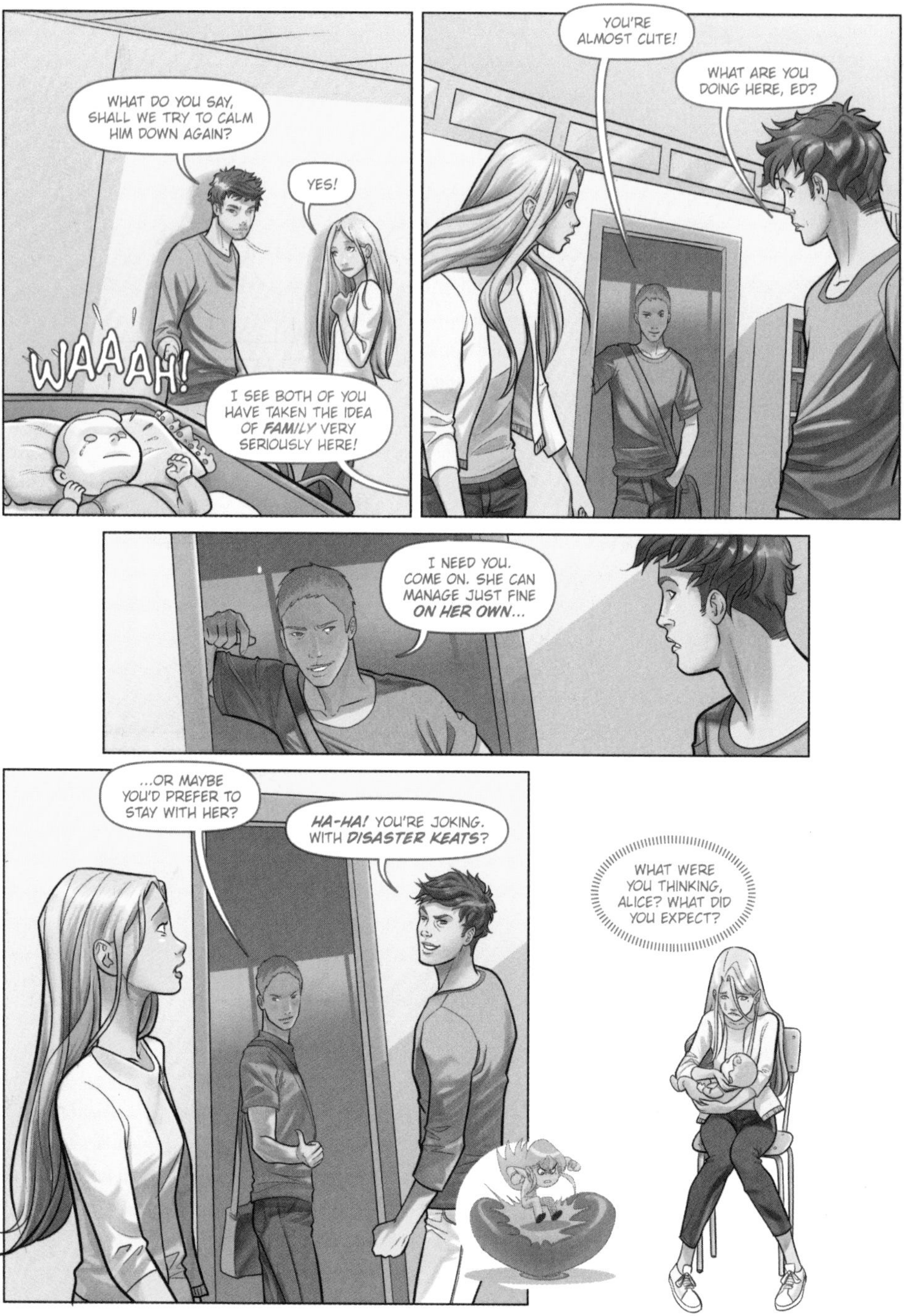
WHAT DO YOU SAY, SHALL WE TRY TO CALM HIM DOWN AGAIN?
YES!
WAAAH!
I SEE BOTH OF YOU HAVE TAKEN THE IDEA OF FAMILY VERY SERIOUSLY HERE!
YOU'RE ALMOST CUTE!
WHAT ARE YOU DOING HERE, ED?
I NEED YOU. COME ON. SHE CAN MANAGE JUST FINE ON HER OWN...
...OR MAYBE YOU'D PREFER TO STAY WITH HER?
HA-HA! YOU'RE JOKING. WITH DISASTER KEATS?
WHAT WERE YOU THINKING, ALICE? WHAT DID YOU EXPECT?

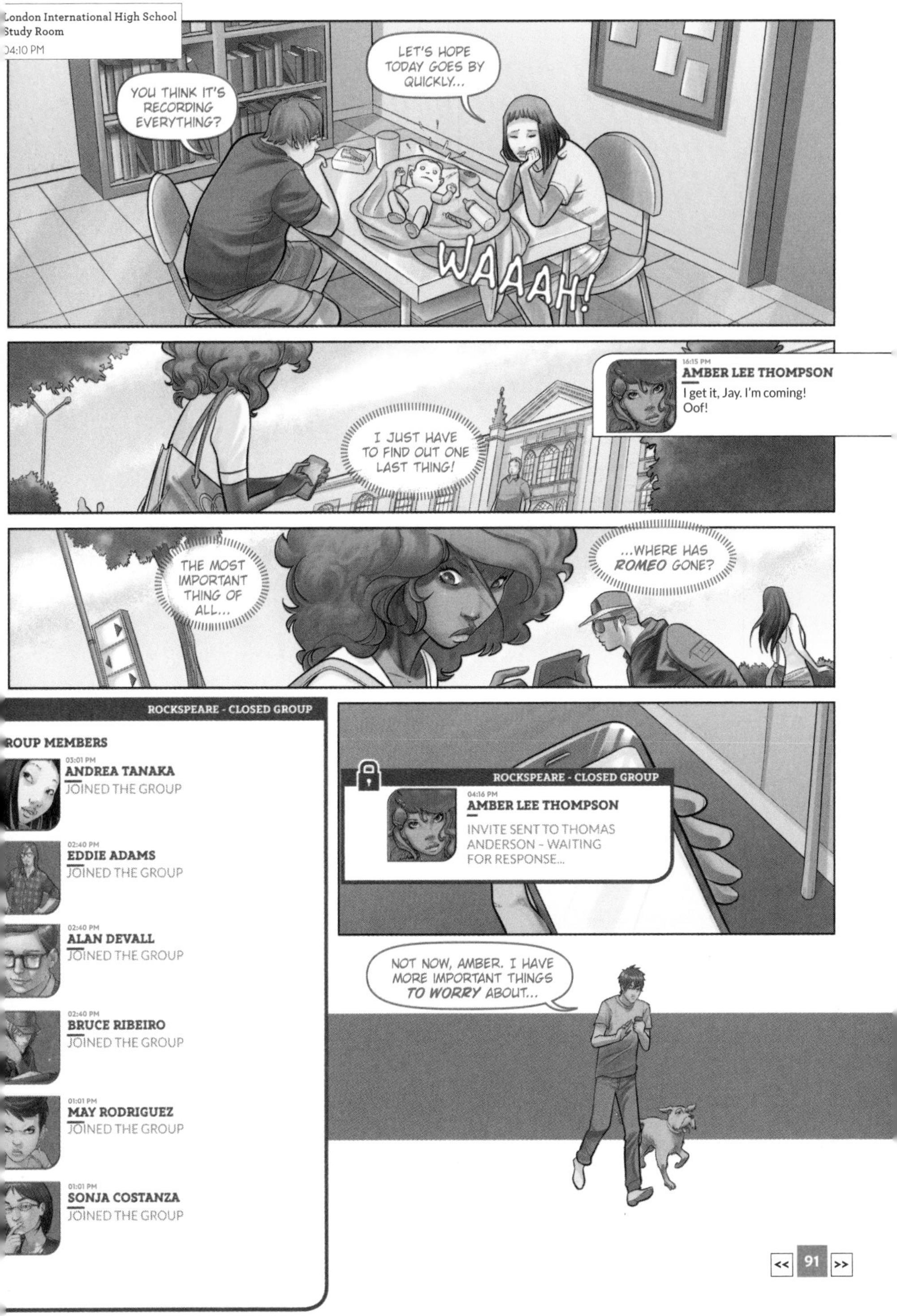

London International High School
Study Room
04:10 PM
YOU THINK IT'S RECORDING EVERYTHING?
LET'S HOPE TODAY GOES BY QUICKLY...
WAAAAH!
I JUST HAVE TO FIND OUT ONE LAST THING!
16:15 PM
AMBER LEE THOMPSON
I get it, Jay. I'm coming! Oof!
THE MOST IMPORTANT THING OF ALL...
...WHERE HAS ROMEO GONE?
ROCKSPEARE - CLOSED GROUP
ROUP MEMBERS
03:01 PM
ANDREA TANAKA
JOINED THE GROUP
02:40 PM
EDDIE ADAMS
JOINED THE GROUP
02:40 PM
ALAN DEVALL
JOINED THE GROUP
02:40 PM
BRUCE RIBEIRO
JOINED THE GROUP
01:01 PM
MAY RODRIGUEZ
JOINED THE GROUP
01:01 PM
SONJA COSTANZA
JOINED THE GROUP
ROCKSPEARE - CLOSED GROUP
04:16 PM
AMBER LEE THOMPSON
INVITE SENT TO THOMAS ANDERSON - WAITING FOR RESPONSE...
NOT NOW, AMBER. I HAVE MORE IMPORTANT THINGS TO WORRY ABOUT...

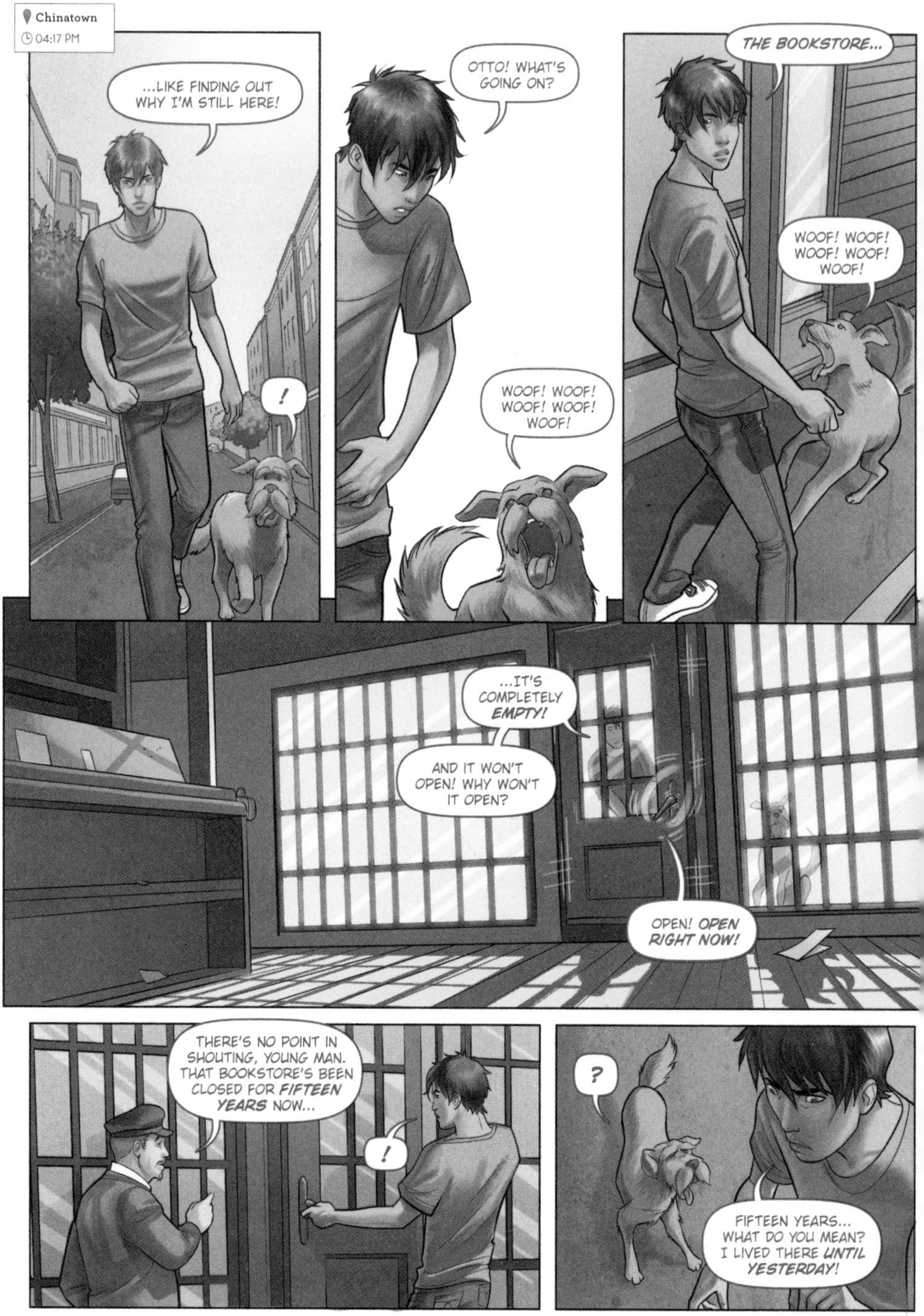
Chinatown
04:17 PM
...LIKE FINDING OUT WHY I'M STILL HERE!
!
OTTO! WHAT'S GOING ON?
WOOF! WOOF! WOOF! WOOF! WOOF!
THE BOOKSTORE...
WOOF! WOOF! WOOF! WOOF! WOOF!
...IT'S COMPLETELY EMPTY!
AND IT WON'T OPEN! WHY WON'T IT OPEN?
OPEN! OPEN RIGHT NOW!
THERE'S NO POINT IN SHOUTING, YOUNG MAN. THAT BOOKSTORE'S BEEN CLOSED FOR FIFTEEN YEARS NOW...
!
?
FIFTEEN YEARS... WHAT DO YOU MEAN? I LIVED THERE UNTIL YESTERDAY!

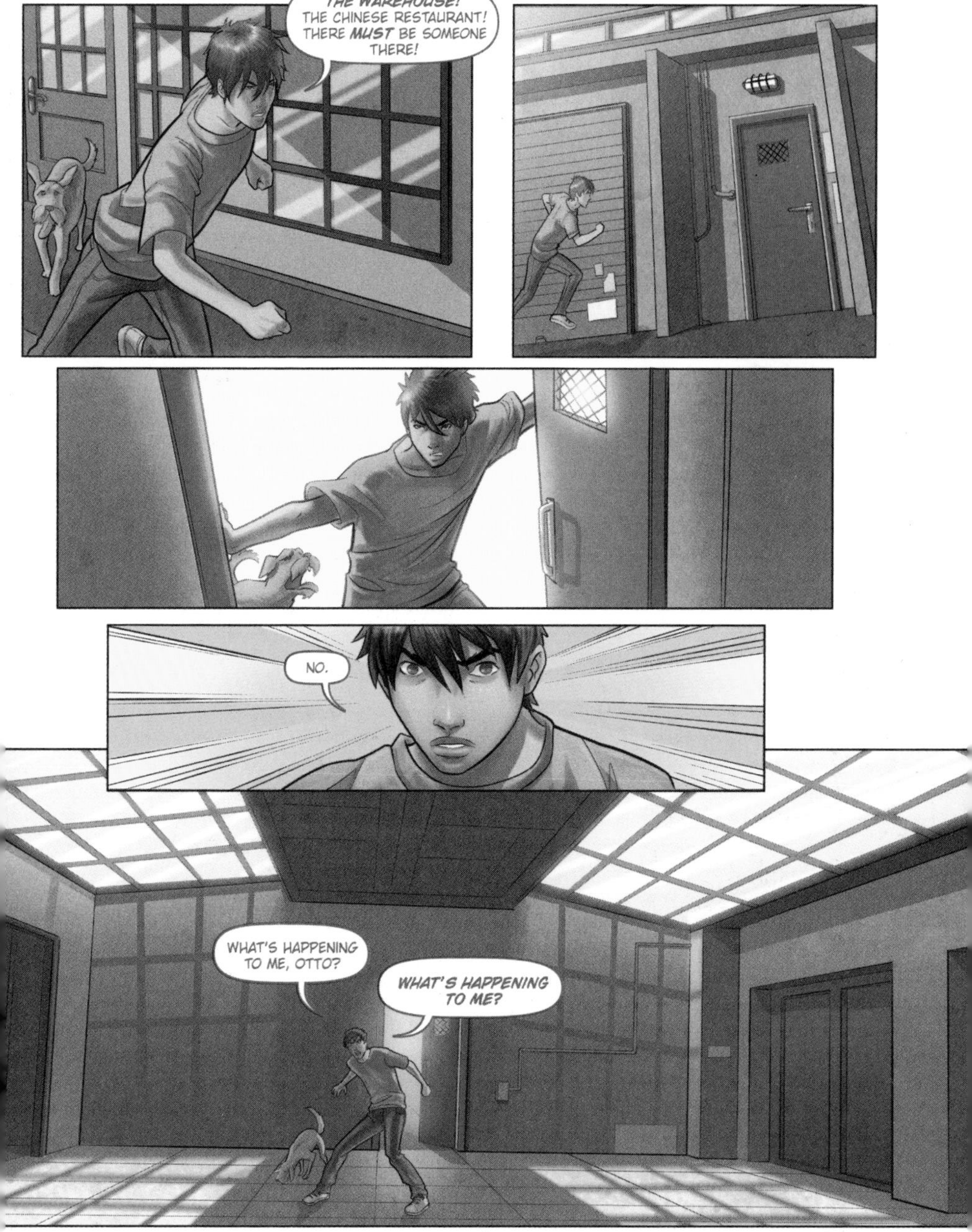
THE WAREHOUSE! THE CHINESE RESTAURANT! THERE MUST BE SOMEONE THERE!
NO.
WHAT'S HAPPENING TO ME, OTTO?
WHAT'S HAPPENING TO ME?

END OF CHAPTER 23

CHAPTER 24

SECRET SUMMIT

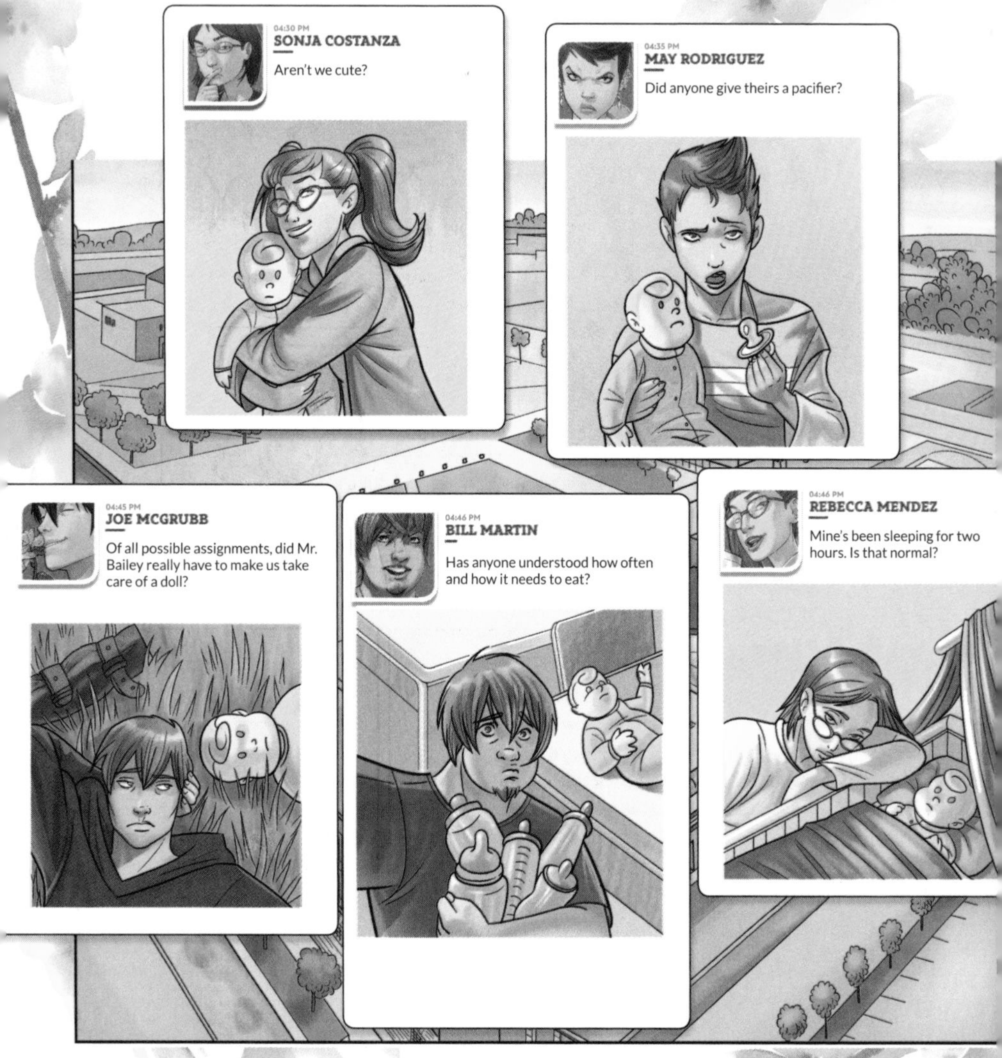
04:30 PM
SONJA COSTANZA
Aren't we cute?
04:35 PM
MAY RODRIGUEZ
Did anyone give theirs a pacifier?
04:45 PM
JOE MCGRUBB
Of all possible assignments, did Mr. Bailey really have to make us take care of a doll?
04:46 PM
BILL MARTIN
Has anyone understood how often and how it needs to eat?
04:46 PM
REBECCA MENDEZ
Mine's been sleeping for two hours. Is that normal?

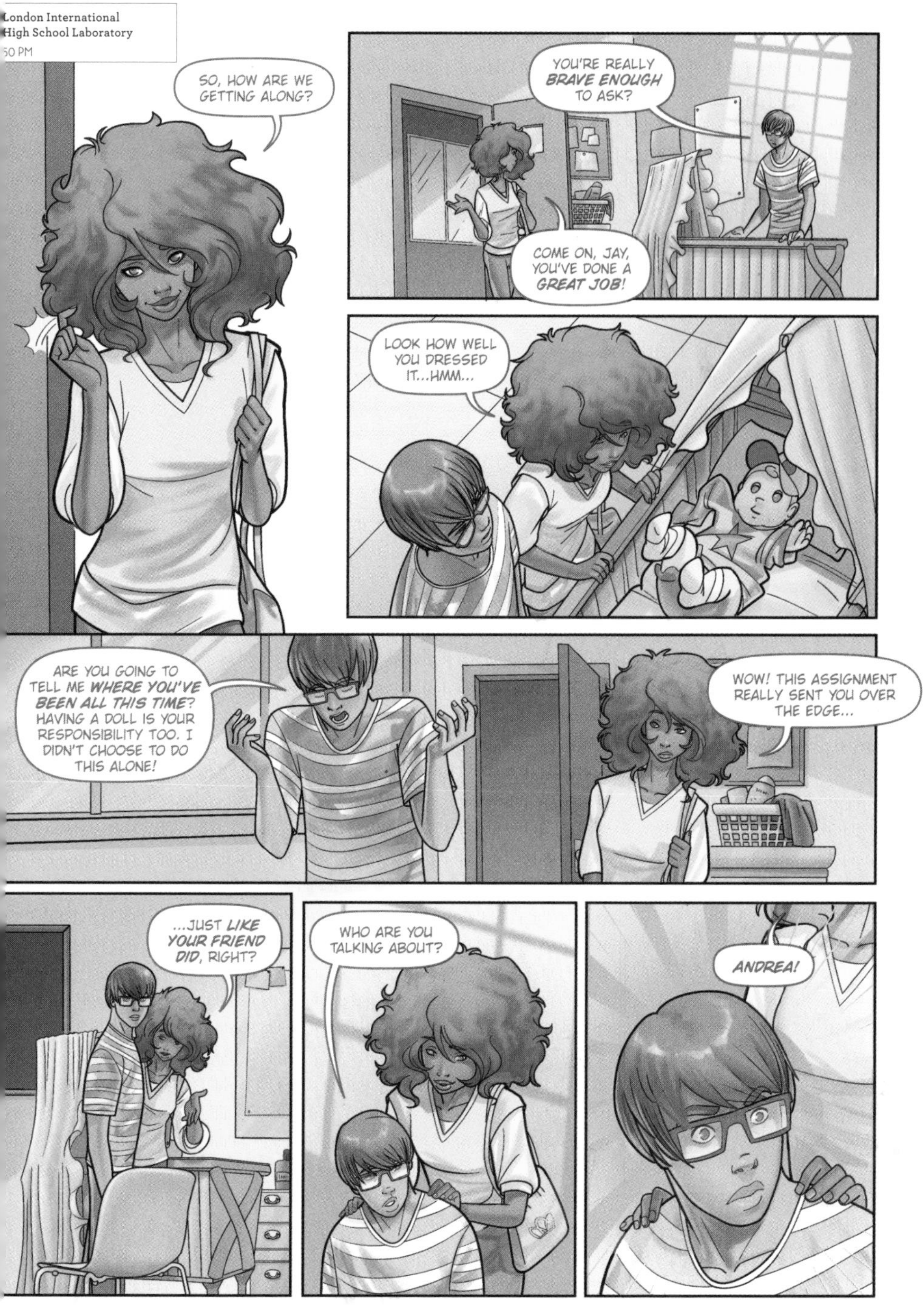
London International
High School Laboratory
50 PM
SO, HOW ARE WE GETTING ALONG?
YOU'RE REALLY BRAVE ENOUGH TO ASK?
COME ON, JAY, YOU'VE DONE A GREAT JOB!
LOOK HOW WELL YOU DRESSED IT...HMM...
ARE YOU GOING TO TELL ME WHERE YOU'VE BEEN ALL THIS TIME? HAVING A DOLL IS YOUR RESPONSIBILITY TOO. I DIDN'T CHOOSE TO DO THIS ALONE!
WOW! THIS ASSIGNMENT REALLY SENT YOU OVER THE EDGE...
...JUST LIKE YOUR FRIEND DID, RIGHT?
WHO ARE YOU TALKING ABOUT?
ANDREA!

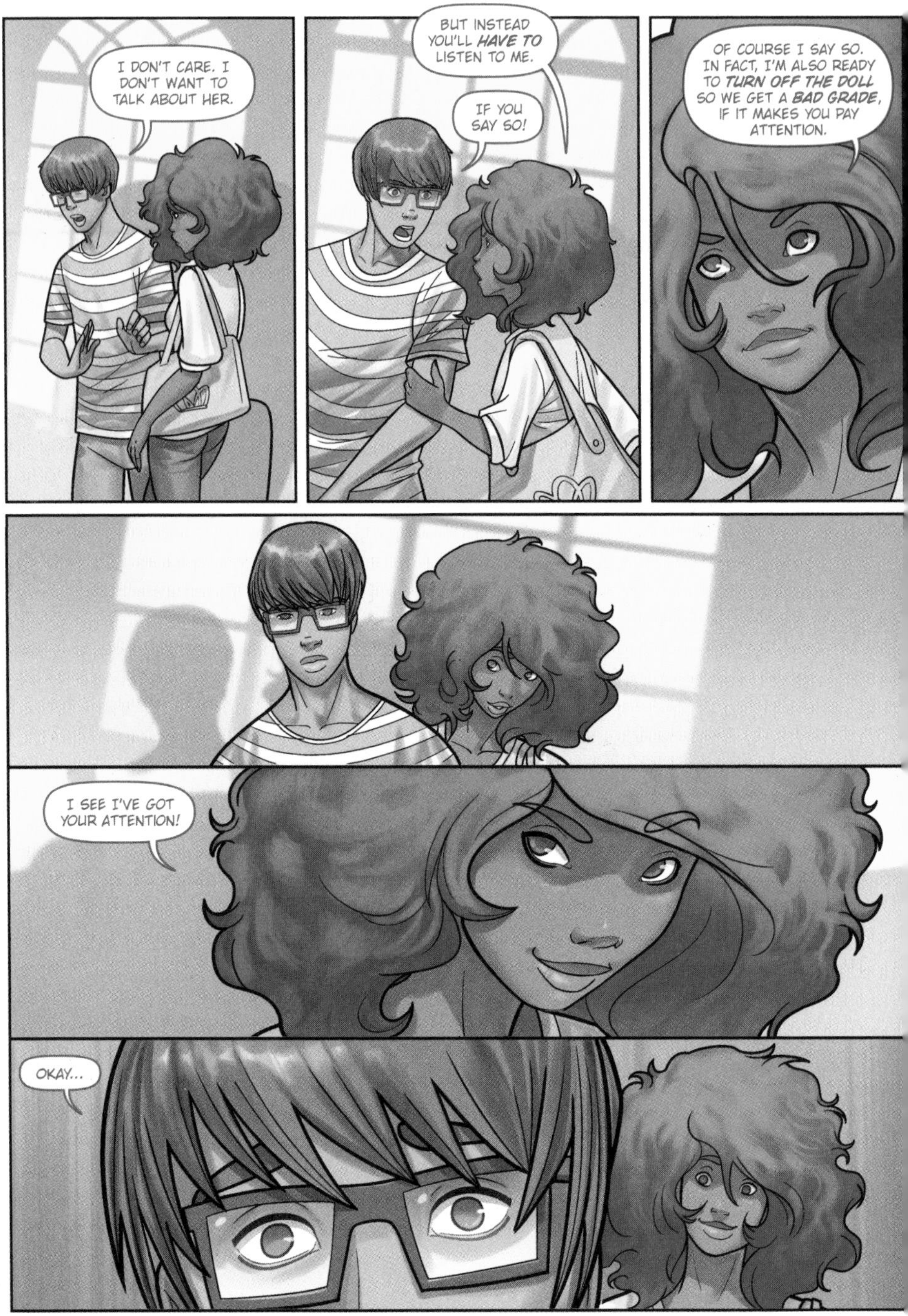
I DON'T CARE. I DON'T WANT TO TALK ABOUT HER.
IF YOU SAY SO!
BUT INSTEAD YOU'LL **HAVE TO** LISTEN TO ME.
OF COURSE I SAY SO. IN FACT, I'M ALSO READY TO **TURN OFF THE DOLL** SO WE GET A **BAD GRADE**, IF IT MAKES YOU PAY ATTENTION.
I SEE I'VE GOT YOUR ATTENTION!
OKAY...

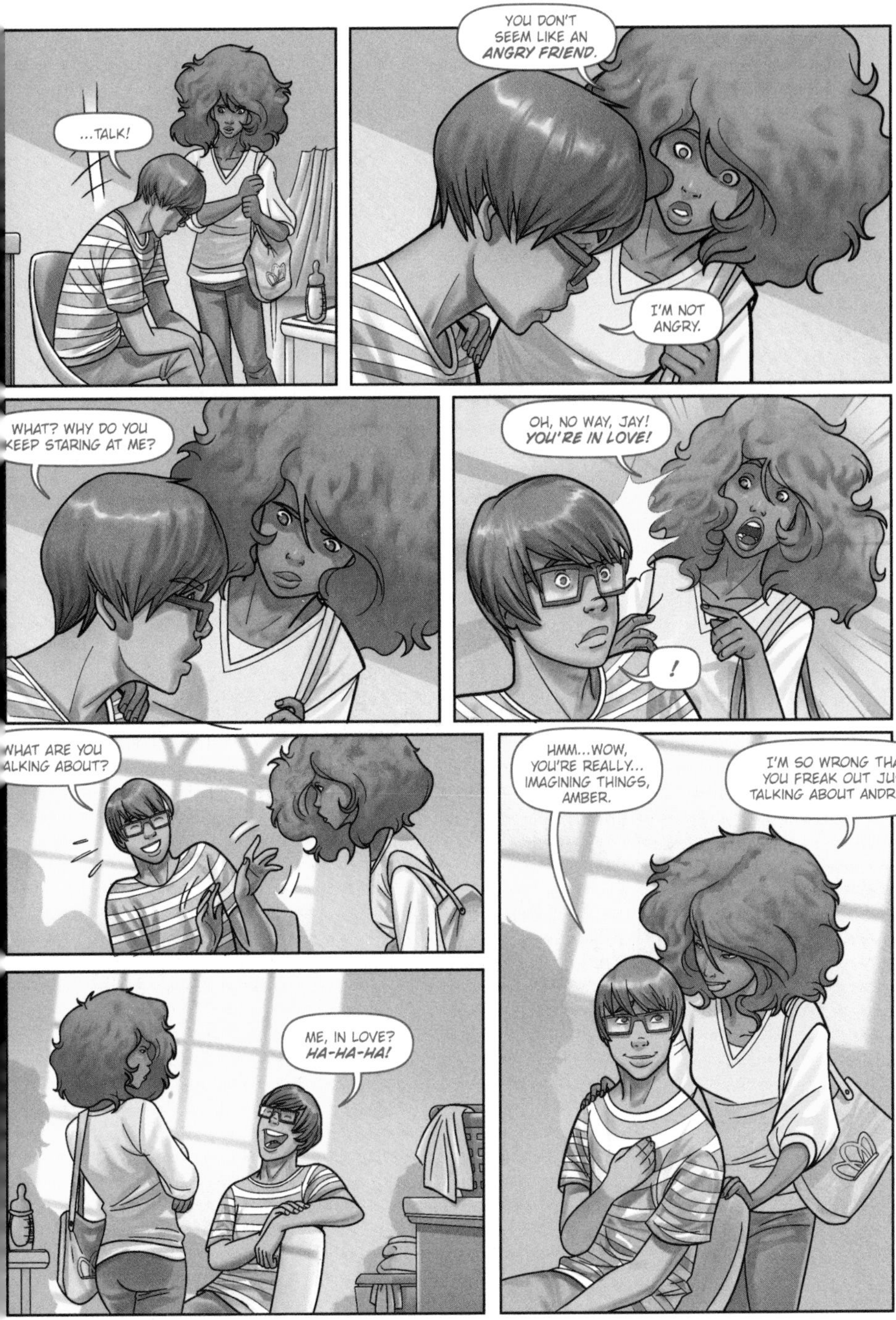
...TALK!
YOU DON'T SEEM LIKE AN ANGRY FRIEND.
I'M NOT ANGRY.
WHAT? WHY DO YOU KEEP STARING AT ME?
OH, NO WAY, JAY! YOU'RE IN LOVE!
!
WHAT ARE YOU TALKING ABOUT?
ME, IN LOVE? HA-HA-HA!
HMM...WOW, YOU'RE REALLY... IMAGINING THINGS, AMBER.
I'M SO WRONG THAT YOU FREAK OUT JUST TALKING ABOUT ANDREA...

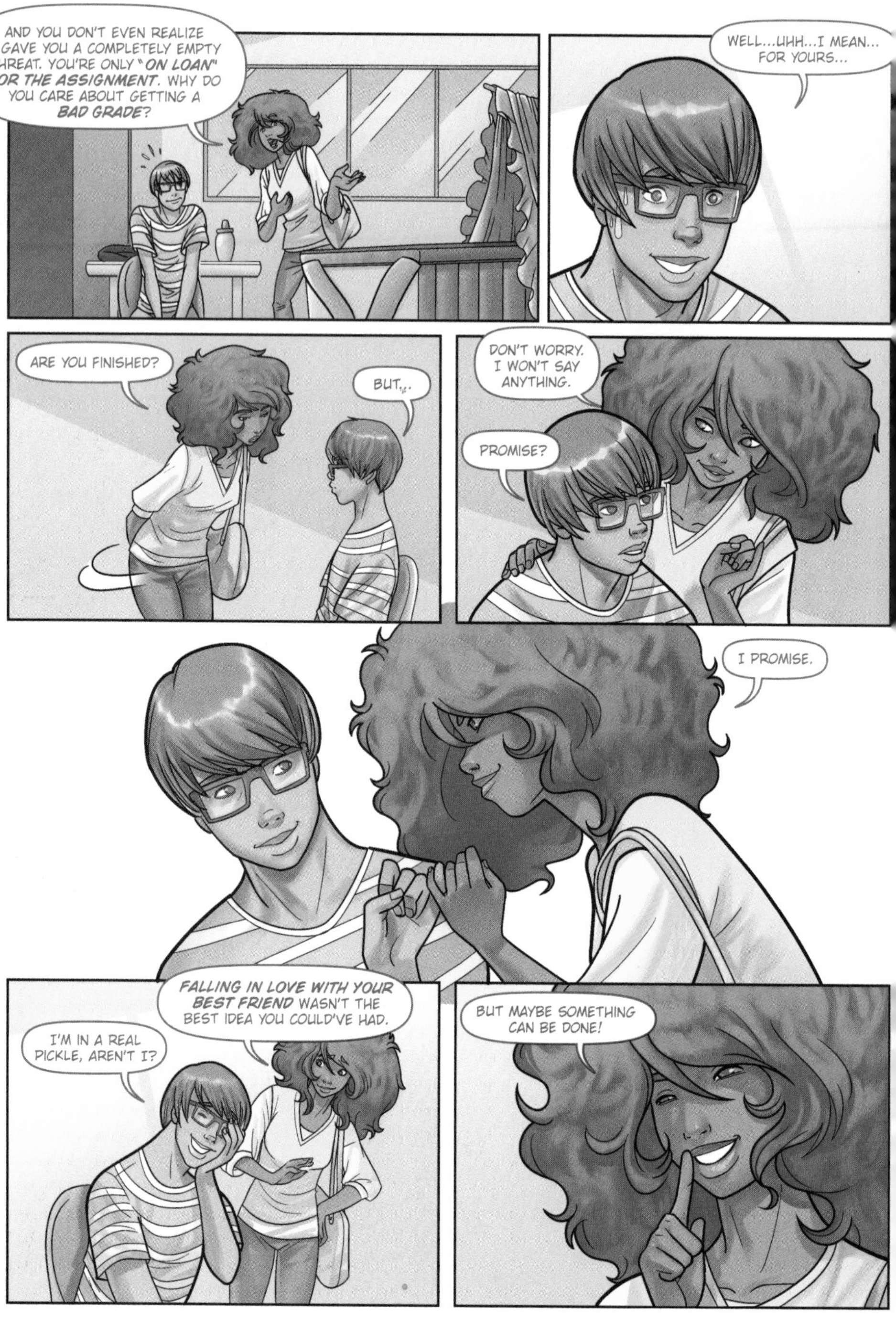

AND YOU DON'T EVEN REALIZE I GAVE YOU A COMPLETELY EMPTY THREAT. YOU'RE ONLY "ON LOAN" FOR THE ASSIGNMENT. WHY DO YOU CARE ABOUT GETTING A BAD GRADE?
WELL...UHH...I MEAN... FOR YOURS...
ARE YOU FINISHED?
BUT...
DON'T WORRY. I WON'T SAY ANYTHING.
PROMISE?
I PROMISE.
I'M IN A REAL PICKLE, AREN'T I?
FALLING IN LOVE WITH YOUR BEST FRIEND WASN'T THE BEST IDEA YOU COULD'VE HAD.
BUT MAYBE SOMETHING CAN BE DONE!

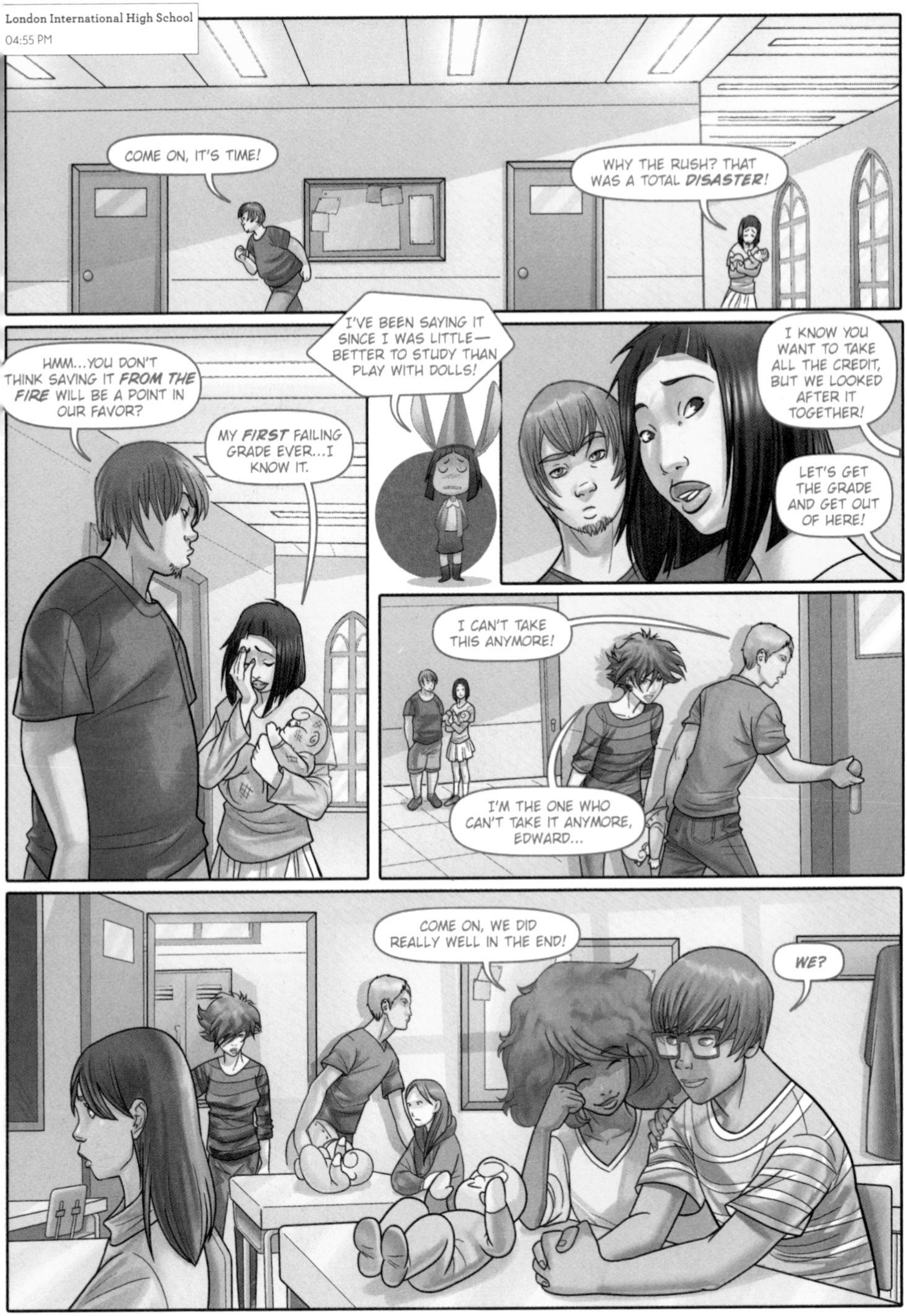
London International High School
04:55 PM
COME ON, IT'S TIME!
WHY THE RUSH? THAT WAS A TOTAL DISASTER!
HMM...YOU DON'T THINK SAVING IT FROM THE FIRE WILL BE A POINT IN OUR FAVOR?
MY FIRST FAILING GRADE EVER...I KNOW IT.
I'VE BEEN SAYING IT SINCE I WAS LITTLE—BETTER TO STUDY THAN PLAY WITH DOLLS!
I KNOW YOU WANT TO TAKE ALL THE CREDIT, BUT WE LOOKED AFTER IT TOGETHER!
LET'S GET THE GRADE AND GET OUT OF HERE!
I CAN'T TAKE THIS ANYMORE!
I'M THE ONE WHO CAN'T TAKE IT ANYMORE, EDWARD...
COME ON, WE DID REALLY WELL IN THE END!
WE?

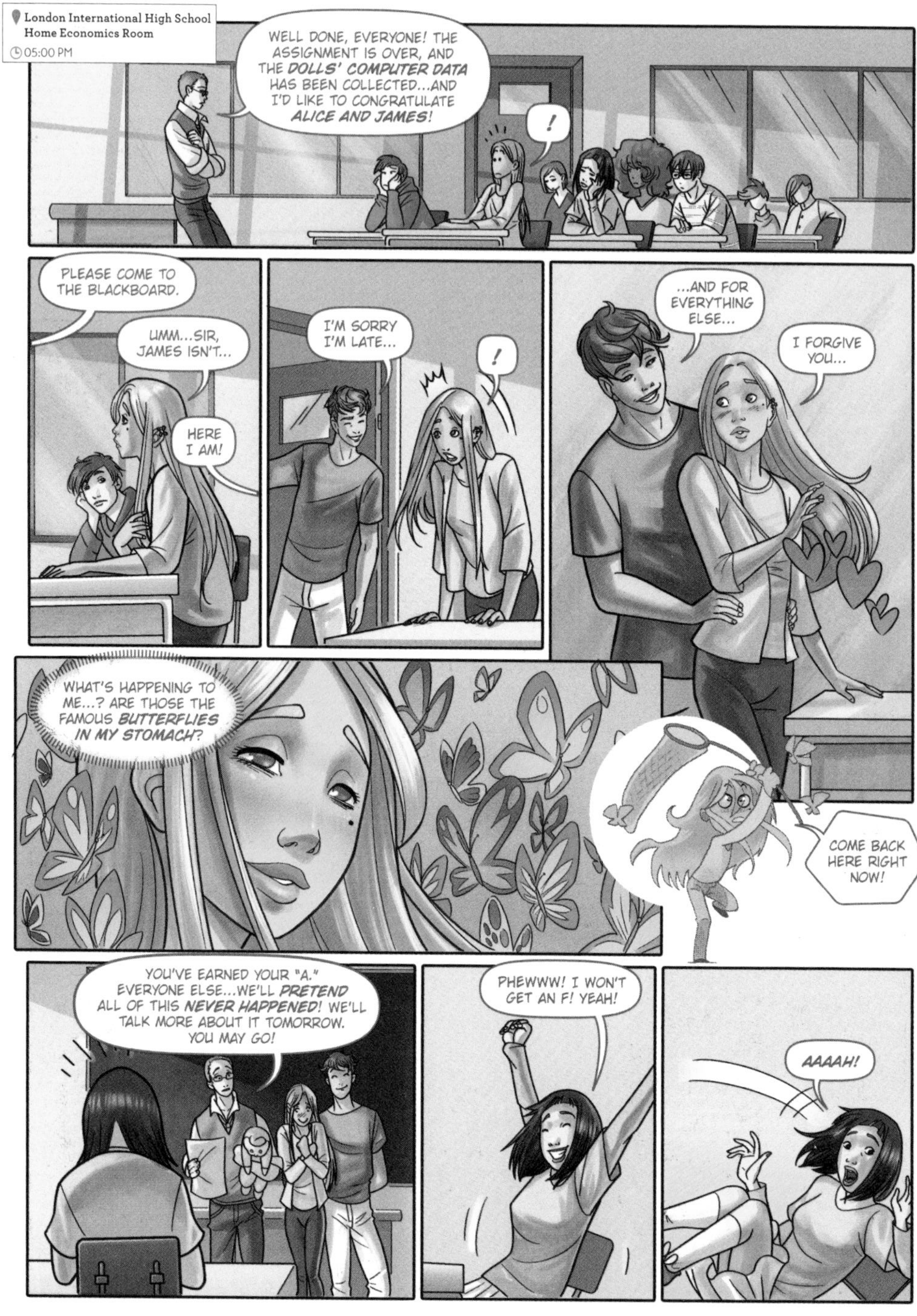
London International High School
Home Economics Room
05:00 PM
WELL DONE, EVERYONE! THE ASSIGNMENT IS OVER, AND THE DOLLS' COMPUTER DATA HAS BEEN COLLECTED...AND I'D LIKE TO CONGRATULATE ALICE AND JAMES!
!
PLEASE COME TO THE BLACKBOARD.
UMM...SIR, JAMES ISN'T...
HERE I AM!
I'M SORRY I'M LATE...
!
...AND FOR EVERYTHING ELSE...
I FORGIVE YOU...
WHAT'S HAPPENING TO ME...? ARE THOSE THE FAMOUS BUTTERFLIES IN MY STOMACH?
COME BACK HERE RIGHT NOW!
YOU'VE EARNED YOUR "A." EVERYONE ELSE...WE'LL PRETEND ALL OF THIS NEVER HAPPENED! WE'LL TALK MORE ABOUT IT TOMORROW. YOU MAY GO!
PHEWWW! I WON'T GET AN F! YEAH!
AAAAH!

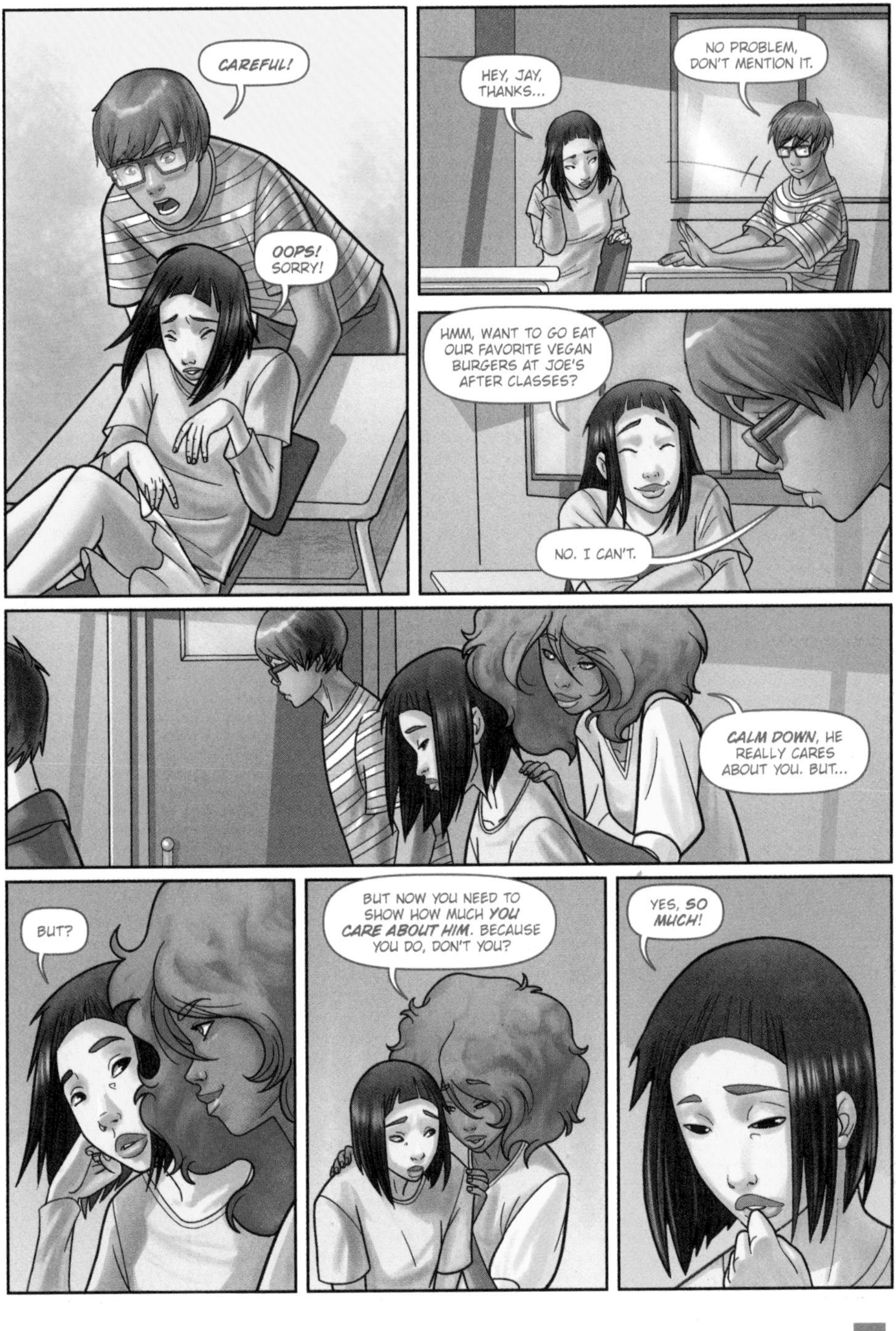
CAREFUL!
OOPS! SORRY!
HEY, JAY, THANKS...
NO PROBLEM, DON'T MENTION IT.
HMM, WANT TO GO EAT OUR FAVORITE VEGAN BURGERS AT JOE'S AFTER CLASSES?
NO. I CAN'T.
CALM DOWN, HE REALLY CARES ABOUT YOU. BUT...
BUT?
BUT NOW YOU NEED TO SHOW HOW MUCH YOU CARE ABOUT HIM. BECAUSE YOU DO, DON'T YOU?
YES, SO MUCH!

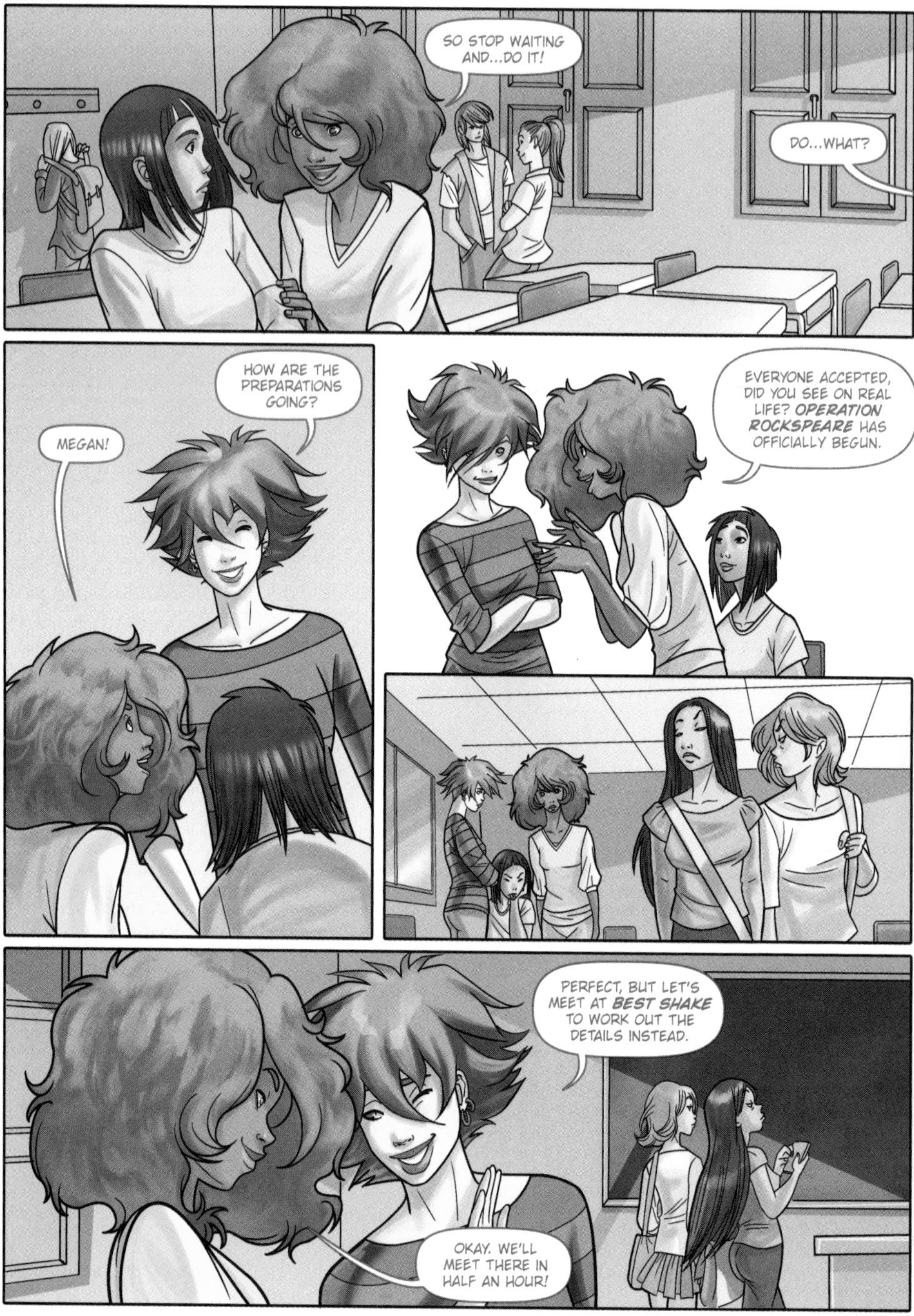
SO STOP WAITING AND...DO IT!
DO...WHAT?
HOW ARE THE PREPARATIONS GOING?
MEGAN!
EVERYONE ACCEPTED, DID YOU SEE ON REAL LIFE? OPERATION ROCKSPEARE HAS OFFICIALLY BEGUN.
PERFECT, BUT LET'S MEET AT BEST SHAKE TO WORK OUT THE DETAILS INSTEAD.
OKAY. WE'LL MEET THERE IN HALF AN HOUR!

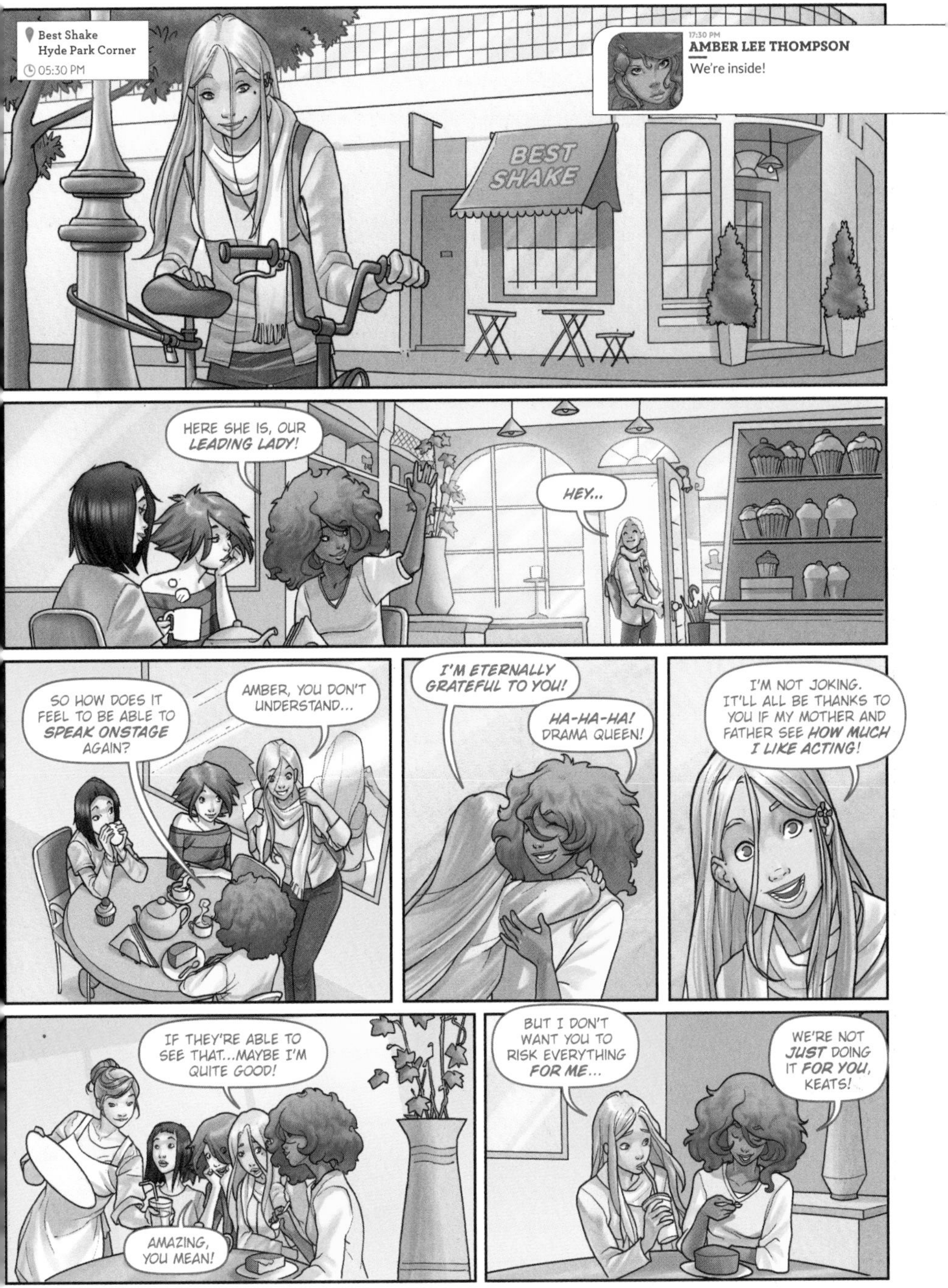

Best Shake
Hyde Park Corner
05:30 PM
17:30 PM
AMBER LEE THOMPSON
We're inside!
BEST SHAKE
HERE SHE IS, OUR LEADING LADY!
HEY...
SO HOW DOES IT FEEL TO BE ABLE TO SPEAK ONSTAGE AGAIN?
AMBER, YOU DON'T UNDERSTAND...
I'M ETERNALLY GRATEFUL TO YOU!
HA-HA-HA! DRAMA QUEEN!
I'M NOT JOKING. IT'LL ALL BE THANKS TO YOU IF MY MOTHER AND FATHER SEE HOW MUCH I LIKE ACTING!
IF THEY'RE ABLE TO SEE THAT...MAYBE I'M QUITE GOOD!
AMAZING, YOU MEAN!
BUT I DON'T WANT YOU TO RISK EVERYTHING FOR ME...
WE'RE NOT JUST DOING IT FOR YOU, KEATS!

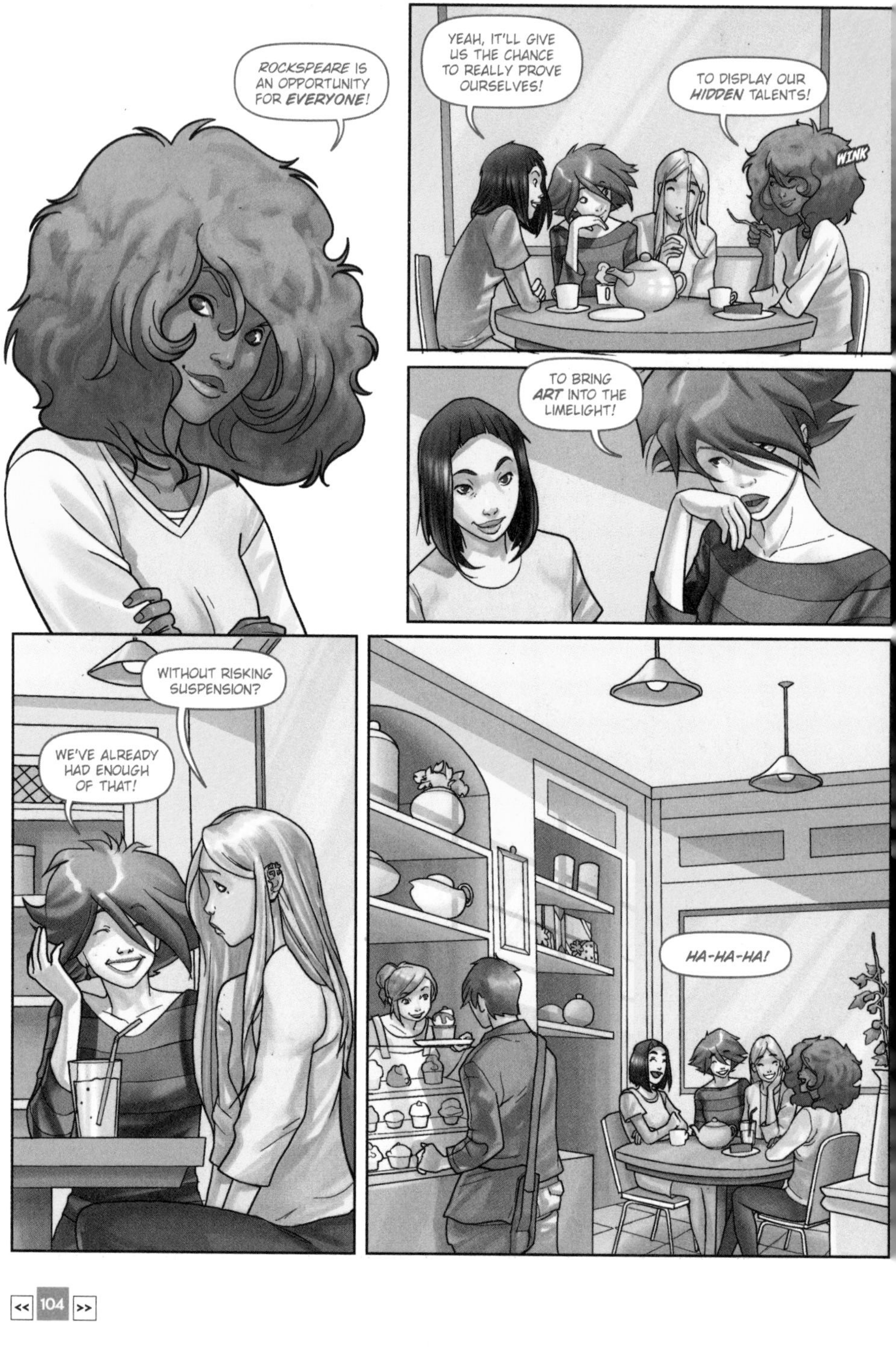

ROCKSPEARE IS AN OPPORTUNITY FOR EVERYONE!
YEAH, IT'LL GIVE US THE CHANCE TO REALLY PROVE OURSELVES!
TO DISPLAY OUR HIDDEN TALENTS!
WINK
TO BRING ART INTO THE LIMELIGHT!
WITHOUT RISKING SUSPENSION?
WE'VE ALREADY HAD ENOUGH OF THAT!
HA-HA-HA!

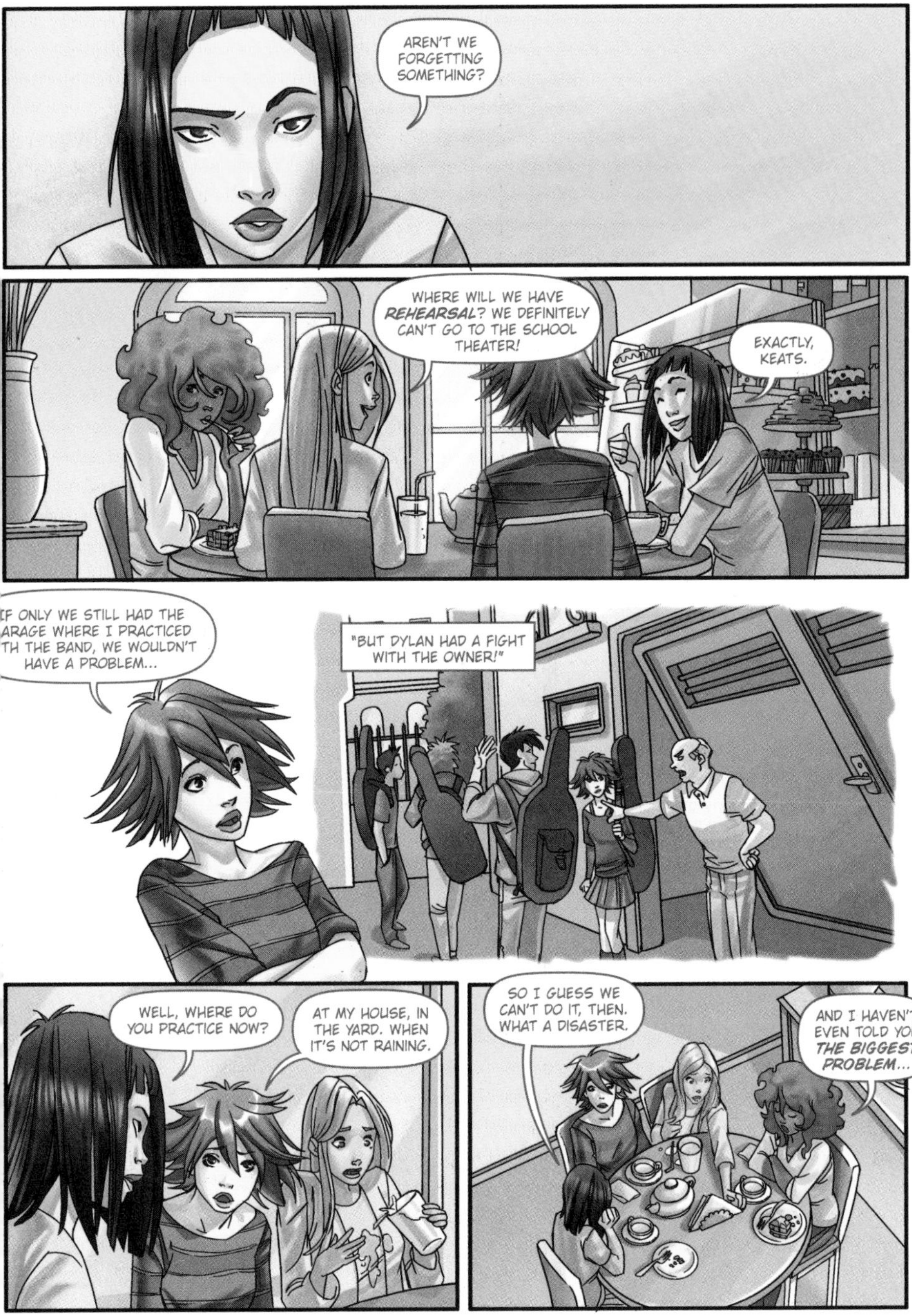

AREN'T WE FORGETTING SOMETHING?
WHERE WILL WE HAVE **REHEARSAL**? WE DEFINITELY CAN'T GO TO THE SCHOOL THEATER!
EXACTLY, KEATS.
IF ONLY WE STILL HAD THE ARAGE WHERE I PRACTICED TH THE BAND, WE WOULDN'T HAVE A PROBLEM...
"BUT DYLAN HAD A FIGHT WITH THE OWNER!"
WELL, WHERE DO YOU PRACTICE NOW?
AT MY HOUSE, IN THE YARD. WHEN IT'S NOT RAINING.
SO I GUESS WE CAN'T DO IT, THEN. WHAT A DISASTER.
AND I HAVEN'T EVEN TOLD YOU **THE BIGGEST PROBLEM...**

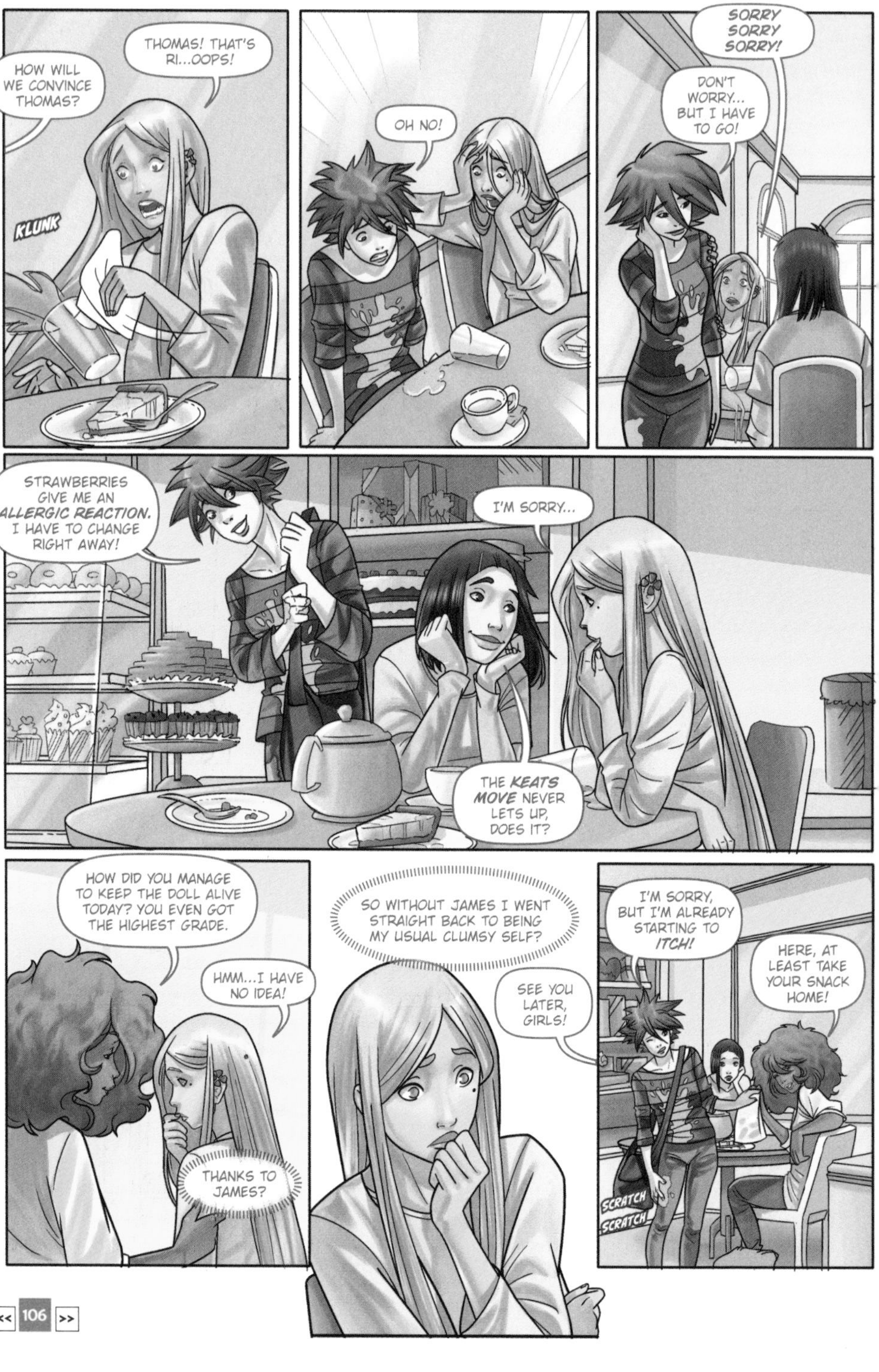
HOW WILL WE CONVINCE THOMAS?
THOMAS! THAT'S RI...OOPS!
KLUNK
OH NO!
SORRY SORRY SORRY!
DON'T WORRY... BUT I HAVE TO GO!
STRAWBERRIES GIVE ME AN ALLERGIC REACTION. I HAVE TO CHANGE RIGHT AWAY!
I'M SORRY...
THE KEATS MOVE NEVER LETS UP, DOES IT?
HOW DID YOU MANAGE TO KEEP THE DOLL ALIVE TODAY? YOU EVEN GOT THE HIGHEST GRADE.
HMM...I HAVE NO IDEA!
THANKS TO JAMES?
SO WITHOUT JAMES I WENT STRAIGHT BACK TO BEING MY USUAL CLUMSY SELF?
SEE YOU LATER, GIRLS!
I'M SORRY, BUT I'M ALREADY STARTING TO ITCH!
HERE, AT LEAST TAKE YOUR SNACK HOME!
SCRATCH
SCRATCH

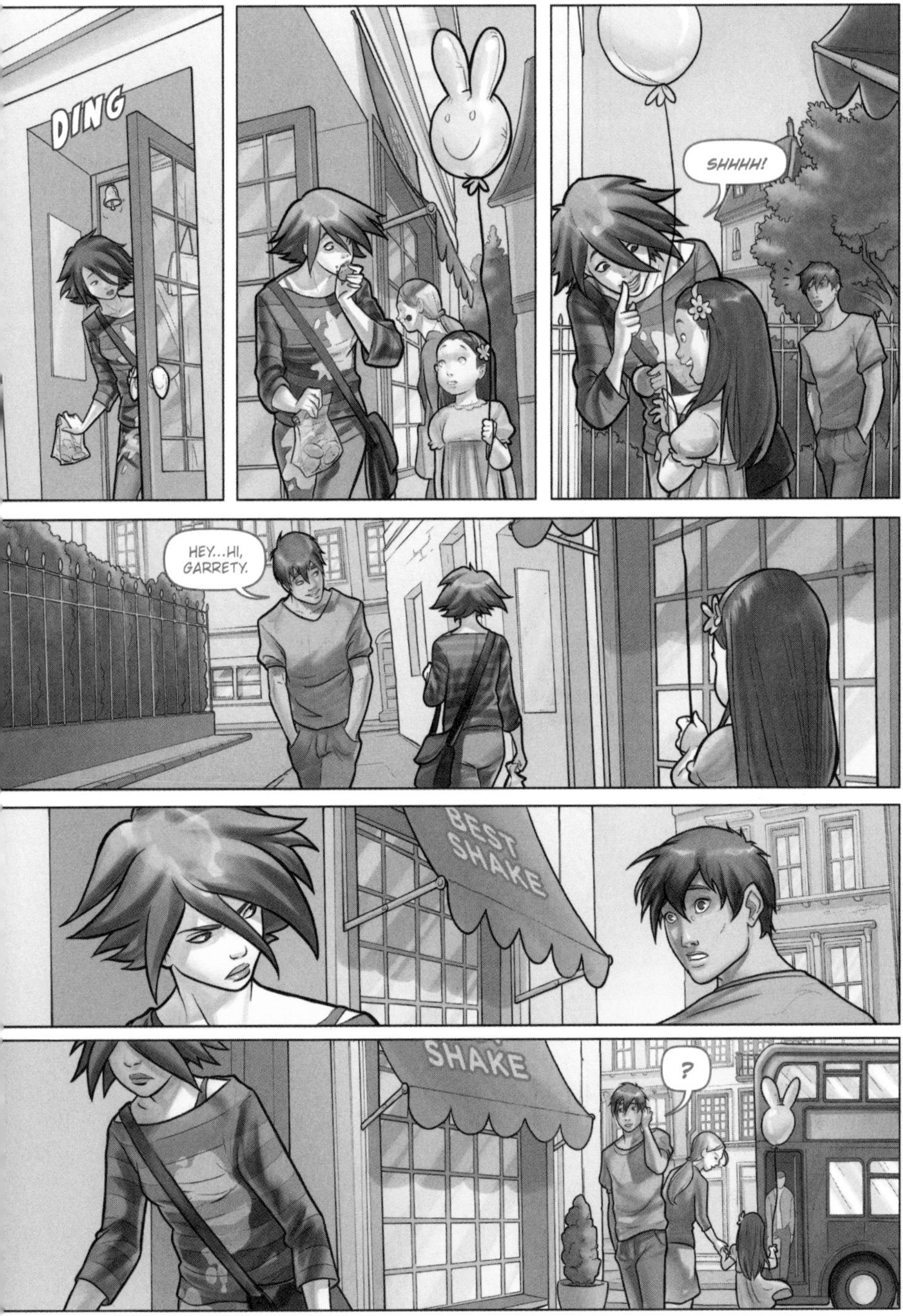
DING
SHHHH!
HEY...HI, GARRETY.
BEST SHAKE
SHAKE
?

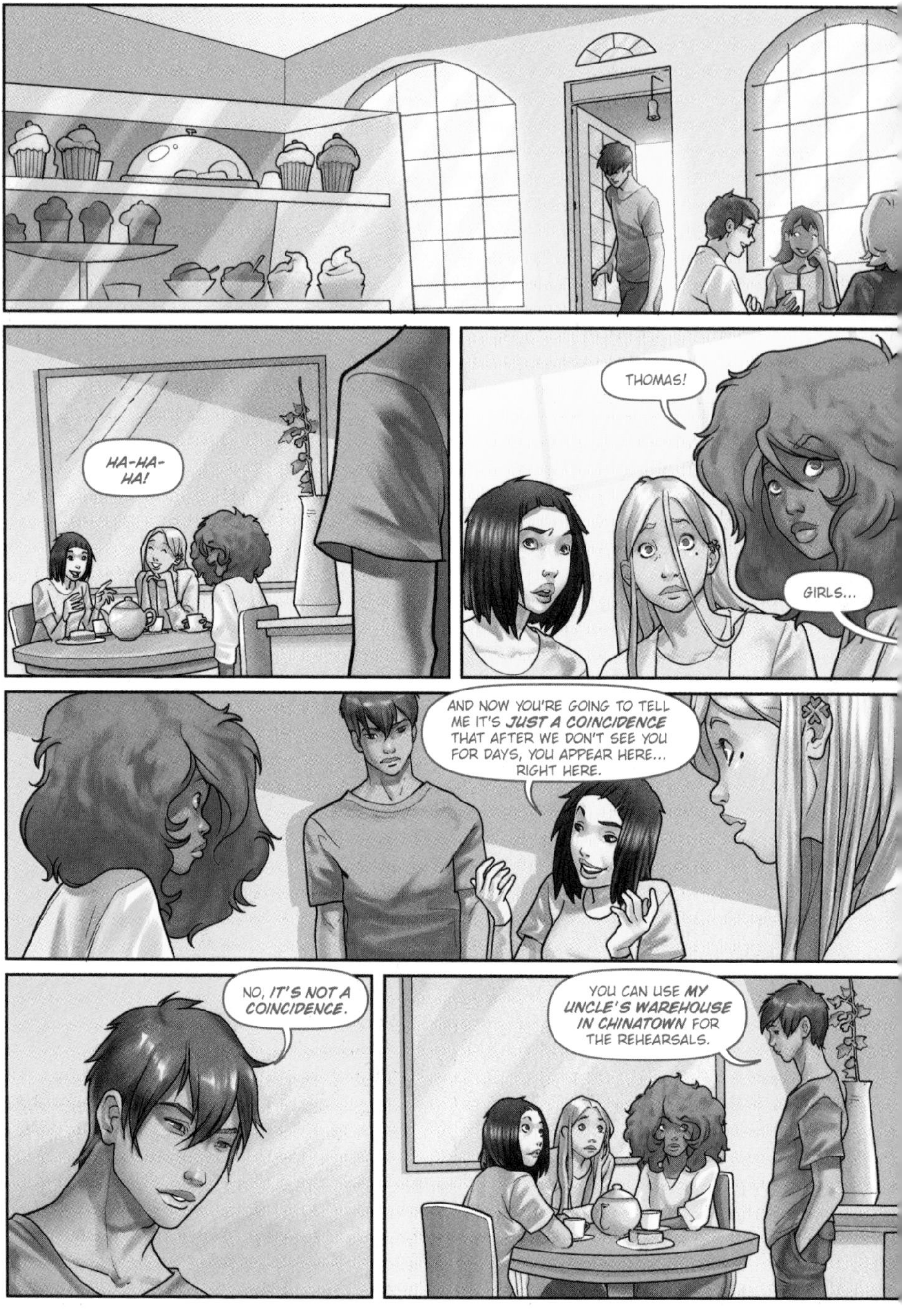
HA-HA-HA!
THOMAS!
GIRLS...
AND NOW YOU'RE GOING TO TELL ME IT'S JUST A COINCIDENCE THAT AFTER WE DON'T SEE YOU FOR DAYS, YOU APPEAR HERE... RIGHT HERE.
NO, IT'S NOT A COINCIDENCE.
YOU CAN USE MY UNCLE'S WAREHOUSE IN CHINATOWN FOR THE REHEARSALS.

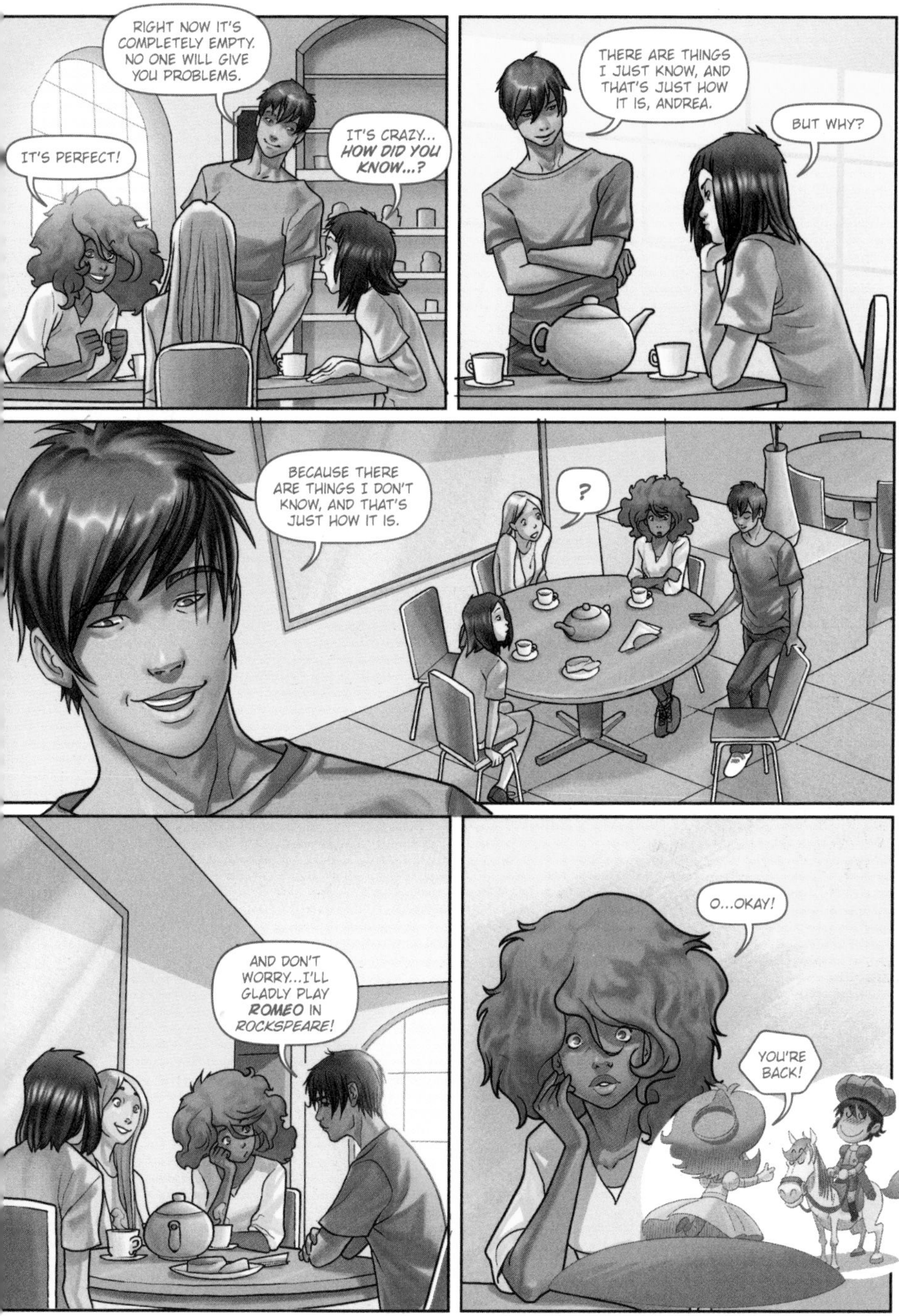
RIGHT NOW IT'S COMPLETELY EMPTY. NO ONE WILL GIVE YOU PROBLEMS.
IT'S PERFECT!
IT'S CRAZY... HOW DID YOU KNOW...?
THERE ARE THINGS I JUST KNOW, AND THAT'S JUST HOW IT IS, ANDREA.
BUT WHY?
BECAUSE THERE ARE THINGS I DON'T KNOW, AND THAT'S JUST HOW IT IS.
?
AND DON'T WORRY...I'LL GLADLY PLAY ROMEO IN ROCKSPEARE!
O...OKAY!
YOU'RE BACK!

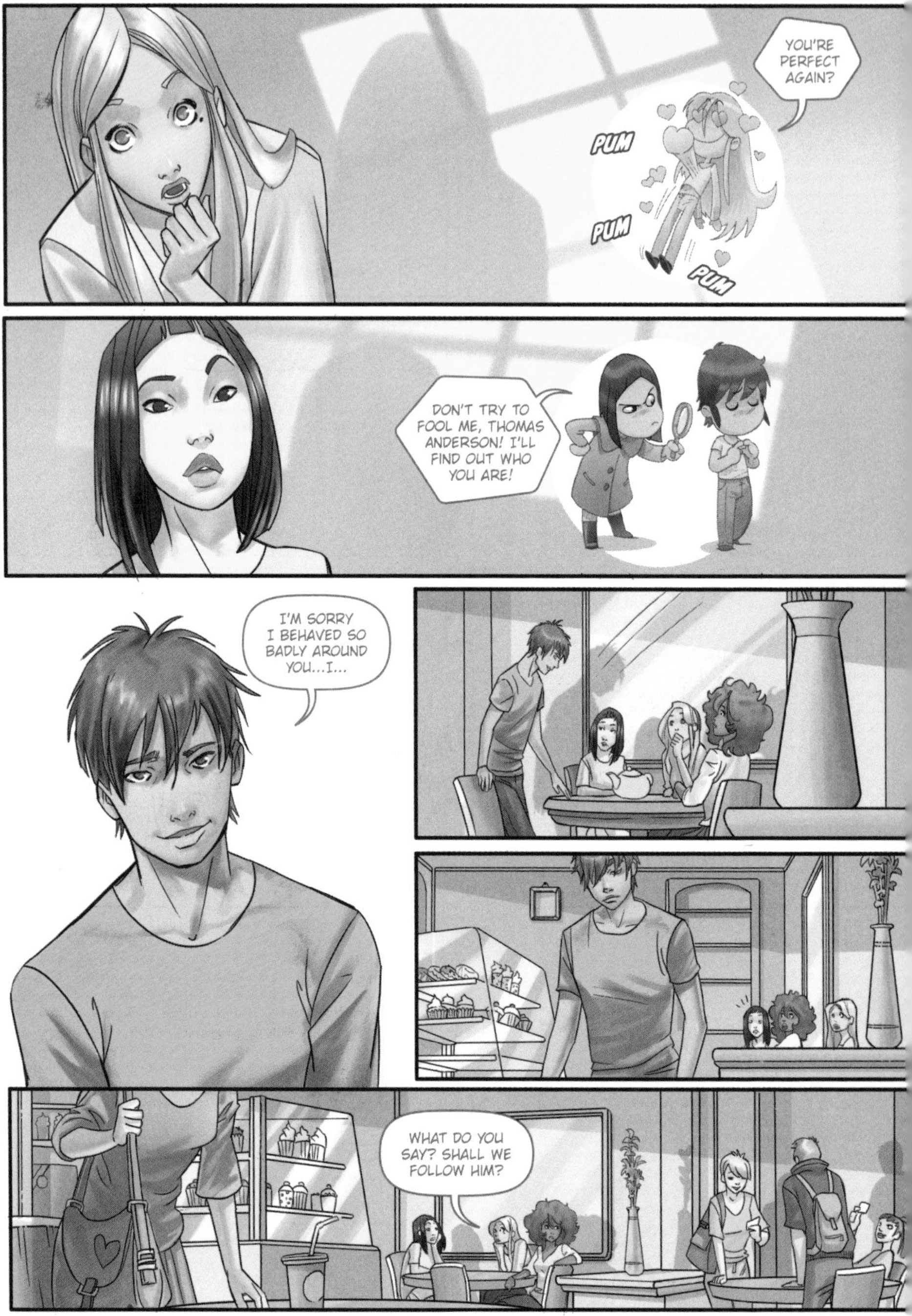
YOU'RE PERFECT AGAIN?
PUM
PUM
PUM
DON'T TRY TO FOOL ME, THOMAS ANDERSON! I'LL FIND OUT WHO YOU ARE!
I'M SORRY I BEHAVED SO BADLY AROUND YOU...I...
WHAT DO YOU SAY? SHALL WE FOLLOW HIM?

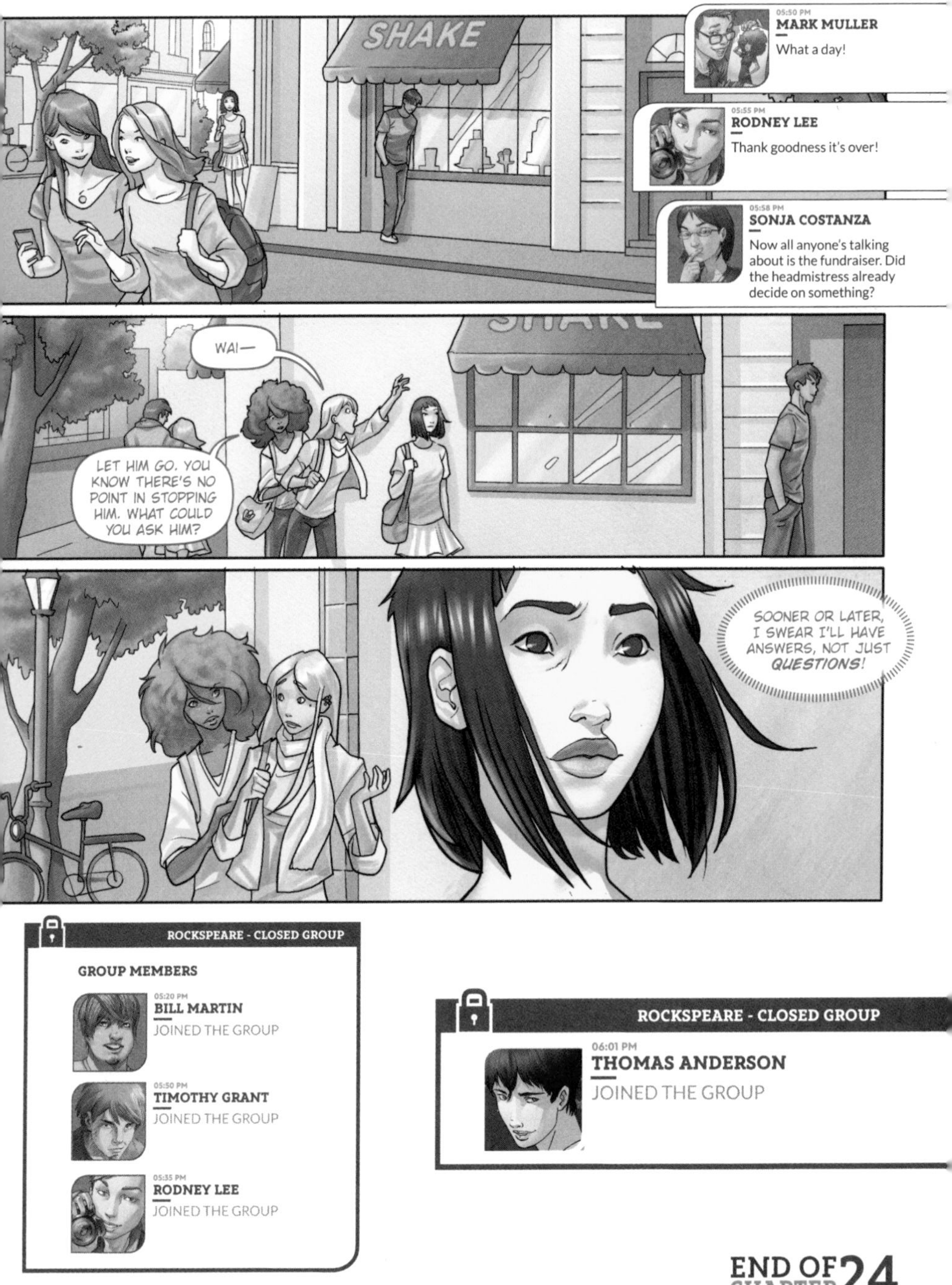

SHAKE
05:50 PM
MARK MULLER
What a day!
05:55 PM
RODNEY LEE
Thank goodness it's over!
05:58 PM
SONJA COSTANZA
Now all anyone's talking about is the fundraiser. Did the headmistress already decide on something?
WAI—
LET HIM GO. YOU KNOW THERE'S NO POINT IN STOPPING HIM. WHAT COULD YOU ASK HIM?
SOONER OR LATER, I SWEAR I'LL HAVE ANSWERS, NOT JUST QUESTIONS!
ROCKSPEARE - CLOSED GROUP
GROUP MEMBERS
05:20 PM
BILL MARTIN
JOINED THE GROUP
05:50 PM
TIMOTHY GRANT
JOINED THE GROUP
05:35 PM
RODNEY LEE
JOINED THE GROUP
ROCKSPEARE - CLOSED GROUP
06:01 PM
THOMAS ANDERSON
JOINED THE GROUP

END OF CHAPTER 24

real life #8

#RockSpeare

Plot: Alessandro Ferrari
Script: Silvia Gianatti
Layout: Giada Perissinotto, Elena Pianta
Cleanup: Egoduo, Marco Dominici
Emotidolls: Andrea Scoppetta
Color: Massimo Rocca, Pierluigi Casolino, Andrea Scoppetta, Mario Perrotta, Slava Panarin, Giuseppe Fontana, Gianluca Barone, Cristina Toniolo, Barbara Bargiggia, Francesca Mengozzi, Giovanni Marcora, Mario Perrotta, Paco Desiato, Antonia Angrisani, MAD5 Factory
Watercolor backgrounds: Valeria Turati
Translation: Edizioni BD and Erin Brady
Lettering and Infographic: Edizioni BD

COVER
Layout and cleanup: Alberto Zanon
Color: Slava Panarin

CONTRIBUTORS
Tomatofarm

Original project developed by Disney Publishing with the contribution of Barbar Baraldi, Paola Barbato, Micol Beltramini and Diana Tomatozombie

#9

#A Night at the Theatre

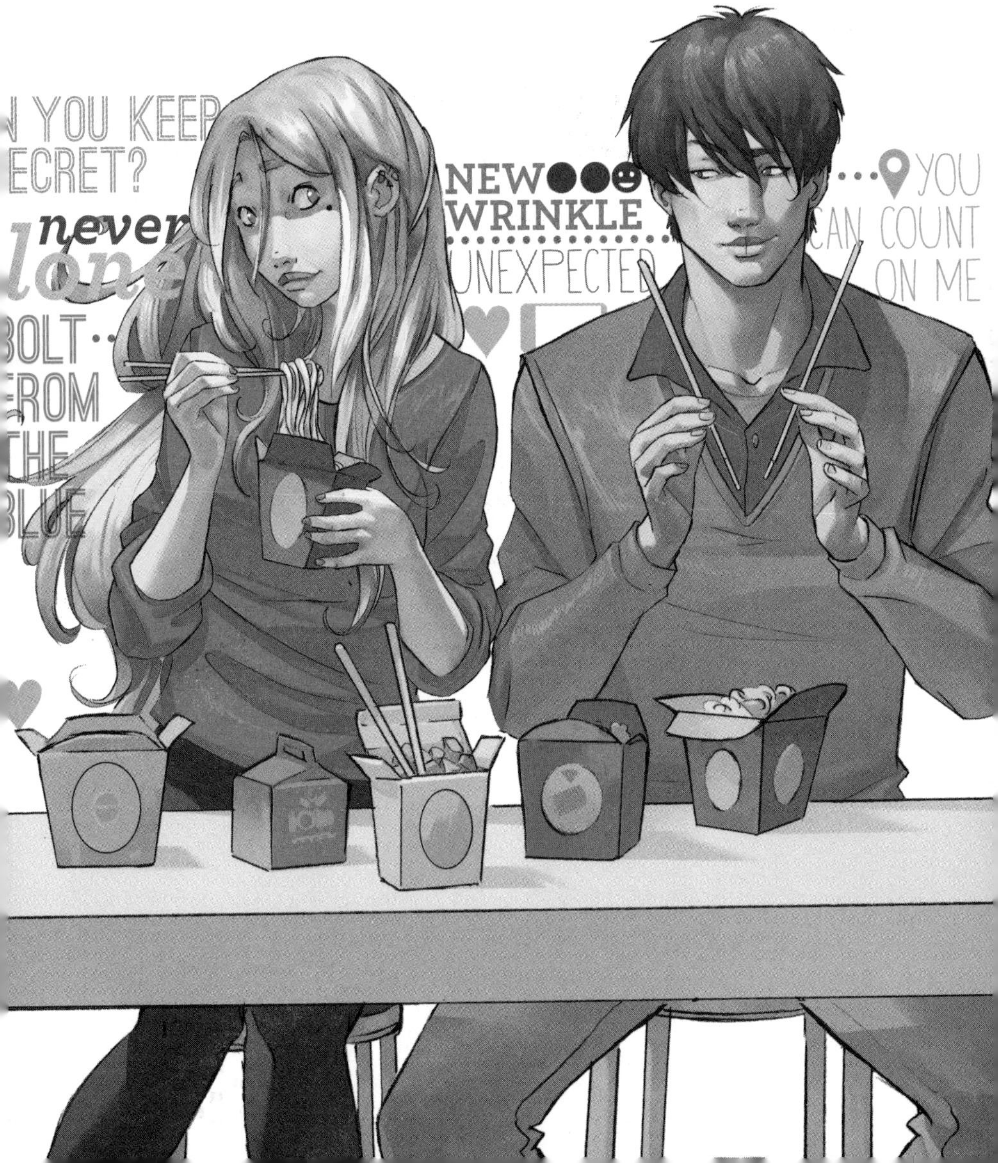
never
NEW
WRINKLE
UNEXPECTED
YOU CAN COUNT ON ME

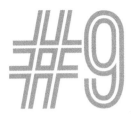

A perfect MISE-EN-SCÈNE

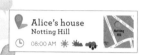

Alice's house
Notting Hill
08:00 AM

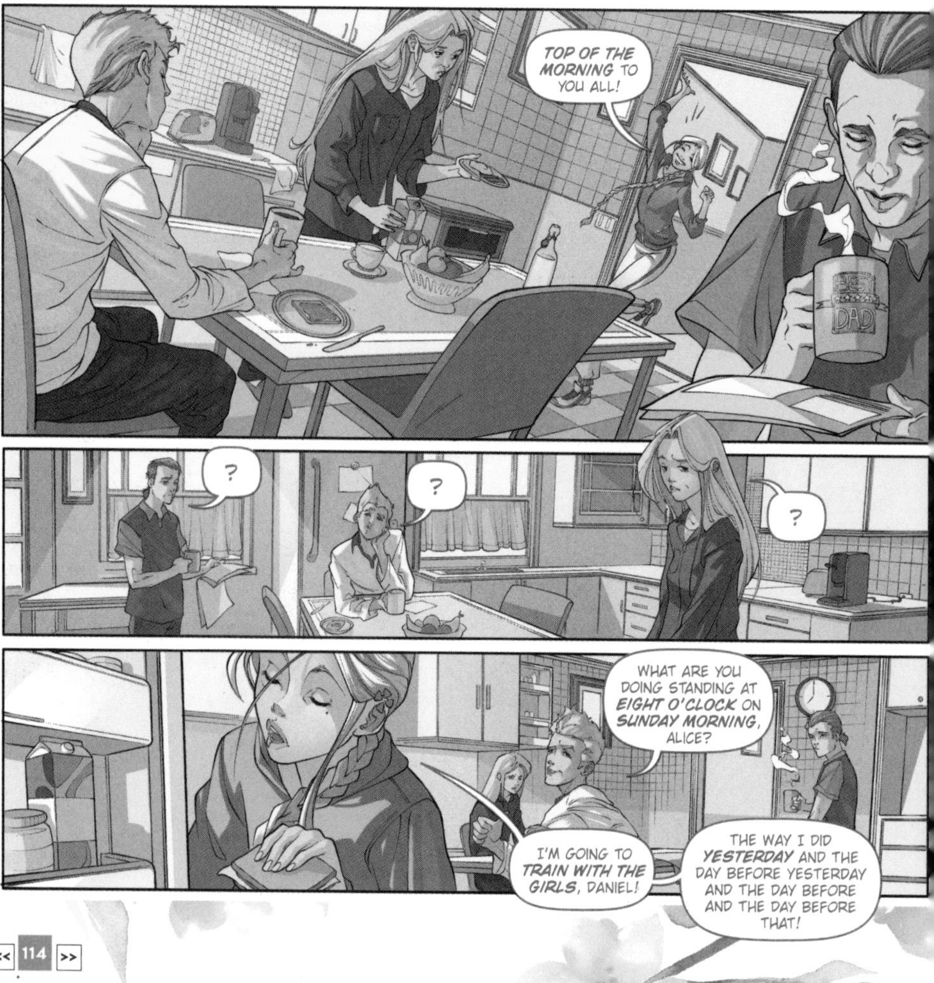
TOP OF THE MORNING TO YOU ALL!
?
?
?
WHAT ARE YOU DOING STANDING AT EIGHT O'CLOCK ON SUNDAY MORNING, ALICE?
I'M GOING TO TRAIN WITH THE GIRLS, DANIEL!
THE WAY I DID YESTERDAY AND THE DAY BEFORE YESTERDAY AND THE DAY BEFORE AND THE DAY BEFORE THAT!

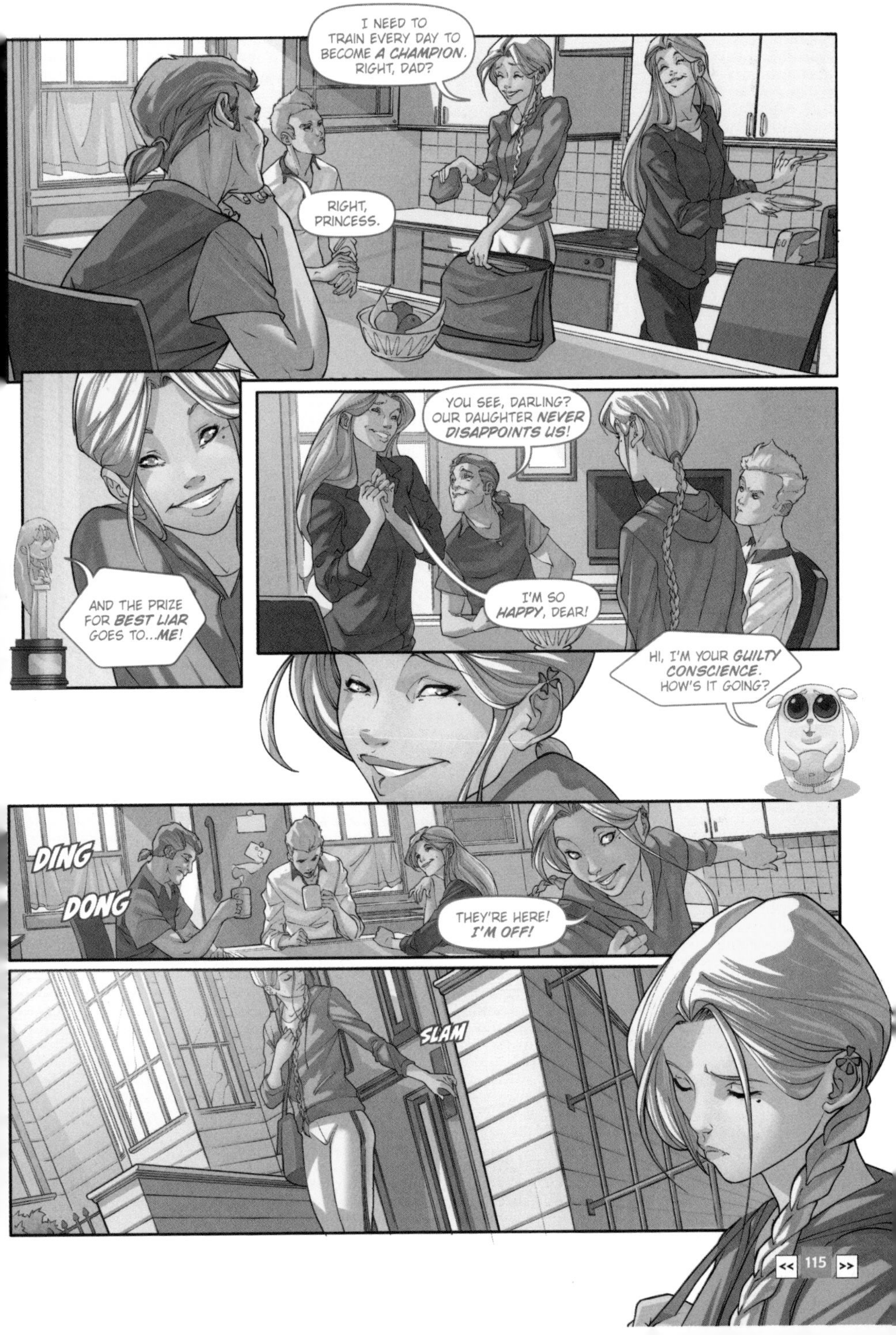
I NEED TO TRAIN EVERY DAY TO BECOME A CHAMPION. RIGHT, DAD?
RIGHT, PRINCESS.
AND THE PRIZE FOR BEST LIAR GOES TO...ME!
YOU SEE, DARLING? OUR DAUGHTER NEVER DISAPPOINTS US!
I'M SO HAPPY, DEAR!
HI, I'M YOUR GUILTY CONSCIENCE. HOW'S IT GOING?
DING
DONG
THEY'RE HERE! I'M OFF!
SLAM

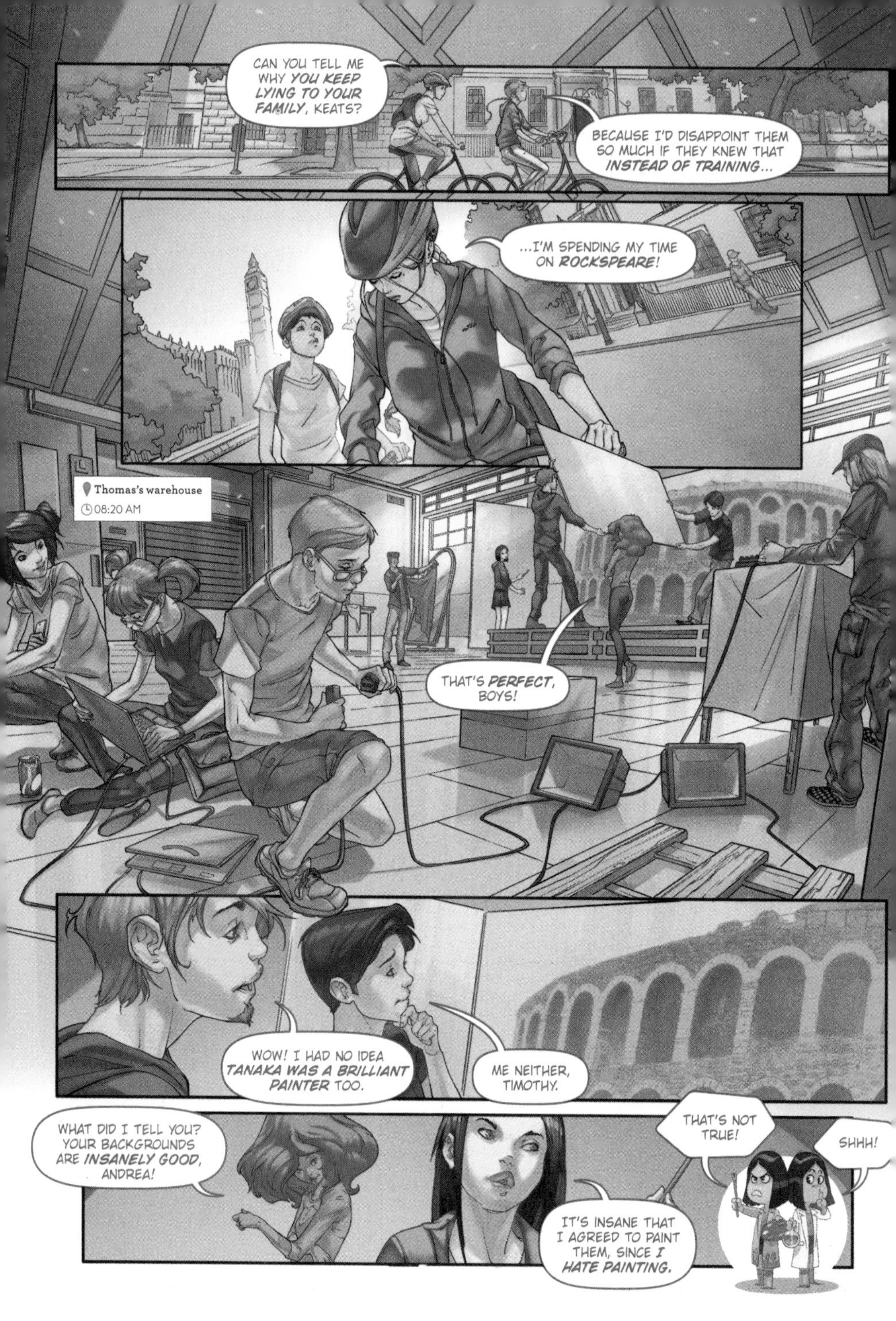

CAN YOU TELL ME WHY YOU KEEP LYING TO YOUR FAMILY, KEATS?
BECAUSE I'D DISAPPOINT THEM SO MUCH IF THEY KNEW THAT INSTEAD OF TRAINING...
...I'M SPENDING MY TIME ON ROCKSPEARE!
Thomas's warehouse
08:20 AM
THAT'S PERFECT, BOYS!
WOW! I HAD NO IDEA TANAKA WAS A BRILLIANT PAINTER TOO.
ME NEITHER, TIMOTHY.
WHAT DID I TELL YOU? YOUR BACKGROUNDS ARE INSANELY GOOD, ANDREA!
IT'S INSANE THAT I AGREED TO PAINT THEM, SINCE I HATE PAINTING.
THAT'S NOT TRUE!
SHHH!

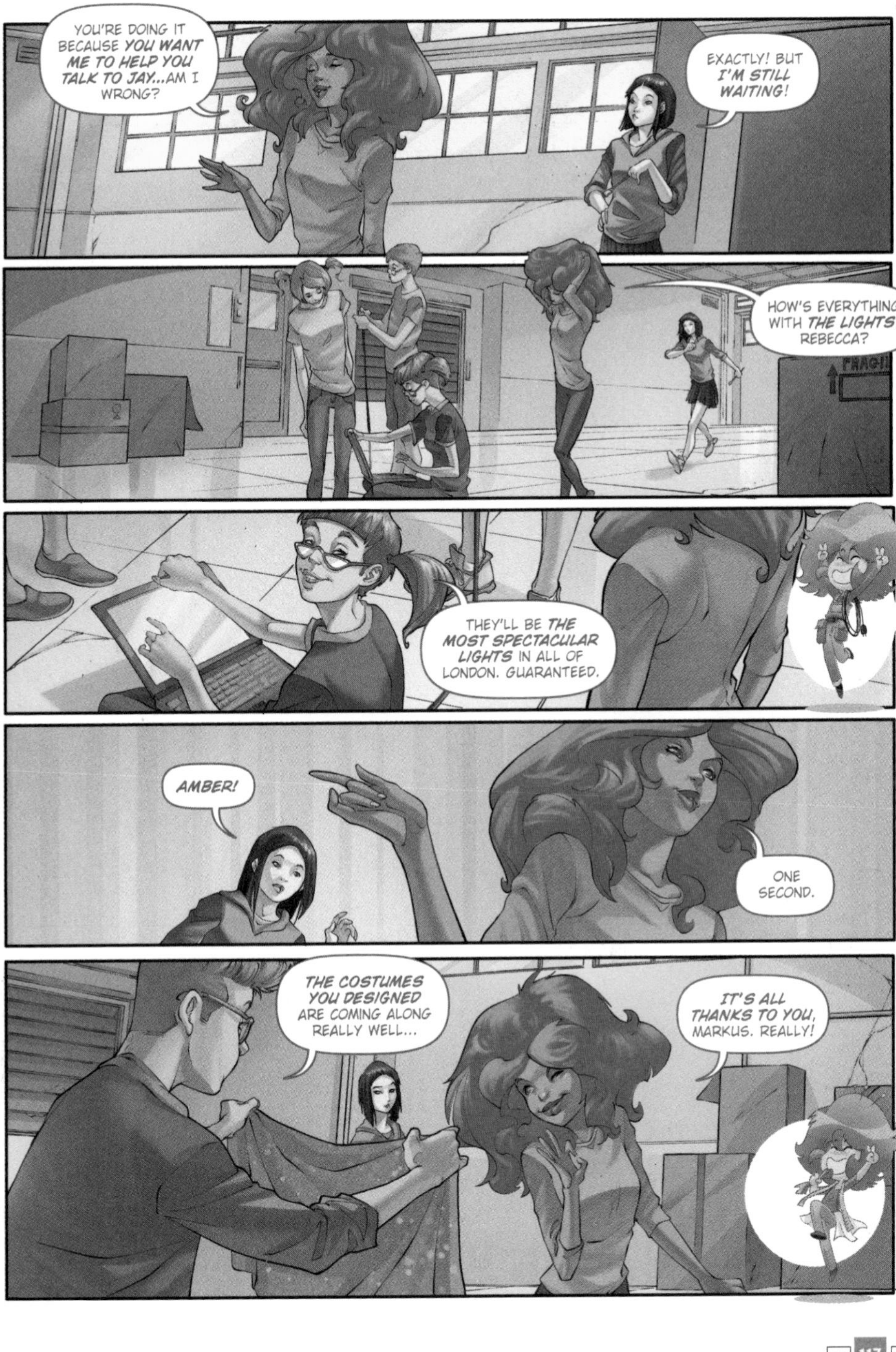
YOU'RE DOING IT BECAUSE YOU WANT ME TO HELP YOU TALK TO JAY...AM I WRONG?
EXACTLY! BUT I'M STILL WAITING!
HOW'S EVERYTHING WITH THE LIGHTS, REBECCA?
THEY'LL BE THE MOST SPECTACULAR LIGHTS IN ALL OF LONDON. GUARANTEED.
AMBER!
ONE SECOND.
THE COSTUMES YOU DESIGNED ARE COMING ALONG REALLY WELL...
IT'S ALL THANKS TO YOU, MARKUS. REALLY!

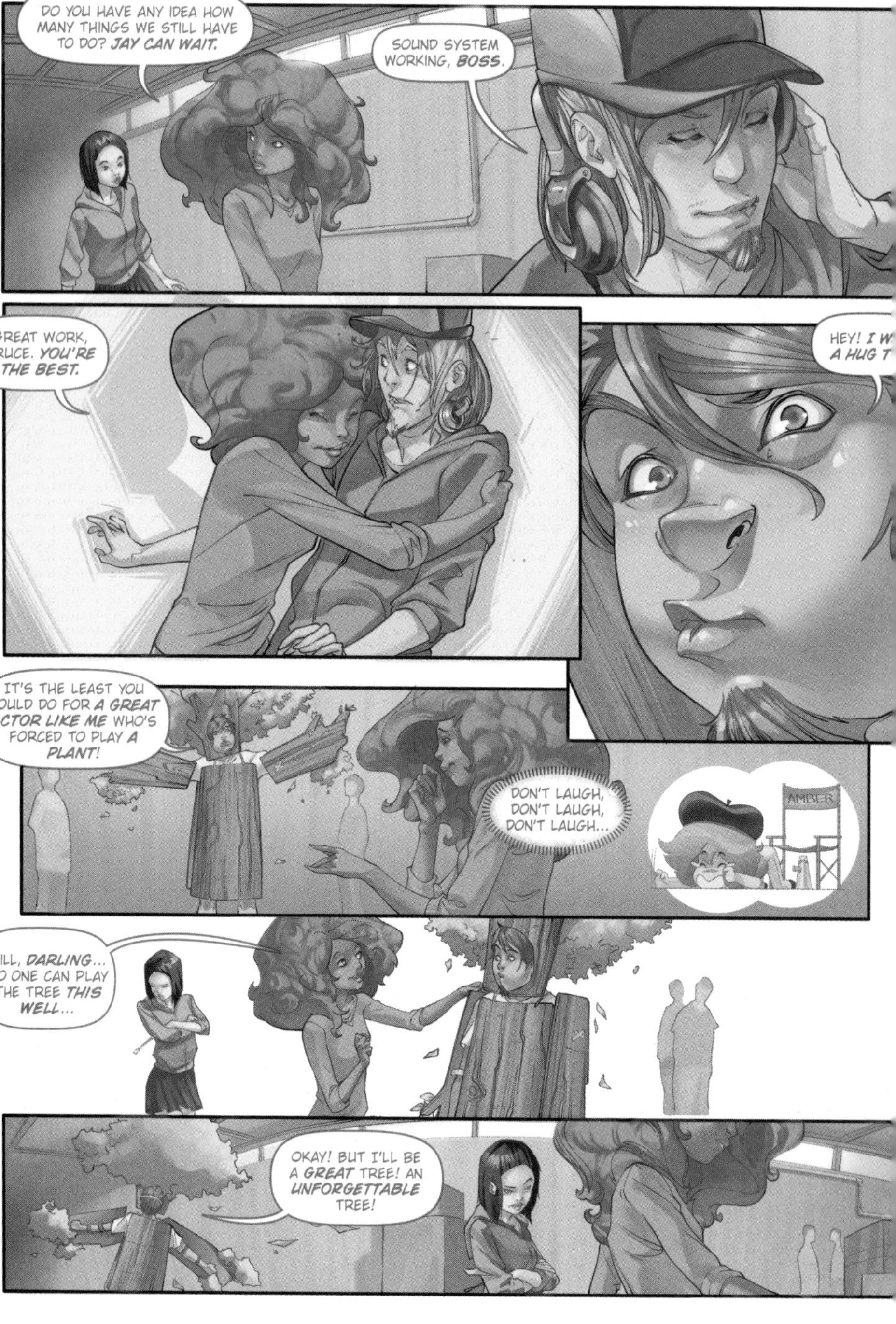
DO YOU HAVE ANY IDEA HOW MANY THINGS WE STILL HAVE TO DO? JAY CAN WAIT.
SOUND SYSTEM WORKING, BOSS.
GREAT WORK, BRUCE. YOU'RE THE BEST.
IT'S THE LEAST YOU COULD DO FOR A GREAT ACTOR LIKE ME WHO'S FORCED TO PLAY A PLANT!
DON'T LAUGH, DON'T LAUGH, DON'T LAUGH...
AMBER
BILL, DARLING... NO ONE CAN PLAY THE TREE THIS WELL...
OKAY! BUT I'LL BE A GREAT TREE! AN UNFORGETTABLE TREE!

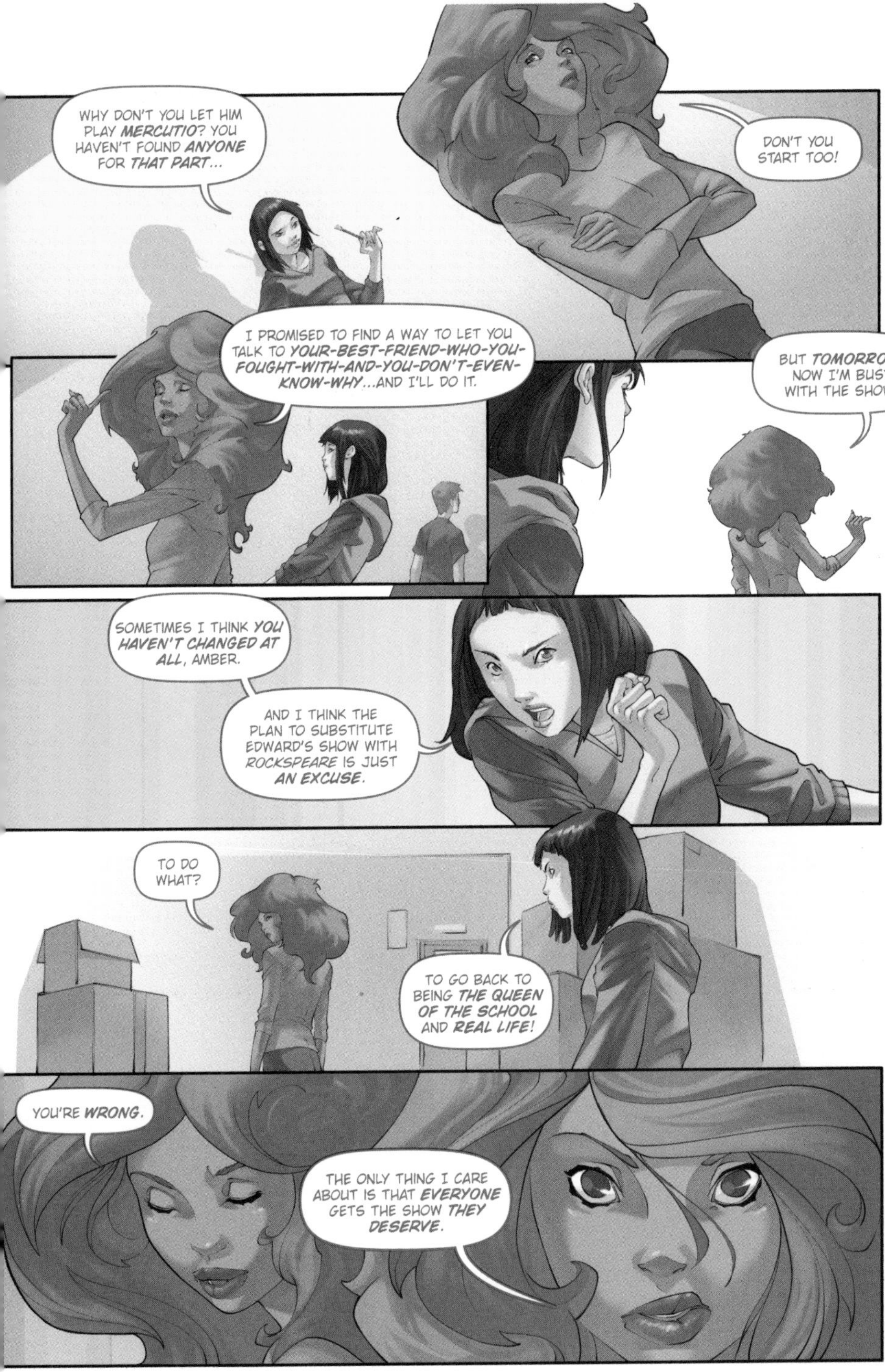
WHY DON'T YOU LET HIM PLAY MERCUTIO? YOU HAVEN'T FOUND ANYONE FOR THAT PART...
DON'T YOU START TOO!
I PROMISED TO FIND A WAY TO LET YOU TALK TO YOUR-BEST-FRIEND-WHO-YOU-FOUGHT-WITH-AND-YOU-DON'T-EVEN-KNOW-WHY...AND I'LL DO IT.
BUT TOMORROW. NOW I'M BUSY WITH THE SHOW!
SOMETIMES I THINK YOU HAVEN'T CHANGED AT ALL, AMBER.
AND I THINK THE PLAN TO SUBSTITUTE EDWARD'S SHOW WITH ROCKSPEARE IS JUST AN EXCUSE.
TO DO WHAT?
TO GO BACK TO BEING THE QUEEN OF THE SCHOOL AND REAL LIFE!
YOU'RE WRONG.
THE ONLY THING I CARE ABOUT IS THAT EVERYONE GETS THE SHOW THEY DESERVE.

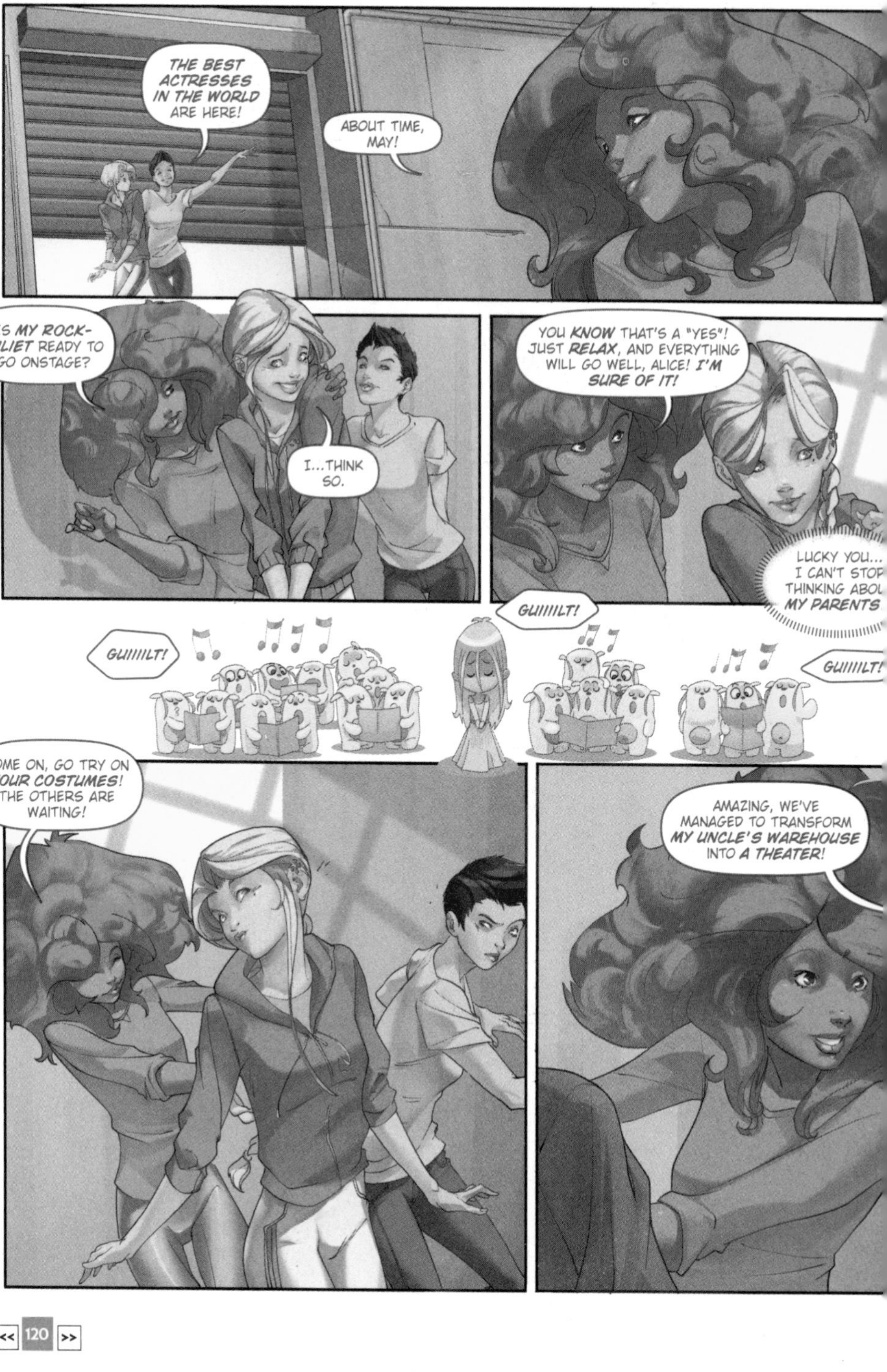
THE BEST ACTRESSES IN THE WORLD ARE HERE!
ABOUT TIME, MAY!
IS MY ROCK-JULIET READY TO GO ONSTAGE?
I...THINK SO.
YOU KNOW THAT'S A "YES"! JUST RELAX, AND EVERYTHING WILL GO WELL, ALICE! I'M SURE OF IT!
LUCKY YOU... I CAN'T STOP THINKING ABOU MY PARENTS
GUIIIILT!
GUIIIILT!
GUIIIILT!
COME ON, GO TRY ON YOUR COSTUMES! THE OTHERS ARE WAITING!
AMAZING, WE'VE MANAGED TO TRANSFORM MY UNCLE'S WAREHOUSE INTO A THEATER!

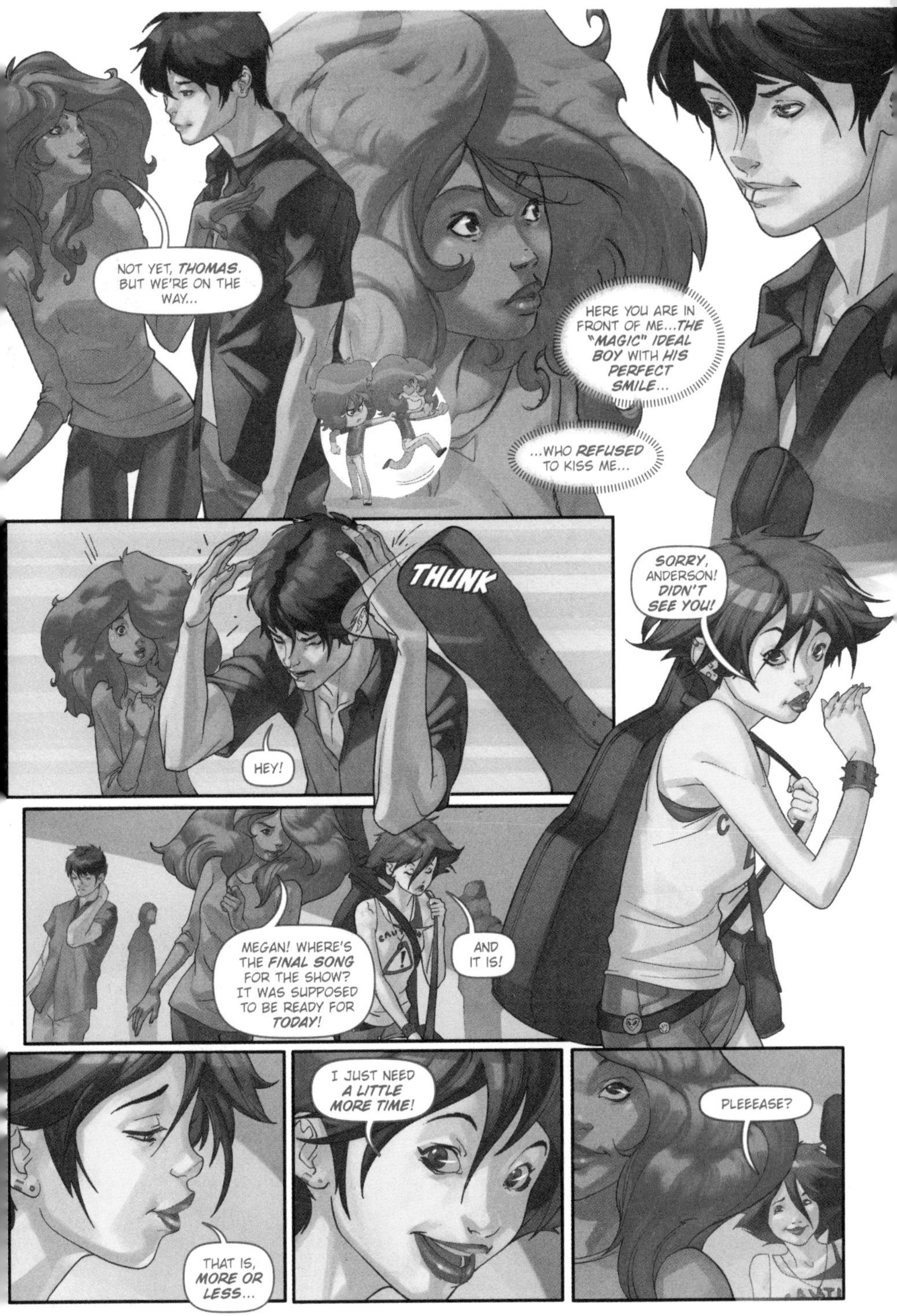
NOT YET, THOMAS. BUT WE'RE ON THE WAY...
HERE YOU ARE IN FRONT OF ME...THE "MAGIC" IDEAL BOY WITH HIS PERFECT SMILE...
...WHO REFUSED TO KISS ME...
THUNK
HEY!
SORRY, ANDERSON! DIDN'T SEE YOU!
MEGAN! WHERE'S THE FINAL SONG FOR THE SHOW? IT WAS SUPPOSED TO BE READY FOR TODAY!
AND IT IS!
THAT IS, MORE OR LESS...
I JUST NEED A LITTLE MORE TIME!
PLEEEASE?

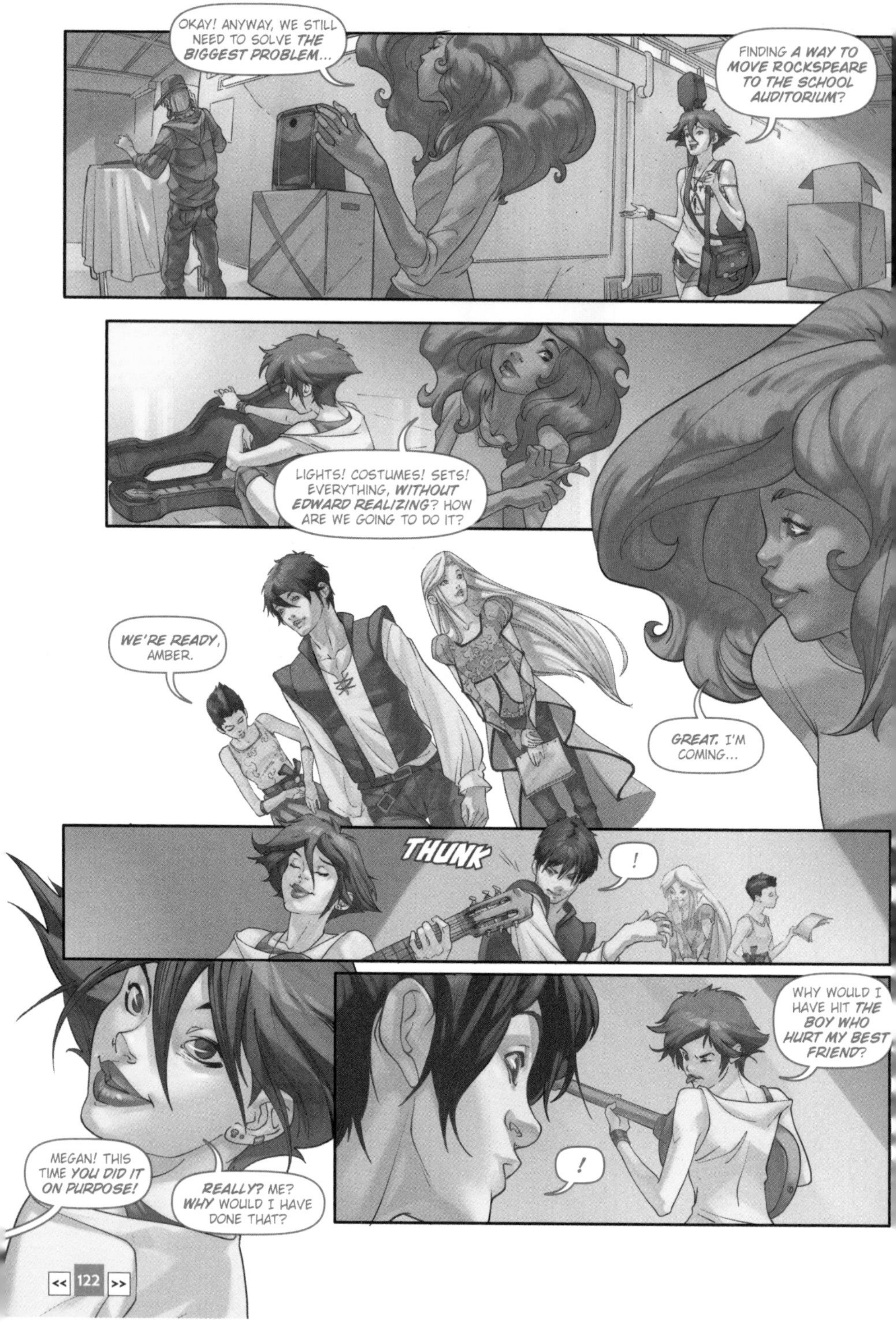
OKAY! ANYWAY, WE STILL NEED TO SOLVE THE BIGGEST PROBLEM...
FINDING A WAY TO MOVE ROCKSPEARE TO THE SCHOOL AUDITORIUM?
LIGHTS! COSTUMES! SETS! EVERYTHING, WITHOUT EDWARD REALIZING? HOW ARE WE GOING TO DO IT?
WE'RE READY, AMBER.
GREAT. I'M COMING...
THUNK
!
WHY WOULD I HAVE HIT THE BOY WHO HURT MY BEST FRIEND?
!
MEGAN! THIS TIME YOU DID IT ON PURPOSE!
REALLY? ME? WHY WOULD I HAVE DONE THAT?

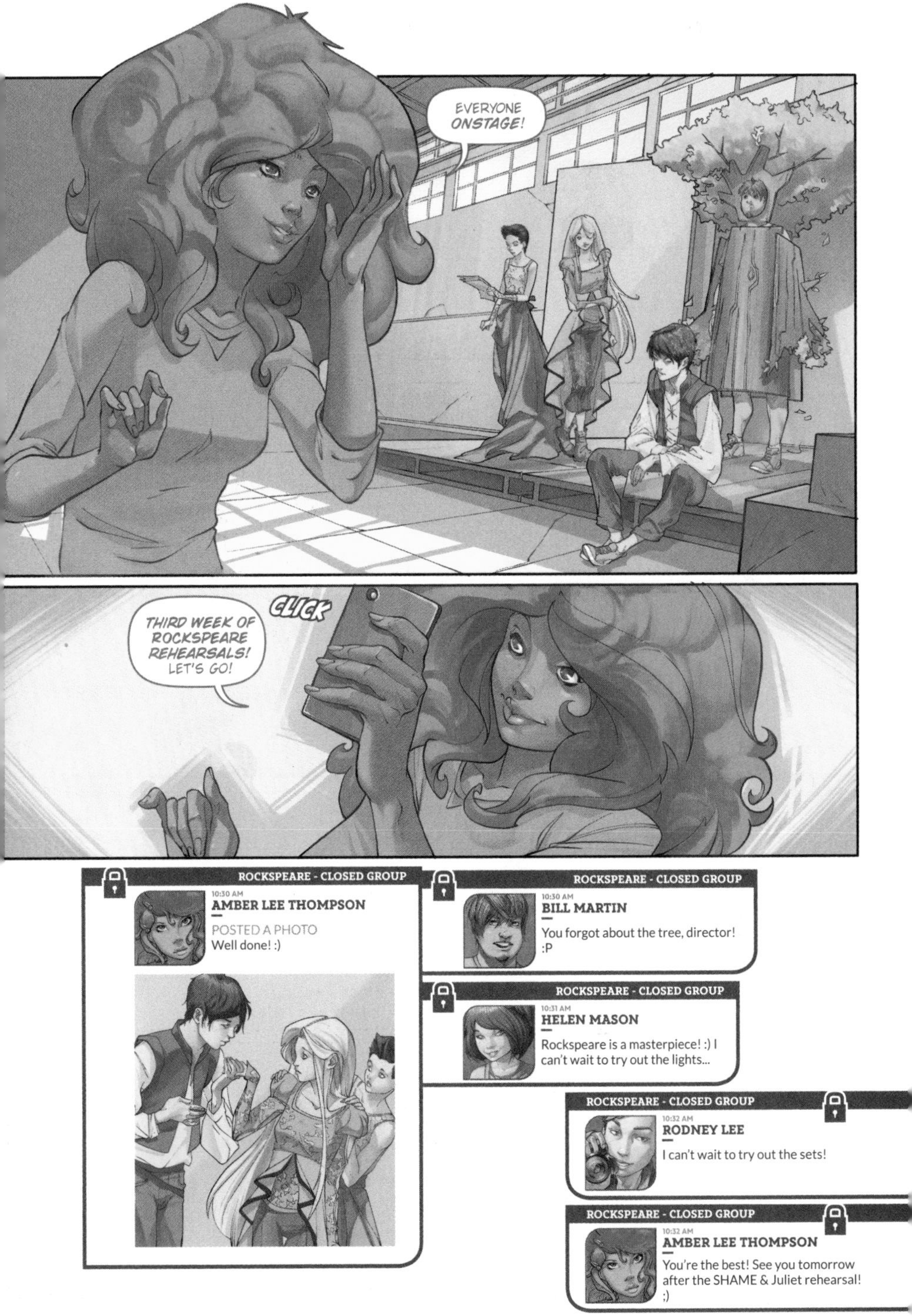
EVERYONE ONSTAGE!
CLICK
THIRD WEEK OF ROCKSPEARE REHEARSALS! LET'S GO!
ROCKSPEARE - CLOSED GROUP
10:30 AM
AMBER LEE THOMPSON
POSTED A PHOTO
Well done! :)
ROCKSPEARE - CLOSED GROUP
10:30 AM
BILL MARTIN
You forgot about the tree, director! :P
ROCKSPEARE - CLOSED GROUP
10:31 AM
HELEN MASON
Rockspeare is a masterpiece! :) I can't wait to try out the lights...
ROCKSPEARE - CLOSED GROUP
10:32 AM
RODNEY LEE
I can't wait to try out the sets!
ROCKSPEARE - CLOSED GROUP
10:32 AM
AMBER LEE THOMPSON
You're the best! See you tomorrow after the SHAME & Juliet rehearsal! ;)

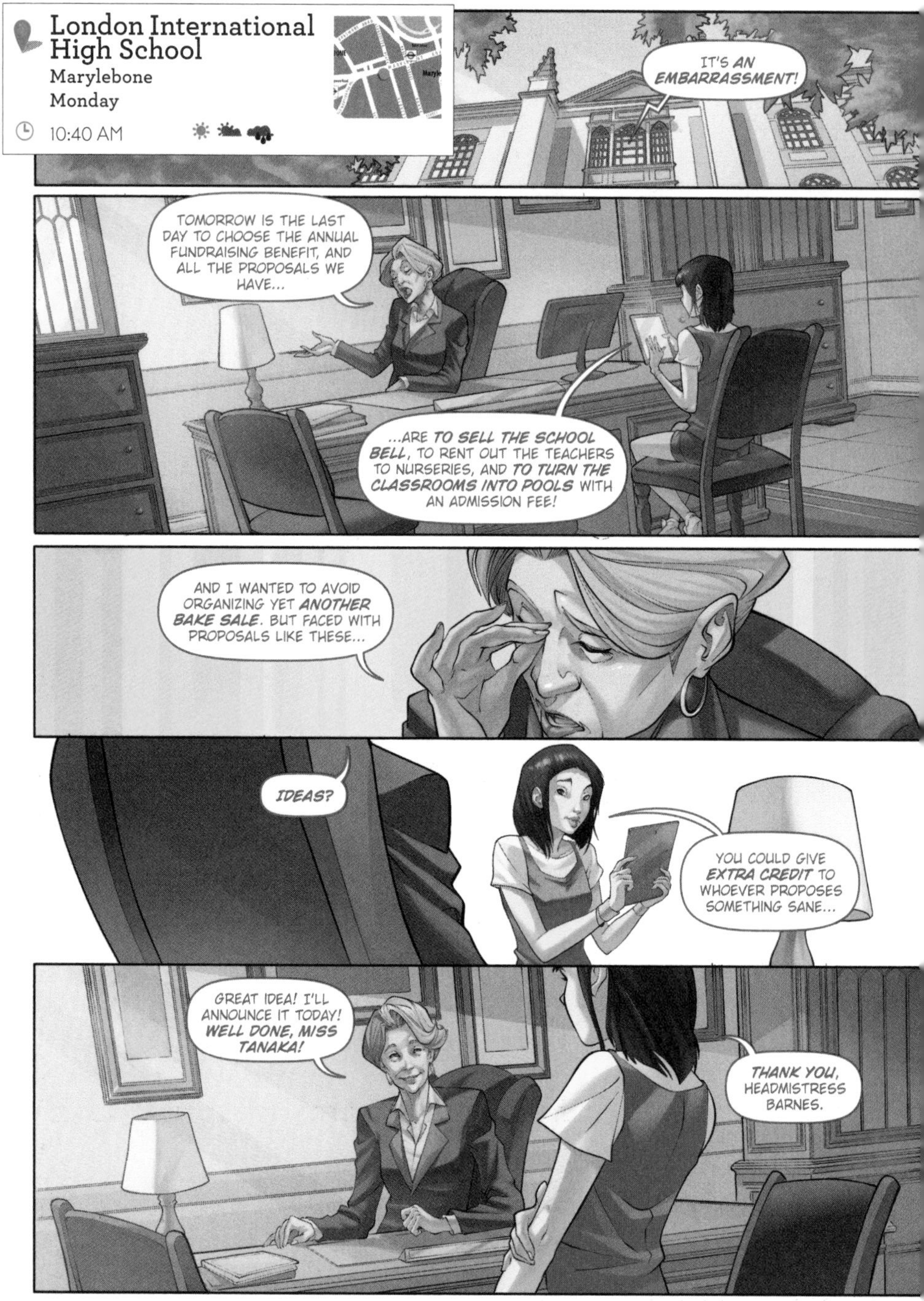
London International High School
Marylebone
Monday
10:40 AM
IT'S AN EMBARRASSMENT!
TOMORROW IS THE LAST DAY TO CHOOSE THE ANNUAL FUNDRAISING BENEFIT, AND ALL THE PROPOSALS WE HAVE...
...ARE TO SELL THE SCHOOL BELL, TO RENT OUT THE TEACHERS TO NURSERIES, AND TO TURN THE CLASSROOMS INTO POOLS WITH AN ADMISSION FEE!
AND I WANTED TO AVOID ORGANIZING YET ANOTHER BAKE SALE. BUT FACED WITH PROPOSALS LIKE THESE...
IDEAS?
YOU COULD GIVE EXTRA CREDIT TO WHOEVER PROPOSES SOMETHING SANE...
GREAT IDEA! I'LL ANNOUNCE IT TODAY! WELL DONE, MISS TANAKA!
THANK YOU, HEADMISTRESS BARNES.

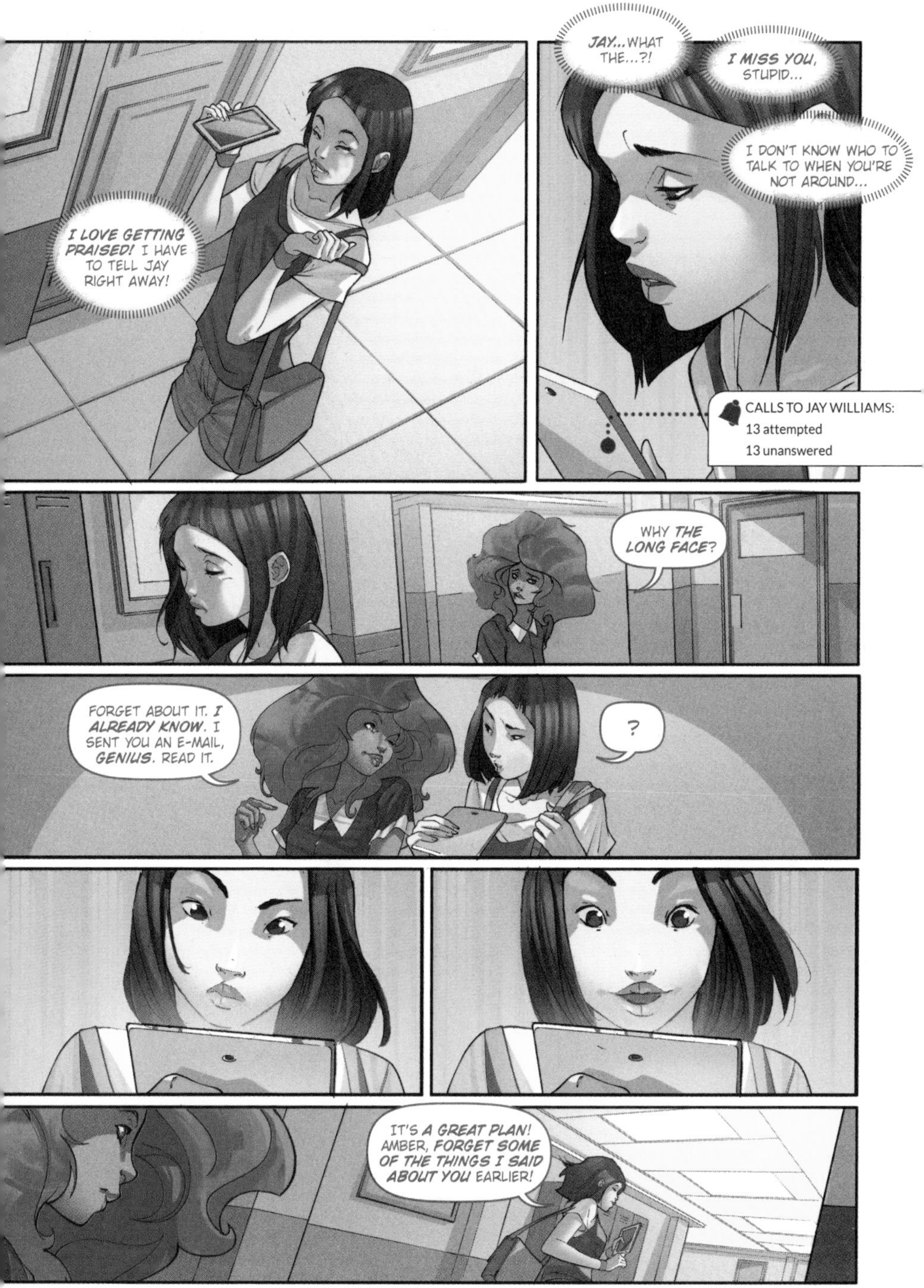
I LOVE GETTING PRAISED! I HAVE TO TELL JAY RIGHT AWAY!
JAY... WHAT THE...?!
I MISS YOU, STUPID...
I DON'T KNOW WHO TO TALK TO WHEN YOU'RE NOT AROUND...
CALLS TO JAY WILLIAMS:
13 attempted
13 unanswered
WHY THE LONG FACE?
FORGET ABOUT IT. I ALREADY KNOW. I SENT YOU AN E-MAIL, GENIUS. READ IT.
?
IT'S A GREAT PLAN! AMBER, FORGET SOME OF THE THINGS I SAID ABOUT YOU EARLIER!

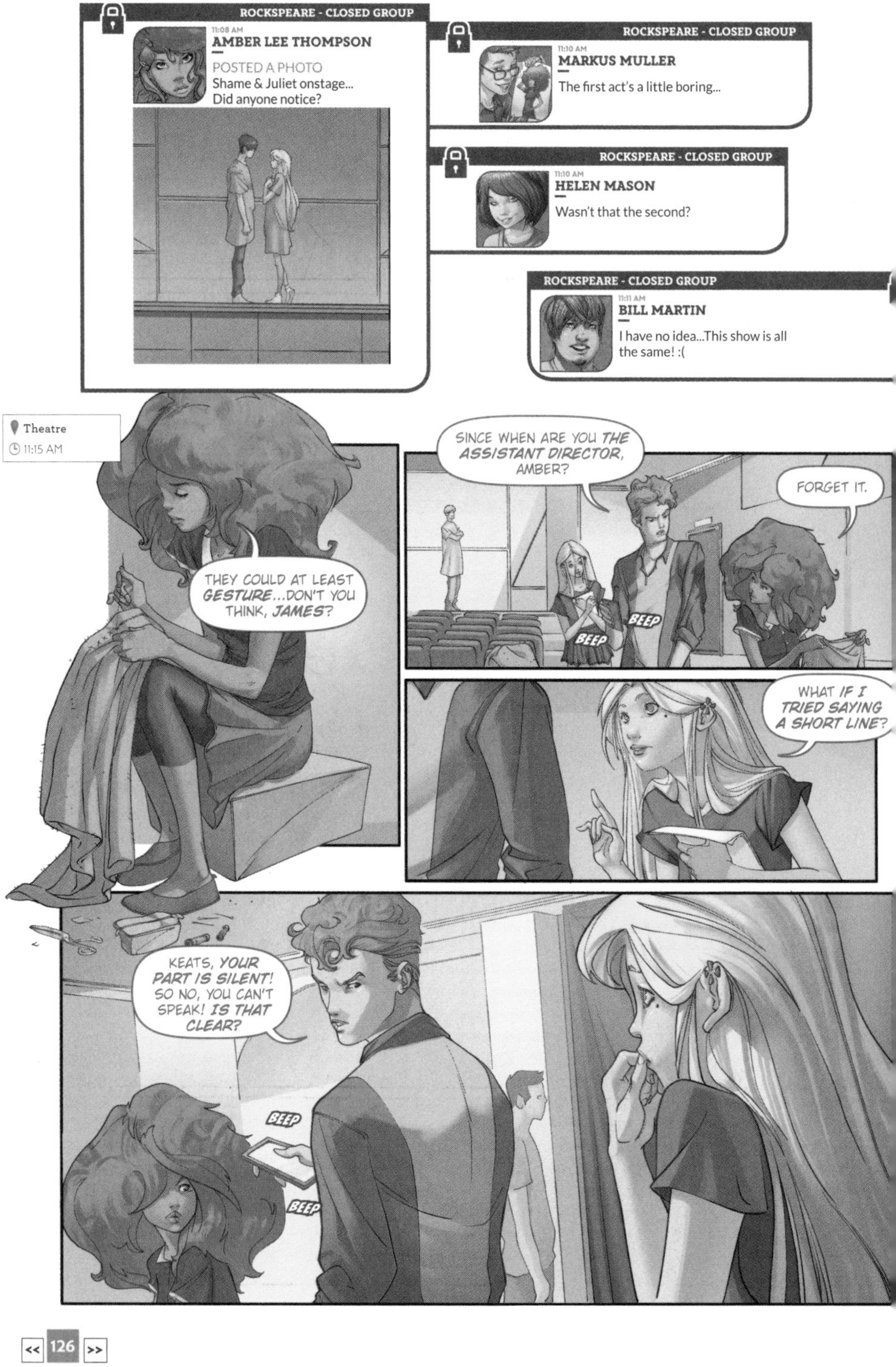
ROCKSPEARE - CLOSED GROUP
11:08 AM
AMBER LEE THOMPSON
POSTED A PHOTO
Shame & Juliet onstage...
Did anyone notice?
ROCKSPEARE - CLOSED GROUP
11:10 AM
MARKUS MULLER
The first act's a little boring...
ROCKSPEARE - CLOSED GROUP
11:10 AM
HELEN MASON
Wasn't that the second?
ROCKSPEARE - CLOSED GROUP
11:11 AM
BILL MARTIN
I have no idea...This show is all the same! :(
Theatre
11:15 AM
THEY COULD AT LEAST GESTURE...DON'T YOU THINK, JAMES?
SINCE WHEN ARE YOU THE ASSISTANT DIRECTOR, AMBER?
FORGET IT.
BEEP
BEEP
WHAT IF I TRIED SAYING A SHORT LINE?
KEATS, YOUR PART IS SILENT! SO NO, YOU CAN'T SPEAK! IS THAT CLEAR?
BEEP
BEEP

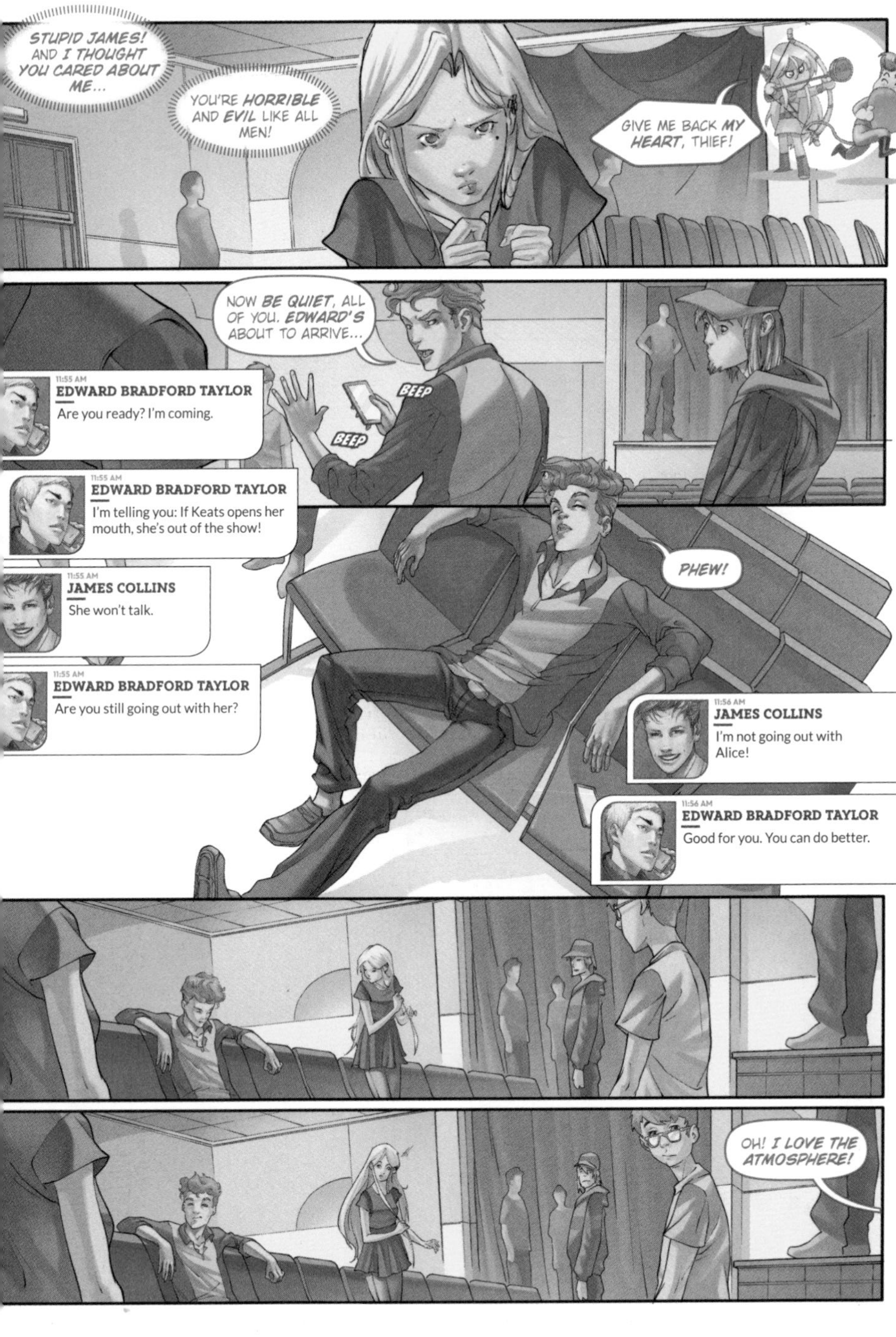

STUPID JAMES! AND I THOUGHT YOU CARED ABOUT ME...
YOU'RE HORRIBLE AND EVIL LIKE ALL MEN!
GIVE ME BACK MY HEART, THIEF!
NOW BE QUIET, ALL OF YOU. EDWARD'S ABOUT TO ARRIVE...
BEEP
BEEP
11:55 AM
EDWARD BRADFORD TAYLOR
Are you ready? I'm coming.
11:55 AM
EDWARD BRADFORD TAYLOR
I'm telling you: If Keats opens her mouth, she's out of the show!
11:55 AM
JAMES COLLINS
She won't talk.
11:55 AM
EDWARD BRADFORD TAYLOR
Are you still going out with her?
PHEW!
11:56 AM
JAMES COLLINS
I'm not going out with Alice!
11:56 AM
EDWARD BRADFORD TAYLOR
Good for you. You can do better.
OH! I LOVE THE ATMOSPHERE!

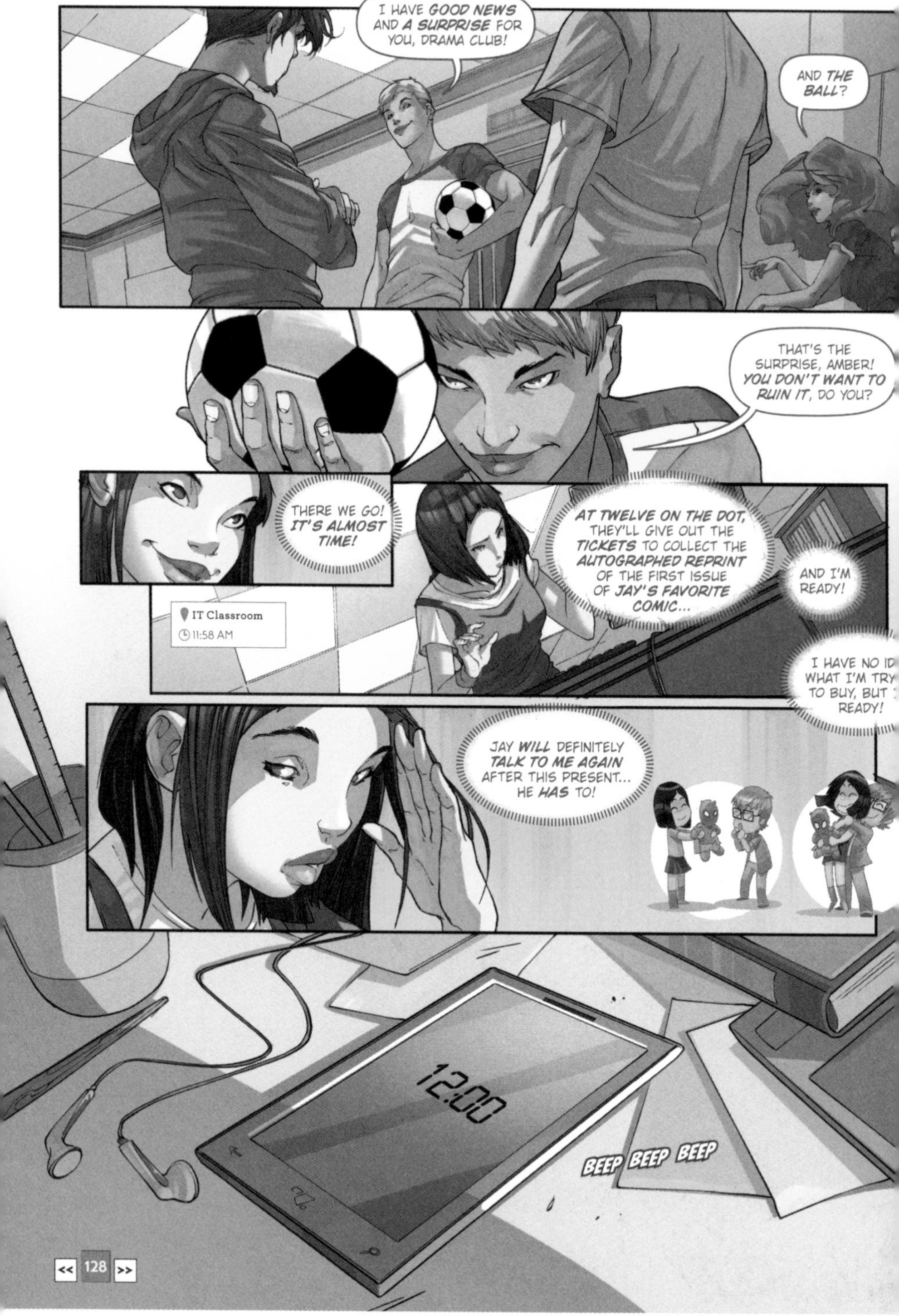
I HAVE GOOD NEWS AND A SURPRISE FOR YOU, DRAMA CLUB!
AND THE BALL?
THAT'S THE SURPRISE, AMBER! YOU DON'T WANT TO RUIN IT, DO YOU?
THERE WE GO! IT'S ALMOST TIME!
IT Classroom
11:58 AM
AT TWELVE ON THE DOT, THEY'LL GIVE OUT THE TICKETS TO COLLECT THE AUTOGRAPHED REPRINT OF THE FIRST ISSUE OF JAY'S FAVORITE COMIC...
AND I'M READY!
JAY WILL DEFINITELY TALK TO ME AGAIN AFTER THIS PRESENT... HE HAS TO!
12:00
BEEP BEEP BEEP

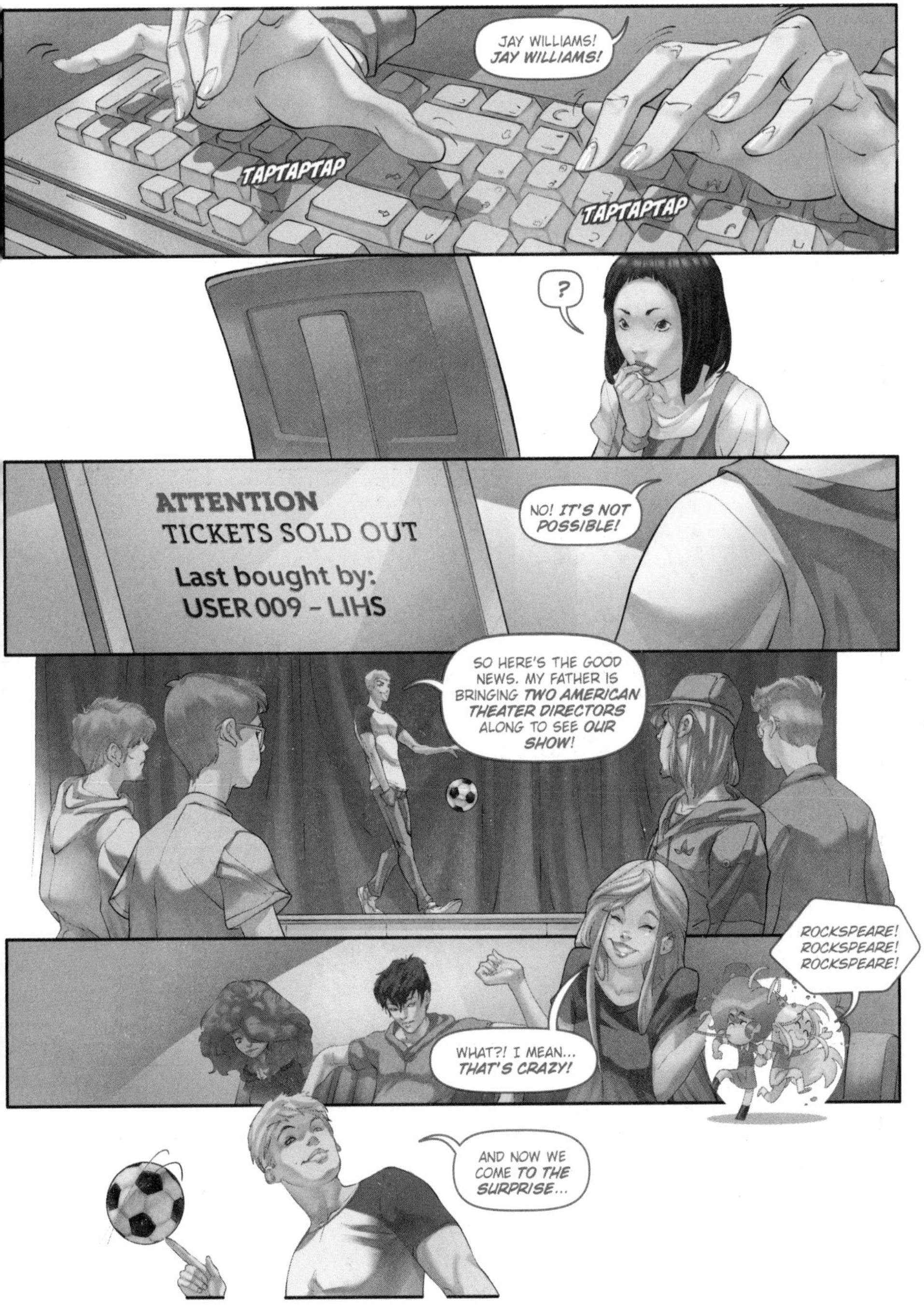
JAY WILLIAMS!
JAY WILLIAMS!
TAPTAPTAP
TAPTAPTAP
?
ATTENTION
TICKETS SOLD OUT
Last bought by:
USER 009 – LIHS
NO! IT'S NOT POSSIBLE!
SO HERE'S THE GOOD NEWS. MY FATHER IS BRINGING TWO AMERICAN THEATER DIRECTORS ALONG TO SEE OUR SHOW!
ROCKSPEARE! ROCKSPEARE! ROCKSPEARE!
WHAT?! I MEAN... THAT'S CRAZY!
AND NOW WE COME TO THE SURPRISE...

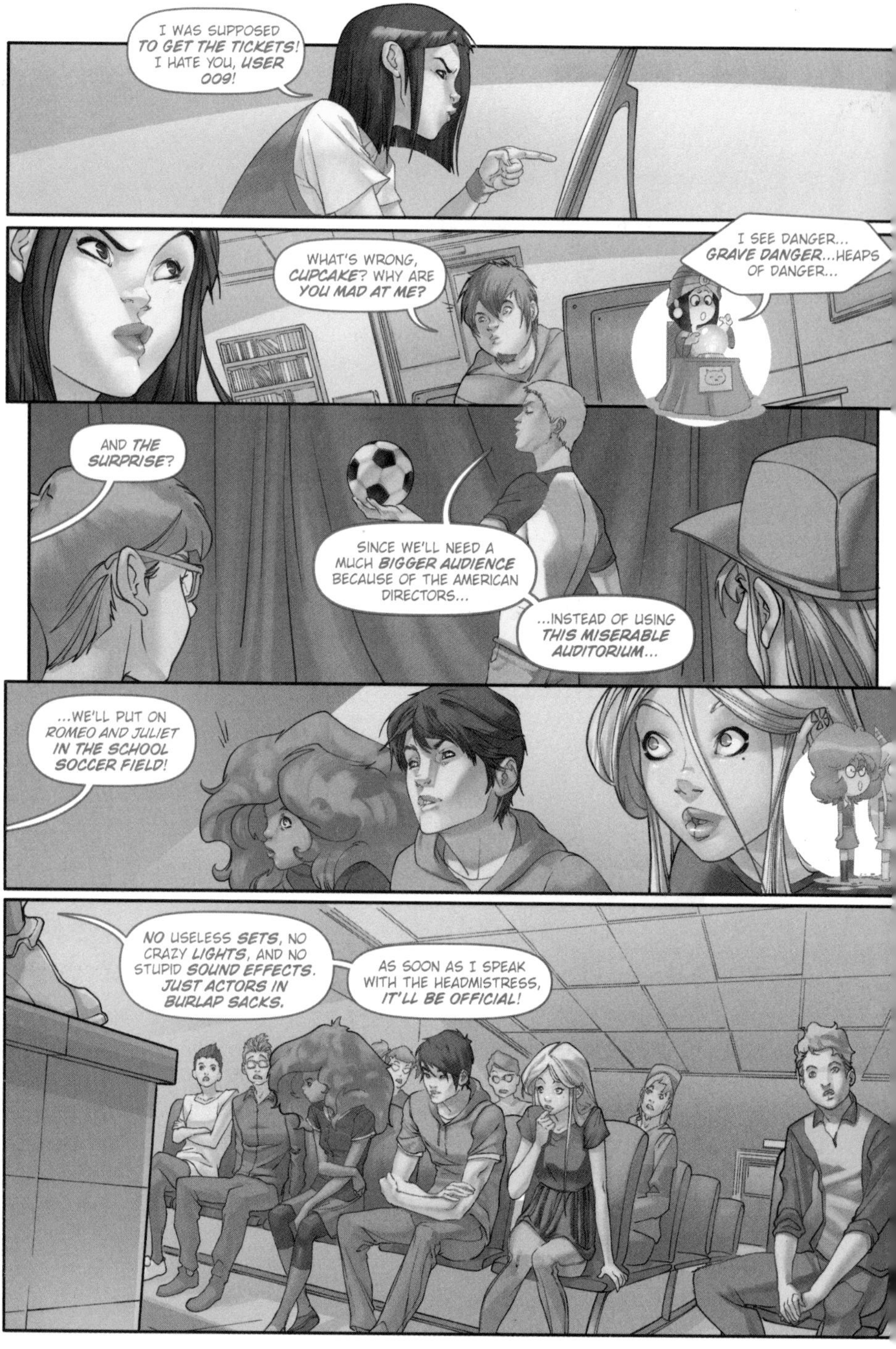
I WAS SUPPOSED TO GET THE TICKETS! I HATE YOU, USER 009!
WHAT'S WRONG, CUPCAKE? WHY ARE YOU MAD AT ME?
I SEE DANGER... GRAVE DANGER...HEAPS OF DANGER...
AND THE SURPRISE?
SINCE WE'LL NEED A MUCH BIGGER AUDIENCE BECAUSE OF THE AMERICAN DIRECTORS...
...INSTEAD OF USING THIS MISERABLE AUDITORIUM...
...WE'LL PUT ON ROMEO AND JULIET IN THE SCHOOL SOCCER FIELD!
NO USELESS SETS, NO CRAZY LIGHTS, AND NO STUPID SOUND EFFECTS. JUST ACTORS IN BURLAP SACKS.
AS SOON AS I SPEAK WITH THE HEADMISTRESS, IT'LL BE OFFICIAL!

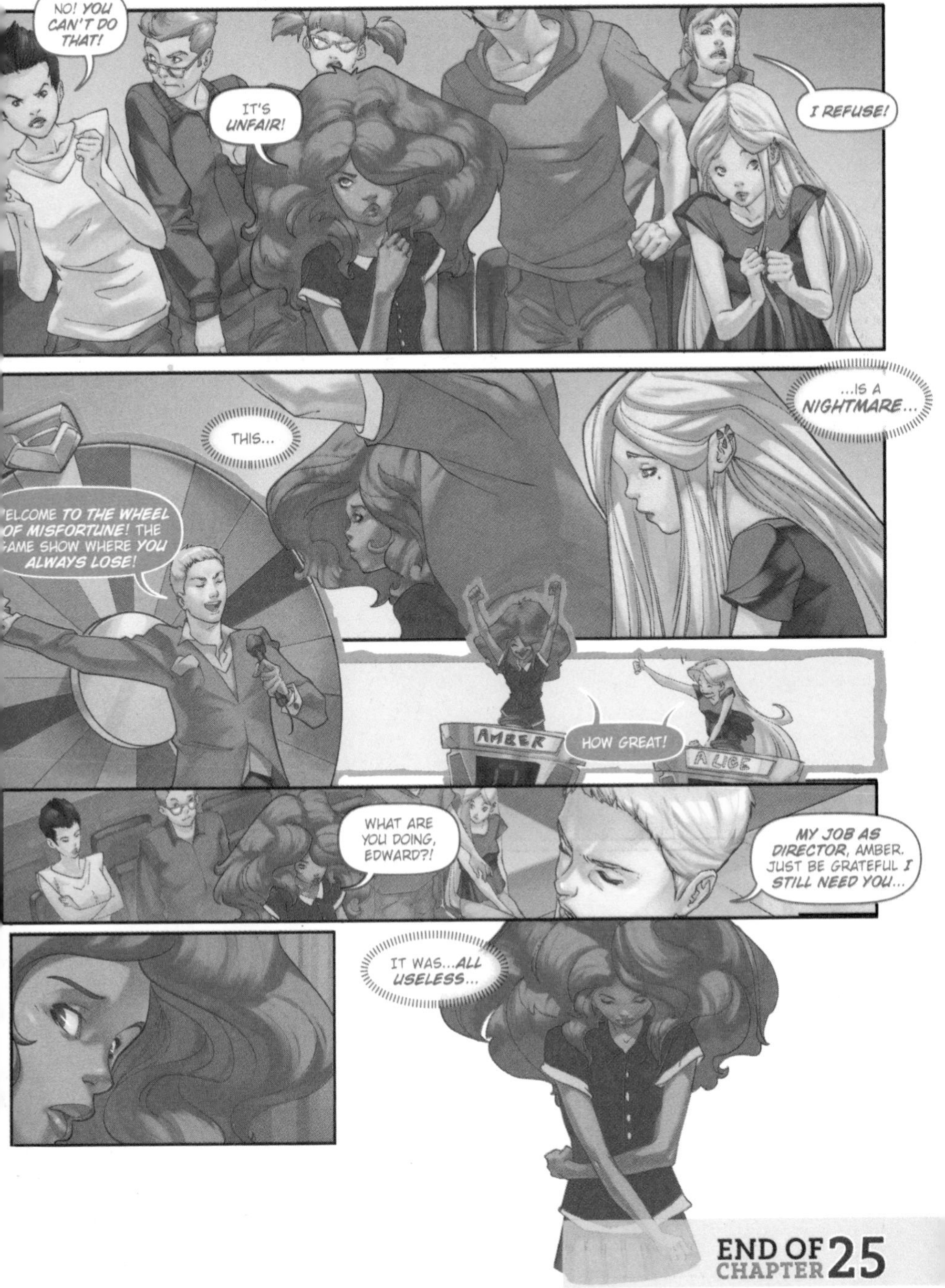
NO! YOU CAN'T DO THAT!
IT'S UNFAIR!
I REFUSE!
THIS...
...IS A NIGHTMARE...
ELCOME TO THE WHEEL OF MISFORTUNE! THE AME SHOW WHERE YOU ALWAYS LOSE!
AMBER
HOW GREAT!
ALICE
WHAT ARE YOU DOING, EDWARD?!
MY JOB AS DIRECTOR, AMBER. JUST BE GRATEFUL I STILL NEED YOU...
IT WAS...ALL USELESS...

END OF CHAPTER 25

CHAPTER 26

NEVER GIVE UP

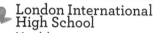

London International High School
Marylebone
02:00 PM

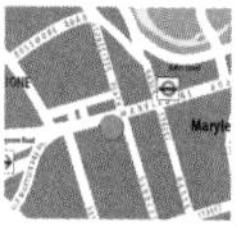

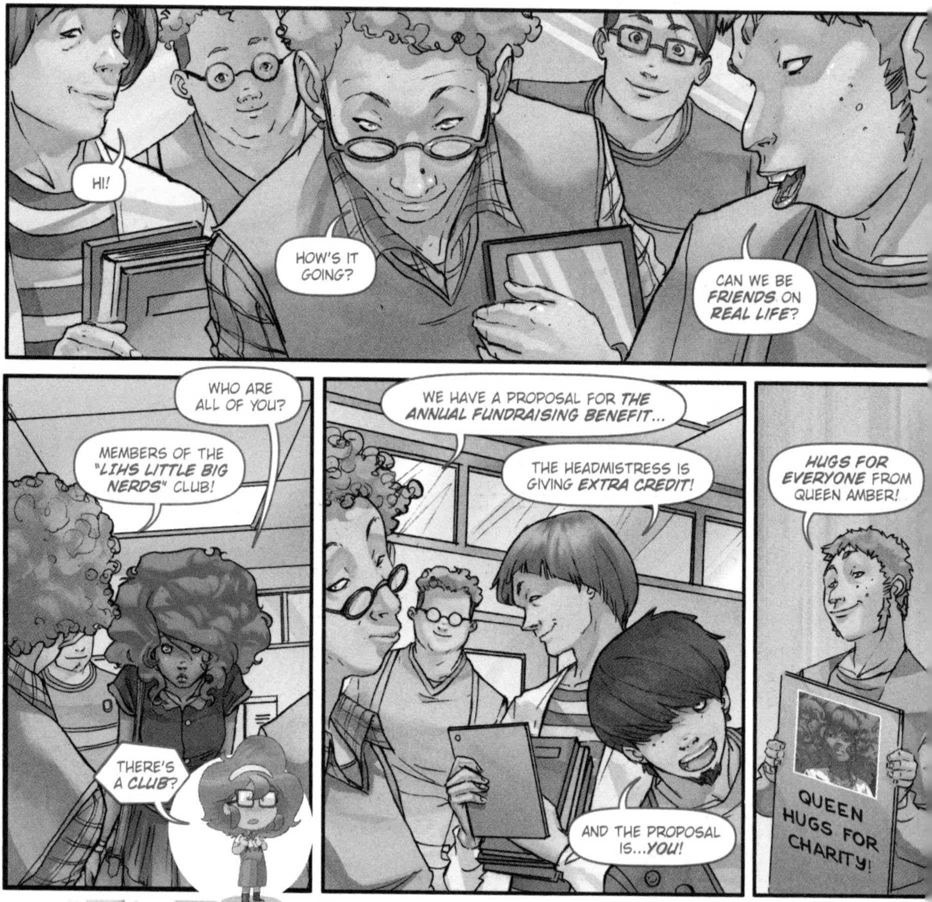
HI!
HOW'S IT GOING?
CAN WE BE *FRIENDS* ON *REAL LIFE*?
WHO ARE ALL OF YOU?
MEMBERS OF THE "*LIHS LITTLE BIG NERDS*" CLUB!
THERE'S A *CLUB*?
WE HAVE A PROPOSAL FOR *THE ANNUAL FUNDRAISING BENEFIT*...
THE HEADMISTRESS IS GIVING *EXTRA CREDIT*!
AND THE PROPOSAL IS...*YOU*!
HUGS FOR EVERYONE FROM QUEEN AMBER!
QUEEN HUGS FOR CHARITY!

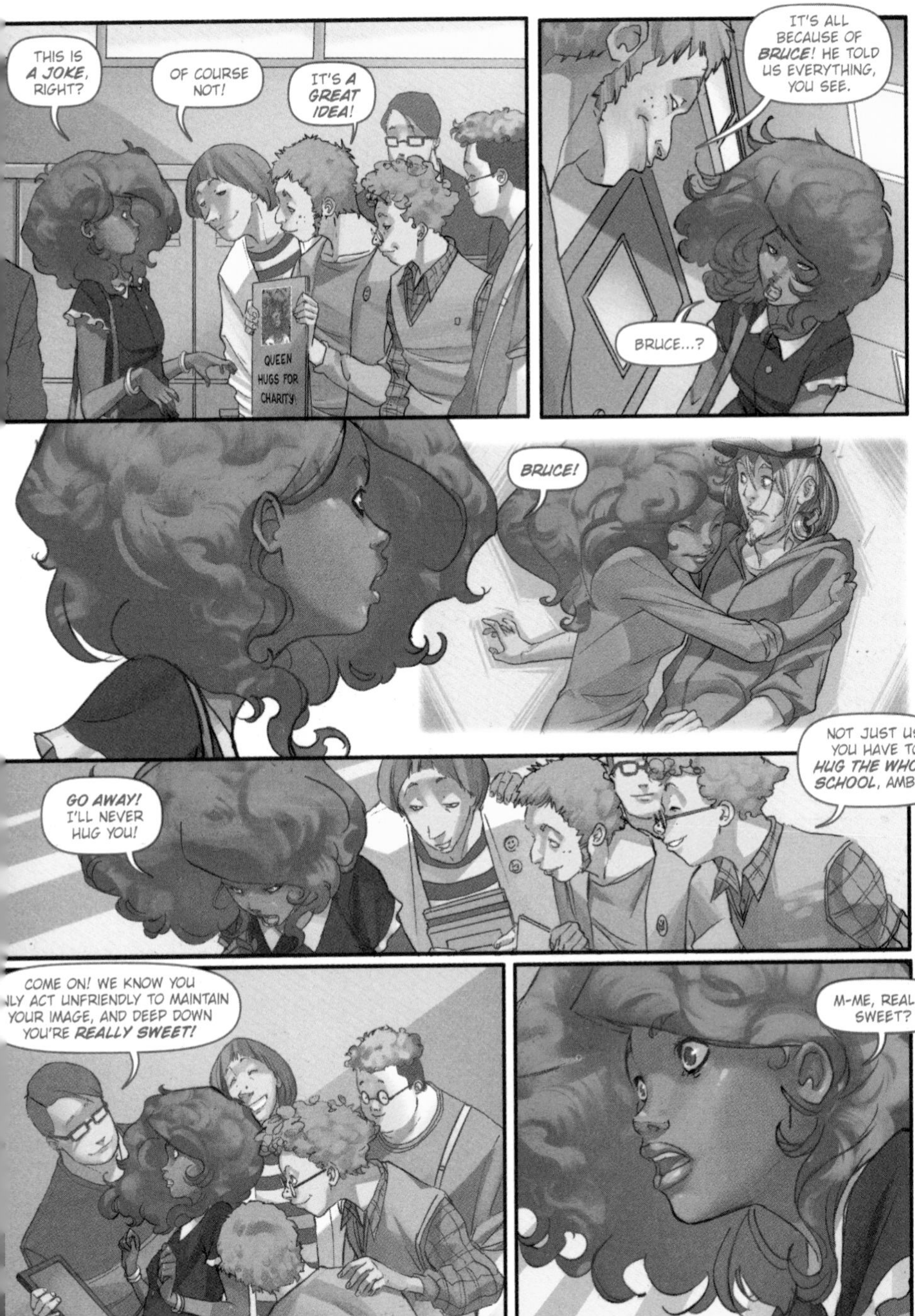
THIS IS A JOKE, RIGHT?
OF COURSE NOT!
IT'S A GREAT IDEA!
QUEEN HUGS FOR CHARITY!
IT'S ALL BECAUSE OF BRUCE! HE TOLD US EVERYTHING, YOU SEE.
BRUCE...?
BRUCE!
GO AWAY! I'LL NEVER HUG YOU!
NOT JUST US, YOU HAVE TO HUG THE WHOLE SCHOOL, AMBER!
COME ON! WE KNOW YOU NLY ACT UNFRIENDLY TO MAINTAIN YOUR IMAGE, AND DEEP DOWN YOU'RE REALLY SWEET!
M-ME, REALLY SWEET?

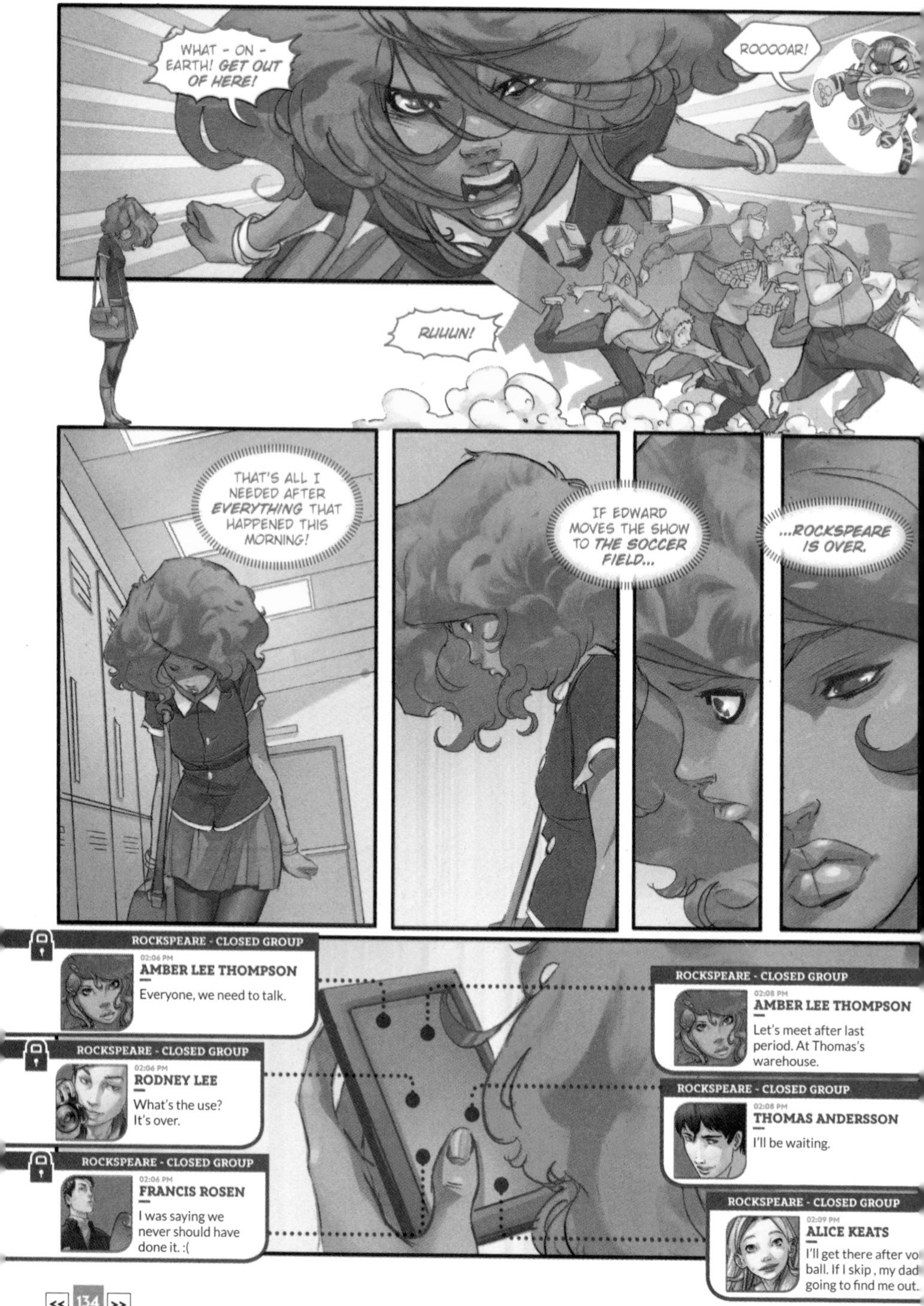

WHAT - ON - EARTH! GET OUT OF HERE!
ROOOOAR!
RUUUN!
THAT'S ALL I NEEDED AFTER EVERYTHING THAT HAPPENED THIS MORNING!
IF EDWARD MOVES THE SHOW TO THE SOCCER FIELD...
...ROCKSPEARE IS OVER.
ROCKSPEARE - CLOSED GROUP
02:06 PM
AMBER LEE THOMPSON
Everyone, we need to talk.
ROCKSPEARE - CLOSED GROUP
02:06 PM
RODNEY LEE
What's the use? It's over.
ROCKSPEARE - CLOSED GROUP
02:06 PM
FRANCIS ROSEN
I was saying we never should have done it. :(
ROCKSPEARE - CLOSED GROUP
02:08 PM
AMBER LEE THOMPSON
Let's meet after last period. At Thomas's warehouse.
ROCKSPEARE - CLOSED GROUP
02:08 PM
THOMAS ANDERSSON
I'll be waiting.
ROCKSPEARE - CLOSED GROUP
02:09 PM
ALICE KEATS
I'll get there after vo ball. If I skip, my dad going to find me out.

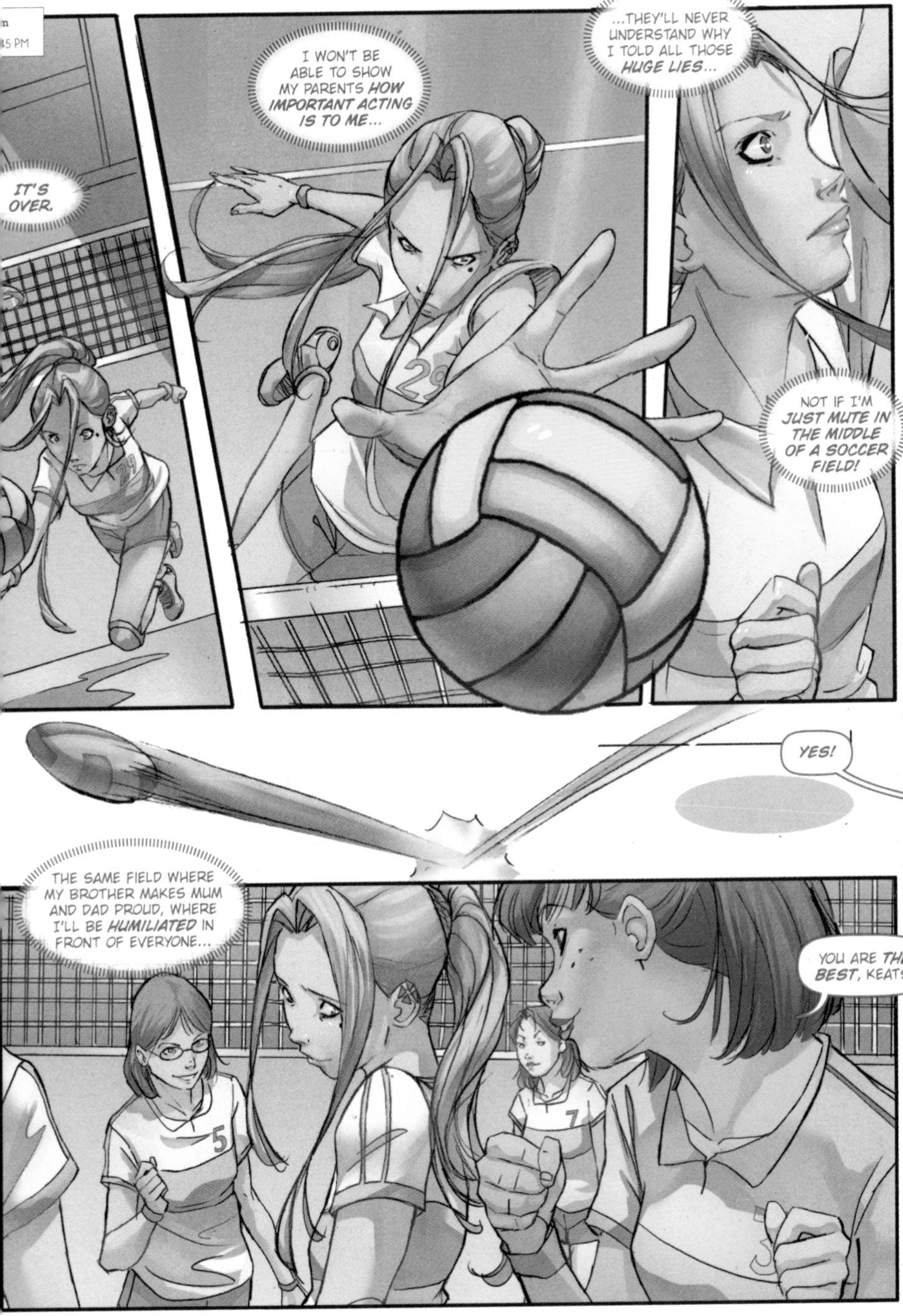
IT'S OVER.
I WON'T BE ABLE TO SHOW MY PARENTS HOW IMPORTANT ACTING IS TO ME...
...THEY'LL NEVER UNDERSTAND WHY I TOLD ALL THOSE HUGE LIES...
NOT IF I'M JUST MUTE IN THE MIDDLE OF A SOCCER FIELD!
YES!
THE SAME FIELD WHERE MY BROTHER MAKES MUM AND DAD PROUD, WHERE I'LL BE HUMILIATED IN FRONT OF EVERYONE...
YOU ARE THE BEST, KEATS!

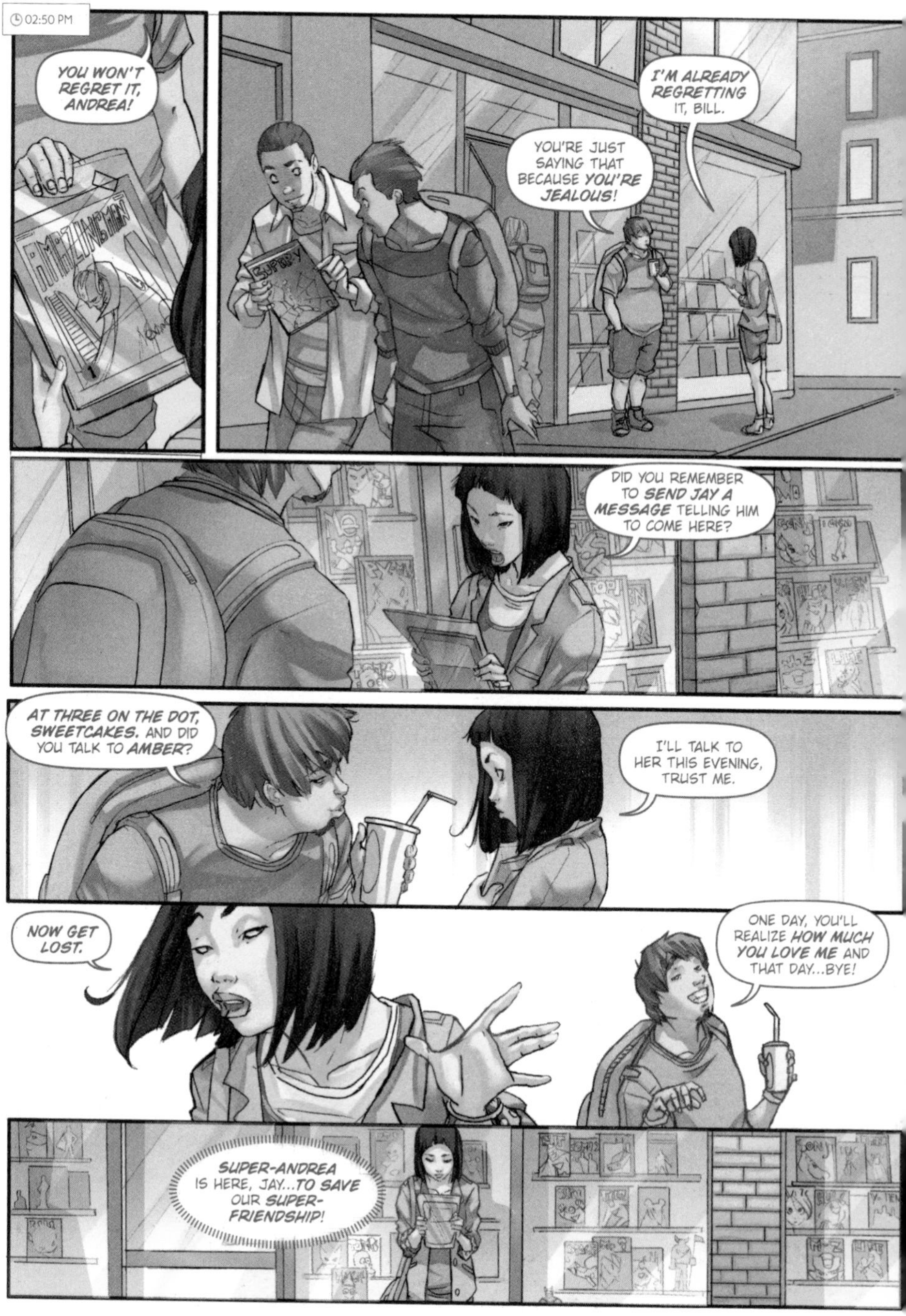

02:50 PM
YOU WON'T REGRET IT, ANDREA!
YOU'RE JUST SAYING THAT BECAUSE YOU'RE JEALOUS!
I'M ALREADY REGRETTING IT, BILL.
DID YOU REMEMBER TO SEND JAY A MESSAGE TELLING HIM TO COME HERE?
AT THREE ON THE DOT, SWEETCAKES. AND DID YOU TALK TO AMBER?
I'LL TALK TO HER THIS EVENING, TRUST ME.
NOW GET LOST.
ONE DAY, YOU'LL REALIZE HOW MUCH YOU LOVE ME AND THAT DAY...BYE!
SUPER-ANDREA IS HERE, JAY...TO SAVE OUR SUPER-FRIENDSHIP!

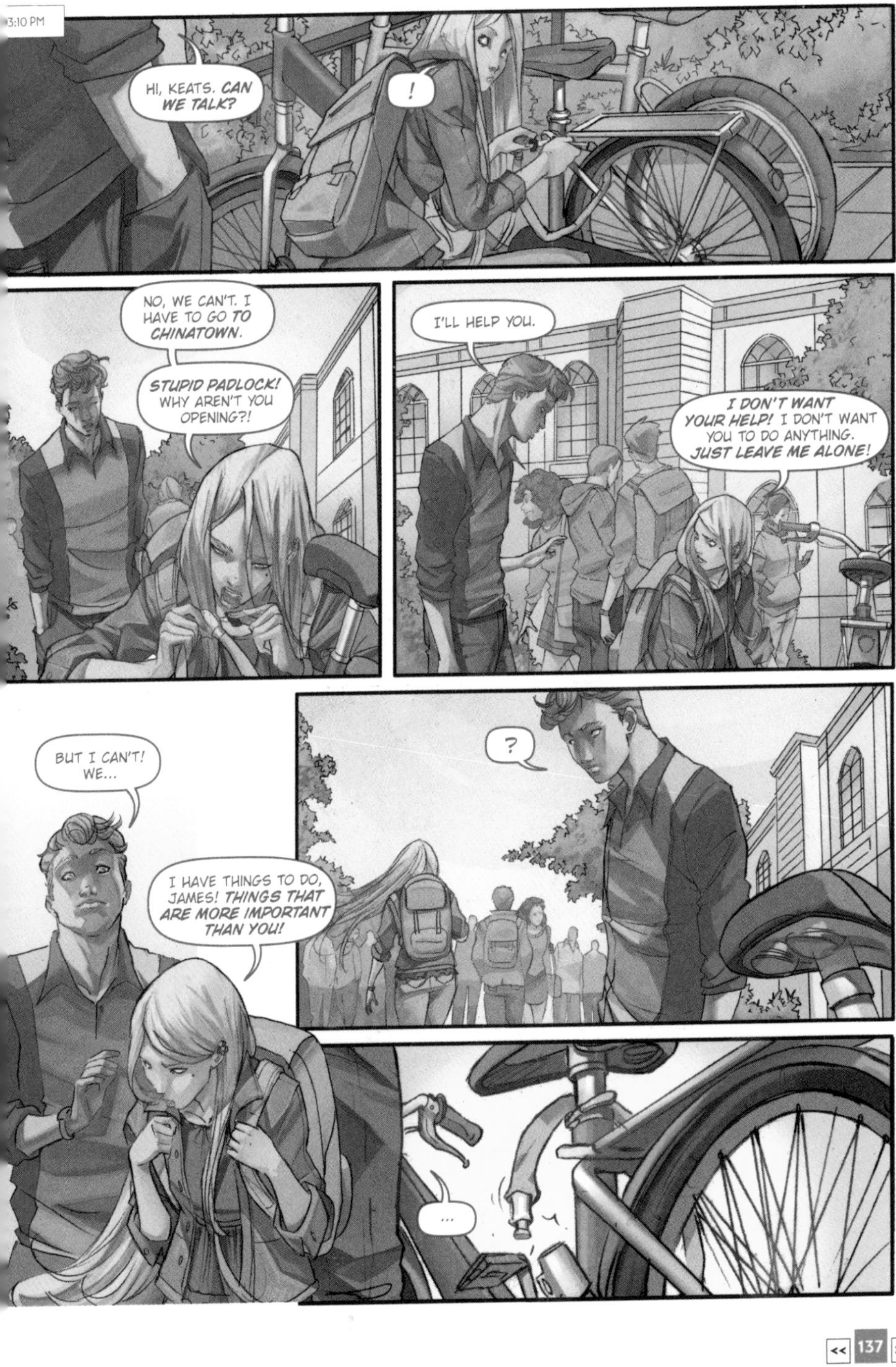
HI, KEATS. CAN WE TALK?
!
NO, WE CAN'T. I HAVE TO GO TO CHINATOWN.
STUPID PADLOCK! WHY AREN'T YOU OPENING?!
I'LL HELP YOU.
I DON'T WANT YOUR HELP! I DON'T WANT YOU TO DO ANYTHING. JUST LEAVE ME ALONE!
BUT I CAN'T! WE...
I HAVE THINGS TO DO, JAMES! THINGS THAT ARE MORE IMPORTANT THAN YOU!
?
...

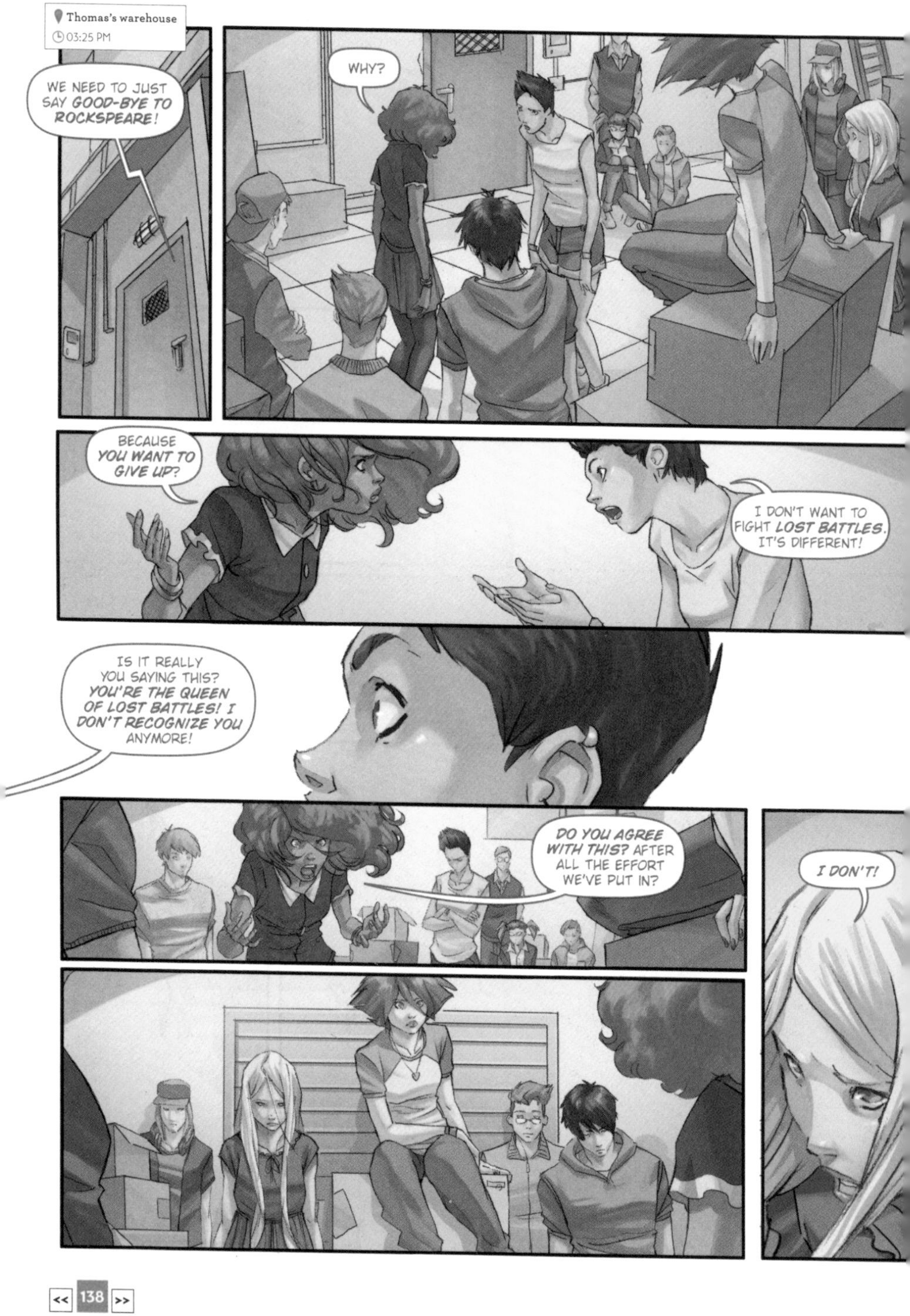
Thomas's warehouse
03:25 PM
WE NEED TO JUST SAY GOOD-BYE TO ROCKSPEARE!
WHY?
BECAUSE YOU WANT TO GIVE UP?
I DON'T WANT TO FIGHT LOST BATTLES. IT'S DIFFERENT!
IS IT REALLY YOU SAYING THIS? YOU'RE THE QUEEN OF LOST BATTLES! I DON'T RECOGNIZE YOU ANYMORE!
DO YOU AGREE WITH THIS? AFTER ALL THE EFFORT WE'VE PUT IN?
I DON'T!

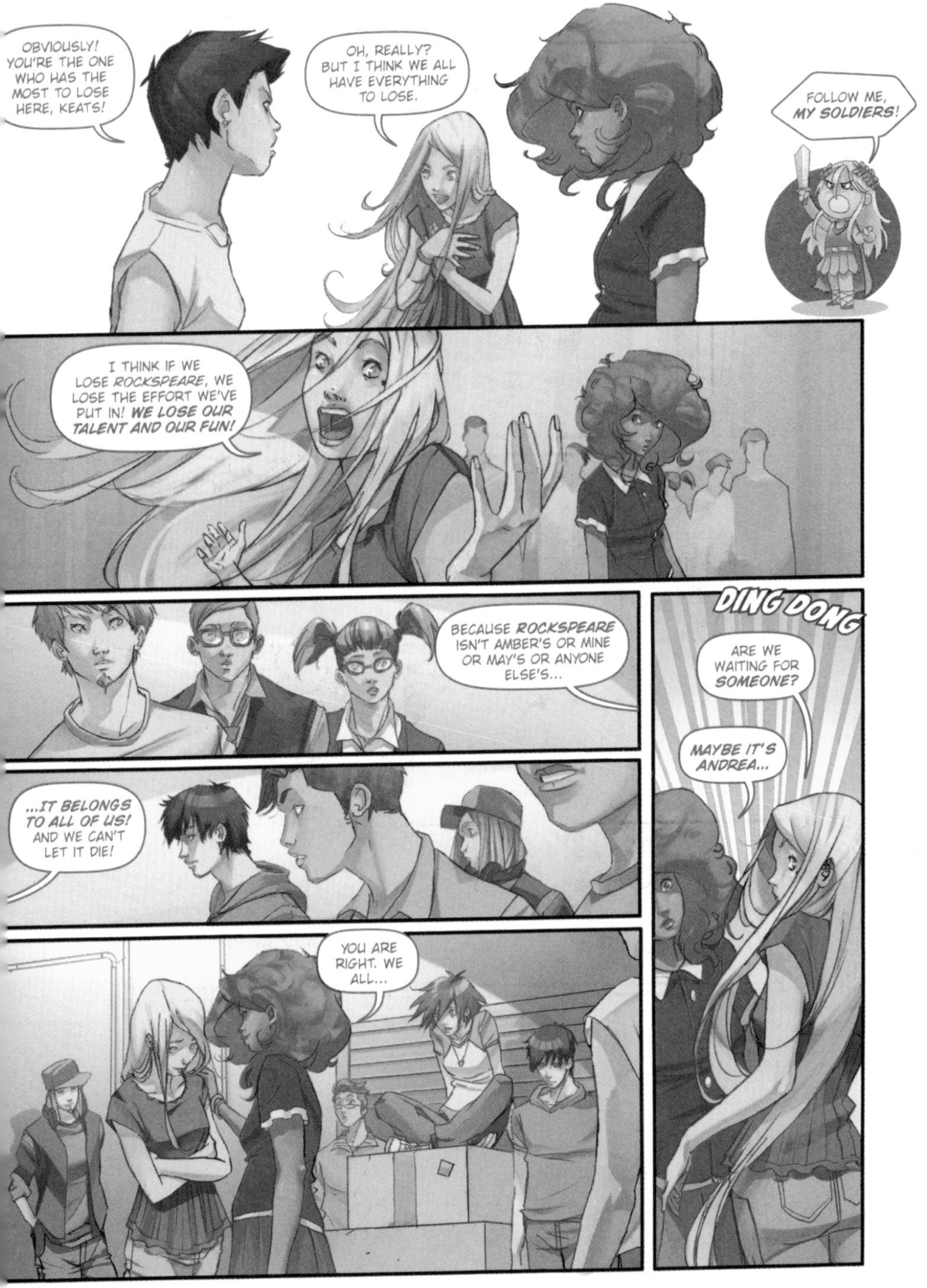
OBVIOUSLY! YOU'RE THE ONE WHO HAS THE MOST TO LOSE HERE, KEATS!
OH, REALLY? BUT I THINK WE ALL HAVE EVERYTHING TO LOSE.
FOLLOW ME, MY SOLDIERS!
I THINK IF WE LOSE ROCKSPEARE, WE LOSE THE EFFORT WE'VE PUT IN! WE LOSE OUR TALENT AND OUR FUN!
BECAUSE ROCKSPEARE ISN'T AMBER'S OR MINE OR MAY'S OR ANYONE ELSE'S...
...IT BELONGS TO ALL OF US! AND WE CAN'T LET IT DIE!
YOU ARE RIGHT. WE ALL...
DING DONG
ARE WE WAITING FOR SOMEONE?
MAYBE IT'S ANDREA...

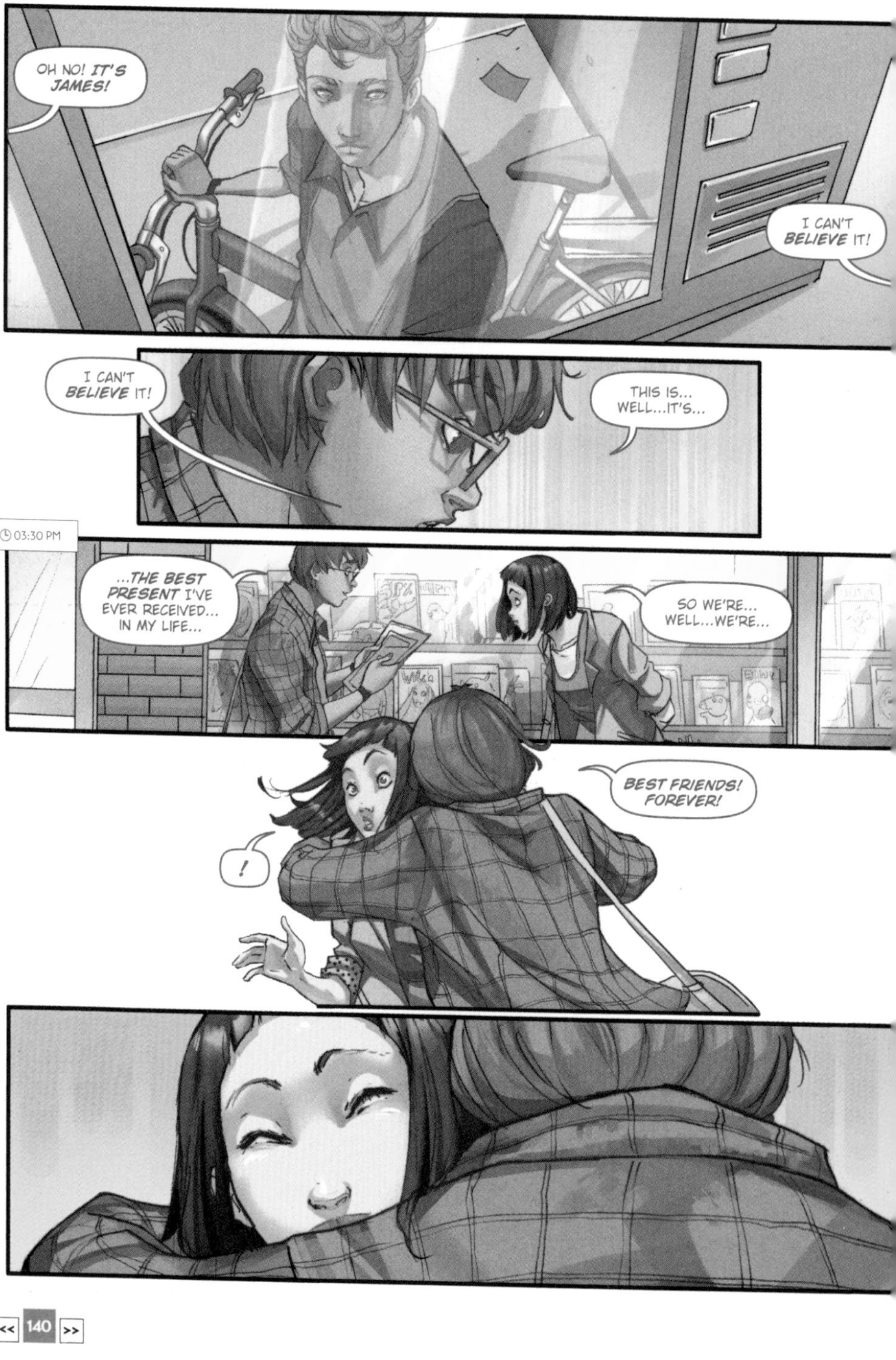
OH NO! IT'S JAMES!
I CAN'T BELIEVE IT!
I CAN'T BELIEVE IT!
THIS IS... WELL...IT'S...
03:30 PM
...THE BEST PRESENT I'VE EVER RECEIVED... IN MY LIFE...
SO WE'RE... WELL...WE'RE...
BEST FRIENDS! FOREVER!
!

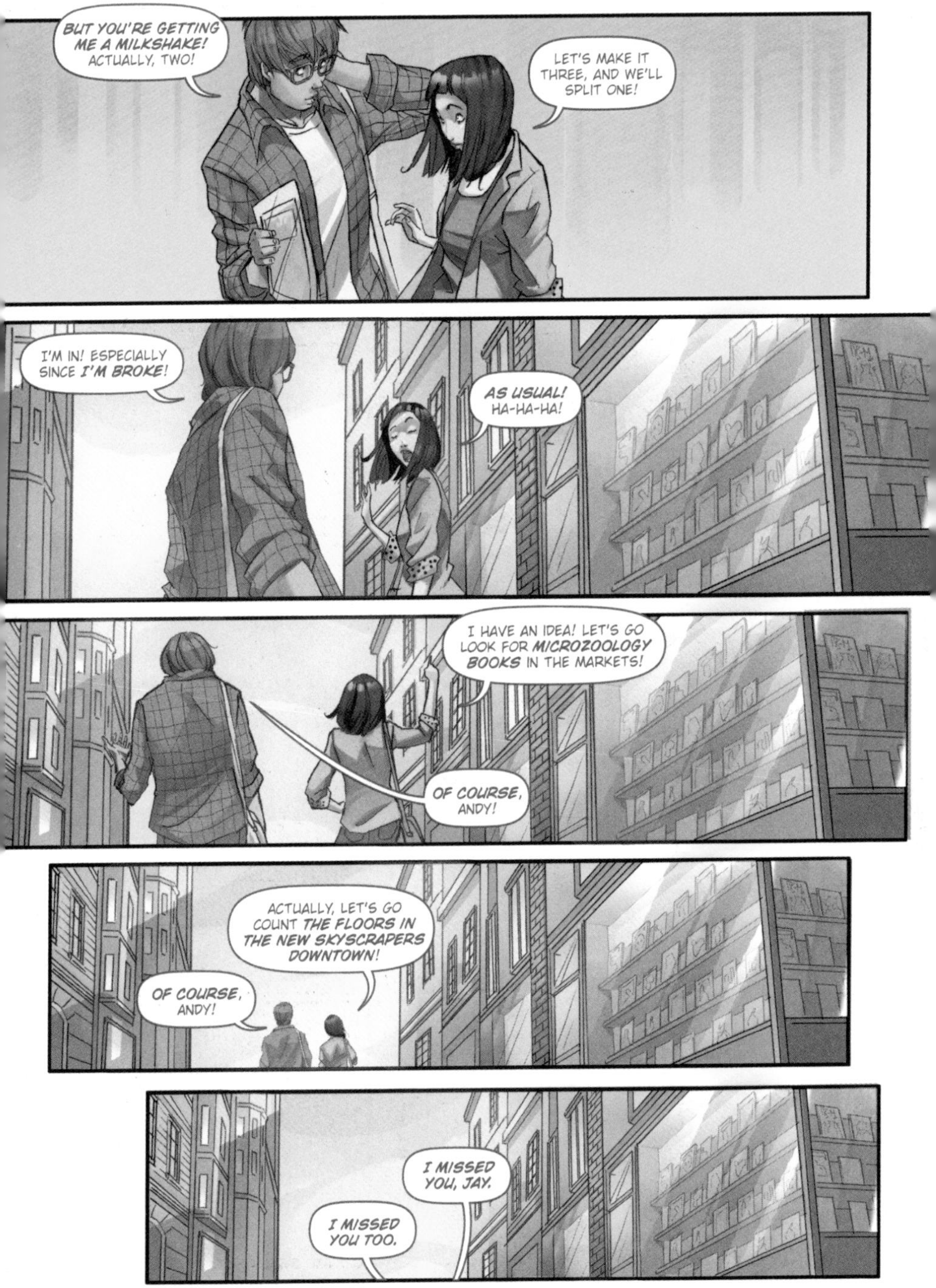
BUT YOU'RE GETTING ME A MILKSHAKE! ACTUALLY, TWO!
LET'S MAKE IT THREE, AND WE'LL SPLIT ONE!
I'M IN! ESPECIALLY SINCE I'M BROKE!
AS USUAL! HA-HA-HA!
I HAVE AN IDEA! LET'S GO LOOK FOR MICROZOOLOGY BOOKS IN THE MARKETS!
OF COURSE, ANDY!
ACTUALLY, LET'S GO COUNT THE FLOORS IN THE NEW SKYSCRAPERS DOWNTOWN!
OF COURSE, ANDY!
I MISSED YOU, JAY.
I MISSED YOU TOO.

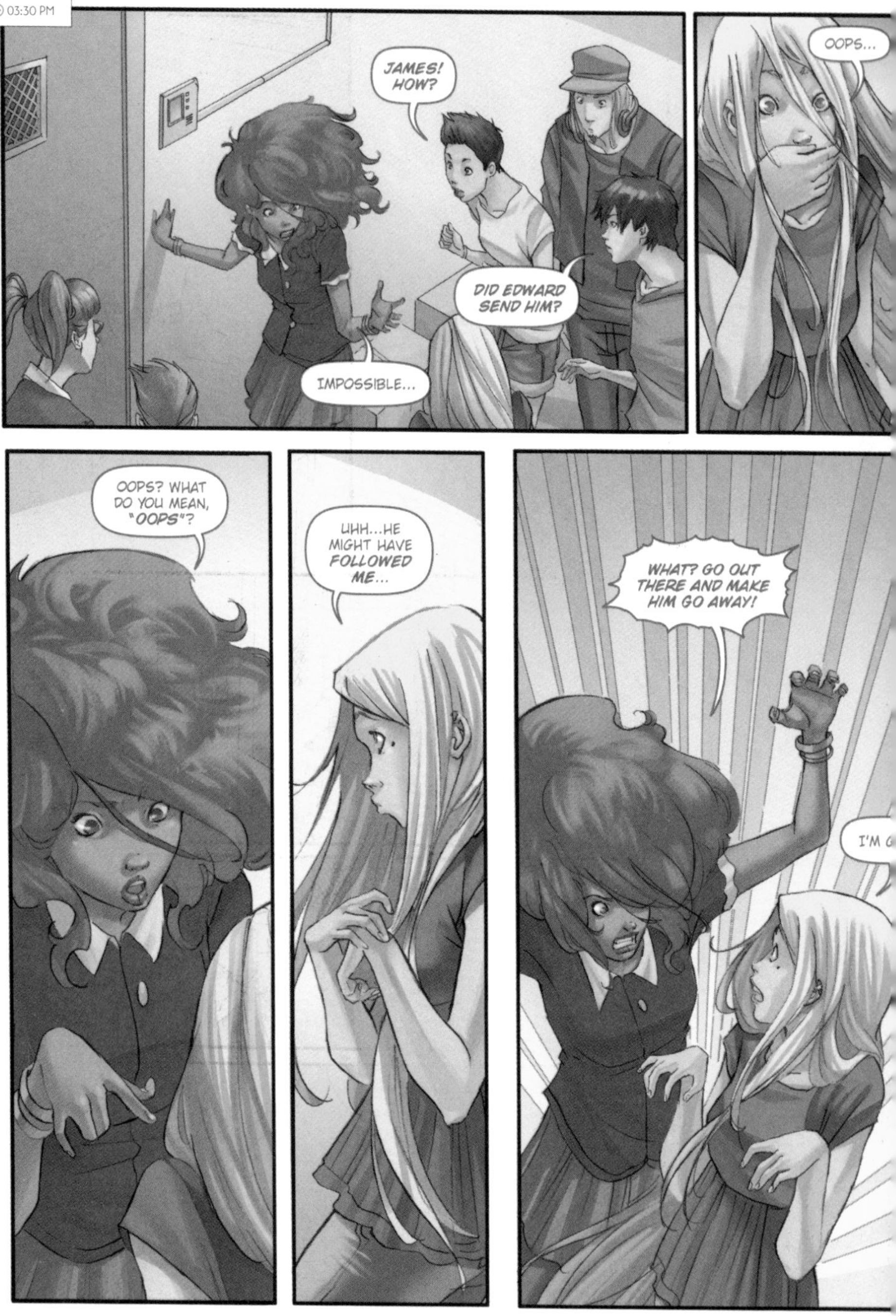
JAMES! HOW?
DID EDWARD SEND HIM?
IMPOSSIBLE...
OOPS...
OOPS? WHAT DO YOU MEAN, "OOPS"?
UHH...HE MIGHT HAVE FOLLOWED ME...
WHAT? GO OUT THERE AND MAKE HIM GO AWAY!

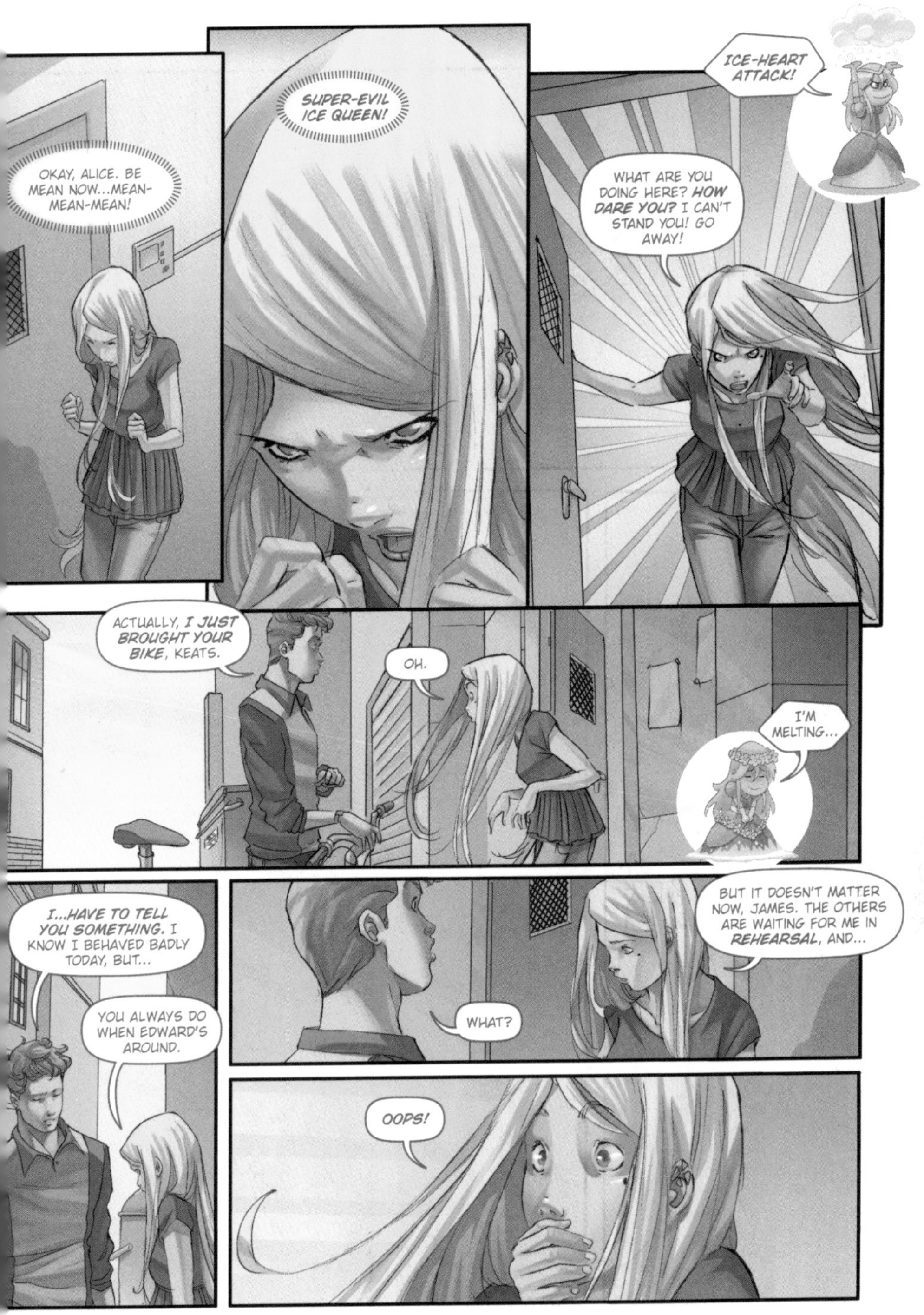
OKAY, ALICE. BE MEAN NOW...MEAN-MEAN-MEAN!
SUPER-EVIL ICE QUEEN!
ICE-HEART ATTACK!
WHAT ARE YOU DOING HERE? HOW DARE YOU? I CAN'T STAND YOU! GO AWAY!
ACTUALLY, I JUST BROUGHT YOUR BIKE, KEATS.
OH.
I'M MELTING...
I...HAVE TO TELL YOU SOMETHING. I KNOW I BEHAVED BADLY TODAY, BUT...
YOU ALWAYS DO WHEN EDWARD'S AROUND.
BUT IT DOESN'T MATTER NOW, JAMES. THE OTHERS ARE WAITING FOR ME IN REHEARSAL, AND...
WHAT?
OOPS!

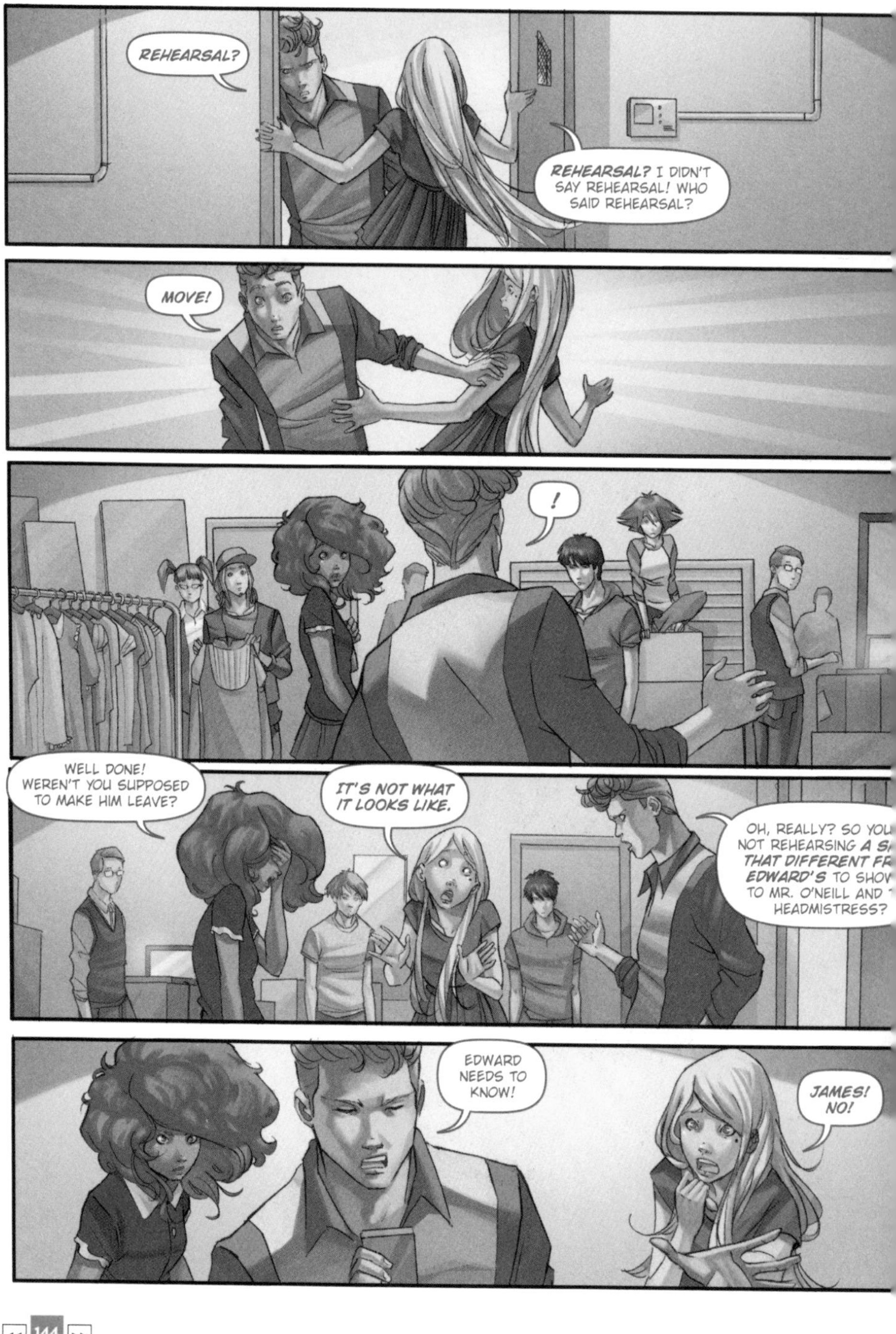
REHEARSAL?
REHEARSAL? I DIDN'T SAY REHEARSAL! WHO SAID REHEARSAL?
MOVE!
!
WELL DONE! WEREN'T YOU SUPPOSED TO MAKE HIM LEAVE?
IT'S NOT WHAT IT LOOKS LIKE.
OH, REALLY? SO YOU NOT REHEARSING A S THAT DIFFERENT F EDWARD'S TO SHOW TO MR. O'NEILL AND HEADMISTRESS?
EDWARD NEEDS TO KNOW!
JAMES! NO!

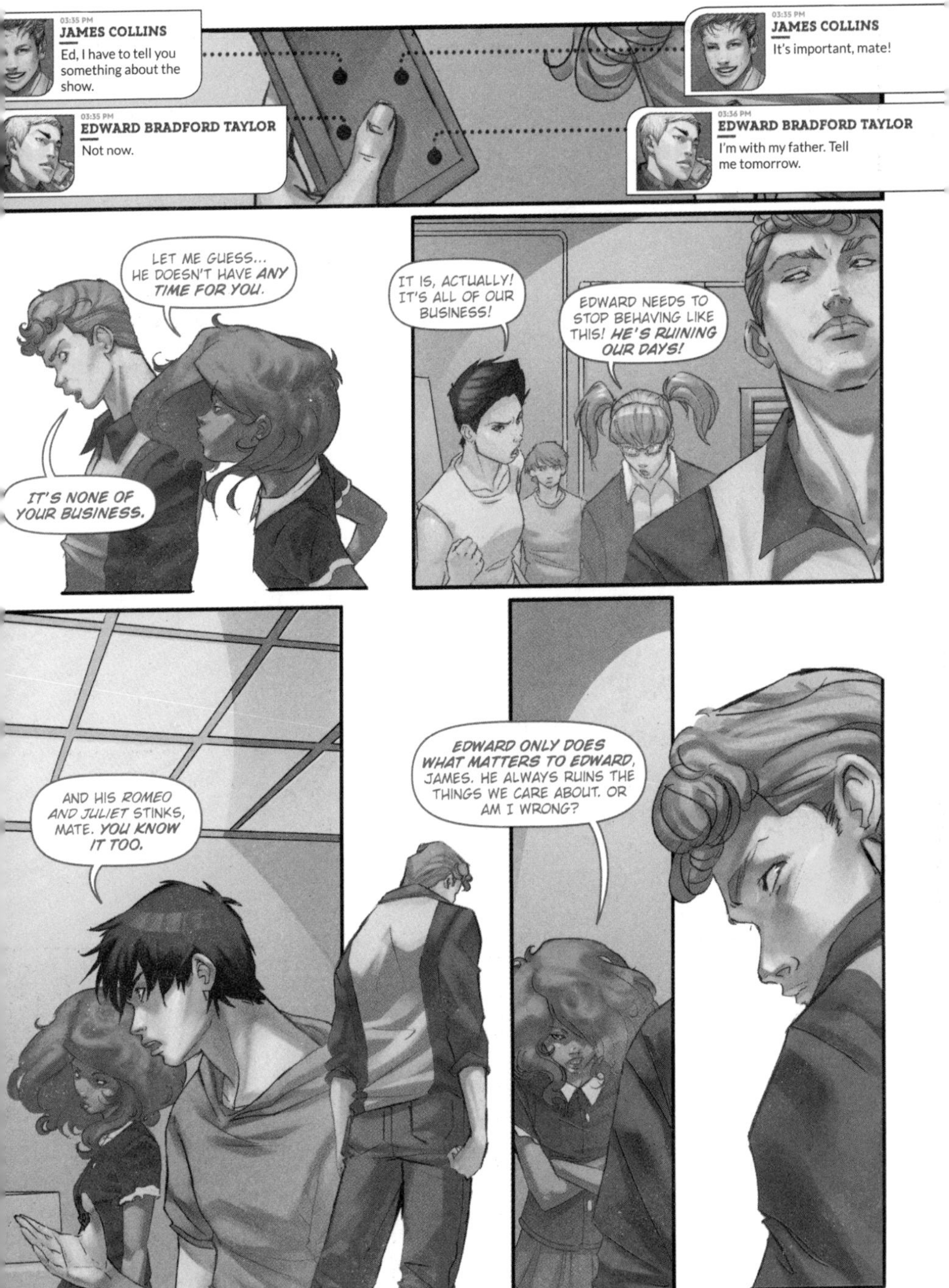

03:35 PM
JAMES COLLINS
Ed, I have to tell you something about the show.
03:35 PM
EDWARD BRADFORD TAYLOR
Not now.
03:35 PM
JAMES COLLINS
It's important, mate!
03:36 PM
EDWARD BRADFORD TAYLOR
I'm with my father. Tell me tomorrow.
LET ME GUESS... HE DOESN'T HAVE ANY TIME FOR YOU.
IT'S NONE OF YOUR BUSINESS.
IT IS, ACTUALLY! IT'S ALL OF OUR BUSINESS!
EDWARD NEEDS TO STOP BEHAVING LIKE THIS! HE'S RUINING OUR DAYS!
AND HIS ROMEO AND JULIET STINKS, MATE. YOU KNOW IT TOO.
EDWARD ONLY DOES WHAT MATTERS TO EDWARD, JAMES. HE ALWAYS RUINS THE THINGS WE CARE ABOUT. OR AM I WRONG?

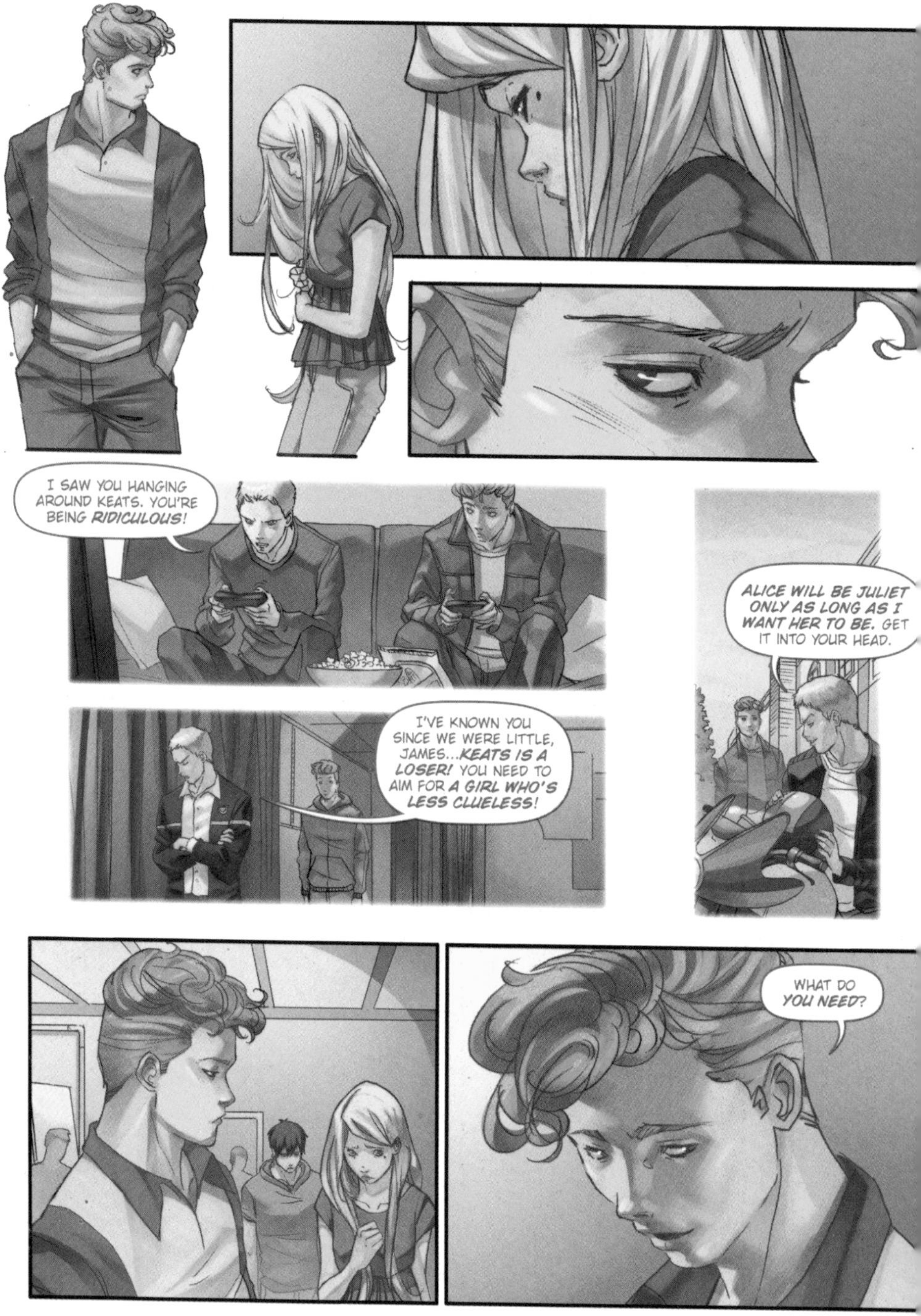
I SAW YOU HANGING AROUND KEATS. YOU'RE BEING RIDICULOUS!
I'VE KNOWN YOU SINCE WE WERE LITTLE, JAMES...KEATS IS A LOSER! YOU NEED TO AIM FOR A GIRL WHO'S LESS CLUELESS!
ALICE WILL BE JULIET ONLY AS LONG AS I WANT HER TO BE. GET IT INTO YOUR HEAD.
WHAT DO YOU NEED?

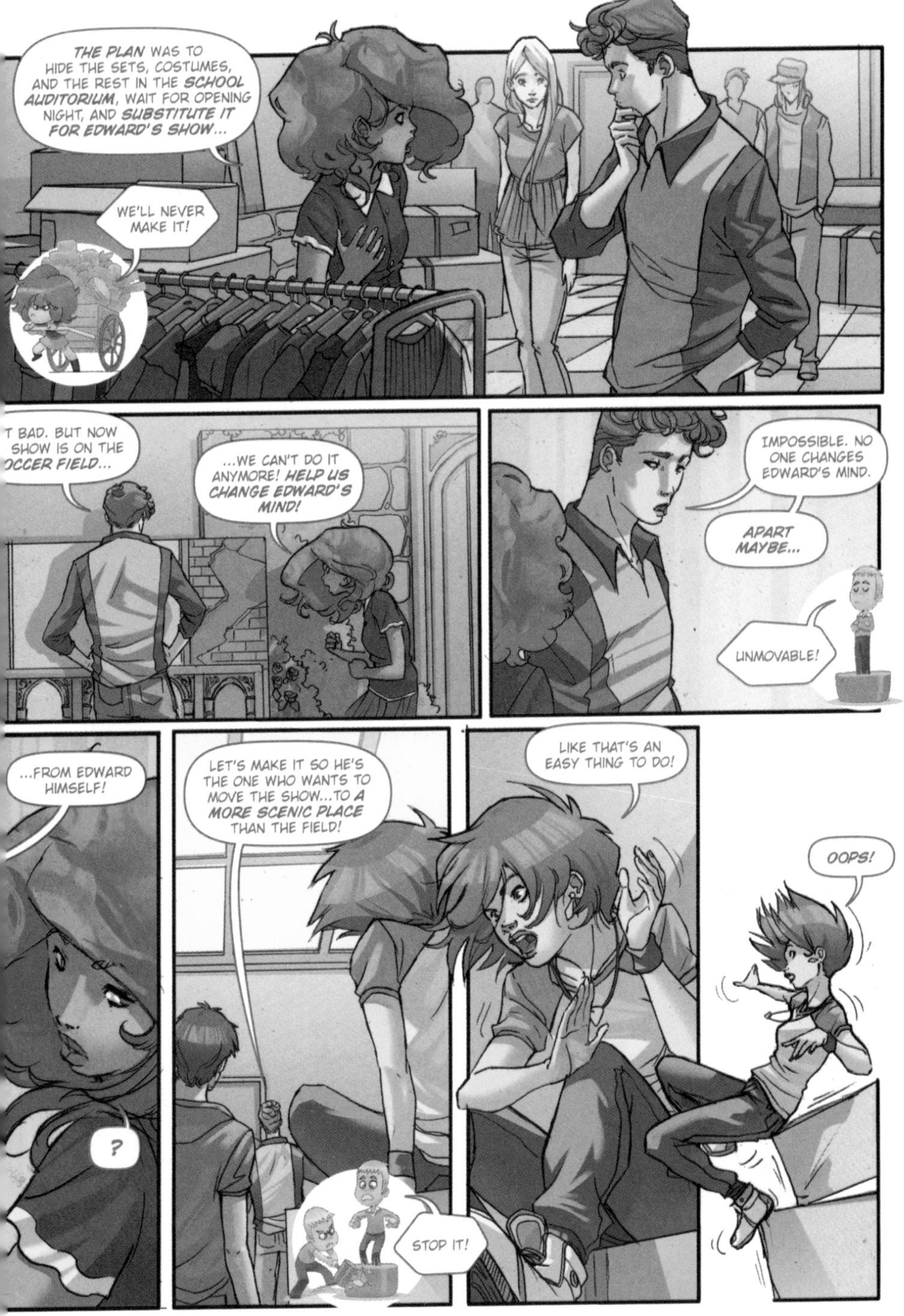
THE PLAN WAS TO HIDE THE SETS, COSTUMES, AND THE REST IN THE SCHOOL AUDITORIUM, WAIT FOR OPENING NIGHT, AND SUBSTITUTE IT FOR EDWARD'S SHOW...
WE'LL NEVER MAKE IT!
T BAD. BUT NOW SHOW IS ON THE OCCER FIELD...
...WE CAN'T DO IT ANYMORE! HELP US CHANGE EDWARD'S MIND!
IMPOSSIBLE. NO ONE CHANGES EDWARD'S MIND.
APART MAYBE...
UNMOVABLE!
...FROM EDWARD HIMSELF!
?
LET'S MAKE IT SO HE'S THE ONE WHO WANTS TO MOVE THE SHOW...TO A MORE SCENIC PLACE THAN THE FIELD!
STOP IT!
LIKE THAT'S AN EASY THING TO DO!
OOPS!

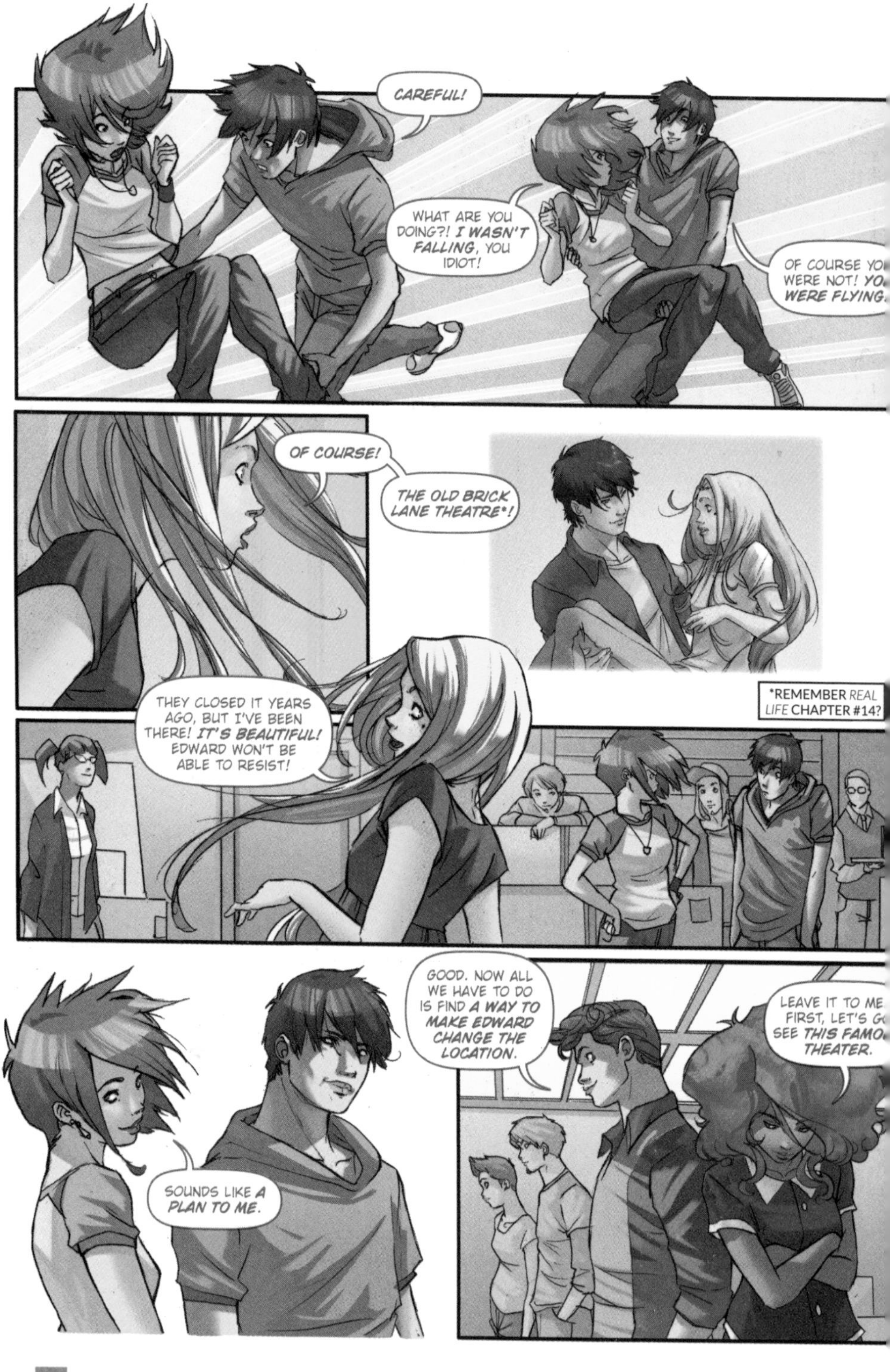
CAREFUL!
WHAT ARE YOU DOING?! I WASN'T FALLING, YOU IDIOT!
OF COURSE YO WERE NOT! YO WERE FLYING.
OF COURSE!
THE OLD BRICK LANE THEATRE*!
THEY CLOSED IT YEARS AGO, BUT I'VE BEEN THERE! IT'S BEAUTIFUL! EDWARD WON'T BE ABLE TO RESIST!
*REMEMBER REAL LIFE CHAPTER #14?
SOUNDS LIKE A PLAN TO ME.
GOOD. NOW ALL WE HAVE TO DO IS FIND A WAY TO MAKE EDWARD CHANGE THE LOCATION.
LEAVE IT TO ME FIRST, LET'S G SEE THIS FAMO THEATER.

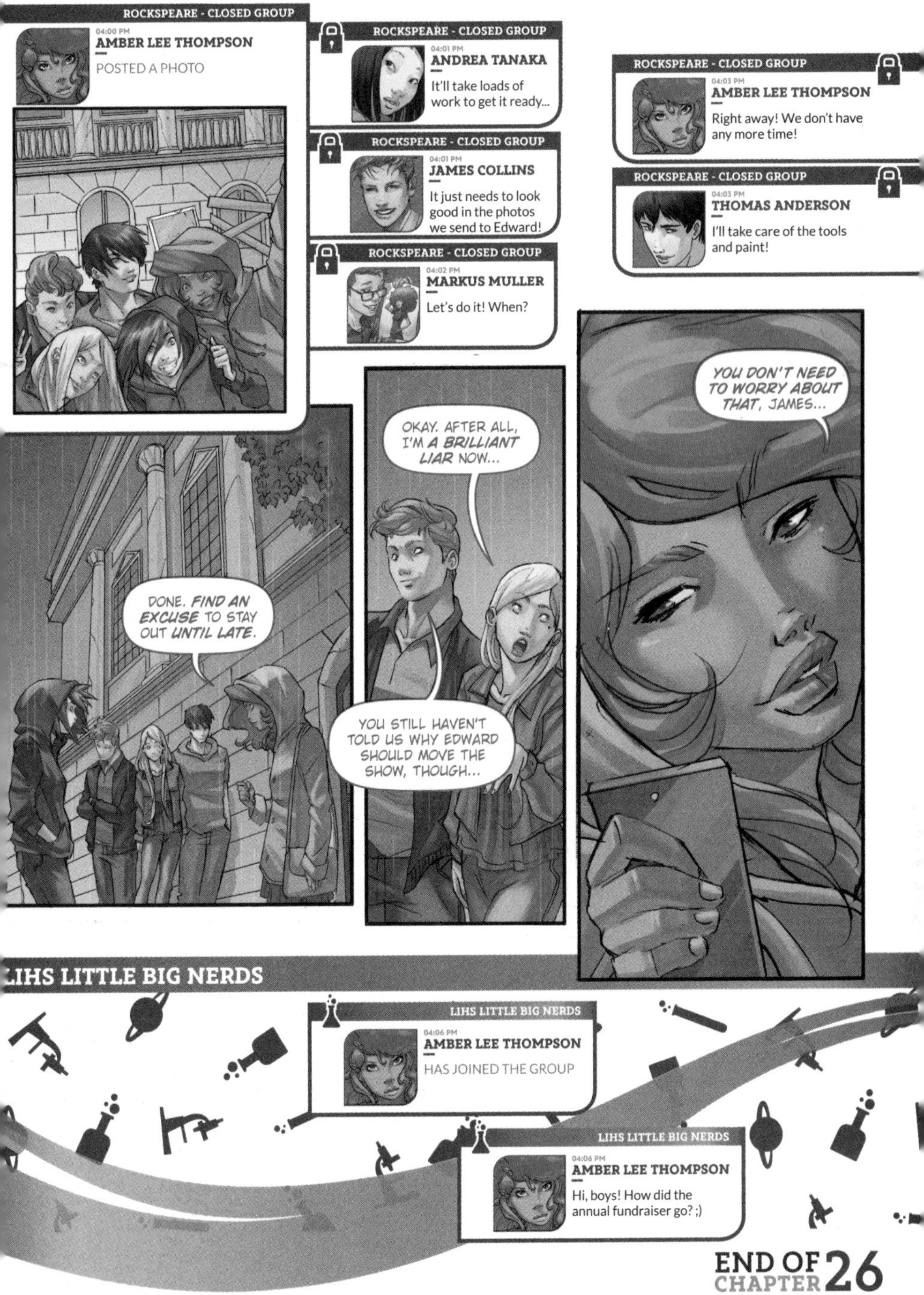

ROCKSPEARE - CLOSED GROUP
04:00 PM
AMBER LEE THOMPSON
POSTED A PHOTO
ROCKSPEARE - CLOSED GROUP
04:01 PM
ANDREA TANAKA
It'll take loads of work to get it ready...
ROCKSPEARE - CLOSED GROUP
04:01 PM
JAMES COLLINS
It just needs to look good in the photos we send to Edward!
ROCKSPEARE - CLOSED GROUP
04:02 PM
MARKUS MULLER
Let's do it! When?
ROCKSPEARE - CLOSED GROUP
04:03 PM
AMBER LEE THOMPSON
Right away! We don't have any more time!
ROCKSPEARE - CLOSED GROUP
04:03 PM
THOMAS ANDERSON
I'll take care of the tools and paint!
DONE. FIND AN EXCUSE TO STAY OUT UNTIL LATE.
OKAY. AFTER ALL, I'M A BRILLIANT LIAR NOW...
YOU STILL HAVEN'T TOLD US WHY EDWARD SHOULD MOVE THE SHOW, THOUGH...
YOU DON'T NEED TO WORRY ABOUT THAT, JAMES...
LIHS LITTLE BIG NERDS
LIHS LITTLE BIG NERDS
04:06 PM
AMBER LEE THOMPSON
HAS JOINED THE GROUP
LIHS LITTLE BIG NERDS
04:06 PM
AMBER LEE THOMPSON
Hi, boys! How did the annual fundraiser go? ;)

END OF CHAPTER 26

WE will ROCK together

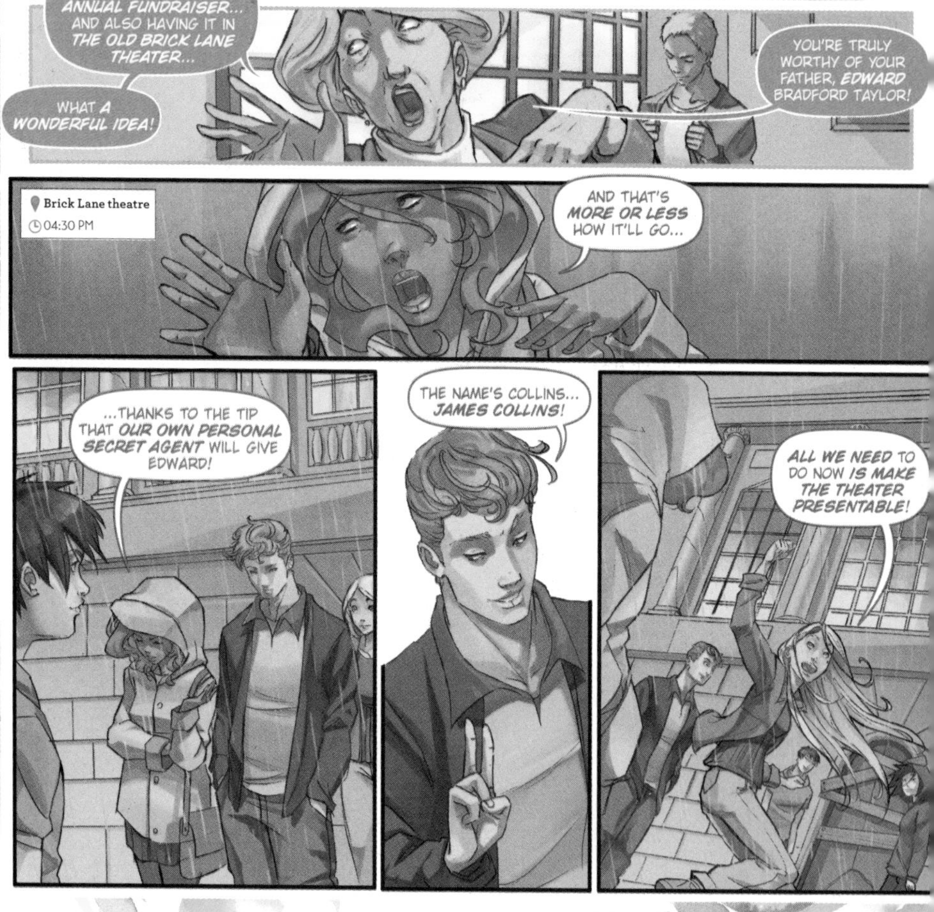
TURNING THE DRAMA CLASS SHOW INTO THE ANNUAL FUNDRAISER... AND ALSO HAVING IT IN THE OLD BRICK LANE THEATER...
WHAT A WONDERFUL IDEA!
YOU'RE TRULY WORTHY OF YOUR FATHER, EDWARD BRADFORD TAYLOR!
Brick Lane theatre
04:30 PM
AND THAT'S MORE OR LESS HOW IT'LL GO...
...THANKS TO THE TIP THAT OUR OWN PERSONAL SECRET AGENT WILL GIVE EDWARD!
THE NAME'S COLLINS... JAMES COLLINS!
ALL WE NEED TO DO NOW IS MAKE THE THEATER PRESENTABLE!

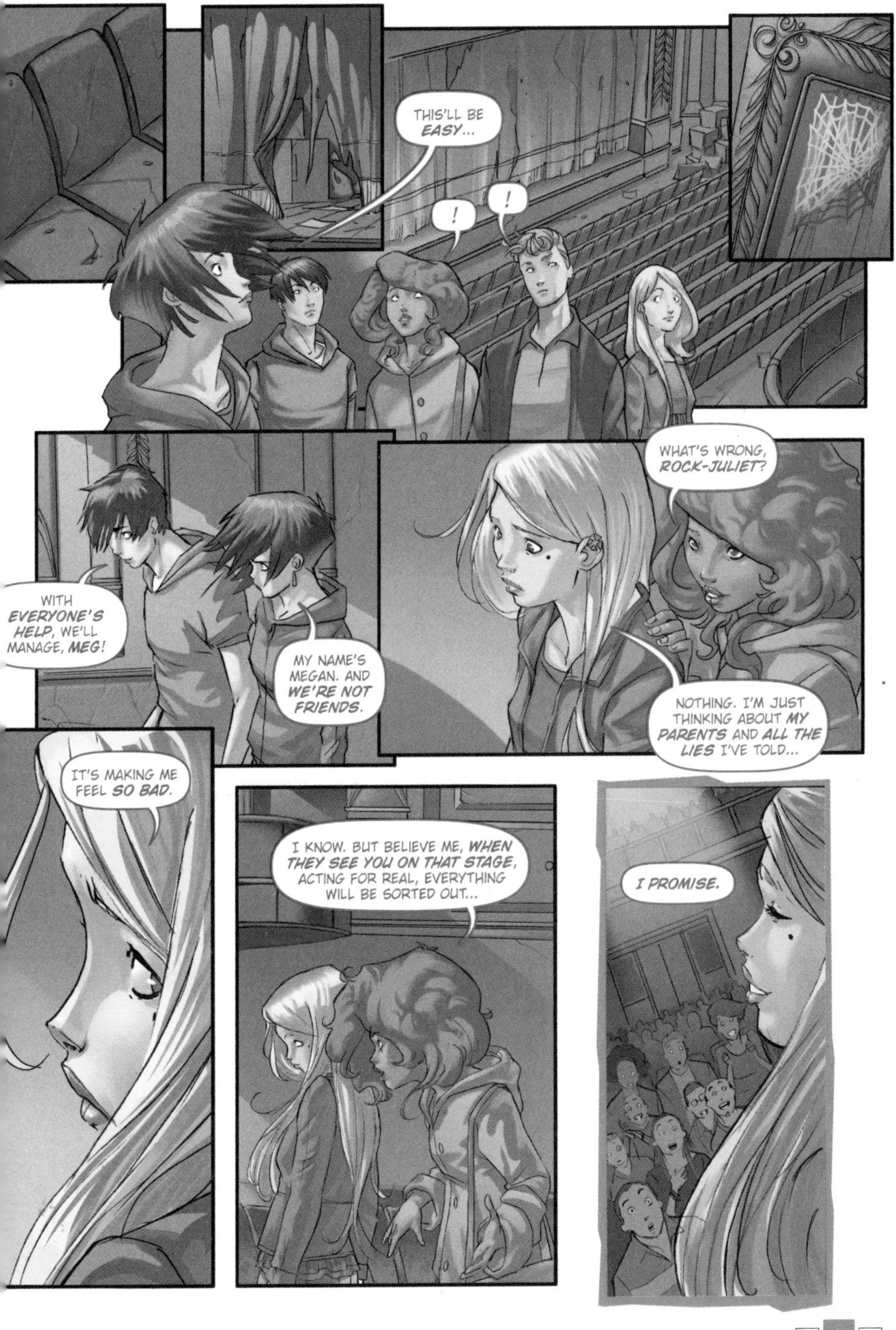
THIS'LL BE EASY...
!
!
WHAT'S WRONG, ROCK-JULIET?
WITH EVERYONE'S HELP, WE'LL MANAGE, MEG!
MY NAME'S MEGAN. AND WE'RE NOT FRIENDS.
NOTHING. I'M JUST THINKING ABOUT MY PARENTS AND ALL THE LIES I'VE TOLD...
IT'S MAKING ME FEEL SO BAD.
I KNOW. BUT BELIEVE ME, WHEN THEY SEE YOU ON THAT STAGE, ACTING FOR REAL, EVERYTHING WILL BE SORTED OUT...
I PROMISE.

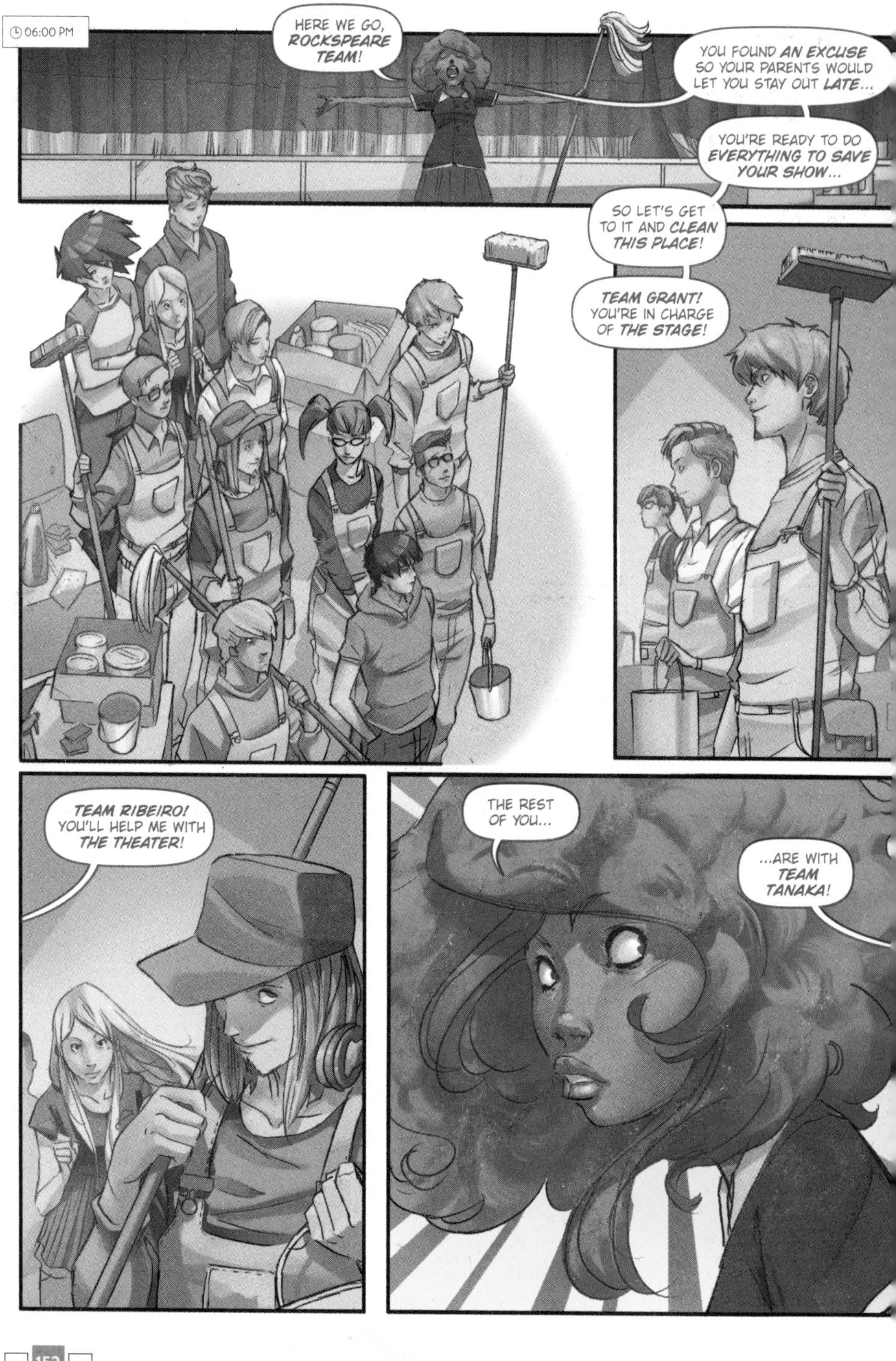
06:00 PM
HERE WE GO, ROCKSPEARE TEAM!
YOU FOUND AN EXCUSE SO YOUR PARENTS WOULD LET YOU STAY OUT LATE...
YOU'RE READY TO DO EVERYTHING TO SAVE YOUR SHOW...
SO LET'S GET TO IT AND CLEAN THIS PLACE!
TEAM GRANT! YOU'RE IN CHARGE OF THE STAGE!
TEAM RIBEIRO! YOU'LL HELP ME WITH THE THEATER!
THE REST OF YOU...
...ARE WITH TEAM TANAKA!

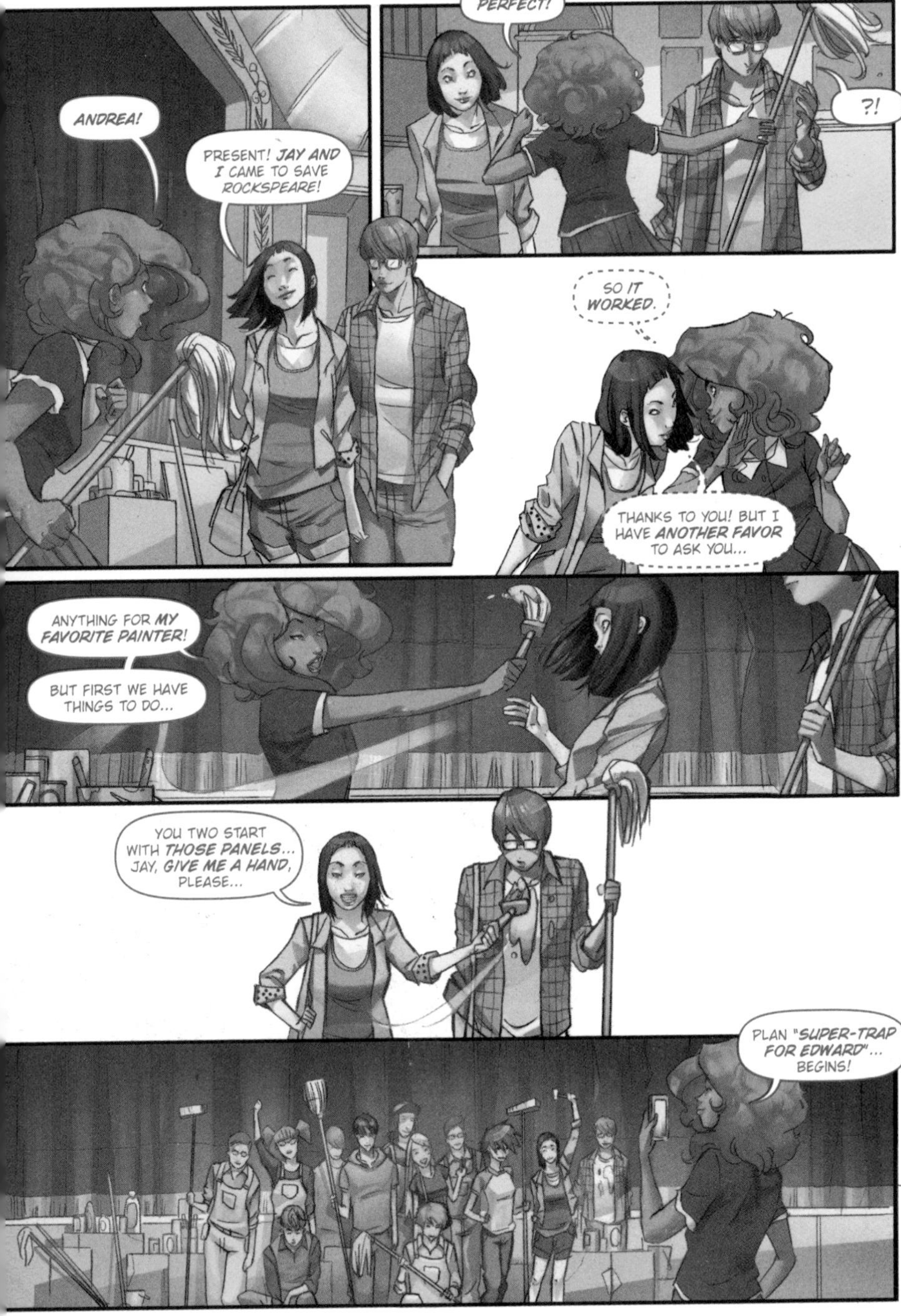

ANDREA!
PRESENT! JAY AND I CAME TO SAVE ROCKSPEARE!
PERFECT!
?!
SO IT WORKED.
THANKS TO YOU! BUT I HAVE ANOTHER FAVOR TO ASK YOU...
ANYTHING FOR MY FAVORITE PAINTER!
BUT FIRST WE HAVE THINGS TO DO...
YOU TWO START WITH THOSE PANELS... JAY, GIVE ME A HAND, PLEASE...
PLAN "SUPER-TRAP FOR EDWARD"... BEGINS!

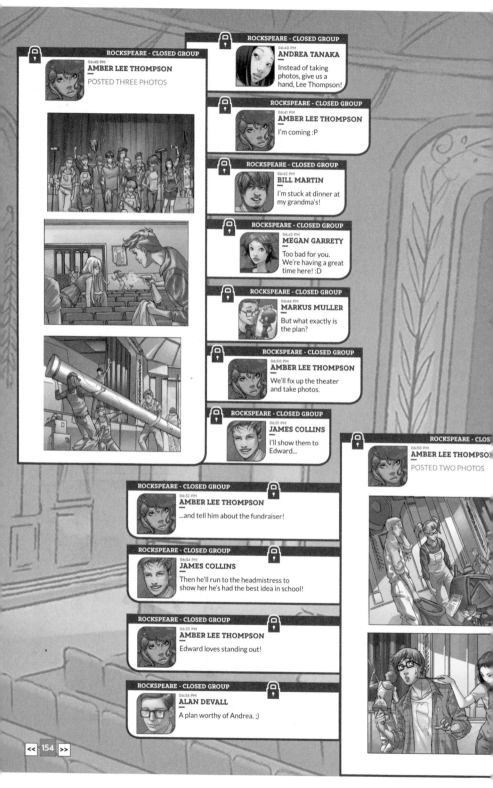

ROCKSPEARE - CLOSED GROUP

06:40 PM
AMBER LEE THOMPSON
POSTED THREE PHOTOS

ROCKSPEARE - CLOSED GROUP

06:40 PM
ANDREA TANAKA
Instead of taking photos, give us a hand, Lee Thompson!

ROCKSPEARE - CLOSED GROUP

06:41 PM
AMBER LEE THOMPSON
I'm coming :P

ROCKSPEARE - CLOSED GROUP

06:42 PM
BILL MARTIN
I'm stuck at dinner at my grandma's!

ROCKSPEARE - CLOSED GROUP

06:43 PM
MEGAN GARRETY
Too bad for you. We're having a great time here! :D

ROCKSPEARE - CLOSED GROUP

06:44 PM
MARKUS MULLER
But what exactly is the plan?

ROCKSPEARE - CLOSED GROUP

06:50 PM
AMBER LEE THOMPSON
We'll fix up the theater and take photos.

ROCKSPEARE - CLOSED GROUP

06:51 PM
JAMES COLLINS
I'll show them to Edward...

ROCKSPEARE - CLOSED GROUP

06:50 PM
AMBER LEE THOMPSON
POSTED TWO PHOTOS

ROCKSPEARE - CLOSED GROUP

06:52 PM
AMBER LEE THOMPSON
...and tell him about the fundraiser!

ROCKSPEARE - CLOSED GROUP

06:54 PM
JAMES COLLINS
Then he'll run to the headmistress to show her he's had the best idea in school!

ROCKSPEARE - CLOSED GROUP

06:55 PM
AMBER LEE THOMPSON
Edward loves standing out!

ROCKSPEARE - CLOSED GROUP

06:56 PM
ALAN DEVALL
A plan worthy of Andrea. ;)

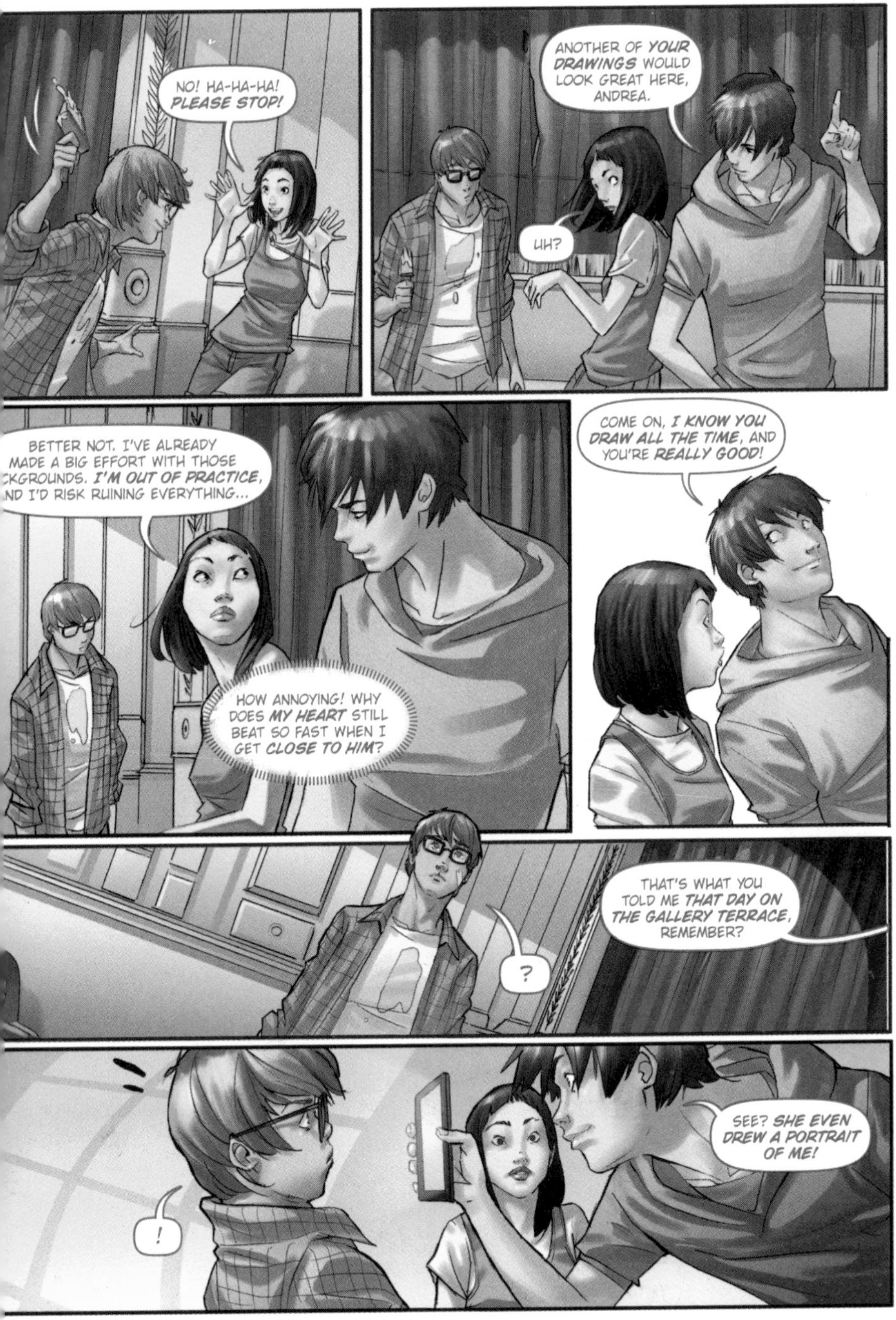
NO! HA-HA-HA! PLEASE STOP!
ANOTHER OF YOUR DRAWINGS WOULD LOOK GREAT HERE, ANDREA.
UH?
BETTER NOT. I'VE ALREADY MADE A BIG EFFORT WITH THOSE CKGROUNDS. I'M OUT OF PRACTICE, ND I'D RISK RUINING EVERYTHING...
HOW ANNOYING! WHY DOES MY HEART STILL BEAT SO FAST WHEN I GET CLOSE TO HIM?
COME ON, I KNOW YOU DRAW ALL THE TIME, AND YOU'RE REALLY GOOD!
?
THAT'S WHAT YOU TOLD ME THAT DAY ON THE GALLERY TERRACE, REMEMBER?
!
SEE? SHE EVEN DREW A PORTRAIT OF ME!

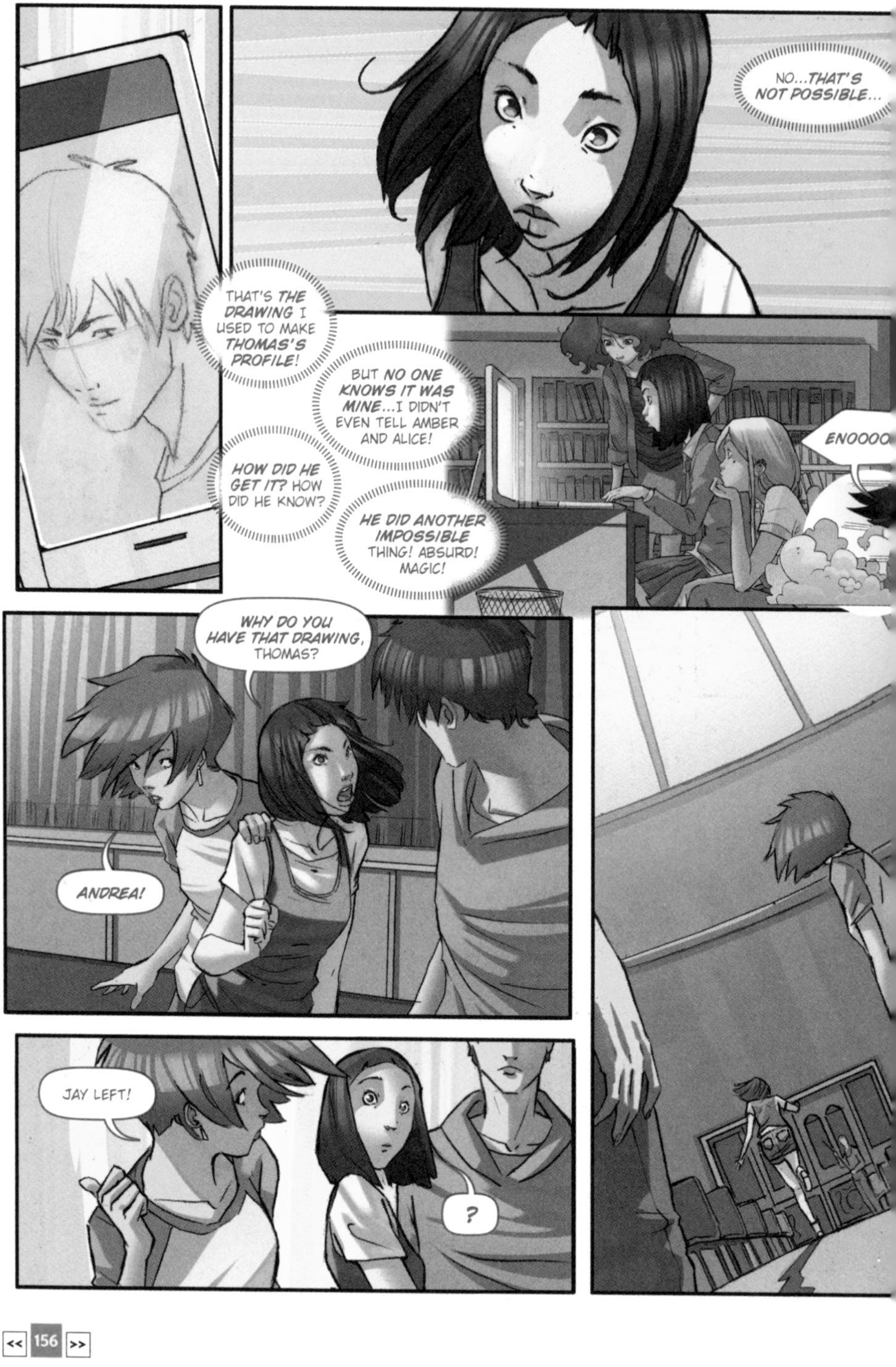
NO...THAT'S NOT POSSIBLE...
THAT'S THE DRAWING I USED TO MAKE THOMAS'S PROFILE!
BUT NO ONE KNOWS IT WAS MINE...I DIDN'T EVEN TELL AMBER AND ALICE!
HOW DID HE GET IT? HOW DID HE KNOW?
HE DID ANOTHER IMPOSSIBLE THING! ABSURD! MAGIC!
ENOOOO
WHY DO YOU HAVE THAT DRAWING, THOMAS?
ANDREA!
JAY LEFT!
?

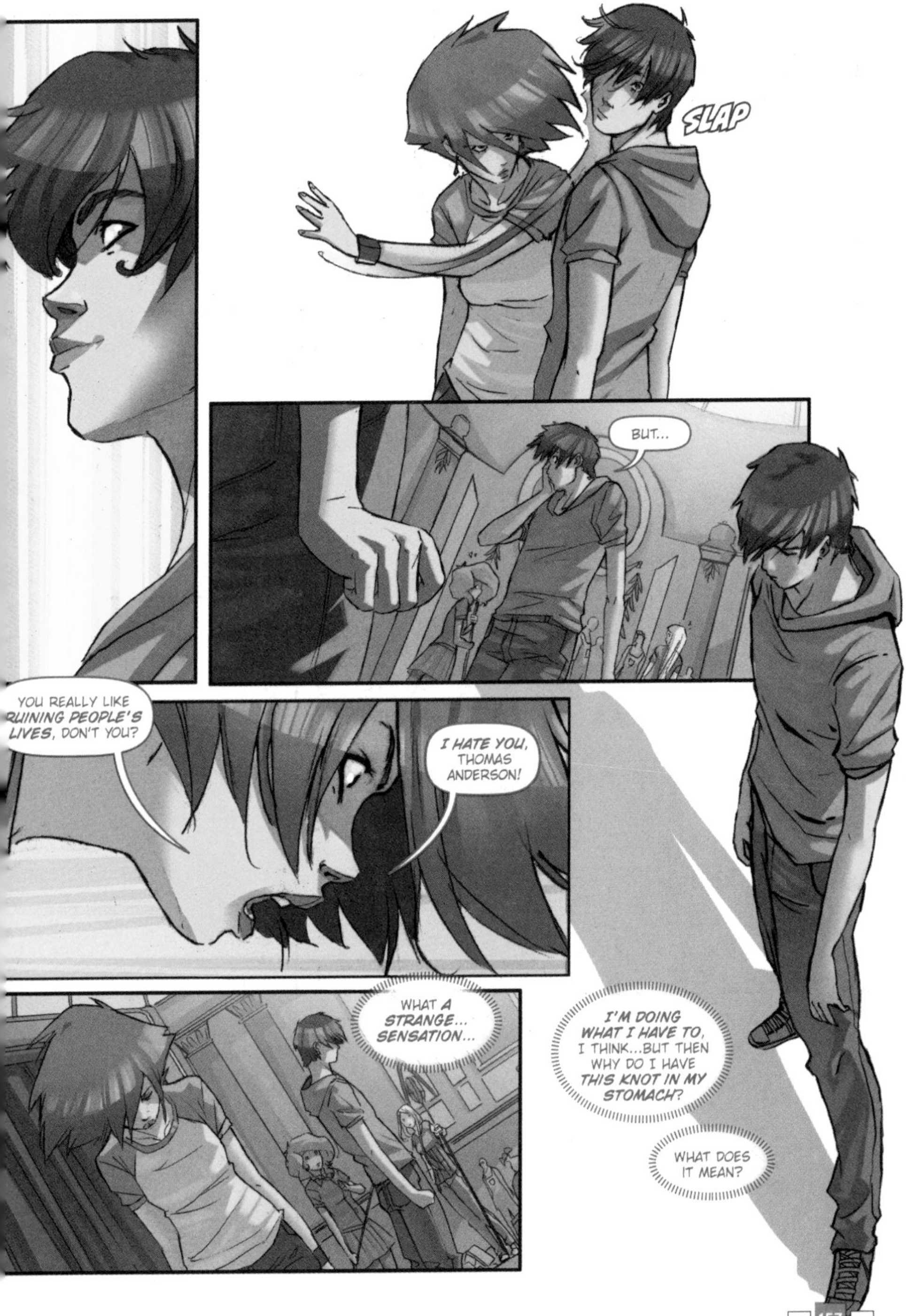
SLAP
BUT...
YOU REALLY LIKE RUINING PEOPLE'S LIVES, DON'T YOU?
I HATE YOU, THOMAS ANDERSON!
WHAT A STRANGE... SENSATION...
I'M DOING WHAT I HAVE TO, I THINK...BUT THEN WHY DO I HAVE THIS KNOT IN MY STOMACH?
WHAT DOES IT MEAN?

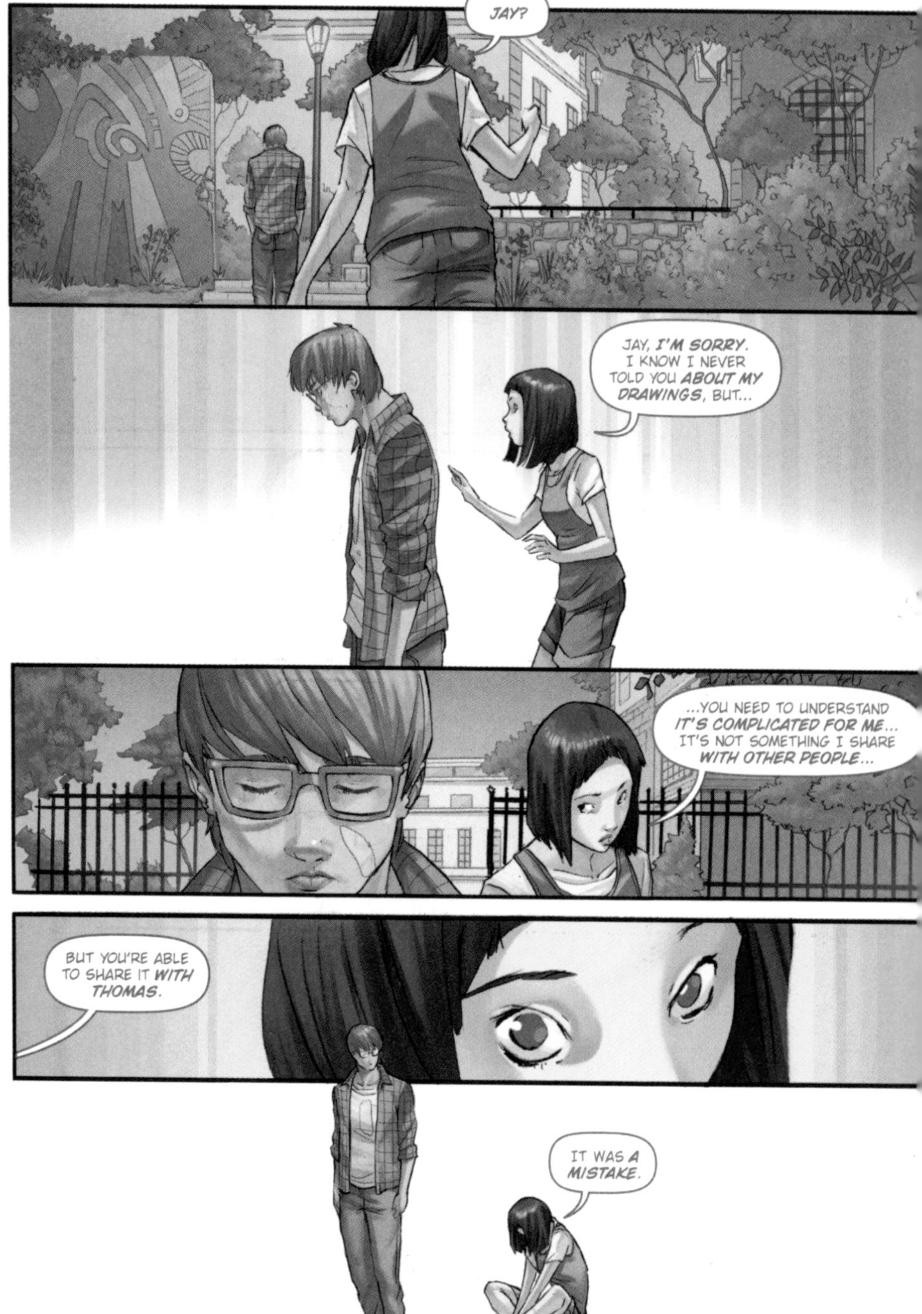
JAY?
JAY, I'M SORRY. I KNOW I NEVER TOLD YOU ABOUT MY DRAWINGS, BUT...
...YOU NEED TO UNDERSTAND IT'S COMPLICATED FOR ME... IT'S NOT SOMETHING I SHARE WITH OTHER PEOPLE...
BUT YOU'RE ABLE TO SHARE IT WITH THOMAS.
IT WAS A MISTAKE.

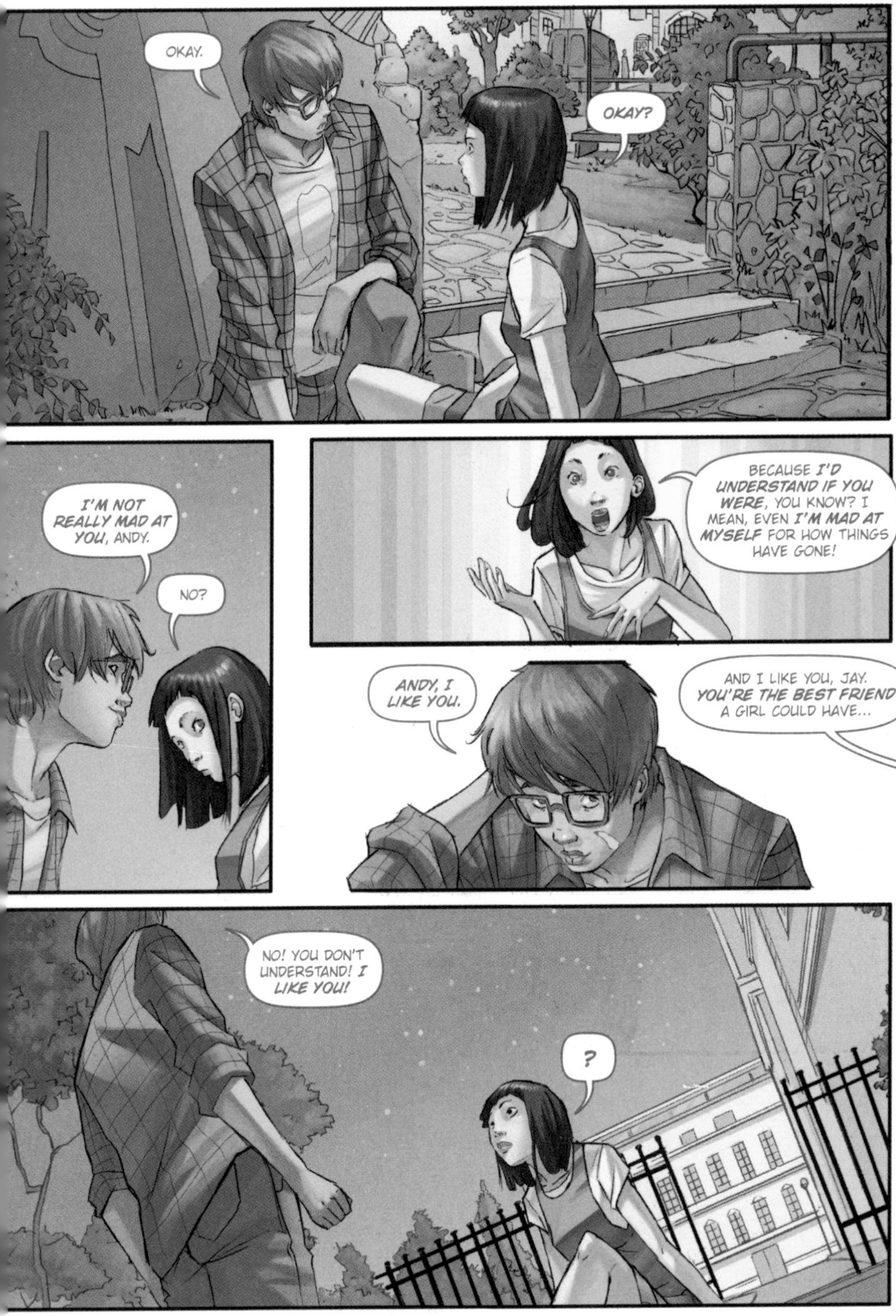
OKAY.
OKAY?
I'M NOT REALLY MAD AT YOU, ANDY.
NO?
BECAUSE I'D UNDERSTAND IF YOU WERE, YOU KNOW? I MEAN, EVEN I'M MAD AT MYSELF FOR HOW THINGS HAVE GONE!
ANDY, I LIKE YOU.
AND I LIKE YOU, JAY. YOU'RE THE BEST FRIEND A GIRL COULD HAVE...
NO! YOU DON'T UNDERSTAND! I LIKE YOU!
?

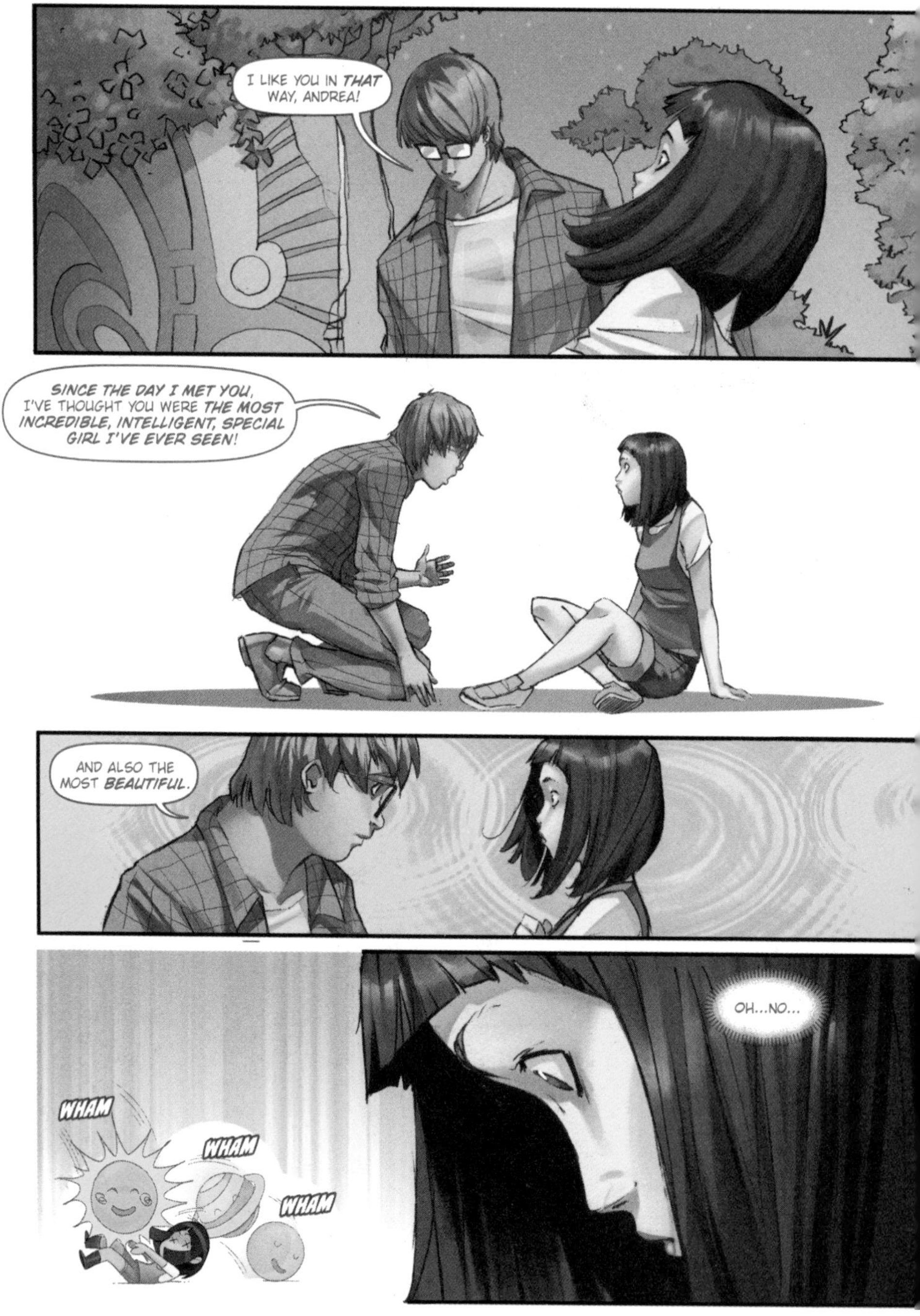
I LIKE YOU IN *THAT* WAY, ANDREA!
SINCE THE DAY I MET YOU, I'VE THOUGHT YOU WERE *THE MOST INCREDIBLE, INTELLIGENT, SPECIAL GIRL I'VE EVER SEEN!*
AND ALSO THE MOST *BEAUTIFUL.*
OH...NO...
WHAM
WHAM
WHAM

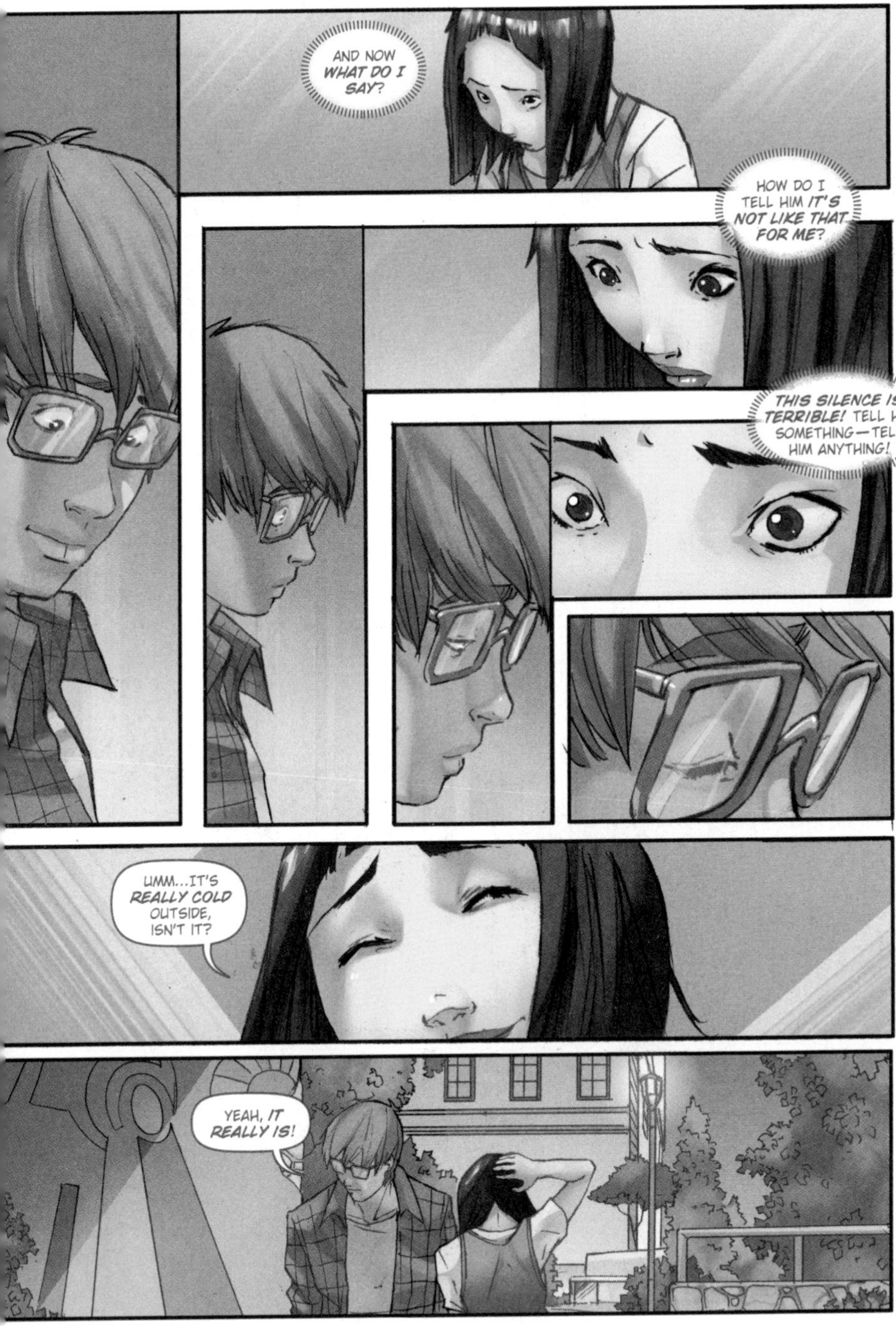
AND NOW WHAT DO I SAY?
HOW DO I TELL HIM IT'S NOT LIKE THAT FOR ME?
THIS SILENCE IS TERRIBLE! TELL HIM SOMETHING—TELL HIM ANYTHING!
UMM...IT'S REALLY COLD OUTSIDE, ISN'T IT?
YEAH, IT REALLY IS!

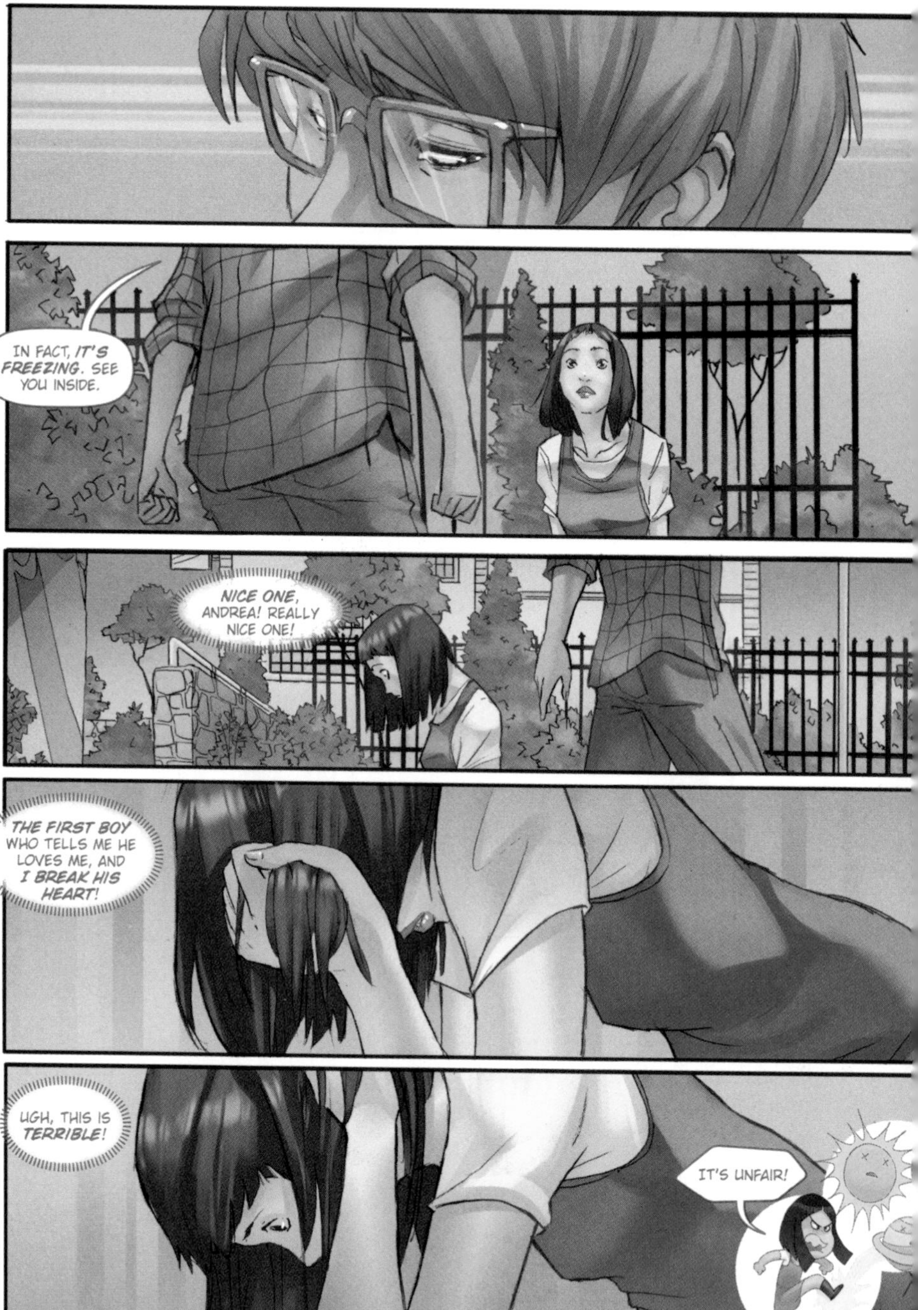
IN FACT, *IT'S FREEZING*. SEE YOU INSIDE.
NICE ONE, ANDREA! REALLY NICE ONE!
THE FIRST BOY WHO TELLS ME HE LOVES ME, AND *I BREAK HIS HEART*!
UGH, THIS IS *TERRIBLE*!
IT'S UNFAIR!

EDWARD BRADFORD TAYLOR
08:11 PM

The best, like always!

JAMES COLLINS
08:13 PM

You did it! :)

EDWARD BRADFORD TAYLOR
08:16 PM

Did you think I wouldn't?

EDWARD BRADFORD TAYLOR'S
ROMEO & JULIET
A MINIMALIST PRODUCTION

JAMES COLLINS
08:20 PM

ONSTAGE AT THE OLD BRICK LANE THEATER!

ALICE KEATS
08:22 PM

What happened to the soccer field?

VANESSA AUSTIN
08:25 PM

Now this is news! :D

RODNEY LEE
08:27 PM

So we can put the sets and everything else back together?

EDWARD BRADFORD TAYLOR
08:30 PM

Yes, for now, Rod.

ROCKSPEARE - CLOSED GROUP

AMBER LEE THOMPSON
08:33 PM

Plan successful!

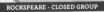

ROCKSPEARE - CLOSED GROUP

JAMES COLLINS
08:35 PM

The headmistress made her decision! No one'll take the theater away from us!

ROCKSPEARE - CLOSED GROUP

MARKUS MULLER
08:37 PM

I'm so happy!

ROCKSPEARE - CLOSED GROUP

REBECCA MENDEZ
08:39 PM

All the effort was worth it!

ROCKSPEARE - CLOSED GROUP

BRUCE RIBEIRO
08:42 PM

I can't wait to start working on Rockspeare again!

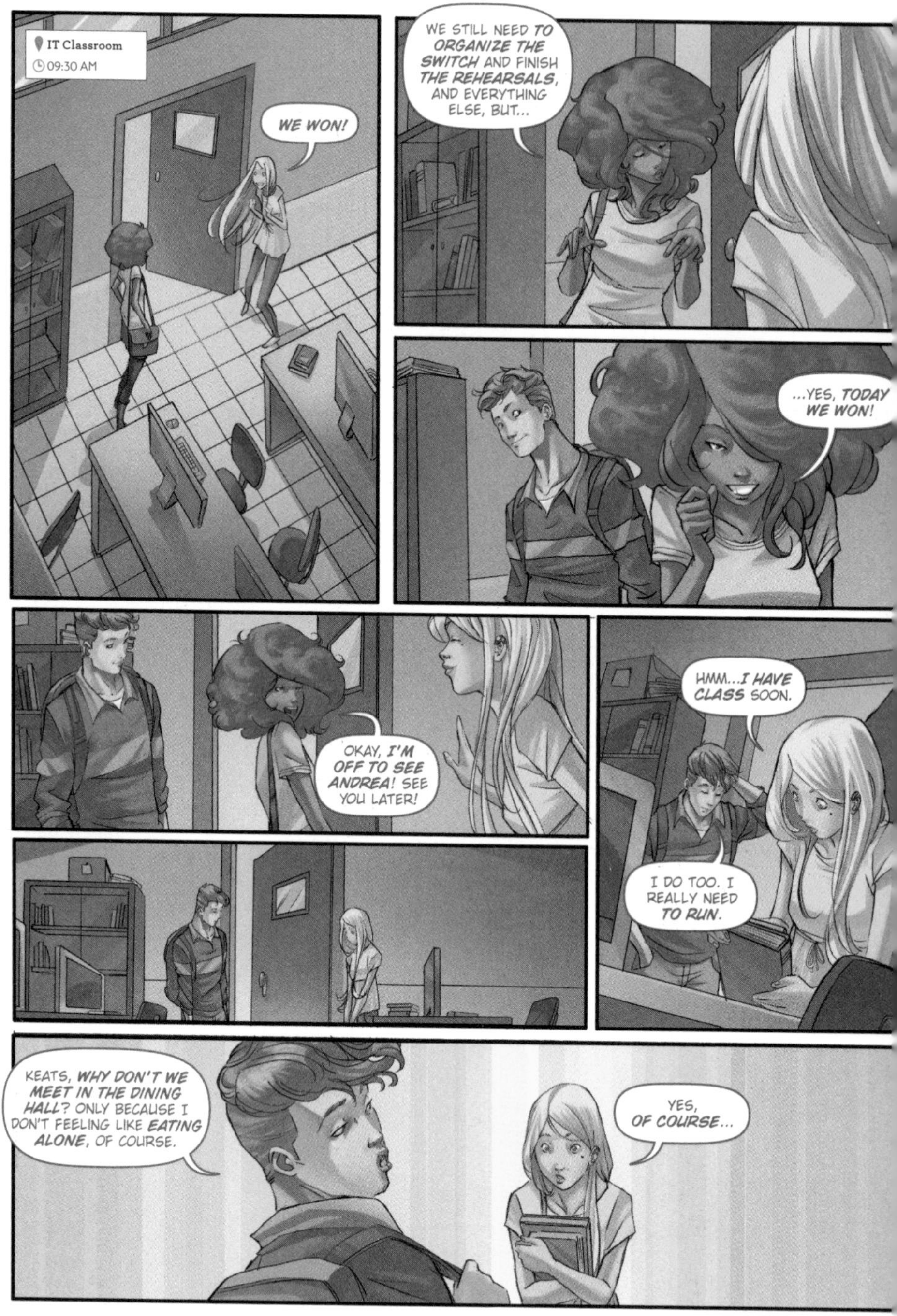
IT Classroom
09:30 AM
WE WON!
WE STILL NEED TO ORGANIZE THE SWITCH AND FINISH THE REHEARSALS, AND EVERYTHING ELSE, BUT...
...YES, TODAY WE WON!
OKAY, I'M OFF TO SEE ANDREA! SEE YOU LATER!
HMM...I HAVE CLASS SOON.
I DO TOO. I REALLY NEED TO RUN.
KEATS, WHY DON'T WE MEET IN THE DINING HALL? ONLY BECAUSE I DON'T FEELING LIKE EATING ALONE, OF COURSE.
YES, OF COURSE...

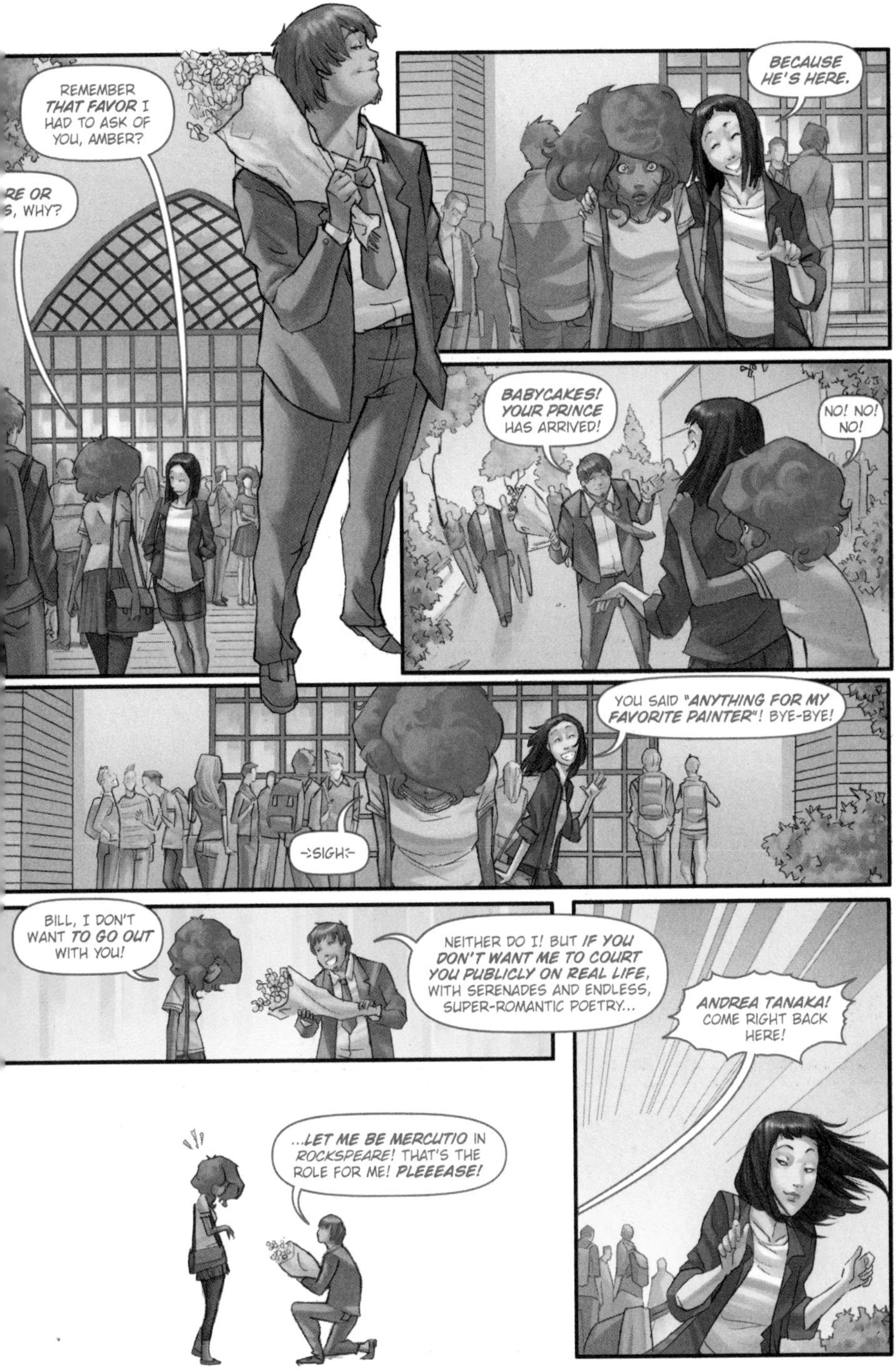

REMEMBER THAT FAVOR I HAD TO ASK OF YOU, AMBER?
RE OR
S, WHY?
BECAUSE HE'S HERE.
BABYCAKES! YOUR PRINCE HAS ARRIVED!
NO! NO! NO!
YOU SAID "ANYTHING FOR MY FAVORITE PAINTER"! BYE-BYE!
-SIGH-
BILL, I DON'T WANT TO GO OUT WITH YOU!
NEITHER DO I! BUT IF YOU DON'T WANT ME TO COURT YOU PUBLICLY ON REAL LIFE, WITH SERENADES AND ENDLESS, SUPER-ROMANTIC POETRY...
...LET ME BE MERCUTIO IN ROCKSPEARE! THAT'S THE ROLE FOR ME! PLEEEASE!
ANDREA TANAKA! COME RIGHT BACK HERE!

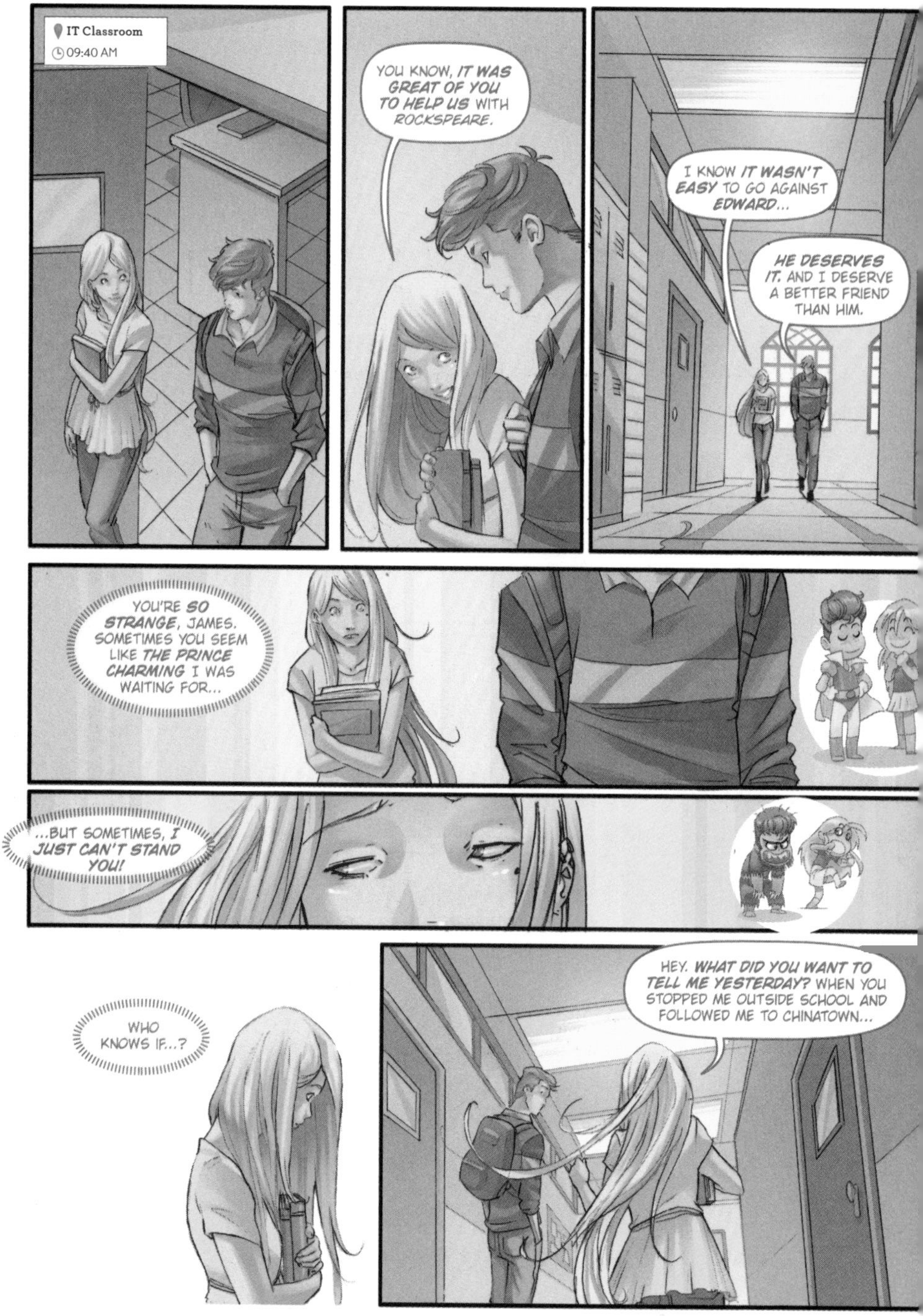

IT Classroom
09:40 AM
YOU KNOW, IT WAS GREAT OF YOU TO HELP US WITH ROCKSPEARE.
I KNOW IT WASN'T EASY TO GO AGAINST EDWARD...
HE DESERVES IT. AND I DESERVE A BETTER FRIEND THAN HIM.
YOU'RE SO STRANGE, JAMES. SOMETIMES YOU SEEM LIKE THE PRINCE CHARMING I WAS WAITING FOR...
...BUT SOMETIMES, I JUST CAN'T STAND YOU!
WHO KNOWS IF...?
HEY. WHAT DID YOU WANT TO TELL ME YESTERDAY? WHEN YOU STOPPED ME OUTSIDE SCHOOL AND FOLLOWED ME TO CHINATOWN...

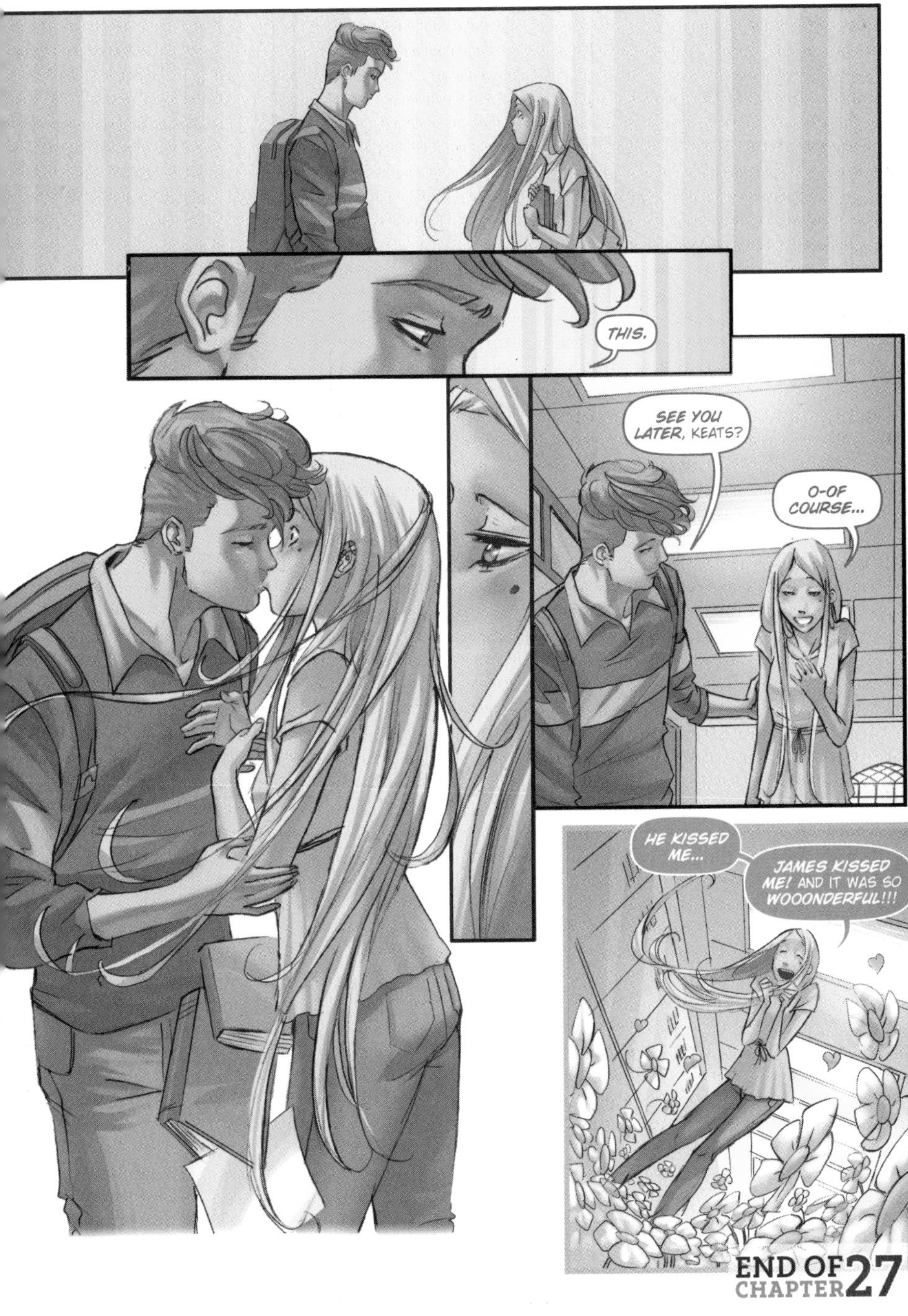
THIS.
SEE YOU LATER, KEATS?
O-OF COURSE...
HE KISSED ME...
JAMES KISSED ME! AND IT WAS SO WOOONDERFUL!!!
END OF CHAPTER 27

#A Night at the Theatre

Plot: Alessandro Ferrari
Script: Alessandro Ferrari
Layout: Simone Buonfantino, Alberto Zanon
Cleanup: Simone Buonfantino, Alberto Zanon
Emotidolls: Andrea Scoppetta, Massimo Rocca
Color: Pierluigi Casolino, Mario Perrotta, Antonia
Emanuela Angrisani, Francesca Mengozzi/
Giovanni Marcora, Giuseppe Fontana
Watercolor backgrounds: Valeria Turati
Translation: Edizioni BD and Erin Brady
Lettering and Infographic: Edizioni BD

COVER
Layout and cleanup: Alberto Zanon
Color: Slava Panarin

CONTRIBUTORS
Tomatofarm

Original project developed by Disney
Publishing with the contribution of Barba
Baraldi, Paola Barbato, Micol Beltramini
and Diana Tomatozombie

#10

#This Song for You

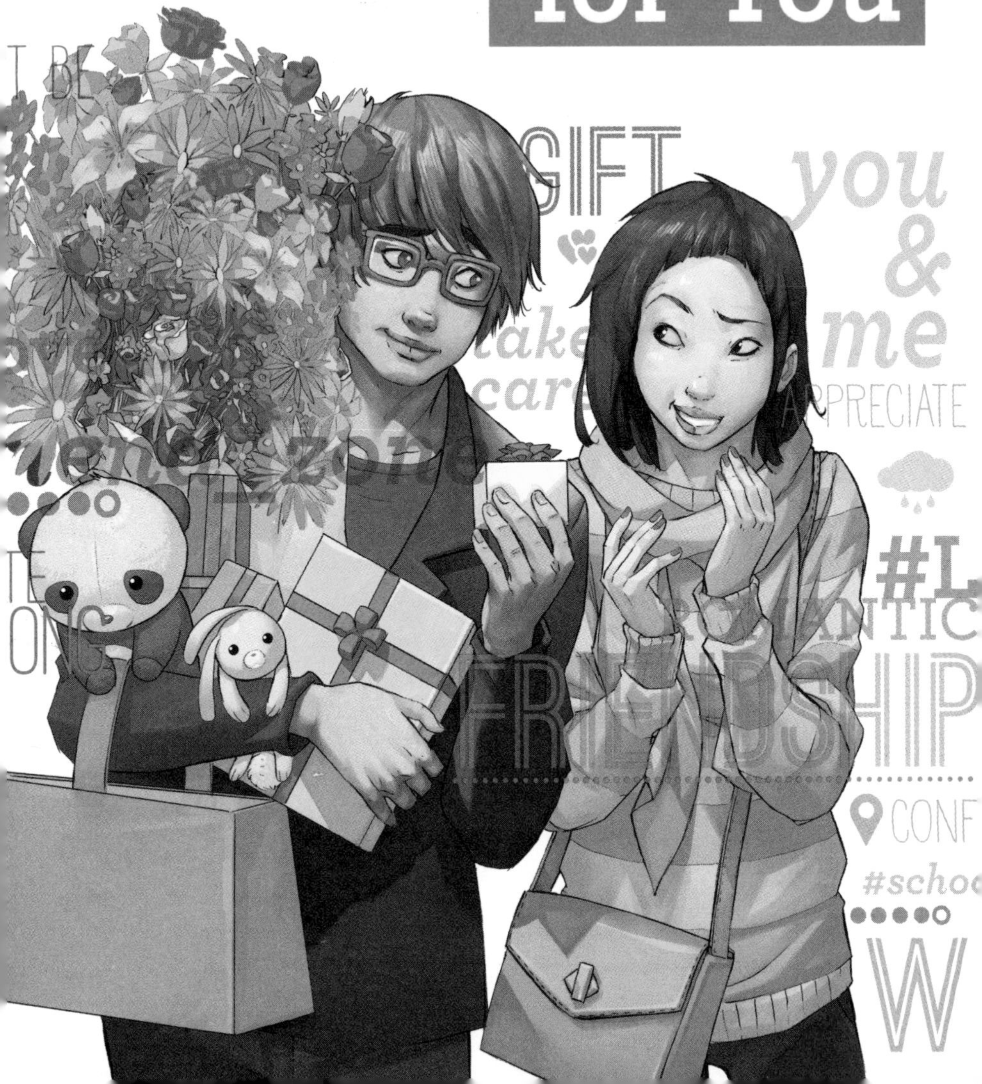
GIFT
you
&
me
FRIENDSHIP

CHAPTER 28

Planning DIVERSION

London International High School
Marylebone
01:05 PM

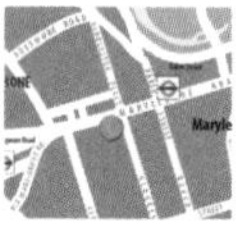

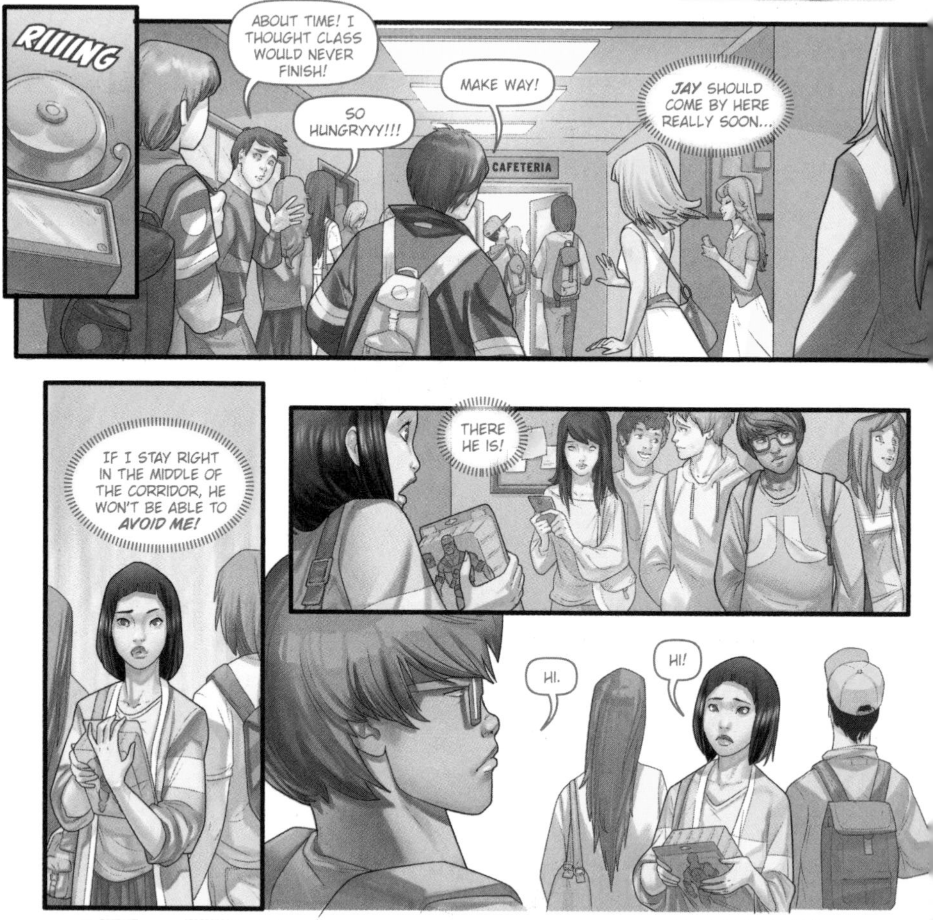

RIIIING
ABOUT TIME! I THOUGHT CLASS WOULD NEVER FINISH!
SO HUNGRYYY!!!
MAKE WAY!
CAFETERIA
JAY SHOULD COME BY HERE REALLY SOON...
IF I STAY RIGHT IN THE MIDDLE OF THE CORRIDOR, HE WON'T BE ABLE TO AVOID ME!
THERE HE IS!
HI.
HI!

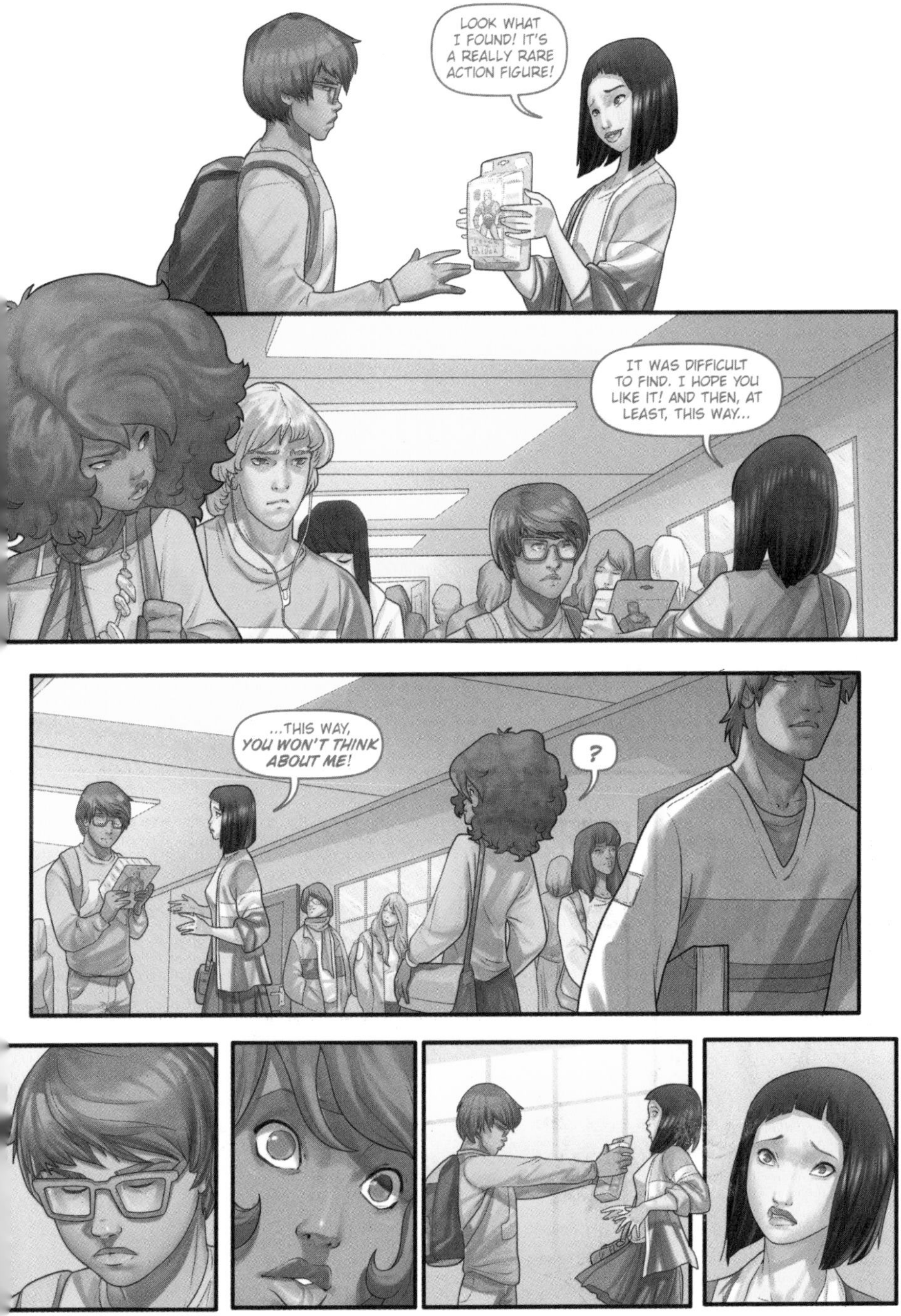
LOOK WHAT I FOUND! IT'S A REALLY RARE ACTION FIGURE!
IT WAS DIFFICULT TO FIND. I HOPE YOU LIKE IT! AND THEN, AT LEAST, THIS WAY...
...THIS WAY, *YOU WON'T THINK ABOUT ME!*
?

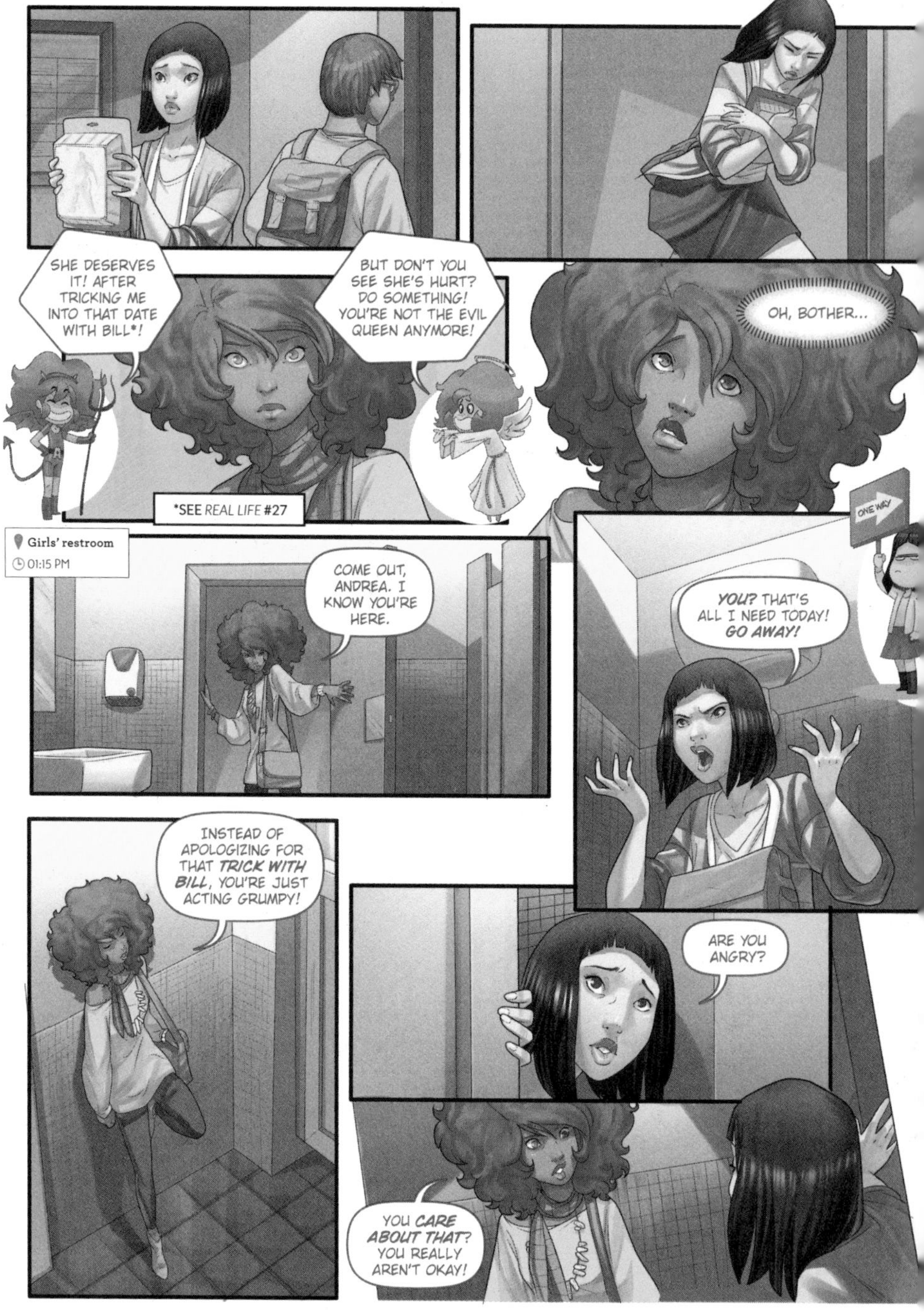
SHE DESERVES IT! AFTER TRICKING ME INTO THAT DATE WITH BILL*!
BUT DON'T YOU SEE SHE'S HURT? DO SOMETHING! YOU'RE NOT THE EVIL QUEEN ANYMORE!
OH, BOTHER...
*SEE REAL LIFE #27
Girls' restroom
01:15 PM
COME OUT, ANDREA. I KNOW YOU'RE HERE.
ONE WAY
YOU? THAT'S ALL I NEED TODAY! GO AWAY!
INSTEAD OF APOLOGIZING FOR THAT TRICK WITH BILL, YOU'RE JUST ACTING GRUMPY!
ARE YOU ANGRY?
YOU CARE ABOUT THAT? YOU REALLY AREN'T OKAY!

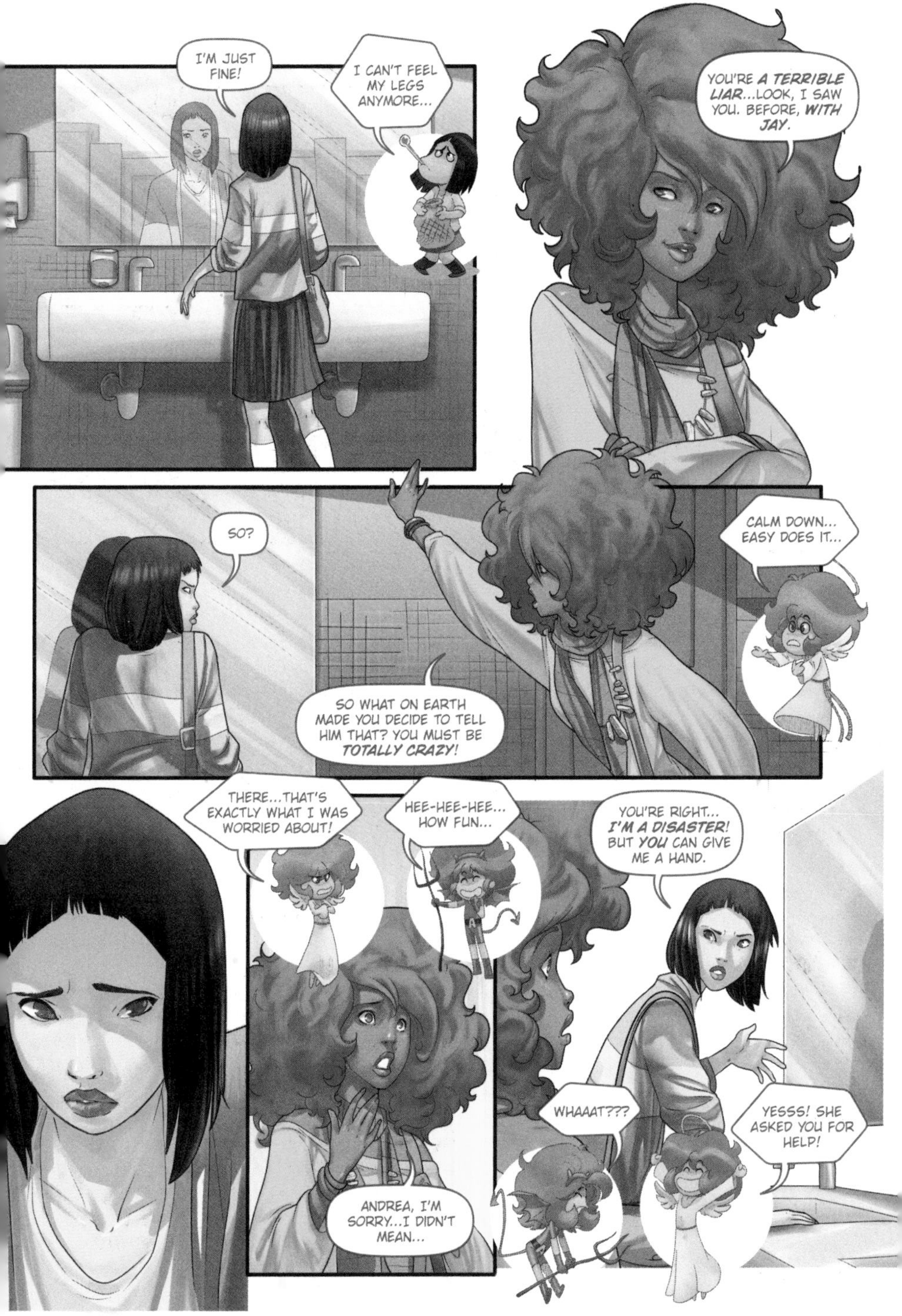
I'M JUST FINE!
I CAN'T FEEL MY LEGS ANYMORE...
YOU'RE A TERRIBLE LIAR...LOOK, I SAW YOU. BEFORE, WITH JAY.
SO?
SO WHAT ON EARTH MADE YOU DECIDE TO TELL HIM THAT? YOU MUST BE TOTALLY CRAZY!
CALM DOWN... EASY DOES IT...
THERE...THAT'S EXACTLY WHAT I WAS WORRIED ABOUT!
HEE-HEE-HEE... HOW FUN...
ANDREA, I'M SORRY...I DIDN'T MEAN...
YOU'RE RIGHT... I'M A DISASTER! BUT YOU CAN GIVE ME A HAND.
WHAAAT???
YESSS! SHE ASKED YOU FOR HELP!

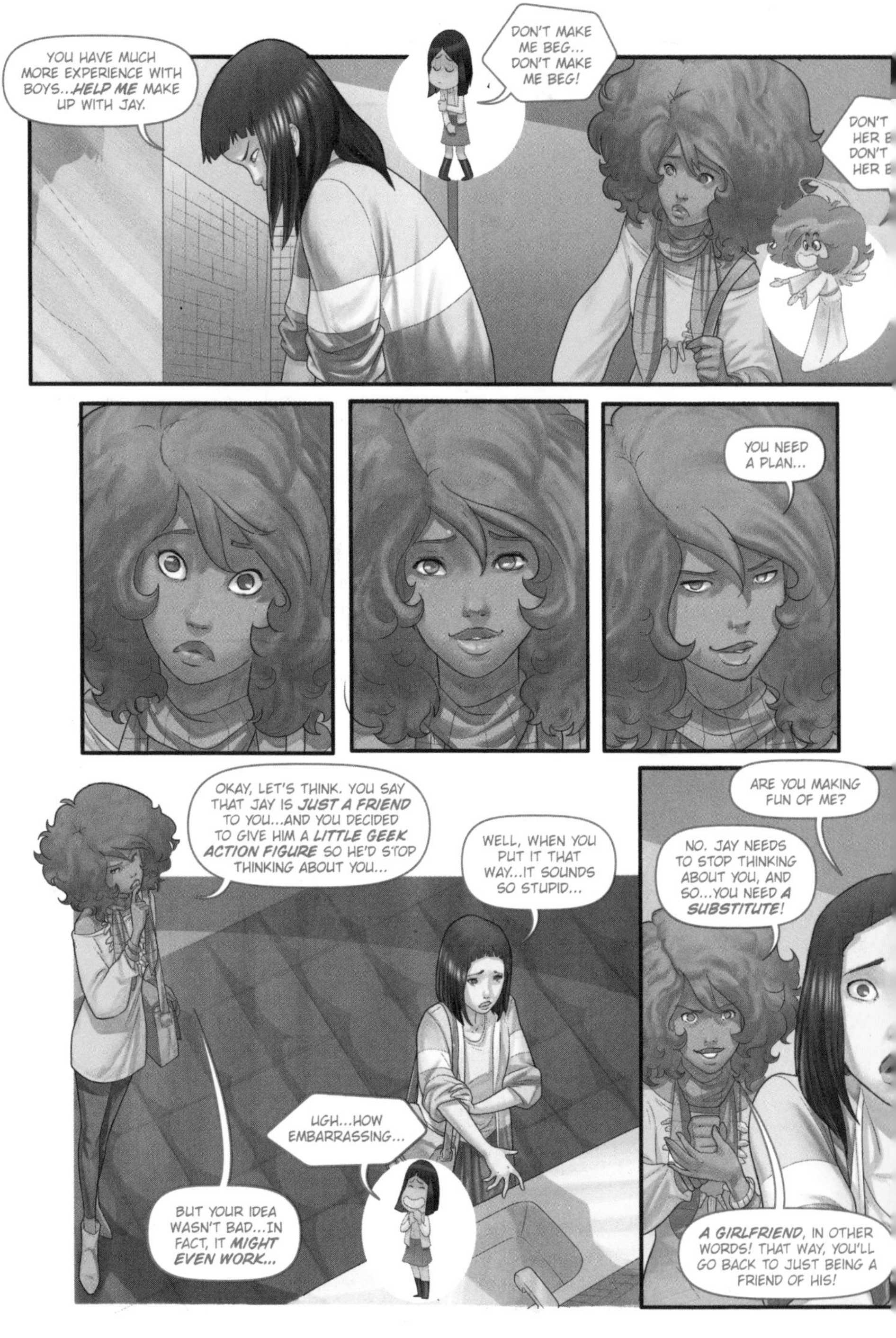
YOU HAVE MUCH MORE EXPERIENCE WITH BOYS...**HELP ME** MAKE UP WITH JAY.
DON'T MAKE ME BEG... DON'T MAKE ME BEG!
YOU NEED A PLAN...
OKAY, LET'S THINK. YOU SAY THAT JAY IS **JUST A FRIEND** TO YOU...AND YOU DECIDED TO GIVE HIM A **LITTLE GEEK ACTION FIGURE** SO HE'D STOP THINKING ABOUT YOU...
WELL, WHEN YOU PUT IT THAT WAY...IT SOUNDS SO STUPID...
UGH...HOW EMBARRASSING...
BUT YOUR IDEA WASN'T BAD...IN FACT, IT **MIGHT EVEN WORK...**
ARE YOU MAKING FUN OF ME?
NO. JAY NEEDS TO STOP THINKING ABOUT YOU, AND SO...YOU NEED **A SUBSTITUTE**!
A GIRLFRIEND, IN OTHER WORDS! THAT WAY, YOU'LL GO BACK TO JUST BEING A FRIEND OF HIS!

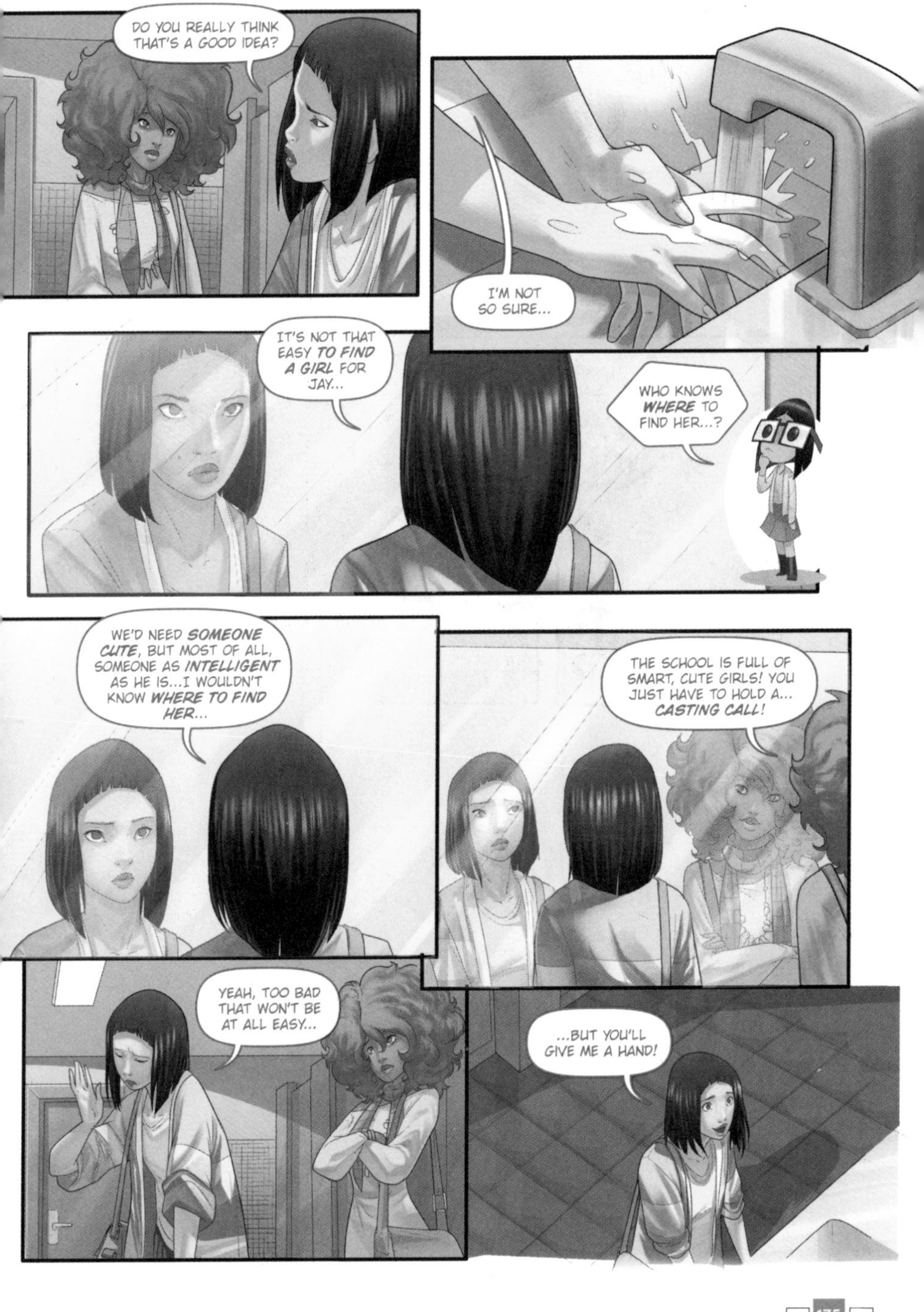
DO YOU REALLY THINK THAT'S A GOOD IDEA?
I'M NOT SO SURE...
IT'S NOT THAT EASY TO FIND A GIRL FOR JAY...
WHO KNOWS WHERE TO FIND HER...?
WE'D NEED SOMEONE CUTE, BUT MOST OF ALL, SOMEONE AS INTELLIGENT AS HE IS...I WOULDN'T KNOW WHERE TO FIND HER...
THE SCHOOL IS FULL OF SMART, CUTE GIRLS! YOU JUST HAVE TO HOLD A... CASTING CALL!
YEAH, TOO BAD THAT WON'T BE AT ALL EASY...
...BUT YOU'LL GIVE ME A HAND!

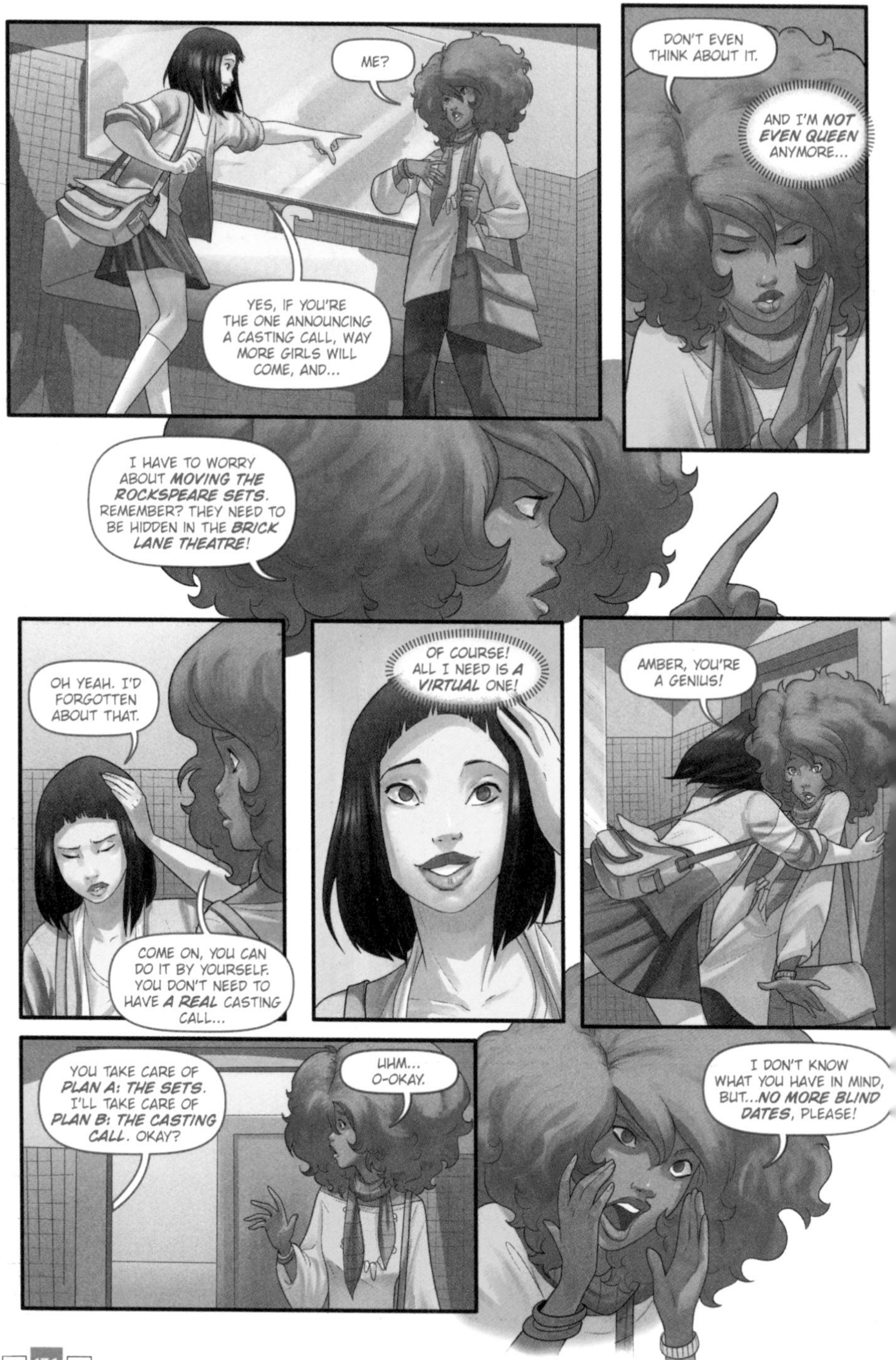

ME?
YES, IF YOU'RE THE ONE ANNOUNCING A CASTING CALL, WAY MORE GIRLS WILL COME, AND...
DON'T EVEN THINK ABOUT IT.
AND I'M **NOT EVEN QUEEN** ANYMORE...
I HAVE TO WORRY ABOUT **MOVING THE ROCKSPEARE SETS**. REMEMBER? THEY NEED TO BE HIDDEN IN THE **BRICK LANE THEATRE**!
OH YEAH. I'D FORGOTTEN ABOUT THAT.
COME ON, YOU CAN DO IT BY YOURSELF. YOU DON'T NEED TO HAVE **A REAL** CASTING CALL...
OF COURSE! ALL I NEED IS **A VIRTUAL** ONE!
AMBER, YOU'RE A GENIUS!
YOU TAKE CARE OF **PLAN A: THE SETS**. I'LL TAKE CARE OF **PLAN B: THE CASTING CALL**. OKAY?
UHM... O-OKAY.
I DON'T KNOW WHAT YOU HAVE IN MIND, BUT...**NO MORE BLIND DATES**, PLEASE!

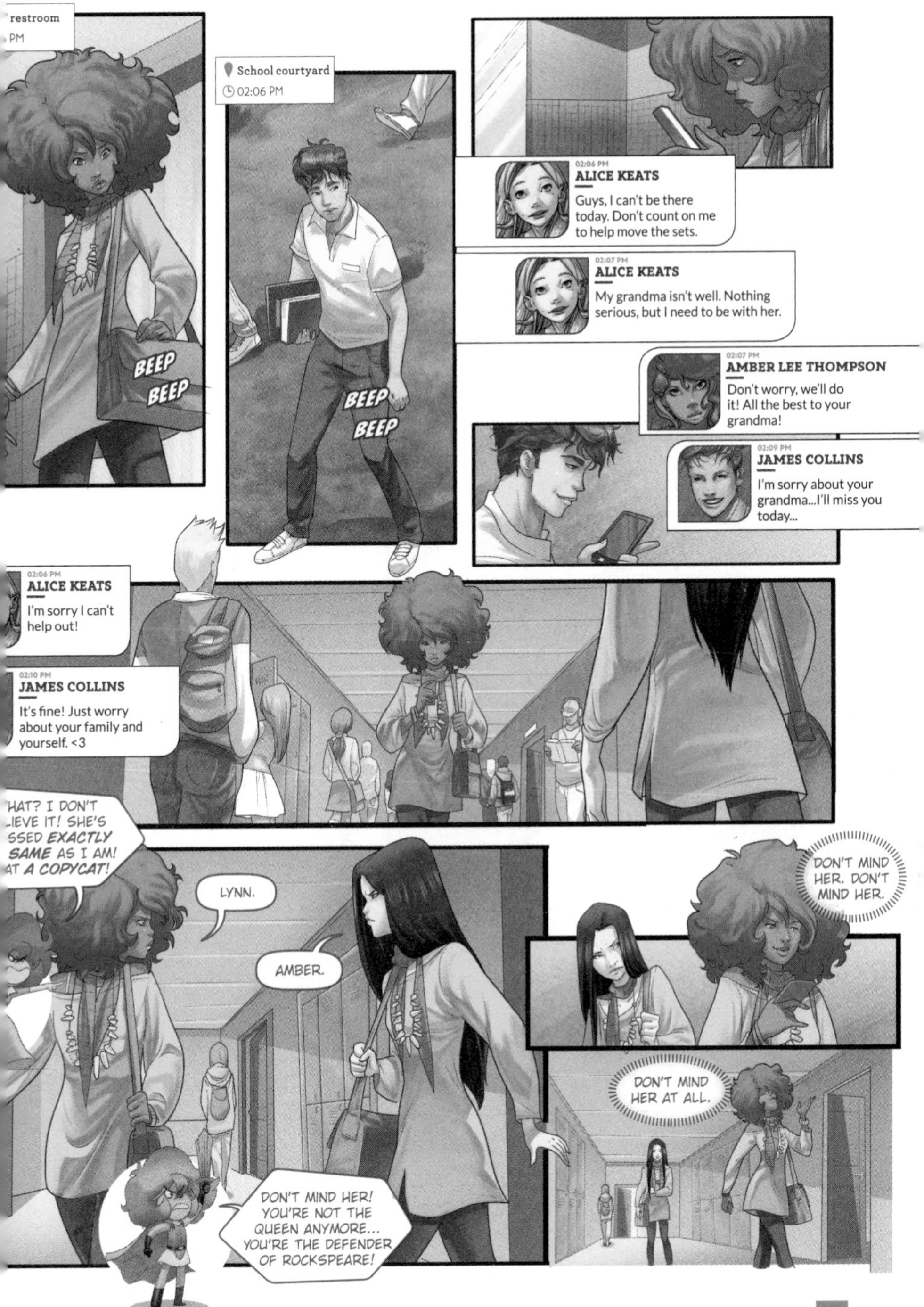
restroom
PM
BEEP
BEEP
School courtyard
02:06 PM
BEEP
BEEP
02:06 PM
ALICE KEATS
Guys, I can't be there today. Don't count on me to help move the sets.
02:07 PM
ALICE KEATS
My grandma isn't well. Nothing serious, but I need to be with her.
02:07 PM
AMBER LEE THOMPSON
Don't worry, we'll do it! All the best to your grandma!
02:09 PM
JAMES COLLINS
I'm sorry about your grandma...I'll miss you today...
02:06 PM
ALICE KEATS
I'm sorry I can't help out!
02:10 PM
JAMES COLLINS
It's fine! Just worry about your family and yourself. <3
HAT? I DON'T LIEVE IT! SHE'S SSED EXACTLY SAME AS I AM! AT A COPYCAT!
LYNN.
AMBER.
DON'T MIND HER! YOU'RE NOT THE QUEEN ANYMORE... YOU'RE THE DEFENDER OF ROCKSPEARE!
DON'T MIND HER. DON'T MIND HER.
DON'T MIND HER AT ALL.

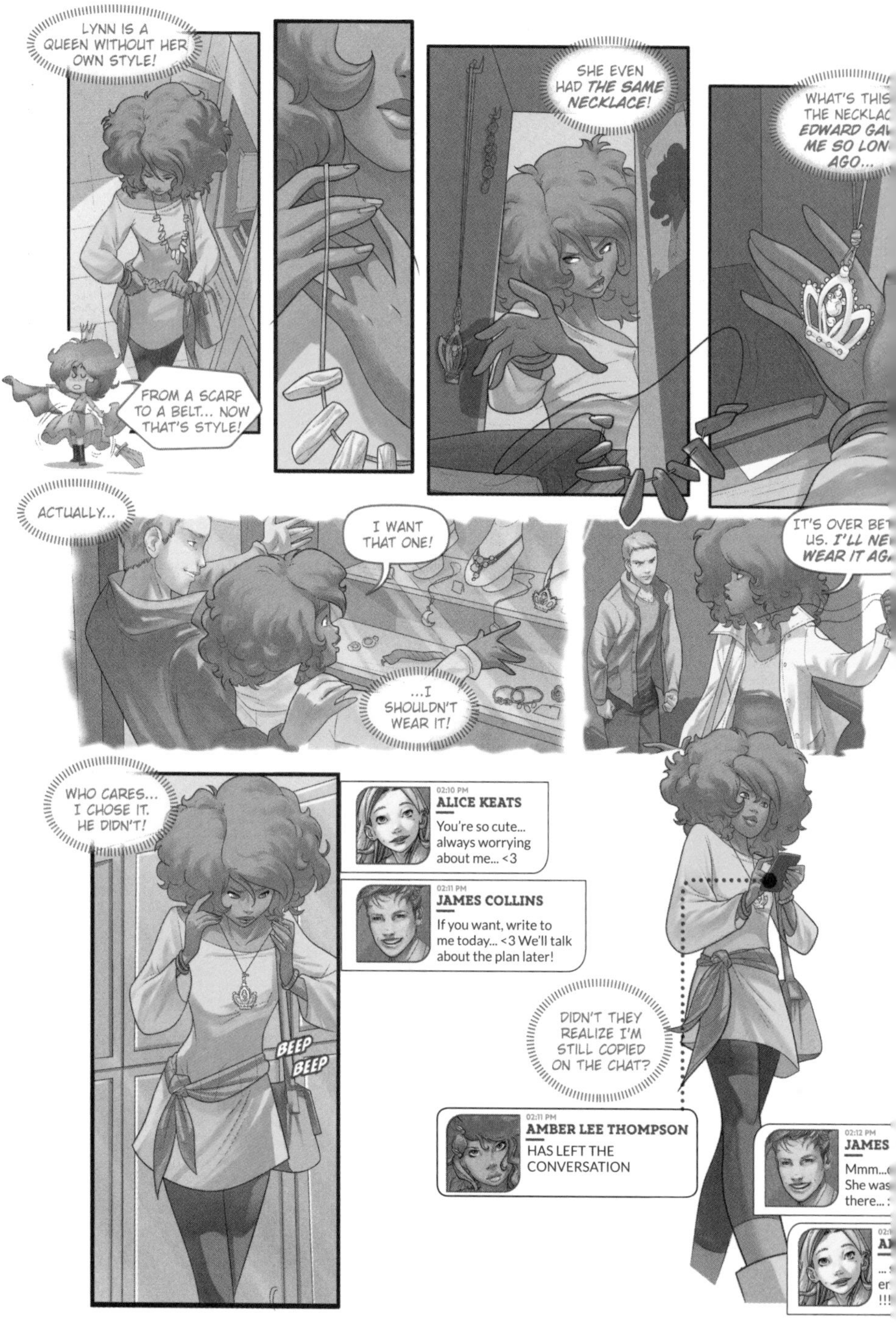

LYNN IS A QUEEN WITHOUT HER OWN STYLE!
FROM A SCARF TO A BELT... NOW THAT'S STYLE!
SHE EVEN HAD THE SAME NECKLACE!
WHAT'S THIS THE NECKLAC EDWARD GA ME SO LON AGO...
ACTUALLY...
I WANT THAT ONE!
...I SHOULDN'T WEAR IT!
IT'S OVER BE US. I'LL NE WEAR IT AG
WHO CARES... I CHOSE IT. HE DIDN'T!
02:10 PM
ALICE KEATS
You're so cute... always worrying about me... <3
02:11 PM
JAMES COLLINS
If you want, write to me today... <3 We'll talk about the plan later!
BEEP
BEEP
DIDN'T THEY REALIZE I'M STILL COPIED ON THE CHAT?
02:11 PM
AMBER LEE THOMPSON
HAS LEFT THE CONVERSATION
02:12 PM
JAMES
Mmm...
She was
there...

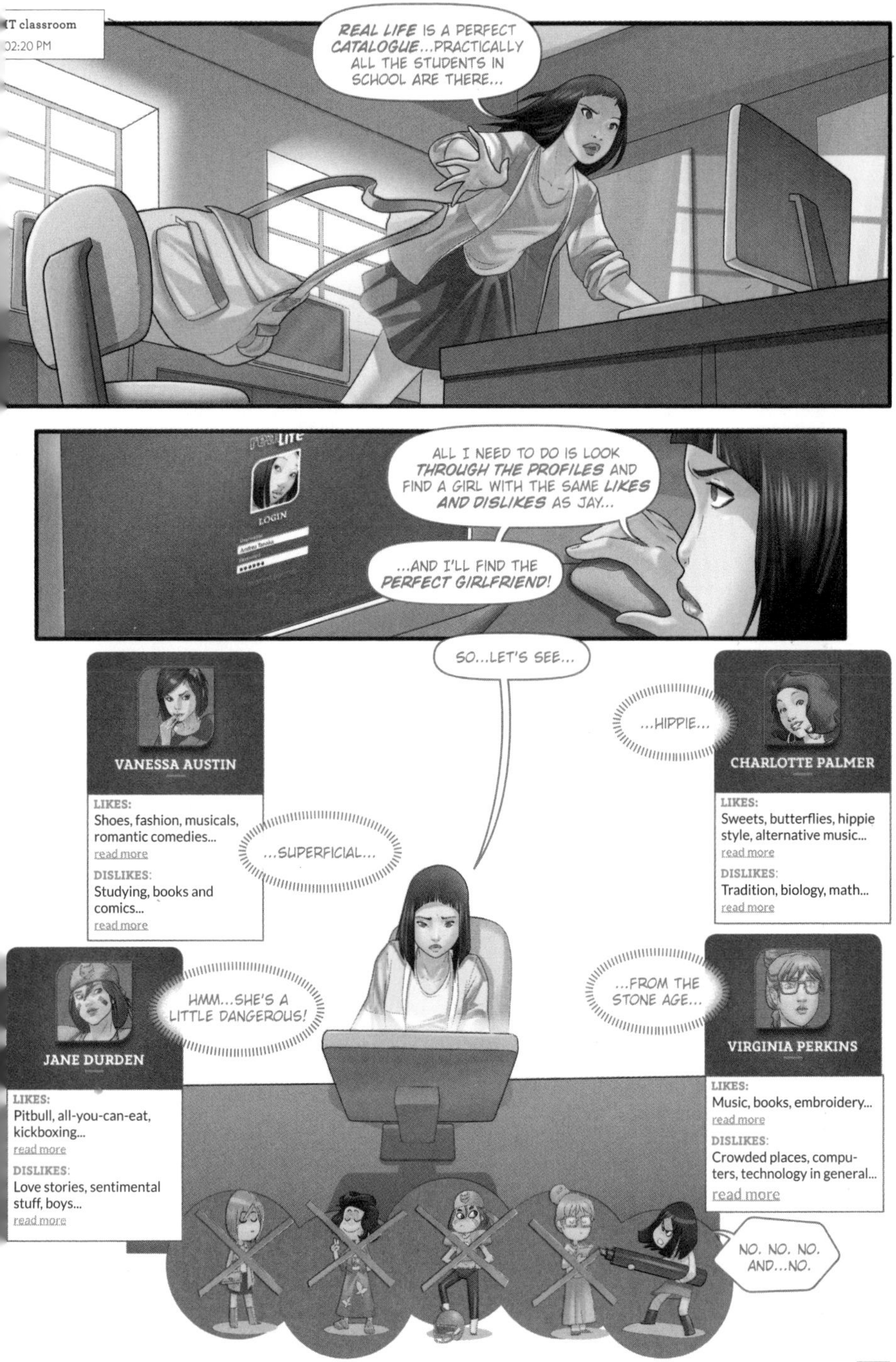

T classroom
02:20 PM
REAL LIFE IS A PERFECT CATALOGUE...PRACTICALLY ALL THE STUDENTS IN SCHOOL ARE THERE...
LOGIN
ALL I NEED TO DO IS LOOK THROUGH THE PROFILES AND FIND A GIRL WITH THE SAME LIKES AND DISLIKES AS JAY...
...AND I'LL FIND THE PERFECT GIRLFRIEND!
SO...LET'S SEE...
VANESSA AUSTIN
LIKES:
Shoes, fashion, musicals, romantic comedies...
read more
DISLIKES:
Studying, books and comics...
read more
...SUPERFICIAL...
...HIPPIE...
CHARLOTTE PALMER
LIKES:
Sweets, butterflies, hippie style, alternative music...
read more
DISLIKES:
Tradition, biology, math...
read more
JANE DURDEN
LIKES:
Pitbull, all-you-can-eat, kickboxing...
read more
DISLIKES:
Love stories, sentimental stuff, boys...
read more
HMM...SHE'S A LITTLE DANGEROUS!
...FROM THE STONE AGE...
VIRGINIA PERKINS
LIKES:
Music, books, embroidery...
read more
DISLIKES:
Crowded places, computers, technology in general...
read more
NO. NO. NO. AND...NO.

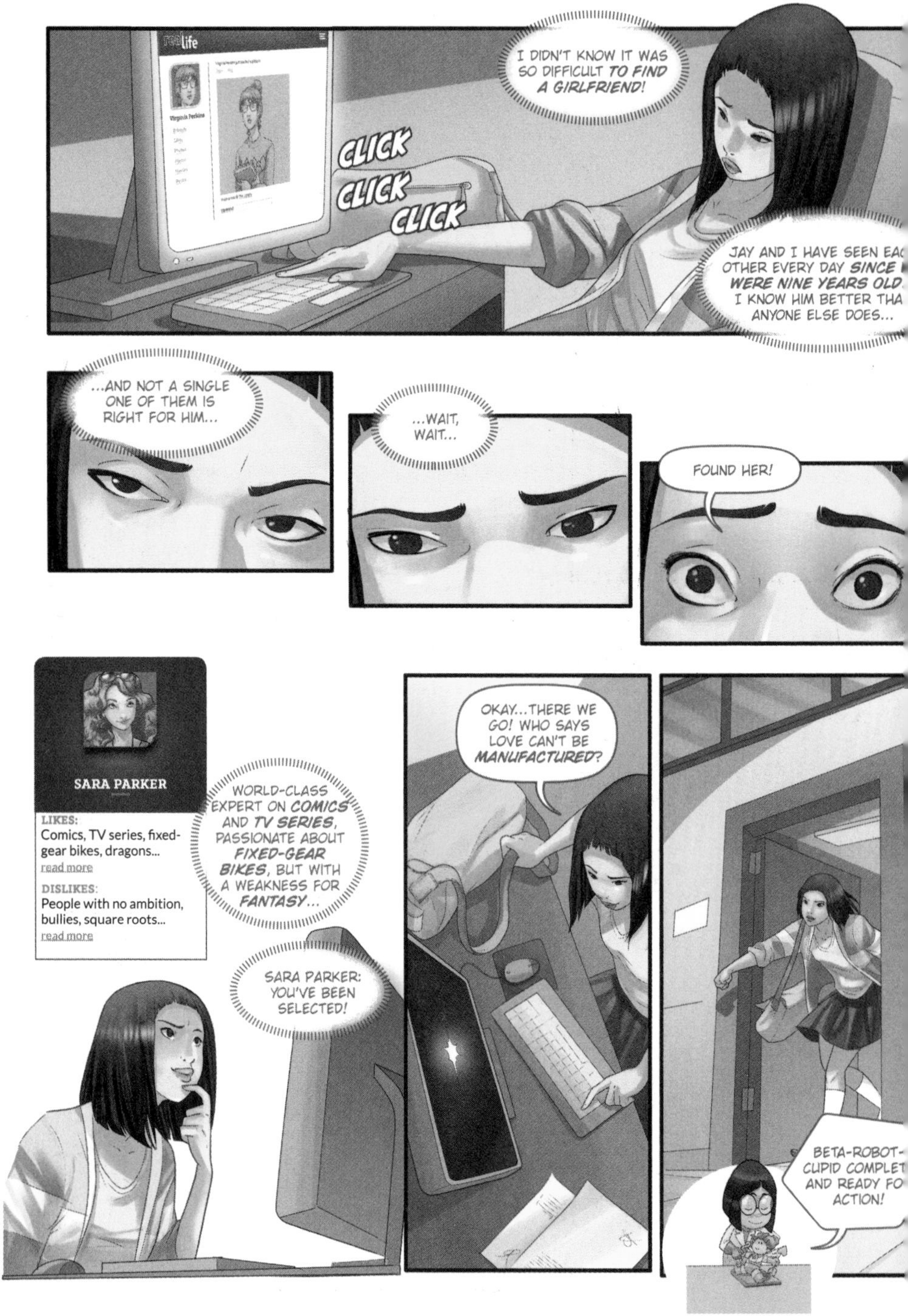
I DIDN'T KNOW IT WAS SO DIFFICULT TO FIND A GIRLFRIEND!
CLICK
CLICK
CLICK
JAY AND I HAVE SEEN EA OTHER EVERY DAY SINCE WERE NINE YEARS OLD I KNOW HIM BETTER THA ANYONE ELSE DOES...
...AND NOT A SINGLE ONE OF THEM IS RIGHT FOR HIM...
...WAIT, WAIT...
FOUND HER!
SARA PARKER
LIKES:
Comics, TV series, fixed-gear bikes, dragons...
read more
DISLIKES:
People with no ambition, bullies, square roots...
read more
WORLD-CLASS EXPERT ON COMICS AND TV SERIES, PASSIONATE ABOUT FIXED-GEAR BIKES, BUT WITH A WEAKNESS FOR FANTASY...
SARA PARKER: YOU'VE BEEN SELECTED!
OKAY...THERE WE GO! WHO SAYS LOVE CAN'T BE MANUFACTURED?
BETA-ROBOT-CUPID COMPLET AND READY FO ACTION!

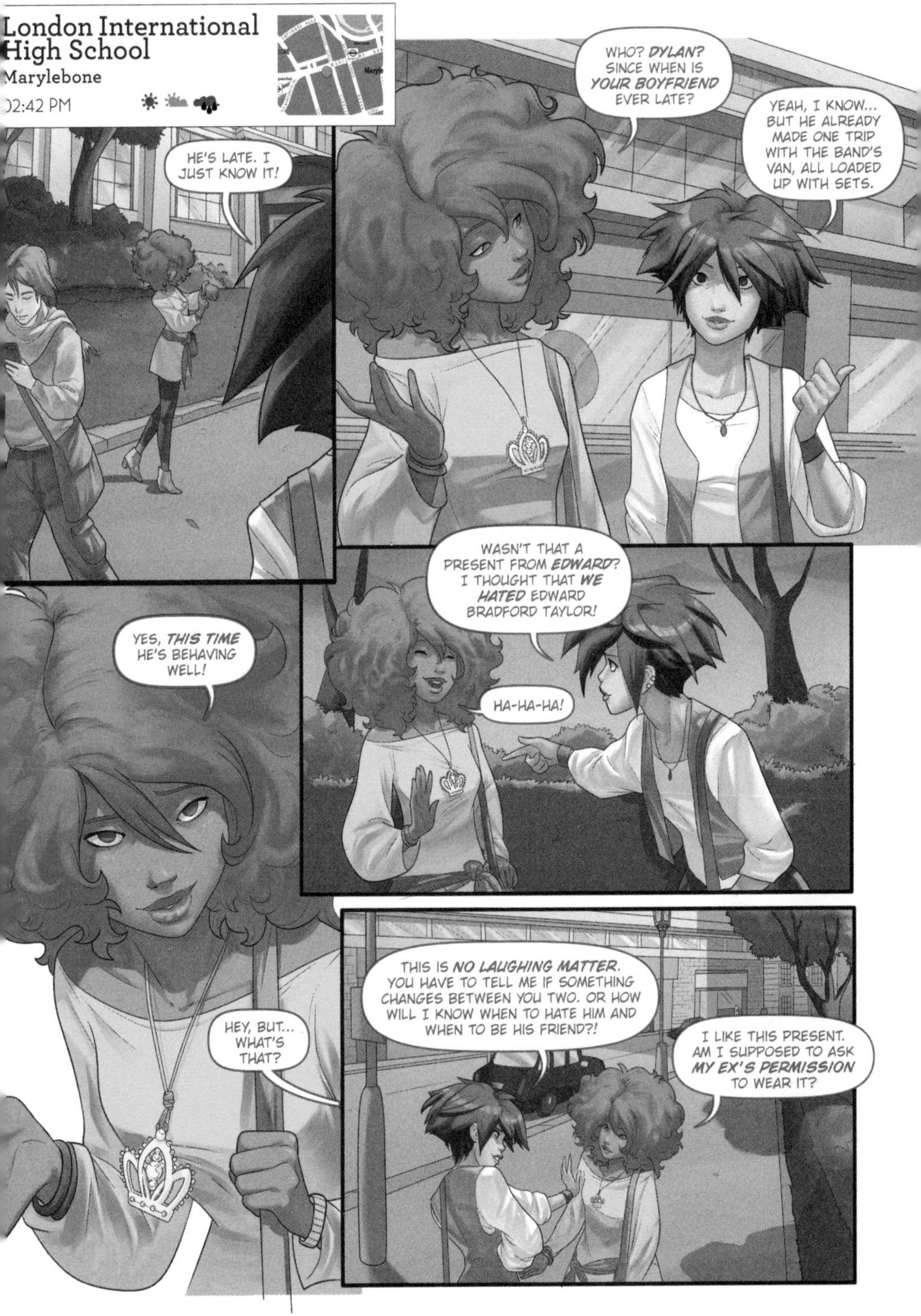
London International High School
Marylebone
02:42 PM
HE'S LATE. I JUST KNOW IT!
WHO? *DYLAN?* SINCE WHEN IS *YOUR BOYFRIEND* EVER LATE?
YEAH, I KNOW... BUT HE ALREADY MADE ONE TRIP WITH THE BAND'S VAN, ALL LOADED UP WITH SETS.
YES, *THIS TIME* HE'S BEHAVING WELL!
WASN'T THAT A PRESENT FROM *EDWARD*? I THOUGHT THAT *WE HATED* EDWARD BRADFORD TAYLOR!
HA-HA-HA!
HEY, BUT... WHAT'S THAT?
THIS IS *NO LAUGHING MATTER*. YOU HAVE TO TELL ME IF SOMETHING CHANGES BETWEEN YOU TWO. OR HOW WILL I KNOW WHEN TO HATE HIM AND WHEN TO BE HIS FRIEND?!
I LIKE THIS PRESENT. AM I SUPPOSED TO ASK *MY EX'S PERMISSION* TO WEAR IT?

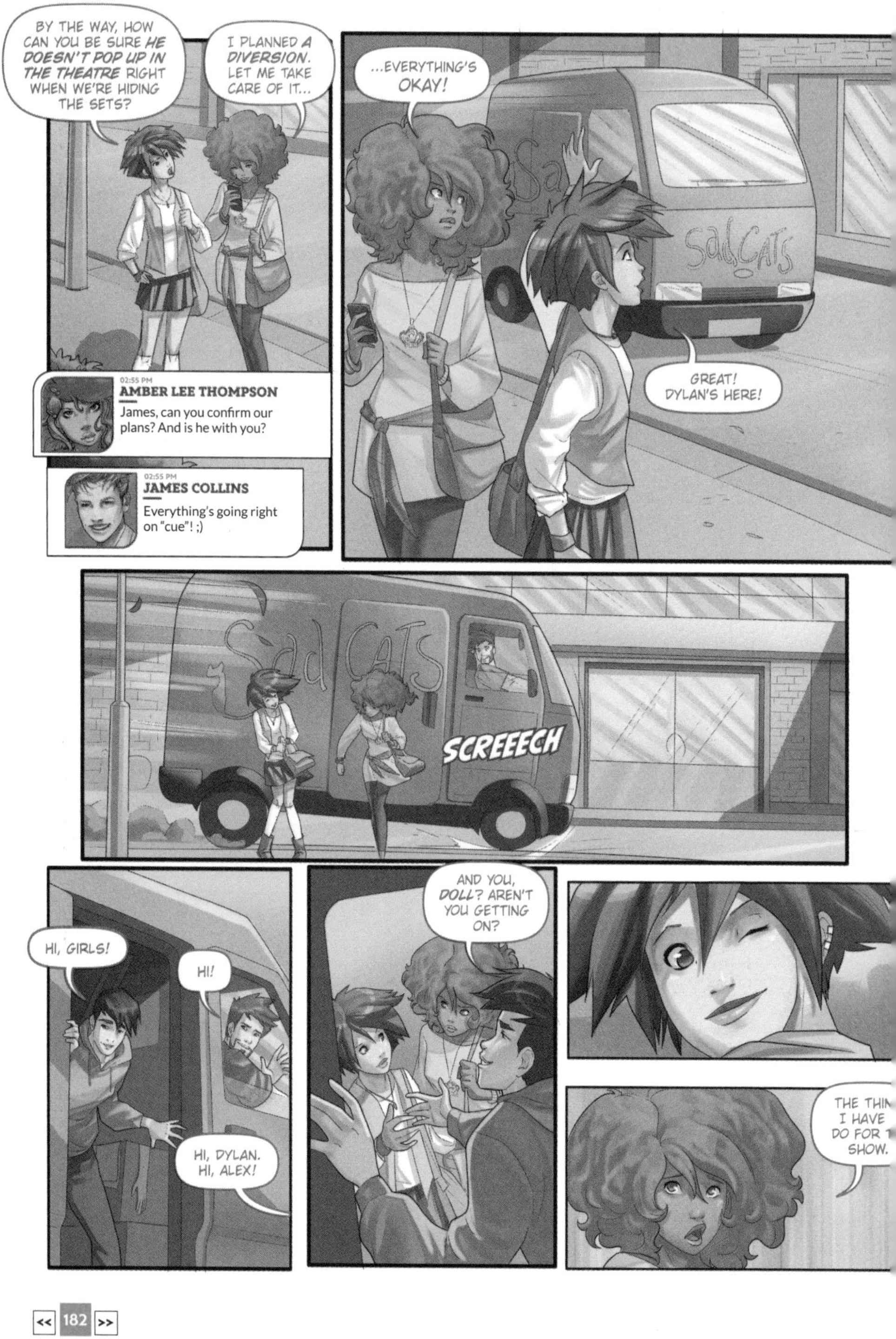
BY THE WAY, HOW CAN YOU BE SURE HE DOESN'T POP UP IN THE THEATRE RIGHT WHEN WE'RE HIDING THE SETS?
I PLANNED A DIVERSION. LET ME TAKE CARE OF IT...
02:55 PM AMBER LEE THOMPSON
James, can you confirm our plans? And is he with you?
02:55 PM JAMES COLLINS
Everything's going right on "cue"! ;)
...EVERYTHING'S OKAY!
GREAT! DYLAN'S HERE!
SAD CATS
SCREEECH
HI, GIRLS!
HI!
HI, DYLAN. HI, ALEX!
AND YOU, DOLL? AREN'T YOU GETTING ON?
THE THI
I HAVE
DO FOR
SHOW.

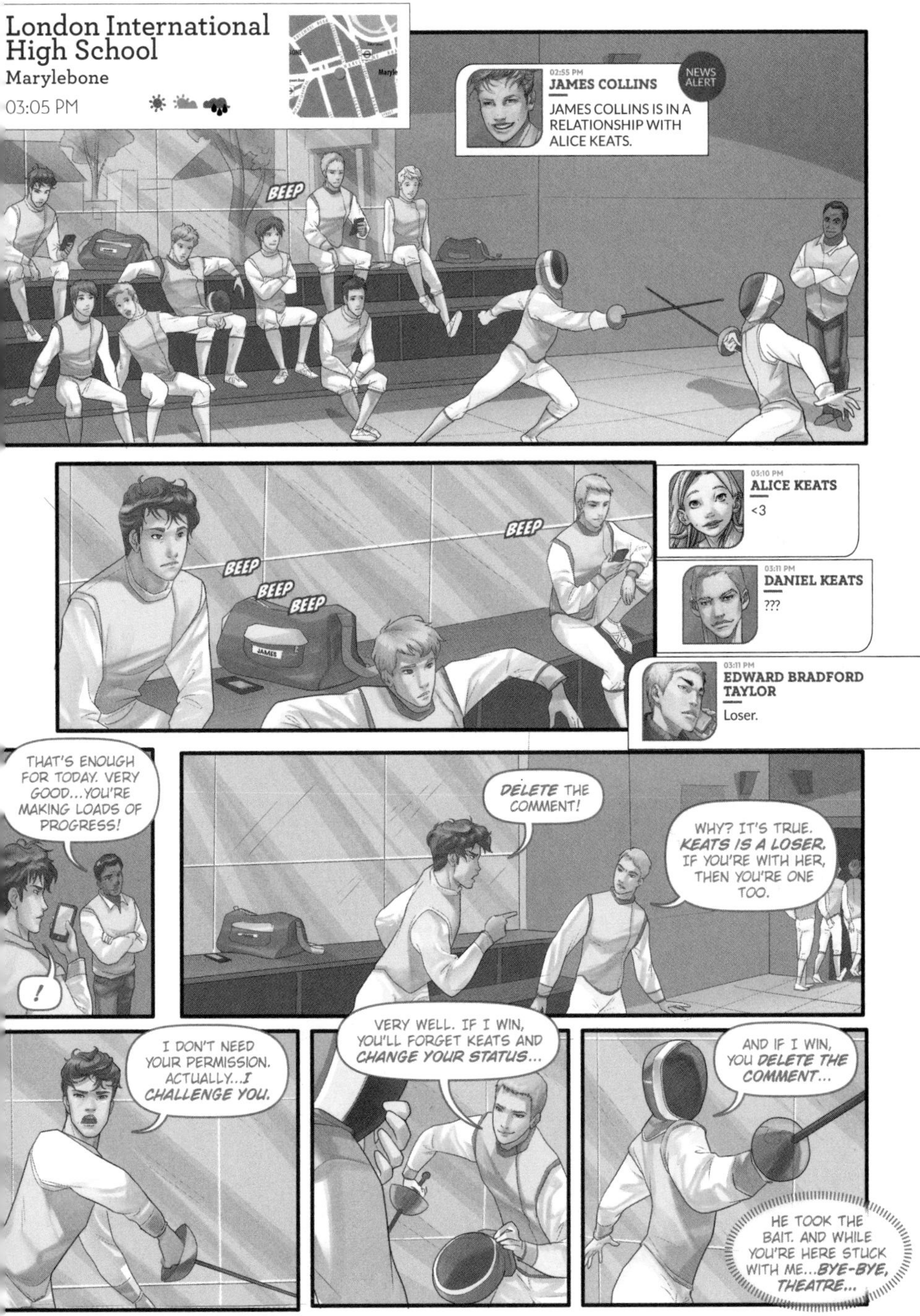
London International High School
Marylebone
03:05 PM
02:55 PM
JAMES COLLINS
NEWS ALERT
JAMES COLLINS IS IN A RELATIONSHIP WITH ALICE KEATS.
BEEP
BEEP
BEEP
BEEP
BEEP
JAMES
03:10 PM
ALICE KEATS
<3
03:11 PM
DANIEL KEATS
???
03:11 PM
EDWARD BRADFORD TAYLOR
Loser.
THAT'S ENOUGH FOR TODAY. VERY GOOD…YOU'RE MAKING LOADS OF PROGRESS!
!
DELETE THE COMMENT!
WHY? IT'S TRUE. KEATS IS A LOSER. IF YOU'RE WITH HER, THEN YOU'RE ONE TOO.
I DON'T NEED YOUR PERMISSION. ACTUALLY…I CHALLENGE YOU.
VERY WELL. IF I WIN, YOU'LL FORGET KEATS AND CHANGE YOUR STATUS…
AND IF I WIN, YOU DELETE THE COMMENT…
HE TOOK THE BAIT. AND WHILE YOU'RE HERE STUCK WITH ME…BYE-BYE, THEATRE…

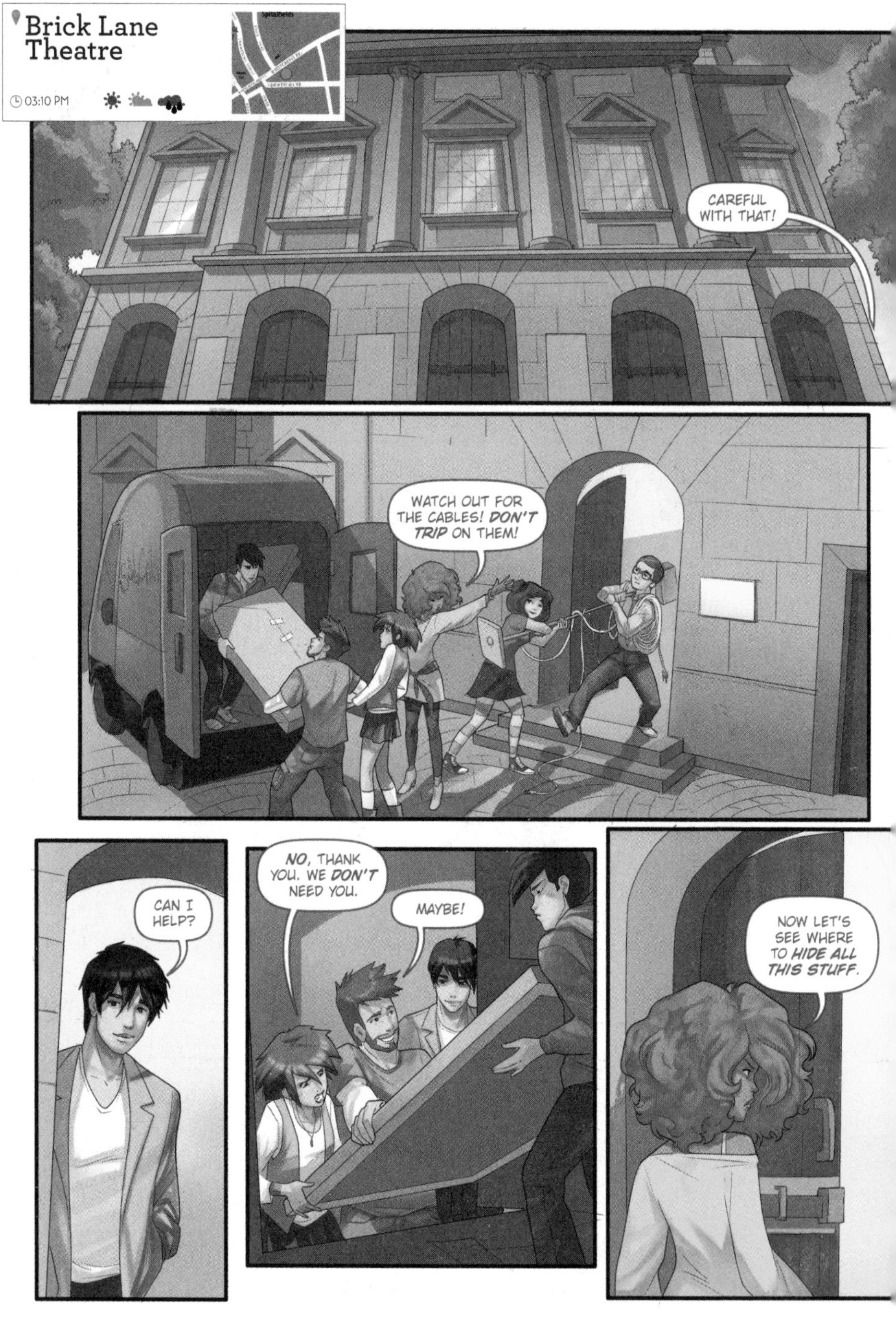
Brick Lane Theatre
03:10 PM
CAREFUL WITH THAT!
WATCH OUT FOR THE CABLES! DON'T TRIP ON THEM!
CAN I HELP?
NO, THANK YOU. WE DON'T NEED YOU.
MAYBE!
NOW LET'S SEE WHERE TO HIDE ALL THIS STUFF.

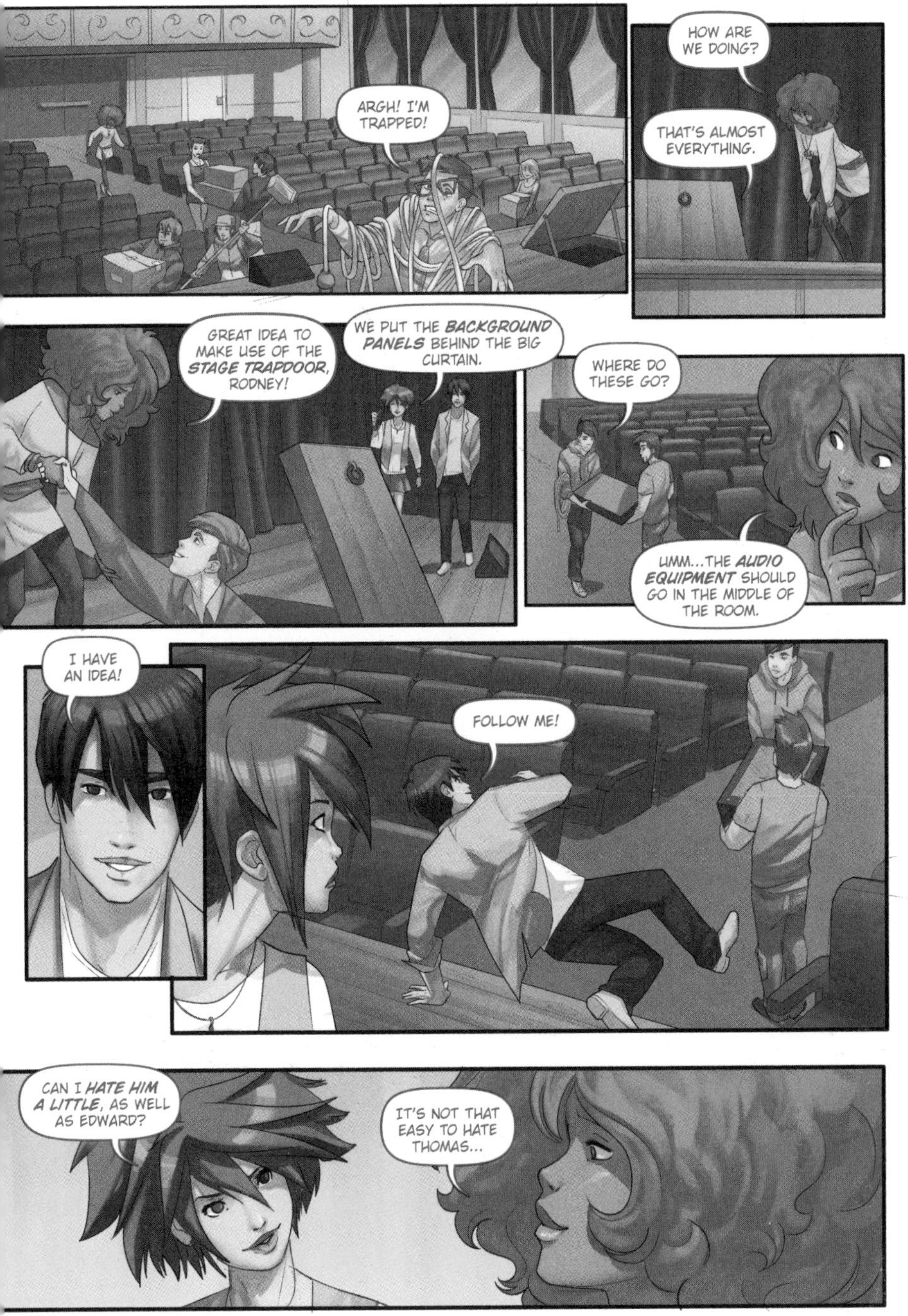
ARGH! I'M TRAPPED!
HOW ARE WE DOING?
THAT'S ALMOST EVERYTHING.
GREAT IDEA TO MAKE USE OF THE STAGE TRAPDOOR, RODNEY!
WE PUT THE BACKGROUND PANELS BEHIND THE BIG CURTAIN.
WHERE DO THESE GO?
UMM...THE AUDIO EQUIPMENT SHOULD GO IN THE MIDDLE OF THE ROOM.
I HAVE AN IDEA!
FOLLOW ME!
CAN I HATE HIM A LITTLE, AS WELL AS EDWARD?
IT'S NOT THAT EASY TO HATE THOMAS...

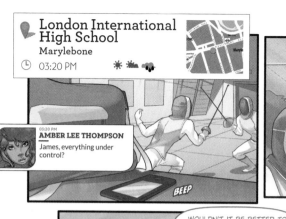

London International High School
Marylebone
03:20 PM
03:20 PM
AMBER LEE THOMPSON
James, everything under control?
BEEP
SURRENDER!
WOULDN'T IT BE BETTER TO JUST ADMIT YOU'RE NO MATCH FOR ME AND SAY GOOD-BYE TO THAT BEANPOLE?
YOU HAVEN'T WON YET, AND STOP TALKING ABOUT ALICE LIKE THAT!
03:20 PM
AMBER LEE THOMPSON
James! Please answer me! We need you to keep Ed away from the theater!
BEEP
JAMES
DON'T TELL ME YOU REALLY LIKE HER! PLEASE, GET A GRIP!
I TOLD YOU...
...TO STOP IT!
CLINK
EDDIE!

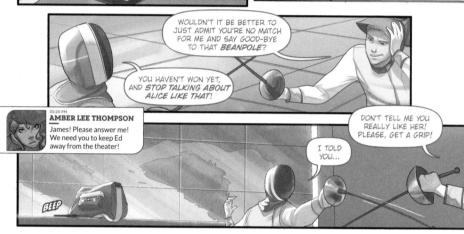

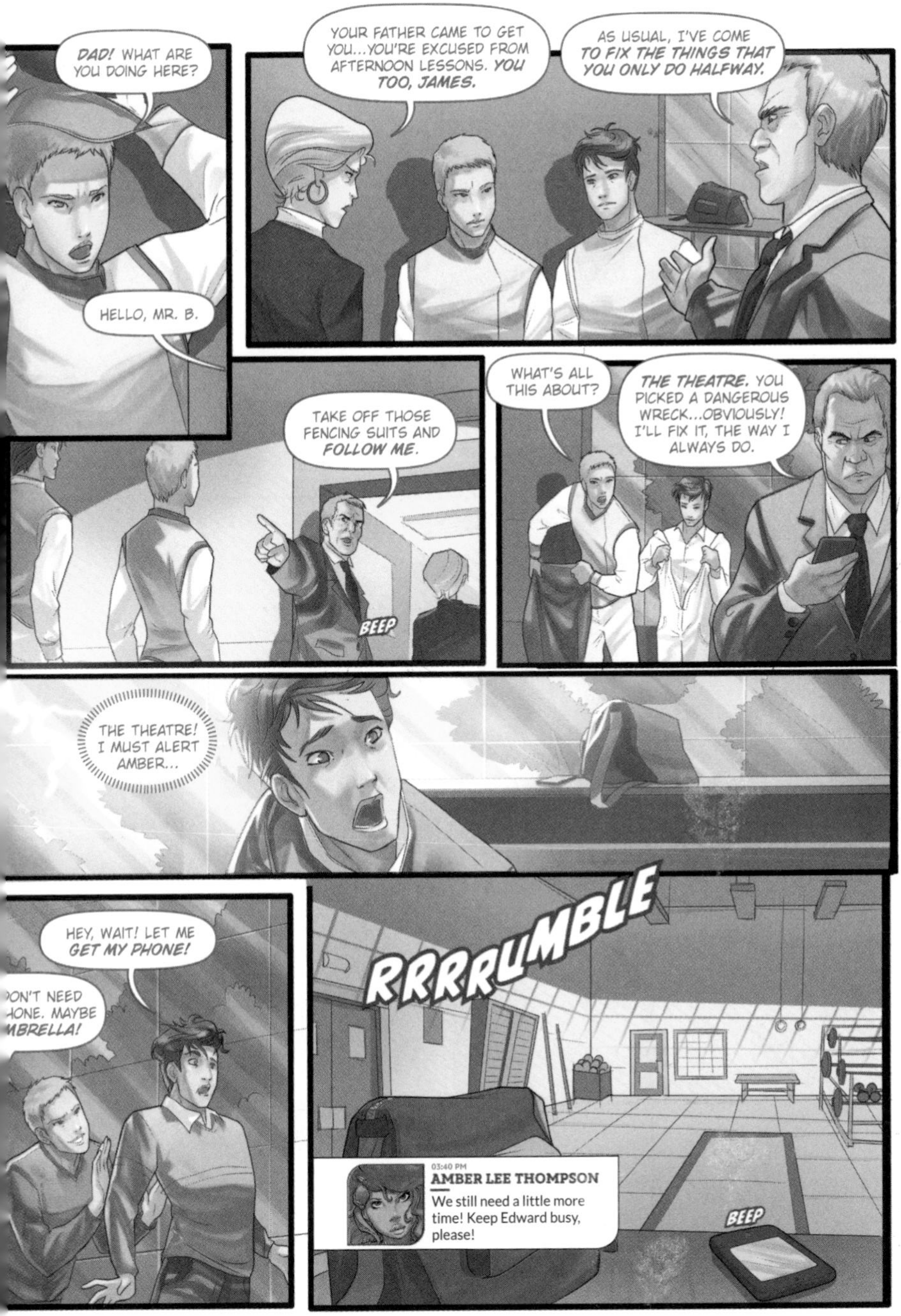
DAD! WHAT ARE YOU DOING HERE?
HELLO, MR. B.
YOUR FATHER CAME TO GET YOU...YOU'RE EXCUSED FROM AFTERNOON LESSONS. YOU TOO, JAMES.
AS USUAL, I'VE COME TO FIX THE THINGS THAT YOU ONLY DO HALFWAY.
TAKE OFF THOSE FENCING SUITS AND FOLLOW ME.
BEEP
WHAT'S ALL THIS ABOUT?
THE THEATRE. YOU PICKED A DANGEROUS WRECK...OBVIOUSLY! I'LL FIX IT, THE WAY I ALWAYS DO.
THE THEATRE! I MUST ALERT AMBER...
HEY, WAIT! LET ME GET MY PHONE!
ON'T NEED
HONE. MAYBE
MBRELLA!
RRRRUMBLE
03:40 PM
AMBER LEE THOMPSON
We still need a little more time! Keep Edward busy, please!
BEEP

END OF CHAPTER 28

CHAPTER 29

HERO of the Day

London International High School
Marylebone
03:45 PM

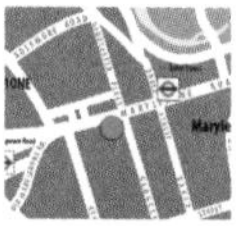

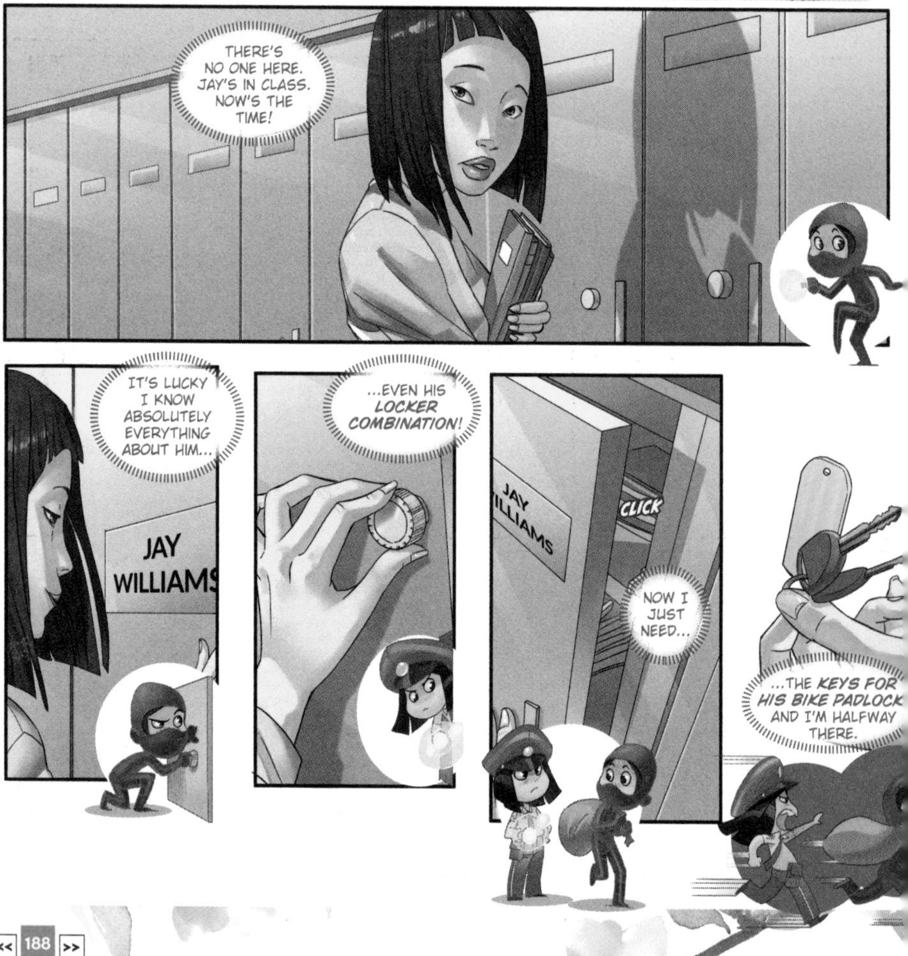
THERE'S NO ONE HERE. JAY'S IN CLASS. NOW'S THE TIME!
IT'S LUCKY I KNOW ABSOLUTELY EVERYTHING ABOUT HIM...
JAY WILLIAMS
...EVEN HIS LOCKER COMBINATION!
JAY WILLIAMS
CLICK
NOW I JUST NEED...
...THE KEYS FOR HIS BIKE PADLOCK AND I'M HALFWAY THERE.

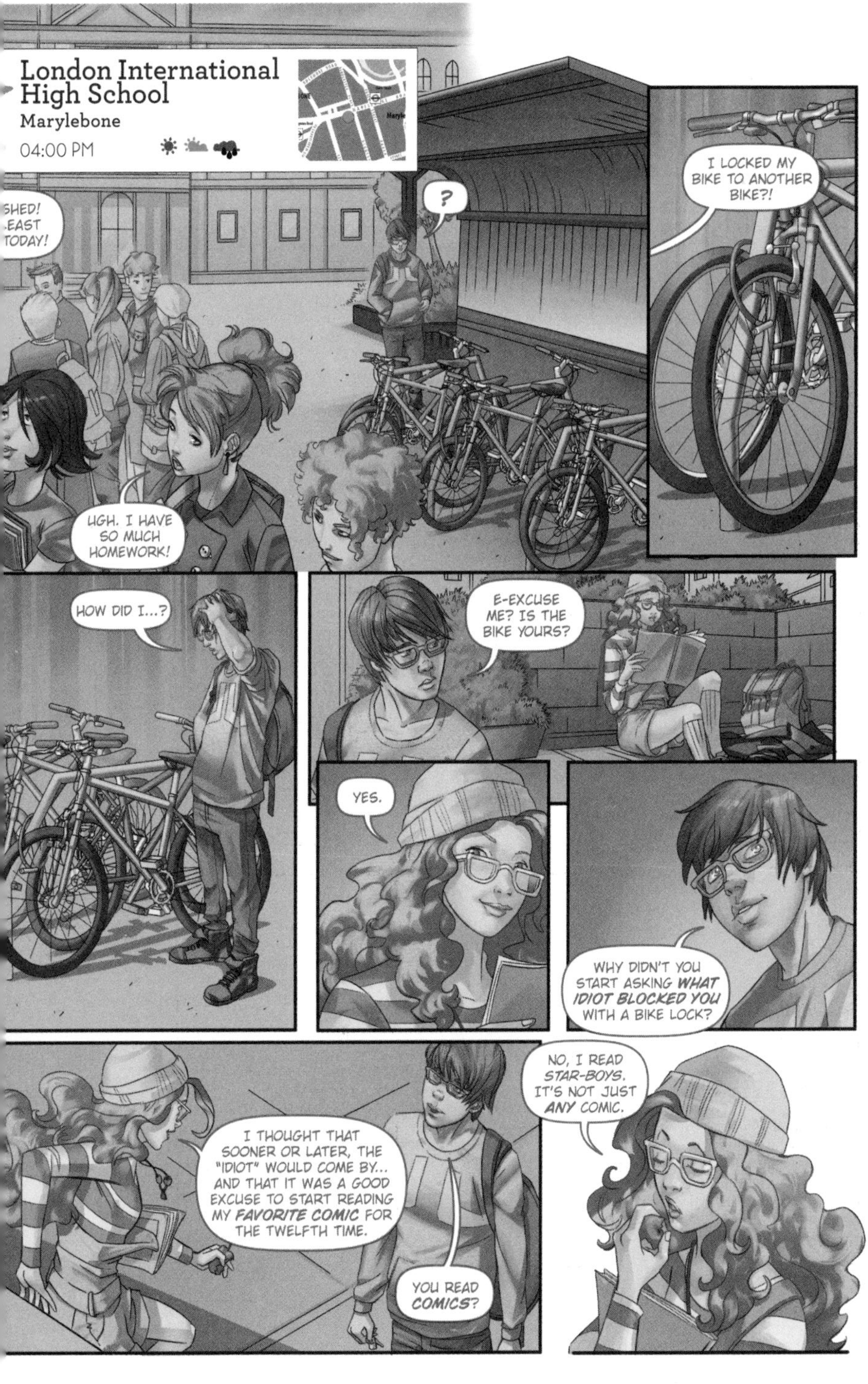
London International High School
Marylebone
04:00 PM
SHED!
EAST
TODAY!
?
UGH. I HAVE SO MUCH HOMEWORK!
I LOCKED MY BIKE TO ANOTHER BIKE?!
HOW DID I...?
E-EXCUSE ME? IS THE BIKE YOURS?
YES.
WHY DIDN'T YOU START ASKING WHAT IDIOT BLOCKED YOU WITH A BIKE LOCK?
I THOUGHT THAT SOONER OR LATER, THE "IDIOT" WOULD COME BY... AND THAT IT WAS A GOOD EXCUSE TO START READING MY FAVORITE COMIC FOR THE TWELFTH TIME.
YOU READ COMICS?
NO, I READ STAR-BOYS. IT'S NOT JUST ANY COMIC.

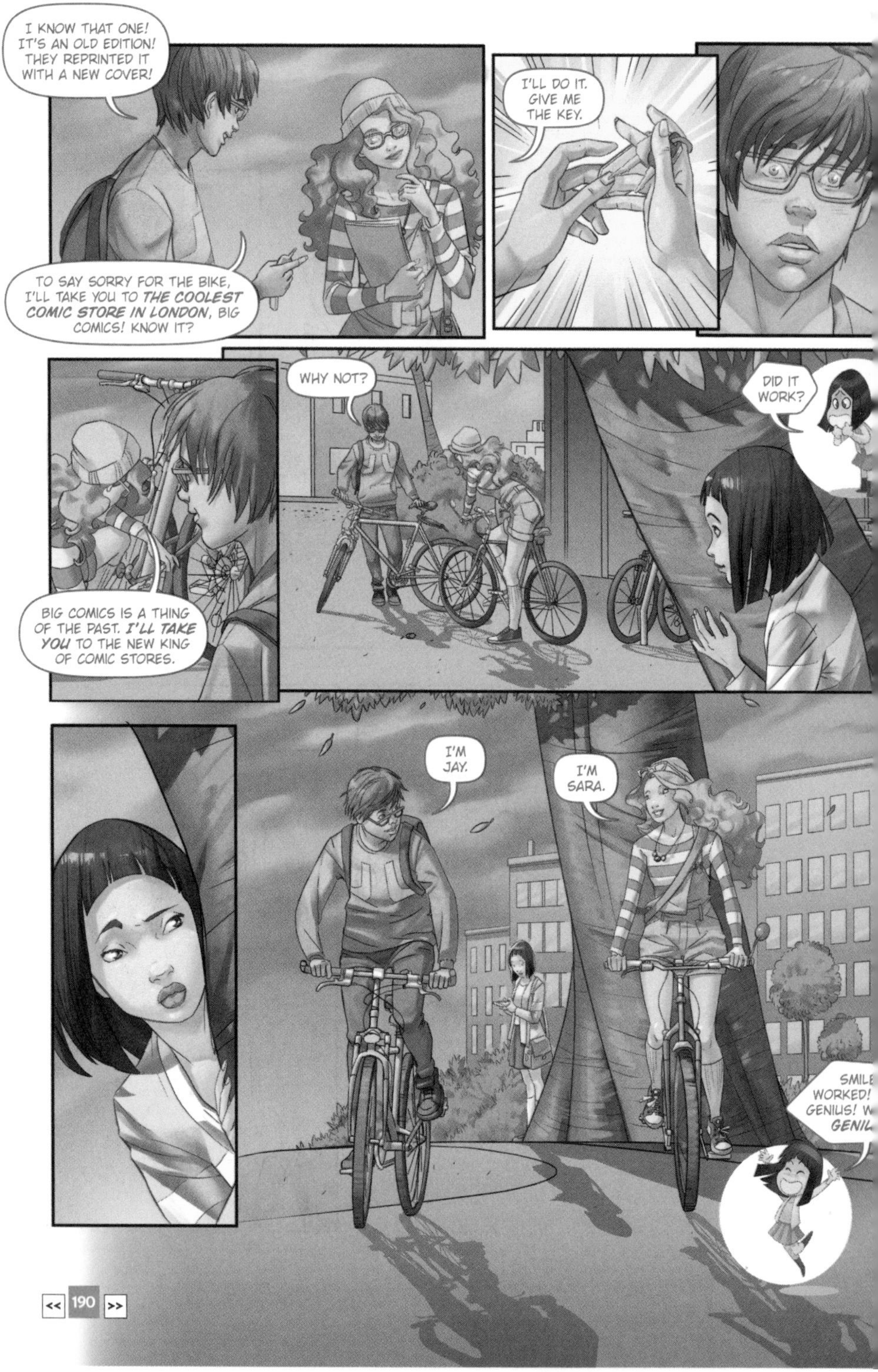
I KNOW THAT ONE! IT'S AN OLD EDITION! THEY REPRINTED IT WITH A NEW COVER!
TO SAY SORRY FOR THE BIKE, I'LL TAKE YOU TO ***THE COOLEST COMIC STORE IN LONDON***, BIG COMICS! KNOW IT?
I'LL DO IT. GIVE ME THE KEY.
BIG COMICS IS A THING OF THE PAST. ***I'LL TAKE YOU*** TO THE NEW KING OF COMIC STORES.
WHY NOT?
DID IT WORK?
I'M JAY.
I'M SARA.
SMIL
WORKED!
GENIUS! W
GENIU

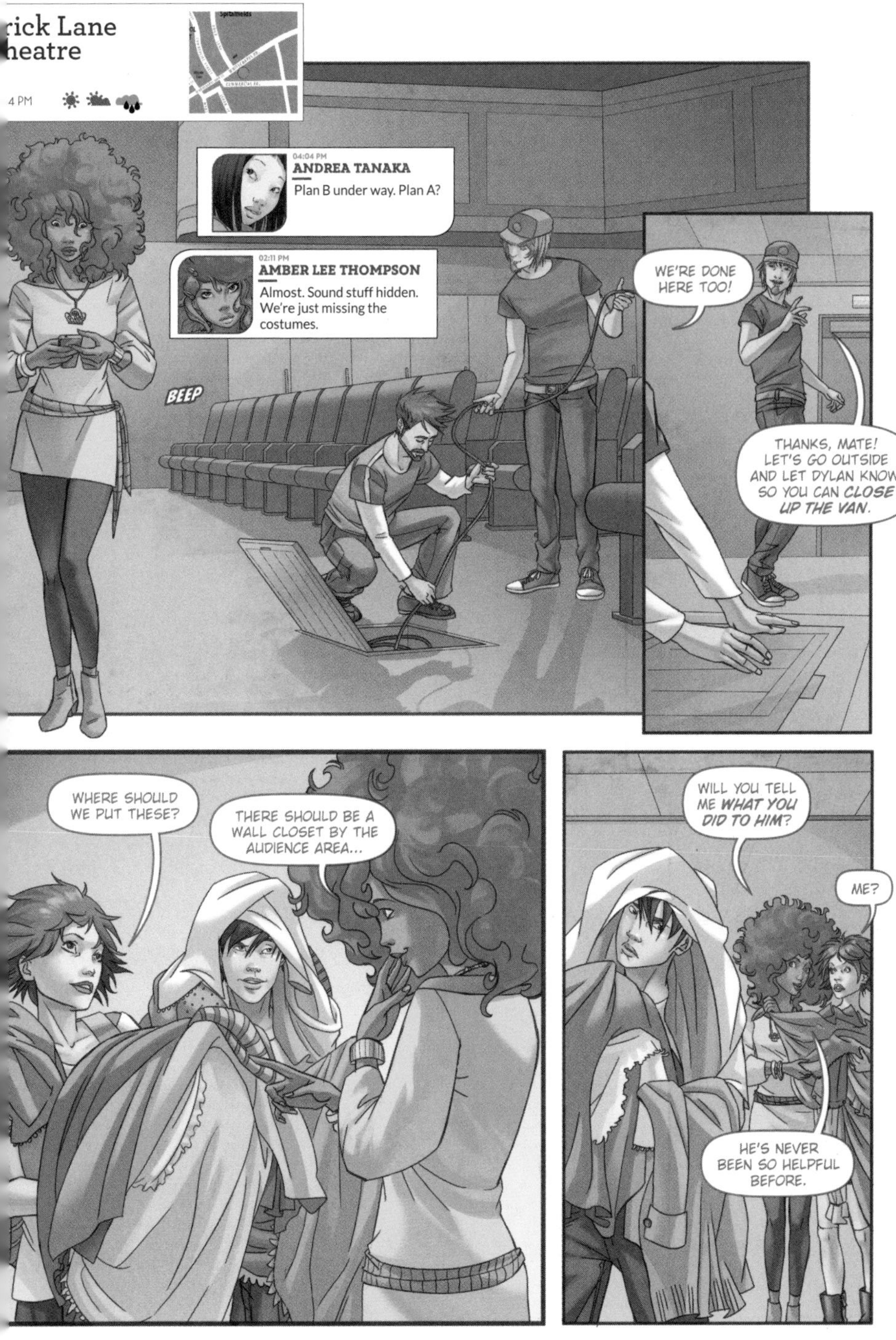
rick Lane
heatre
4 PM
04:04 PM
ANDREA TANAKA
Plan B under way. Plan A?
02:11 PM
AMBER LEE THOMPSON
Almost. Sound stuff hidden. We're just missing the costumes.
BEEP
WE'RE DONE HERE TOO!
THANKS, MATE! LET'S GO OUTSIDE AND LET DYLAN KNOW, SO YOU CAN CLOSE UP THE VAN.
WHERE SHOULD WE PUT THESE?
THERE SHOULD BE A WALL CLOSET BY THE AUDIENCE AREA...
WILL YOU TELL ME WHAT YOU DID TO HIM?
ME?
HE'S NEVER BEEN SO HELPFUL BEFORE.

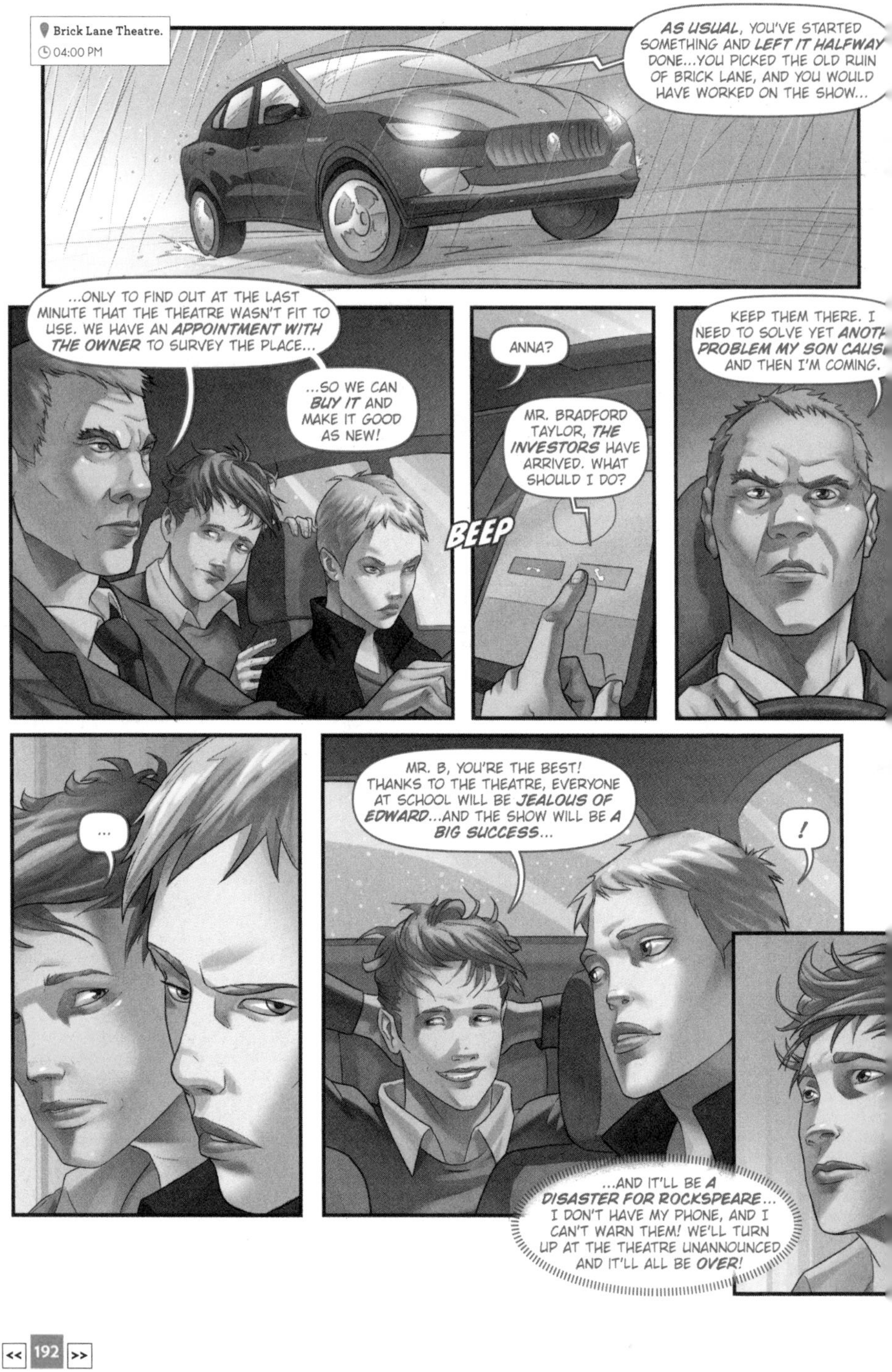
Brick Lane Theatre.
04:00 PM
AS USUAL, YOU'VE STARTED SOMETHING AND LEFT IT HALFWAY DONE...YOU PICKED THE OLD RUIN OF BRICK LANE, AND YOU WOULD HAVE WORKED ON THE SHOW...
...ONLY TO FIND OUT AT THE LAST MINUTE THAT THE THEATRE WASN'T FIT TO USE. WE HAVE AN APPOINTMENT WITH THE OWNER TO SURVEY THE PLACE...
...SO WE CAN BUY IT AND MAKE IT GOOD AS NEW!
BEEP
ANNA?
MR. BRADFORD TAYLOR, THE INVESTORS HAVE ARRIVED. WHAT SHOULD I DO?
KEEP THEM THERE. I NEED TO SOLVE YET ANOTH PROBLEM MY SON CAUS AND THEN I'M COMING.
...
MR. B, YOU'RE THE BEST! THANKS TO THE THEATRE, EVERYONE AT SCHOOL WILL BE JEALOUS OF EDWARD...AND THE SHOW WILL BE A BIG SUCCESS...
!
...AND IT'LL BE A DISASTER FOR ROCKSPEARE... I DON'T HAVE MY PHONE, AND I CAN'T WARN THEM! WE'LL TURN UP AT THE THEATRE UNANNOUNCED AND IT'LL ALL BE OVER!

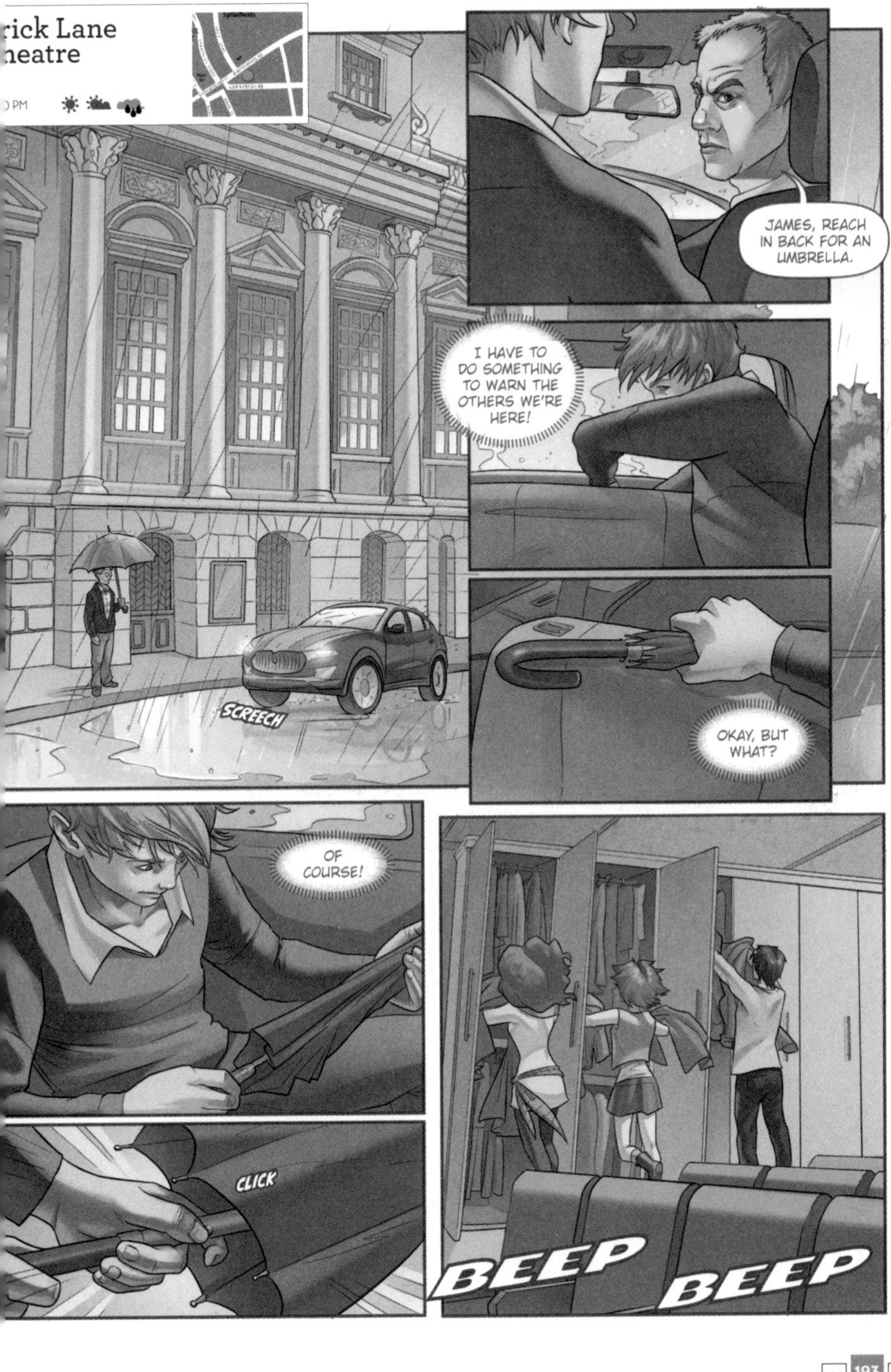
rick Lane
heatre
) PM
JAMES, REACH IN BACK FOR AN UMBRELLA.
I HAVE TO DO SOMETHING TO WARN THE OTHERS WE'RE HERE!
SCREECH
OKAY, BUT WHAT?
OF COURSE!
CLICK
BEEP
BEEP

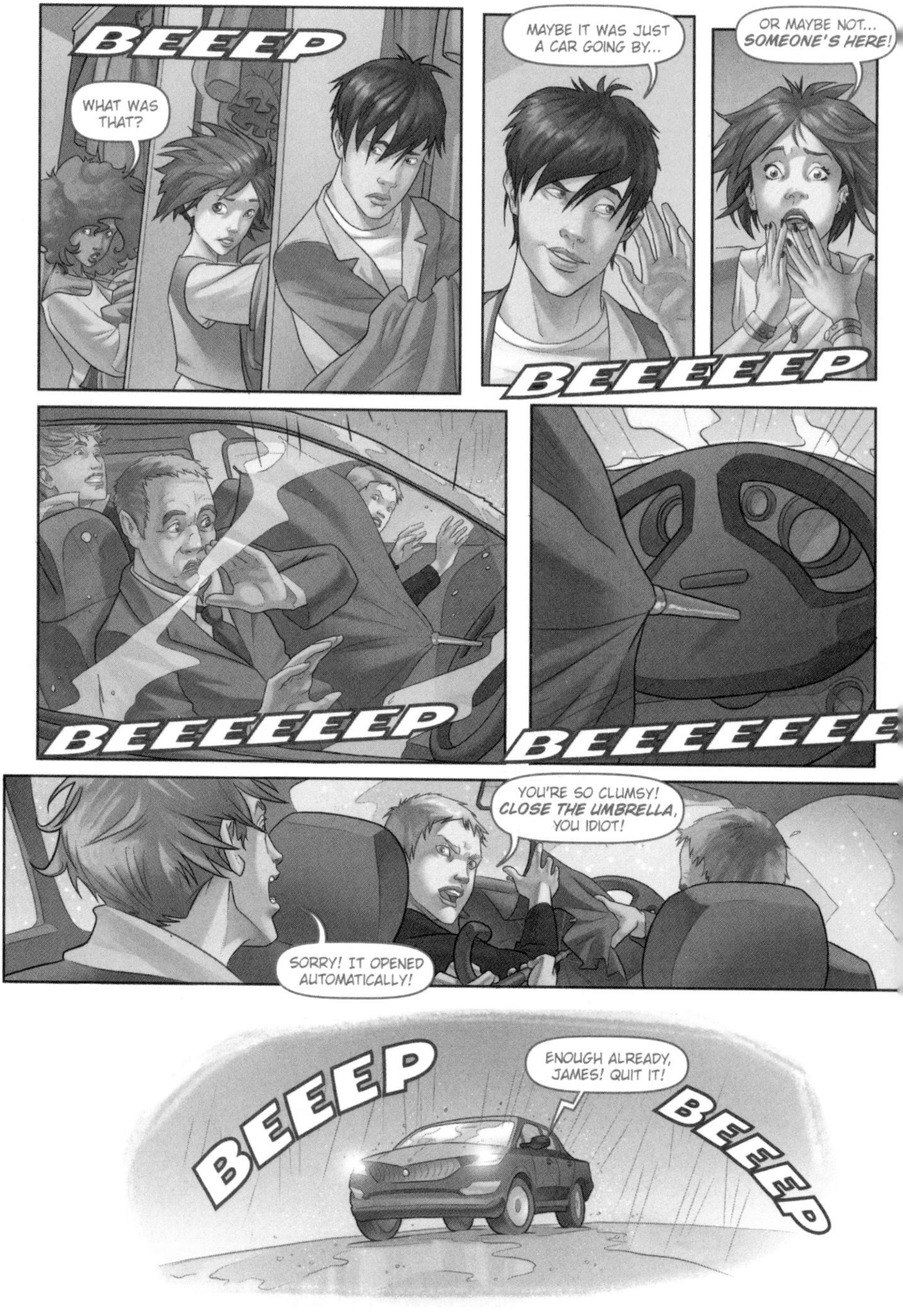
BEEEP
WHAT WAS THAT?
MAYBE IT WAS JUST A CAR GOING BY...
OR MAYBE NOT... SOMEONE'S HERE!
BEEEEEP
BEEEEEEEP
BEEEEEEEE
YOU'RE SO CLUMSY! CLOSE THE UMBRELLA, YOU IDIOT!
SORRY! IT OPENED AUTOMATICALLY!
BEEEP
ENOUGH ALREADY, JAMES! QUIT IT!
BEEEEP

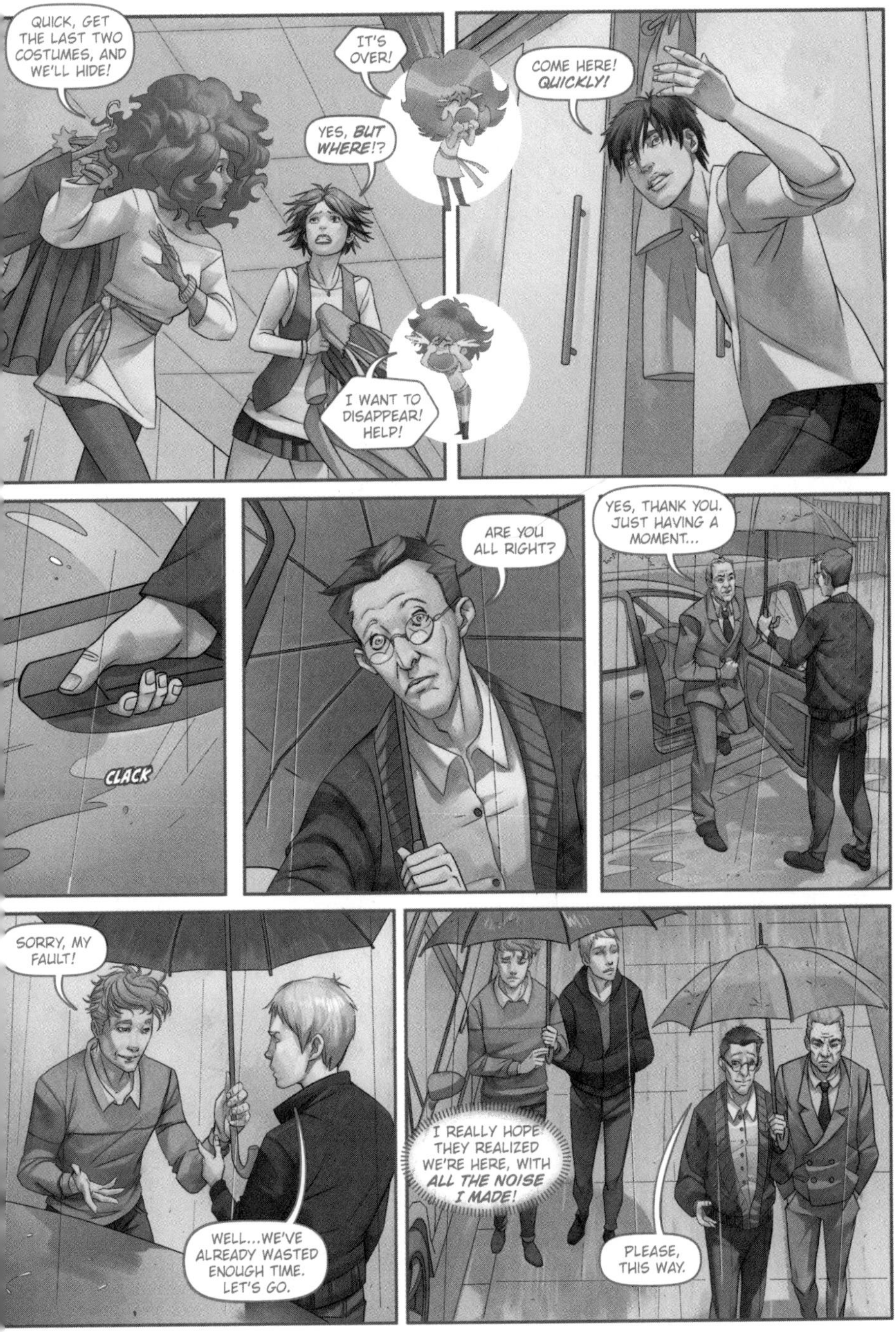

QUICK, GET THE LAST TWO COSTUMES, AND WE'LL HIDE!
IT'S OVER!
YES, BUT WHERE!?
I WANT TO DISAPPEAR! HELP!
COME HERE! QUICKLY!
CLACK
ARE YOU ALL RIGHT?
YES, THANK YOU. JUST HAVING A MOMENT...
SORRY, MY FAULT!
WELL...WE'VE ALREADY WASTED ENOUGH TIME. LET'S GO.
I REALLY HOPE THEY REALIZED WE'RE HERE, WITH ALL THE NOISE I MADE!
PLEASE, THIS WAY.

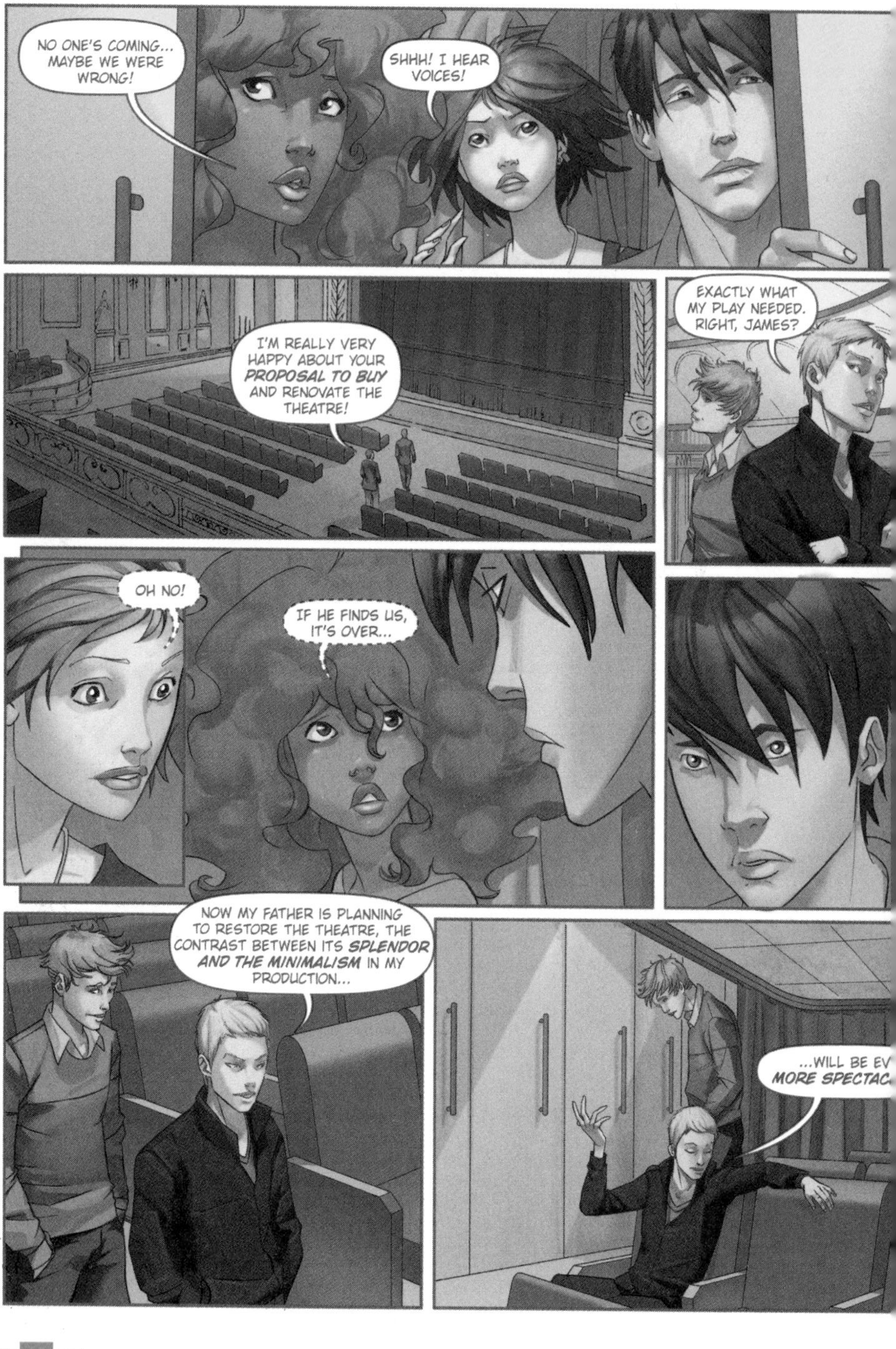
NO ONE'S COMING... MAYBE WE WERE WRONG!
SHHH! I HEAR VOICES!
I'M REALLY VERY HAPPY ABOUT YOUR **PROPOSAL TO BUY** AND RENOVATE THE THEATRE!
EXACTLY WHAT MY PLAY NEEDED. RIGHT, JAMES?
OH NO!
IF HE FINDS US, IT'S OVER...
NOW MY FATHER IS PLANNING TO RESTORE THE THEATRE, THE CONTRAST BETWEEN ITS **SPLENDOR AND THE MINIMALISM** IN MY PRODUCTION...
...WILL BE EV
MORE SPECTAC

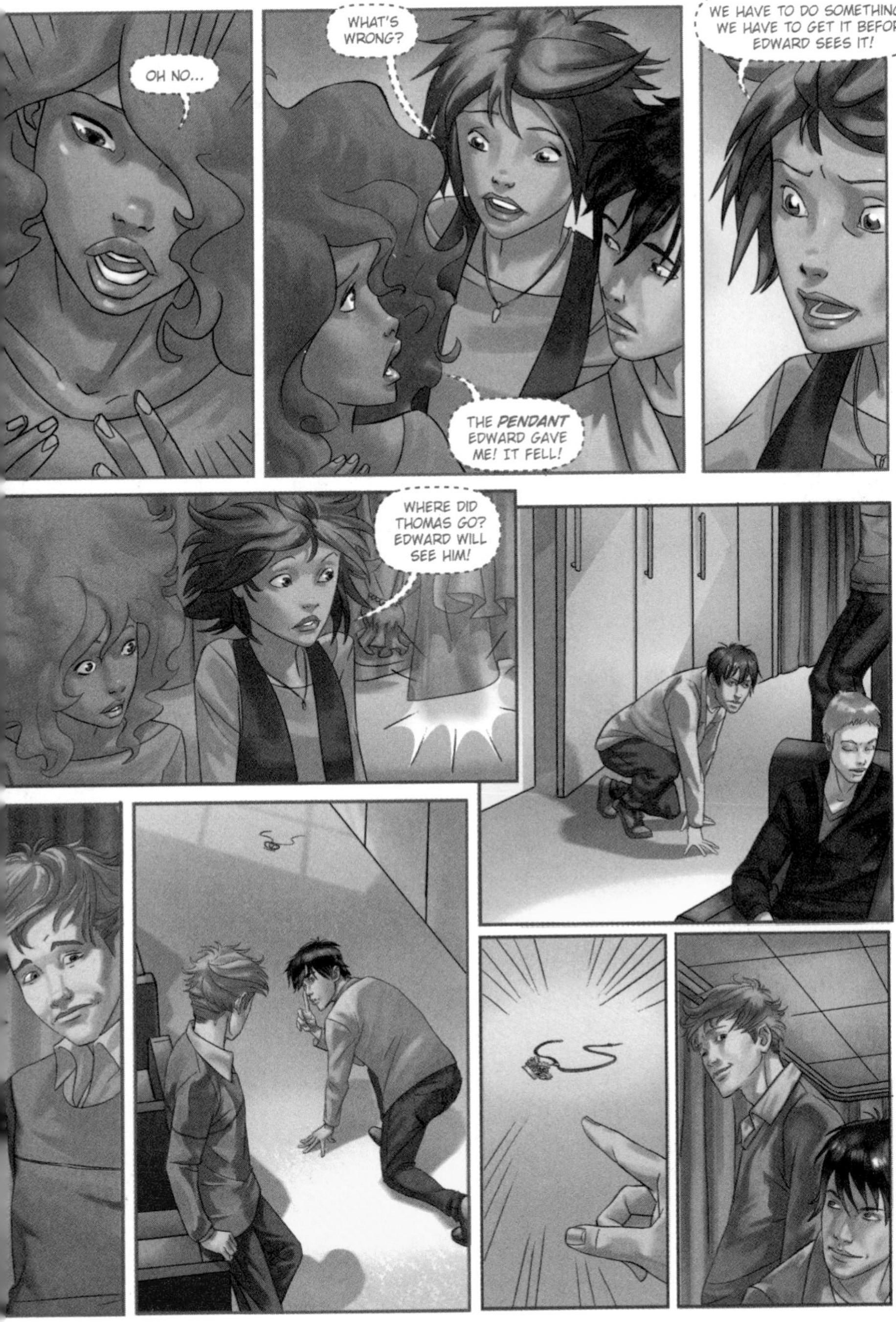
OH NO...
WHAT'S WRONG?
THE *PENDANT* EDWARD GAVE ME! IT FELL!
WE HAVE TO DO SOMETHING... WE HAVE TO GET IT BEFORE EDWARD SEES IT!
WHERE DID THOMAS GO? EDWARD WILL SEE HIM!

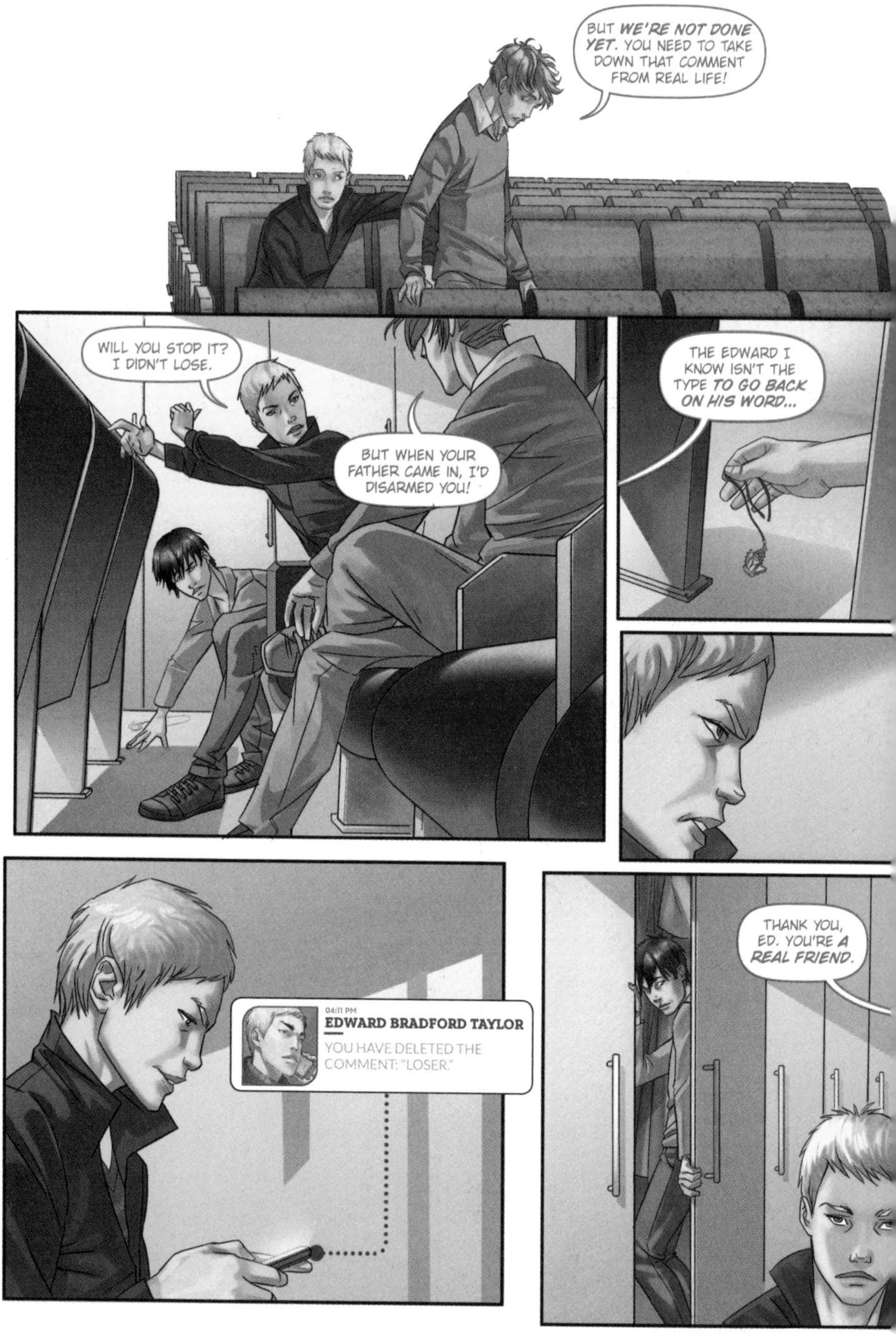
BUT WE'RE NOT DONE YET. YOU NEED TO TAKE DOWN THAT COMMENT FROM REAL LIFE!
WILL YOU STOP IT? I DIDN'T LOSE.
BUT WHEN YOUR FATHER CAME IN, I'D DISARMED YOU!
THE EDWARD I KNOW ISN'T THE TYPE TO GO BACK ON HIS WORD...
04:11 PM
EDWARD BRADFORD TAYLOR
YOU HAVE DELETED THE COMMENT: "LOSER."
THANK YOU, ED. YOU'RE A REAL FRIEND.

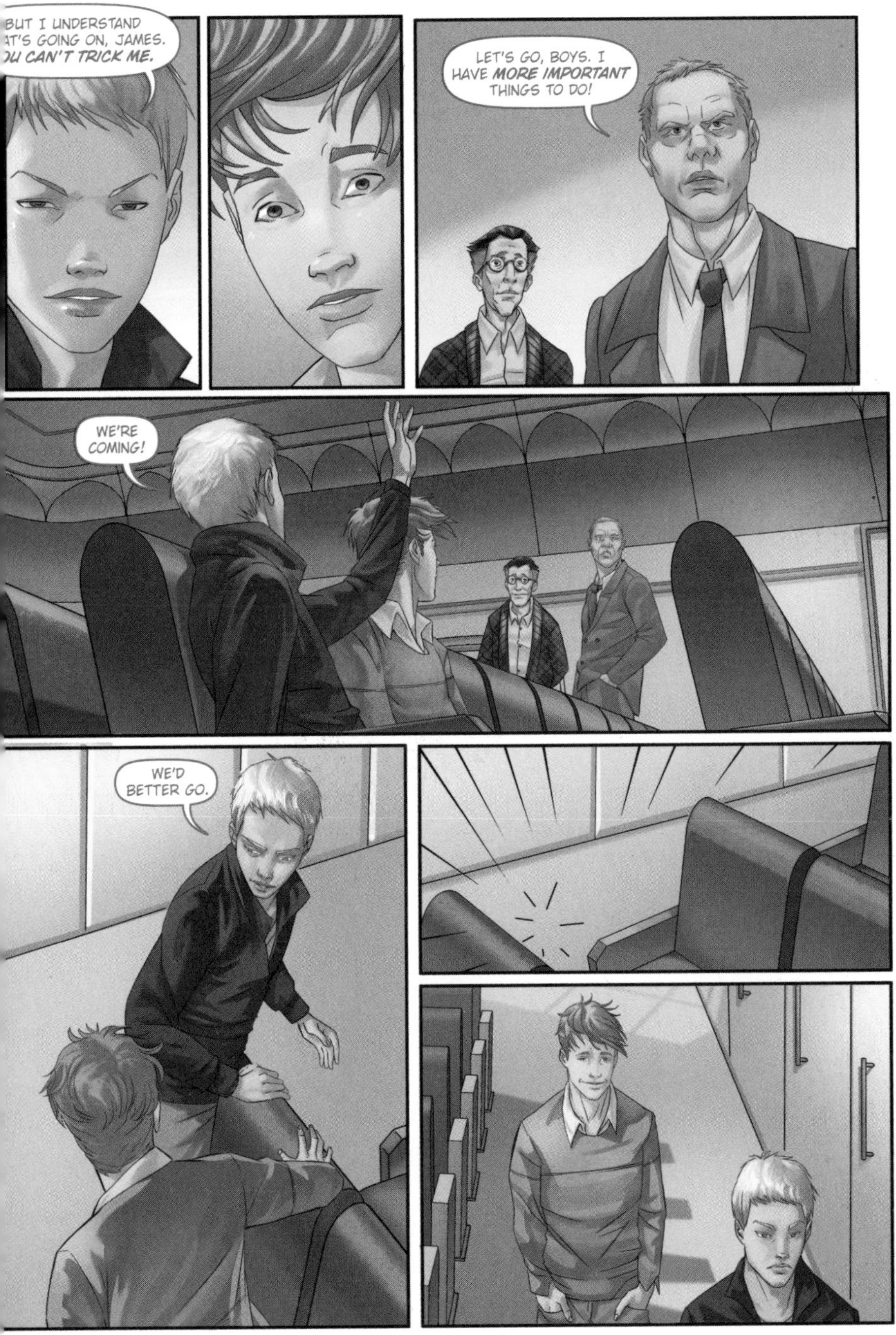
BUT I UNDERSTAND
AT'S GOING ON, JAMES.
OU CAN'T TRICK ME.
LET'S GO, BOYS. I HAVE MORE IMPORTANT THINGS TO DO!
WE'RE COMING!
WE'D BETTER GO.

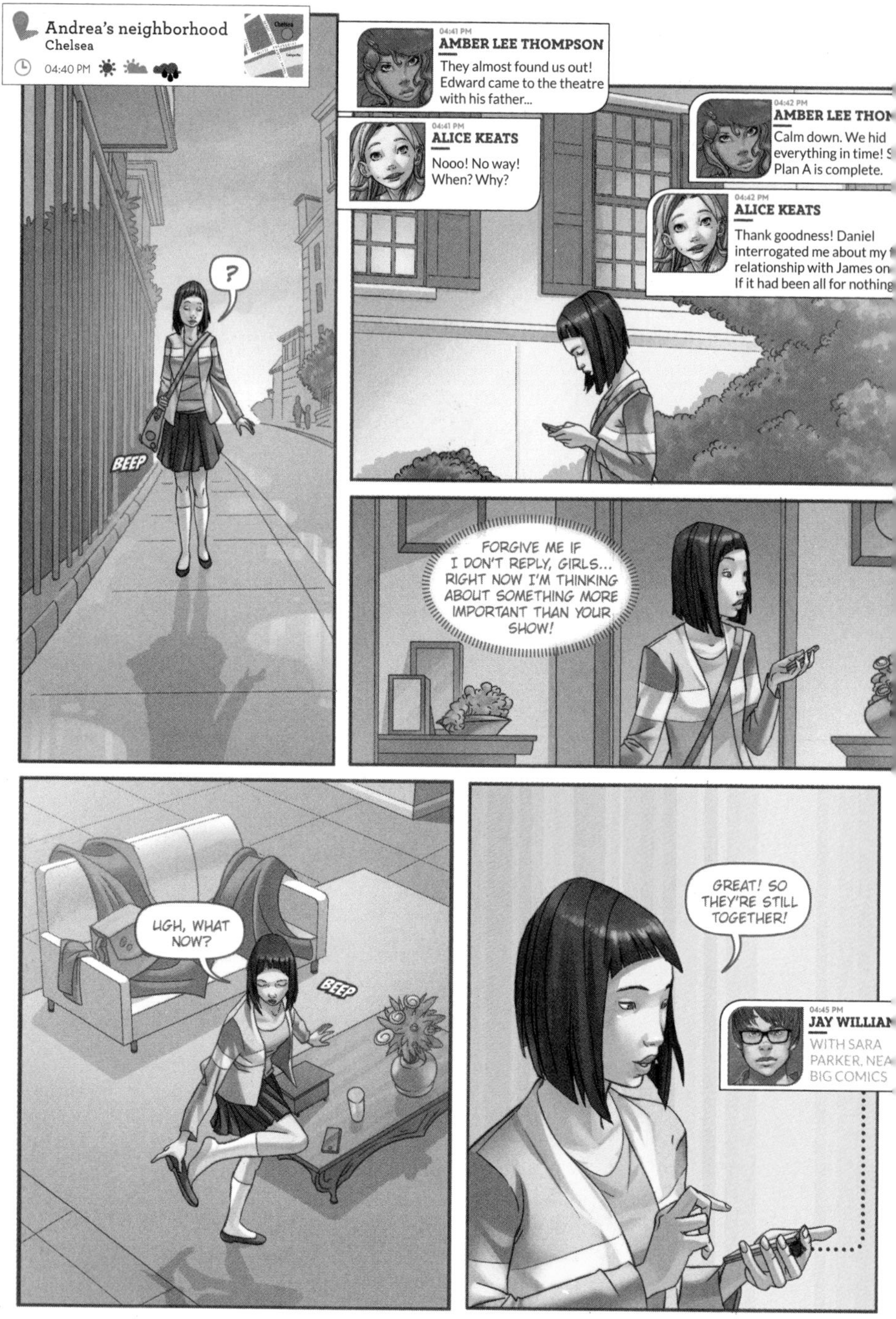
Andrea's neighborhood
Chelsea
04:40 PM
Chelsea
?
BEEP
04:41 PM
AMBER LEE THOMPSON
They almost found us out! Edward came to the theatre with his father...
04:41 PM
ALICE KEATS
Nooo! No way! When? Why?
04:42 PM
AMBER LEE THOM
Calm down. We hid everything in time!
Plan A is complete.
04:42 PM
ALICE KEATS
Thank goodness! Daniel interrogated me about my
relationship with James on
If it had been all for nothing
FORGIVE ME IF I DON'T REPLY, GIRLS... RIGHT NOW I'M THINKING ABOUT SOMETHING MORE IMPORTANT THAN YOUR SHOW!
UGH, WHAT NOW?
BEEP
GREAT! SO THEY'RE STILL TOGETHER!
04:45 PM
JAY WILLIA
WITH SARA
PARKER, NEA
BIG COMICS

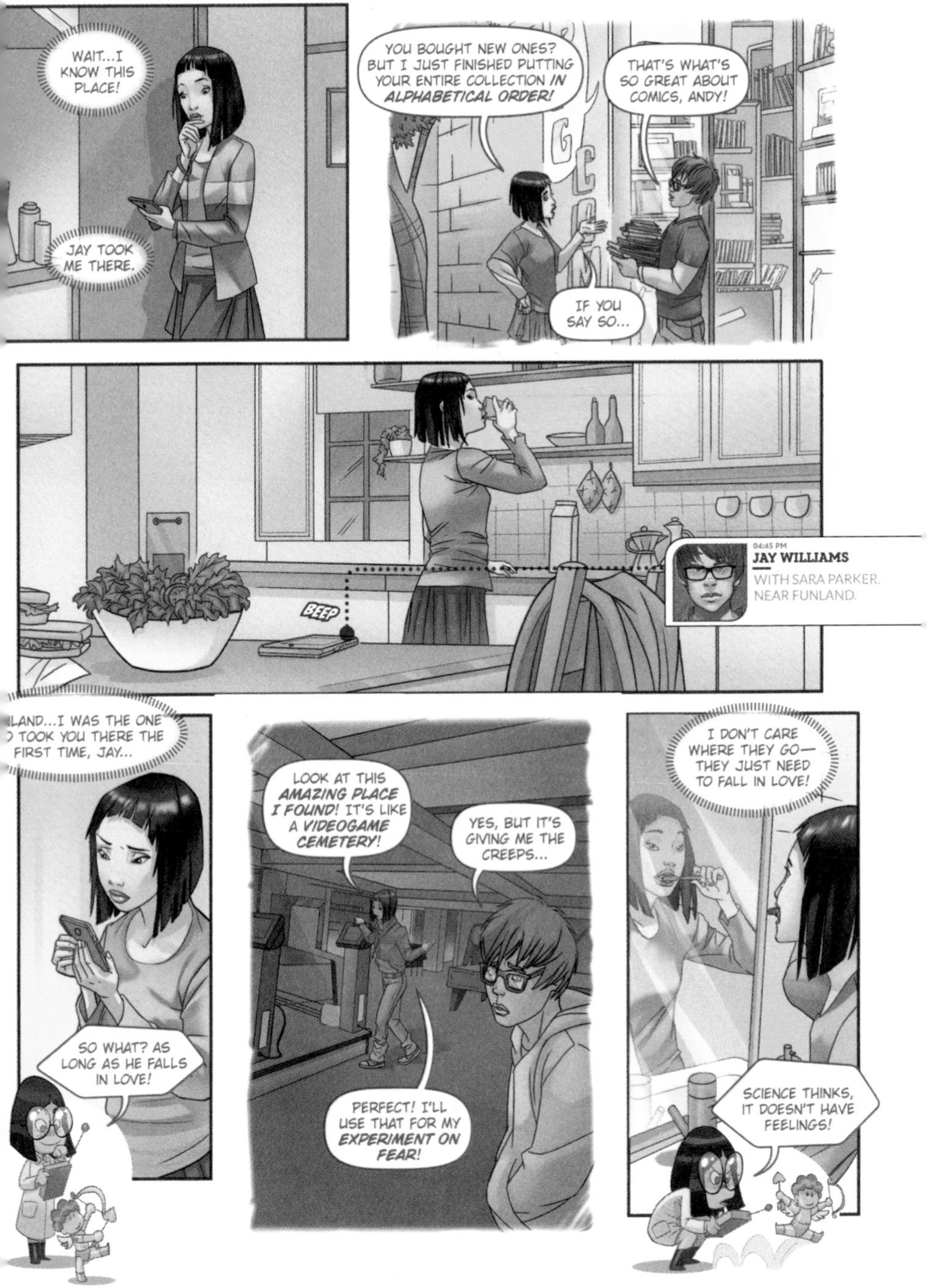
WAIT...I KNOW THIS PLACE!
JAY TOOK ME THERE.
YOU BOUGHT NEW ONES? BUT I JUST FINISHED PUTTING YOUR ENTIRE COLLECTION IN ALPHABETICAL ORDER!
THAT'S WHAT'S SO GREAT ABOUT COMICS, ANDY!
IF YOU SAY SO...
BEEP
04:45 PM
JAY WILLIAMS
WITH SARA PARKER. NEAR FUNLAND.
LAND...I WAS THE ONE O TOOK YOU THERE THE FIRST TIME, JAY...
SO WHAT? AS LONG AS HE FALLS IN LOVE!
LOOK AT THIS AMAZING PLACE I FOUND! IT'S LIKE A VIDEOGAME CEMETERY!
YES, BUT IT'S GIVING ME THE CREEPS...
PERFECT! I'LL USE THAT FOR MY EXPERIMENT ON FEAR!
I DON'T CARE WHERE THEY GO—THEY JUST NEED TO FALL IN LOVE!
SCIENCE THINKS, IT DOESN'T HAVE FEELINGS!

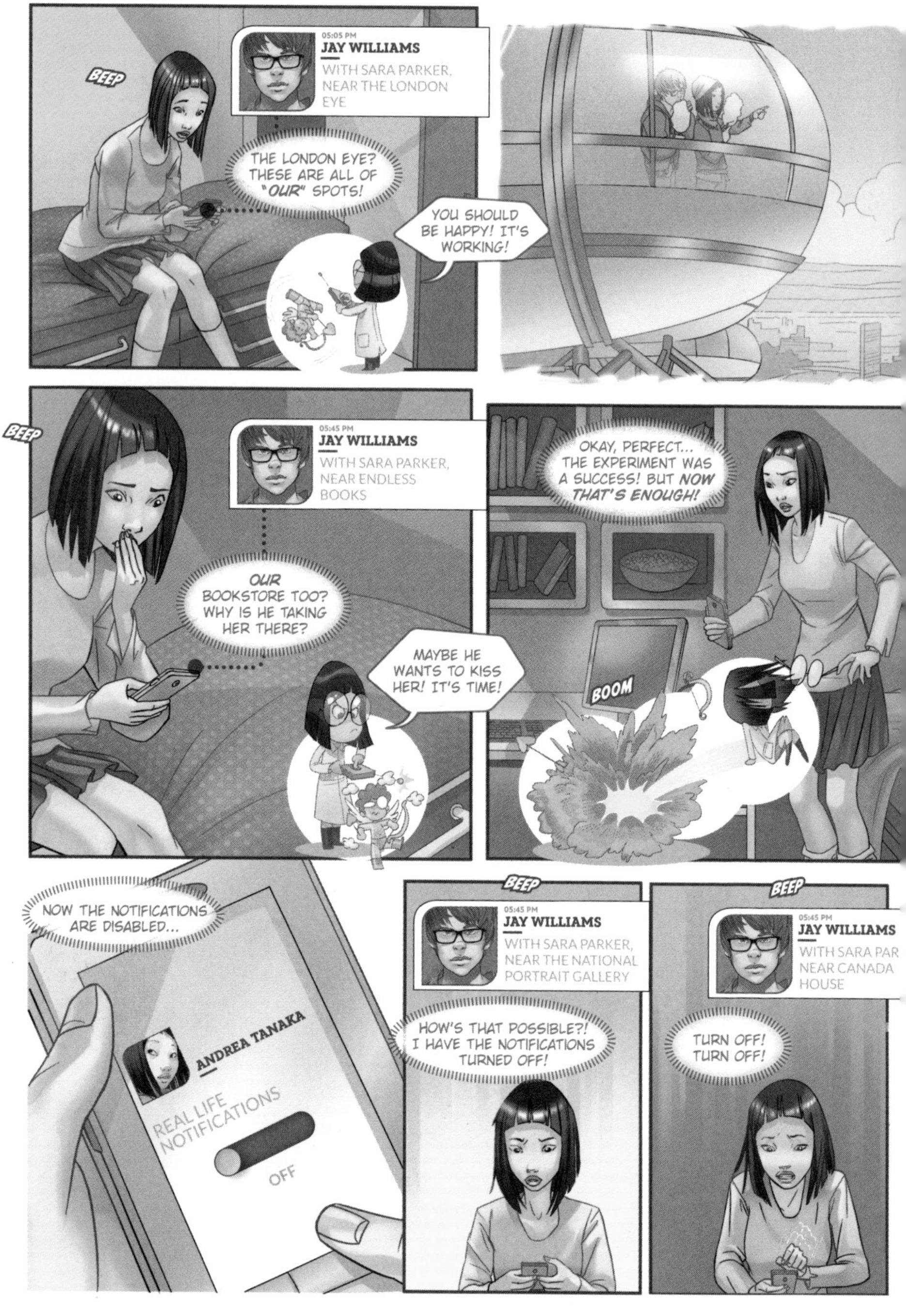
BEEP
05:05 PM
JAY WILLIAMS
WITH SARA PARKER, NEAR THE LONDON EYE
THE LONDON EYE? THESE ARE ALL OF "OUR" SPOTS!
YOU SHOULD BE HAPPY! IT'S WORKING!
BEEP
05:45 PM
JAY WILLIAMS
WITH SARA PARKER, NEAR ENDLESS BOOKS
OUR BOOKSTORE TOO? WHY IS HE TAKING HER THERE?
MAYBE HE WANTS TO KISS HER! IT'S TIME!
OKAY, PERFECT... THE EXPERIMENT WAS A SUCCESS! BUT NOW THAT'S ENOUGH!
BOOM
NOW THE NOTIFICATIONS ARE DISABLED...
ANDREA TANAKA
REAL LIFE NOTIFICATIONS
OFF
BEEP
05:45 PM
JAY WILLIAMS
WITH SARA PARKER, NEAR THE NATIONAL PORTRAIT GALLERY
HOW'S THAT POSSIBLE?! I HAVE THE NOTIFICATIONS TURNED OFF!
BEEP
05:45 PM
JAY WILLIAMS
WITH SARA PAR
NEAR CANADA HOUSE
TURN OFF! TURN OFF!

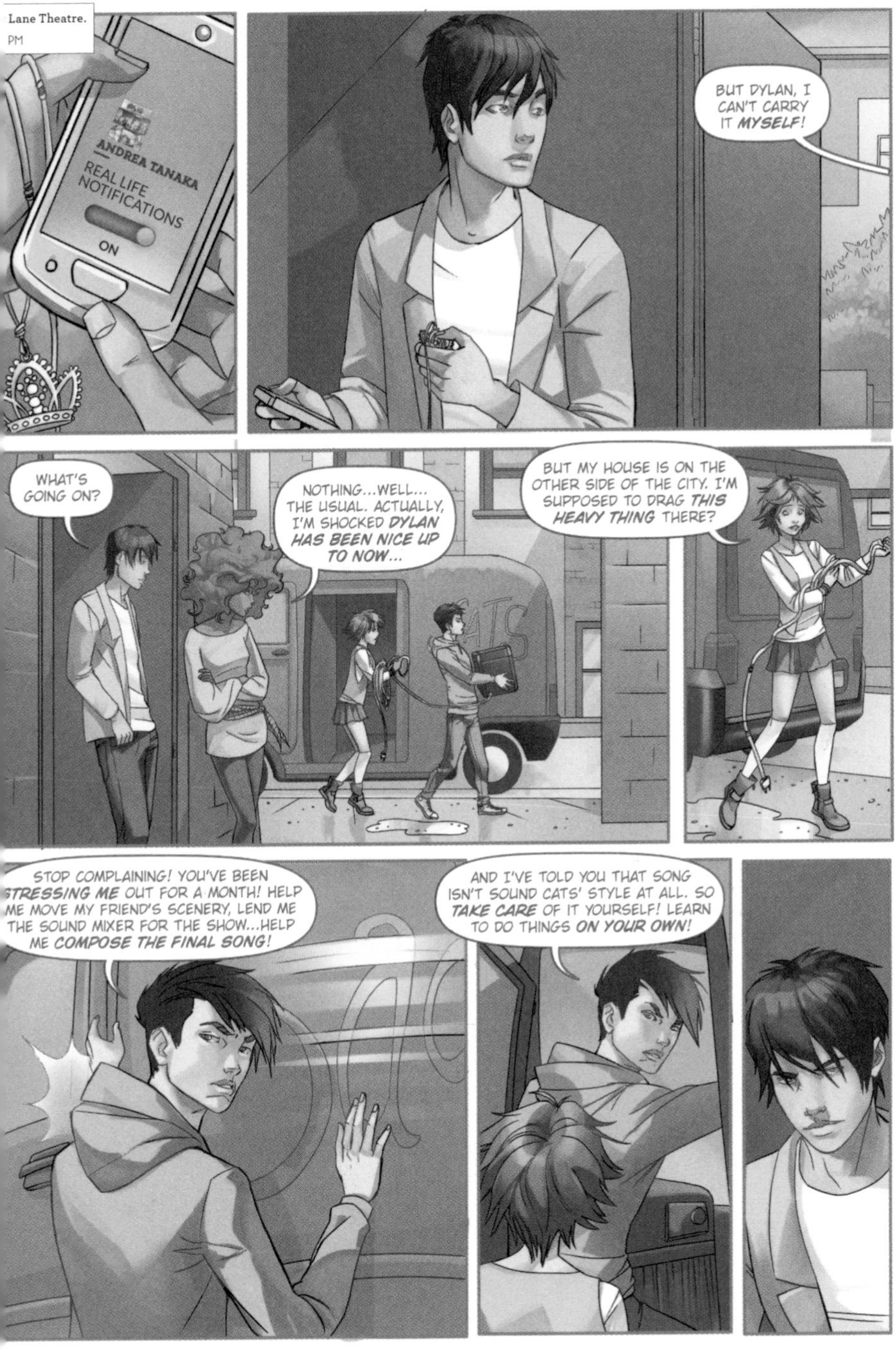
Lane Theatre.
PM
ANDREA TANAKA
REAL LIFE NOTIFICATIONS
ON
BUT DYLAN, I CAN'T CARRY IT *MYSELF*!
WHAT'S GOING ON?
NOTHING...WELL... THE USUAL. ACTUALLY, I'M SHOCKED *DYLAN HAS BEEN NICE UP TO NOW*...
BUT MY HOUSE IS ON THE OTHER SIDE OF THE CITY. I'M SUPPOSED TO DRAG *THIS HEAVY THING* THERE?
STOP COMPLAINING! YOU'VE BEEN *STRESSING ME* OUT FOR A MONTH! HELP ME MOVE MY FRIEND'S SCENERY, LEND ME THE SOUND MIXER FOR THE SHOW...HELP ME *COMPOSE THE FINAL SONG*!
AND I'VE TOLD YOU THAT SONG ISN'T SOUND CATS' STYLE AT ALL. SO *TAKE CARE* OF IT YOURSELF! LEARN TO DO THINGS *ON YOUR OWN*!

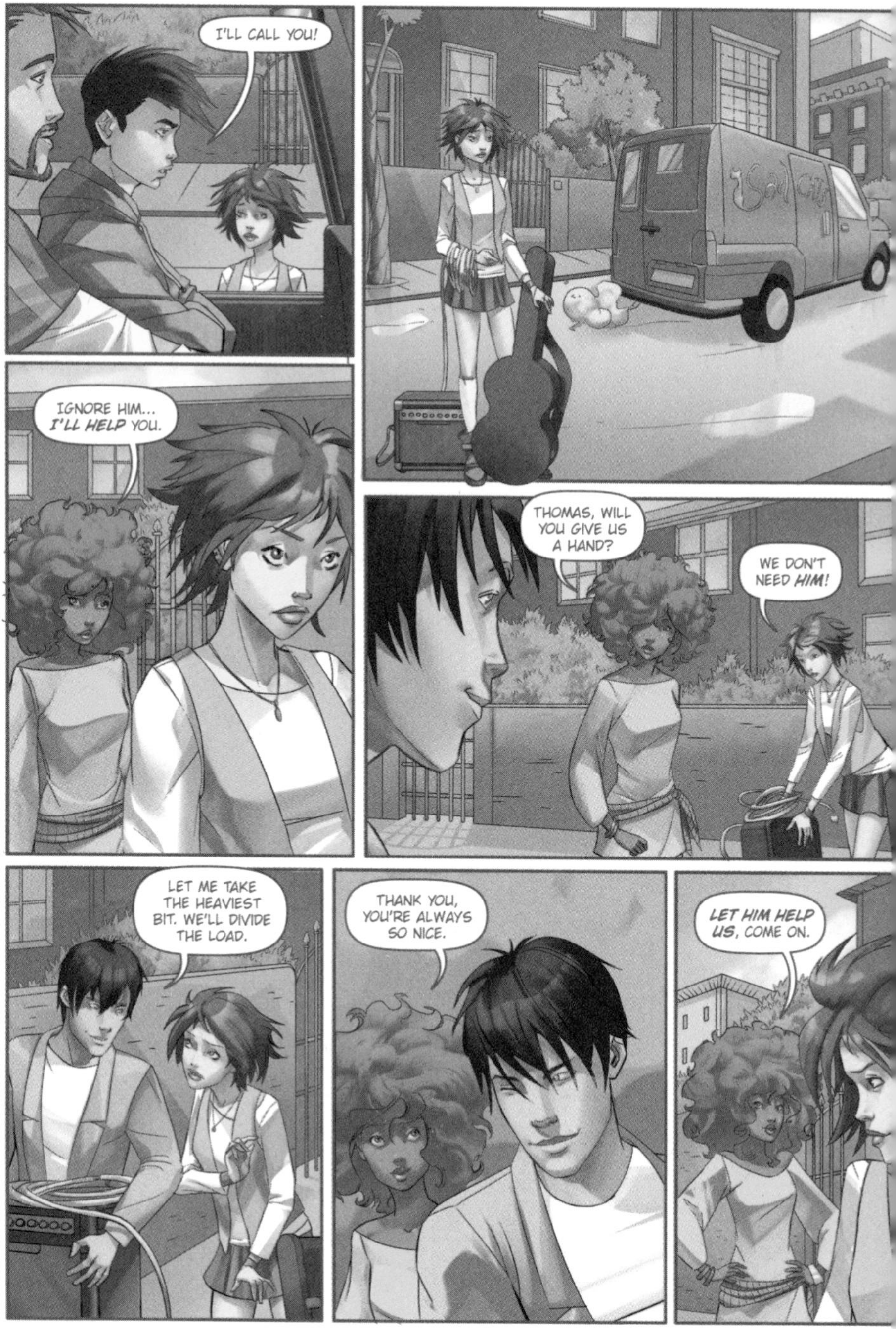
I'LL CALL YOU!
IGNORE HIM... I'LL HELP YOU.
THOMAS, WILL YOU GIVE US A HAND?
WE DON'T NEED HIM!
LET ME TAKE THE HEAVIEST BIT. WE'LL DIVIDE THE LOAD.
THANK YOU, YOU'RE ALWAYS SO NICE.
LET HIM HELP US, COME ON.

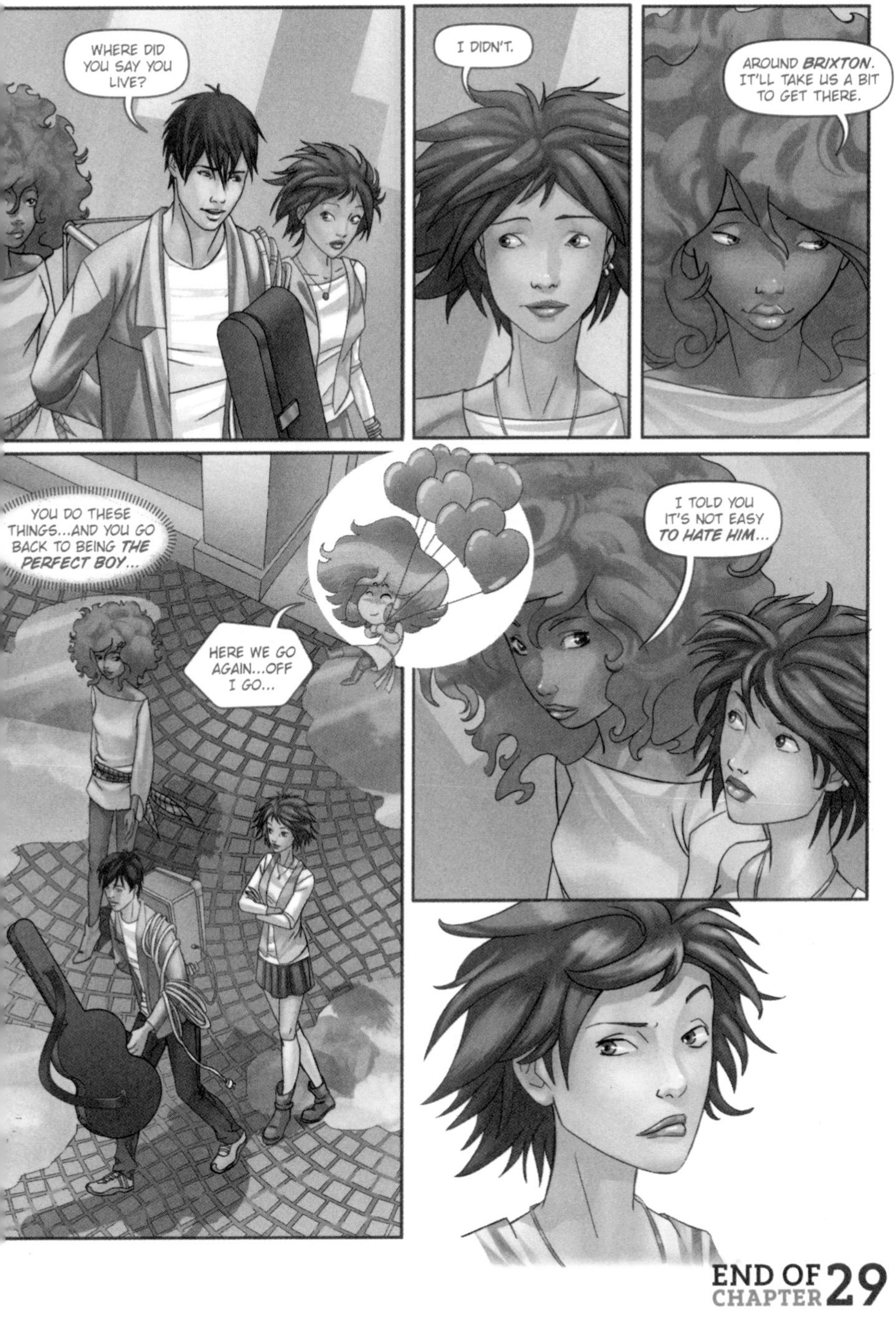

WHERE DID YOU SAY YOU LIVE?
I DIDN'T.
AROUND **BRIXTON**. IT'LL TAKE US A BIT TO GET THERE.
YOU DO THESE THINGS...AND YOU GO BACK TO BEING ***THE PERFECT BOY***...
HERE WE GO AGAIN...OFF I GO...
I TOLD YOU IT'S NOT EASY ***TO HATE HIM***...

END OF CHAPTER 29

CHAPTER 30

Surprising FEELING

Folgate st.
London

05:55 PM

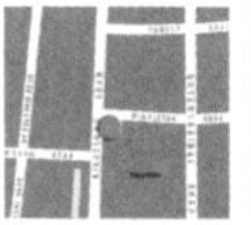

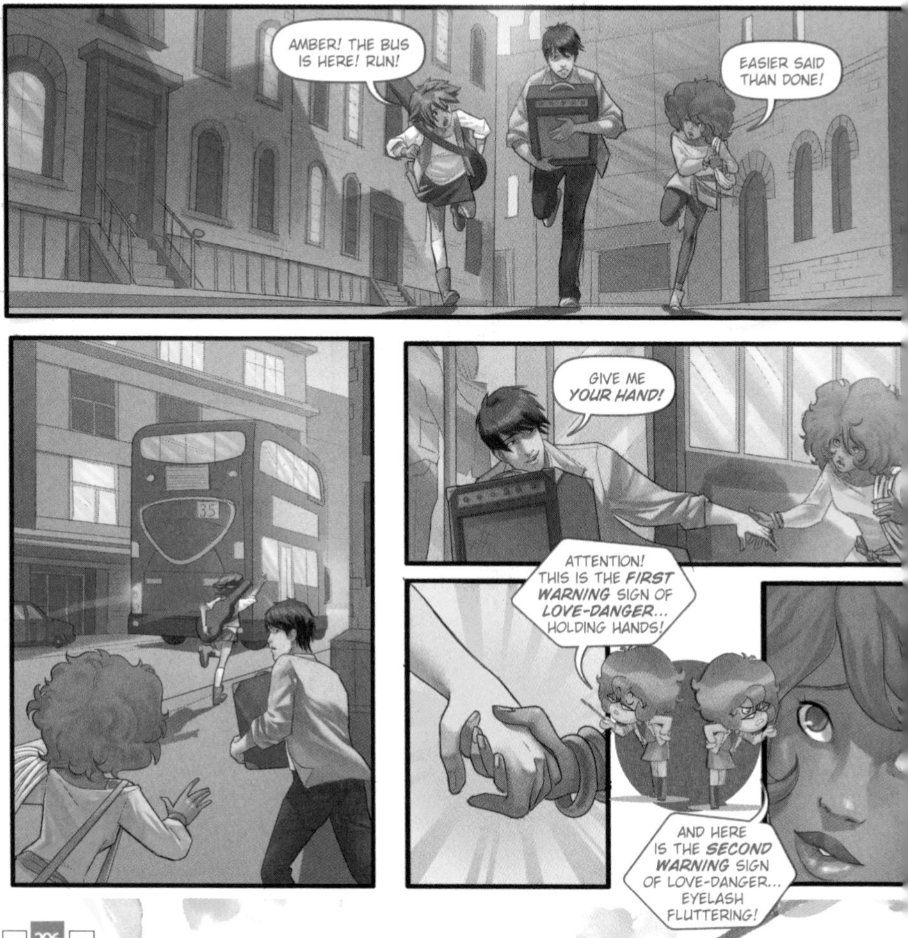
AMBER! THE BUS IS HERE! RUN!
EASIER SAID THAN DONE!
GIVE ME *YOUR HAND!*
ATTENTION! THIS IS THE *FIRST WARNING* SIGN OF *LOVE-DANGER...* HOLDING HANDS!
AND HERE IS THE *SECOND WARNING* SIGN OF LOVE-DANGER... EYELASH FLUTTERING!

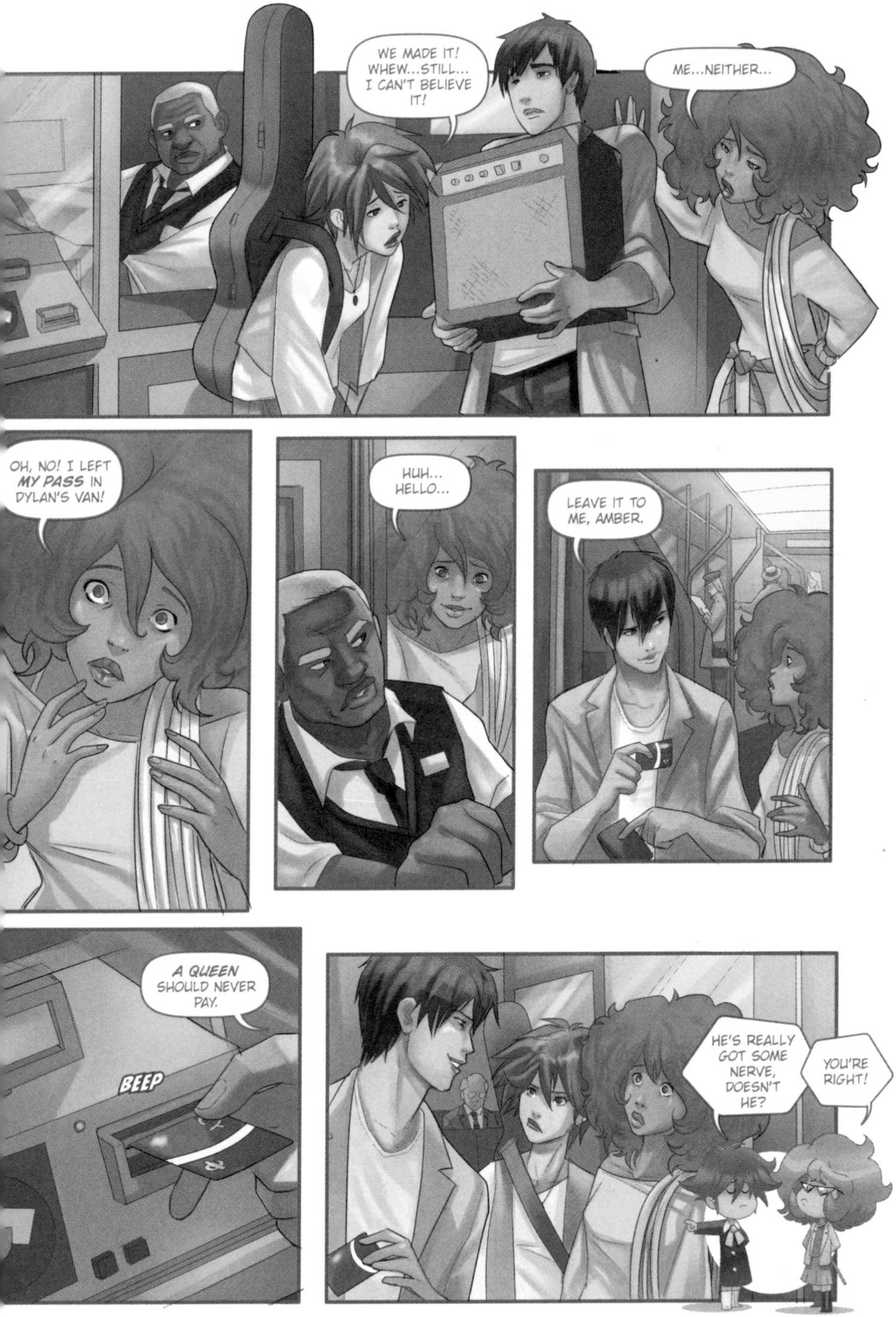
WE MADE IT! WHEW...STILL... I CAN'T BELIEVE IT!
ME...NEITHER...
OH, NO! I LEFT MY PASS IN DYLAN'S VAN!
HUH... HELLO...
LEAVE IT TO ME, AMBER.
A QUEEN SHOULD NEVER PAY.
BEEP
HE'S REALLY GOT SOME NERVE, DOESN'T HE?
YOU'RE RIGHT!

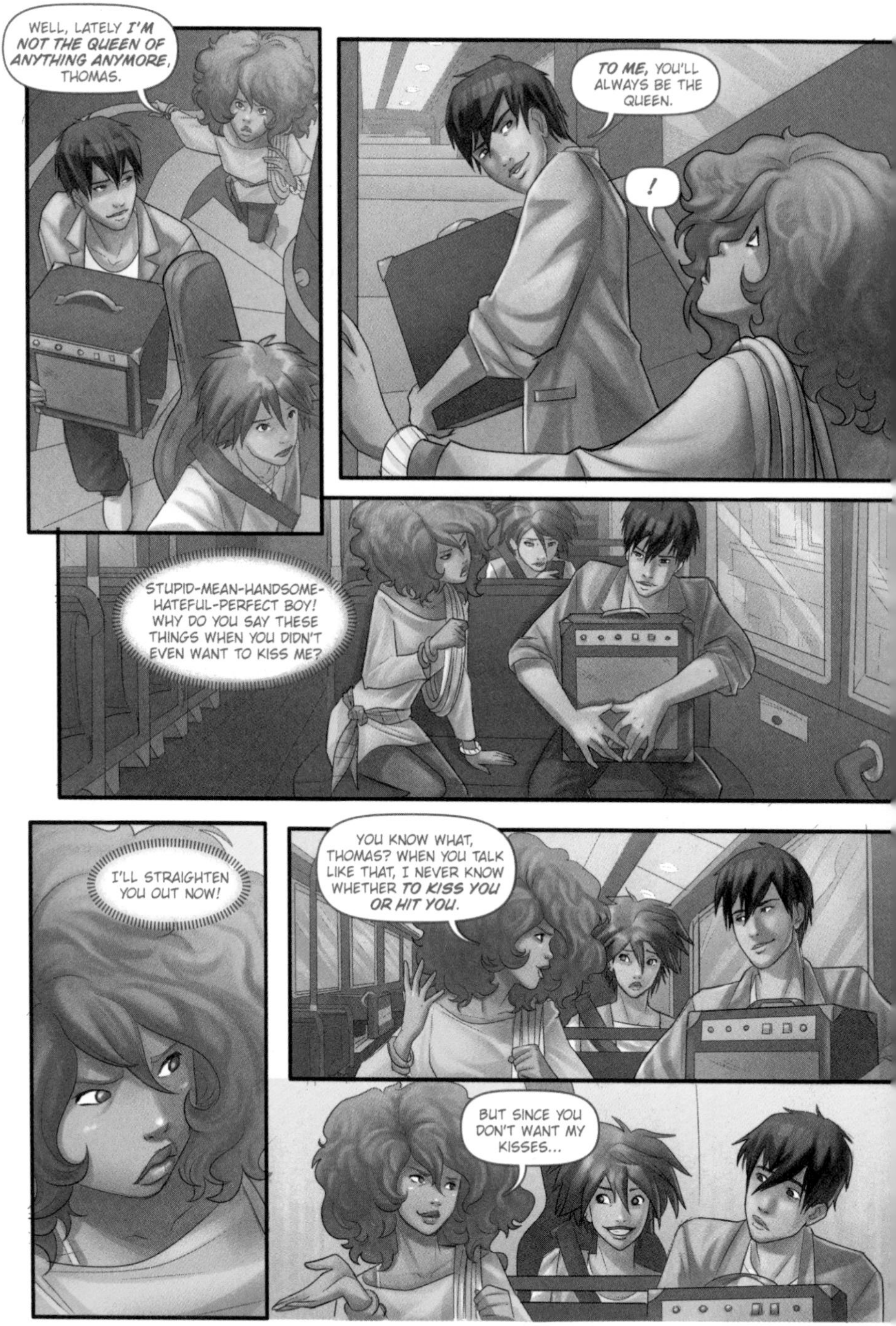
WELL, LATELY I'M NOT THE QUEEN OF ANYTHING ANYMORE, THOMAS.
TO ME, YOU'LL ALWAYS BE THE QUEEN.
!
STUPID-MEAN-HANDSOME-HATEFUL-PERFECT BOY! WHY DO YOU SAY THESE THINGS WHEN YOU DIDN'T EVEN WANT TO KISS ME?
I'LL STRAIGHTEN YOU OUT NOW!
YOU KNOW WHAT, THOMAS? WHEN YOU TALK LIKE THAT, I NEVER KNOW WHETHER TO KISS YOU OR HIT YOU.
BUT SINCE YOU DON'T WANT MY KISSES...

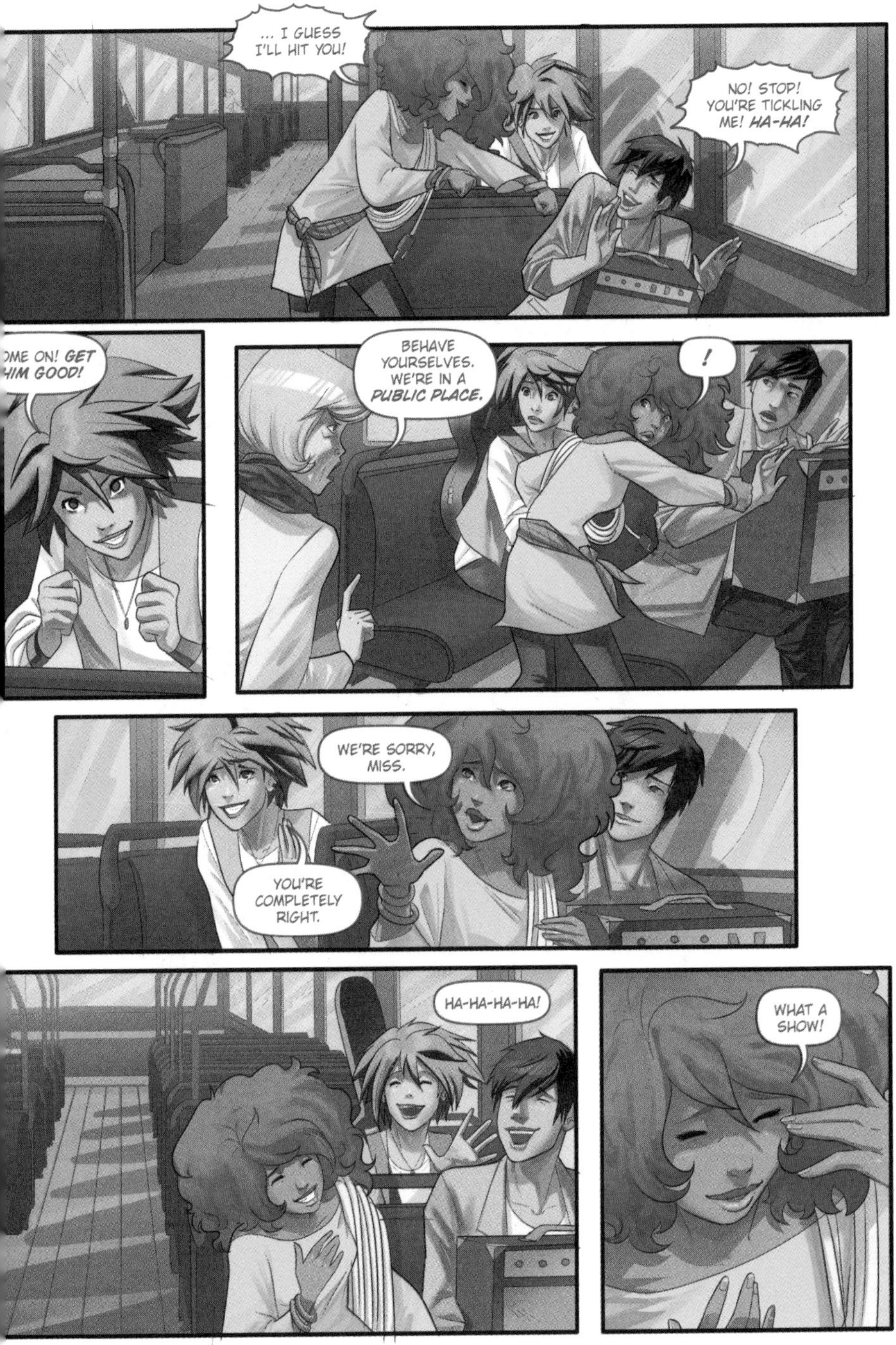
... I GUESS I'LL HIT YOU!
NO! STOP! YOU'RE TICKLING ME! HA-HA!
OME ON! GET HIM GOOD!
BEHAVE YOURSELVES. WE'RE IN A PUBLIC PLACE.
!
WE'RE SORRY, MISS.
YOU'RE COMPLETELY RIGHT.
HA-HA-HA-HA!
WHAT A SHOW!

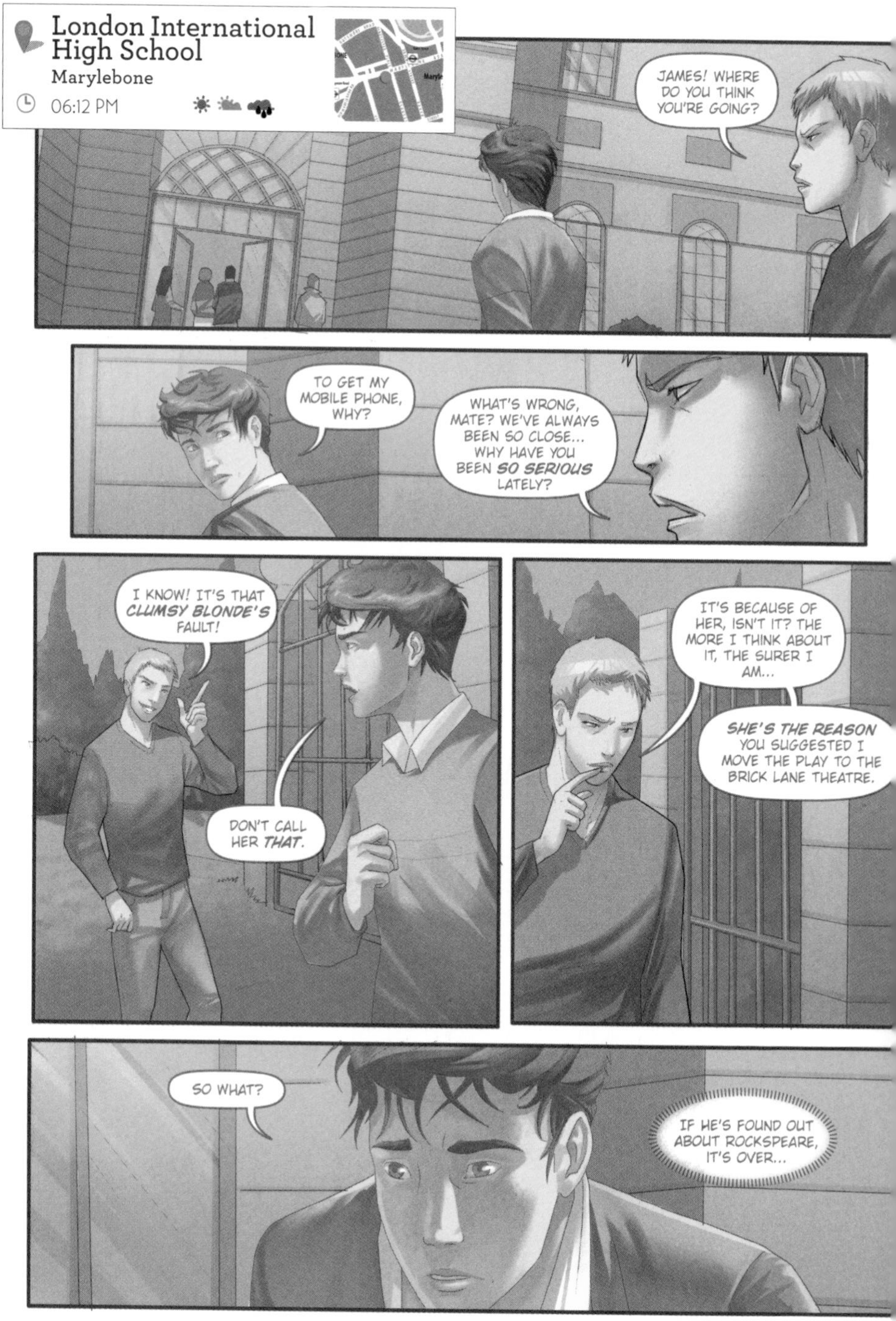
London International High School
Marylebone
06:12 PM
JAMES! WHERE DO YOU THINK YOU'RE GOING?
TO GET MY MOBILE PHONE, WHY?
WHAT'S WRONG, MATE? WE'VE ALWAYS BEEN SO CLOSE... WHY HAVE YOU BEEN SO SERIOUS LATELY?
I KNOW! IT'S THAT CLUMSY BLONDE'S FAULT!
DON'T CALL HER THAT.
IT'S BECAUSE OF HER, ISN'T IT? THE MORE I THINK ABOUT IT, THE SURER I AM...
SHE'S THE REASON YOU SUGGESTED I MOVE THE PLAY TO THE BRICK LANE THEATRE.
SO WHAT?
IF HE'S FOUND OUT ABOUT ROCKSPEARE, IT'S OVER...

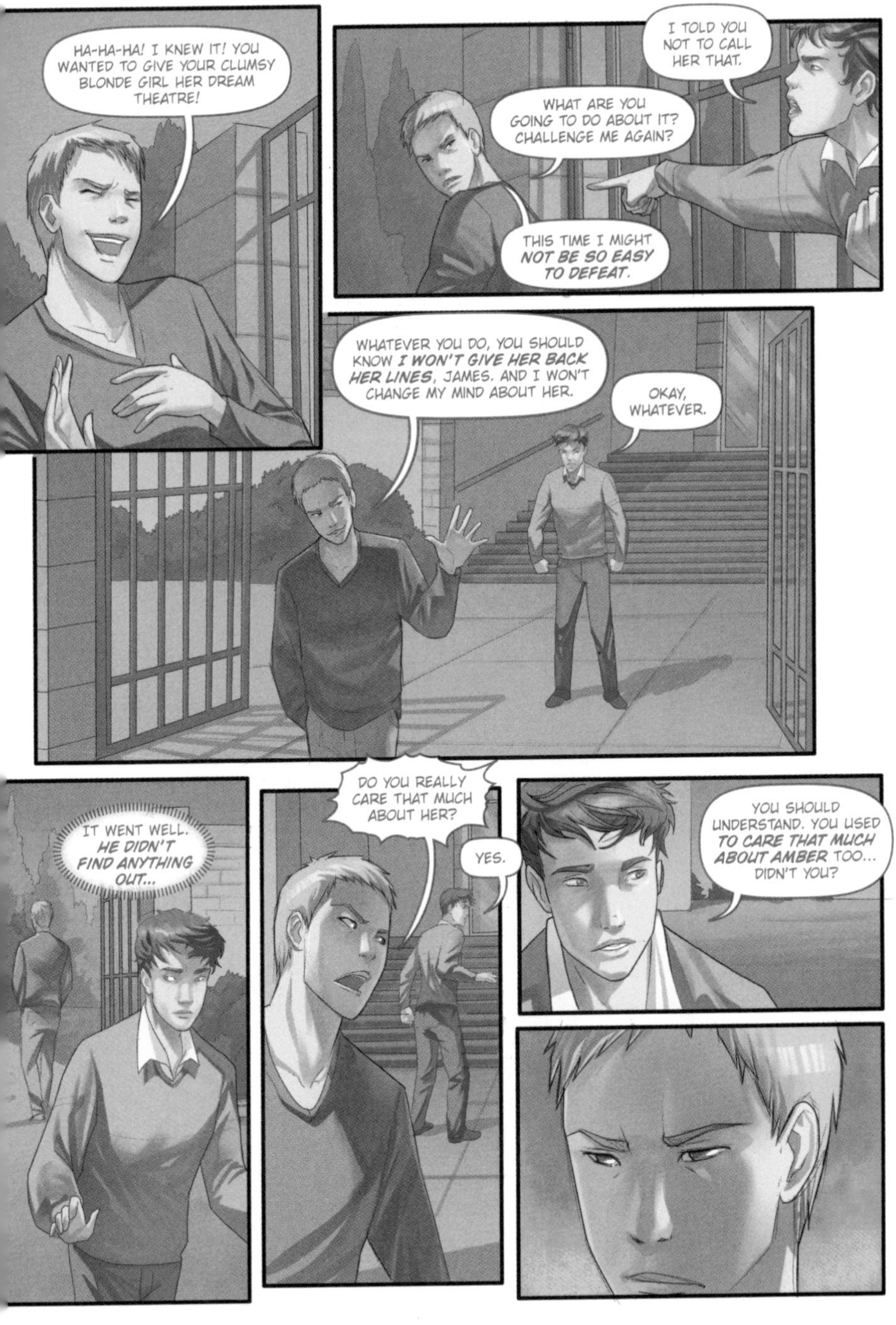
HA-HA-HA! I KNEW IT! YOU WANTED TO GIVE YOUR CLUMSY BLONDE GIRL HER DREAM THEATRE!
I TOLD YOU NOT TO CALL HER THAT.
WHAT ARE YOU GOING TO DO ABOUT IT? CHALLENGE ME AGAIN?
THIS TIME I MIGHT NOT BE SO EASY TO DEFEAT.
WHATEVER YOU DO, YOU SHOULD KNOW I WON'T GIVE HER BACK HER LINES, JAMES. AND I WON'T CHANGE MY MIND ABOUT HER.
OKAY, WHATEVER.
IT WENT WELL. HE DIDN'T FIND ANYTHING OUT...
DO YOU REALLY CARE THAT MUCH ABOUT HER?
YES.
YOU SHOULD UNDERSTAND. YOU USED TO CARE THAT MUCH ABOUT AMBER TOO... DIDN'T YOU?

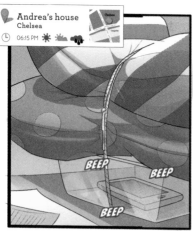

BEEP

BEEP

BEEP

...ELIZABETH I ASCENDED THE THRONE ON NOVEMBER 17 1558, AND WAS CROWNED IN JANUARY 1559...

...THE CONFLICT WITH PHILLIP II OF SPAIN BEGAN IN 1569...

RRRRR

...AT THE SAME TIME, THE FAMOUS NINE YEARS' WAR HAD BEGUN...

RRRRRR

...BOTH SPANISH EXPEDITIONS WERE STOPPED IN SUPPORT OF THE REBELLION.

RRRRRR

...THE FIRST CEASEFIRE WAS PROPOSED IN 1598...

OLÉ.

RRRRRR

...BUT ONCE THE CEASEFIRE EXPIRED, THE ENGLISH WERE DEFEATED AT THE BATTLE OF...

RRR

RRR

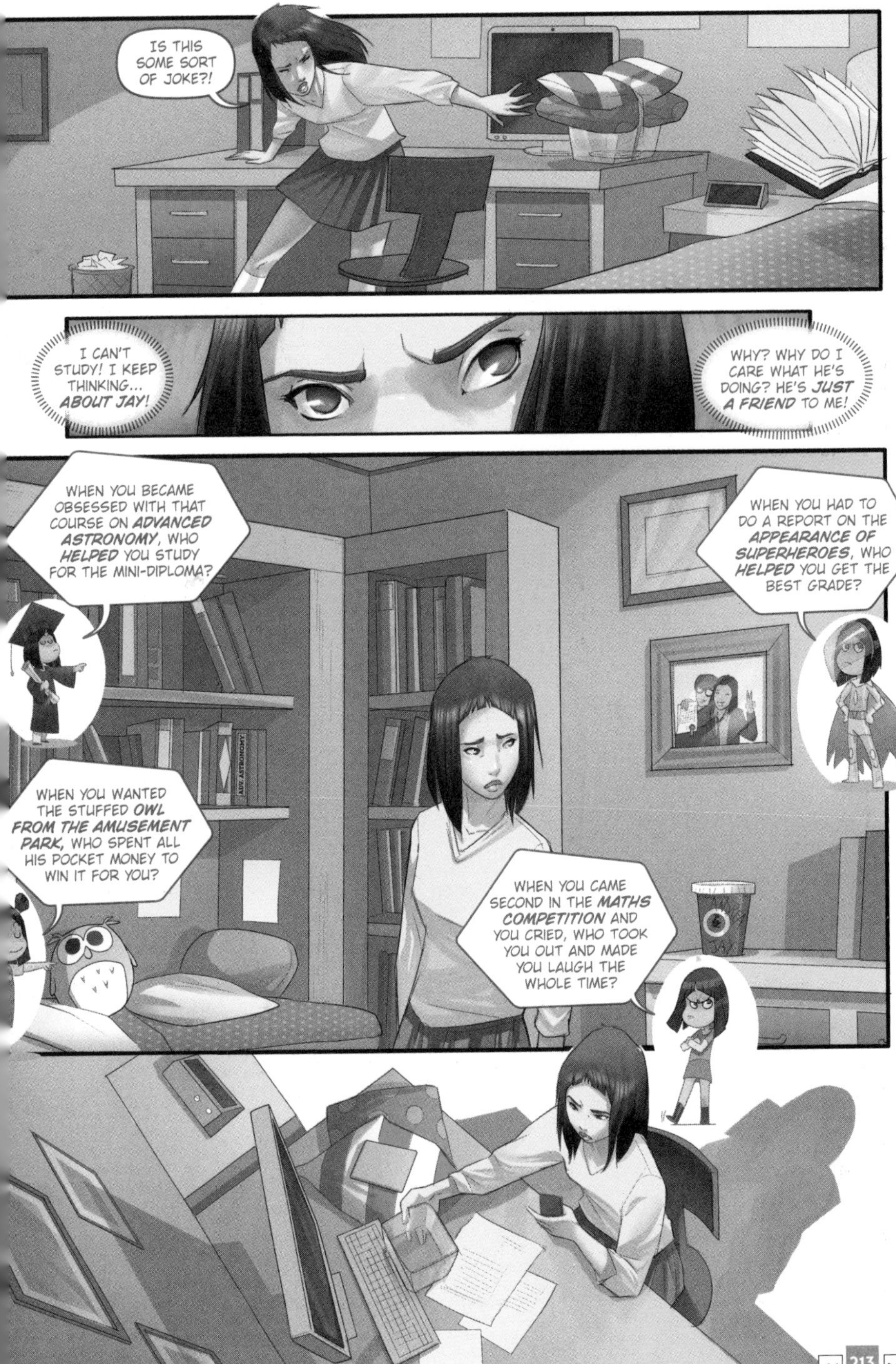
IS THIS SOME SORT OF JOKE?!
I CAN'T STUDY! I KEEP THINKING... ABOUT JAY!
WHY? WHY DO I CARE WHAT HE'S DOING? HE'S JUST A FRIEND TO ME!
WHEN YOU BECAME OBSESSED WITH THAT COURSE ON ADVANCED ASTRONOMY, WHO HELPED YOU STUDY FOR THE MINI-DIPLOMA?
WHEN YOU HAD TO DO A REPORT ON THE APPEARANCE OF SUPERHEROES, WHO HELPED YOU GET THE BEST GRADE?
WHEN YOU WANTED THE STUFFED OWL FROM THE AMUSEMENT PARK, WHO SPENT ALL HIS POCKET MONEY TO WIN IT FOR YOU?
WHEN YOU CAME SECOND IN THE MATHS COMPETITION AND YOU CRIED, WHO TOOK YOU OUT AND MADE YOU LAUGH THE WHOLE TIME?
ADV. ASTRONOMY

James's house
06:33 PM

06:53 PM
JAMES COLLINS
Hi! I'm at home now... :)

06:33 PM
ALICE KEATS
I was just talking about you with my grandma!

06:34 PM
JAMES
Oh, no! did you

06:34 PM
ALICE KEATS
Not telling you!

06:34 PM
JAMES COLLINS
Well, I talked about you with Edward...

06:35 PM
ALICE KEATS
Ok, I don't want to know anything! :D

06:36 PM
ALICE KEATS
I have to ask you some

06:36 PM
JAMES COLLINS
Fire away, Keats. I'm ready.

06:37 PM
ALICE KEATS
The Real Life status says... the one that says we're in a relationship... now it's not needed to get a rise out of Edward anymore...

06:37 PM
JAMES COLLINS
You want me to take it down?

06:38 PM
ALICE K
Do you?

06:38 PM
JAMES CO
I asked you fi

06:39 PM
ALICE KEATS
I don't, but... if we leave it... well, you know, right?

06:40 PM
JAMES COLLINS
It means we're really together.

06:41 PM
JAMES COLL
So? Are we toge or not, Alice?

<< **214** >>

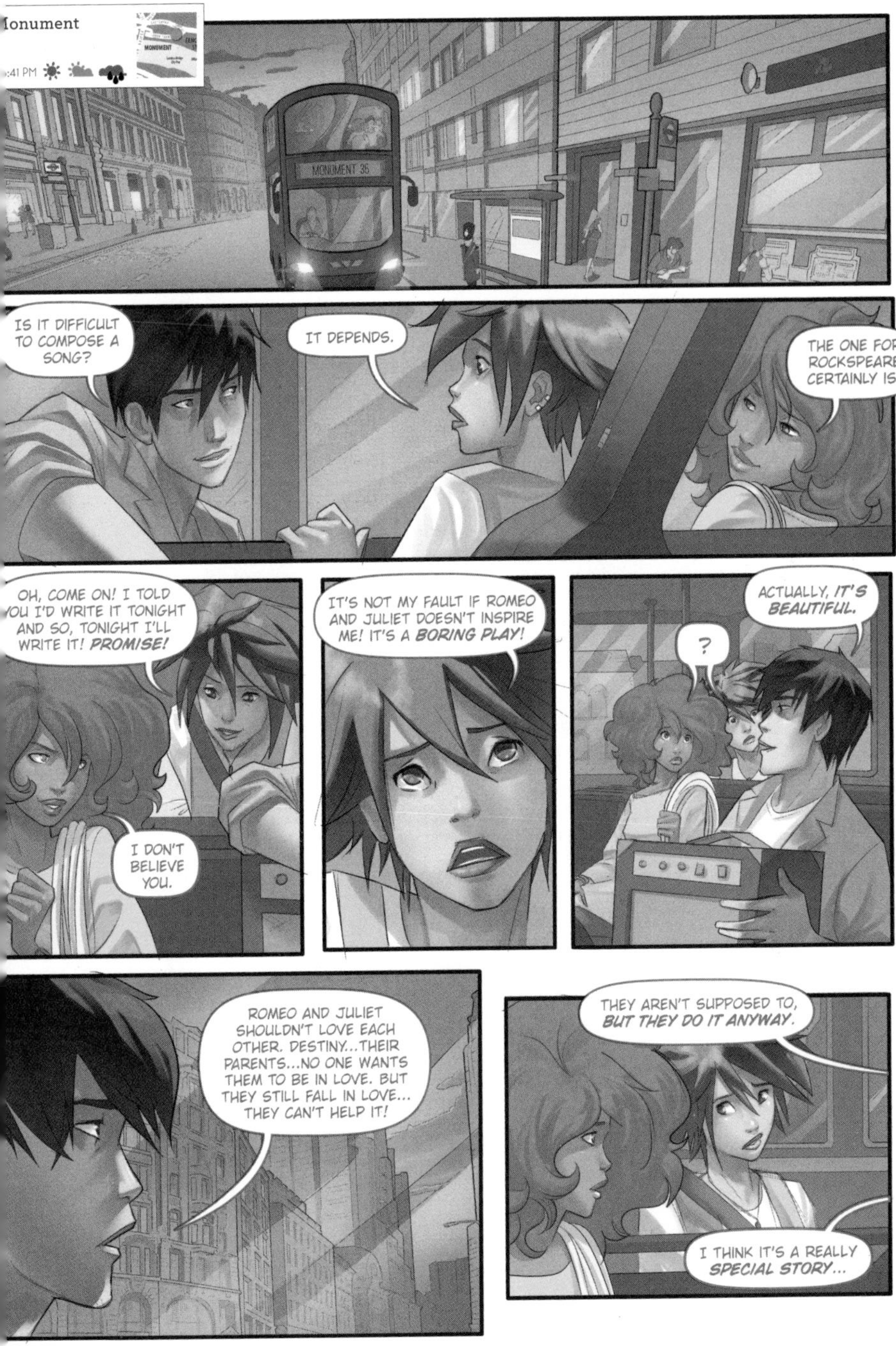
Monument
:41 PM
MONUMENT 35
IS IT DIFFICULT TO COMPOSE A SONG?
IT DEPENDS.
THE ONE FOR ROCKSPEARE CERTAINLY IS!
OH, COME ON! I TOLD YOU I'D WRITE IT TONIGHT AND SO, TONIGHT I'LL WRITE IT! PROMISE!
I DON'T BELIEVE YOU.
IT'S NOT MY FAULT IF ROMEO AND JULIET DOESN'T INSPIRE ME! IT'S A BORING PLAY!
ACTUALLY, IT'S BEAUTIFUL.
?
ROMEO AND JULIET SHOULDN'T LOVE EACH OTHER. DESTINY...THEIR PARENTS...NO ONE WANTS THEM TO BE IN LOVE. BUT THEY STILL FALL IN LOVE... THEY CAN'T HELP IT!
THEY AREN'T SUPPOSED TO, BUT THEY DO IT ANYWAY.
I THINK IT'S A REALLY SPECIAL STORY...

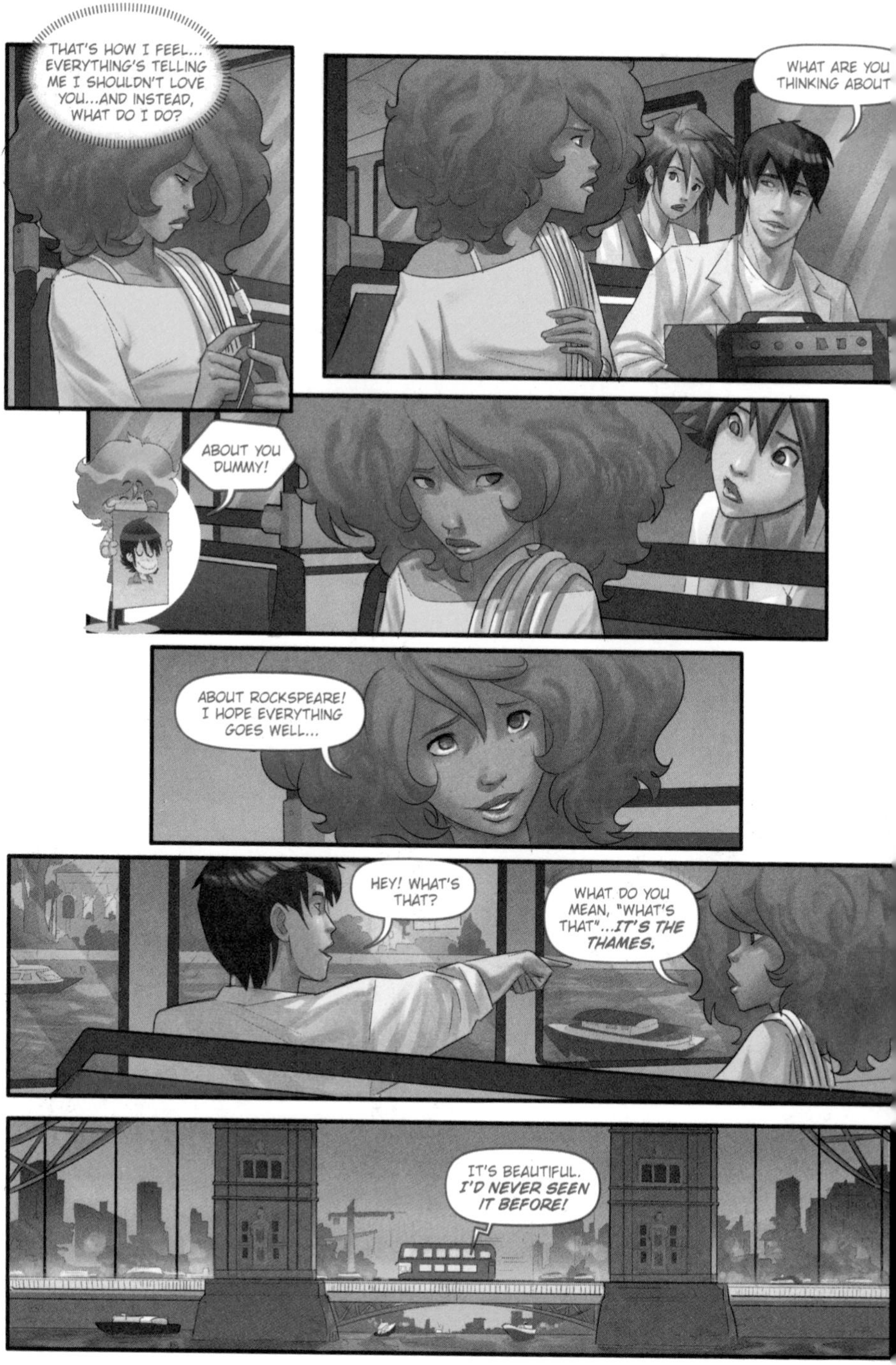
THAT'S HOW I FEEL... EVERYTHING'S TELLING ME I SHOULDN'T LOVE YOU...AND INSTEAD, WHAT DO I DO?
WHAT ARE YOU THINKING ABOUT
ABOUT YOU DUMMY!
ABOUT ROCKSPEARE! I HOPE EVERYTHING GOES WELL...
HEY! WHAT'S THAT?
WHAT DO YOU MEAN, "WHAT'S THAT"...IT'S THE THAMES.
IT'S BEAUTIFUL. I'D NEVER SEEN IT BEFORE!

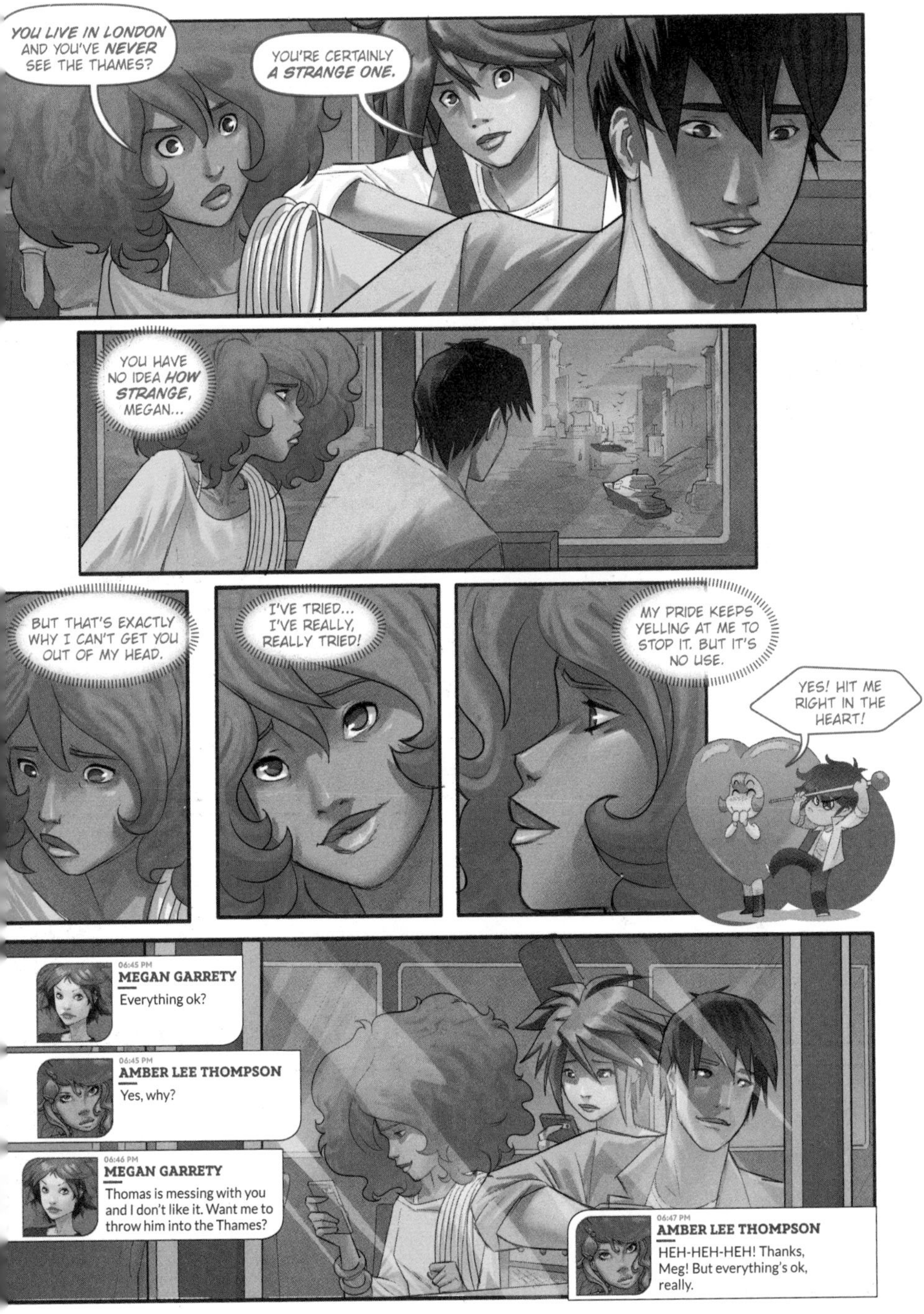

YOU LIVE IN LONDON AND YOU'VE NEVER SEE THE THAMES?
YOU'RE CERTAINLY A STRANGE ONE.
YOU HAVE NO IDEA HOW STRANGE, MEGAN...
BUT THAT'S EXACTLY WHY I CAN'T GET YOU OUT OF MY HEAD.
I'VE TRIED... I'VE REALLY, REALLY TRIED!
MY PRIDE KEEPS YELLING AT ME TO STOP IT. BUT IT'S NO USE.
YES! HIT ME RIGHT IN THE HEART!
06:45 PM
MEGAN GARRETY
Everything ok?
06:45 PM
AMBER LEE THOMPSON
Yes, why?
06:46 PM
MEGAN GARRETY
Thomas is messing with you and I don't like it. Want me to throw him into the Thames?
06:47 PM
AMBER LEE THOMPSON
HEH-HEH-HEH! Thanks, Meg! But everything's ok, really.

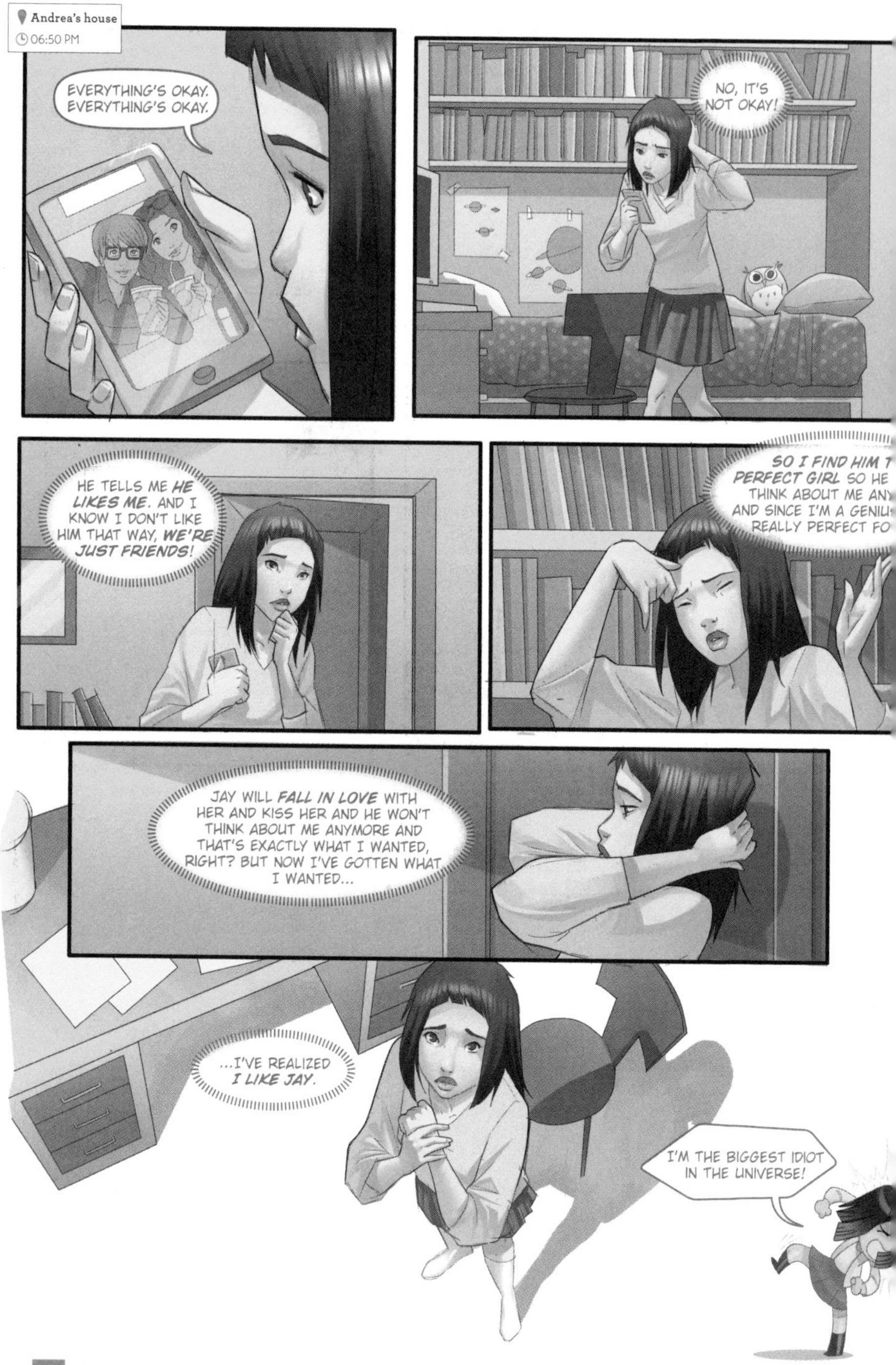
Andrea's house
06:50 PM
EVERYTHING'S OKAY. EVERYTHING'S OKAY.
NO, IT'S NOT OKAY!
HE TELLS ME HE LIKES ME. AND I KNOW I DON'T LIKE HIM THAT WAY, WE'RE JUST FRIENDS!
SO I FIND HIM PERFECT GIRL SO HE THINK ABOUT ME AND SINCE I'M A REALLY PERFECT
JAY WILL FALL IN LOVE WITH HER AND KISS HER AND HE WON'T THINK ABOUT ME ANYMORE AND THAT'S EXACTLY WHAT I WANTED, RIGHT? BUT NOW I'VE GOTTEN WHAT I WANTED...
...I'VE REALIZED I LIKE JAY.
I'M THE BIGGEST IDIOT IN THE UNIVERSE!

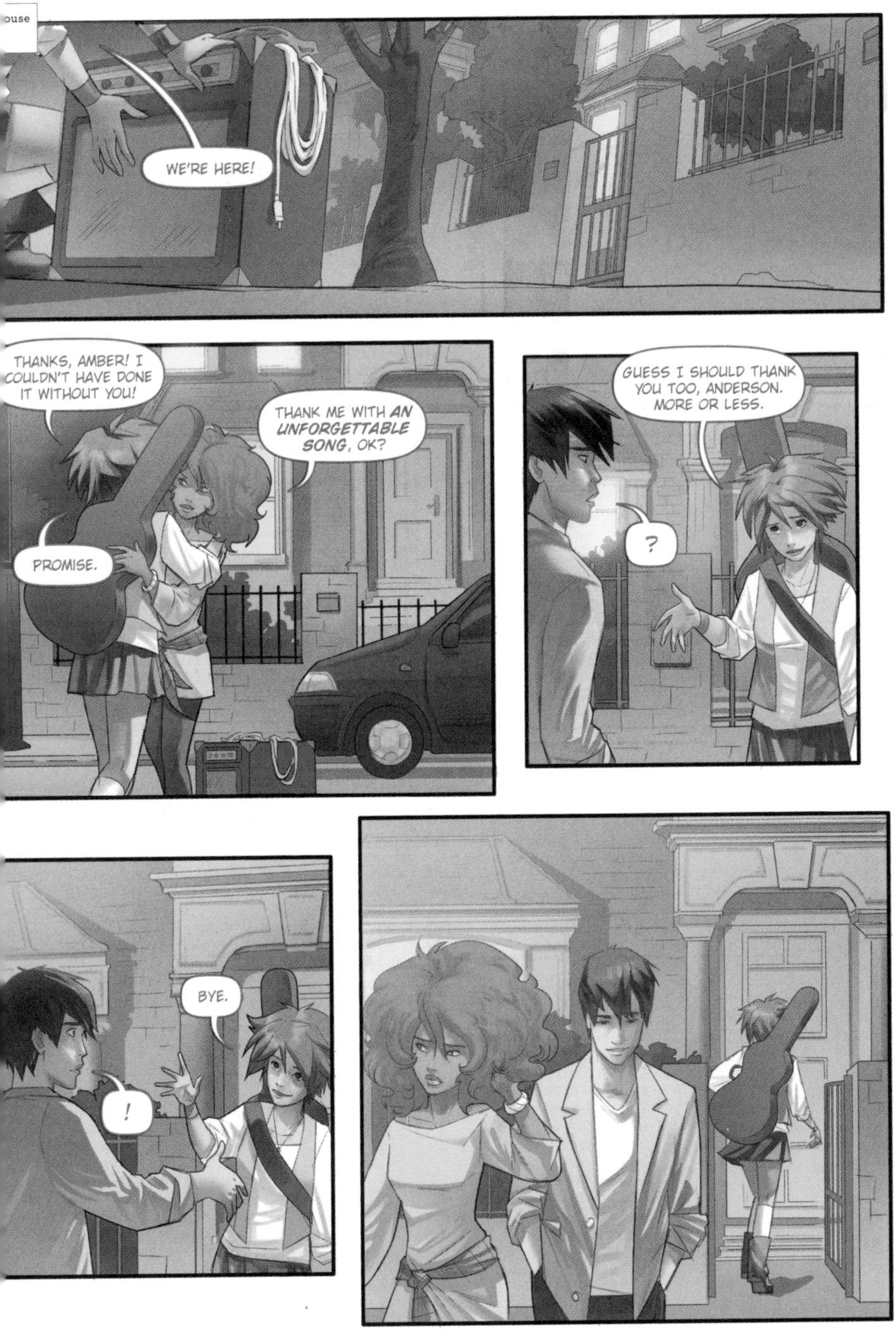
WE'RE HERE!
THANKS, AMBER! I COULDN'T HAVE DONE IT WITHOUT YOU!
THANK ME WITH **AN UNFORGETTABLE SONG**, OK?
PROMISE.
GUESS I SHOULD THANK YOU TOO, ANDERSON. MORE OR LESS.
?
BYE.
!

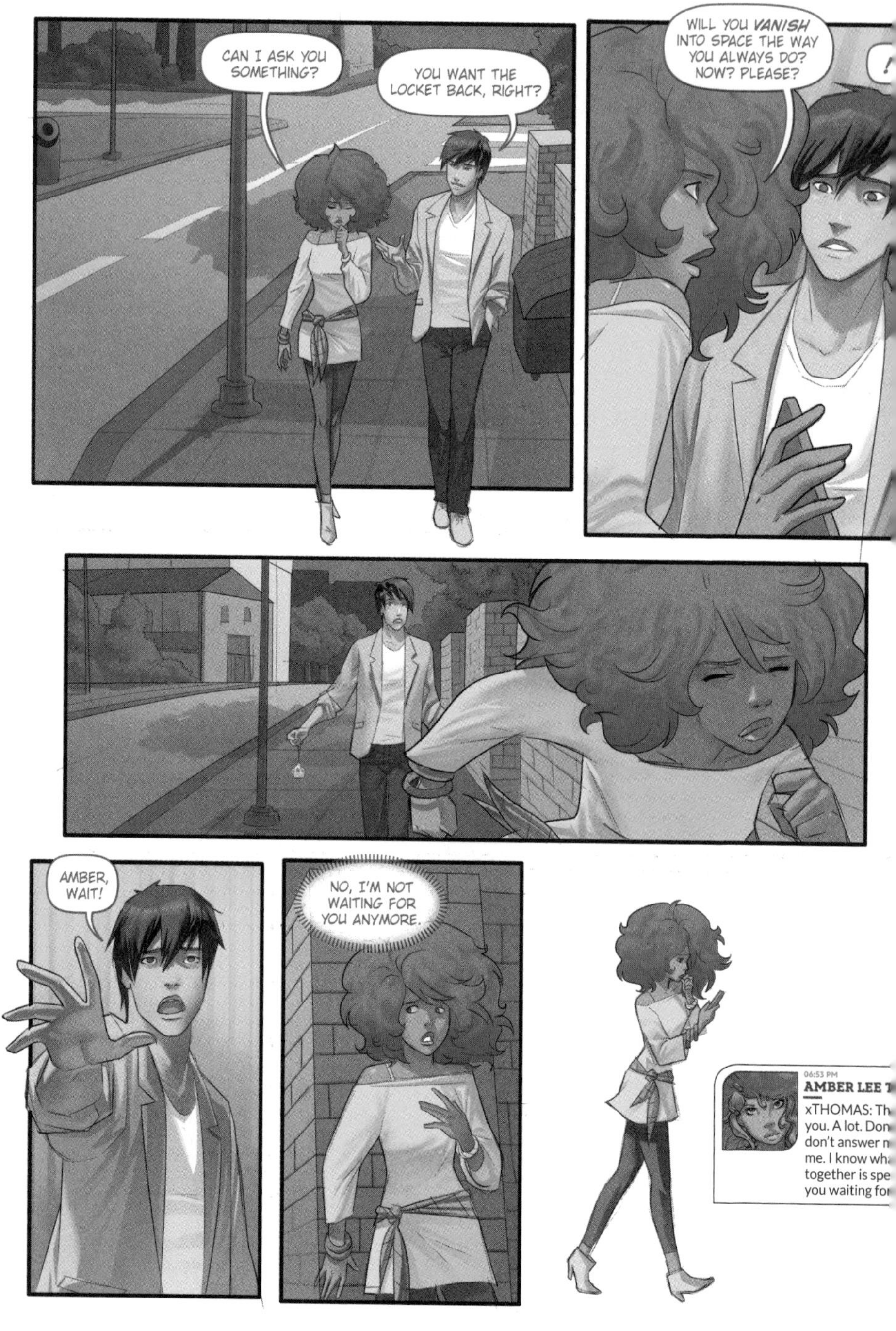
CAN I ASK YOU SOMETHING?
YOU WANT THE LOCKET BACK, RIGHT?
WILL YOU VANISH INTO SPACE THE WAY YOU ALWAYS DO? NOW? PLEASE?
!
AMBER, WAIT!
NO, I'M NOT WAITING FOR YOU ANYMORE.
06:53 PM
AMBER LEE
xTHOMAS: Th
you. A lot. Don
don't answer m
me. I know wh
together is spe
you waiting fo

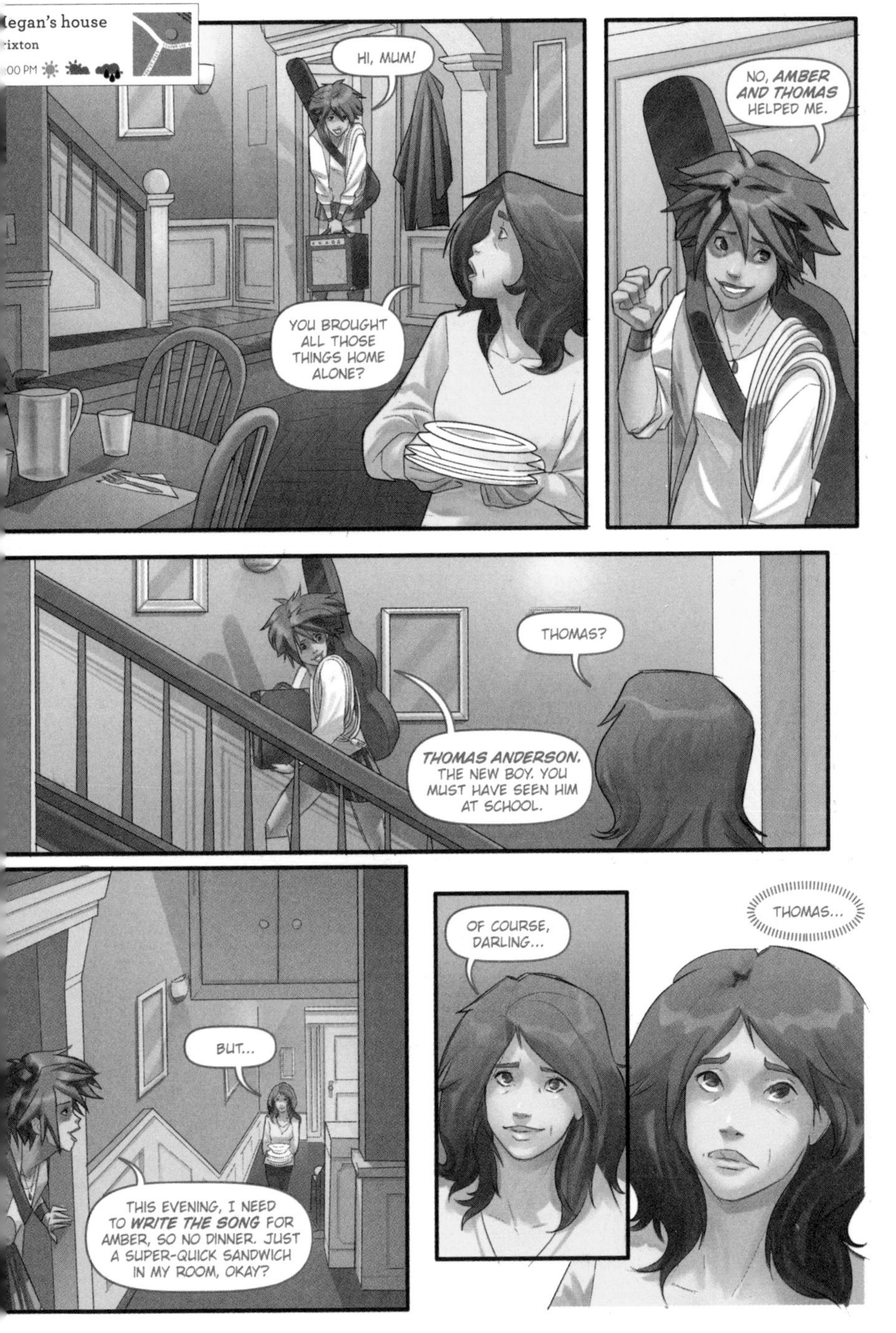
HI, MUM!
YOU BROUGHT ALL THOSE THINGS HOME ALONE?
NO, **AMBER AND THOMAS** HELPED ME.
THOMAS?
THOMAS ANDERSON. THE NEW BOY. YOU MUST HAVE SEEN HIM AT SCHOOL.
BUT...
THIS EVENING, I NEED TO ***WRITE THE SONG*** FOR AMBER, SO NO DINNER. JUST A SUPER-QUICK SANDWICH IN MY ROOM, OKAY?
OF COURSE, DARLING...
THOMAS...

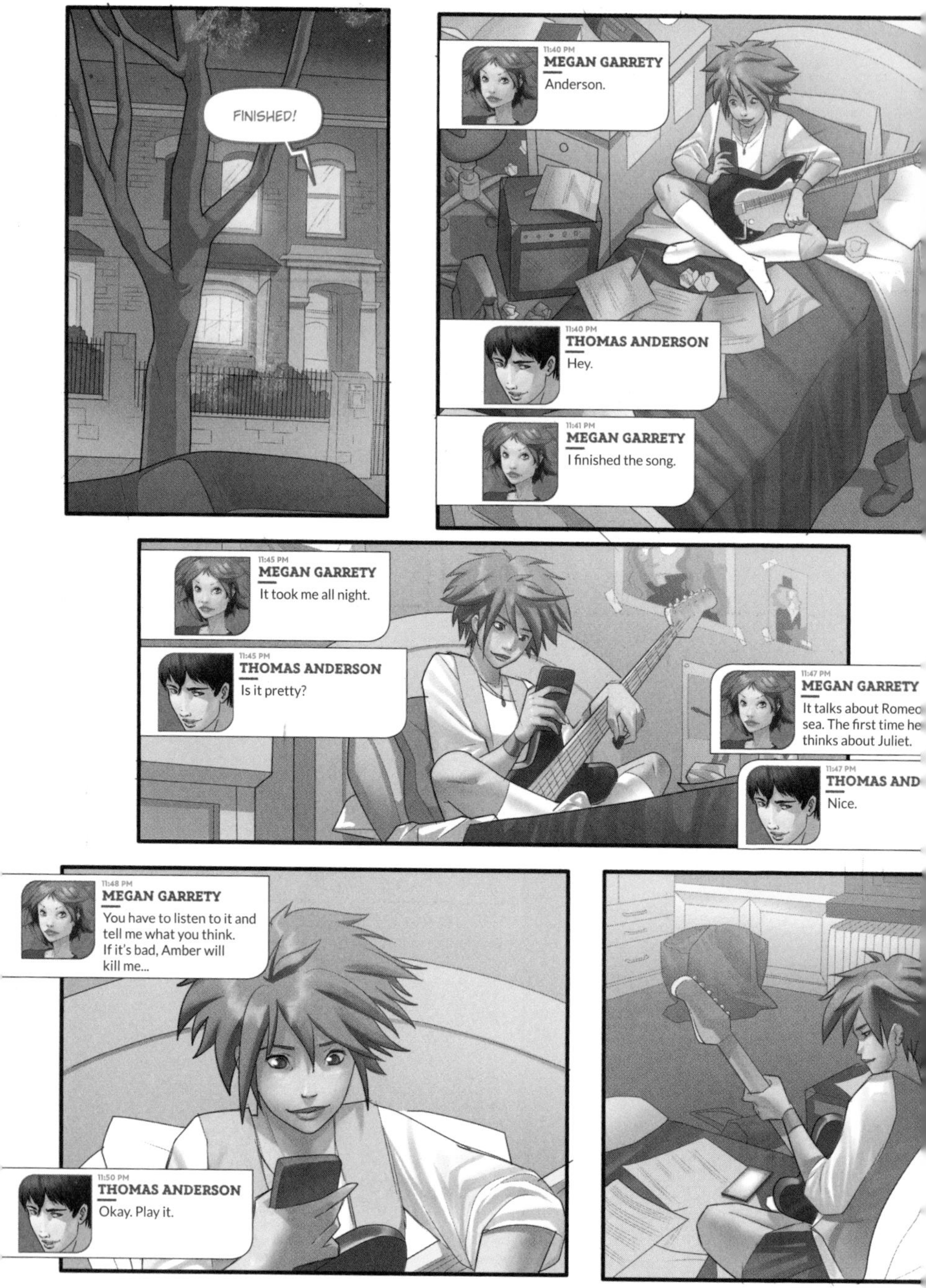

FINISHED!
11:40 PM
MEGAN GARRETY
Anderson.
11:40 PM
THOMAS ANDERSON
Hey.
11:41 PM
MEGAN GARRETY
I finished the song.
11:45 PM
MEGAN GARRETY
It took me all night.
11:45 PM
THOMAS ANDERSON
Is it pretty?
11:47 PM
MEGAN GARRETY
It talks about Romeo
sea. The first time he
thinks about Juliet.
11:47 PM
THOMAS AND
Nice.
11:48 PM
MEGAN GARRETY
You have to listen to it and
tell me what you think.
If it's bad, Amber will
kill me...
11:50 PM
THOMAS ANDERSON
Okay. Play it.

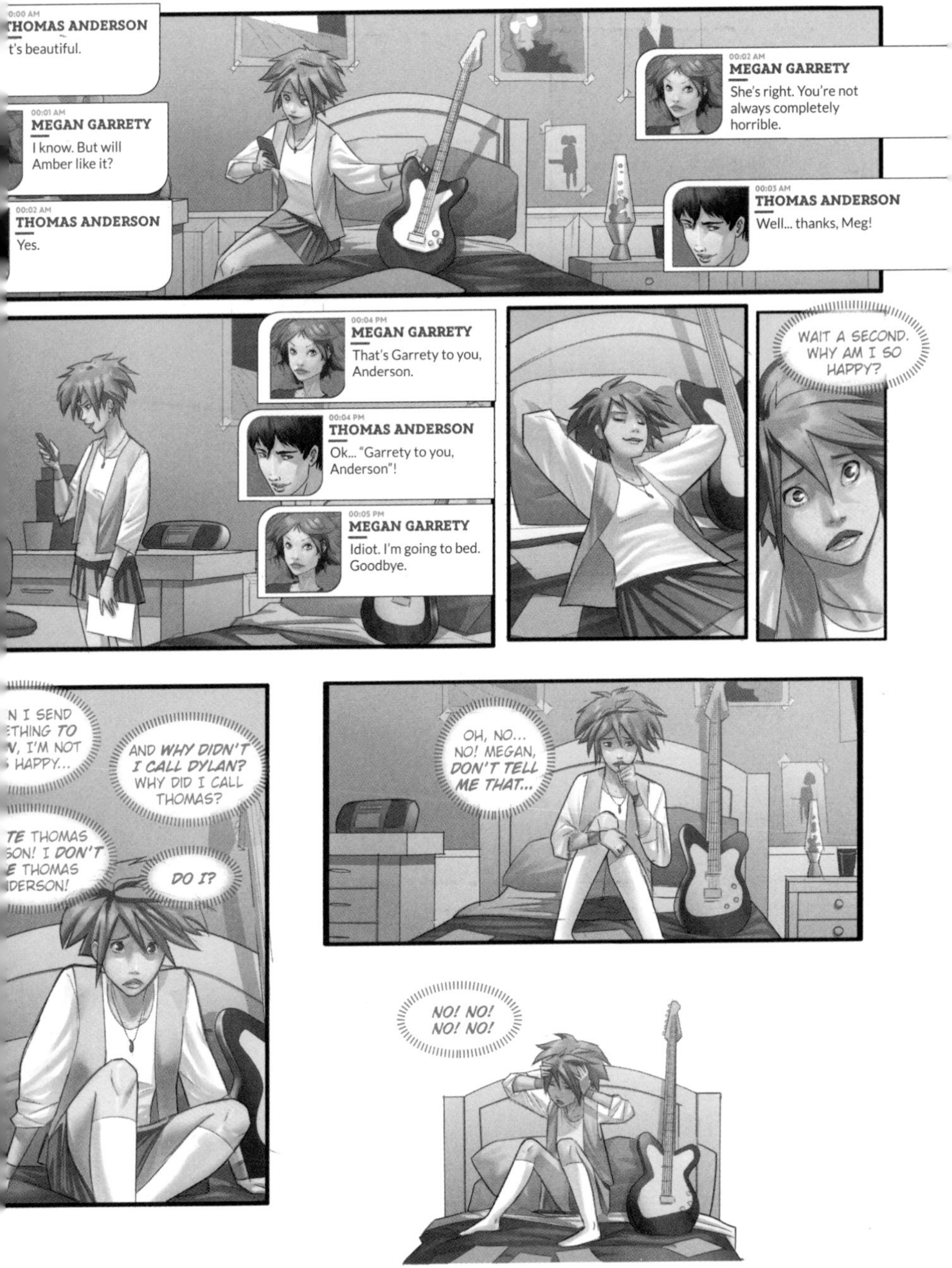

0:00 AM
THOMAS ANDERSON
t's beautiful.
00:01 AM
MEGAN GARRETY
I know. But will Amber like it?
00:02 AM
THOMAS ANDERSON
Yes.
00:02 AM
MEGAN GARRETY
She's right. You're not always completely horrible.
00:03 AM
THOMAS ANDERSON
Well... thanks, Meg!
00:04 PM
MEGAN GARRETY
That's Garrety to you, Anderson.
00:04 PM
THOMAS ANDERSON
Ok... "Garrety to you, Anderson"!
00:05 PM
MEGAN GARRETY
Idiot. I'm going to bed. Goodbye.
WAIT A SECOND. WHY AM I SO HAPPY?
N I SEND ETHING TO V, I'M NOT S HAPPY...
AND WHY DIDN'T I CALL DYLAN? WHY DID I CALL THOMAS?
TE THOMAS SON! I DON'T E THOMAS DERSON!
DO I?
OH, NO... NO! MEGAN, DON'T TELL ME THAT...
NO! NO! NO! NO!

END OF CHAPTER 30

#This Song for You

Plot: Alessandro Ferrari
Script: Chantal Pericoli
Layout: Emilio Urbano, Monica Catalano
Cleanup: Arianna Robustelli, Egoduo,
Romina Moranelli, Luigi Aimè
Emotidolls: Andrea Scoppetta
Color: Arancia Studio e Pierluigi
Casolino, Mario Perrotta, Massimo Rocca,
Francesca Mengozzi, Giovanni Marcora,
Antonia Angrisani e Cristina Toniolo.
Watercolor backgrounds: Valeria Turati
Translation: Edizioni BD and Erin Brady
Lettering and Infographic: Edizioni BD

COVER
Layout and cleanup: Alberto Zanon
Color: Slava Panarin

CONTRIBUTORS
Tomatofarm

Original project developed by Disney
Publishing with the contribution of Bar
Baraldi, Paola Barbato, Micol Beltramin
and Diana Tomatozombie

#11

#Our Tune

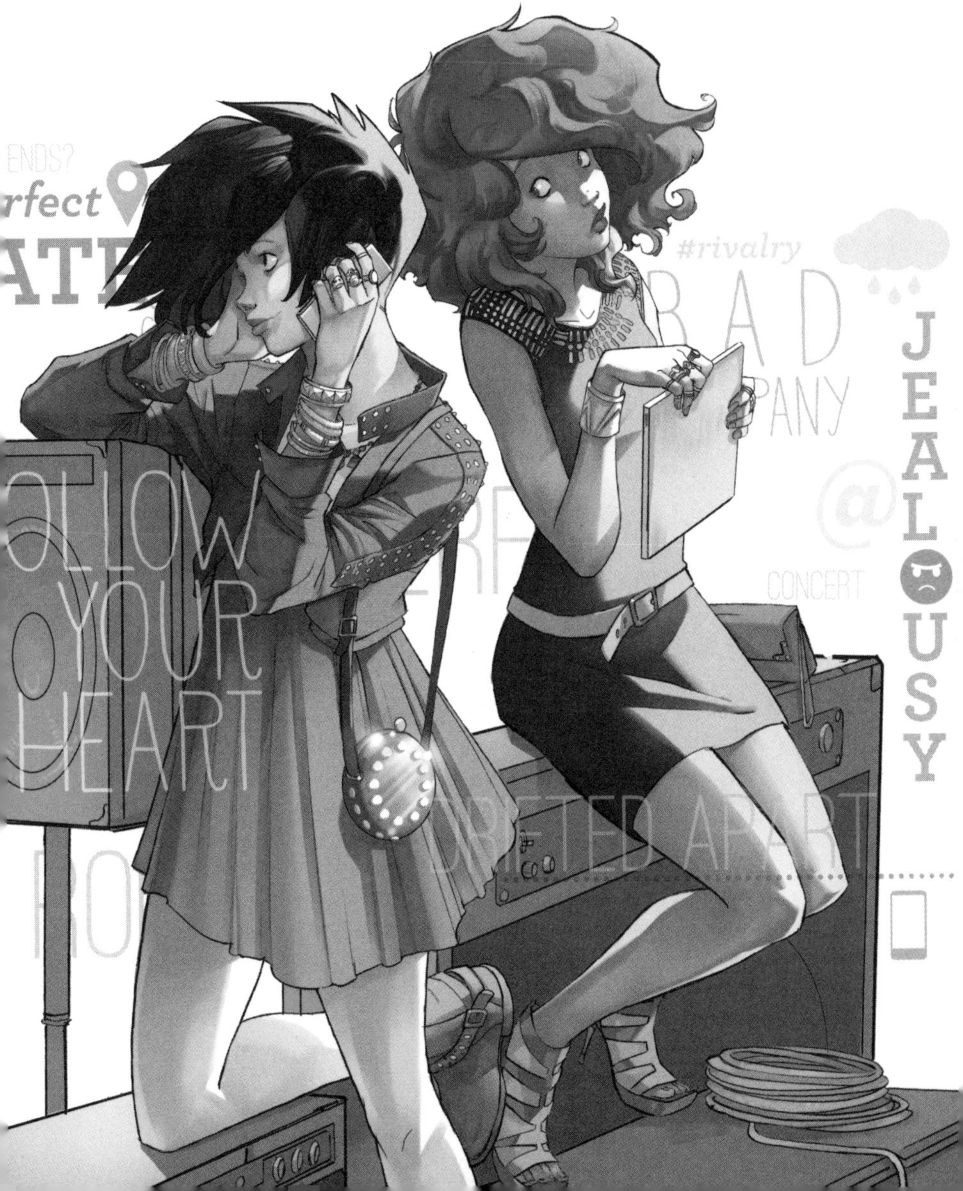
ENDS?
rfect
#rivalry
BAD
PANY
CONCERT
JEALOUSY
OLLOW
YOUR
HEART

CHAPTER 31

Time to CHOOSE

Alice's house
Notting Hill
05:45 PM

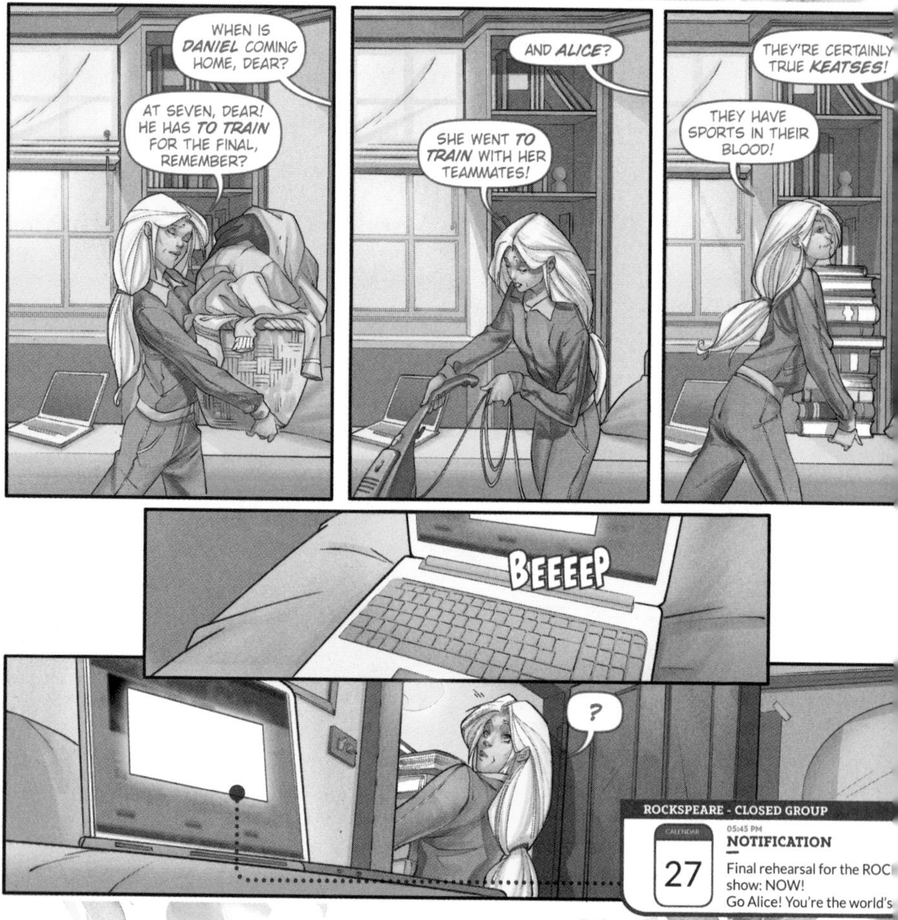

WHEN IS DANIEL COMING HOME, DEAR?
AT SEVEN, DEAR! HE HAS TO TRAIN FOR THE FINAL, REMEMBER?
AND ALICE?
SHE WENT TO TRAIN WITH HER TEAMMATES!
THEY'RE CERTAINLY TRUE KEATSES!
THEY HAVE SPORTS IN THEIR BLOOD!
BEEEEP
?
ROCKSPEARE - CLOSED GROUP
05:45 PM
NOTIFICATION
27
Final rehearsal for the
show: NOW!
Go Alice! You're the world's

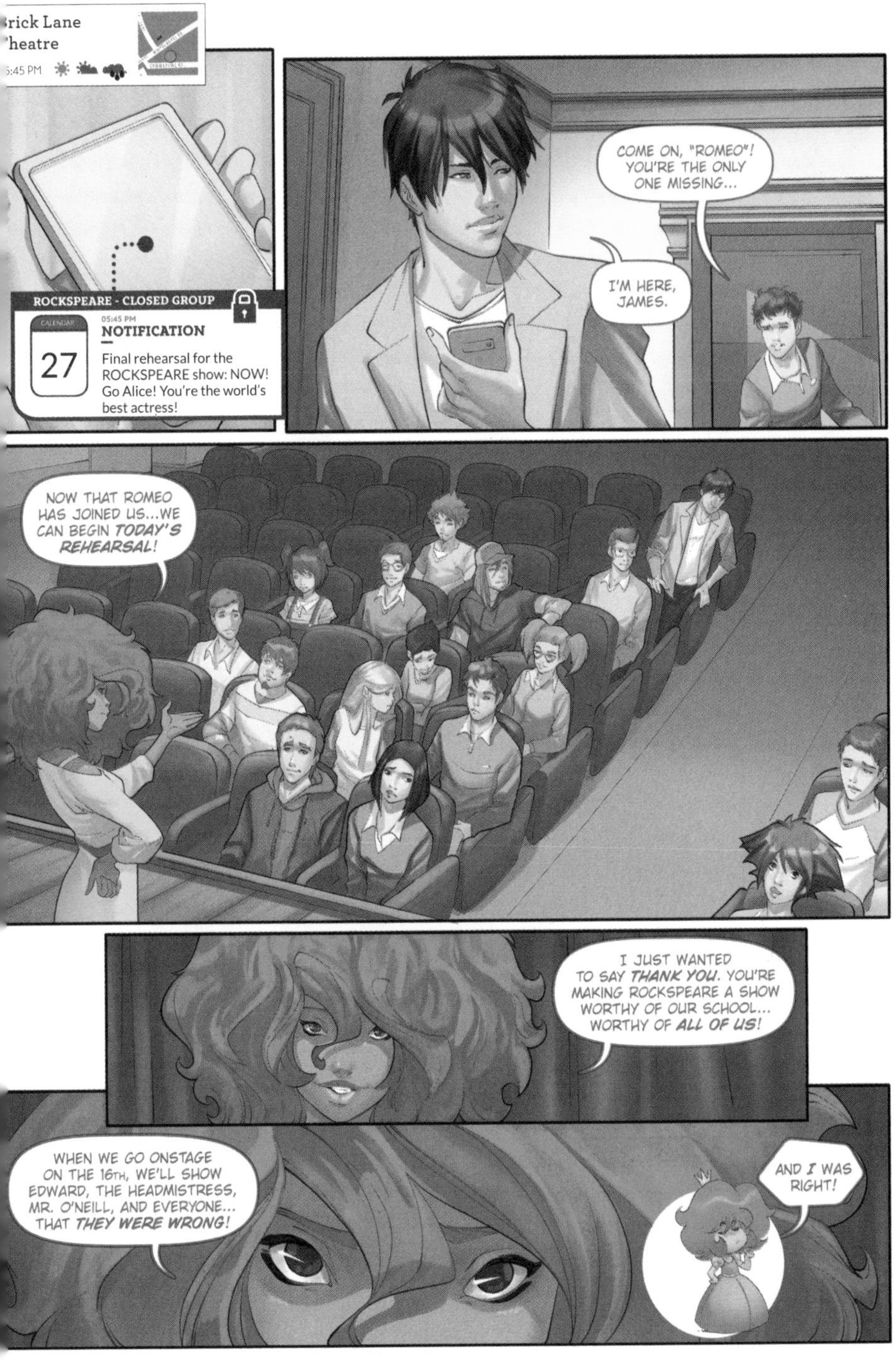
Brick Lane
Theatre
5:45 PM
ROCKSPEARE - CLOSED GROUP
CALENDAR
27
05:45 PM
NOTIFICATION
Final rehearsal for the ROCKSPEARE show: NOW! Go Alice! You're the world's best actress!
COME ON, "ROMEO"! YOU'RE THE ONLY ONE MISSING...
I'M HERE, JAMES.
NOW THAT ROMEO HAS JOINED US...WE CAN BEGIN TODAY'S REHEARSAL!
I JUST WANTED TO SAY THANK YOU. YOU'RE MAKING ROCKSPEARE A SHOW WORTHY OF OUR SCHOOL... WORTHY OF ALL OF US!
WHEN WE GO ONSTAGE ON THE 16TH, WE'LL SHOW EDWARD, THE HEADMISTRESS, MR. O'NEILL, AND EVERYONE... THAT THEY WERE WRONG!
AND I WAS RIGHT!

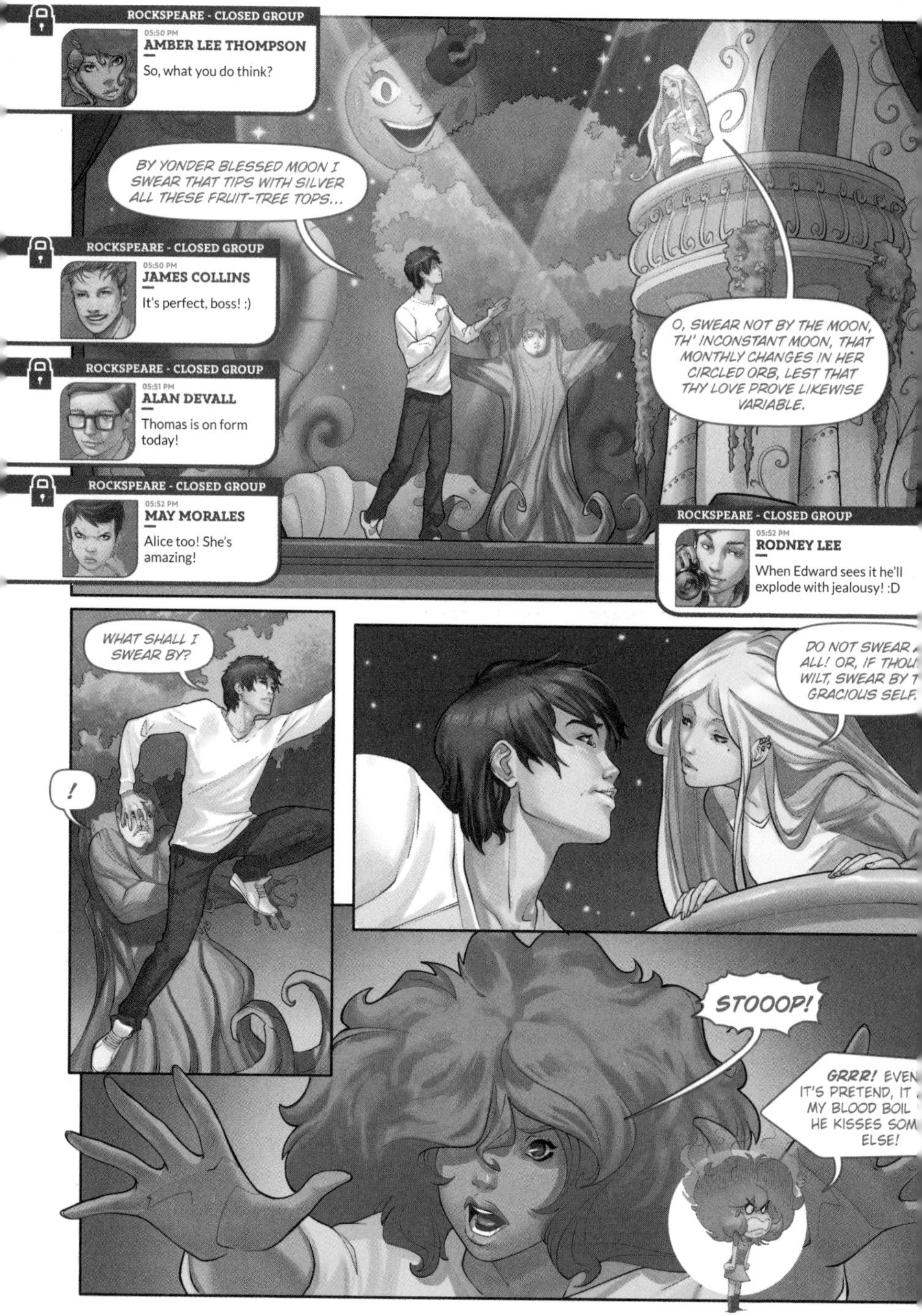
ROCKSPEARE - CLOSED GROUP
05:50 PM
AMBER LEE THOMPSON
So, what you do think?
BY YONDER BLESSED MOON I SWEAR THAT TIPS WITH SILVER ALL THESE FRUIT-TREE TOPS...
ROCKSPEARE - CLOSED GROUP
05:50 PM
JAMES COLLINS
It's perfect, boss! :)
O, SWEAR NOT BY THE MOON, TH' INCONSTANT MOON, THAT MONTHLY CHANGES IN HER CIRCLED ORB, LEST THAT THY LOVE PROVE LIKEWISE VARIABLE.
ROCKSPEARE - CLOSED GROUP
05:51 PM
ALAN DEVALL
Thomas is on form today!
ROCKSPEARE - CLOSED GROUP
05:52 PM
MAY MORALES
Alice too! She's amazing!
ROCKSPEARE - CLOSED GROUP
05:52 PM
RODNEY LEE
When Edward sees it he'll explode with jealousy! :D
WHAT SHALL I SWEAR BY?
!
STOOOP!

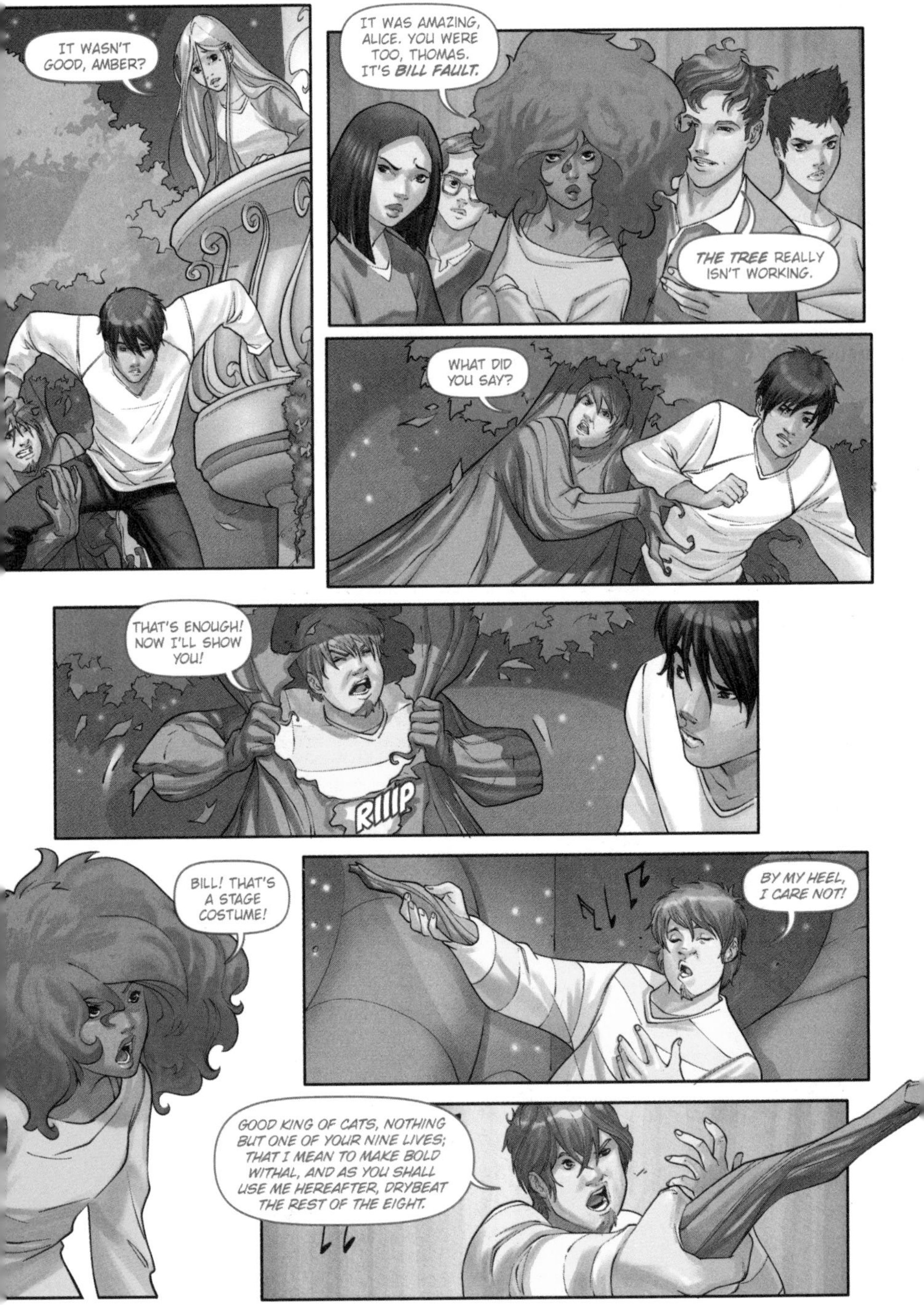
IT WASN'T GOOD, AMBER?
IT WAS AMAZING, ALICE. YOU WERE TOO, THOMAS. IT'S BILL FAULT.
THE TREE REALLY ISN'T WORKING.
WHAT DID YOU SAY?
THAT'S ENOUGH! NOW I'LL SHOW YOU!
RIIIP
BILL! THAT'S A STAGE COSTUME!
BY MY HEEL, I CARE NOT!
GOOD KING OF CATS, NOTHING BUT ONE OF YOUR NINE LIVES; THAT I MEAN TO MAKE BOLD WITHAL, AND AS YOU SHALL USE ME HEREAFTER, DRYBEAT THE REST OF THE EIGHT.

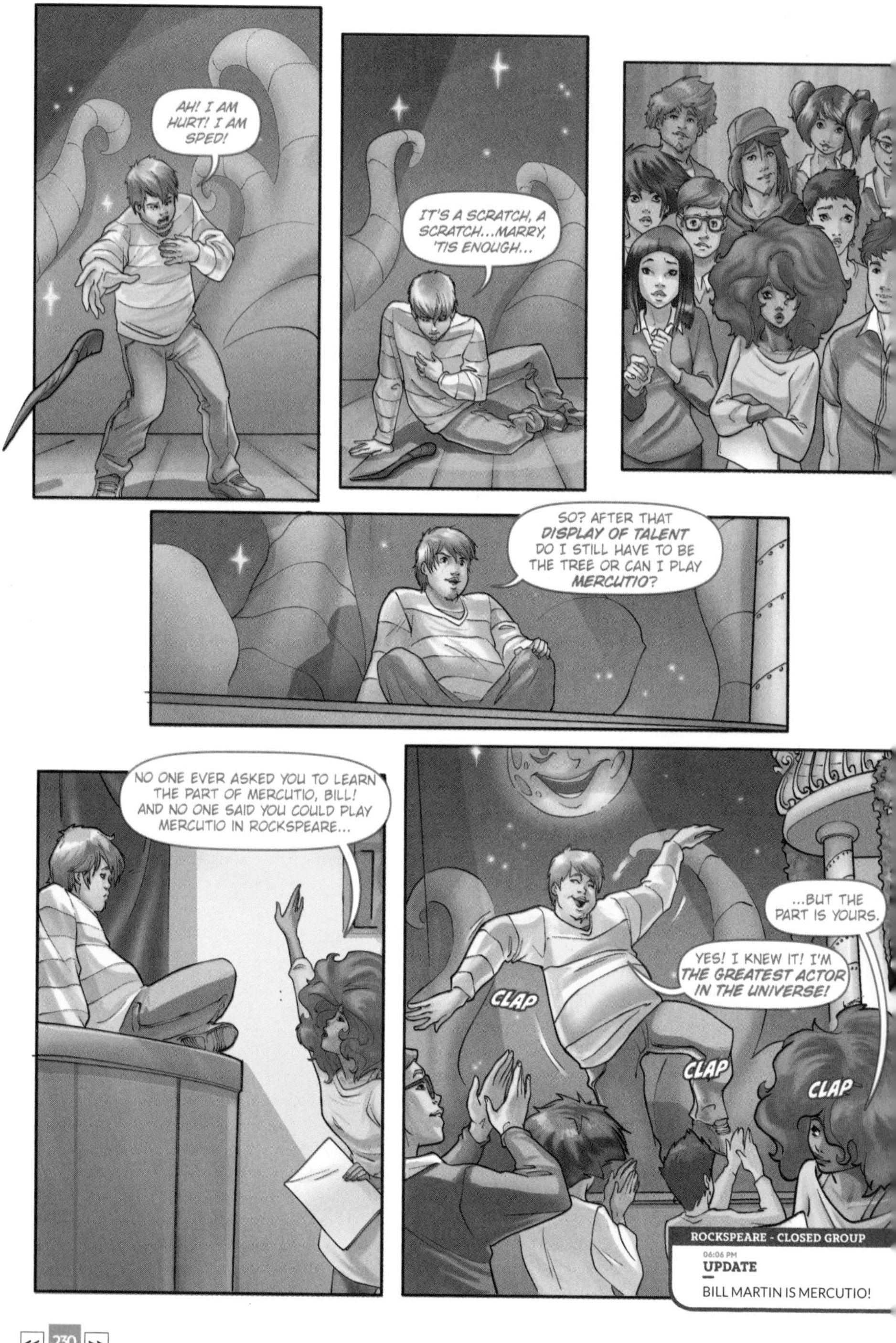
AH! I AM HURT! I AM SPED!
IT'S A SCRATCH, A SCRATCH...MARRY, 'TIS ENOUGH...
SO? AFTER THAT DISPLAY OF TALENT DO I STILL HAVE TO BE THE TREE OR CAN I PLAY MERCUTIO?
NO ONE EVER ASKED YOU TO LEARN THE PART OF MERCUTIO, BILL! AND NO ONE SAID YOU COULD PLAY MERCUTIO IN ROCKSPEARE...
...BUT THE PART IS YOURS.
YES! I KNEW IT! I'M THE GREATEST ACTOR IN THE UNIVERSE!
CLAP
CLAP
CLAP
ROCKSPEARE - CLOSED GROUP
06:06 PM
UPDATE
BILL MARTIN IS MERCUTIO!

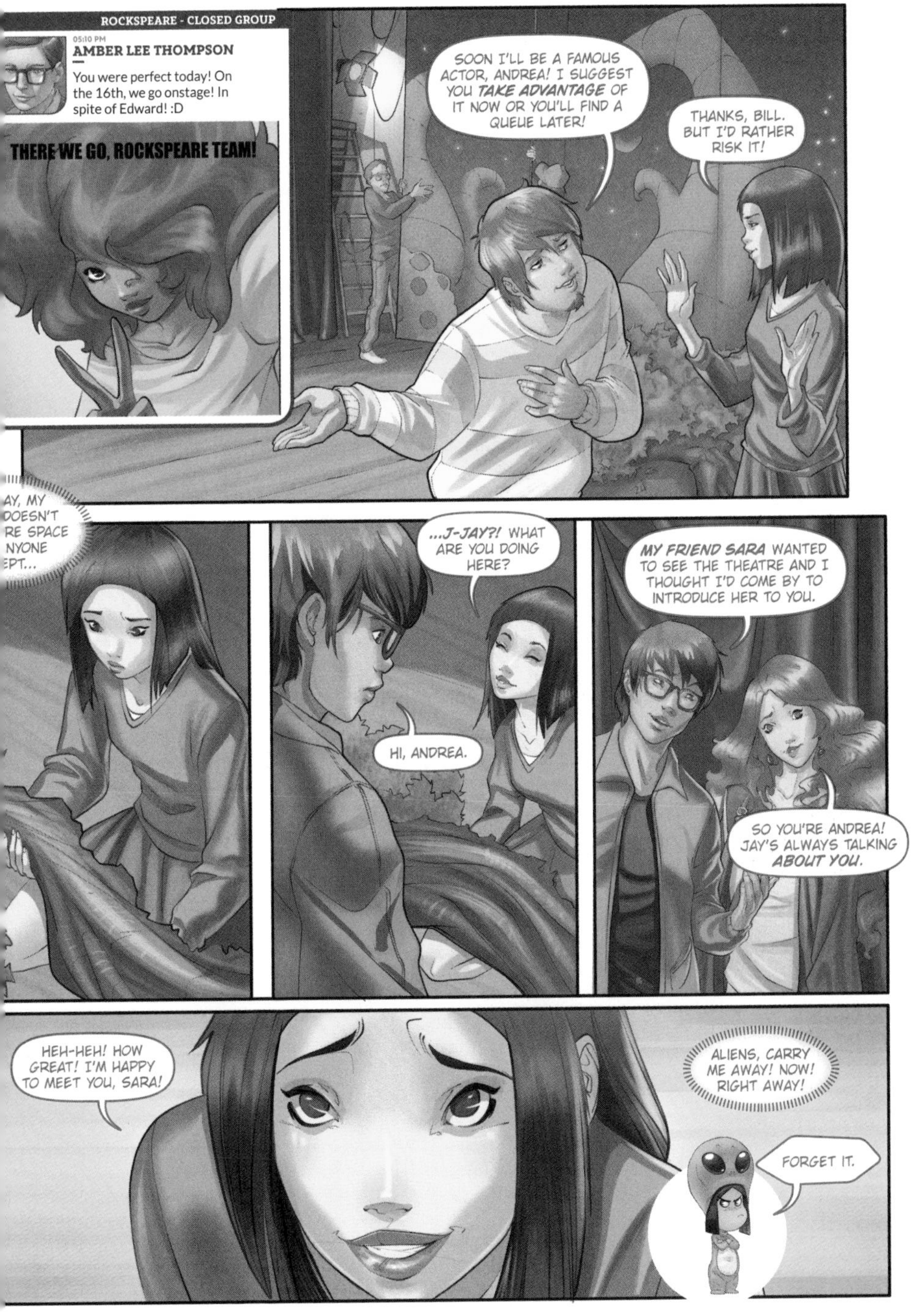
ROCKSPEARE - CLOSED GROUP
05:10 PM
AMBER LEE THOMPSON
You were perfect today! On the 16th, we go onstage! In spite of Edward! :D
THERE WE GO, ROCKSPEARE TEAM!
SOON I'LL BE A FAMOUS ACTOR, ANDREA! I SUGGEST YOU TAKE ADVANTAGE OF IT NOW OR YOU'LL FIND A QUEUE LATER!
THANKS, BILL. BUT I'D RATHER RISK IT!
AY, MY DOESN'T RE SPACE NYONE EPT...
...J-JAY?! WHAT ARE YOU DOING HERE?
HI, ANDREA.
MY FRIEND SARA WANTED TO SEE THE THEATRE AND I THOUGHT I'D COME BY TO INTRODUCE HER TO YOU.
SO YOU'RE ANDREA! JAY'S ALWAYS TALKING ABOUT YOU.
HEH-HEH! HOW GREAT! I'M HAPPY TO MEET YOU, SARA!
ALIENS, CARRY ME AWAY! NOW! RIGHT AWAY!
FORGET IT.

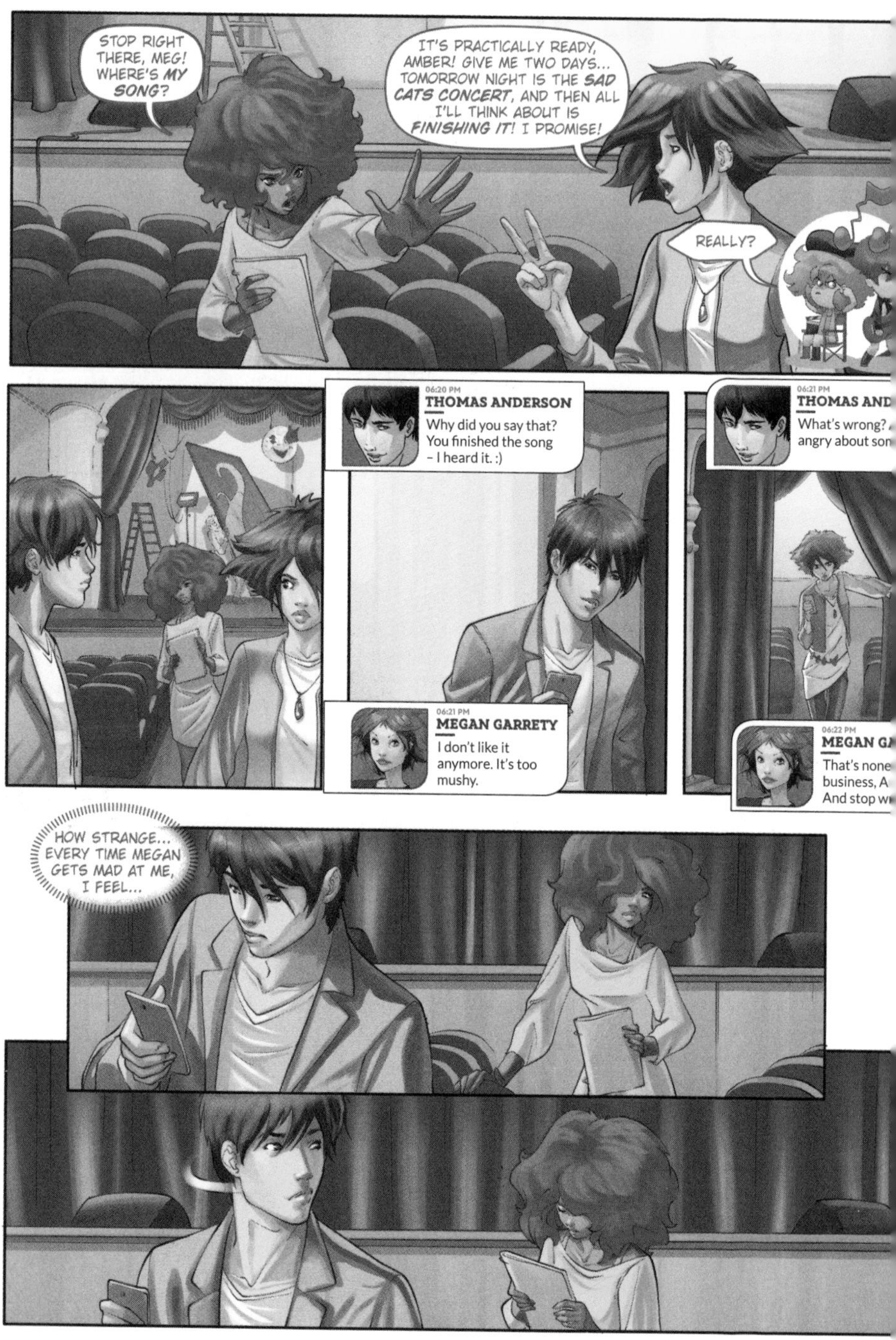

STOP RIGHT THERE, MEG! WHERE'S MY SONG?
IT'S PRACTICALLY READY, AMBER! GIVE ME TWO DAYS... TOMORROW NIGHT IS THE SAD CATS CONCERT, AND THEN ALL I'LL THINK ABOUT IS FINISHING IT! I PROMISE!
REALLY?
06:20 PM
THOMAS ANDERSON
Why did you say that? You finished the song – I heard it. :)
06:21 PM
MEGAN GARRETY
I don't like it anymore. It's too mushy.
06:21 PM
THOMAS AND
What's wrong?
angry about som
06:22 PM
MEGAN GA
That's none
business, A
And stop w
HOW STRANGE... EVERY TIME MEGAN GETS MAD AT ME, I FEEL...

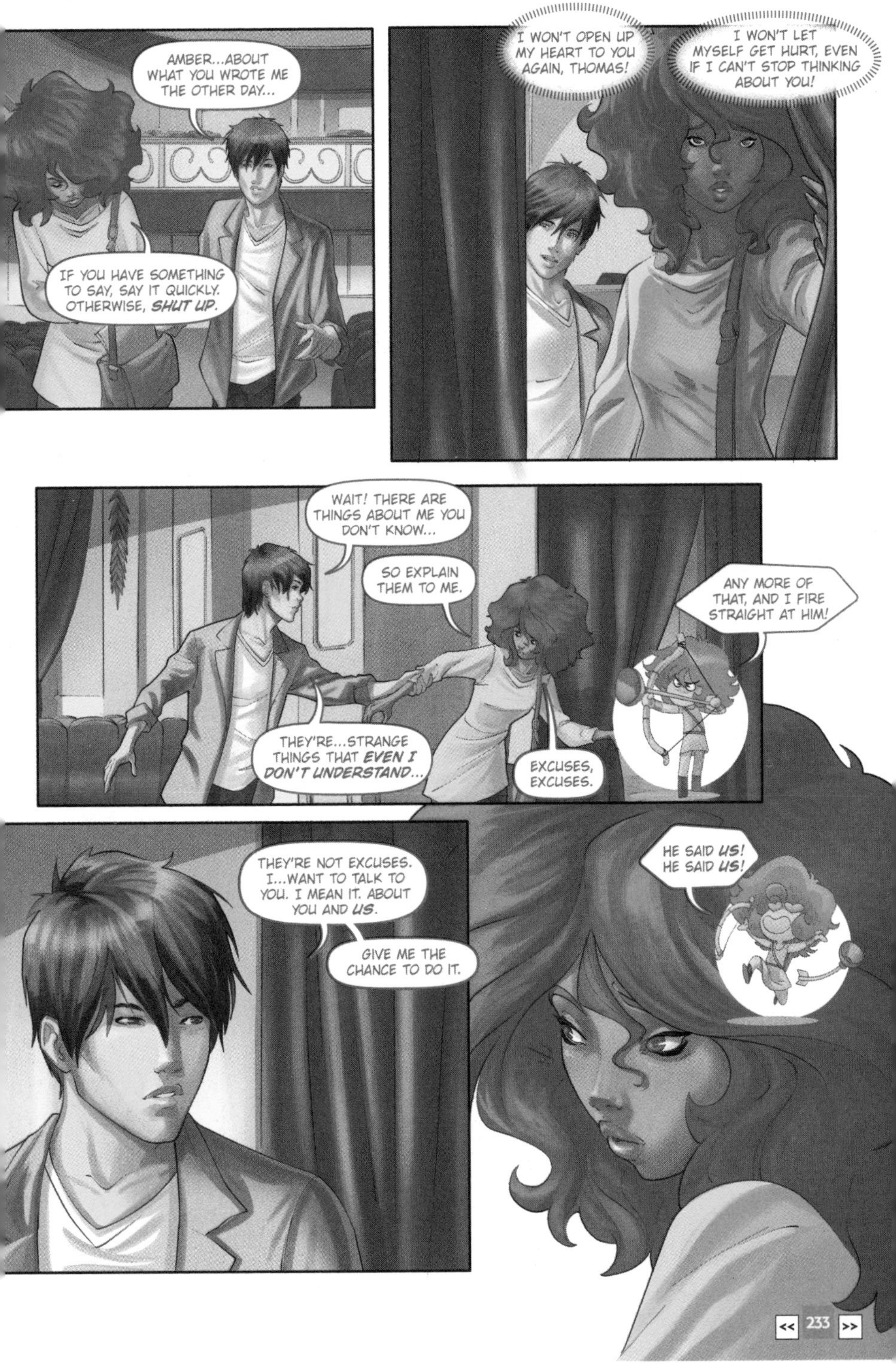
AMBER...ABOUT WHAT YOU WROTE ME THE OTHER DAY...
IF YOU HAVE SOMETHING TO SAY, SAY IT QUICKLY. OTHERWISE, SHUT UP.
I WON'T OPEN UP MY HEART TO YOU AGAIN, THOMAS!
I WON'T LET MYSELF GET HURT, EVEN IF I CAN'T STOP THINKING ABOUT YOU!
WAIT! THERE ARE THINGS ABOUT ME YOU DON'T KNOW...
SO EXPLAIN THEM TO ME.
ANY MORE OF THAT, AND I FIRE STRAIGHT AT HIM!
THEY'RE...STRANGE THINGS THAT EVEN I DON'T UNDERSTAND...
EXCUSES, EXCUSES.
THEY'RE NOT EXCUSES. I...WANT TO TALK TO YOU. I MEAN IT. ABOUT YOU AND US.
GIVE ME THE CHANCE TO DO IT.
HE SAID US! HE SAID US!

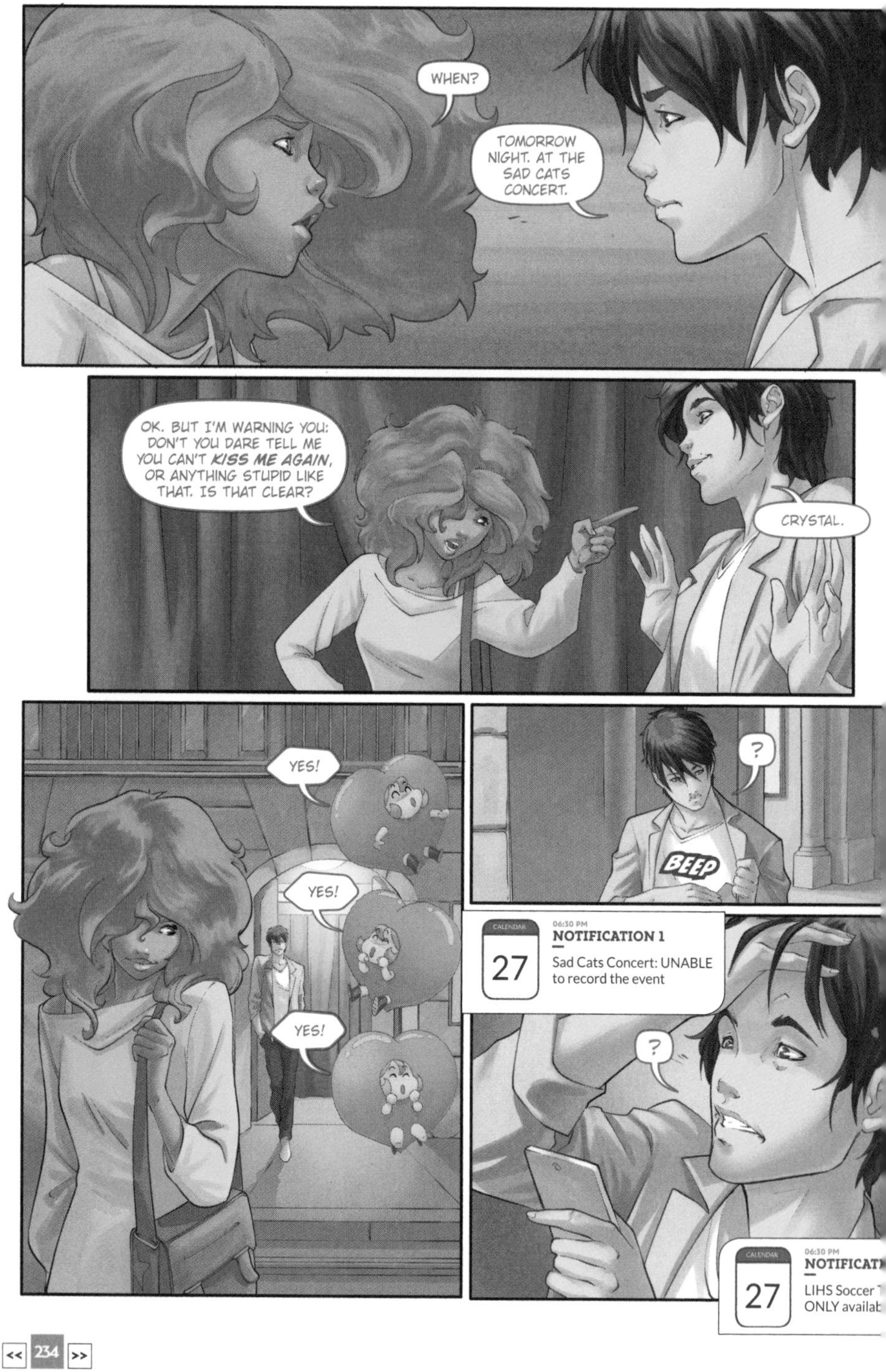

WHEN?
TOMORROW NIGHT. AT THE SAD CATS CONCERT.
OK. BUT I'M WARNING YOU: DON'T YOU DARE TELL ME YOU CAN'T KISS ME AGAIN, OR ANYTHING STUPID LIKE THAT. IS THAT CLEAR?
CRYSTAL.
YES!
YES!
YES!
?
BEEP
CALENDAR
27
06:30 PM
NOTIFICATION 1
Sad Cats Concert: UNABLE to record the event
?
CALENDAR
27
06:30 PM
LIHS Soccer
ONLY

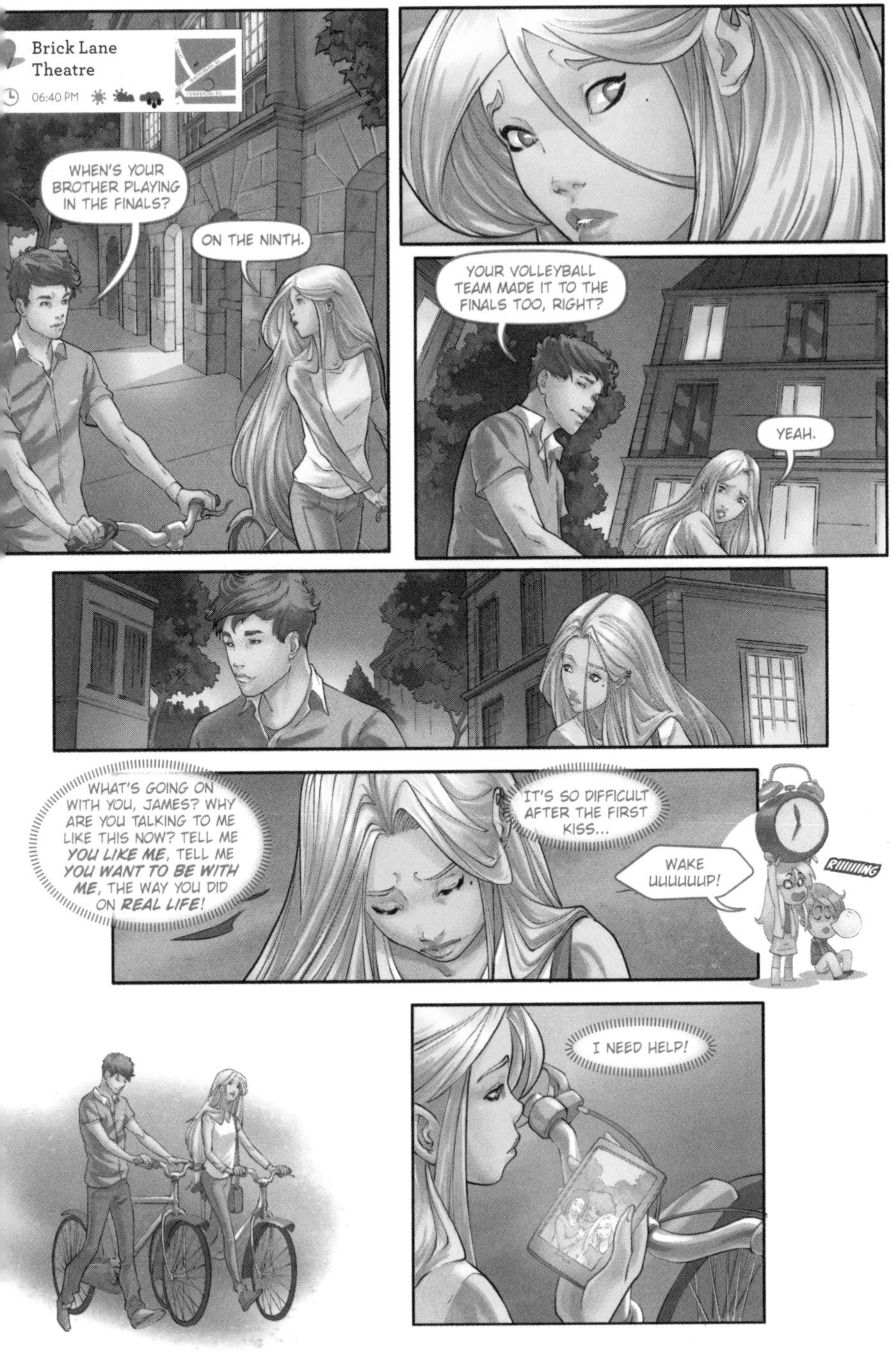
Brick Lane
Theatre
06:40 PM
WHEN'S YOUR BROTHER PLAYING IN THE FINALS?
ON THE NINTH.
YOUR VOLLEYBALL TEAM MADE IT TO THE FINALS TOO, RIGHT?
YEAH.
WHAT'S GOING ON WITH YOU, JAMES? WHY ARE YOU TALKING TO ME LIKE THIS NOW? TELL ME *YOU LIKE ME*, TELL ME *YOU WANT TO BE WITH ME*, THE WAY YOU DID ON *REAL LIFE*!
IT'S SO DIFFICULT AFTER THE FIRST KISS...
WAKE UUUUUUP!
RIIIIIING
I NEED HELP!

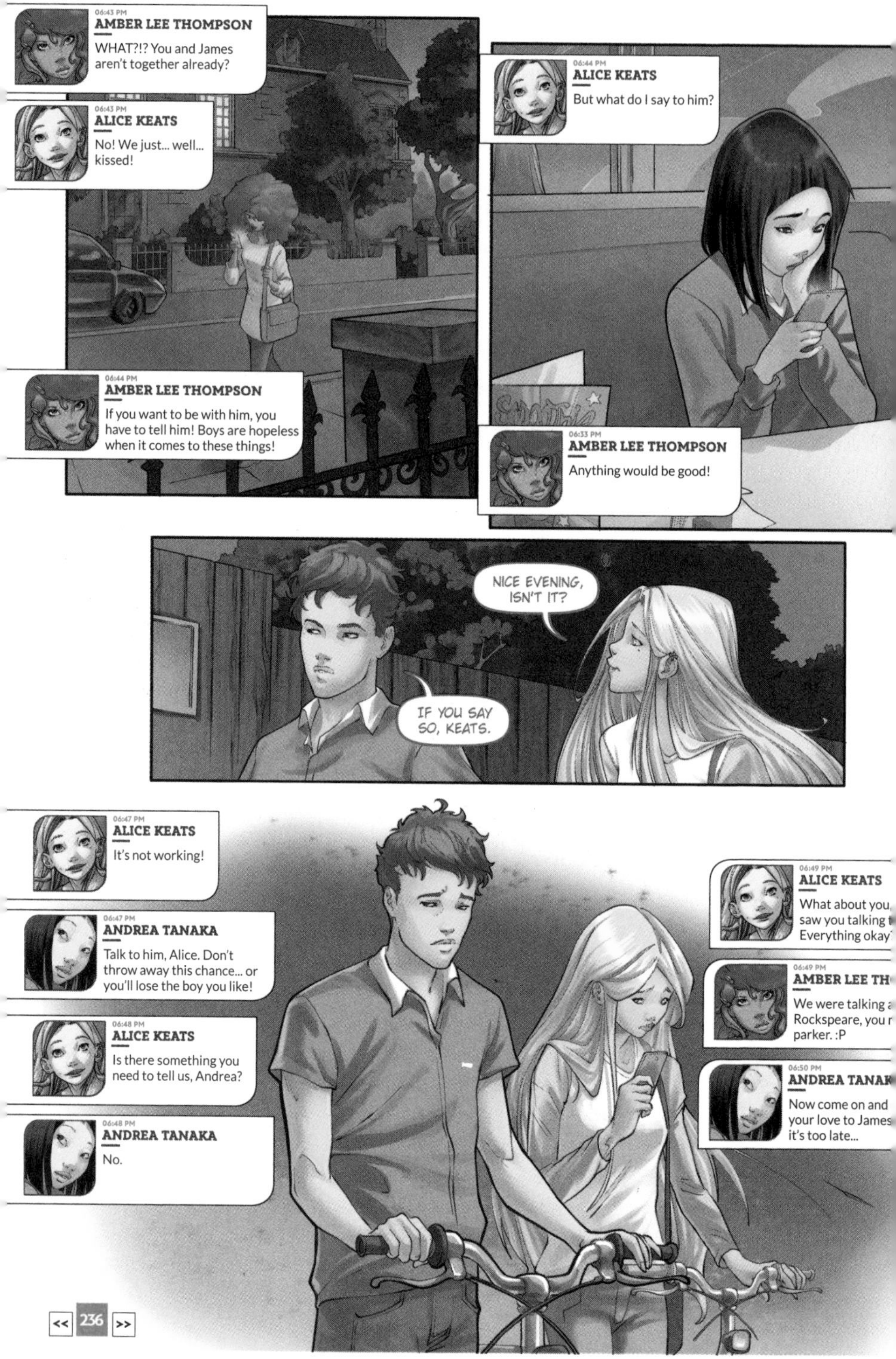
06:43 PM
AMBER LEE THOMPSON
WHAT?!? You and James aren't together already?
06:43 PM
ALICE KEATS
No! We just... well... kissed!
06:44 PM
AMBER LEE THOMPSON
If you want to be with him, you have to tell him! Boys are hopeless when it comes to these things!
06:44 PM
ALICE KEATS
But what do I say to him?
06:33 PM
AMBER LEE THOMPSON
Anything would be good!
NICE EVENING, ISN'T IT?
IF YOU SAY SO, KEATS.
06:47 PM
ALICE KEATS
It's not working!
06:47 PM
ANDREA TANAKA
Talk to him, Alice. Don't throw away this chance... or you'll lose the boy you like!
06:48 PM
ALICE KEATS
Is there something you need to tell us, Andrea?
06:48 PM
ANDREA TANAKA
No.
06:49 PM
ALICE KEATS
What about you
saw you talking
Everything okay
06:49 PM
AMBER LEE TH
We were talking
Rockspeare, you
parker. :P
06:50 PM
ANDREA TANAK
Now come on and
your love to James
it's too late...

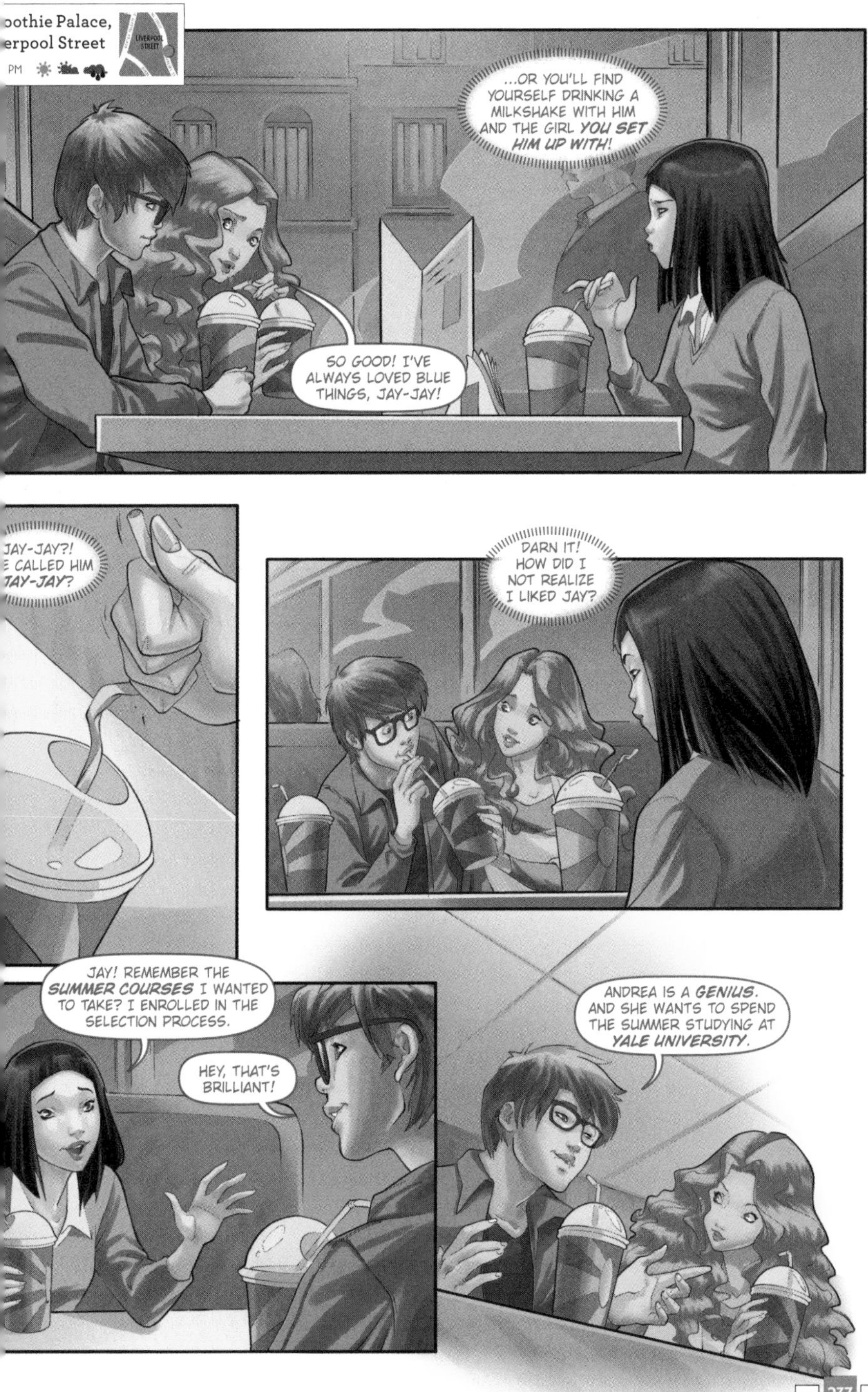
oothie Palace,
erpool Street
PM
LIVERPOOL STREET
...OR YOU'LL FIND YOURSELF DRINKING A MILKSHAKE WITH HIM AND THE GIRL **YOU SET HIM UP WITH**!
SO GOOD! I'VE ALWAYS LOVED BLUE THINGS, JAY-JAY!
JAY-JAY?! E CALLED HIM **JAY-JAY**?
DARN IT! HOW DID I NOT REALIZE I LIKED JAY?
JAY! REMEMBER THE **SUMMER COURSES** I WANTED TO TAKE? I ENROLLED IN THE SELECTION PROCESS.
HEY, THAT'S BRILLIANT!
ANDREA IS A **GENIUS**. AND SHE WANTS TO SPEND THE SUMMER STUDYING AT **YALE UNIVERSITY**.

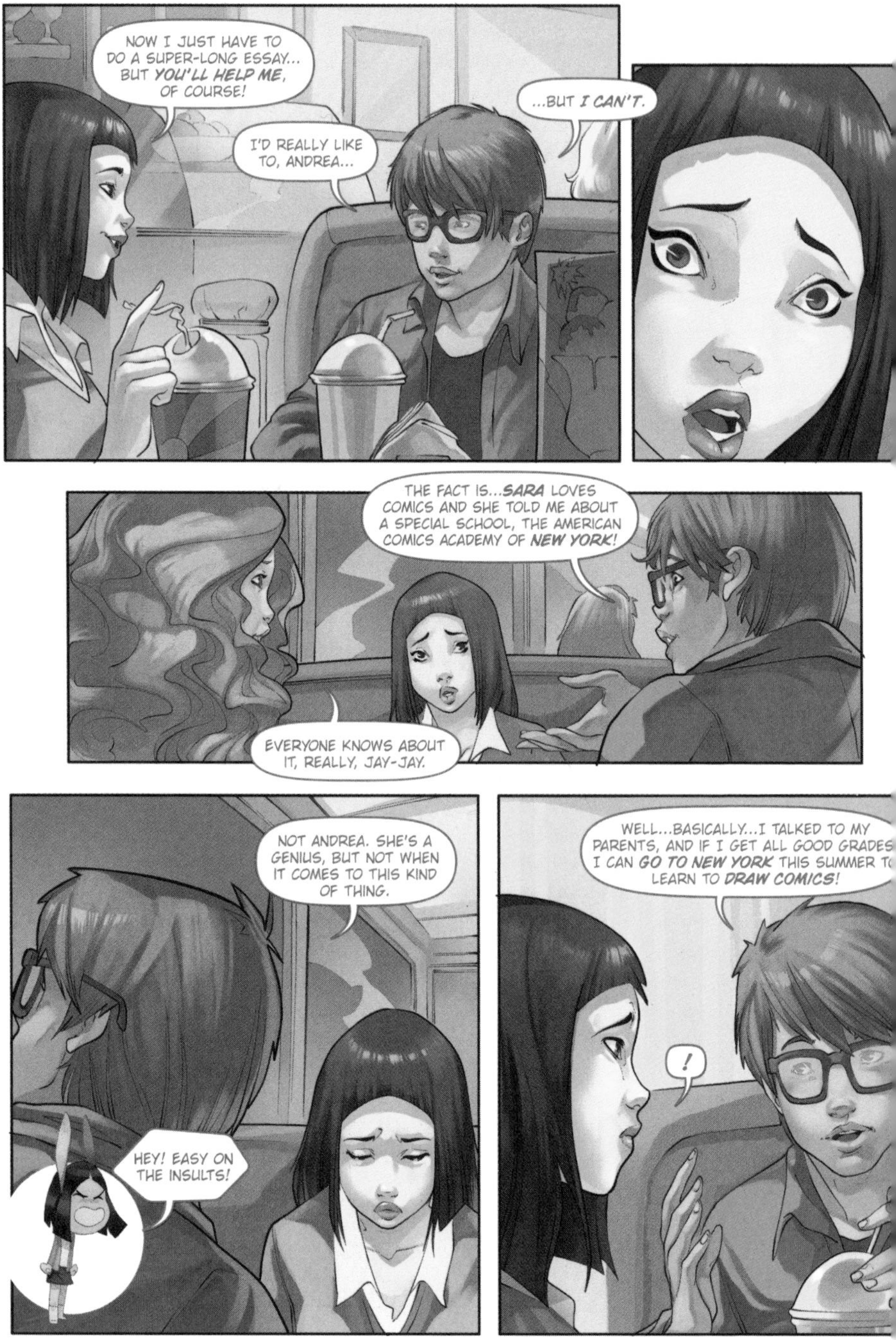
NOW I JUST HAVE TO DO A SUPER-LONG ESSAY... BUT YOU'LL HELP ME, OF COURSE!
I'D REALLY LIKE TO, ANDREA...
...BUT I CAN'T.
THE FACT IS...SARA LOVES COMICS AND SHE TOLD ME ABOUT A SPECIAL SCHOOL, THE AMERICAN COMICS ACADEMY OF NEW YORK!
EVERYONE KNOWS ABOUT IT, REALLY, JAY-JAY.
NOT ANDREA. SHE'S A GENIUS, BUT NOT WHEN IT COMES TO THIS KIND OF THING.
HEY! EASY ON THE INSULTS!
WELL...BASICALLY...I TALKED TO MY PARENTS, AND IF I GET ALL GOOD GRADES I CAN GO TO NEW YORK THIS SUMMER TO LEARN TO DRAW COMICS!
!

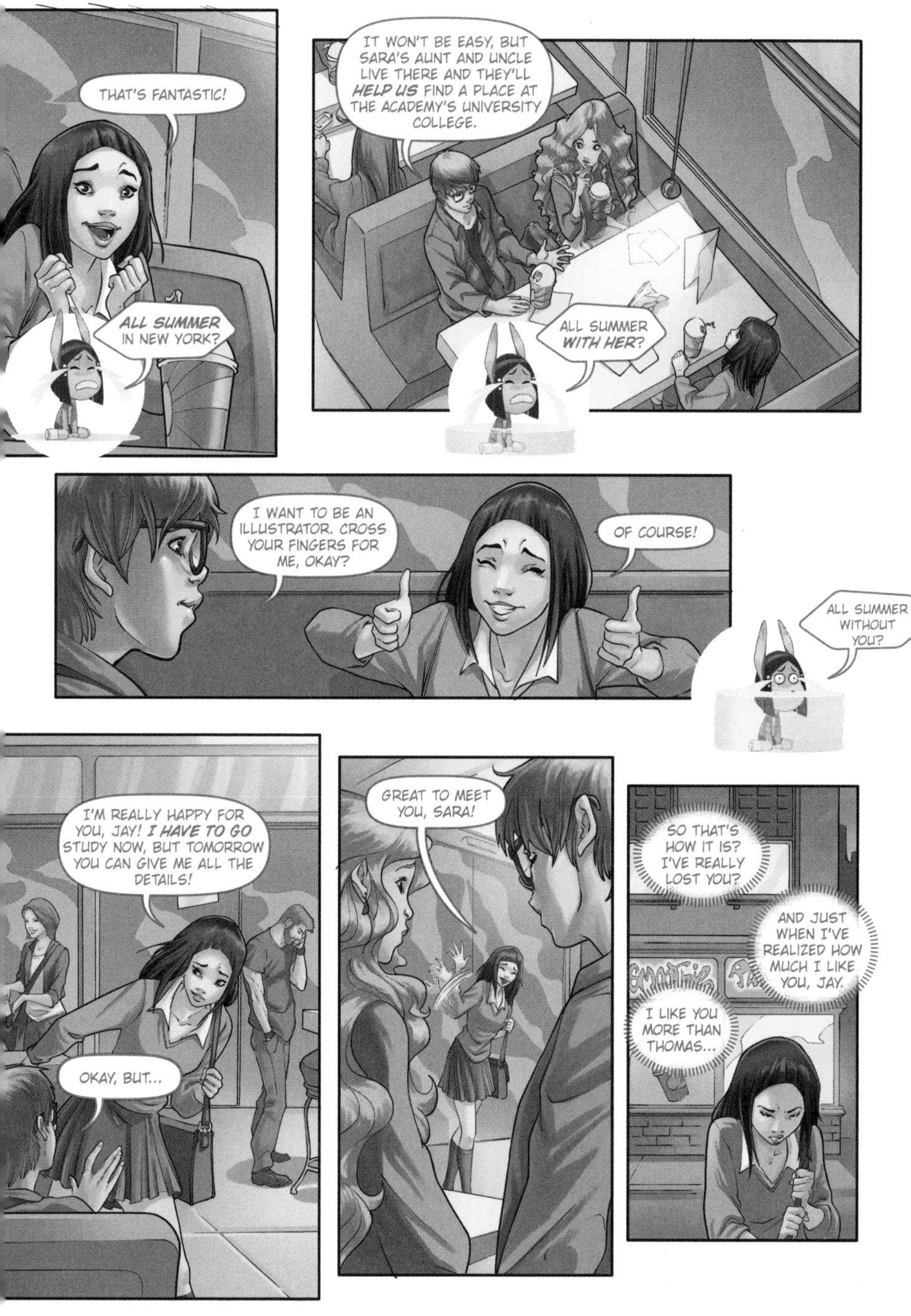
THAT'S FANTASTIC!
ALL SUMMER IN NEW YORK?
IT WON'T BE EASY, BUT SARA'S AUNT AND UNCLE LIVE THERE AND THEY'LL HELP US FIND A PLACE AT THE ACADEMY'S UNIVERSITY COLLEGE.
ALL SUMMER WITH HER?
I WANT TO BE AN ILLUSTRATOR. CROSS YOUR FINGERS FOR ME, OKAY?
OF COURSE!
ALL SUMMER WITHOUT YOU?
I'M REALLY HAPPY FOR YOU, JAY! I HAVE TO GO STUDY NOW, BUT TOMORROW YOU CAN GIVE ME ALL THE DETAILS!
OKAY, BUT...
GREAT TO MEET YOU, SARA!
SO THAT'S HOW IT IS? I'VE REALLY LOST YOU?
AND JUST WHEN I'VE REALIZED HOW MUCH I LIKE YOU, JAY.
I LIKE YOU MORE THAN THOMAS...

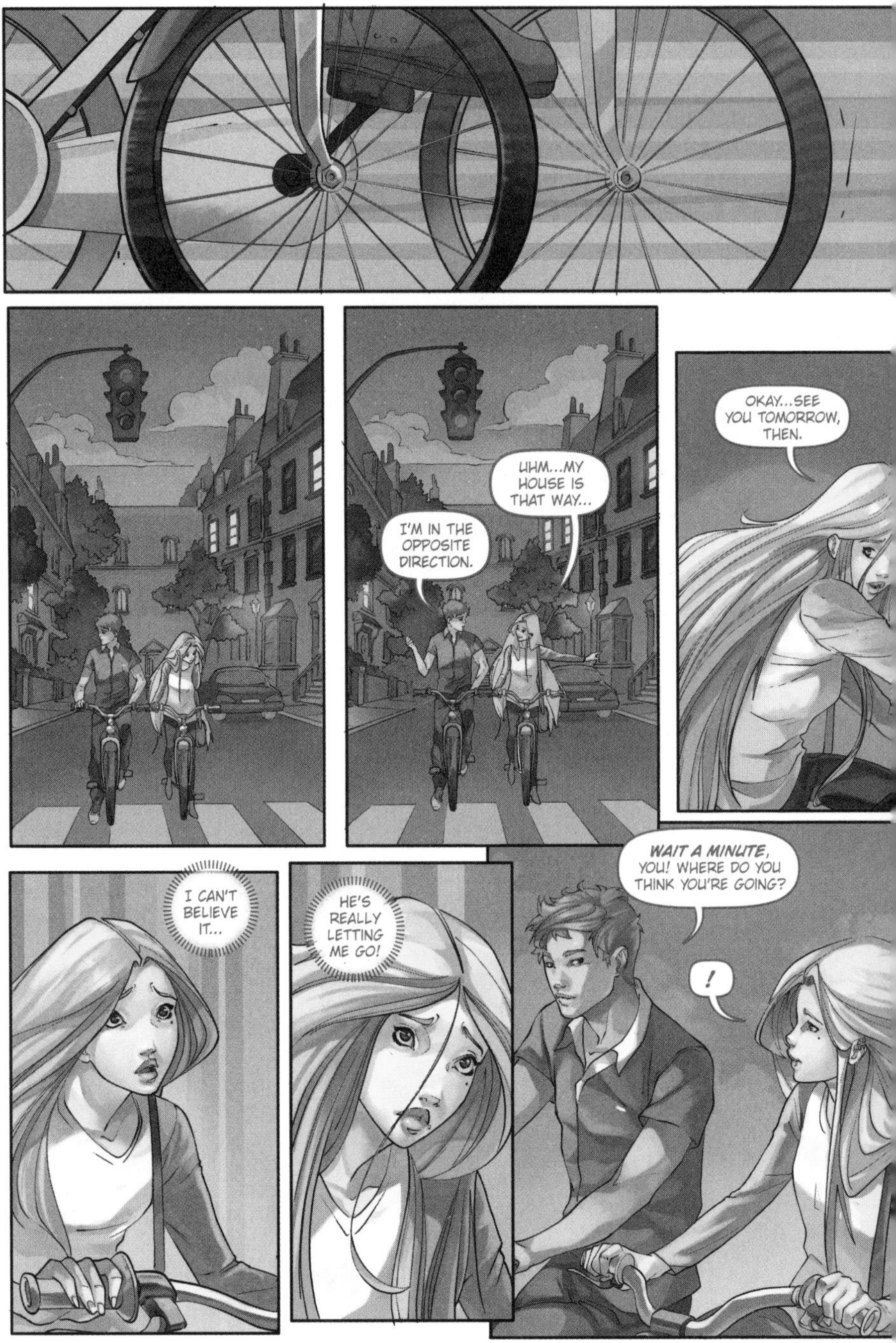
UHM...MY
HOUSE IS
THAT WAY...
I'M IN THE
OPPOSITE
DIRECTION.
OKAY...SEE
YOU TOMORROW,
THEN.
I CAN'T
BELIEVE
IT...
HE'S
REALLY
LETTING
ME GO!
WAIT A MINUTE,
YOU! WHERE DO YOU
THINK YOU'RE GOING?
!

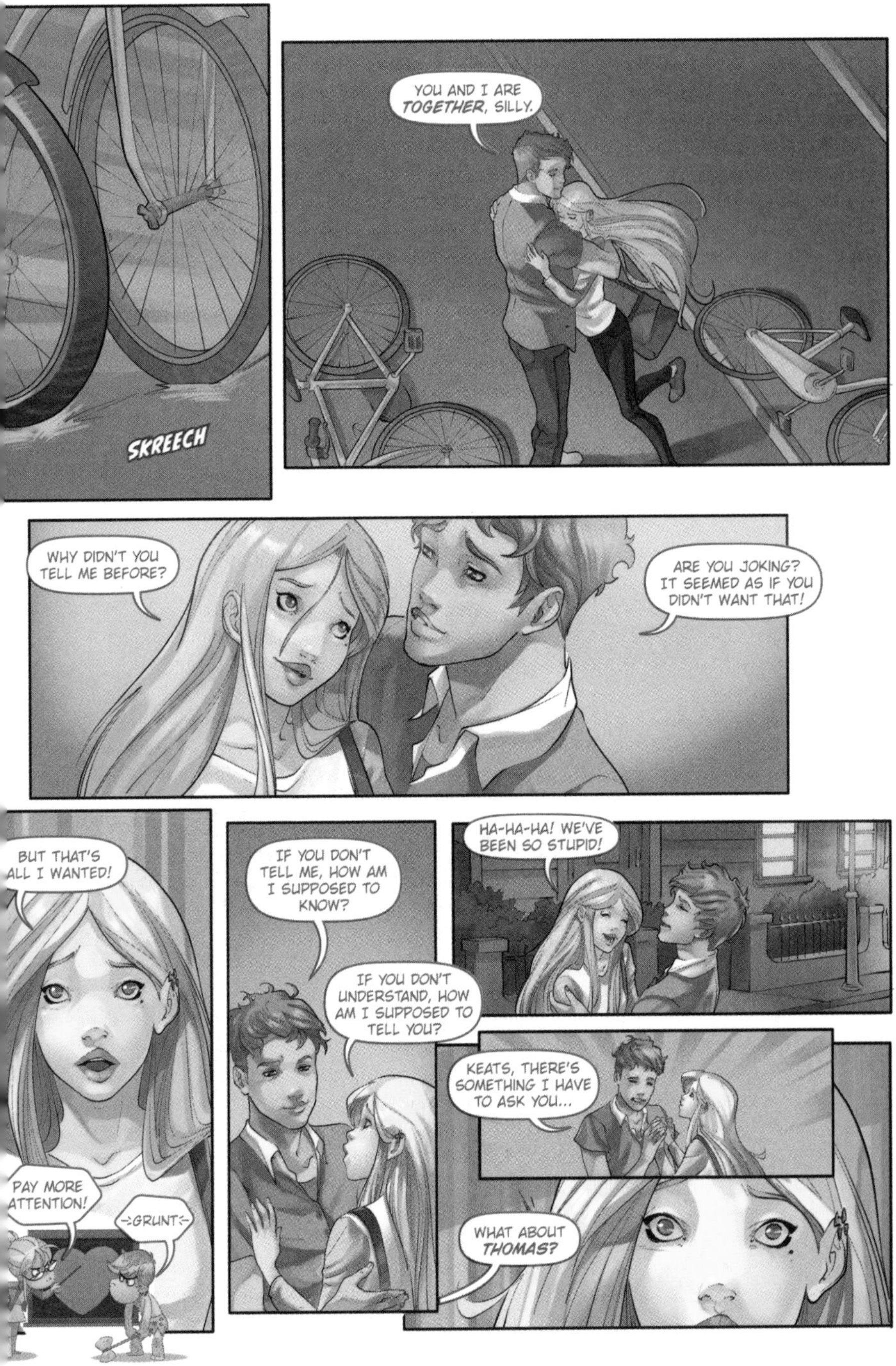
SKREECH
YOU AND I ARE TOGETHER, SILLY.
WHY DIDN'T YOU TELL ME BEFORE?
ARE YOU JOKING? IT SEEMED AS IF YOU DIDN'T WANT THAT!
BUT THAT'S ALL I WANTED!
PAY MORE ATTENTION!
-GRUNT-
IF YOU DON'T TELL ME, HOW AM I SUPPOSED TO KNOW?
IF YOU DON'T UNDERSTAND, HOW AM I SUPPOSED TO TELL YOU?
HA-HA-HA! WE'VE BEEN SO STUPID!
KEATS, THERE'S SOMETHING I HAVE TO ASK YOU...
WHAT ABOUT THOMAS?

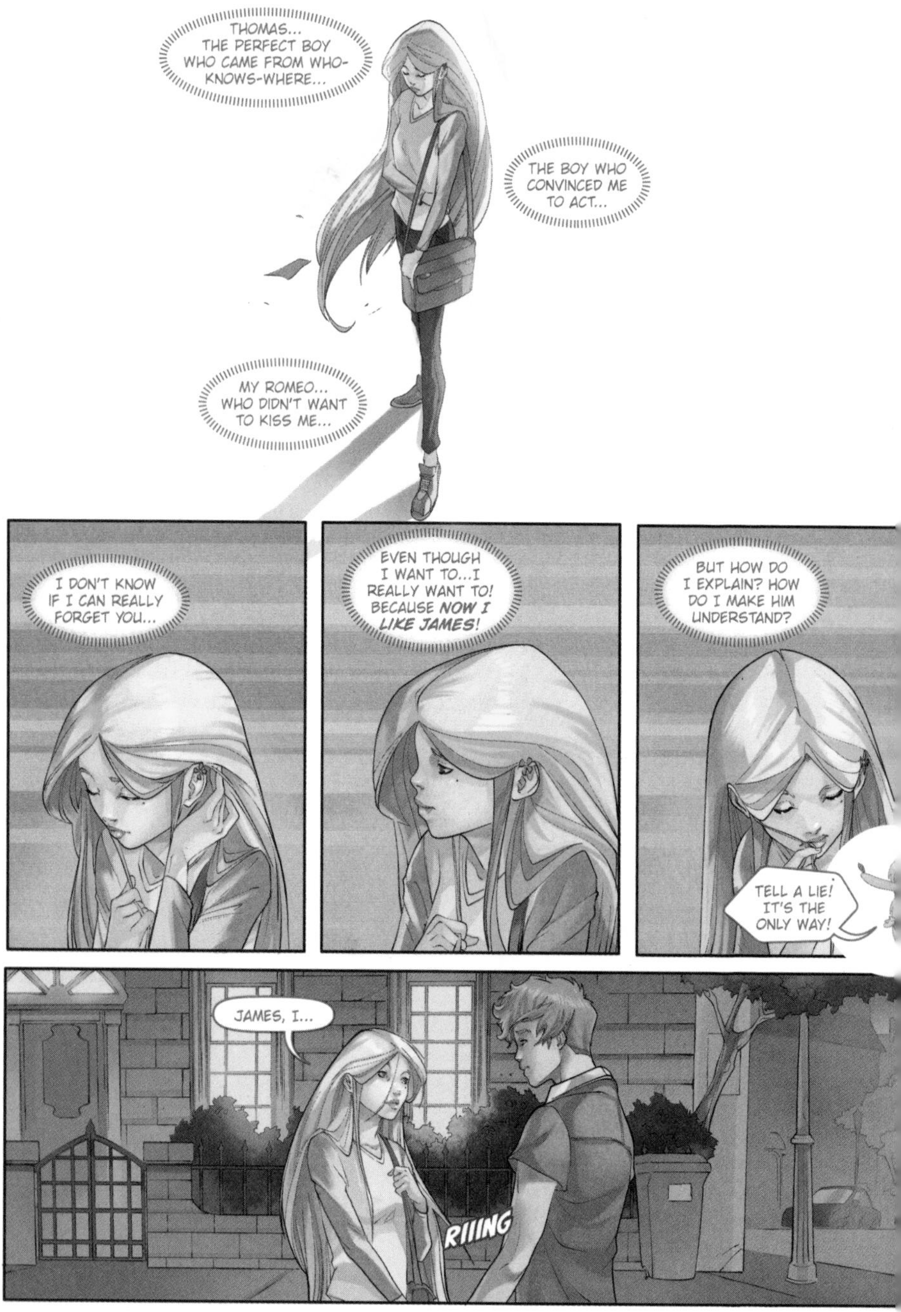
THOMAS... THE PERFECT BOY WHO CAME FROM WHO-KNOWS-WHERE...
THE BOY WHO CONVINCED ME TO ACT...
MY ROMEO... WHO DIDN'T WANT TO KISS ME...
I DON'T KNOW IF I CAN REALLY FORGET YOU...
EVEN THOUGH I WANT TO...I REALLY WANT TO! BECAUSE NOW I LIKE JAMES!
BUT HOW DO I EXPLAIN? HOW DO I MAKE HIM UNDERSTAND?
TELL A LIE! IT'S THE ONLY WAY!
JAMES, I...
RIIING

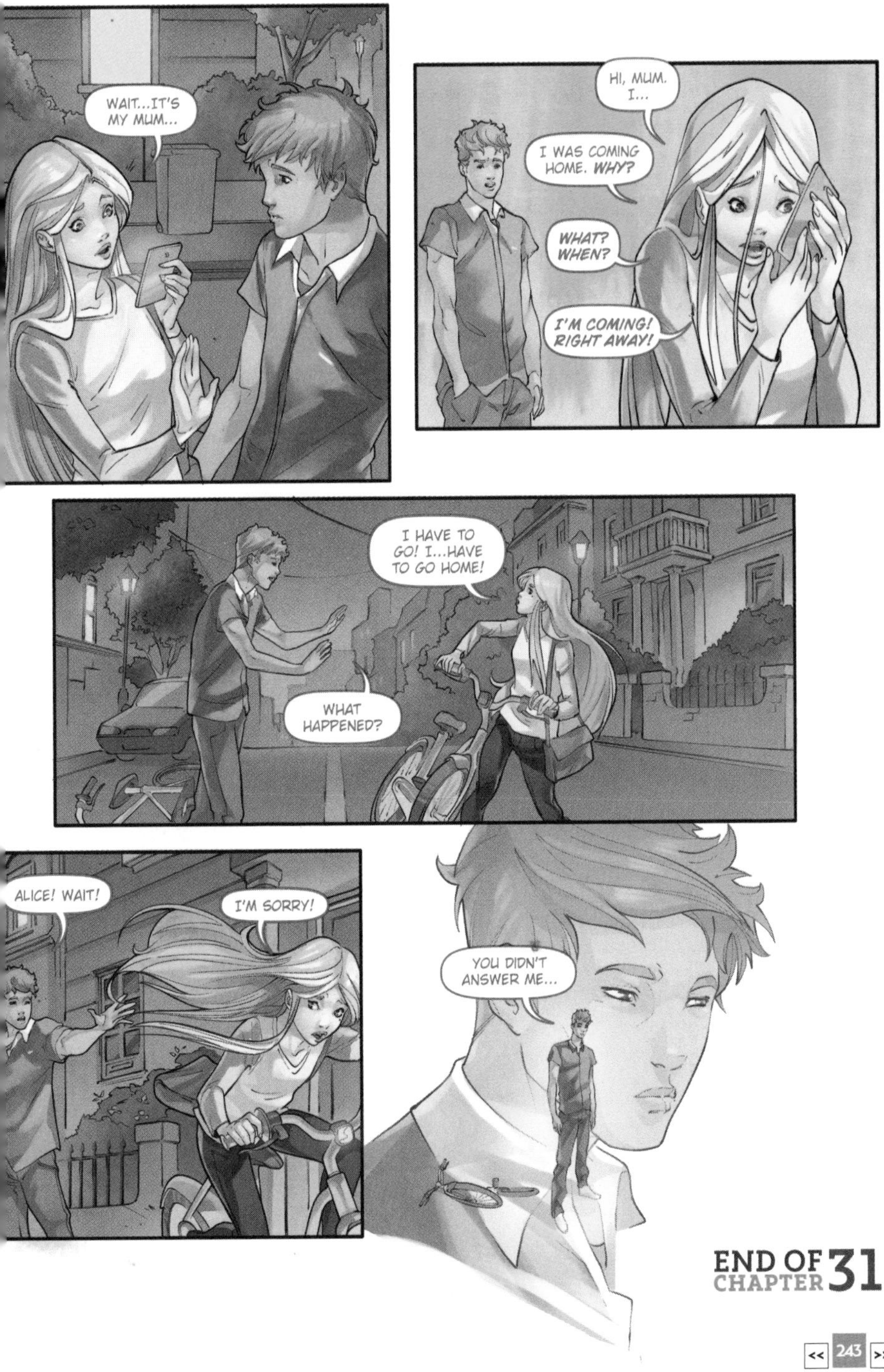
WAIT...IT'S MY MUM...
HI, MUM. I...
I WAS COMING HOME. WHY?
WHAT? WHEN?
I'M COMING! RIGHT AWAY!
I HAVE TO GO! I...HAVE TO GO HOME!
WHAT HAPPENED?
ALICE! WAIT!
I'M SORRY!
YOU DIDN'T ANSWER ME...

END OF CHAPTER 31

CHAPTER 32

A stolen KISS

Alice's house
Notting Hill
07:48 PM

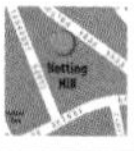

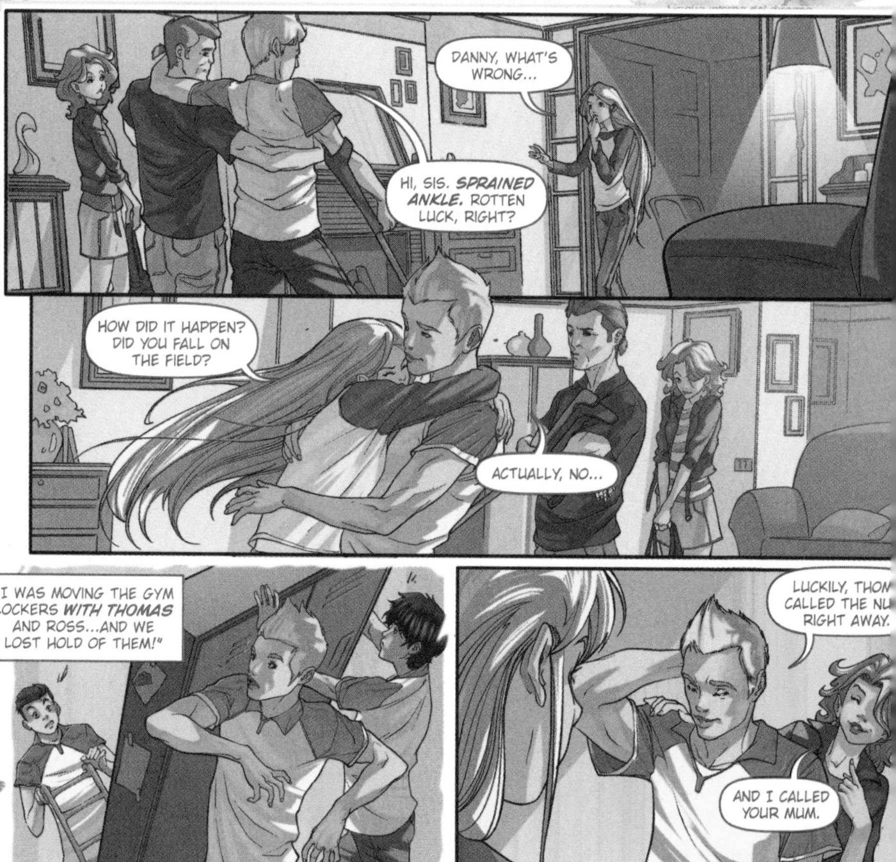
DANNY, WHAT'S WRONG...
HI, SIS. **SPRAINED ANKLE.** ROTTEN LUCK, RIGHT?
HOW DID IT HAPPEN? DID YOU FALL ON THE FIELD?
ACTUALLY, NO...
"I WAS MOVING THE GYM LOCKERS **WITH THOMAS** AND ROSS...AND WE LOST HOLD OF THEM!"
LUCKILY, THOM CALLED THE NU RIGHT AWAY.
AND I CALLED YOUR MUM.

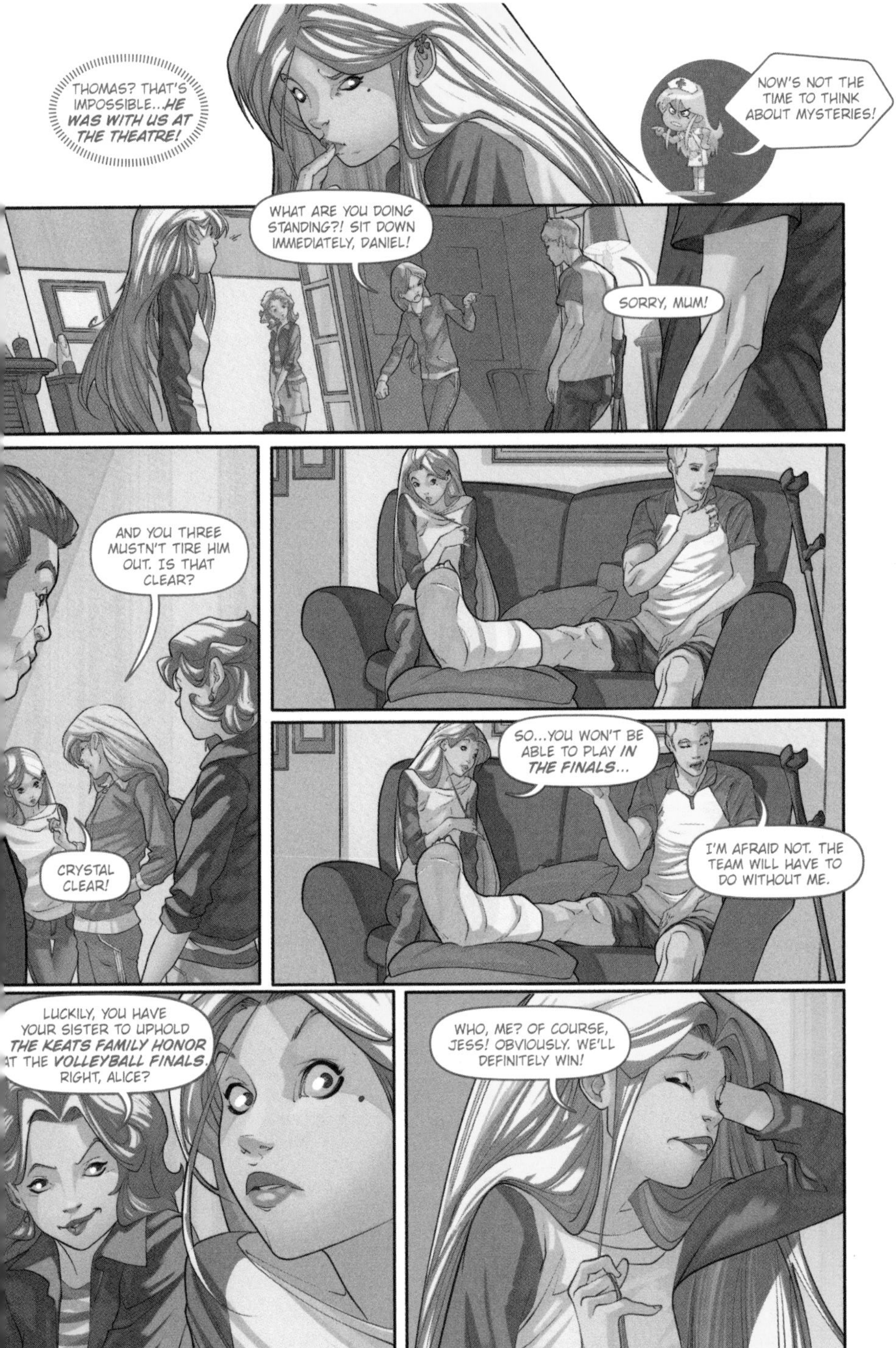
THOMAS? THAT'S IMPOSSIBLE... HE WAS WITH US AT THE THEATRE!
NOW'S NOT THE TIME TO THINK ABOUT MYSTERIES!
WHAT ARE YOU DOING STANDING?! SIT DOWN IMMEDIATELY, DANIEL!
SORRY, MUM!
AND YOU THREE MUSTN'T TIRE HIM OUT. IS THAT CLEAR?
CRYSTAL CLEAR!
SO...YOU WON'T BE ABLE TO PLAY IN THE FINALS...
I'M AFRAID NOT. THE TEAM WILL HAVE TO DO WITHOUT ME.
LUCKILY, YOU HAVE YOUR SISTER TO UPHOLD THE KEATS FAMILY HONOR AT THE VOLLEYBALL FINALS. RIGHT, ALICE?
WHO, ME? OF COURSE, JESS! OBVIOUSLY. WE'LL DEFINITELY WIN!

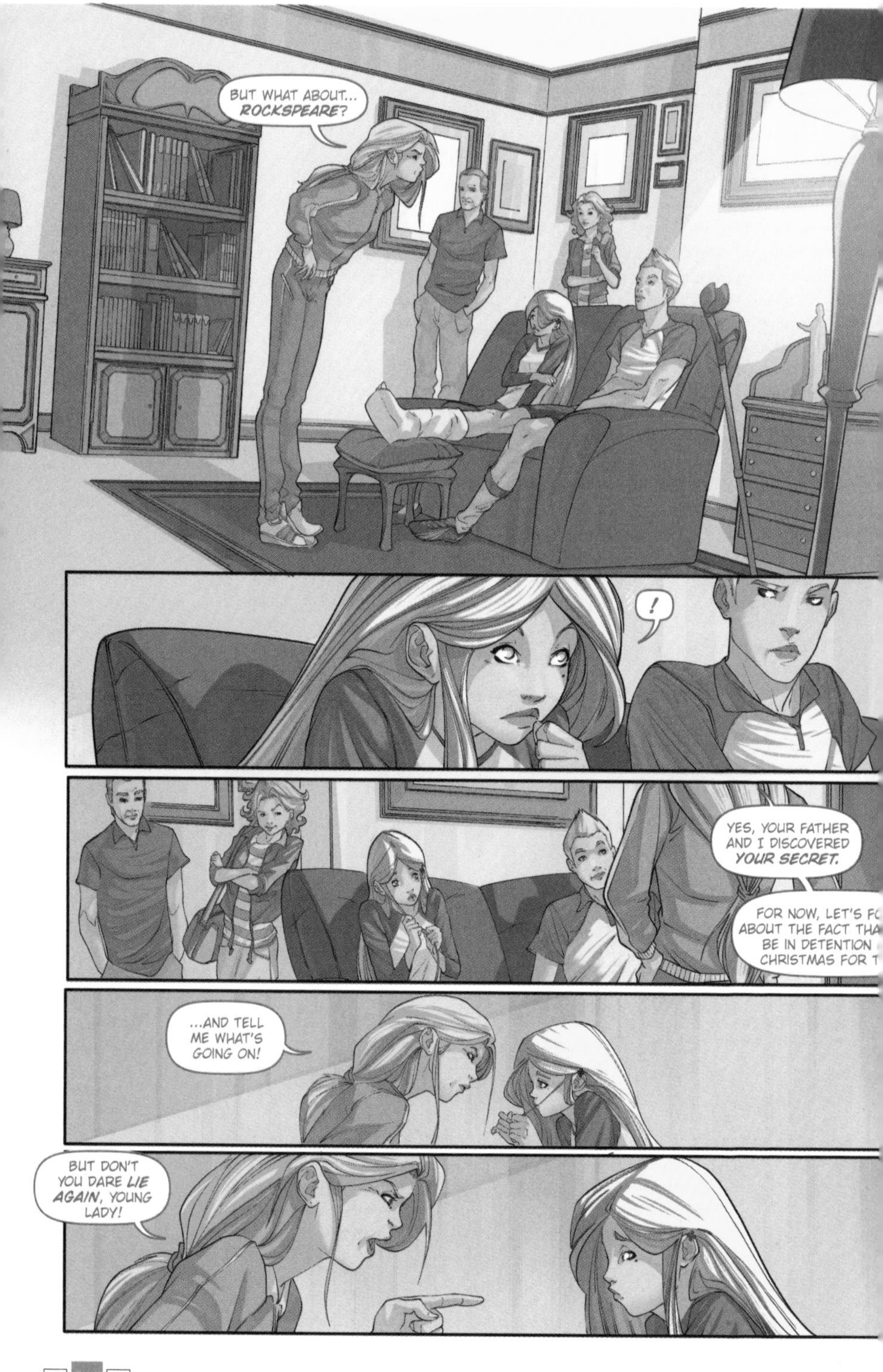
BUT WHAT ABOUT... ROCKSPEARE?
!
YES, YOUR FATHER AND I DISCOVERED YOUR SECRET.
FOR NOW, LET'S FO
ABOUT THE FACT THA
BE IN DETENTION
CHRISTMAS FOR T
...AND TELL ME WHAT'S GOING ON!
BUT DON'T YOU DARE LIE AGAIN, YOUNG LADY!

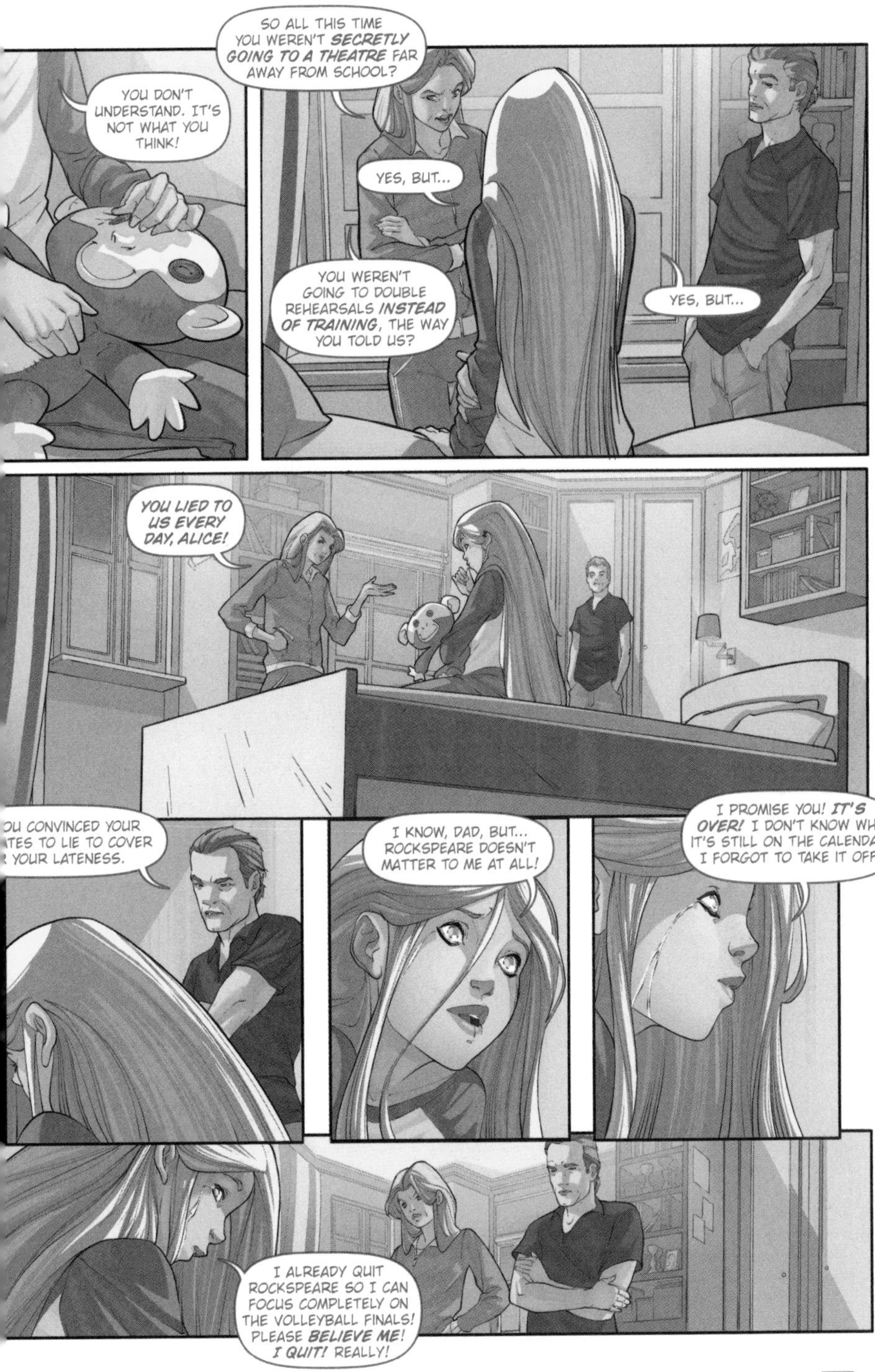
YOU DON'T UNDERSTAND. IT'S NOT WHAT YOU THINK!
SO ALL THIS TIME YOU WEREN'T SECRETLY GOING TO A THEATRE FAR AWAY FROM SCHOOL?
YES, BUT...
YOU WEREN'T GOING TO DOUBLE REHEARSALS INSTEAD OF TRAINING, THE WAY YOU TOLD US?
YES, BUT...
YOU LIED TO US EVERY DAY, ALICE!
OU CONVINCED YOUR
TES TO LIE TO COVER
YOUR LATENESS.
I KNOW, DAD, BUT... ROCKSPEARE DOESN'T MATTER TO ME AT ALL!
I PROMISE YOU! IT'S OVER! I DON'T KNOW WHY IT'S STILL ON THE CALENDAR, I FORGOT TO TAKE IT OFF!
I ALREADY QUIT ROCKSPEARE SO I CAN FOCUS COMPLETELY ON THE VOLLEYBALL FINALS! PLEASE BELIEVE ME! I QUIT! REALLY!

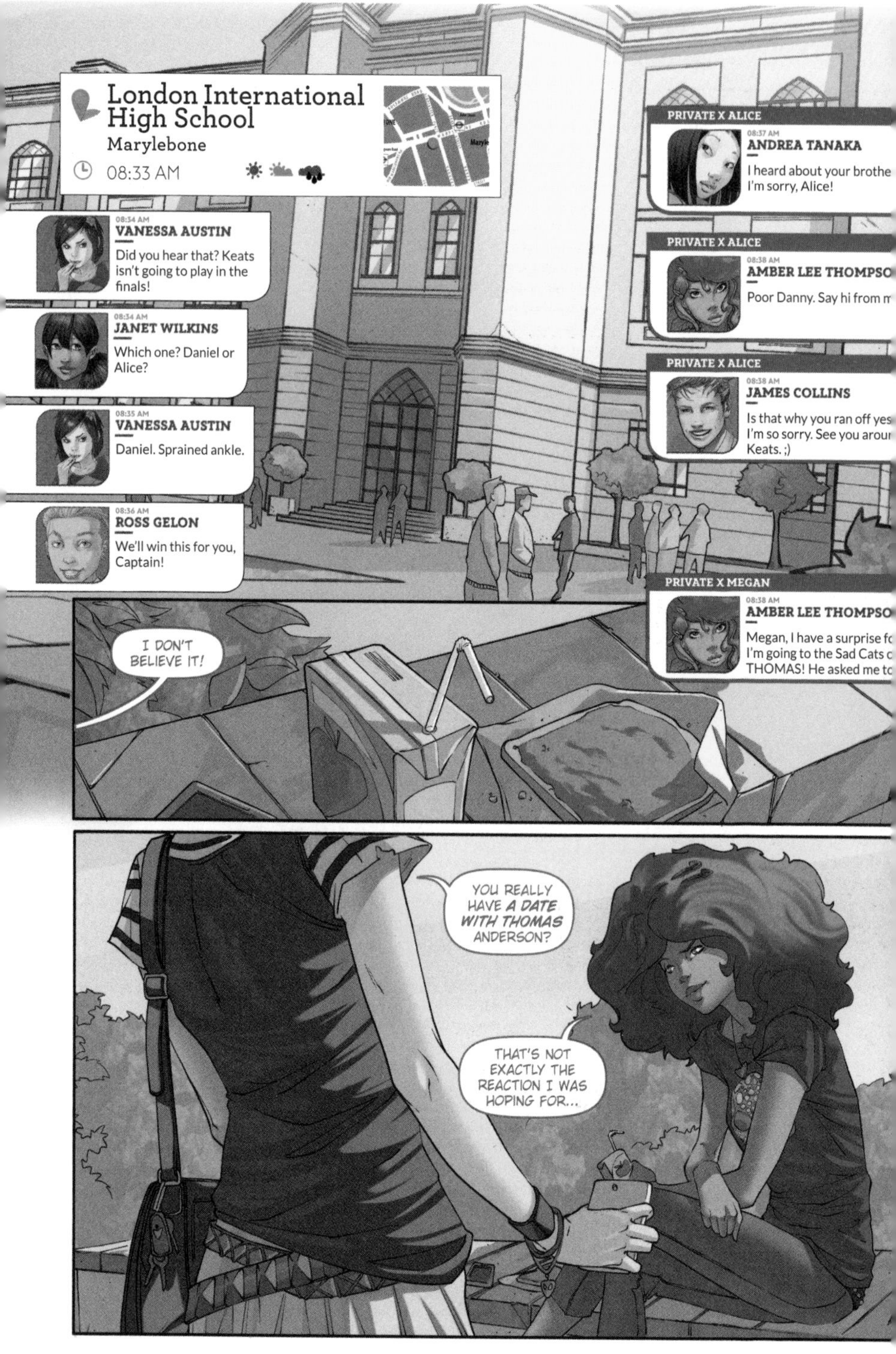

London International High School
Marylebone
08:33 AM
08:34 AM VANESSA AUSTIN Did you hear that? Keats isn't going to play in the finals!
08:34 AM JANET WILKINS Which one? Daniel or Alice?
08:35 AM VANESSA AUSTIN Daniel. Sprained ankle.
08:36 AM ROSS GELON We'll win this for you, Captain!
PRIVATE X ALICE 08:37 AM ANDREA TANAKA I heard about your brothe I'm sorry, Alice!
PRIVATE X ALICE 08:38 AM AMBER LEE THOMPSO Poor Danny. Say hi from m
PRIVATE X ALICE 08:38 AM JAMES COLLINS Is that why you ran off yes I'm so sorry. See you arour Keats. ;)
PRIVATE X MEGAN 08:38 AM AMBER LEE THOMPSO Megan, I have a surprise fo I'm going to the Sad Cats c THOMAS! He asked me to
I DON'T BELIEVE IT!
YOU REALLY HAVE A DATE WITH THOMAS ANDERSON?
THAT'S NOT EXACTLY THE REACTION I WAS HOPING FOR...

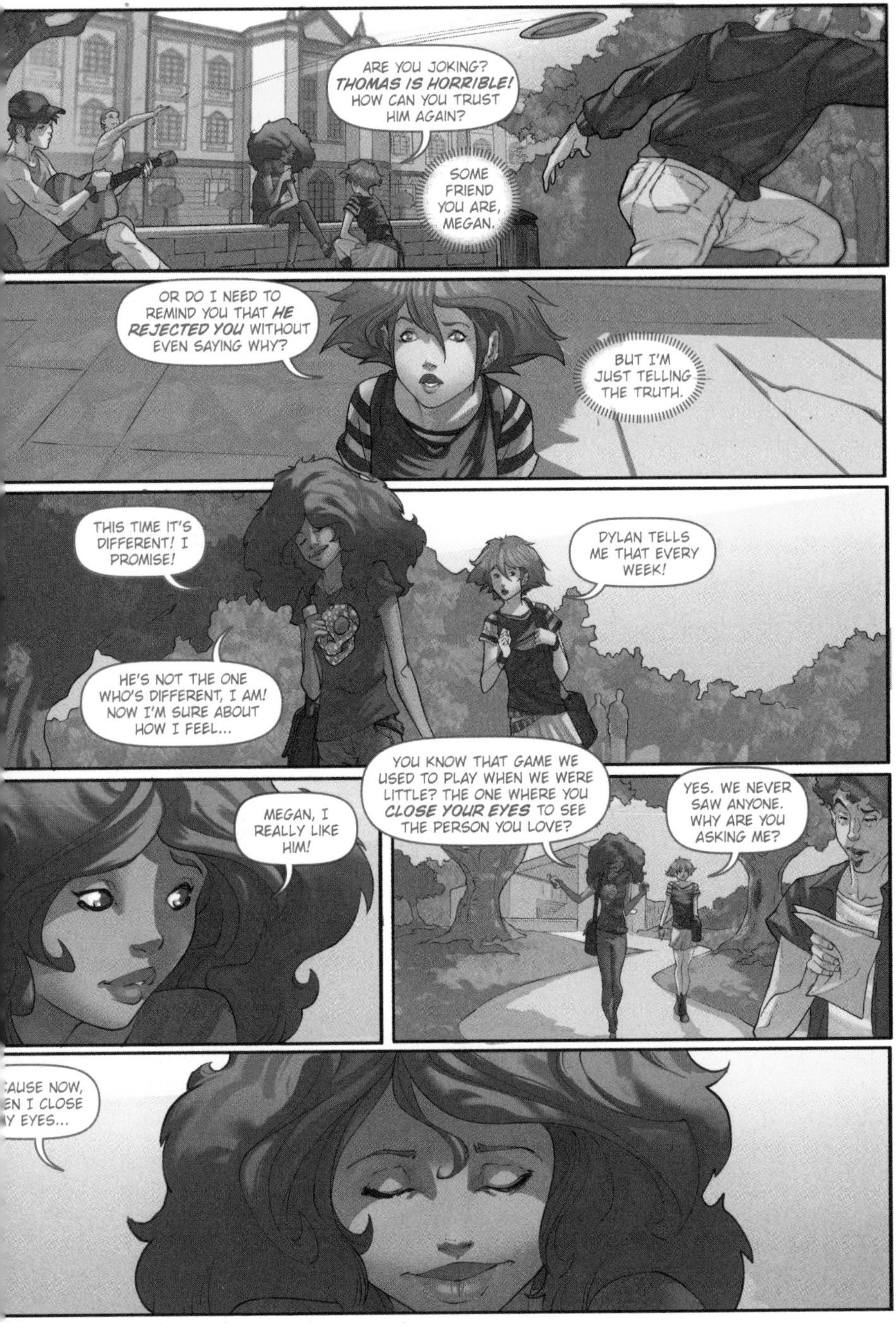
ARE YOU JOKING? THOMAS IS HORRIBLE! HOW CAN YOU TRUST HIM AGAIN?
SOME FRIEND YOU ARE, MEGAN.
OR DO I NEED TO REMIND YOU THAT HE REJECTED YOU WITHOUT EVEN SAYING WHY?
BUT I'M JUST TELLING THE TRUTH.
THIS TIME IT'S DIFFERENT! I PROMISE!
DYLAN TELLS ME THAT EVERY WEEK!
HE'S NOT THE ONE WHO'S DIFFERENT, I AM! NOW I'M SURE ABOUT HOW I FEEL...
MEGAN, I REALLY LIKE HIM!
YOU KNOW THAT GAME WE USED TO PLAY WHEN WE WERE LITTLE? THE ONE WHERE YOU CLOSE YOUR EYES TO SEE THE PERSON YOU LOVE?
YES. WE NEVER SAW ANYONE. WHY ARE YOU ASKING ME?
CAUSE NOW, EN I CLOSE Y EYES...

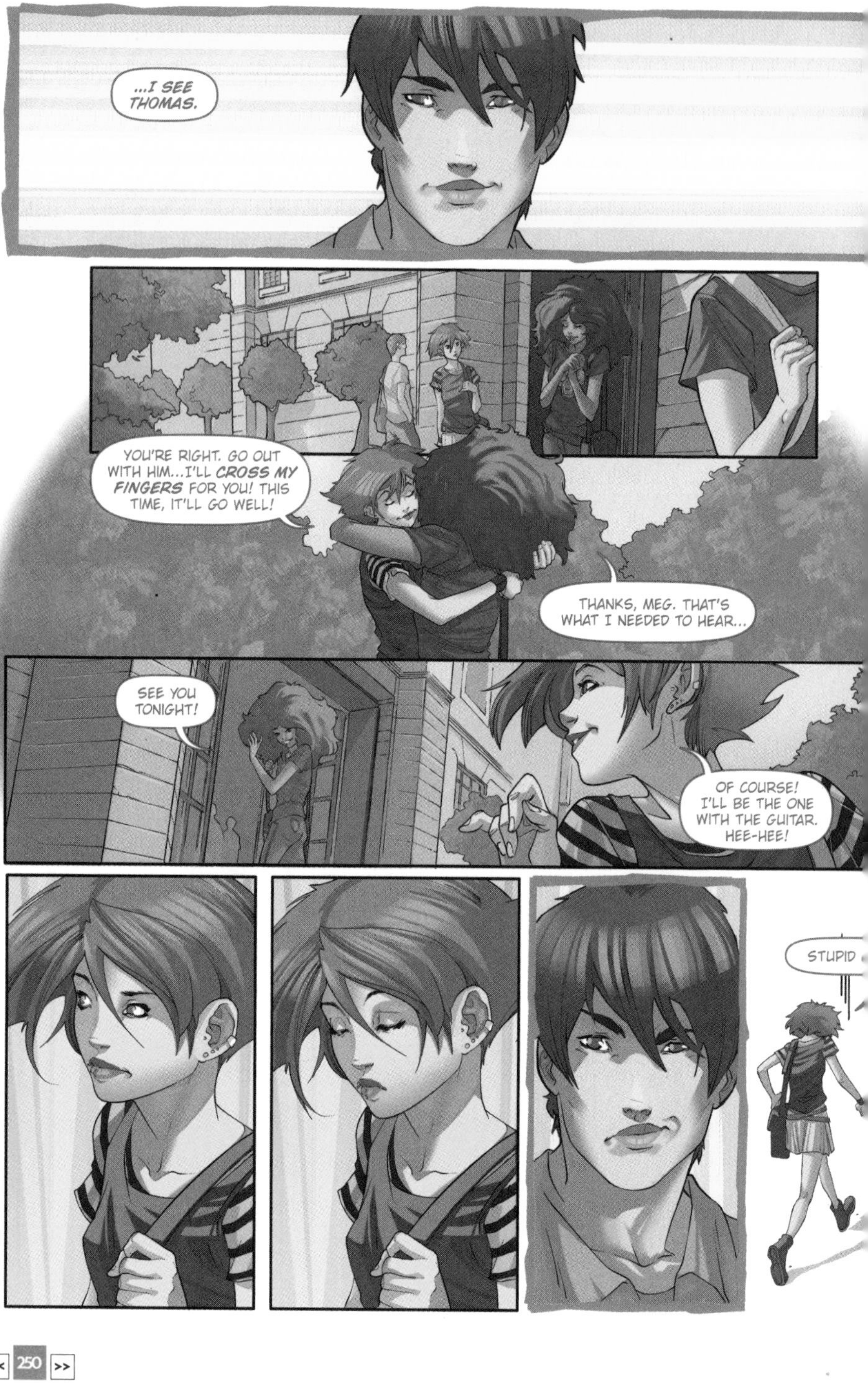

...I SEE THOMAS.
YOU'RE RIGHT. GO OUT WITH HIM...I'LL CROSS MY FINGERS FOR YOU! THIS TIME, IT'LL GO WELL!
THANKS, MEG. THAT'S WHAT I NEEDED TO HEAR...
SEE YOU TONIGHT!
OF COURSE! I'LL BE THE ONE WITH THE GUITAR. HEE-HEE!
STUPID

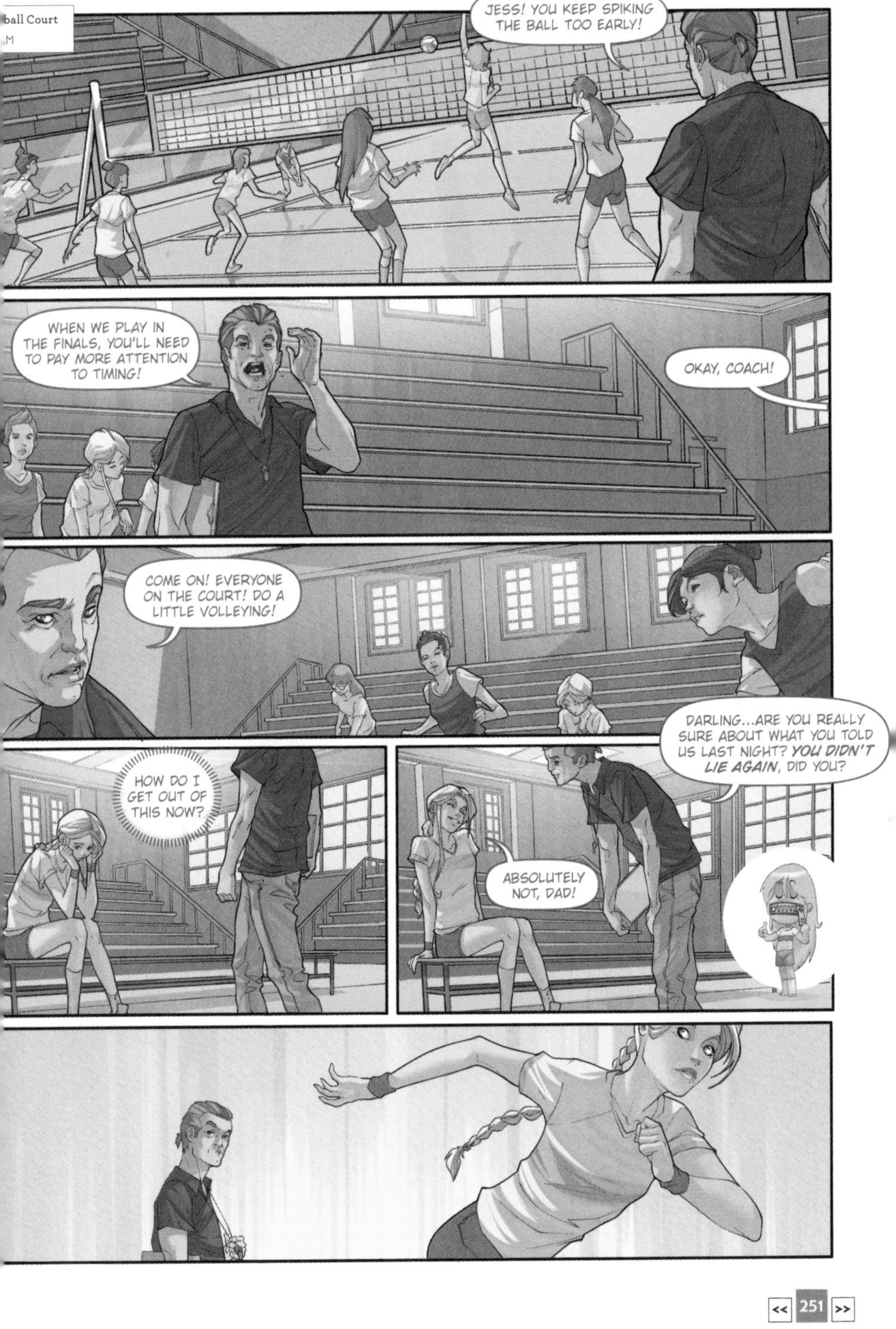

ball Court
JESS! YOU KEEP SPIKING THE BALL TOO EARLY!
WHEN WE PLAY IN THE FINALS, YOU'LL NEED TO PAY MORE ATTENTION TO TIMING!
OKAY, COACH!
COME ON! EVERYONE ON THE COURT! DO A LITTLE VOLLEYING!
HOW DO I GET OUT OF THIS NOW?
DARLING...ARE YOU REALLY SURE ABOUT WHAT YOU TOLD US LAST NIGHT? ***YOU DIDN'T LIE AGAIN***, DID YOU?
ABSOLUTELY NOT, DAD!

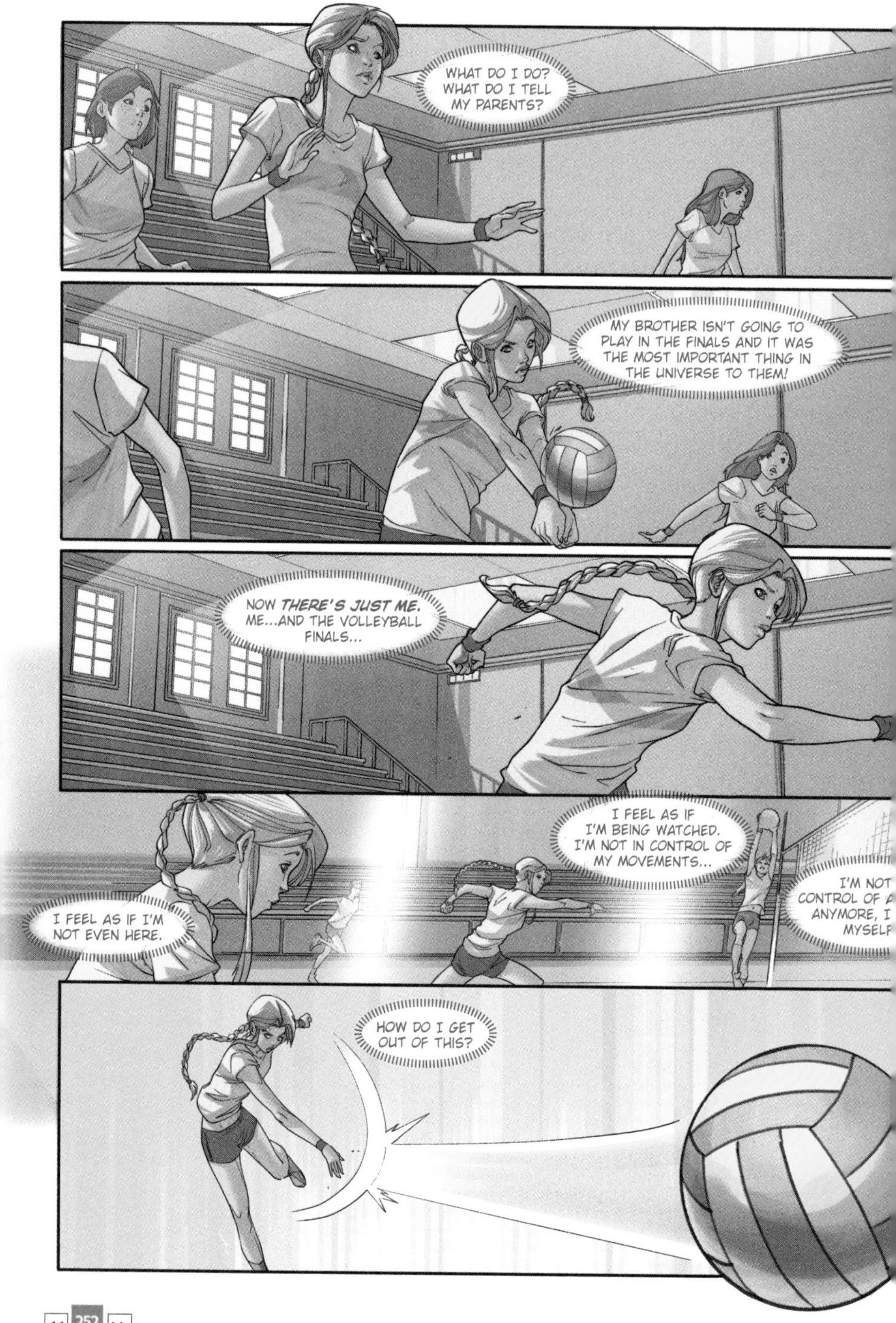

WHAT DO I DO? WHAT DO I TELL MY PARENTS?
MY BROTHER ISN'T GOING TO PLAY IN THE FINALS AND IT WAS THE MOST IMPORTANT THING IN THE UNIVERSE TO THEM!
NOW **THERE'S JUST ME.** ME...AND THE VOLLEYBALL FINALS...
I FEEL AS IF I'M NOT EVEN HERE.
I FEEL AS IF I'M BEING WATCHED. I'M NOT IN CONTROL OF MY MOVEMENTS...
HOW DO I GET OUT OF THIS?

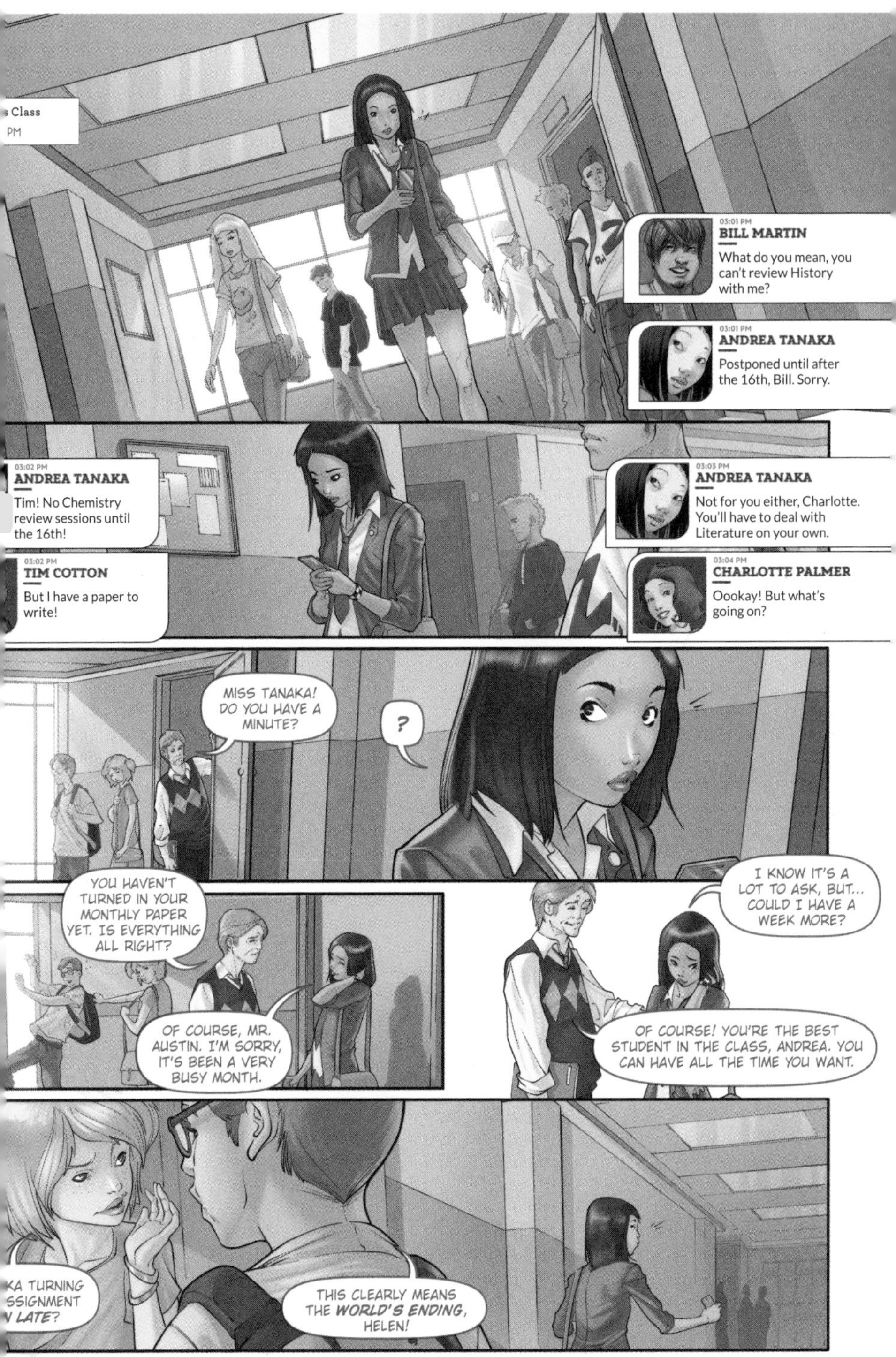
s Class
PM
03:01 PM
BILL MARTIN
What do you mean, you can't review History with me?
03:01 PM
ANDREA TANAKA
Postponed until after the 16th, Bill. Sorry.
03:02 PM
ANDREA TANAKA
Tim! No Chemistry review sessions until the 16th!
03:02 PM
TIM COTTON
But I have a paper to write!
03:03 PM
ANDREA TANAKA
Not for you either, Charlotte. You'll have to deal with Literature on your own.
03:04 PM
CHARLOTTE PALMER
Oookay! But what's going on?
MISS TANAKA! DO YOU HAVE A MINUTE?
?
YOU HAVEN'T TURNED IN YOUR MONTHLY PAPER YET. IS EVERYTHING ALL RIGHT?
OF COURSE, MR. AUSTIN. I'M SORRY, IT'S BEEN A VERY BUSY MONTH.
I KNOW IT'S A LOT TO ASK, BUT... COULD I HAVE A WEEK MORE?
OF COURSE! YOU'RE THE BEST STUDENT IN THE CLASS, ANDREA. YOU CAN HAVE ALL THE TIME YOU WANT.
KA TURNING
SSIGNMENT
LATE?
THIS CLEARLY MEANS THE WORLD'S ENDING, HELEN!

Andrea's House
Sloane Square
05:13 PM

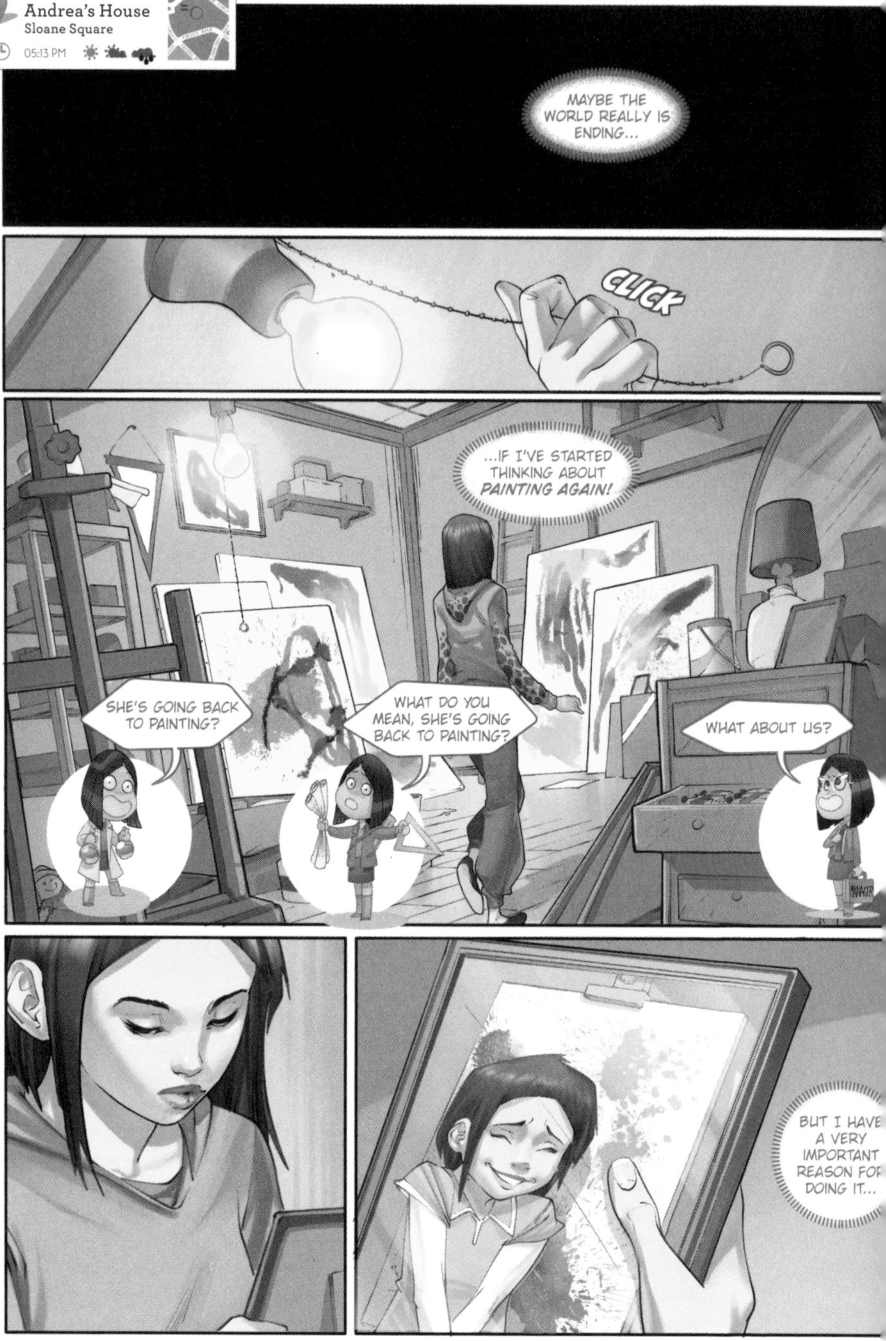

MAYBE THE WORLD REALLY IS ENDING...
CLICK
...IF I'VE STARTED THINKING ABOUT PAINTING AGAIN!
SHE'S GOING BACK TO PAINTING?
WHAT DO YOU MEAN, SHE'S GOING BACK TO PAINTING?
WHAT ABOUT US?
BUT I HAVE A VERY IMPORTANT REASON FOR DOING IT...

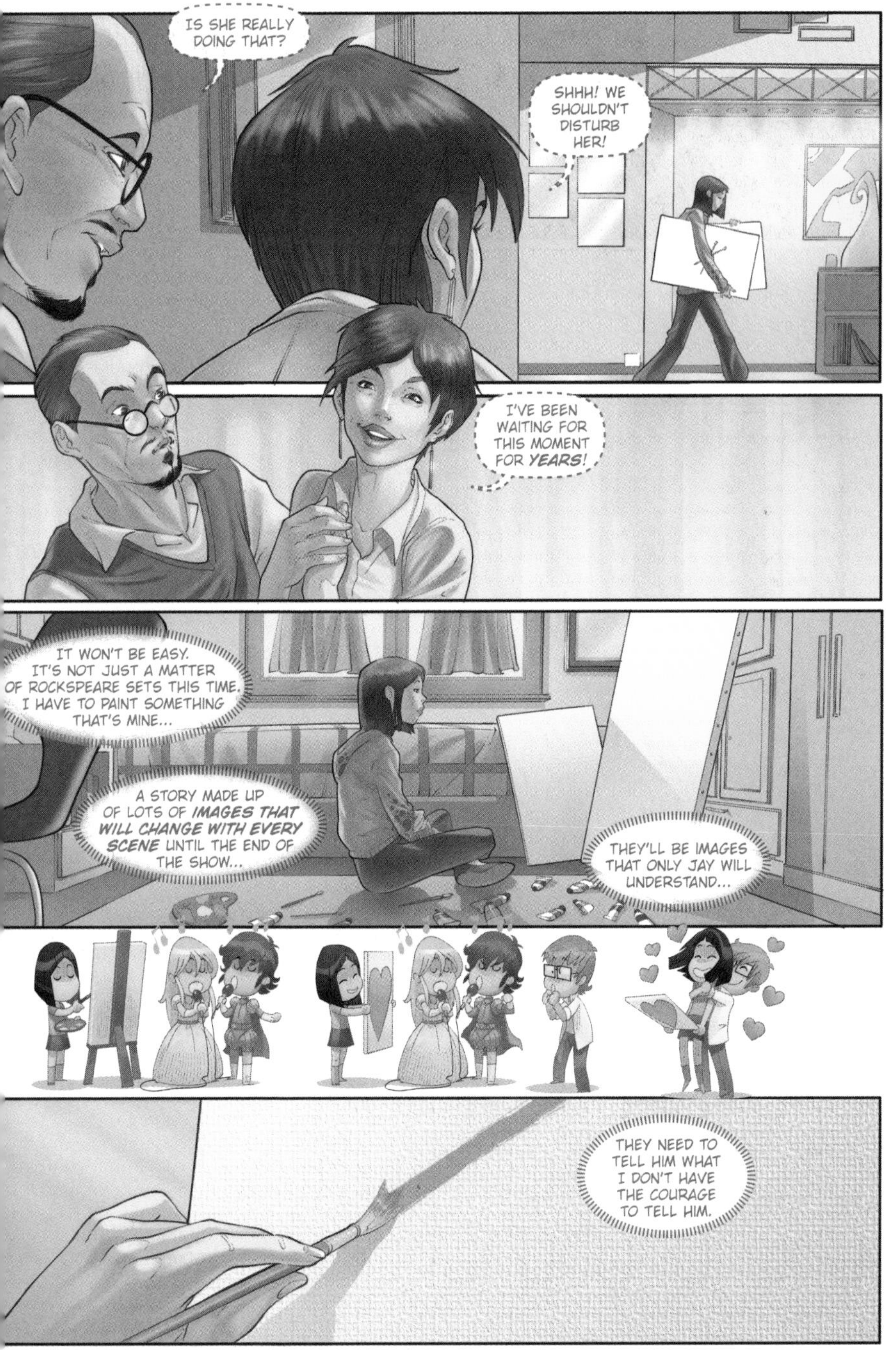
IS SHE REALLY DOING THAT?
SHHH! WE SHOULDN'T DISTURB HER!
I'VE BEEN WAITING FOR THIS MOMENT FOR YEARS!
IT WON'T BE EASY. IT'S NOT JUST A MATTER OF ROCKSPEARE SETS THIS TIME. I HAVE TO PAINT SOMETHING THAT'S MINE...
A STORY MADE UP OF LOTS OF IMAGES THAT WILL CHANGE WITH EVERY SCENE UNTIL THE END OF THE SHOW...
THEY'LL BE IMAGES THAT ONLY JAY WILL UNDERSTAND...
THEY NEED TO TELL HIM WHAT I DON'T HAVE THE COURAGE TO TELL HIM.

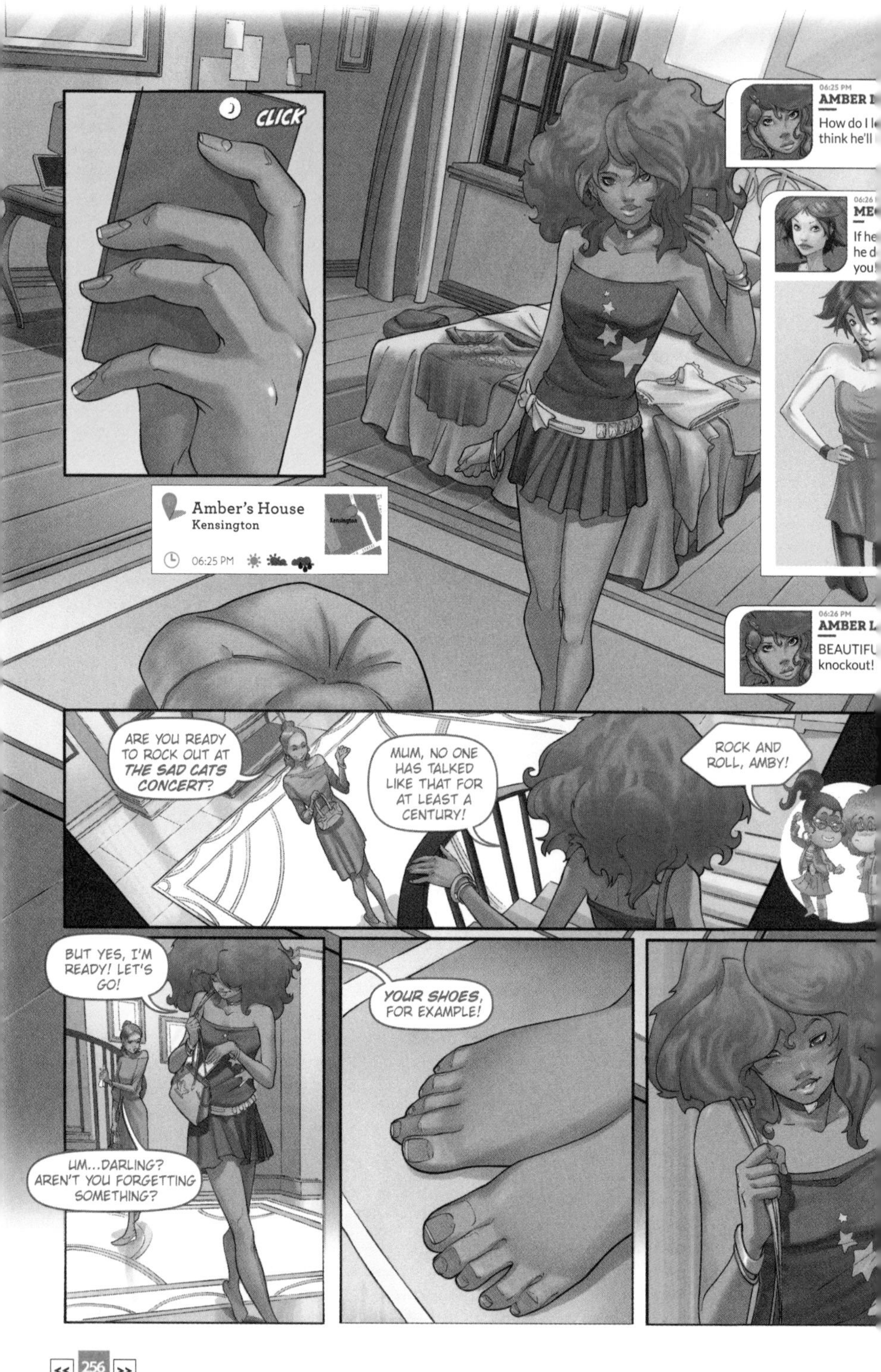

CLICK
06:25 PM
How do I
think he'll
06:26
Amber's House
Kensington
06:25 PM
06:26 PM
knockout!
ARE YOU READY TO ROCK OUT AT THE SAD CATS CONCERT?
MUM, NO ONE HAS TALKED LIKE THAT FOR AT LEAST A CENTURY!
ROCK AND ROLL, AMBY!
BUT YES, I'M READY! LET'S GO!
UM...DARLING? AREN'T YOU FORGETTING SOMETHING?
YOUR SHOES, FOR EXAMPLE!

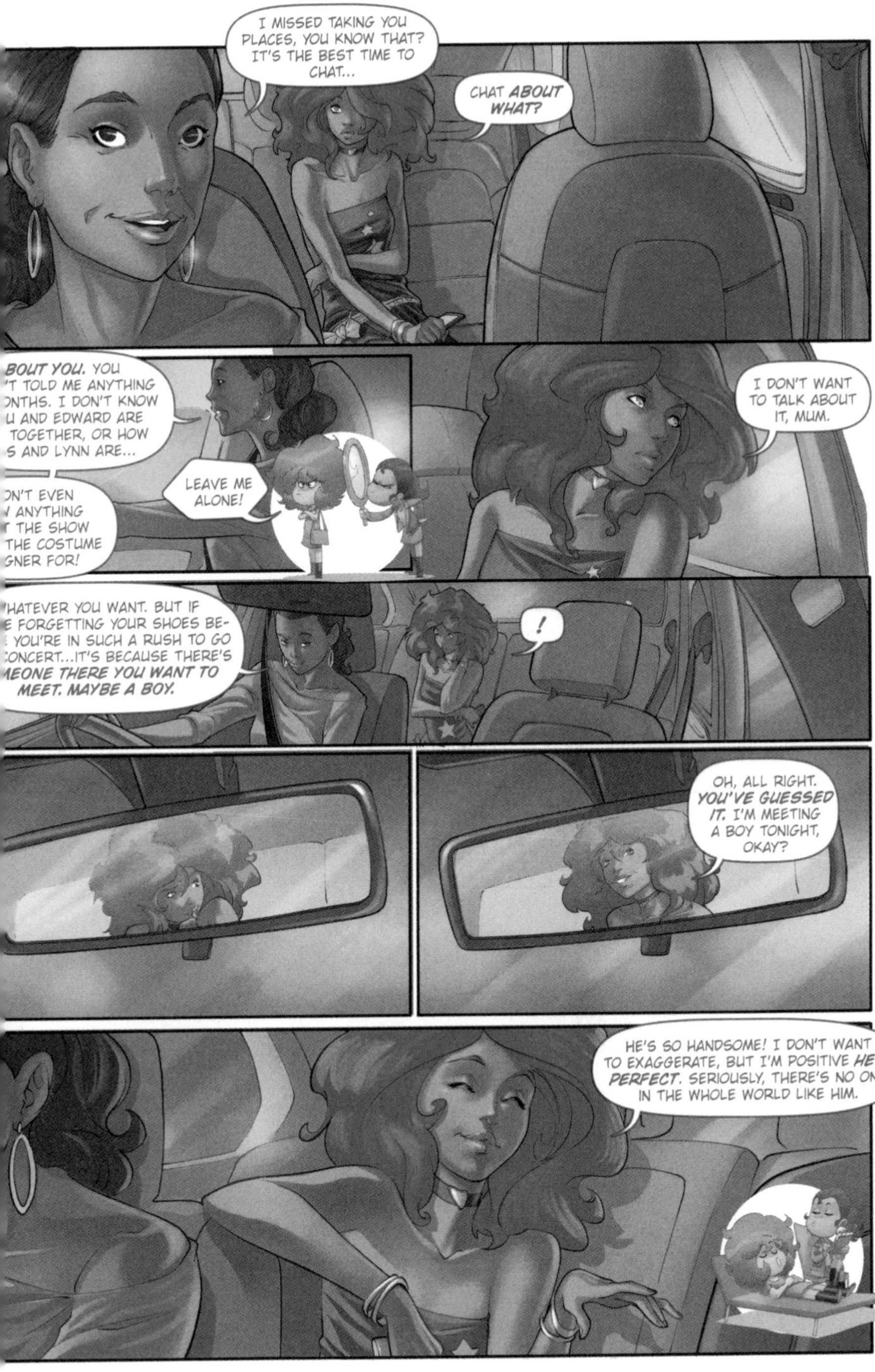
I MISSED TAKING YOU PLACES, YOU KNOW THAT? IT'S THE BEST TIME TO CHAT...
CHAT ABOUT WHAT?
BOUT YOU. YOU 'T TOLD ME ANYTHING ONTHS. I DON'T KNOW U AND EDWARD ARE TOGETHER, OR HOW S AND LYNN ARE...
ON'T EVEN ANYTHING T THE SHOW THE COSTUME GNER FOR!
LEAVE ME ALONE!
I DON'T WANT TO TALK ABOUT IT, MUM.
HATEVER YOU WANT. BUT IF E FORGETTING YOUR SHOES BE- YOU'RE IN SUCH A RUSH TO GO CONCERT...IT'S BECAUSE THERE'S MEONE THERE YOU WANT TO MEET. MAYBE A BOY.
!
OH, ALL RIGHT. YOU'VE GUESSED IT. I'M MEETING A BOY TONIGHT, OKAY?
HE'S SO HANDSOME! I DON'T WANT TO EXAGGERATE, BUT I'M POSITIVE HE'S PERFECT. SERIOUSLY, THERE'S NO ONE IN THE WHOLE WORLD LIKE HIM.

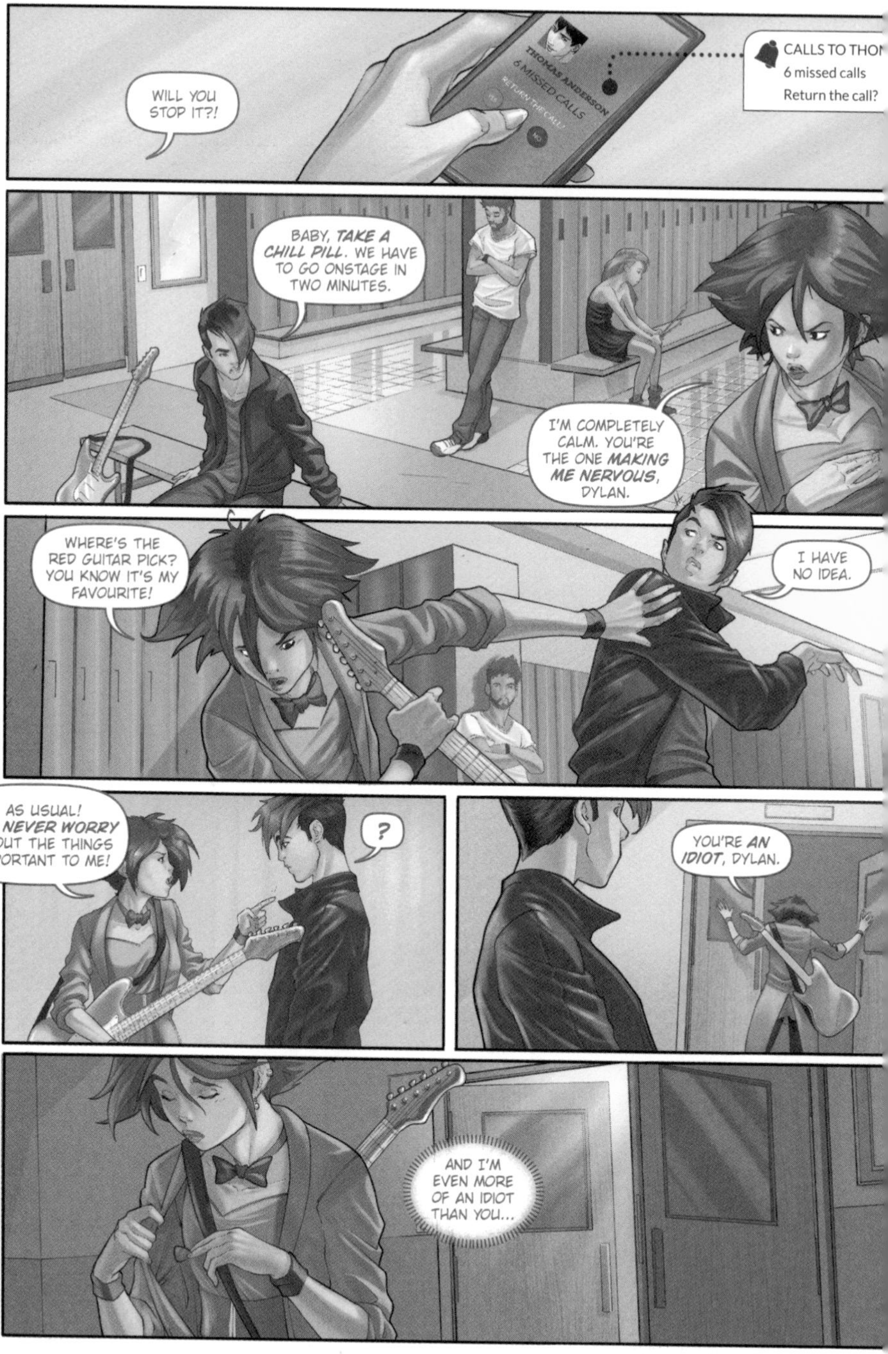
THOMAS ANDERSON
6 MISSED CALLS
RETURN THE CALL?
WILL YOU STOP IT?!
CALLS TO THOM
6 missed calls
Return the call?
BABY, **TAKE A CHILL PILL**. WE HAVE TO GO ONSTAGE IN TWO MINUTES.
I'M COMPLETELY CALM. YOU'RE THE ONE **MAKING ME NERVOUS**, DYLAN.
WHERE'S THE RED GUITAR PICK? YOU KNOW IT'S MY FAVOURITE!
I HAVE NO IDEA.
AS USUAL! YOU **NEVER WORRY** ABOUT THE THINGS IMPORTANT TO ME!
?
YOU'RE **AN IDIOT**, DYLAN.
AND I'M EVEN MORE OF AN IDIOT THAN YOU...

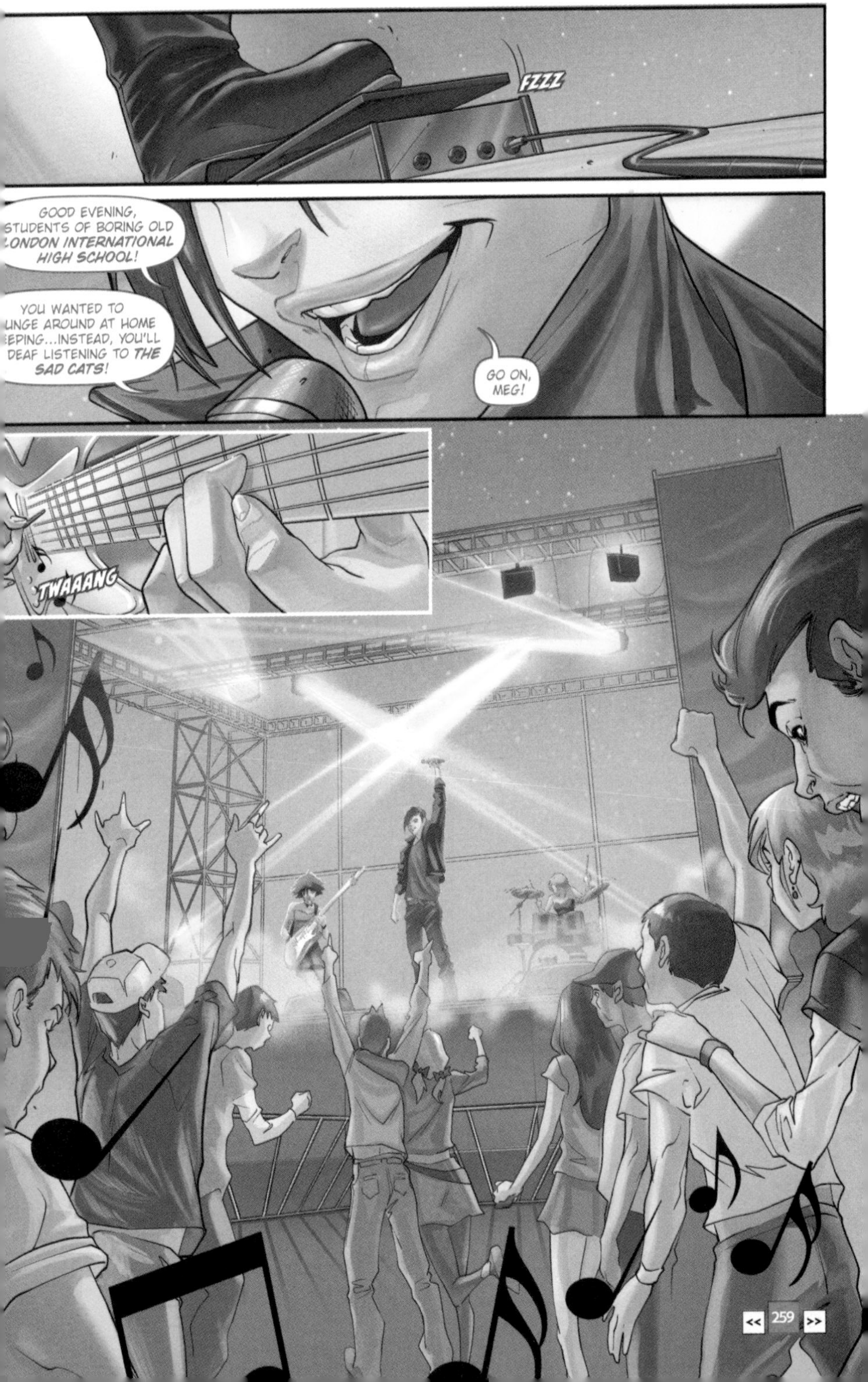
FZZZ
GOOD EVENING, STUDENTS OF BORING OLD LONDON INTERNATIONAL HIGH SCHOOL!
YOU WANTED TO UNGE AROUND AT HOME EEPING...INSTEAD, YOU'LL DEAF LISTENING TO THE SAD CATS!
GO ON, MEG!
TWAAANG

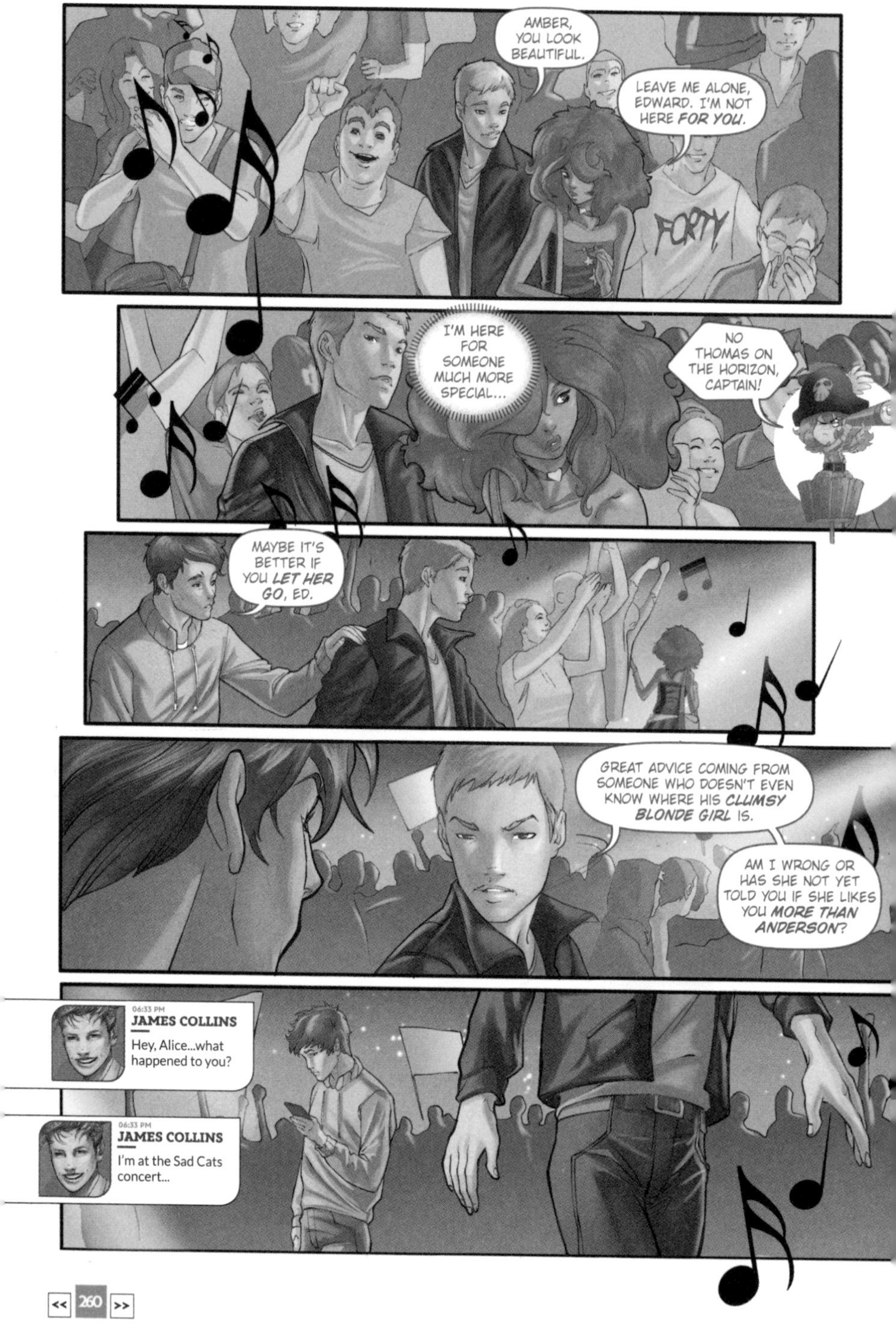
AMBER, YOU LOOK BEAUTIFUL.
LEAVE ME ALONE, EDWARD. I'M NOT HERE FOR YOU.
FORTY
I'M HERE FOR SOMEONE MUCH MORE SPECIAL...
NO THOMAS ON THE HORIZON, CAPTAIN!
MAYBE IT'S BETTER IF YOU LET HER GO, ED.
GREAT ADVICE COMING FROM SOMEONE WHO DOESN'T EVEN KNOW WHERE HIS CLUMSY BLONDE GIRL IS.
AM I WRONG OR HAS SHE NOT YET TOLD YOU IF SHE LIKES YOU MORE THAN ANDERSON?
06:33 PM
JAMES COLLINS
Hey, Alice...what happened to you?
06:33 PM
JAMES COLLINS
I'm at the Sad Cats concert...

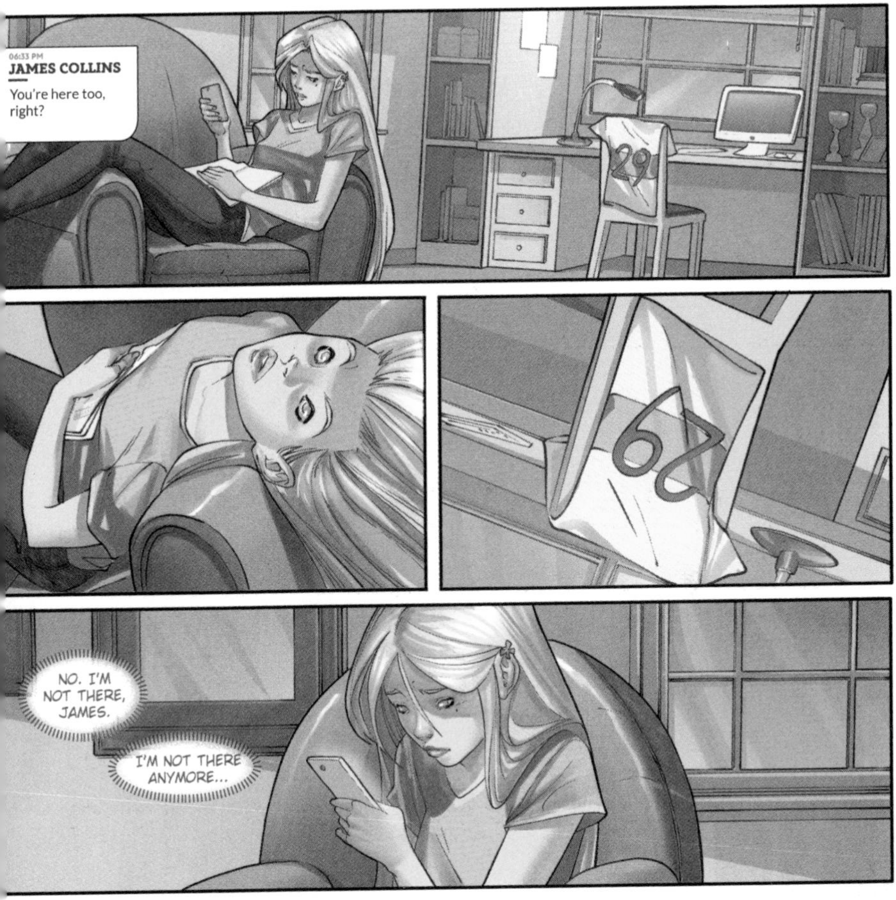
06:33 PM
JAMES COLLINS
You're here too, right?
NO. I'M NOT THERE, JAMES.
I'M NOT THERE ANYMORE...

ROCKSPEARE - CLOSED GROUP

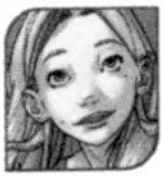

05:50 PM

ALICE KEATS

I don't know how to tell all of you, so I'm just going to say it. I don't want to be your Juliet anymore. I'm quitting Rockspeare, and I'm quitting Edward's play too.

ROCKSPEARE - CLOSED GROUP

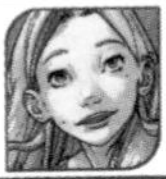

05:50 PM

ALICE KEATS

I'm sorry. Really sorry. Don't call me.

END OF CHAPTER 32

CHAPTER 33

Is this THE END?

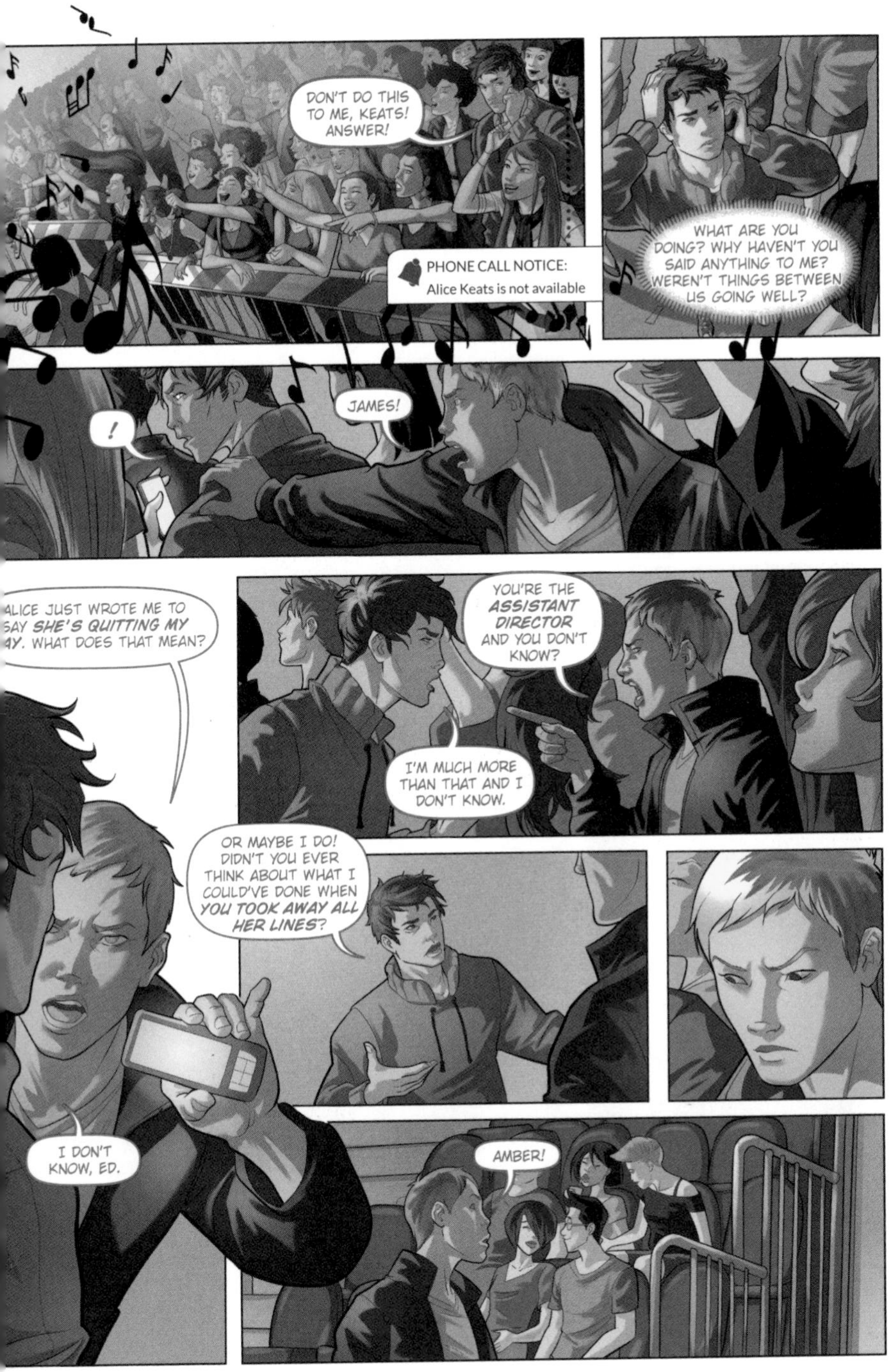
DON'T DO THIS TO ME, KEATS! ANSWER!
PHONE CALL NOTICE:
Alice Keats is not available
WHAT ARE YOU DOING? WHY HAVEN'T YOU SAID ANYTHING TO ME? WEREN'T THINGS BETWEEN US GOING WELL?
!
JAMES!
ALICE JUST WROTE ME TO SAY SHE'S QUITTING MY
AY. WHAT DOES THAT MEAN?
YOU'RE THE ASSISTANT DIRECTOR AND YOU DON'T KNOW?
I'M MUCH MORE THAN THAT AND I DON'T KNOW.
OR MAYBE I DO! DIDN'T YOU EVER THINK ABOUT WHAT I COULD'VE DONE WHEN YOU TOOK AWAY ALL HER LINES?
I DON'T KNOW, ED.
AMBER!

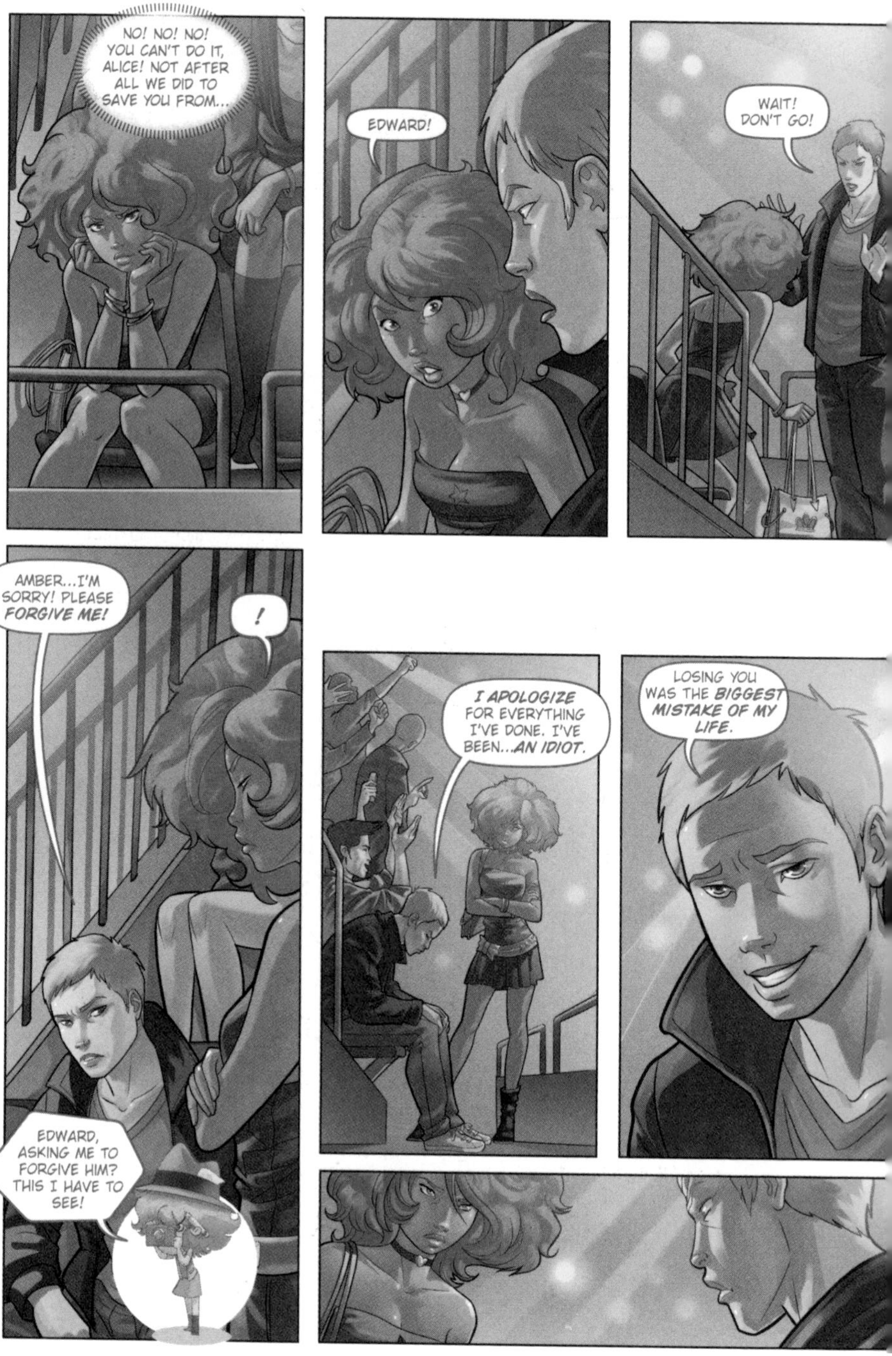
NO! NO! NO! YOU CAN'T DO IT, ALICE! NOT AFTER ALL WE DID TO SAVE YOU FROM...
EDWARD!
WAIT! DON'T GO!
AMBER...I'M SORRY! PLEASE FORGIVE ME!
!
EDWARD, ASKING ME TO FORGIVE HIM? THIS I HAVE TO SEE!
I APOLOGIZE FOR EVERYTHING I'VE DONE. I'VE BEEN...AN IDIOT.
LOSING YOU WAS THE BIGGEST MISTAKE OF MY LIFE.

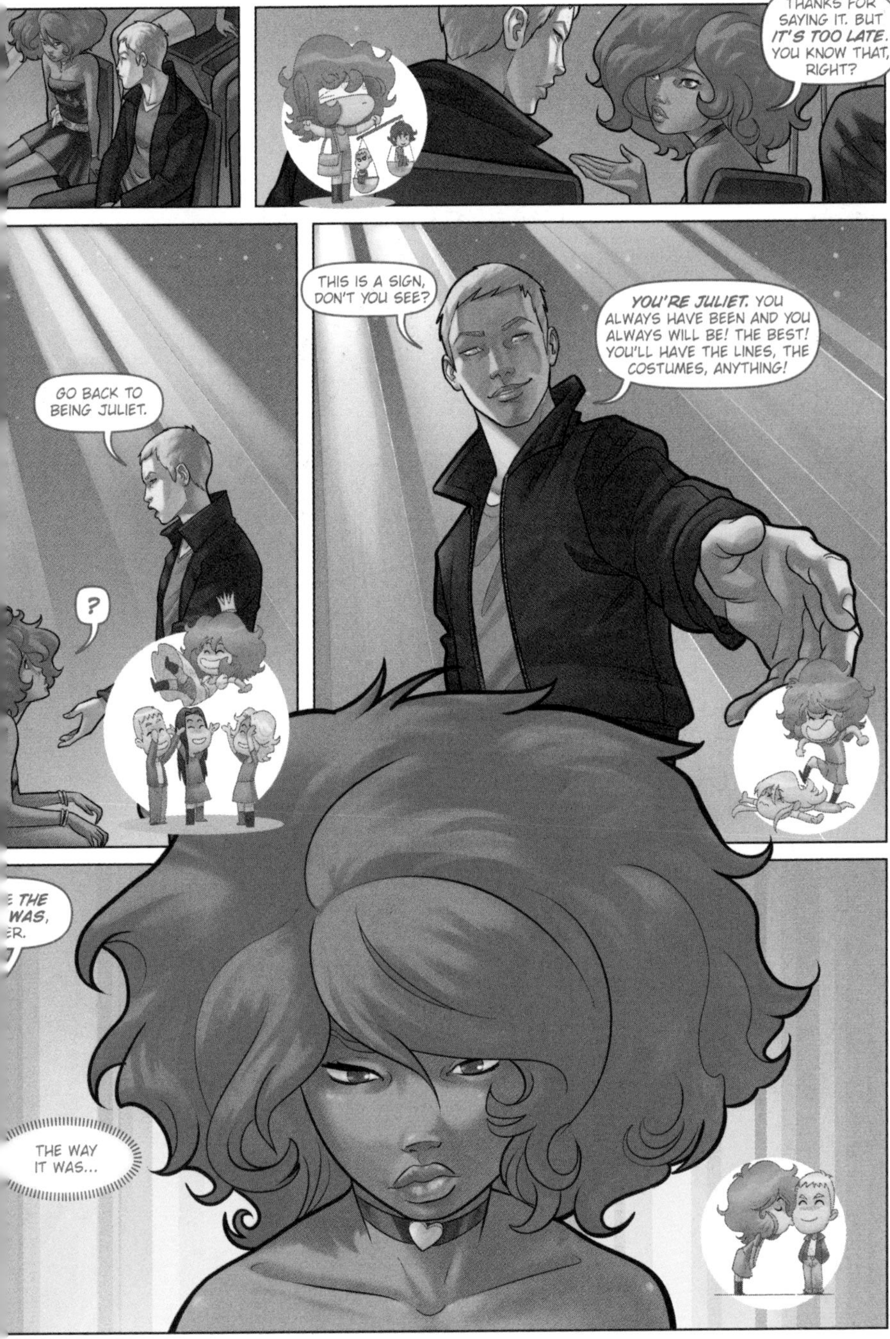
THANKS FOR SAYING IT. BUT *IT'S TOO LATE*. YOU KNOW THAT, RIGHT?
GO BACK TO BEING JULIET.
THIS IS A SIGN, DON'T YOU SEE?
YOU'RE JULIET. YOU ALWAYS HAVE BEEN AND YOU ALWAYS WILL BE! THE BEST! YOU'LL HAVE THE LINES, THE COSTUMES, ANYTHING!
?
THE WAY IT WAS...

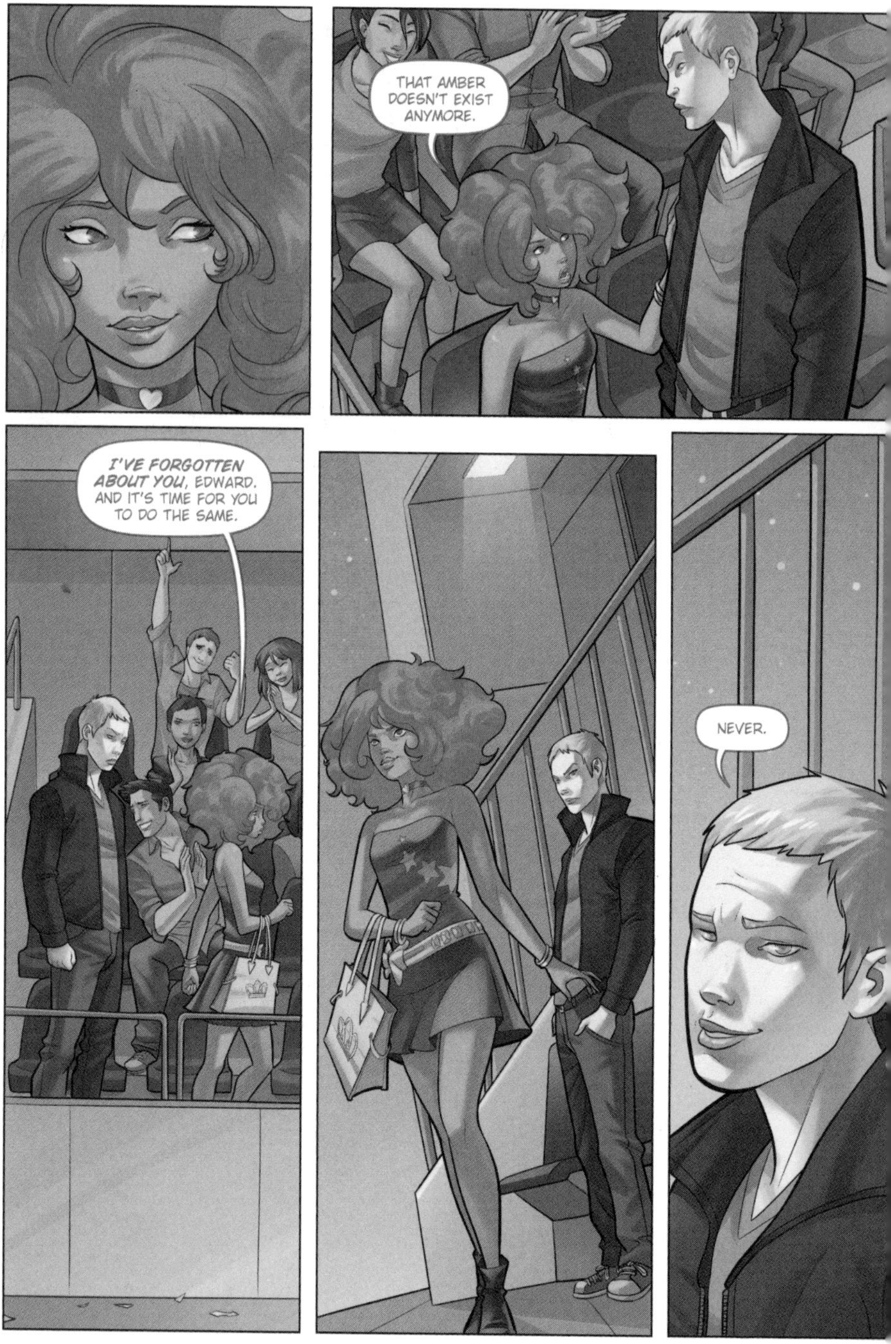
THAT AMBER DOESN'T EXIST ANYMORE.
I'VE FORGOTTEN ABOUT YOU, EDWARD. AND IT'S TIME FOR YOU TO DO THE SAME.
NEVER.

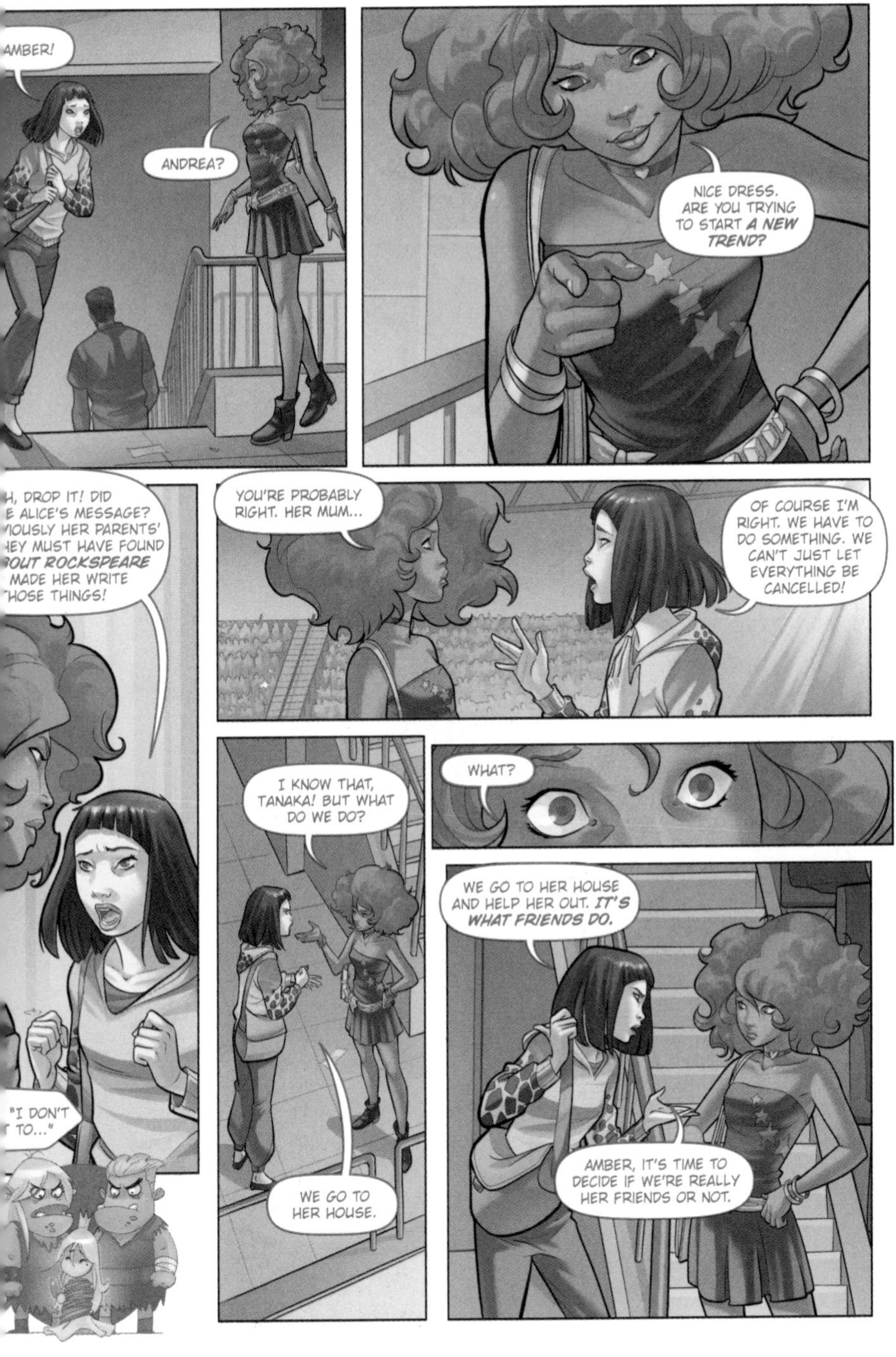
MBER!
ANDREA?
NICE DRESS. ARE YOU TRYING TO START **A NEW TREND?**
H, DROP IT! DID E ALICE'S MESSAGE? VIOUSLY HER PARENTS' HEY MUST HAVE FOUND **BOUT ROCKSPEARE** MADE HER WRITE THOSE THINGS!
"I DON'T T TO..."
YOU'RE PROBABLY RIGHT. HER MUM...
OF COURSE I'M RIGHT. WE HAVE TO DO SOMETHING. WE CAN'T JUST LET EVERYTHING BE CANCELLED!
I KNOW THAT, TANAKA! BUT WHAT DO WE DO?
WE GO TO HER HOUSE.
WHAT?
WE GO TO HER HOUSE AND HELP HER OUT. **IT'S WHAT FRIENDS DO.**
AMBER, IT'S TIME TO DECIDE IF WE'RE REALLY HER FRIENDS OR NOT.

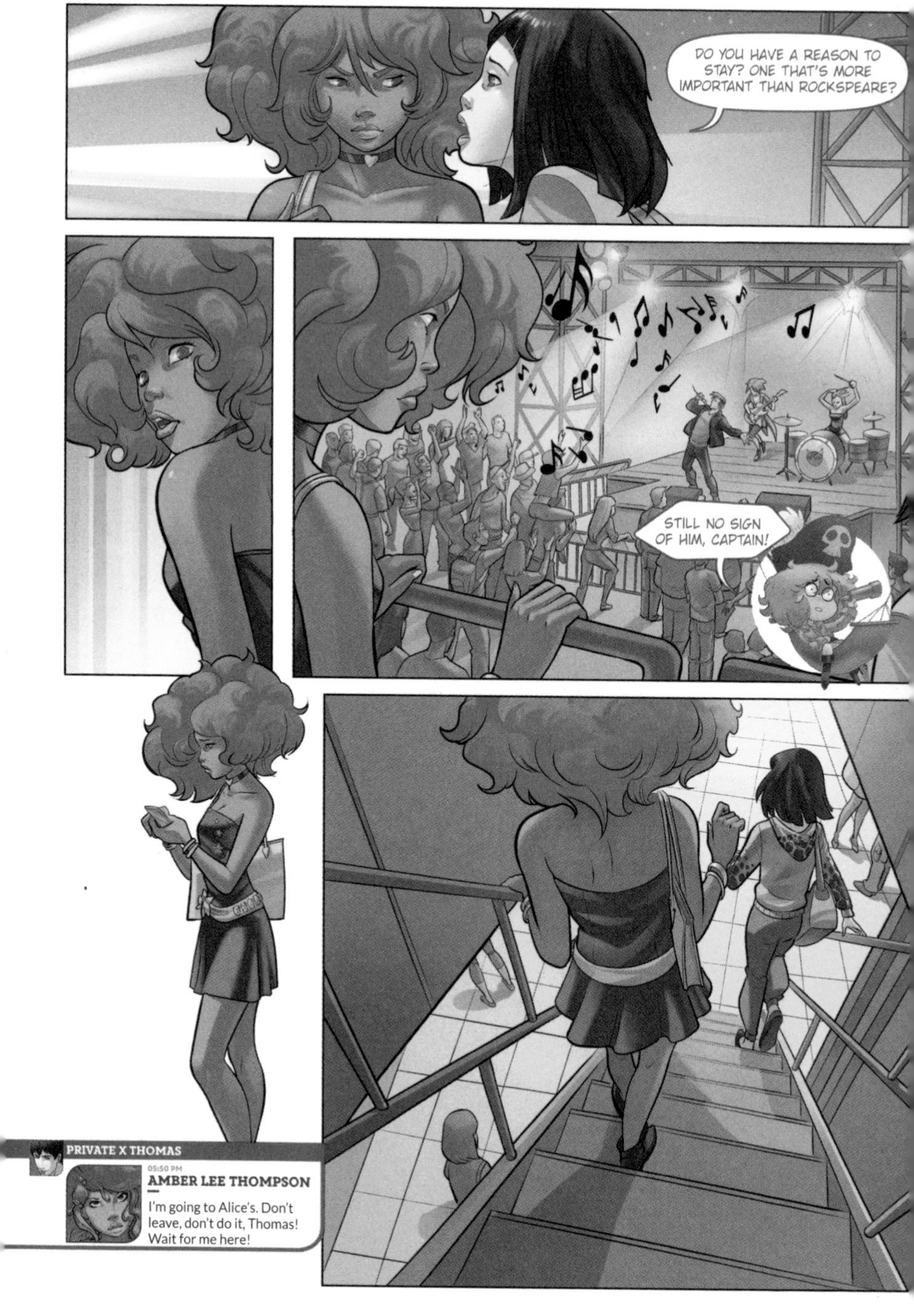
DO YOU HAVE A REASON TO STAY? ONE THAT'S MORE IMPORTANT THAN ROCKSPEARE?
STILL NO SIGN OF HIM, CAPTAIN!
PRIVATE X THOMAS
05:50 PM
AMBER LEE THOMPSON
I'm going to Alice's. Don't leave, don't do it, Thomas! Wait for me here!

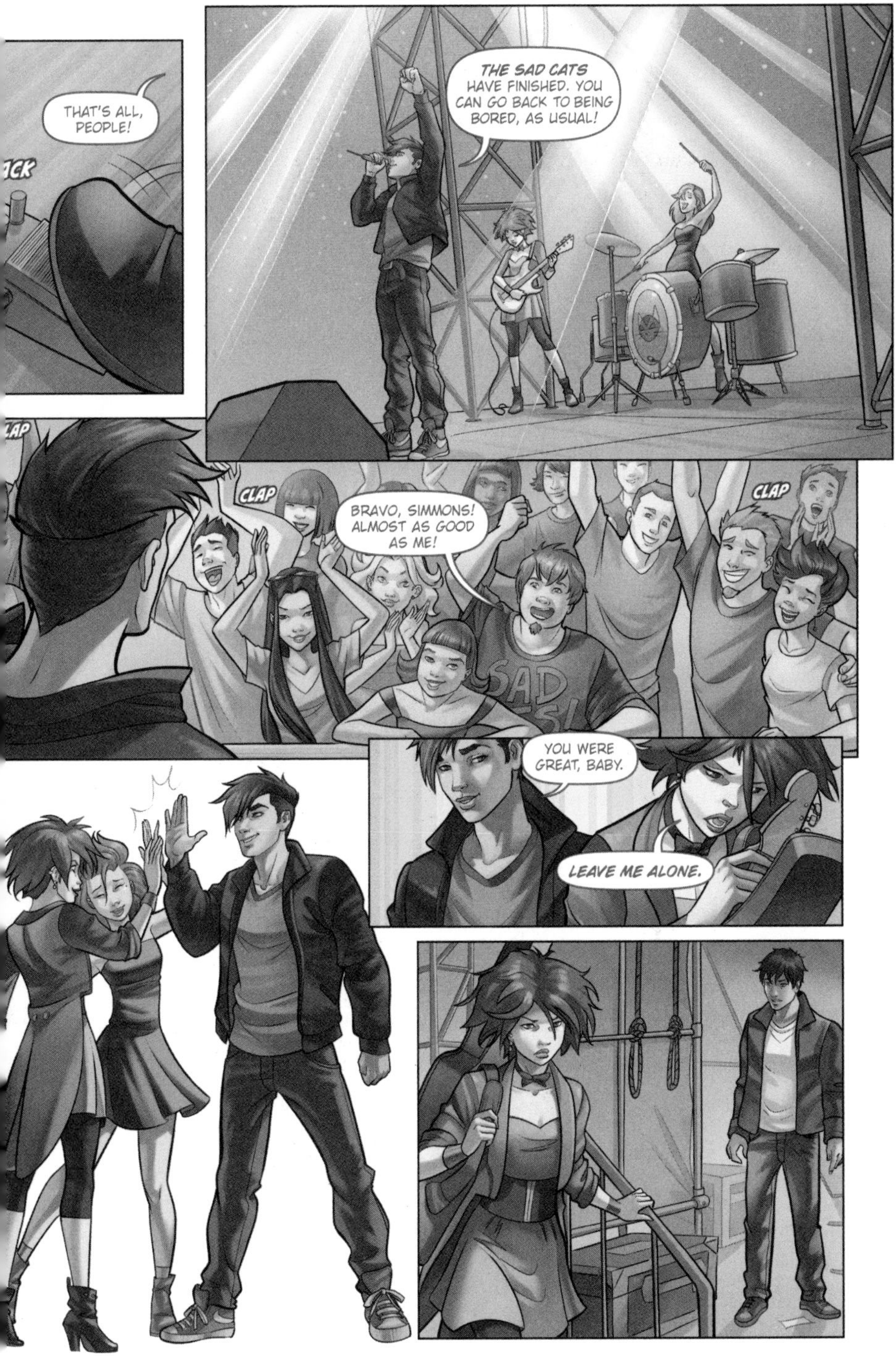
THAT'S ALL, PEOPLE!
THE SAD CATS HAVE FINISHED. YOU CAN GO BACK TO BEING BORED, AS USUAL!
CLAP
CLAP
BRAVO, SIMMONS! ALMOST AS GOOD AS ME!
CLAP
YOU WERE GREAT, BABY.
LEAVE ME ALONE.

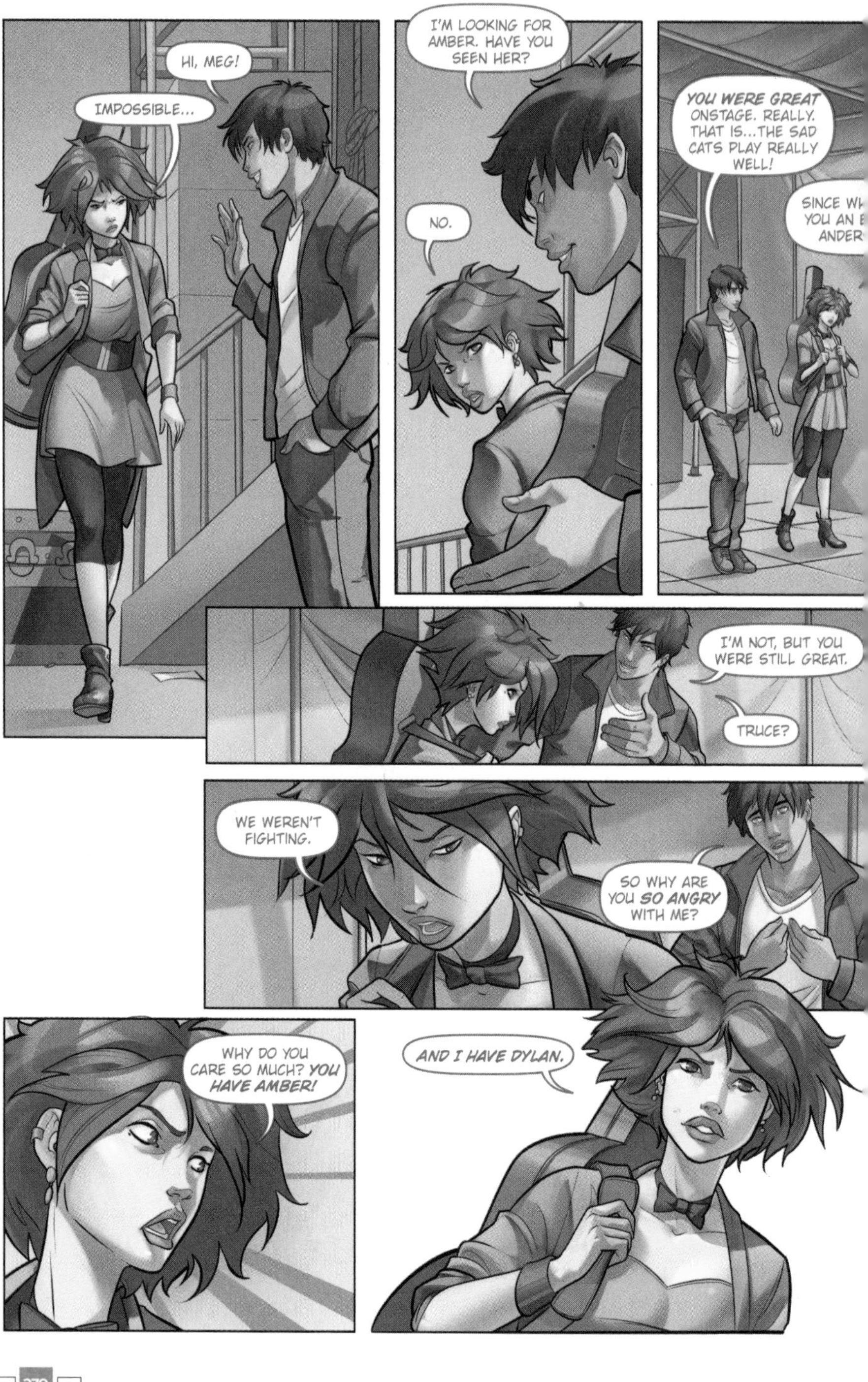
HI, MEG!
IMPOSSIBLE...
I'M LOOKING FOR AMBER. HAVE YOU SEEN HER?
NO.
YOU WERE GREAT ONSTAGE. REALLY. THAT IS...THE SAD CATS PLAY REALLY WELL!
SINCE WH YOU AN E ANDER
I'M NOT, BUT YOU WERE STILL GREAT.
TRUCE?
WE WEREN'T FIGHTING.
SO WHY ARE YOU *SO ANGRY* WITH ME?
WHY DO YOU CARE SO MUCH? *YOU HAVE AMBER!*
AND I HAVE DYLAN.

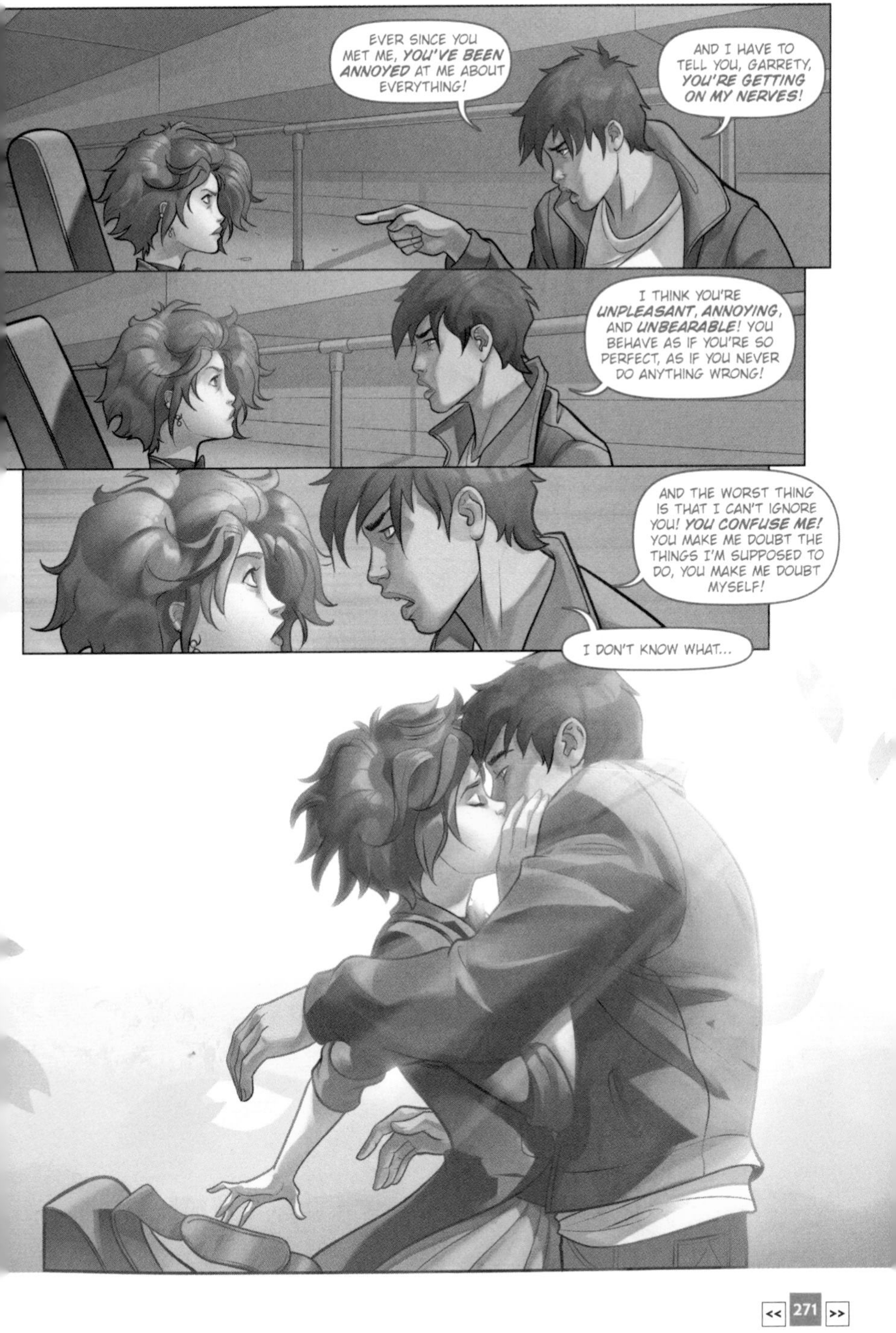
EVER SINCE YOU MET ME, ***YOU'VE BEEN ANNOYED*** AT ME ABOUT EVERYTHING!
AND I HAVE TO TELL YOU, GARRETY, ***YOU'RE GETTING ON MY NERVES!***
I THINK YOU'RE ***UNPLEASANT, ANNOYING***, AND ***UNBEARABLE!*** YOU BEHAVE AS IF YOU'RE SO PERFECT, AS IF YOU NEVER DO ANYTHING WRONG!
AND THE WORST THING IS THAT I CAN'T IGNORE YOU! ***YOU CONFUSE ME!*** YOU MAKE ME DOUBT THE THINGS I'M SUPPOSED TO DO, YOU MAKE ME DOUBT MYSELF!
I DON'T KNOW WHAT...

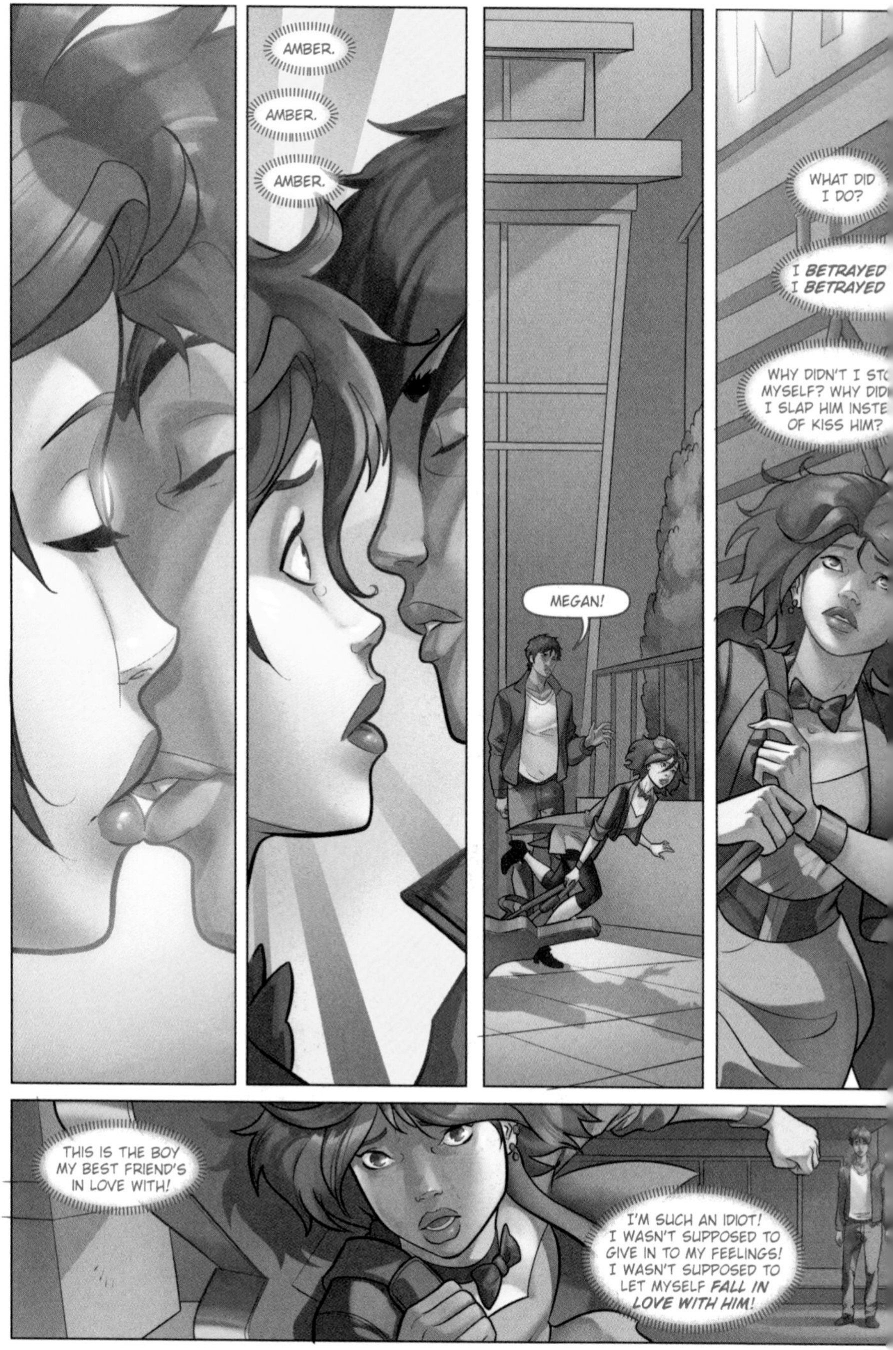
AMBER.
AMBER.
AMBER.
MEGAN!
WHAT DID I DO?
I BETRAYED I BETRAYED
WHY DIDN'T I STO MYSELF? WHY DIDN I SLAP HIM INSTE OF KISS HIM?
THIS IS THE BOY MY BEST FRIEND'S IN LOVE WITH!
I'M SUCH AN IDIOT! I WASN'T SUPPOSED TO GIVE IN TO MY FEELINGS! I WASN'T SUPPOSED TO LET MYSELF FALL IN LOVE WITH HIM!

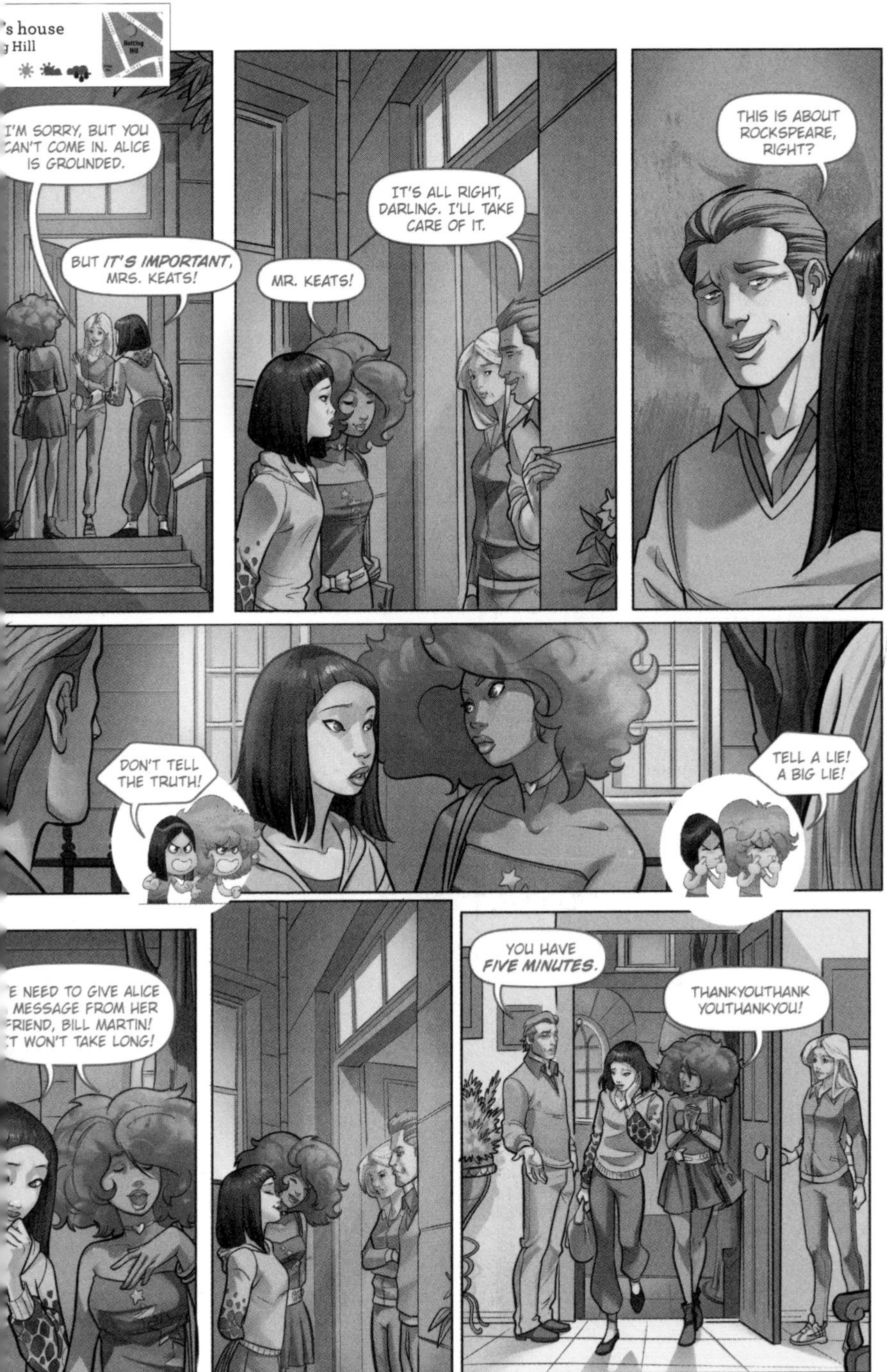
's house
g Hill
Notting Hill
I'M SORRY, BUT YOU CAN'T COME IN. ALICE IS GROUNDED.
BUT IT'S IMPORTANT, MRS. KEATS!
MR. KEATS!
IT'S ALL RIGHT, DARLING. I'LL TAKE CARE OF IT.
THIS IS ABOUT ROCKSPEARE, RIGHT?
DON'T TELL THE TRUTH!
TELL A LIE! A BIG LIE!
E NEED TO GIVE ALICE MESSAGE FROM HER FRIEND, BILL MARTIN! T WON'T TAKE LONG!
YOU HAVE FIVE MINUTES.
THANKYOUTHANK YOUTHANKYOU!

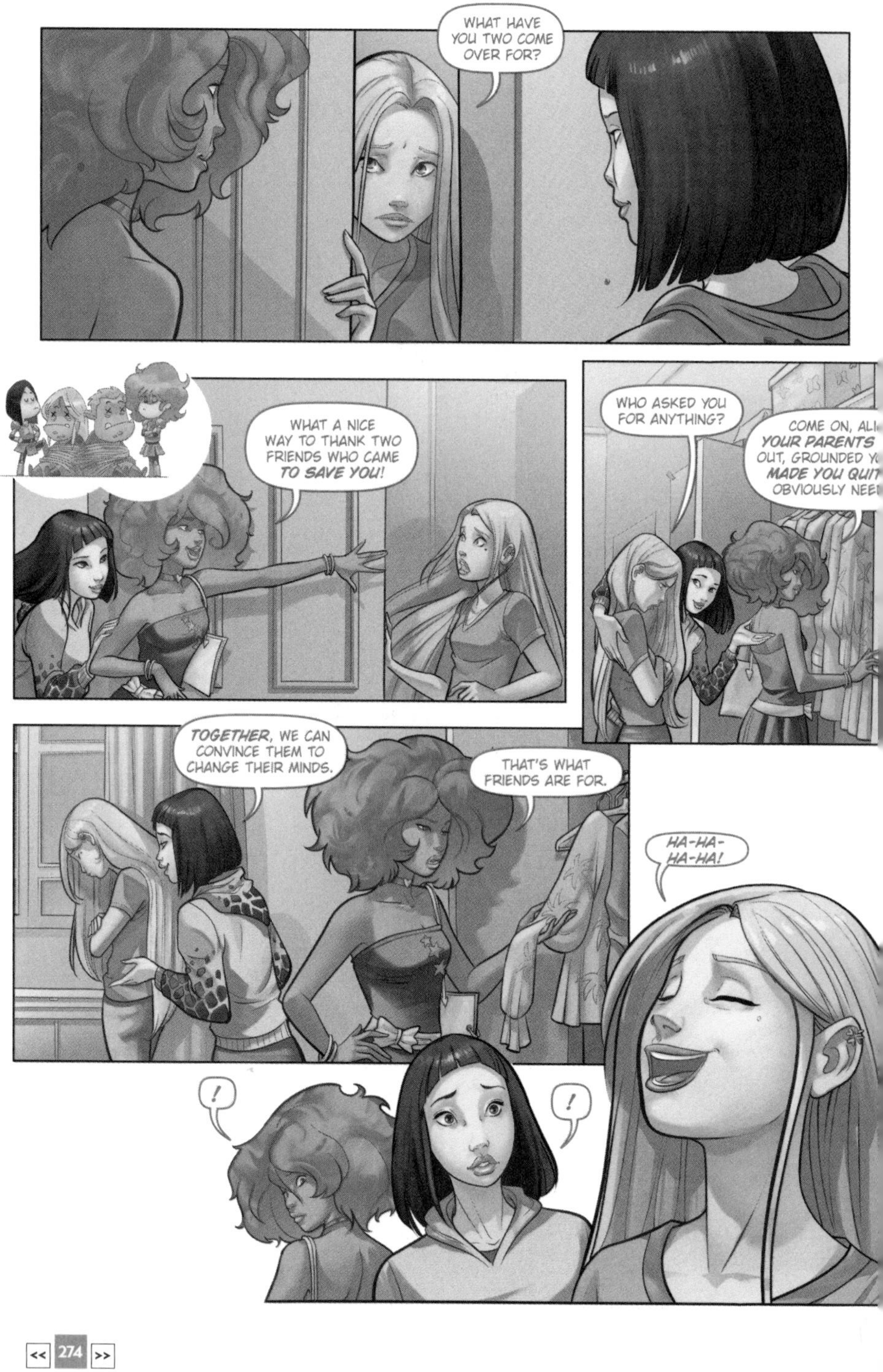
WHAT HAVE YOU TWO COME OVER FOR?
WHAT A NICE WAY TO THANK TWO FRIENDS WHO CAME **TO SAVE YOU**!
WHO ASKED YOU FOR ANYTHING?
COME ON, ALI **YOUR PARENTS** OUT, GROUNDED Y **MADE YOU QUIT** OBVIOUSLY NEE
TOGETHER, WE CAN CONVINCE THEM TO CHANGE THEIR MINDS.
THAT'S WHAT FRIENDS ARE FOR.
HA-HA-HA-HA!
!
!

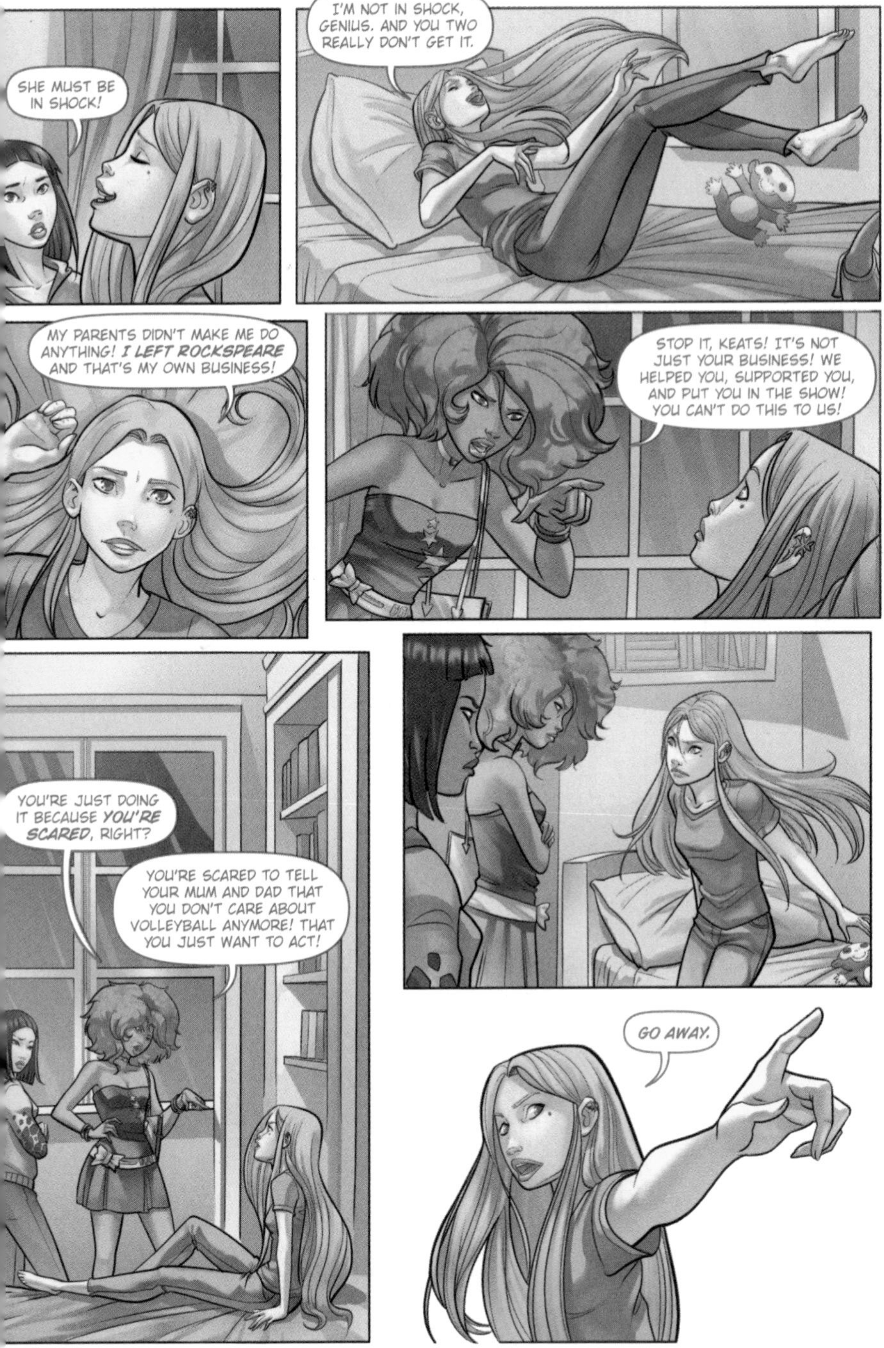
SHE MUST BE IN SHOCK!
I'M NOT IN SHOCK, GENIUS. AND YOU TWO REALLY DON'T GET IT.
MY PARENTS DIDN'T MAKE ME DO ANYTHING! I LEFT ROCKSPEARE AND THAT'S MY OWN BUSINESS!
STOP IT, KEATS! IT'S NOT JUST YOUR BUSINESS! WE HELPED YOU, SUPPORTED YOU, AND PUT YOU IN THE SHOW! YOU CAN'T DO THIS TO US!
YOU'RE JUST DOING IT BECAUSE YOU'RE SCARED, RIGHT?
YOU'RE SCARED TO TELL YOUR MUM AND DAD THAT YOU DON'T CARE ABOUT VOLLEYBALL ANYMORE! THAT YOU JUST WANT TO ACT!
GO AWAY.

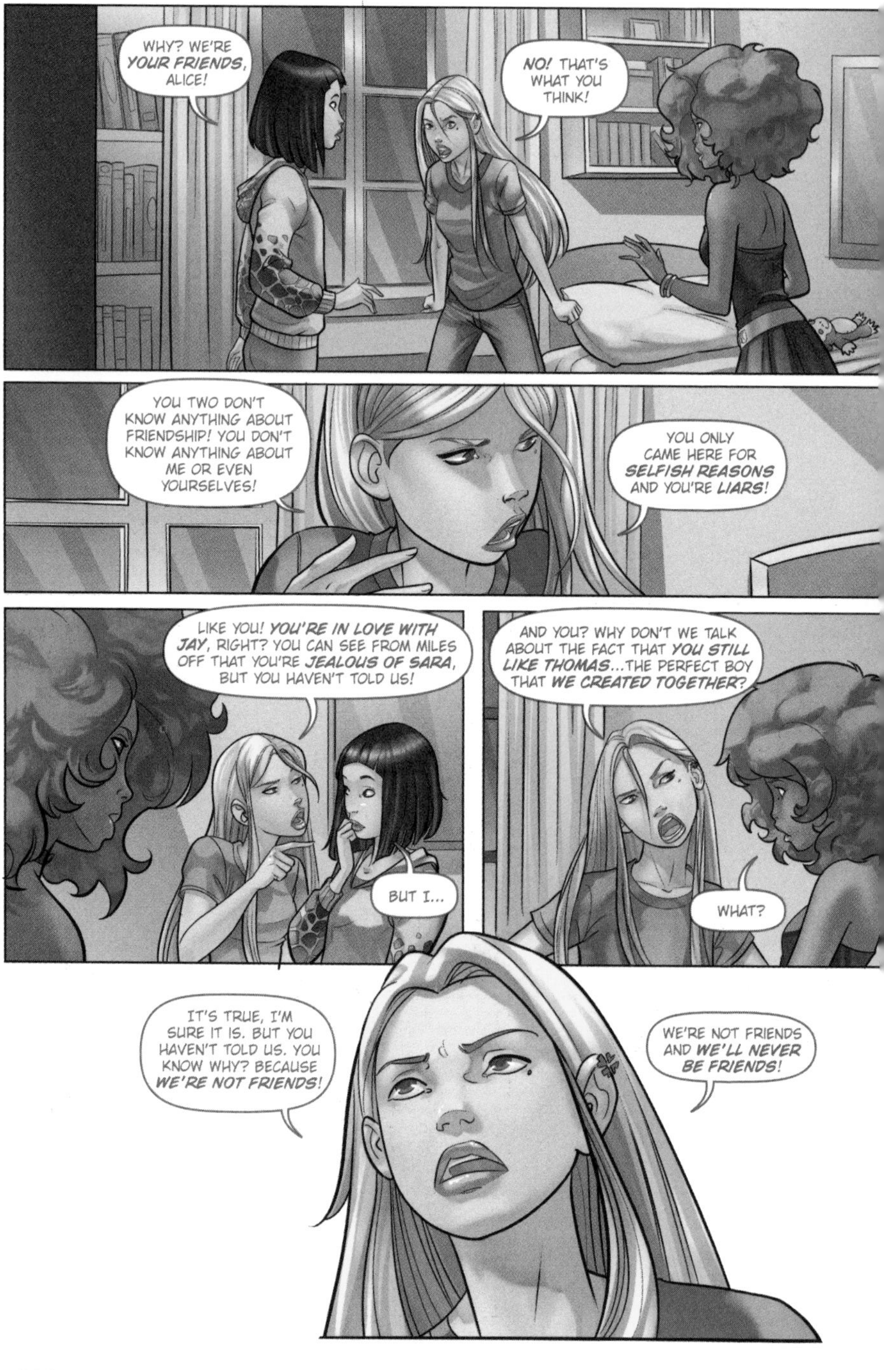
WHY? WE'RE YOUR FRIENDS, ALICE!
NO! THAT'S WHAT YOU THINK!
YOU TWO DON'T KNOW ANYTHING ABOUT FRIENDSHIP! YOU DON'T KNOW ANYTHING ABOUT ME OR EVEN YOURSELVES!
YOU ONLY CAME HERE FOR SELFISH REASONS AND YOU'RE LIARS!
LIKE YOU! YOU'RE IN LOVE WITH JAY, RIGHT? YOU CAN SEE FROM MILES OFF THAT YOU'RE JEALOUS OF SARA, BUT YOU HAVEN'T TOLD US!
BUT I...
AND YOU? WHY DON'T WE TALK ABOUT THE FACT THAT YOU STILL LIKE THOMAS...THE PERFECT BOY THAT WE CREATED TOGETHER?
WHAT?
IT'S TRUE, I'M SURE IT IS. BUT YOU HAVEN'T TOLD US. YOU KNOW WHY? BECAUSE WE'RE NOT FRIENDS!
WE'RE NOT FRIENDS AND WE'LL NEVER BE FRIENDS!

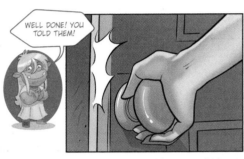

WELL DONE! YOU TOLD THEM!

YEAH, I TOLD THEM...

AMBER AND ANDREA...THE GIRLS THAT CHANGED MY WHOLE YEAR...

...HAVE BEEN REALLY BAD FRIENDS. IT'S TRUE! FIRST BECAUSE OF THOMAS, THEN BECAUSE OF ROCKSPEARE...

I'M RIGHT, I KNOW I'M RIGHT!

BUT BEING RIGHT ISN'T ANY FUN IF YOU'RE LEFT ALONE...

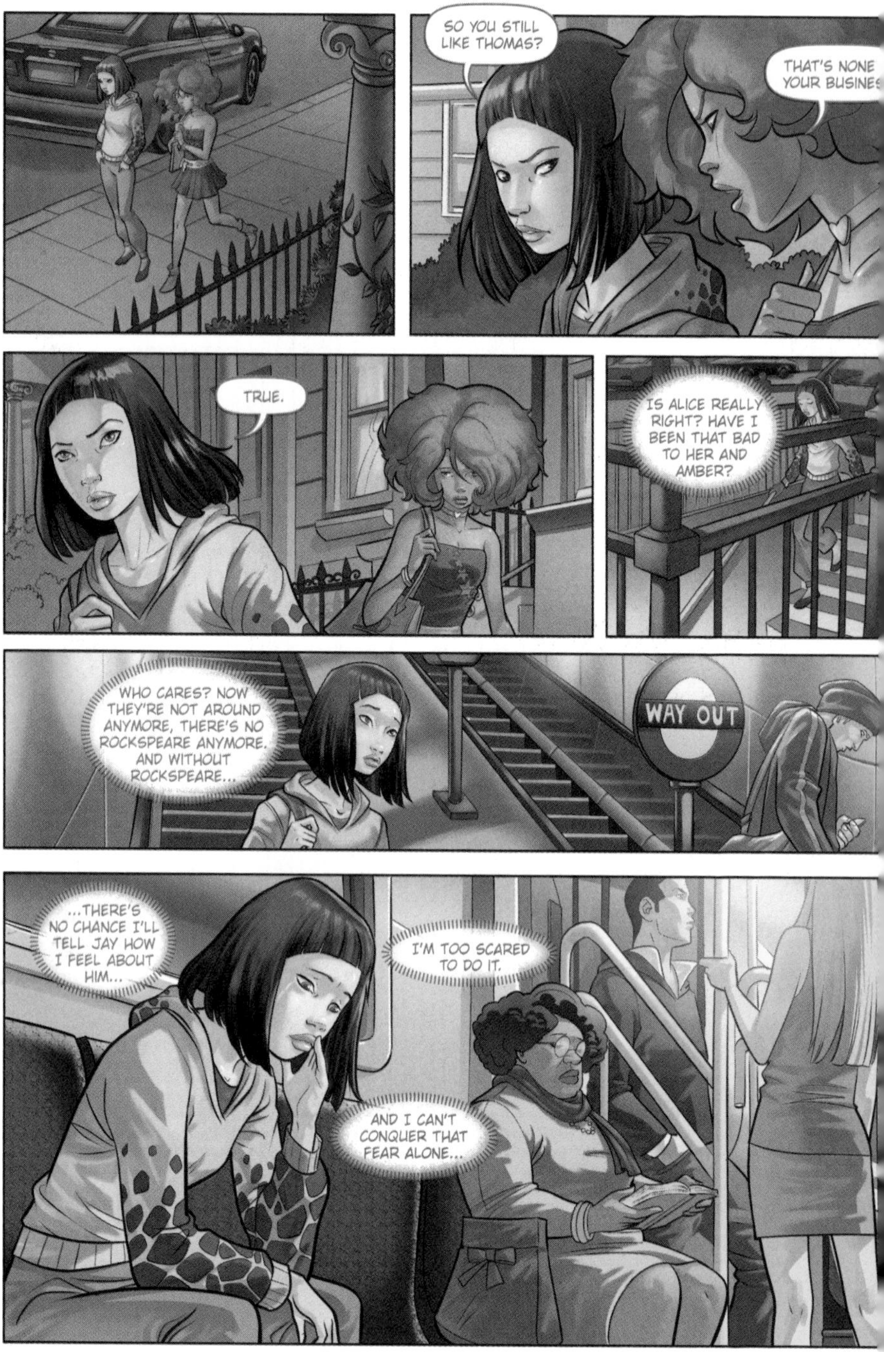
SO YOU STILL LIKE THOMAS?
THAT'S NONE YOUR BUSINES
TRUE.
IS ALICE REALLY RIGHT? HAVE I BEEN THAT BAD TO HER AND AMBER?
WHO CARES? NOW THEY'RE NOT AROUND ANYMORE, THERE'S NO ROCKSPEARE ANYMORE. AND WITHOUT ROCKSPEARE...
WAY OUT
...THERE'S NO CHANCE I'LL TELL JAY HOW I FEEL ABOUT HIM...
I'M TOO SCARED TO DO IT.
AND I CAN'T CONQUER THAT FEAR ALONE...

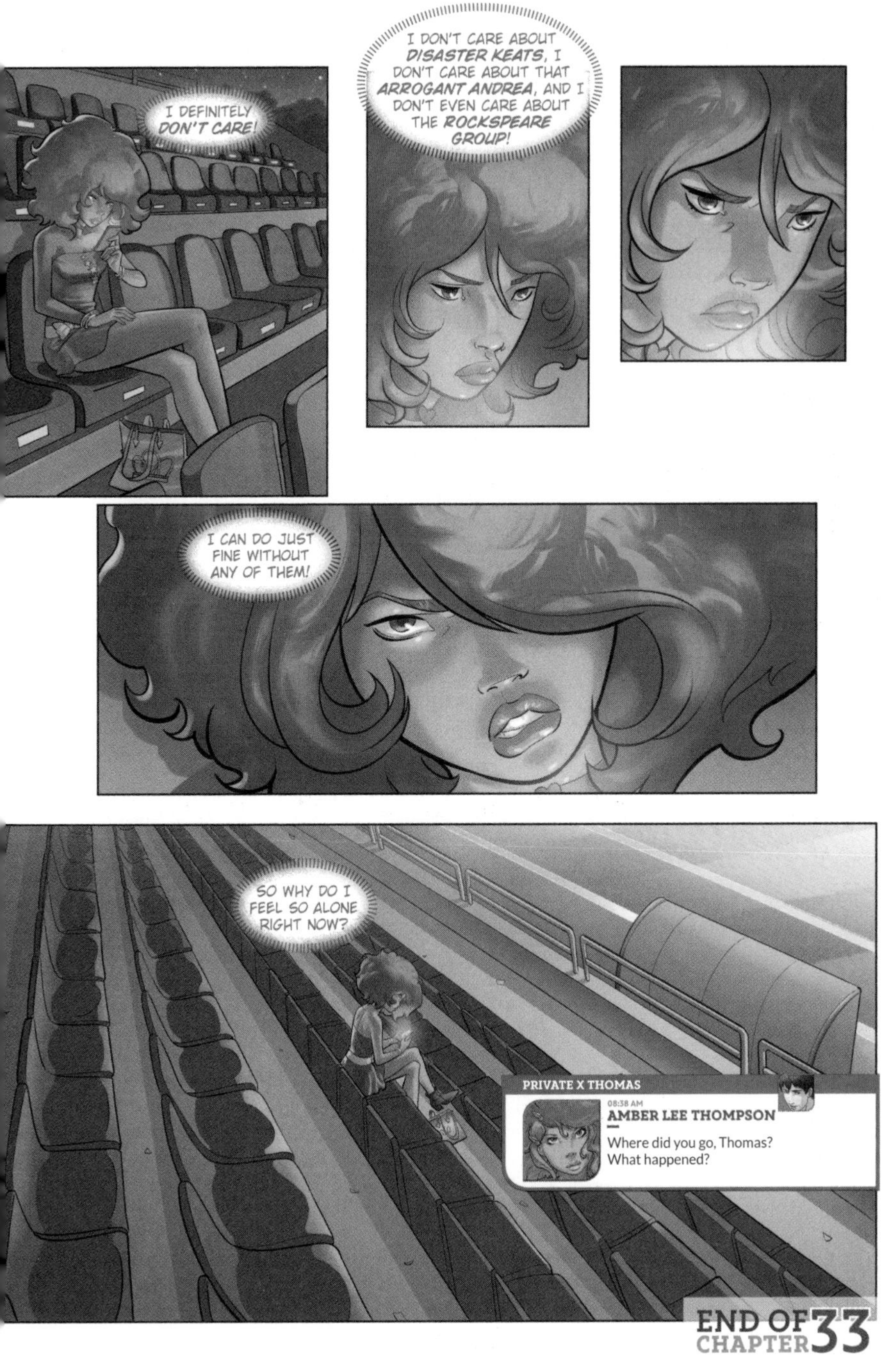
I DEFINITELY DON'T CARE!
I DON'T CARE ABOUT DISASTER KEATS, I DON'T CARE ABOUT THAT ARROGANT ANDREA, AND I DON'T EVEN CARE ABOUT THE ROCKSPEARE GROUP!
I CAN DO JUST FINE WITHOUT ANY OF THEM!
SO WHY DO I FEEL SO ALONE RIGHT NOW?
PRIVATE X THOMAS
08:38 AM
AMBER LEE THOMPSON
Where did you go, Thomas? What happened?

END OF CHAPTER 33

#Our Tune

Script: Alessandro Ferrari
Layout: Emilio Urbano, Simone Buonfantino, Manuela Razzi
Cleanup: Simone Buonfantino, Marco Dominici
Emotidolls: Andrea Scoppetta
Color: Arancia Studio, Giuseppe Fontana, Tomato Farm
Watercolor backgrounds: Valeria Turati
Translation: Edizioni BD and Erin Brady
Lettering and Infographic: Edizioni BD

COVER
Layout and cleanup: Alberto Zanon
Color: Slava Panarin

CONTRIBUTORS
Tomatofarm

Original project developed by Disney Publishing with the contribution of Ba Baraldi, Paola Barbato, Micol Beltrami and Diana Tomatozombie

#12

#Hearts Onstage

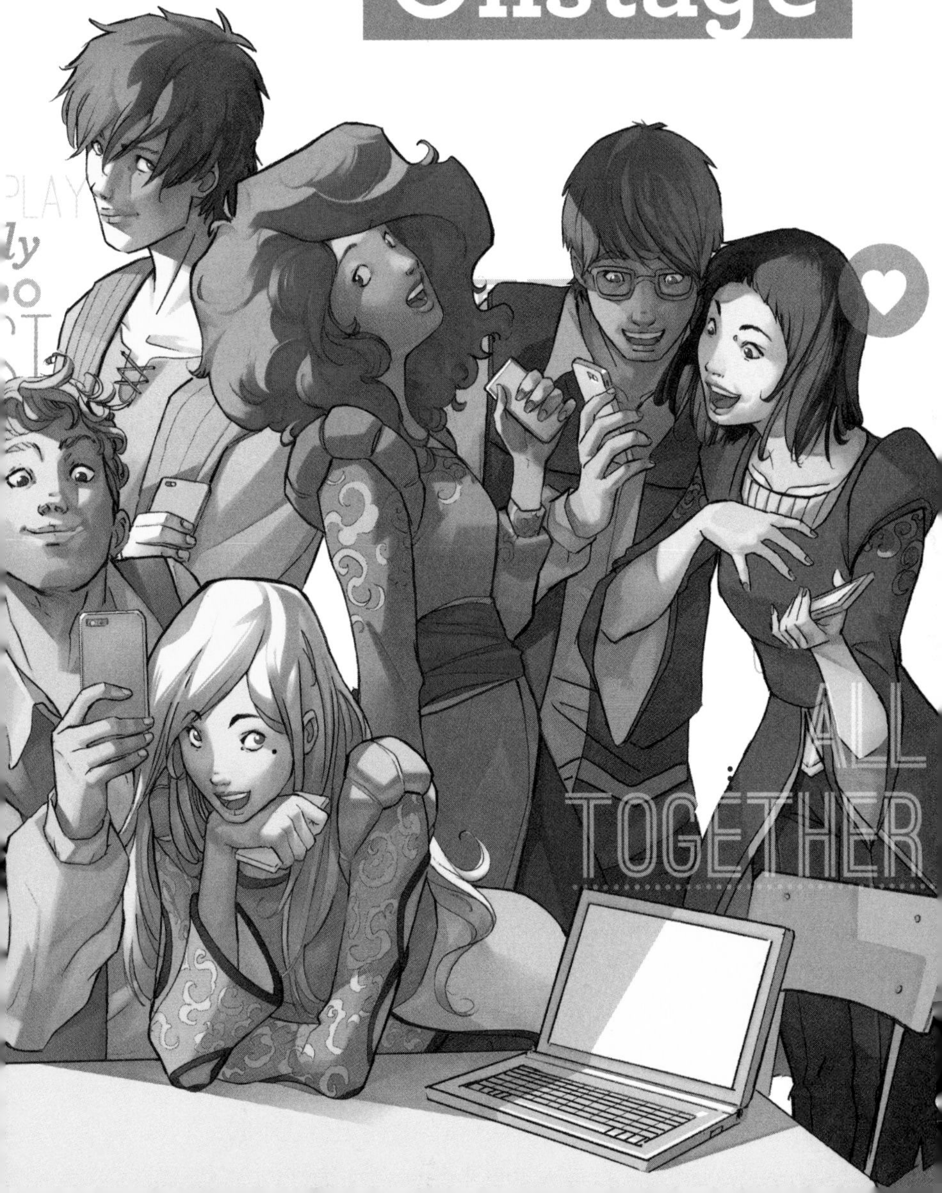
PLAY
ALL TOGETHER

CHAPTER 34

ROCKSPEARE TIME

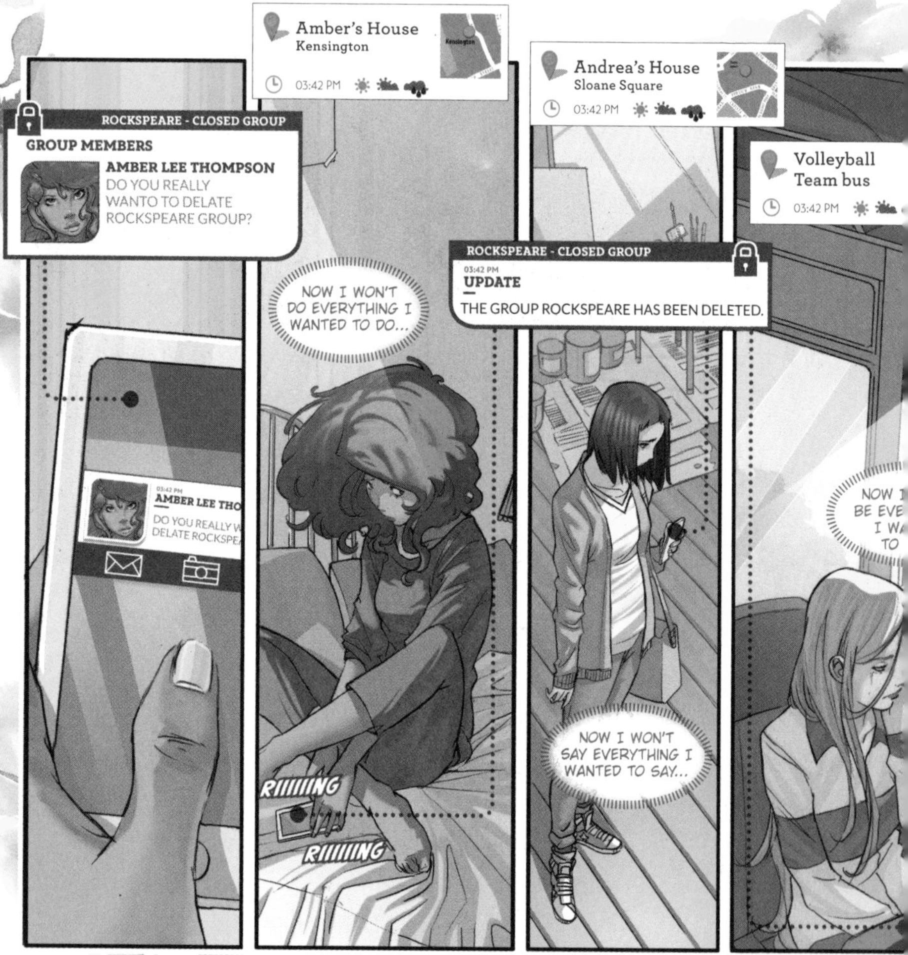

ROCKSPEARE - CLOSED GROUP
GROUP MEMBERS
AMBER LEE THOMPSON
DO YOU REALLY WANTO TO DELATE ROCKSPEARE GROUP?
03:42 PM
AMBER LEE THO
DO YOU REALLY W
DELATE ROCKSPE
Amber's House
Kensington
03:42 PM
NOW I WON'T DO EVERYTHING I WANTED TO DO...
RIIIIING
RIIIIING
Andrea's House
Sloane Square
03:42 PM
ROCKSPEARE - CLOSED GROUP
03:42 PM
UPDATE
THE GROUP ROCKSPEARE HAS BEEN DELETED.
NOW I WON'T SAY EVERYTHING I WANTED TO SAY...
Volleyball Team bus
03:42 PM

Amber's house
03:42 PM

NO, BILL! THERE'S *NO WAY I'M PLAYING JULIET AGAIN*, NOT FOR EDWARD OR FOR ROCKSPEARE!

AND NO! *NOT EVEN YOU* CAN PLAY *HER!* IT DOESN'T MATTER HOW GOOD YOU ARE!

...EO, RE ART MEO?

SOMEONE STOP HIM!

WHAT A DISASTER. EVERYTHING'S GONE WRONG.

CLICK

AND YOU DIDN'T WAIT FOR ME.

I MISS YOU, THOMAS...I *MISS YOU SO MUCH*...

03:43 PM
THOMAS ANDERSON
—
Has a new notification.

TO TELL THE TRUTH, I FEEL LOST WITHOUT YOU.

03:44 PM
THOMAS ANDERSON
—
Has a new notification.

03:44 PM
THOMAS ANDERSON
—
Has a new notification.

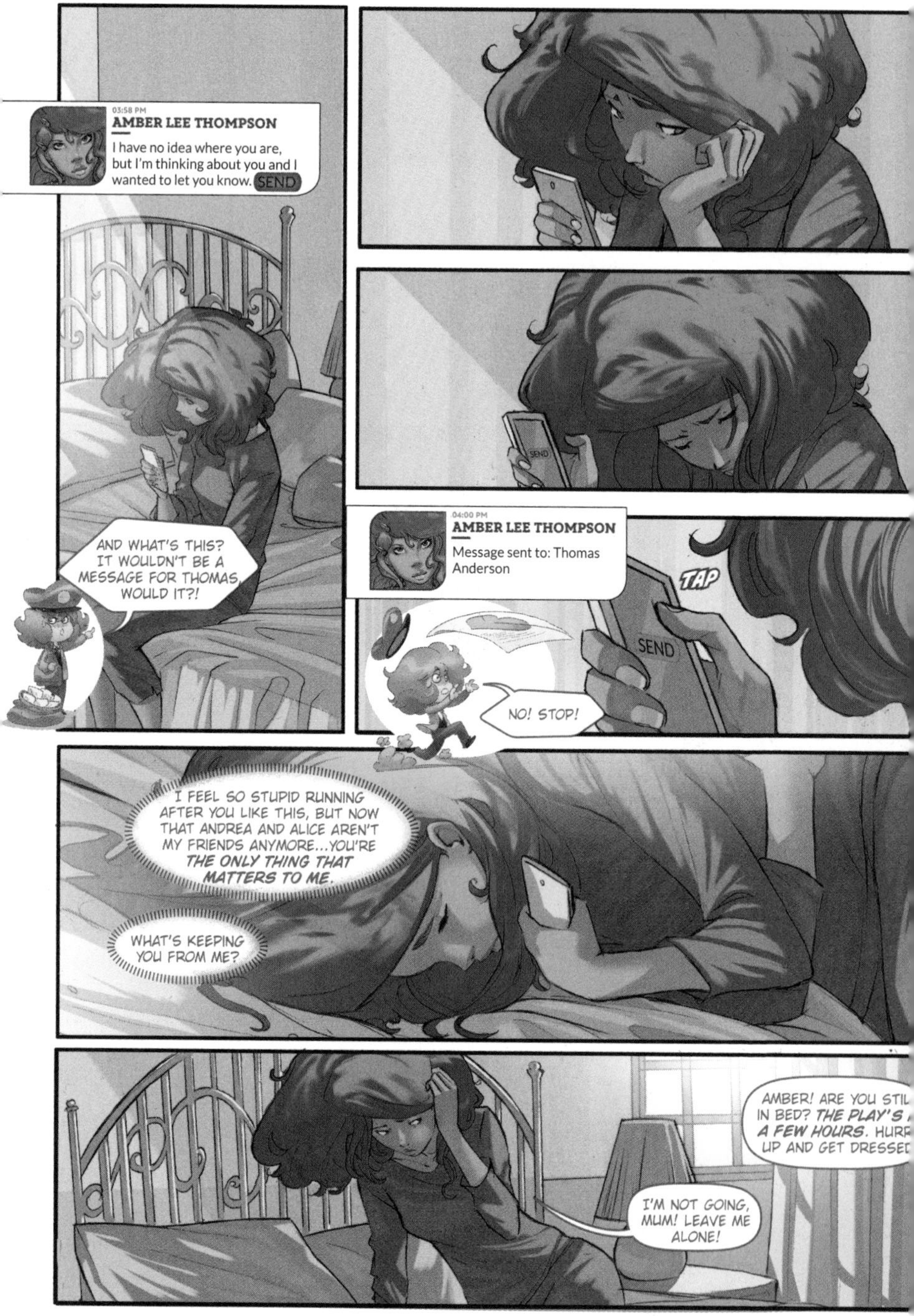
03:58 PM
AMBER LEE THOMPSON
I have no idea where you are, but I'm thinking about you and I wanted to let you know. SEND
AND WHAT'S THIS? IT WOULDN'T BE A MESSAGE FOR THOMAS, WOULD IT?!
SEND
04:00 PM
AMBER LEE THOMPSON
Message sent to: Thomas Anderson
TAP
SEND
NO! STOP!
I FEEL SO STUPID RUNNING AFTER YOU LIKE THIS, BUT NOW THAT ANDREA AND ALICE AREN'T MY FRIENDS ANYMORE...YOU'RE THE ONLY THING THAT MATTERS TO ME.
WHAT'S KEEPING YOU FROM ME?
AMBER! ARE YOU STIL IN BED? THE PLAY'S A FEW HOURS. HURR UP AND GET DRESSED
I'M NOT GOING, MUM! LEAVE ME ALONE!

house

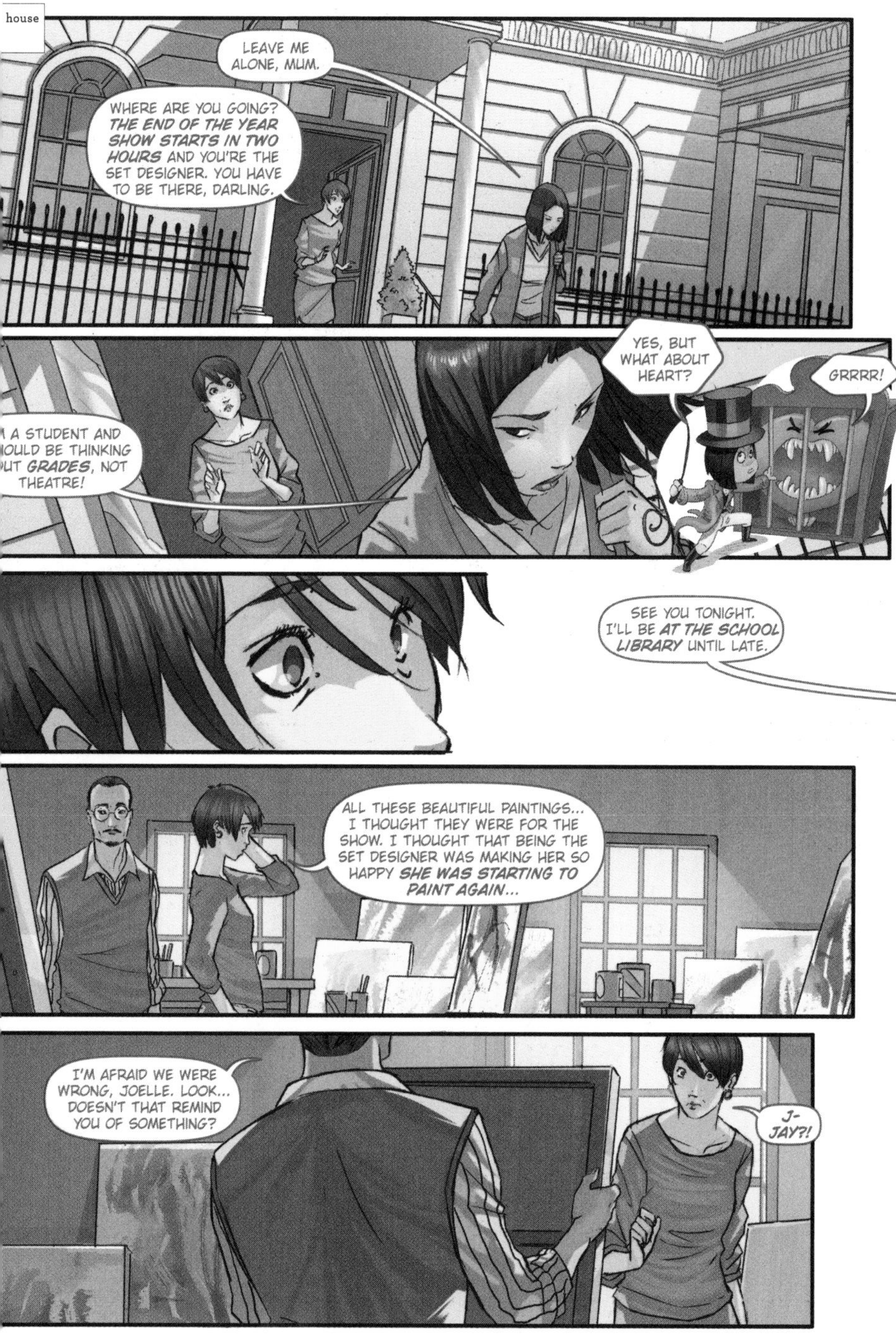

LEAVE ME ALONE, MUM.
WHERE ARE YOU GOING? THE END OF THE YEAR SHOW STARTS IN TWO HOURS AND YOU'RE THE SET DESIGNER. YOU HAVE TO BE THERE, DARLING.
YES, BUT WHAT ABOUT HEART?
GRRRR!
A STUDENT AND OULD BE THINKING UT GRADES, NOT THEATRE!
SEE YOU TONIGHT. I'LL BE AT THE SCHOOL LIBRARY UNTIL LATE.
ALL THESE BEAUTIFUL PAINTINGS... I THOUGHT THEY WERE FOR THE SHOW. I THOUGHT THAT BEING THE SET DESIGNER WAS MAKING HER SO HAPPY SHE WAS STARTING TO PAINT AGAIN...
I'M AFRAID WE WERE WRONG, JOELLE. LOOK... DOESN'T THAT REMIND YOU OF SOMETHING?
J- JAY?!

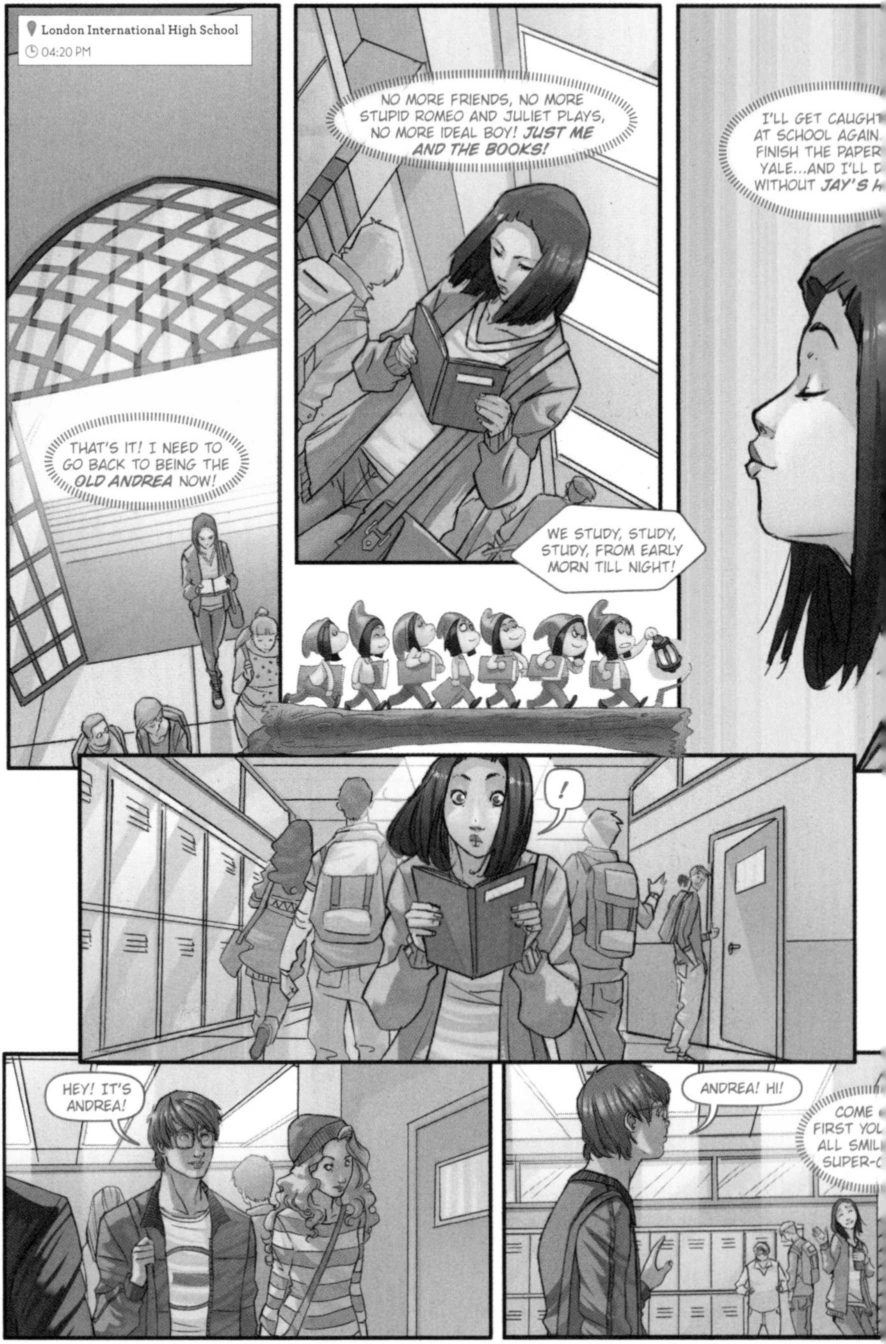

London International High School
04:20 PM
THAT'S IT! I NEED TO GO BACK TO BEING THE OLD ANDREA NOW!
NO MORE FRIENDS, NO MORE STUPID ROMEO AND JULIET PLAYS, NO MORE IDEAL BOY! JUST ME AND THE BOOKS!
WE STUDY, STUDY, STUDY, FROM EARLY MORN TILL NIGHT!
I'LL GET CAUGH
AT SCHOOL AGAIN
FINISH THE PAPER
YALE...AND I'LL
WITHOUT JAY'S
!
HEY! IT'S ANDREA!
ANDREA! HI!
COME
FIRST YO
ALL SMIL
SUPER-

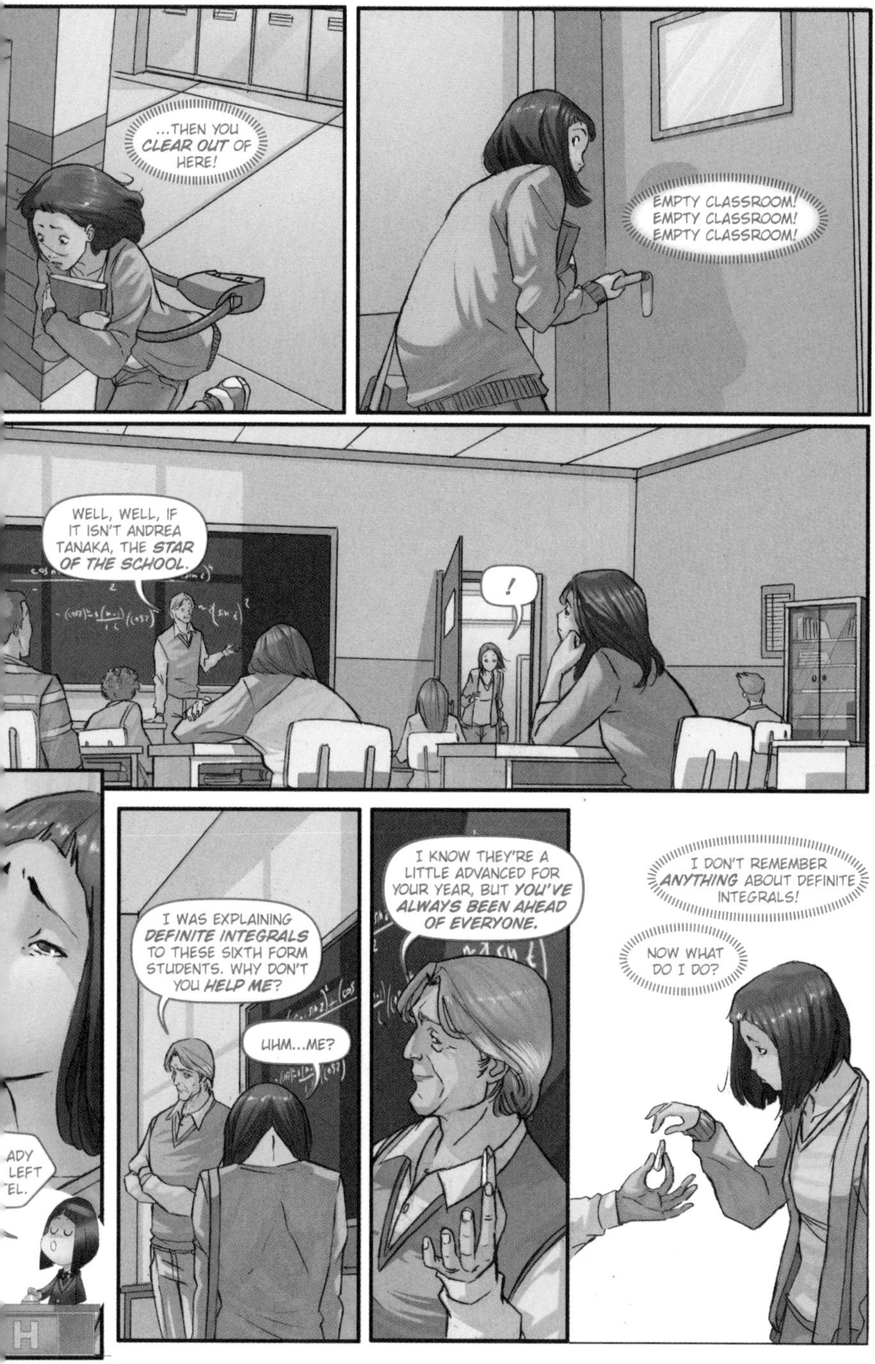

...THEN YOU CLEAR OUT OF HERE!
EMPTY CLASSROOM! EMPTY CLASSROOM! EMPTY CLASSROOM!
WELL, WELL, IF IT ISN'T ANDREA TANAKA, THE STAR OF THE SCHOOL.
!
ADY LEFT EL.
I WAS EXPLAINING DEFINITE INTEGRALS TO THESE SIXTH FORM STUDENTS. WHY DON'T YOU HELP ME?
UHM...ME?
I KNOW THEY'RE A LITTLE ADVANCED FOR YOUR YEAR, BUT YOU'VE ALWAYS BEEN AHEAD OF EVERYONE.
I DON'T REMEMBER ANYTHING ABOUT DEFINITE INTEGRALS!
NOW WHAT DO I DO?

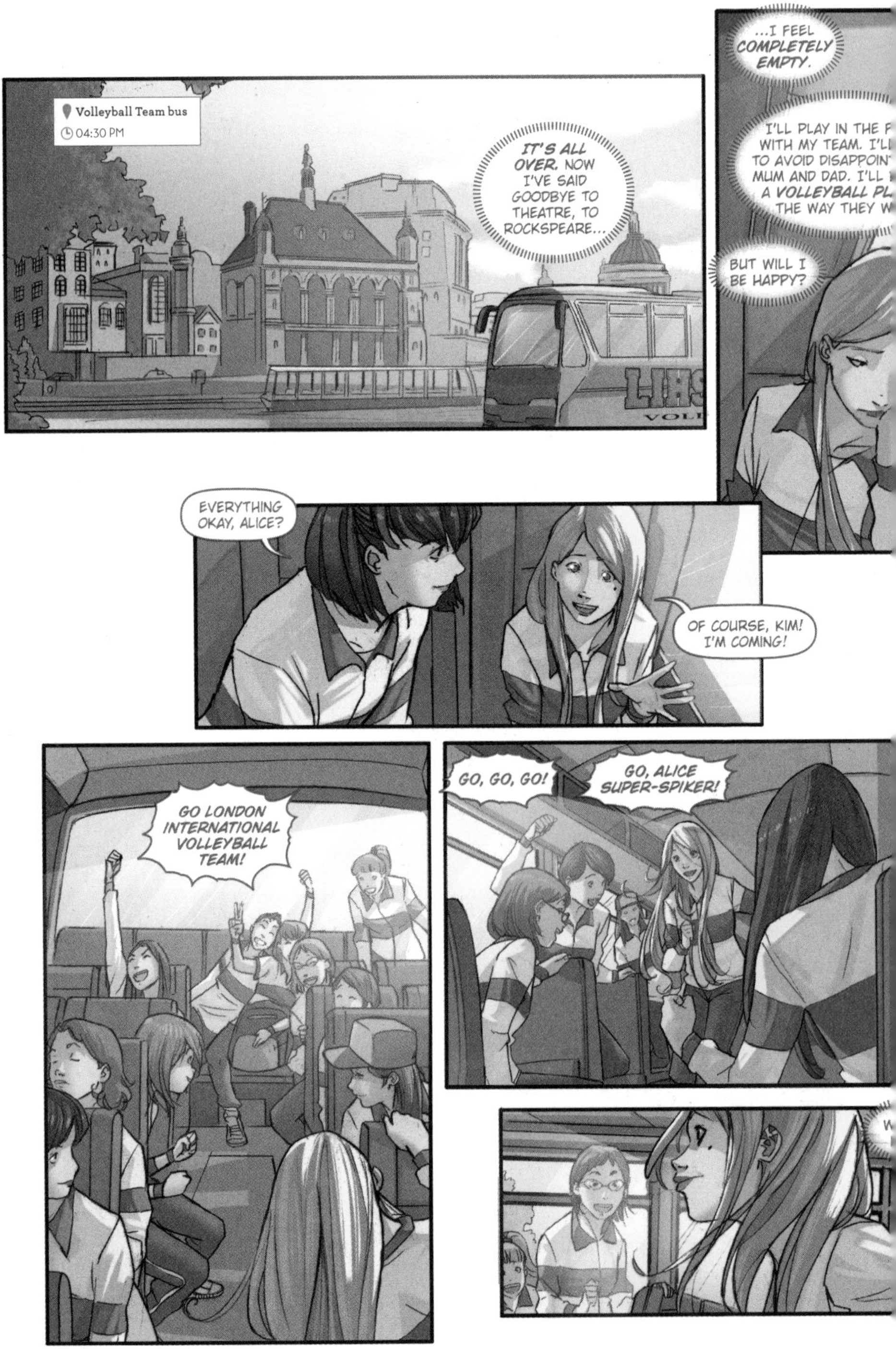
Volleyball Team bus
04:30 PM
IT'S ALL OVER. NOW I'VE SAID GOODBYE TO THEATRE, TO ROCKSPEARE...
LIHS
...I FEEL COMPLETELY EMPTY.
I'LL PLAY IN THE
WITH MY TEAM.
TO AVOID
MUM AND DAD. I'LL
A VOLLEYBALL
THE WAY THEY
BUT WILL I BE HAPPY?
EVERYTHING OKAY, ALICE?
OF COURSE, KIM! I'M COMING!
GO LONDON INTERNATIONAL VOLLEYBALL TEAM!
GO, GO, GO!
GO, ALICE SUPER-SPIKER!

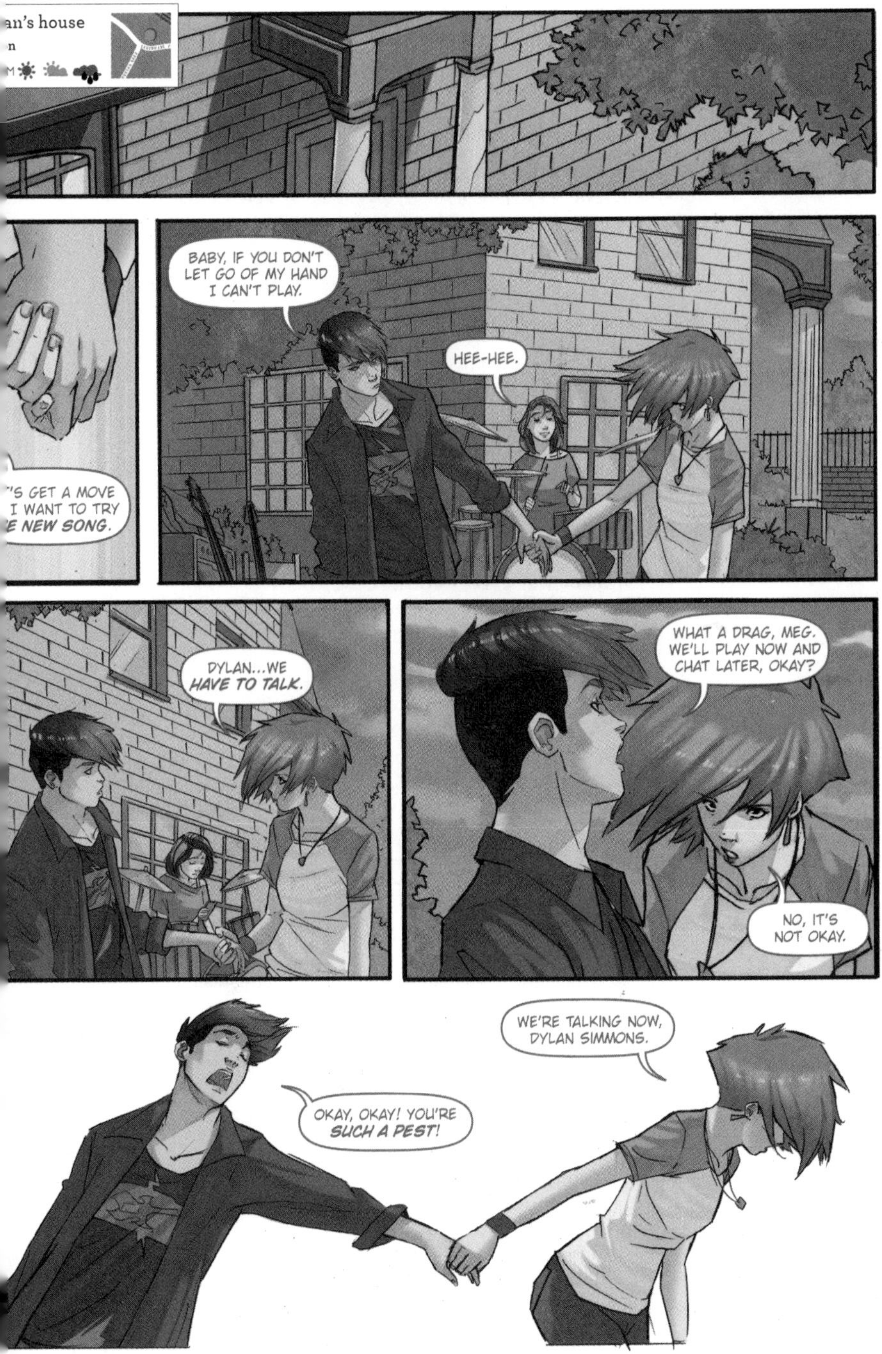
an's house
n
'S GET A MOVE
I WANT TO TRY
E NEW SONG.
BABY, IF YOU DON'T LET GO OF MY HAND I CAN'T PLAY.
HEE-HEE.
DYLAN...WE HAVE TO TALK.
WHAT A DRAG, MEG. WE'LL PLAY NOW AND CHAT LATER, OKAY?
NO, IT'S NOT OKAY.
WE'RE TALKING NOW, DYLAN SIMMONS.
OKAY, OKAY! YOU'RE SUCH A PEST!

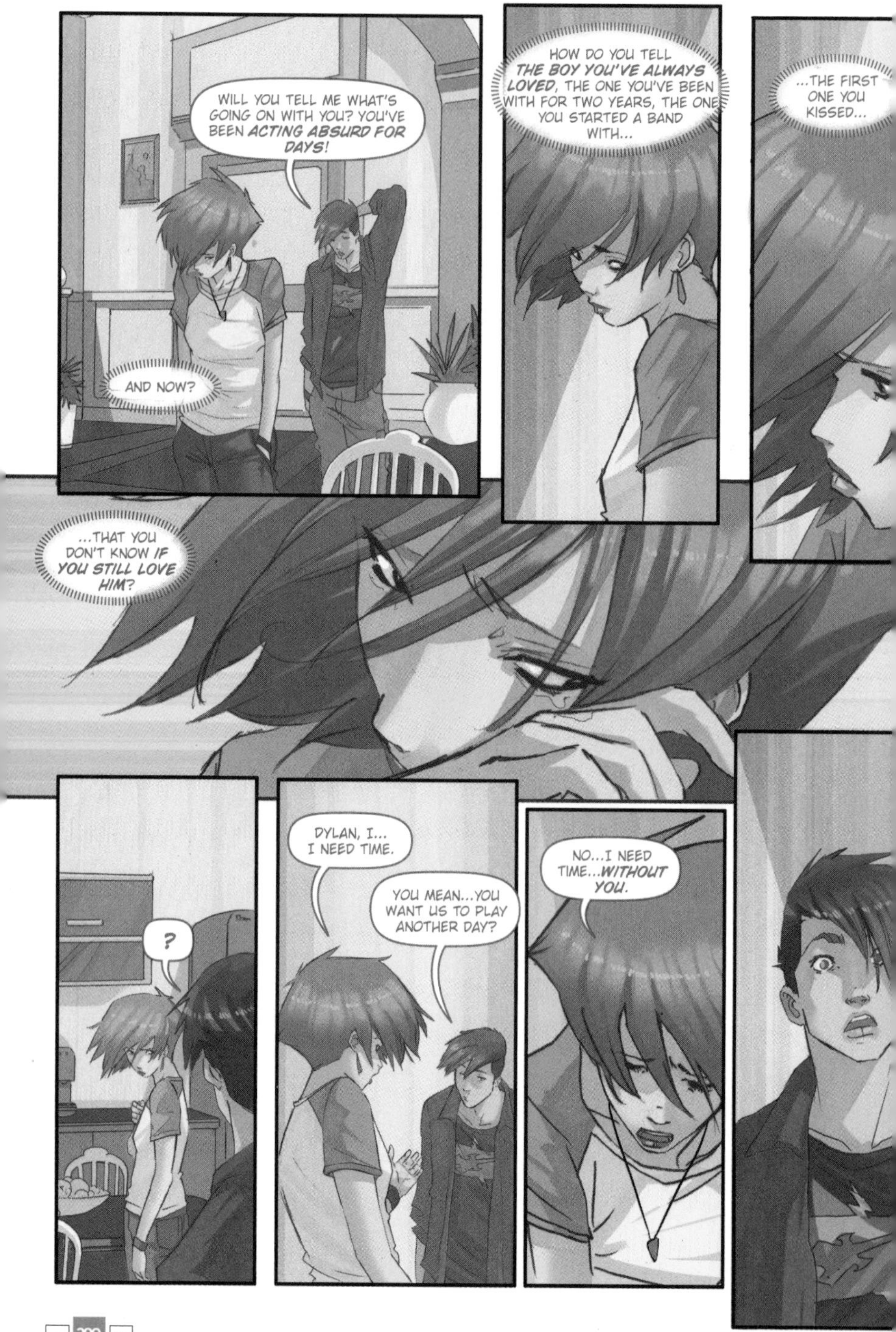
WILL YOU TELL ME WHAT'S GOING ON WITH YOU? YOU'VE BEEN ACTING ABSURD FOR DAYS!
AND NOW?
HOW DO YOU TELL THE BOY YOU'VE ALWAYS LOVED, THE ONE YOU'VE BEEN WITH FOR TWO YEARS, THE ONE YOU STARTED A BAND WITH...
...THE FIRST ONE YOU KISSED...
...THAT YOU DON'T KNOW IF YOU STILL LOVE HIM?
?
DYLAN, I... I NEED TIME.
YOU MEAN...YOU WANT US TO PLAY ANOTHER DAY?
NO...I NEED TIME...WITHOUT YOU.

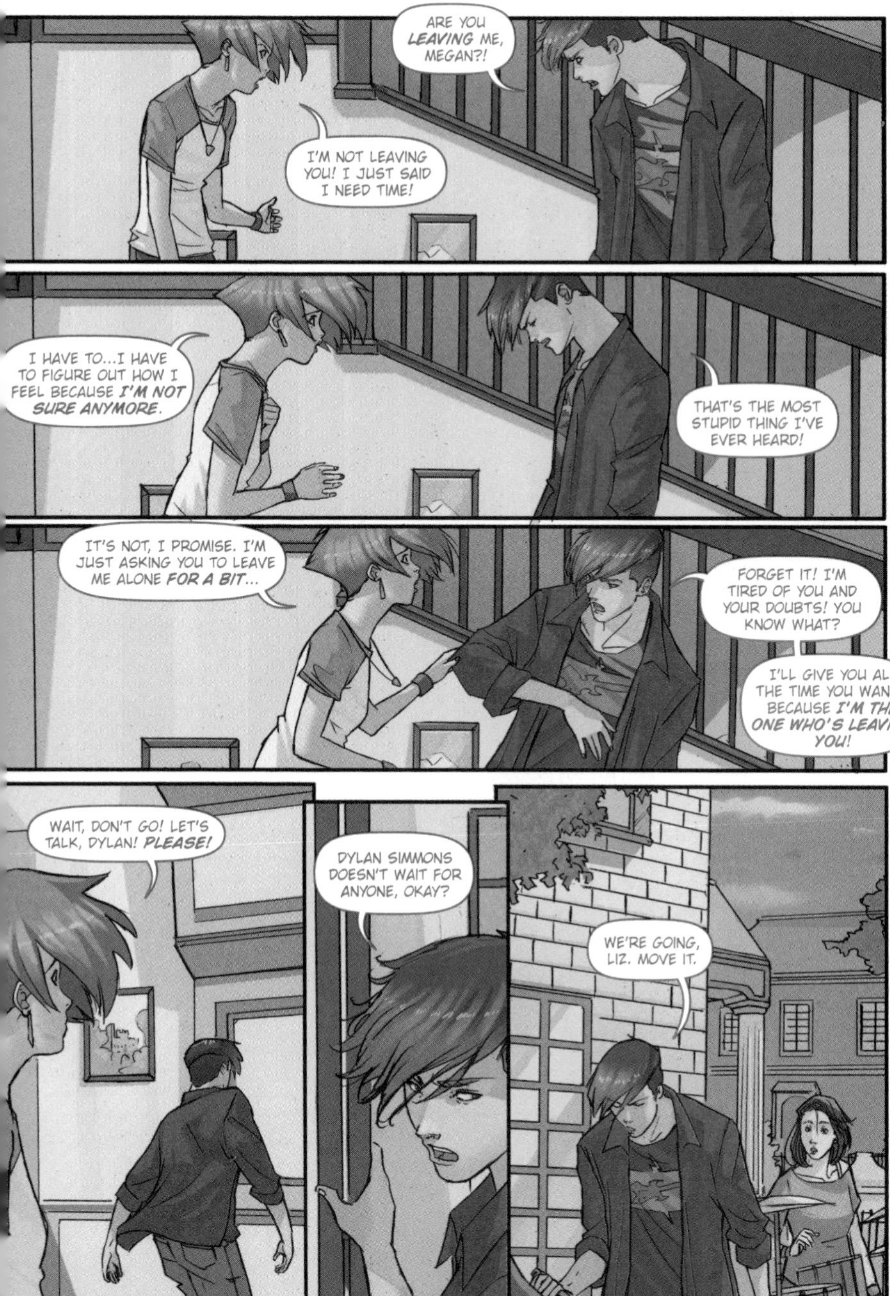
ARE YOU LEAVING ME, MEGAN?!
I'M NOT LEAVING YOU! I JUST SAID I NEED TIME!
I HAVE TO...I HAVE TO FIGURE OUT HOW I FEEL BECAUSE I'M NOT SURE ANYMORE.
THAT'S THE MOST STUPID THING I'VE EVER HEARD!
IT'S NOT, I PROMISE. I'M JUST ASKING YOU TO LEAVE ME ALONE FOR A BIT...
FORGET IT! I'M TIRED OF YOU AND YOUR DOUBTS! YOU KNOW WHAT?
I'LL GIVE YOU ALL THE TIME YOU WANT... BECAUSE I'M THE ONE WHO'S LEAVING YOU!
WAIT, DON'T GO! LET'S TALK, DYLAN! PLEASE!
DYLAN SIMMONS DOESN'T WAIT FOR ANYONE, OKAY?
WE'RE GOING, LIZ. MOVE IT.

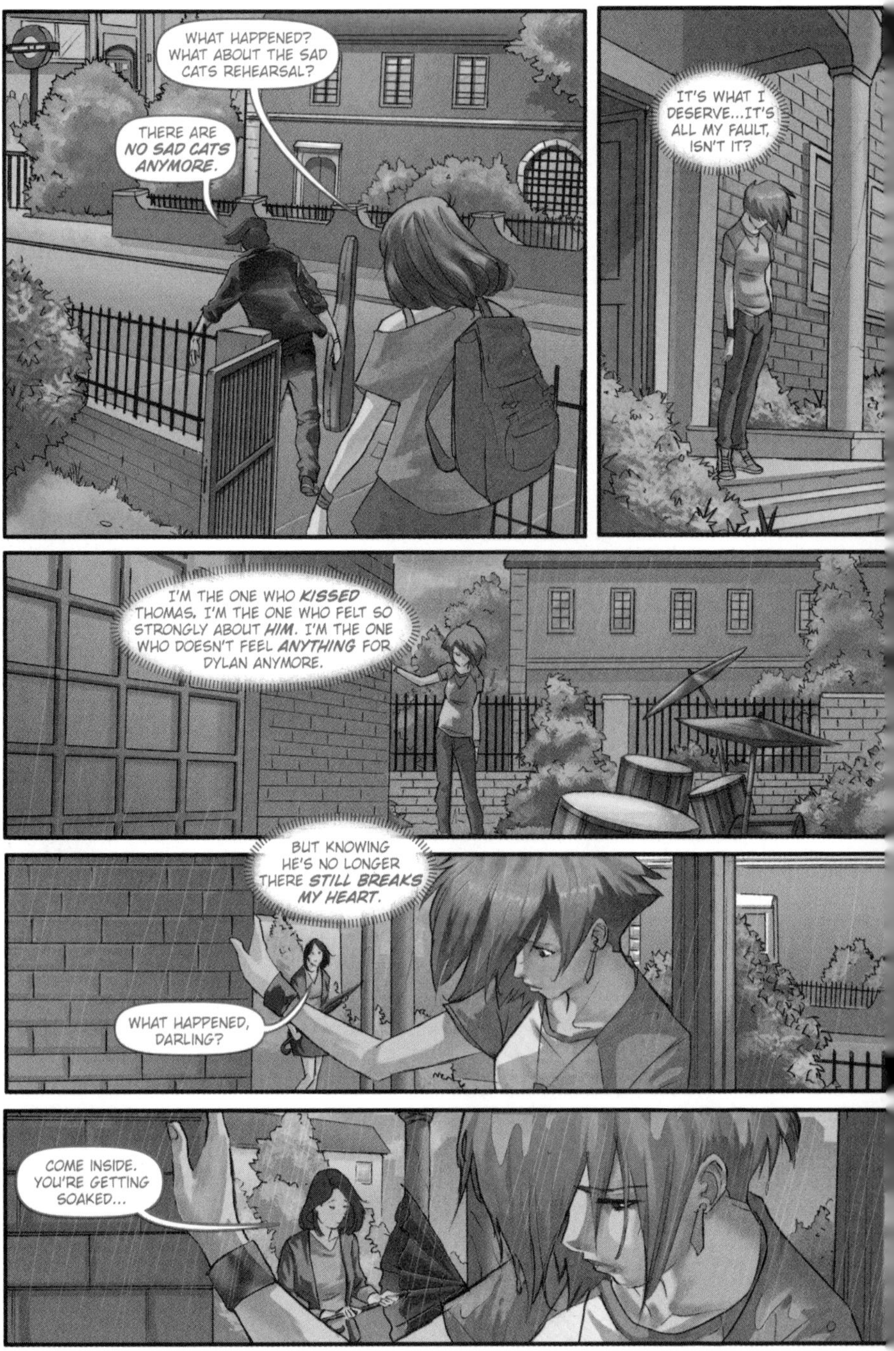
WHAT HAPPENED? WHAT ABOUT THE SAD CATS REHEARSAL?
THERE ARE NO SAD CATS ANYMORE.
IT'S WHAT I DESERVE...IT'S ALL MY FAULT, ISN'T IT?
I'M THE ONE WHO KISSED THOMAS. I'M THE ONE WHO FELT SO STRONGLY ABOUT HIM. I'M THE ONE WHO DOESN'T FEEL ANYTHING FOR DYLAN ANYMORE.
BUT KNOWING HE'S NO LONGER THERE STILL BREAKS MY HEART.
WHAT HAPPENED, DARLING?
COME INSIDE. YOU'RE GETTING SOAKED...

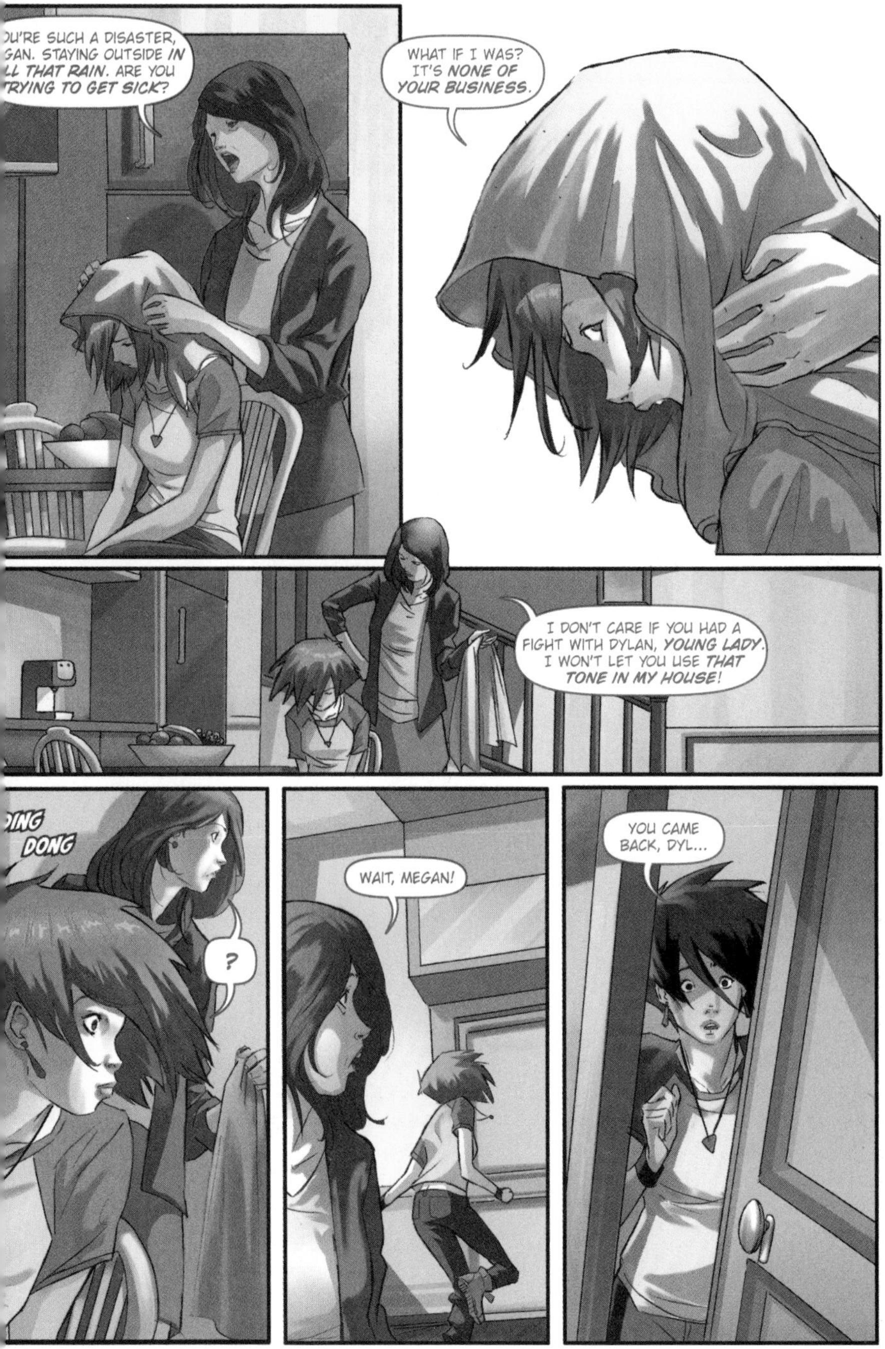

OU'RE SUCH A DISASTER, GAN. STAYING OUTSIDE IN LL THAT RAIN. ARE YOU TRYING TO GET SICK?
WHAT IF I WAS? IT'S NONE OF YOUR BUSINESS.
I DON'T CARE IF YOU HAD A FIGHT WITH DYLAN, YOUNG LADY. I WON'T LET YOU USE THAT TONE IN MY HOUSE!
DING DONG
?
WAIT, MEGAN!
YOU CAME BACK, DYL...

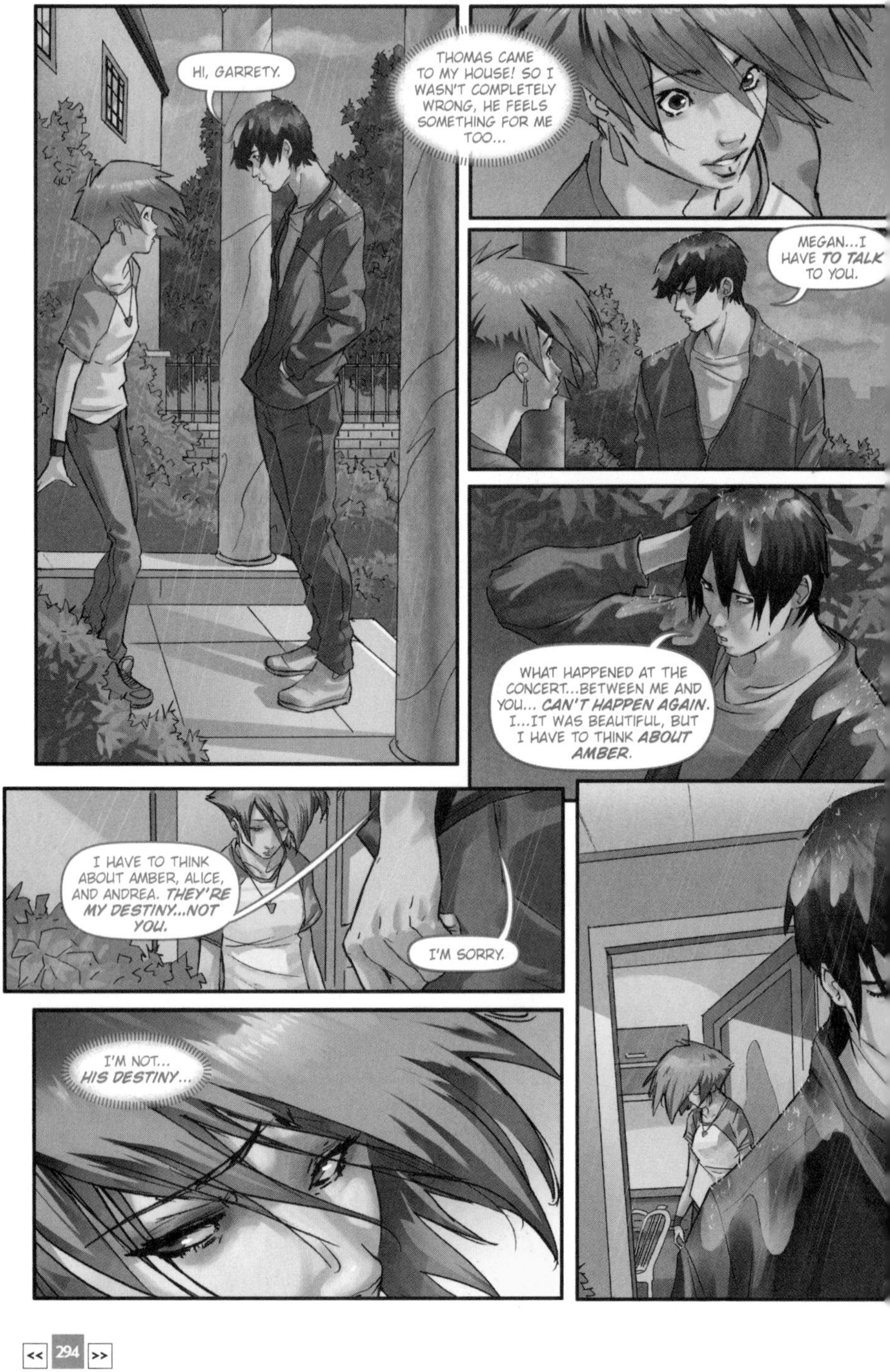
HI, GARRETY.
THOMAS CAME TO MY HOUSE! SO I WASN'T COMPLETELY WRONG, HE FEELS SOMETHING FOR ME TOO...
MEGAN...I HAVE TO TALK TO YOU.
WHAT HAPPENED AT THE CONCERT...BETWEEN ME AND YOU... CAN'T HAPPEN AGAIN. I...IT WAS BEAUTIFUL, BUT I HAVE TO THINK ABOUT AMBER.
I HAVE TO THINK ABOUT AMBER, ALICE, AND ANDREA. THEY'RE MY DESTINY...NOT YOU.
I'M SORRY.
I'M NOT... HIS DESTINY...

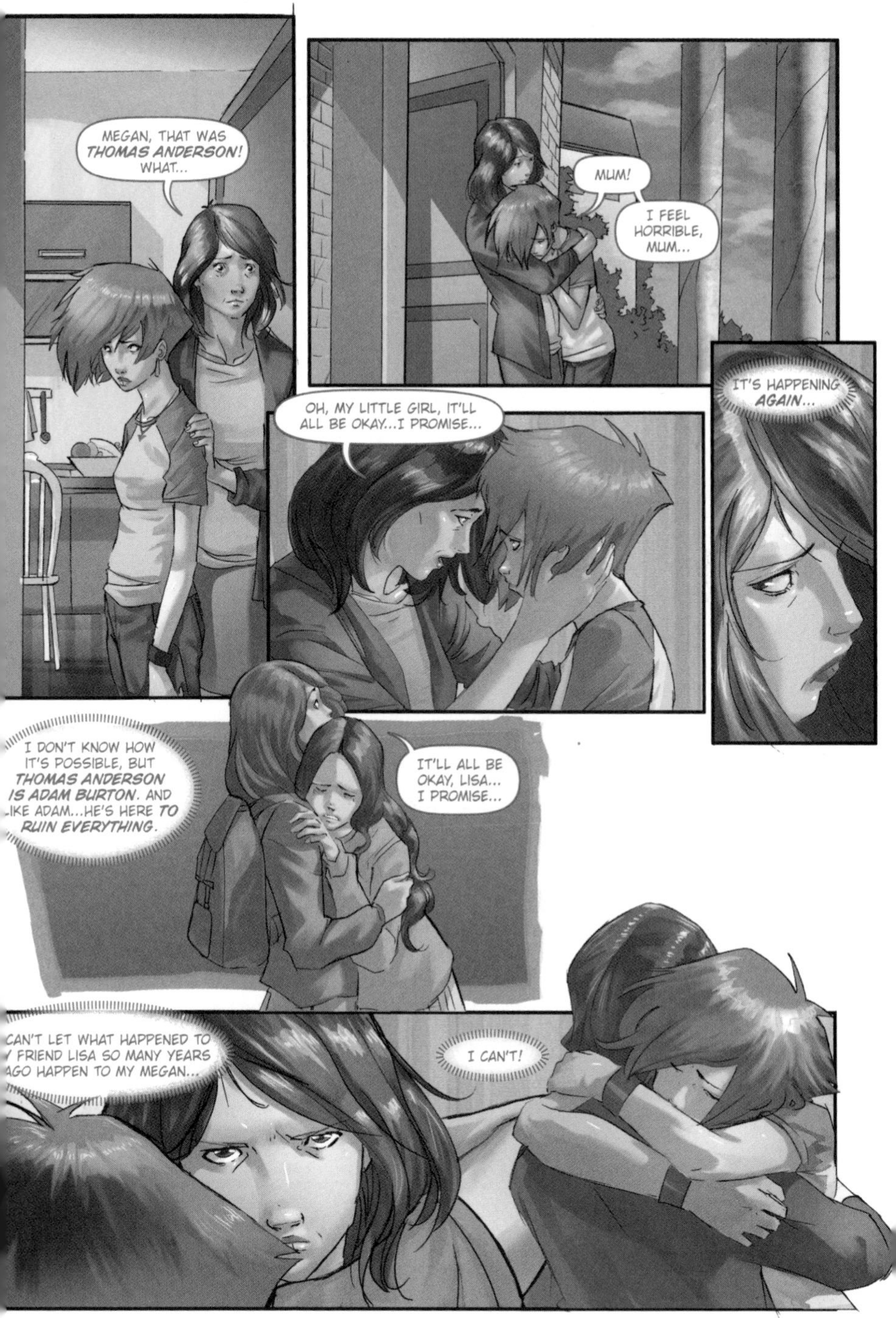
MEGAN, THAT WAS THOMAS ANDERSON! WHAT...
MUM!
I FEEL HORRIBLE, MUM...
OH, MY LITTLE GIRL, IT'LL ALL BE OKAY...I PROMISE...
IT'S HAPPENING AGAIN...
I DON'T KNOW HOW IT'S POSSIBLE, BUT THOMAS ANDERSON IS ADAM BURTON. AND LIKE ADAM...HE'S HERE TO RUIN EVERYTHING.
IT'LL ALL BE OKAY, LISA... I PROMISE...
CAN'T LET WHAT HAPPENED TO Y FRIEND LISA SO MANY YEARS AGO HAPPEN TO MY MEGAN...
I CAN'T!

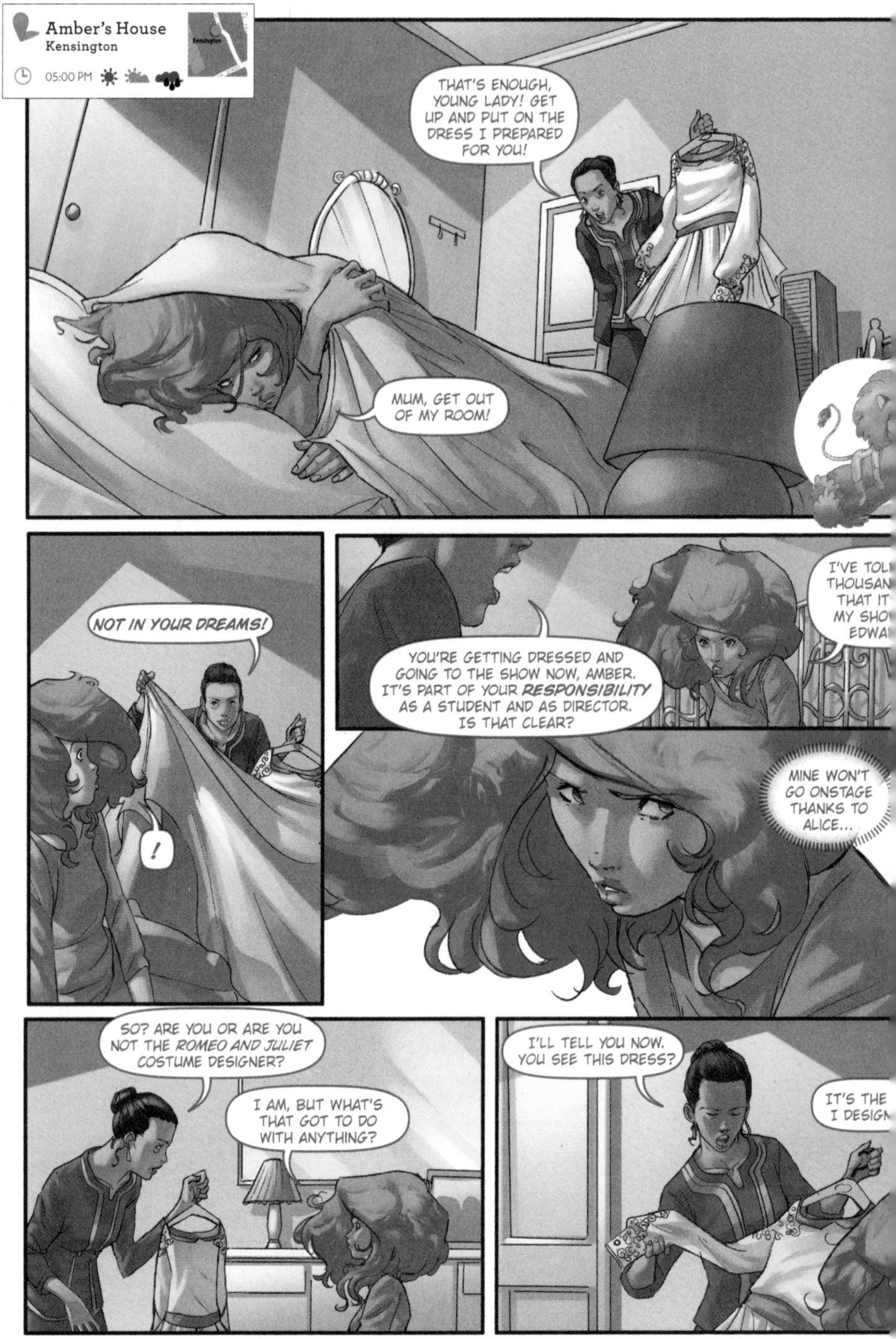

Amber's House
Kensington
05:00 PM
Kensington
THAT'S ENOUGH, YOUNG LADY! GET UP AND PUT ON THE DRESS I PREPARED FOR YOU!
MUM, GET OUT OF MY ROOM!
NOT IN YOUR DREAMS!
!
YOU'RE GETTING DRESSED AND GOING TO THE SHOW NOW, AMBER. IT'S PART OF YOUR *RESPONSIBILITY* AS A STUDENT AND AS DIRECTOR. IS THAT CLEAR?
I'VE TOL THOUSAN THAT IT MY SHO EDWA
MINE WON'T GO ONSTAGE THANKS TO ALICE...
SO? ARE YOU OR ARE YOU NOT THE *ROMEO AND JULIET* COSTUME DESIGNER?
I AM, BUT WHAT'S THAT GOT TO DO WITH ANYTHING?
I'LL TELL YOU NOW. YOU SEE THIS DRESS?
IT'S THE I DESIGN

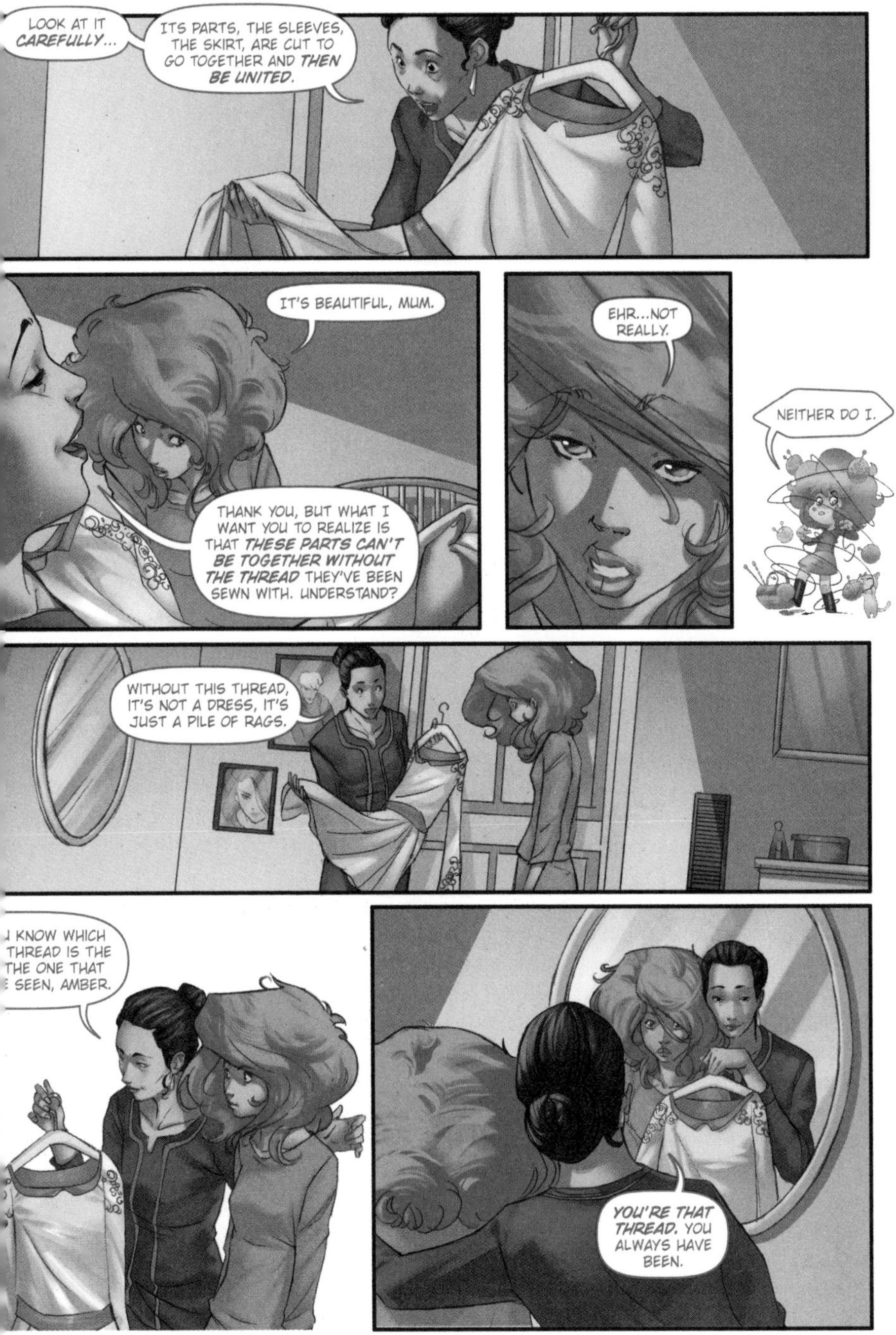
LOOK AT IT *CAREFULLY*...
ITS PARTS, THE SLEEVES, THE SKIRT, ARE CUT TO GO TOGETHER AND *THEN BE UNITED.*
IT'S BEAUTIFUL, MUM.
THANK YOU, BUT WHAT I WANT YOU TO REALIZE IS THAT *THESE PARTS CAN'T BE TOGETHER WITHOUT THE THREAD* THEY'VE BEEN SEWN WITH. UNDERSTAND?
EHR...NOT REALLY.
NEITHER DO I.
WITHOUT THIS THREAD, IT'S NOT A DRESS, IT'S JUST A PILE OF RAGS.
I KNOW WHICH THREAD IS THE THE ONE THAT SEEN, AMBER.
YOU'RE THAT THREAD. YOU ALWAYS HAVE BEEN.

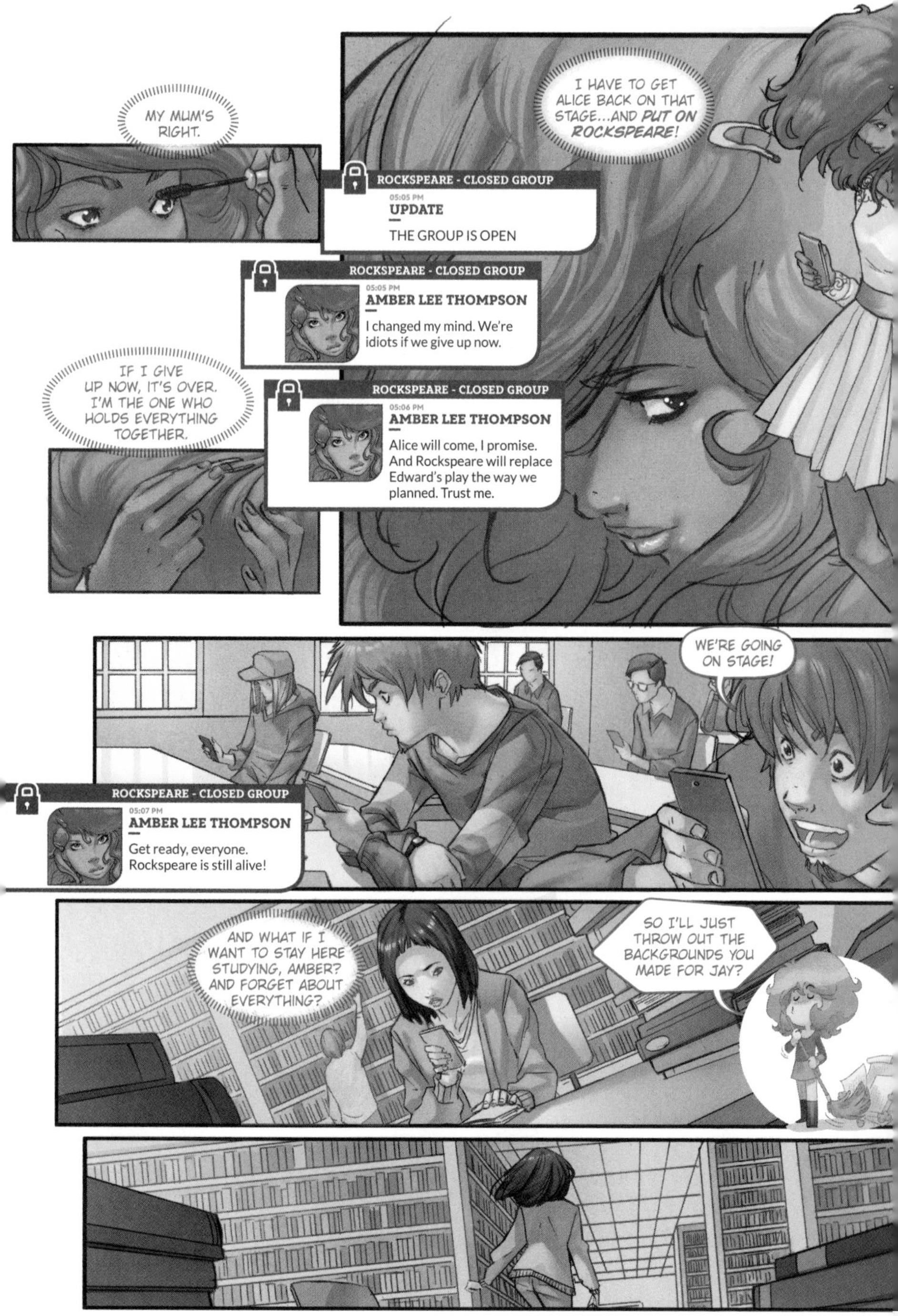
MY MUM'S RIGHT.
I HAVE TO GET ALICE BACK ON THAT STAGE...AND PUT ON ROCKSPEARE!
ROCKSPEARE - CLOSED GROUP
05:05 PM
UPDATE
THE GROUP IS OPEN
ROCKSPEARE - CLOSED GROUP
05:05 PM
AMBER LEE THOMPSON
I changed my mind. We're idiots if we give up now.
IF I GIVE UP NOW, IT'S OVER. I'M THE ONE WHO HOLDS EVERYTHING TOGETHER.
ROCKSPEARE - CLOSED GROUP
05:06 PM
AMBER LEE THOMPSON
Alice will come, I promise. And Rockspeare will replace Edward's play the way we planned. Trust me.
ROCKSPEARE - CLOSED GROUP
05:07 PM
AMBER LEE THOMPSON
Get ready, everyone. Rockspeare is still alive!
WE'RE GOING ON STAGE!
AND WHAT IF I WANT TO STAY HERE STUDYING, AMBER? AND FORGET ABOUT EVERYTHING?
SO I'LL JUST THROW OUT THE BACKGROUNDS YOU MADE FOR JAY?

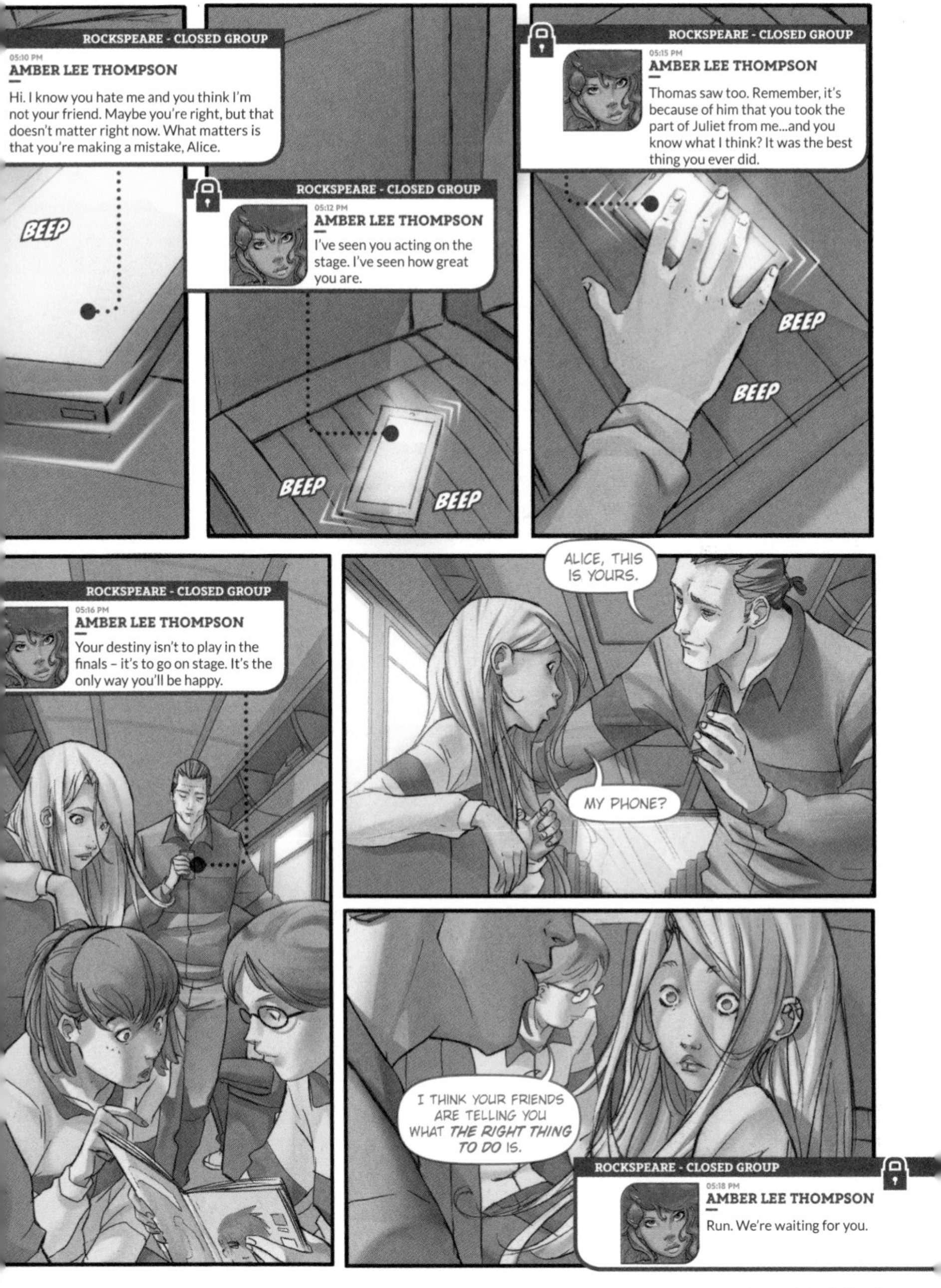
ROCKSPEARE - CLOSED GROUP
05:10 PM
AMBER LEE THOMPSON
Hi. I know you hate me and you think I'm not your friend. Maybe you're right, but that doesn't matter right now. What matters is that you're making a mistake, Alice.
BEEP
ROCKSPEARE - CLOSED GROUP
05:12 PM
AMBER LEE THOMPSON
I've seen you acting on the stage. I've seen how great you are.
BEEP
BEEP
ROCKSPEARE - CLOSED GROUP
05:15 PM
AMBER LEE THOMPSON
Thomas saw too. Remember, it's because of him that you took the part of Juliet from me...and you know what I think? It was the best thing you ever did.
BEEP
BEEP
ROCKSPEARE - CLOSED GROUP
05:16 PM
AMBER LEE THOMPSON
Your destiny isn't to play in the finals – it's to go on stage. It's the only way you'll be happy.
ALICE, THIS IS YOURS.
MY PHONE?
I THINK YOUR FRIENDS ARE TELLING YOU WHAT *THE RIGHT THING TO DO* IS.
ROCKSPEARE - CLOSED GROUP
05:18 PM
AMBER LEE THOMPSON
Run. We're waiting for you.

END OF CHAPTER 34

CHAPTER 35

MAKE YOUR CHOICE

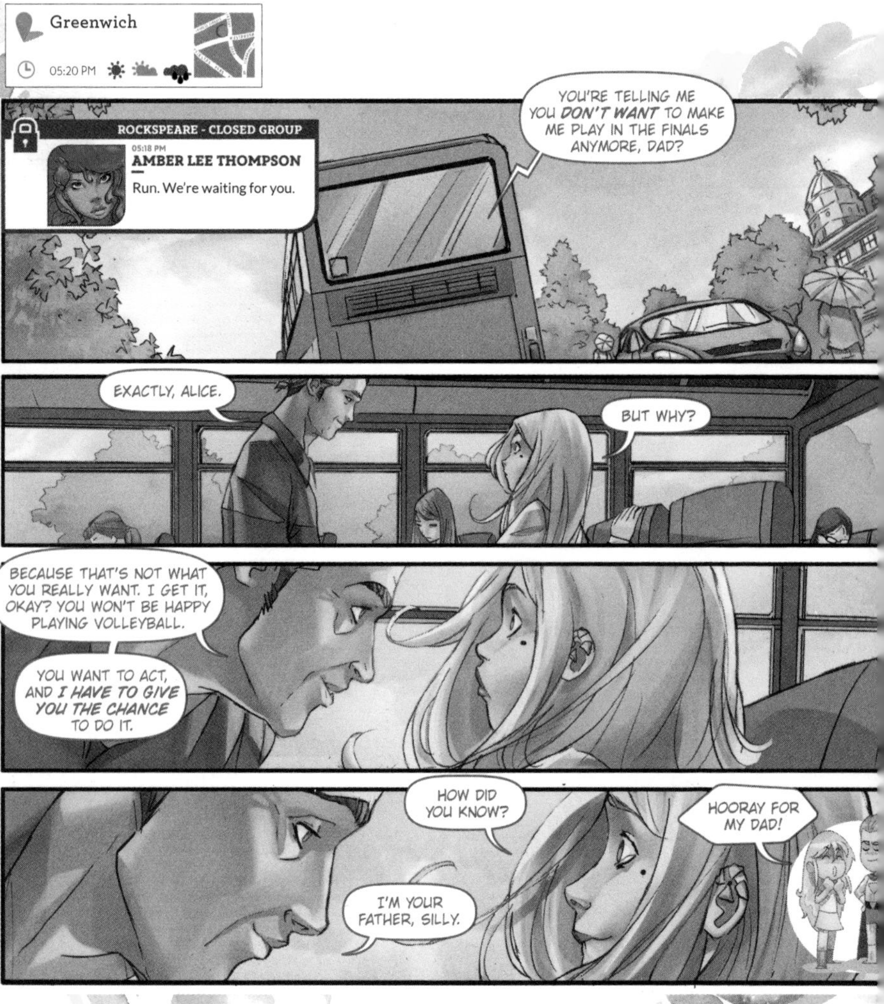

Greenwich
05:20 PM
ROCKSPEARE - CLOSED GROUP
05:18 PM
AMBER LEE THOMPSON
Run. We're waiting for you.
YOU'RE TELLING ME YOU DON'T WANT TO MAKE ME PLAY IN THE FINALS ANYMORE, DAD?
EXACTLY, ALICE.
BUT WHY?
BECAUSE THAT'S NOT WHAT YOU REALLY WANT. I GET IT, OKAY? YOU WON'T BE HAPPY PLAYING VOLLEYBALL.
YOU WANT TO ACT, AND I HAVE TO GIVE YOU THE CHANCE TO DO IT.
HOW DID YOU KNOW?
I'M YOUR FATHER, SILLY.
HOORAY FOR MY DAD!

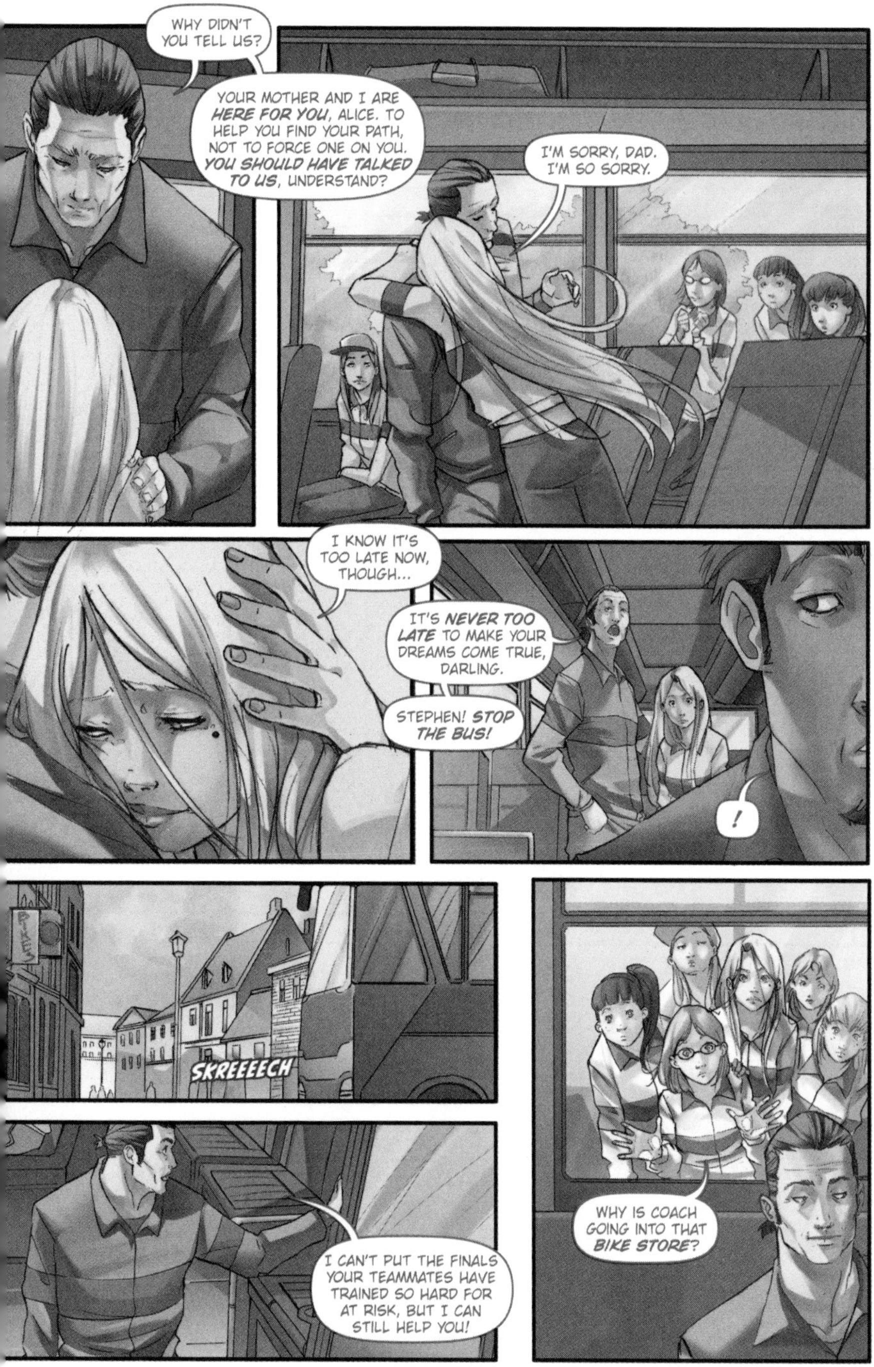
WHY DIDN'T YOU TELL US?
YOUR MOTHER AND I ARE **HERE FOR YOU**, ALICE. TO HELP YOU FIND YOUR PATH, NOT TO FORCE ONE ON YOU. **YOU SHOULD HAVE TALKED TO US**, UNDERSTAND?
I'M SORRY, DAD. I'M SO SORRY.
I KNOW IT'S TOO LATE NOW, THOUGH...
IT'S **NEVER TOO LATE** TO MAKE YOUR DREAMS COME TRUE, DARLING.
STEPHEN! **STOP THE BUS!**
!
SKREEEECH
I CAN'T PUT THE FINALS YOUR TEAMMATES HAVE TRAINED SO HARD FOR AT RISK, BUT I CAN STILL HELP YOU!
WHY IS COACH GOING INTO THAT **BIKE STORE**?

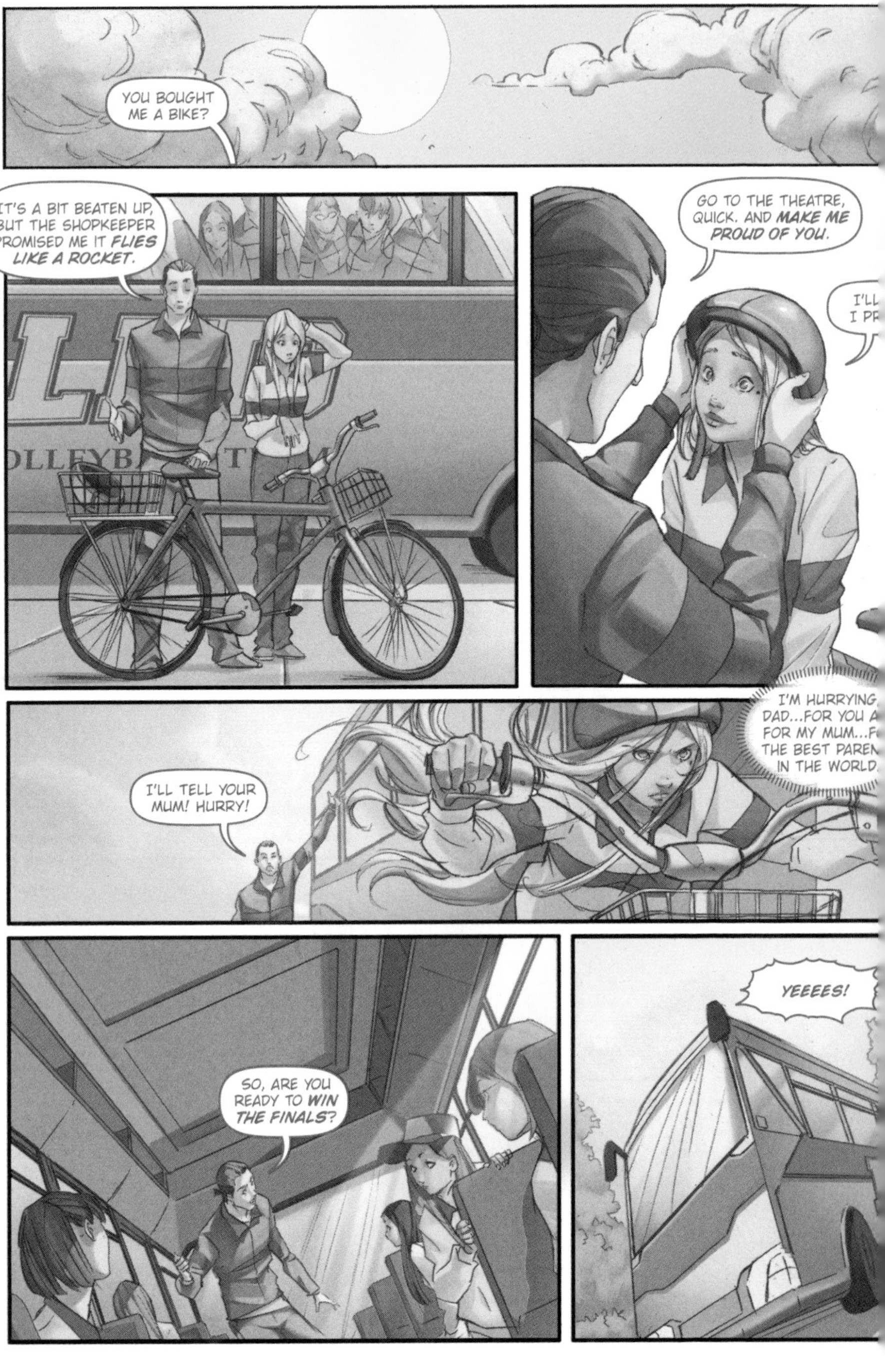

YOU BOUGHT ME A BIKE?
IT'S A BIT BEATEN UP, BUT THE SHOPKEEPER PROMISED ME IT FLIES LIKE A ROCKET.
GO TO THE THEATRE, QUICK. AND MAKE ME PROUD OF YOU.
I'LL TELL YOUR MUM! HURRY!
SO, ARE YOU READY TO WIN THE FINALS?
YEEEES!

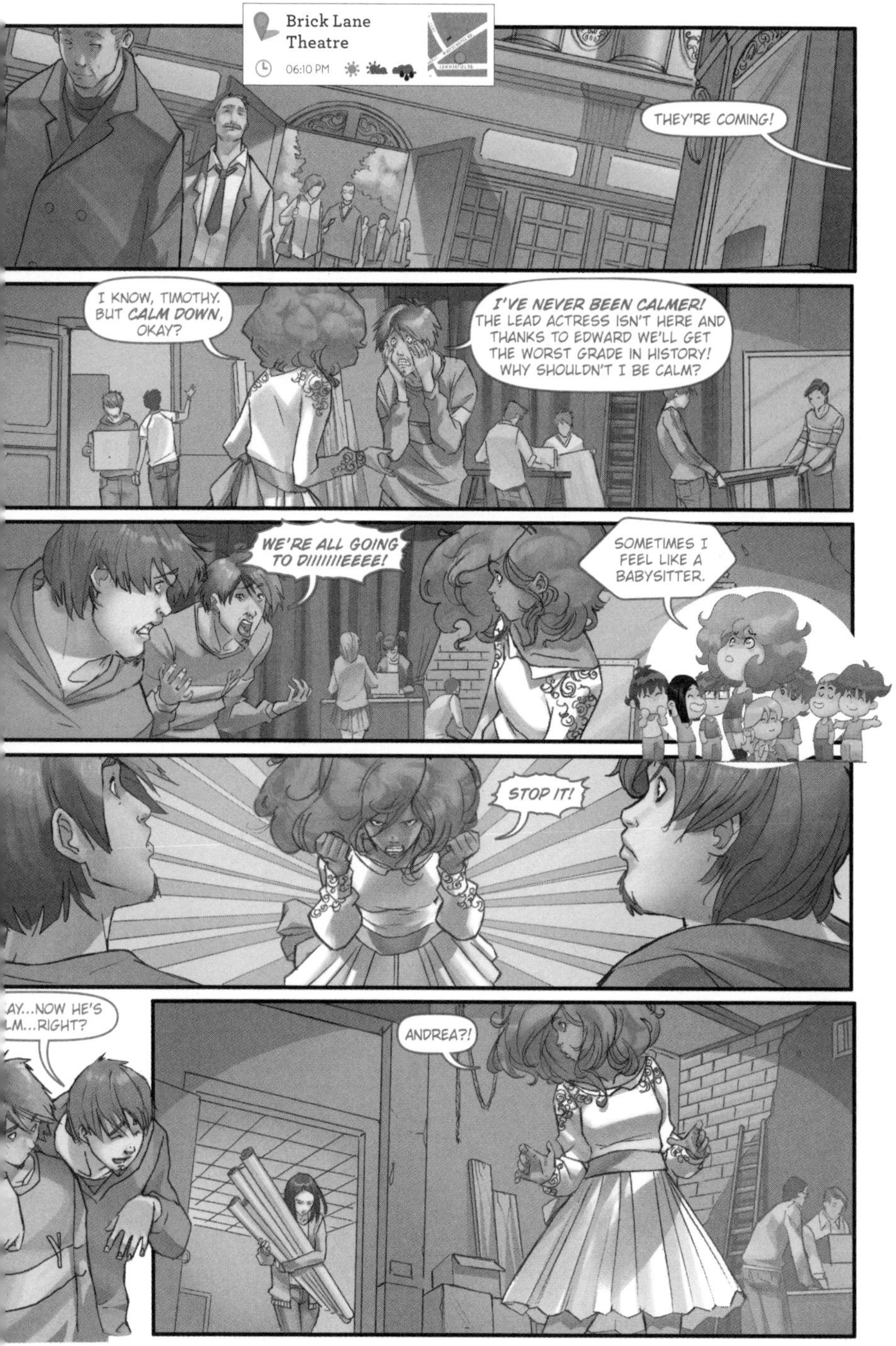
Brick Lane Theatre
06:10 PM
THEY'RE COMING!
I KNOW, TIMOTHY. BUT CALM DOWN, OKAY?
I'VE NEVER BEEN CALMER! THE LEAD ACTRESS ISN'T HERE AND THANKS TO EDWARD WE'LL GET THE WORST GRADE IN HISTORY! WHY SHOULDN'T I BE CALM?
WE'RE ALL GOING TO DIIIIIIEEEE!
SOMETIMES I FEEL LIKE A BABYSITTER.
STOP IT!
AY...NOW HE'S LM...RIGHT?
ANDREA?!

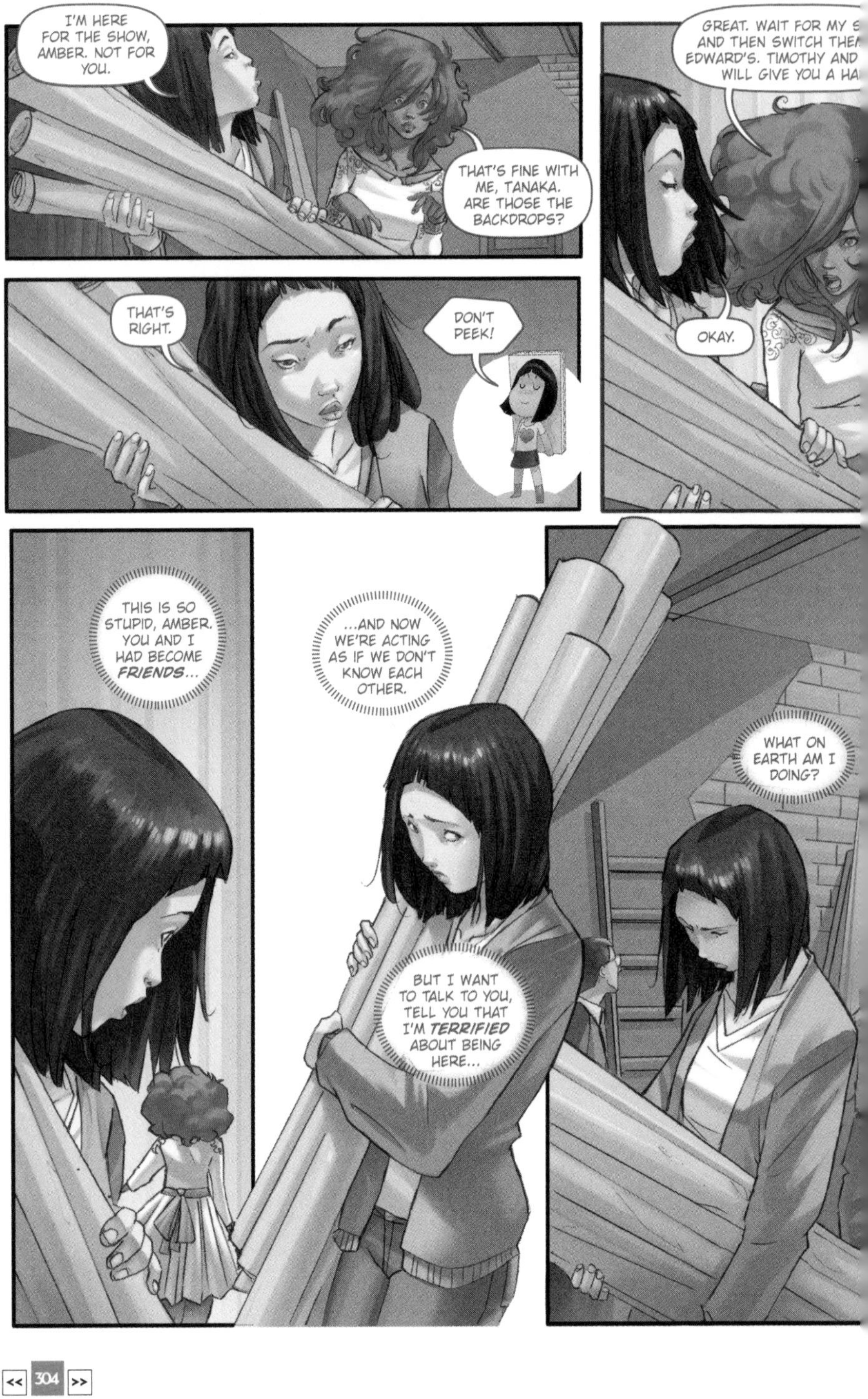

I'M HERE FOR THE SHOW, AMBER. NOT FOR YOU.
THAT'S FINE WITH ME, TANAKA. ARE THOSE THE BACKDROPS?
THAT'S RIGHT.
DON'T PEEK!
GREAT. WAIT FOR MY S AND THEN SWITCH THEM EDWARD'S. TIMOTHY AND WILL GIVE YOU A HA
OKAY.
THIS IS SO STUPID, AMBER. YOU AND I HAD BECOME *FRIENDS*...
...AND NOW WE'RE ACTING AS IF WE DON'T KNOW EACH OTHER.
WHAT ON EARTH AM I DOING?
BUT I WANT TO TALK TO YOU, TELL YOU THAT I'M *TERRIFIED* ABOUT BEING HERE...

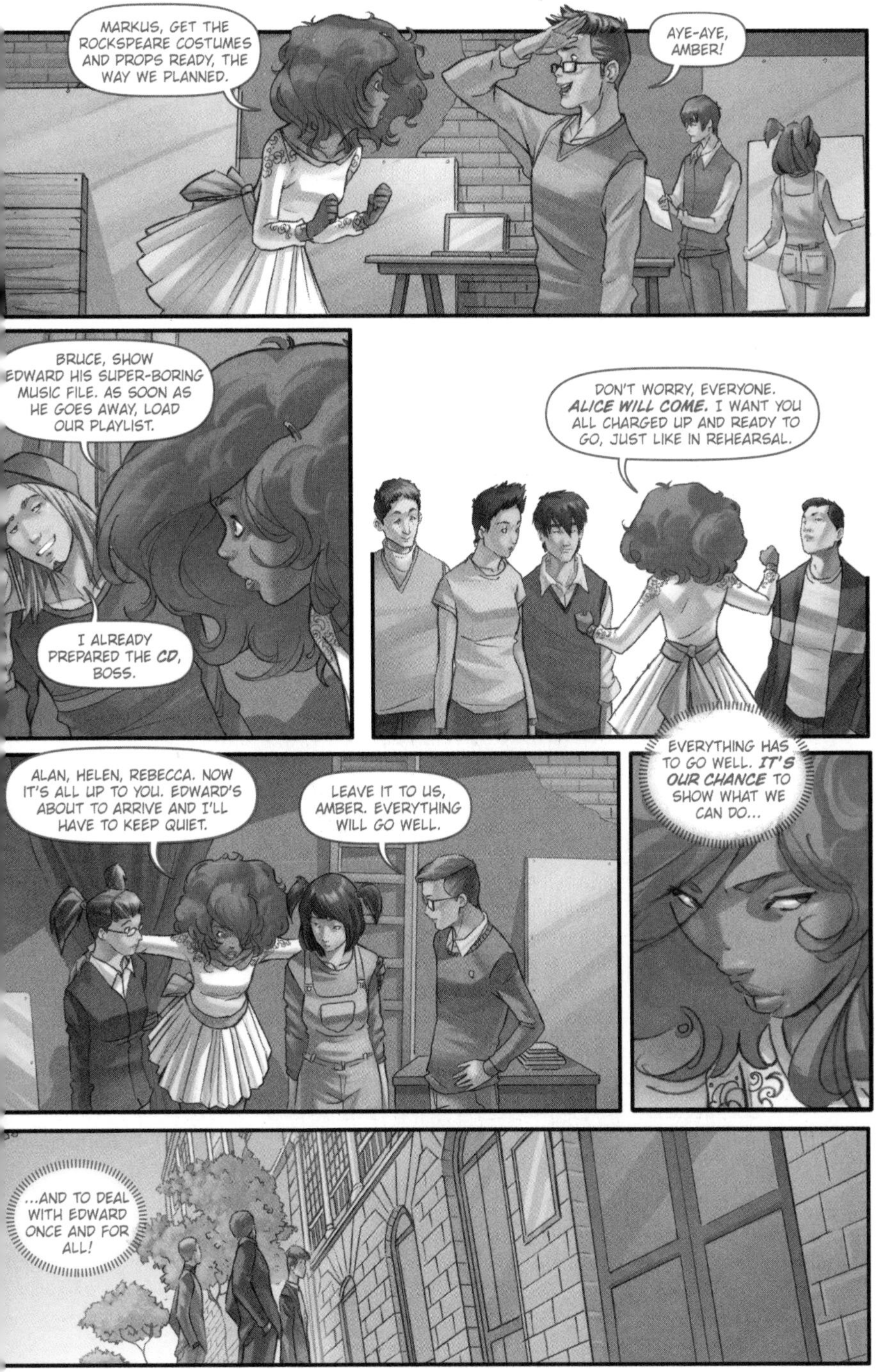
MARKUS, GET THE ROCKSPEARE COSTUMES AND PROPS READY, THE WAY WE PLANNED.
AYE-AYE, AMBER!
BRUCE, SHOW EDWARD HIS SUPER-BORING MUSIC FILE. AS SOON AS HE GOES AWAY, LOAD OUR PLAYLIST.
I ALREADY PREPARED THE *CD*, BOSS.
DON'T WORRY, EVERYONE. ***ALICE WILL COME.*** I WANT YOU ALL CHARGED UP AND READY TO GO, JUST LIKE IN REHEARSAL.
ALAN, HELEN, REBECCA. NOW IT'S ALL UP TO YOU. EDWARD'S ABOUT TO ARRIVE AND I'LL HAVE TO KEEP QUIET.
LEAVE IT TO US, AMBER. EVERYTHING WILL GO WELL.
EVERYTHING HAS TO GO WELL. ***IT'S OUR CHANCE*** TO SHOW WHAT WE CAN DO...
...AND TO DEAL WITH EDWARD ONCE AND FOR ALL!

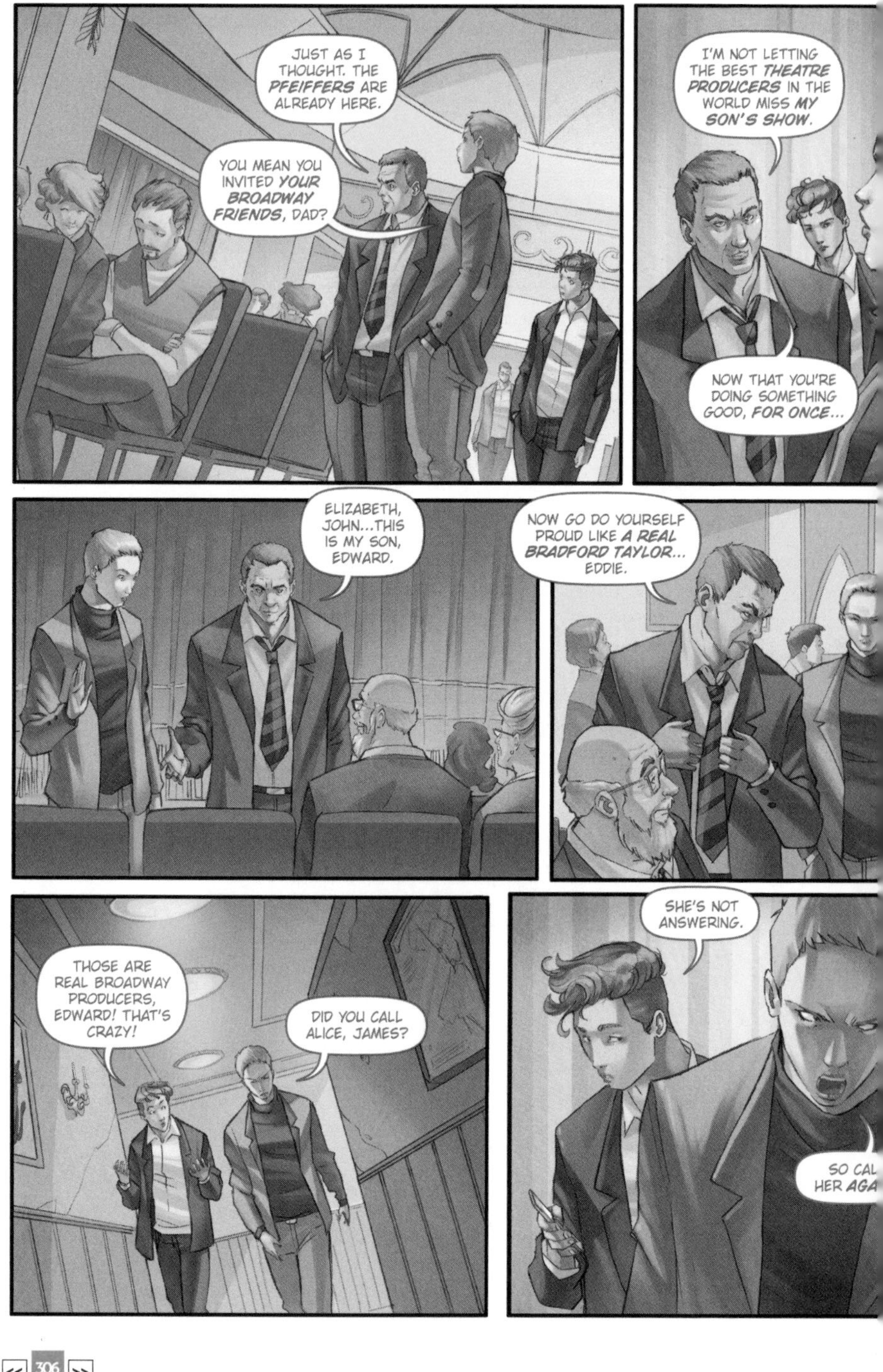

JUST AS I THOUGHT. THE PFEIFFERS ARE ALREADY HERE.
YOU MEAN YOU INVITED YOUR BROADWAY FRIENDS, DAD?
I'M NOT LETTING THE BEST THEATRE PRODUCERS IN THE WORLD MISS MY SON'S SHOW.
NOW THAT YOU'RE DOING SOMETHING GOOD, FOR ONCE...
ELIZABETH, JOHN...THIS IS MY SON, EDWARD.
NOW GO DO YOURSELF PROUD LIKE A REAL BRADFORD TAYLOR... EDDIE.
THOSE ARE REAL BROADWAY PRODUCERS, EDWARD! THAT'S CRAZY!
DID YOU CALL ALICE, JAMES?
SHE'S NOT ANSWERING.

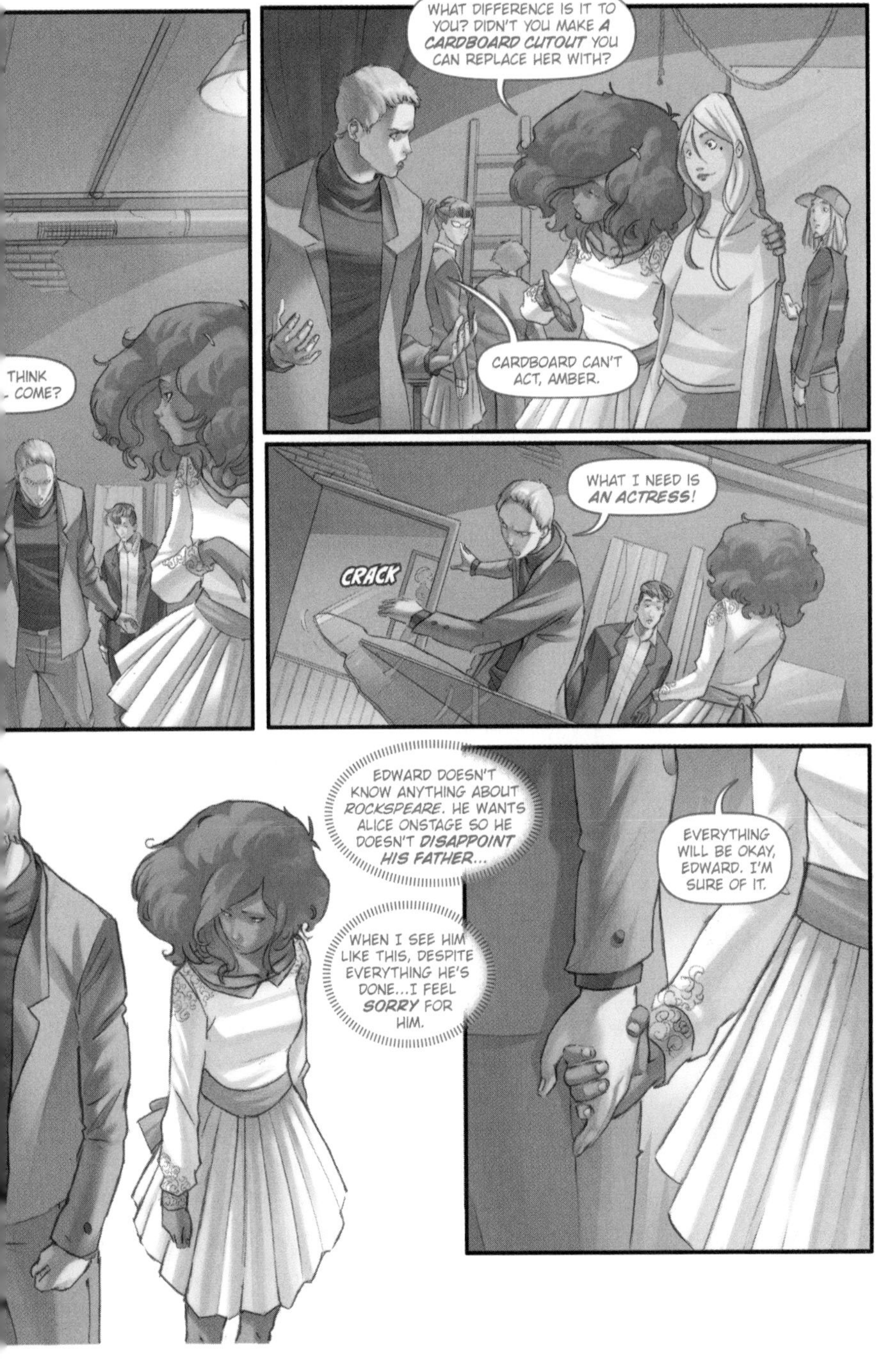
THINK
COME?
WHAT DIFFERENCE IS IT TO YOU? DIDN'T YOU MAKE A CARDBOARD CUTOUT YOU CAN REPLACE HER WITH?
CARDBOARD CAN'T ACT, AMBER.
WHAT I NEED IS AN ACTRESS!
CRACK
EDWARD DOESN'T KNOW ANYTHING ABOUT ROCKSPEARE. HE WANTS ALICE ONSTAGE SO HE DOESN'T DISAPPOINT HIS FATHER...
WHEN I SEE HIM LIKE THIS, DESPITE EVERYTHING HE'S DONE...I FEEL SORRY FOR HIM.
EVERYTHING WILL BE OKAY, EDWARD. I'M SURE OF IT.

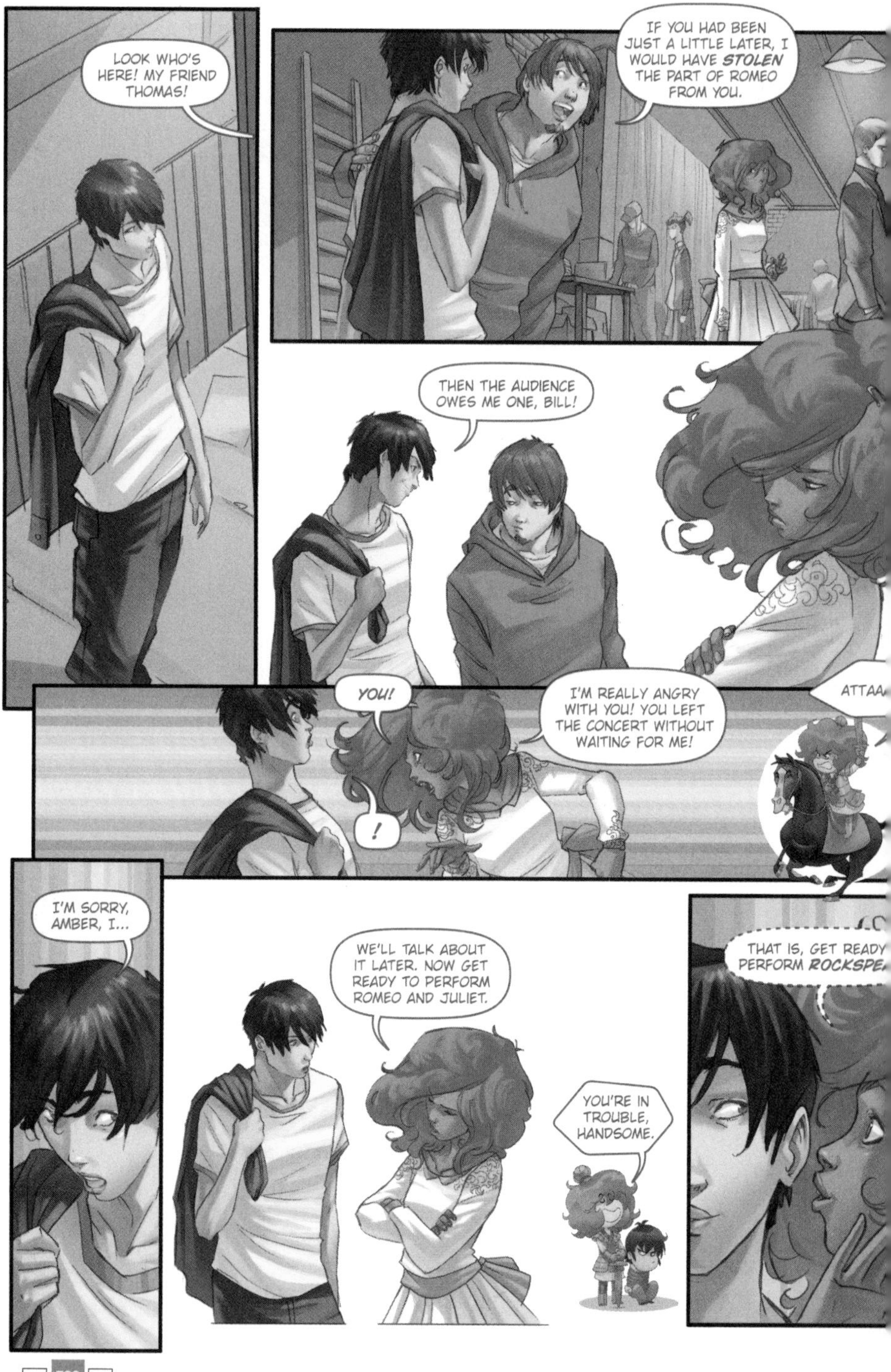
LOOK WHO'S HERE! MY FRIEND THOMAS!
IF YOU HAD BEEN JUST A LITTLE LATER, I WOULD HAVE **STOLEN** THE PART OF ROMEO FROM YOU.
THEN THE AUDIENCE OWES ME ONE, BILL!
YOU!
!
I'M REALLY ANGRY WITH YOU! YOU LEFT THE CONCERT WITHOUT WAITING FOR ME!
I'M SORRY, AMBER, I...
WE'LL TALK ABOUT IT LATER. NOW GET READY TO PERFORM ROMEO AND JULIET.
YOU'RE IN TROUBLE, HANDSOME.

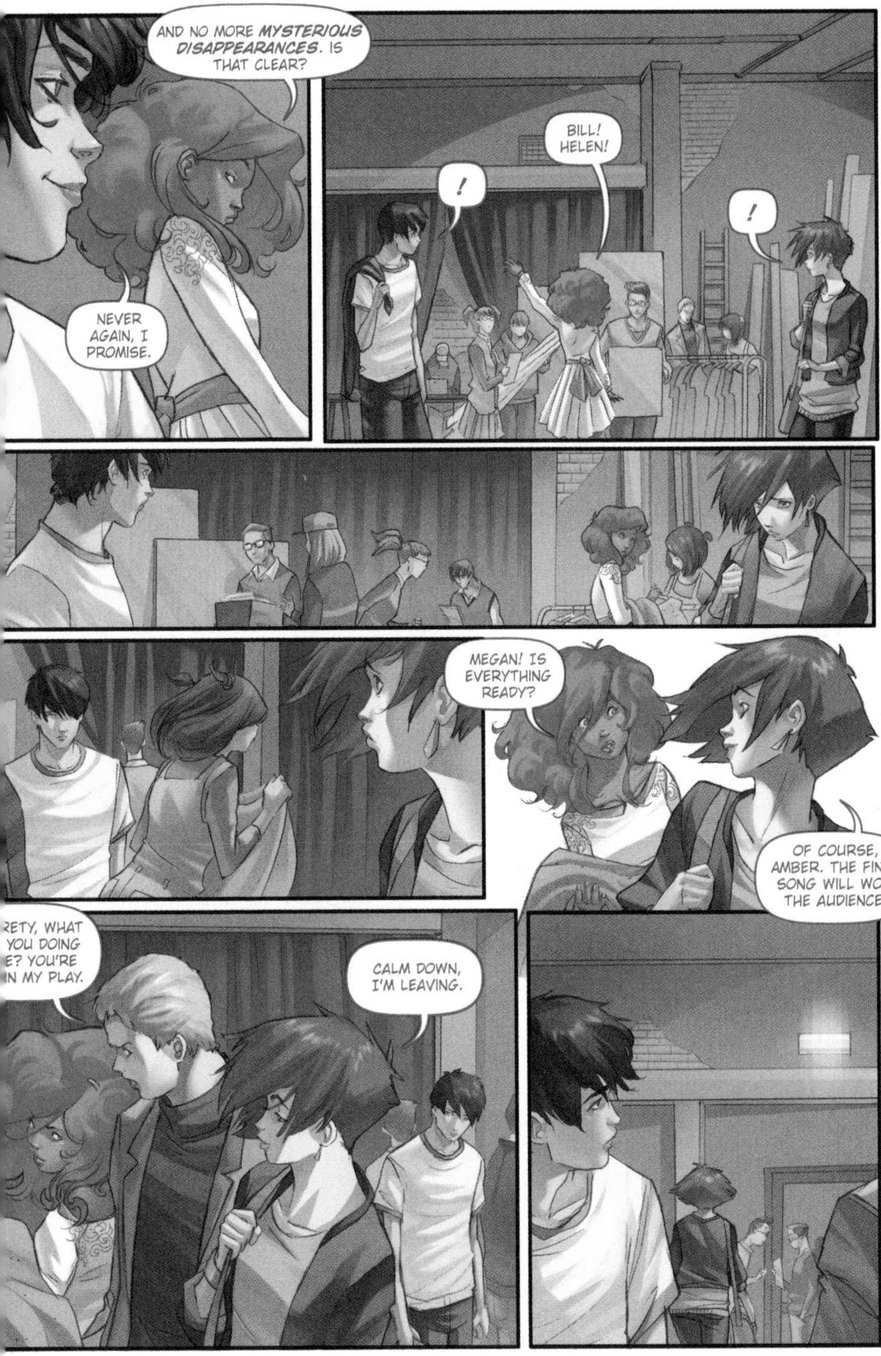
AND NO MORE **MYSTERIOUS DISAPPEARANCES**. IS THAT CLEAR?
NEVER AGAIN, I PROMISE.
!
BILL! HELEN!
!
MEGAN! IS EVERYTHING READY?
OF COURSE, AMBER. THE FINAL SONG WILL WOW THE AUDIENCE!
RETY, WHAT YOU DOING E? YOU'RE N MY PLAY.
CALM DOWN, I'M LEAVING.

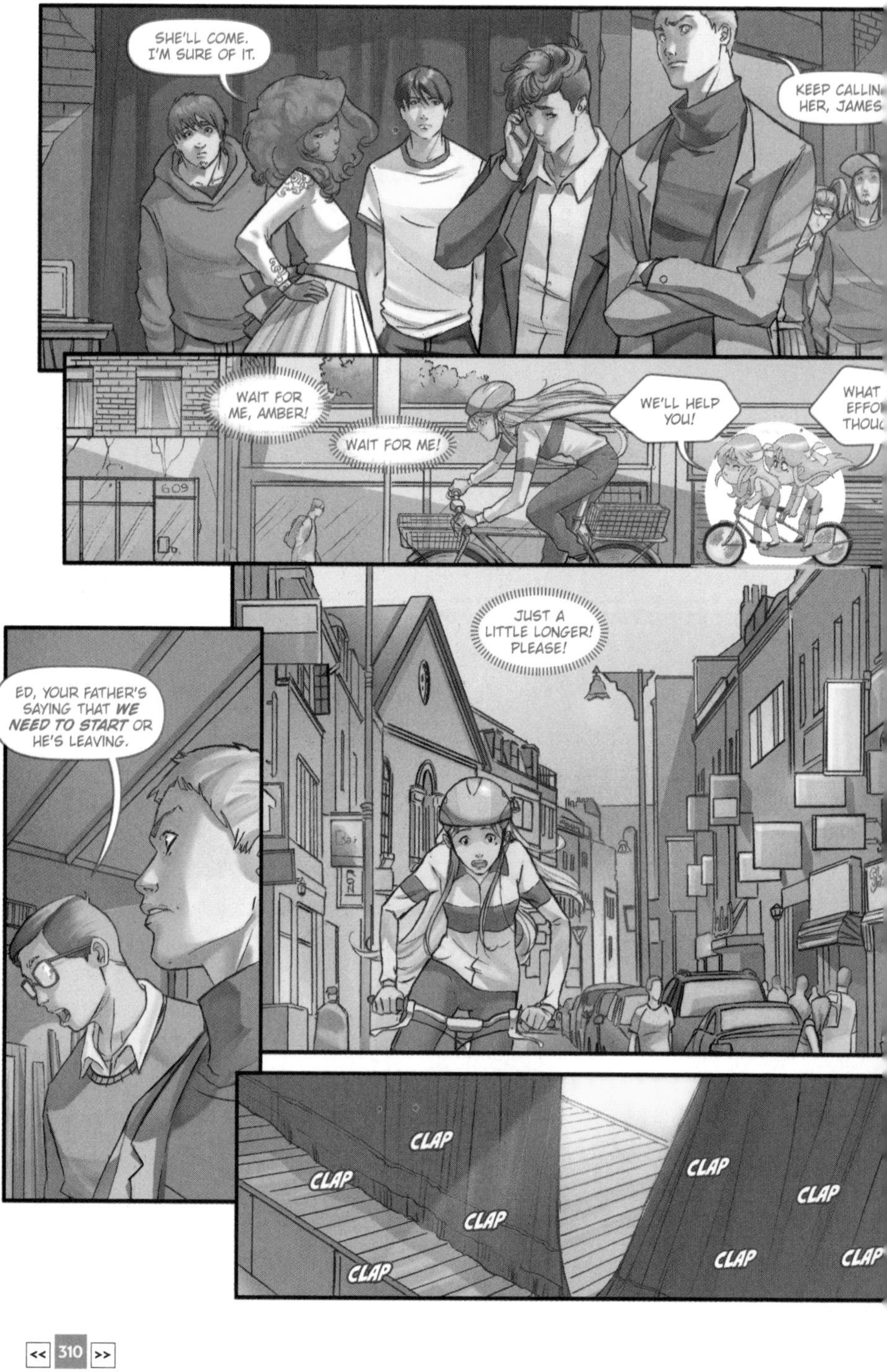

SHE'LL COME. I'M SURE OF IT.
KEEP CALLIN HER, JAMES
WAIT FOR ME, AMBER!
WAIT FOR ME!
WE'LL HELP YOU!
WHAT EFFO THOU
JUST A LITTLE LONGER! PLEASE!
ED, YOUR FATHER'S SAYING THAT WE NEED TO START OR HE'S LEAVING.
CLAP
CLAP
CLAP
CLAP
CLAP
CLAP
CLAP
CLAP

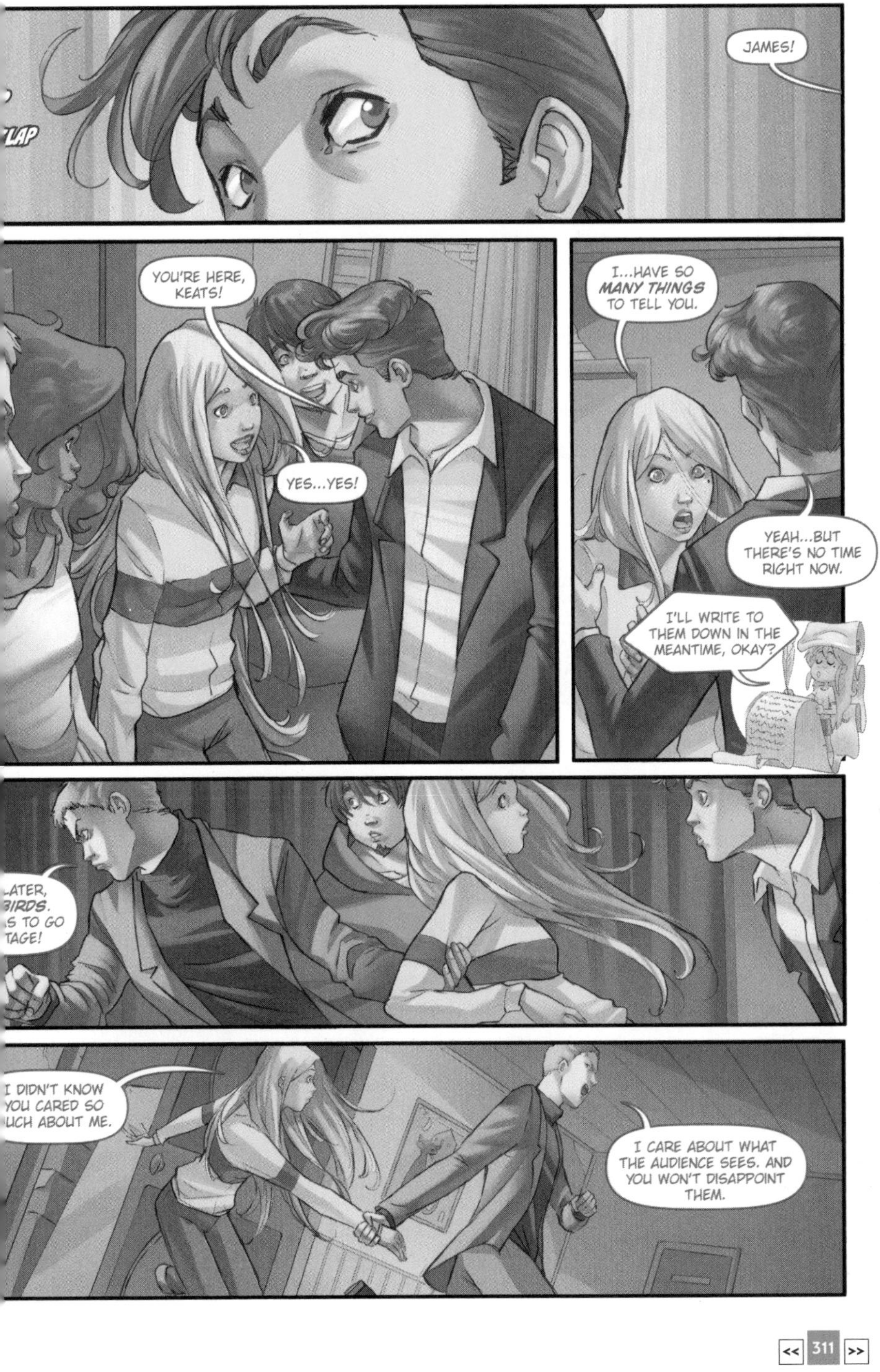

JAMES!
YOU'RE HERE, KEATS!
YES...YES!
I...HAVE SO MANY THINGS TO TELL YOU.
YEAH...BUT THERE'S NO TIME RIGHT NOW.
I'LL WRITE TO THEM DOWN IN THE MEANTIME, OKAY?
ATER, IRDS. S TO GO TAGE!
I DIDN'T KNOW YOU CARED SO UCH ABOUT ME.
I CARE ABOUT WHAT THE AUDIENCE SEES. AND YOU WON'T DISAPPOINT THEM.

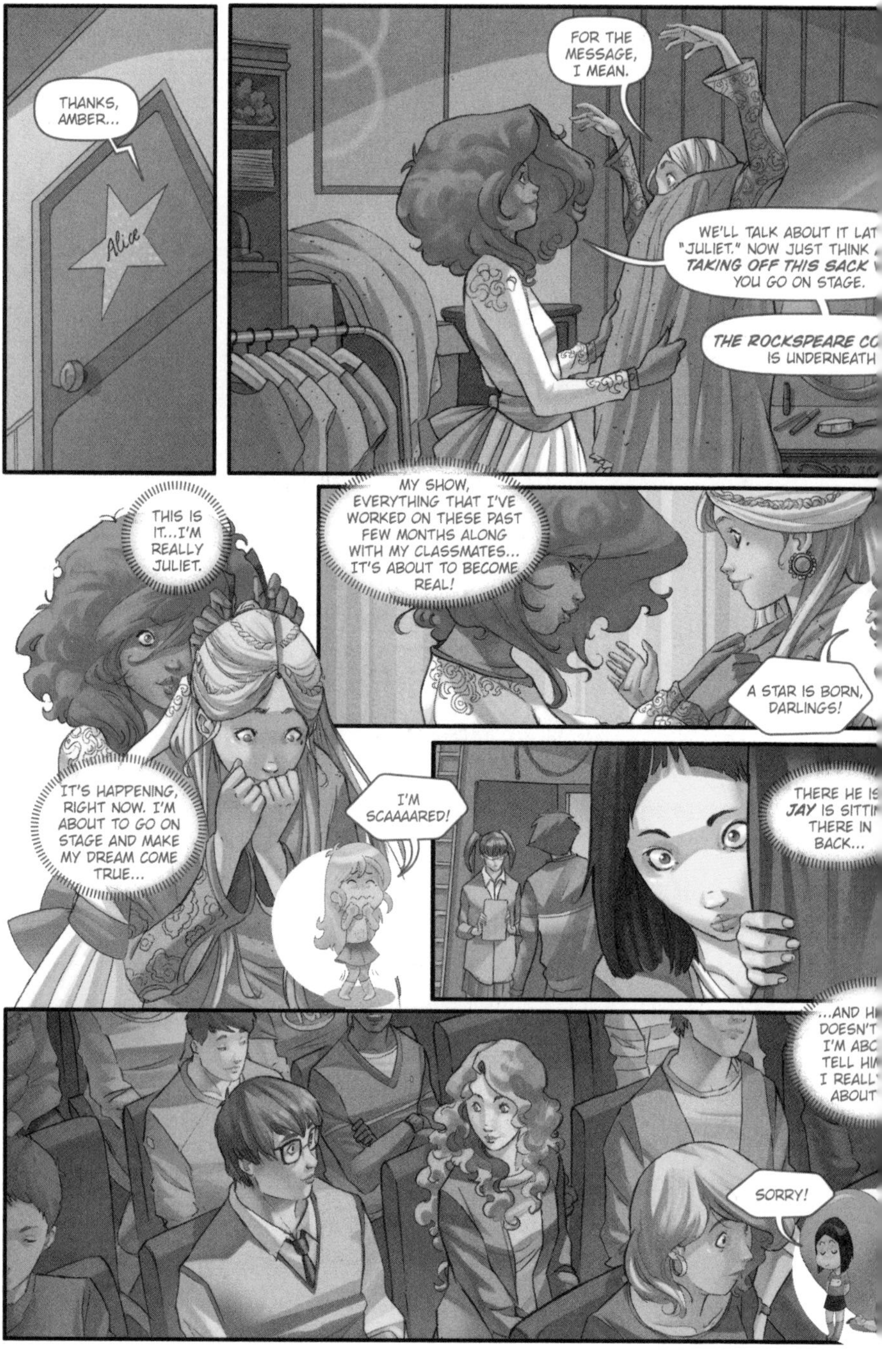
THANKS, AMBER...
Alice
FOR THE MESSAGE, I MEAN.
WE'LL TALK ABOUT IT LAT
"JULIET." NOW JUST THINK
TAKING OFF THIS SACK
YOU GO ON STAGE.
THE ROCKSPEARE CO
IS UNDERNEATH
THIS IS IT...I'M REALLY JULIET.
MY SHOW, EVERYTHING THAT I'VE WORKED ON THESE PAST FEW MONTHS ALONG WITH MY CLASSMATES... IT'S ABOUT TO BECOME REAL!
A STAR IS BORN, DARLINGS!
IT'S HAPPENING, RIGHT NOW. I'M ABOUT TO GO ON STAGE AND MAKE MY DREAM COME TRUE...
I'M SCAAAARED!
THERE HE IS
JAY IS SITTI
THERE IN
BACK...
...AND H
DOESN'T
I'M ABO
TELL HI
I REALL
ABOUT
SORRY!

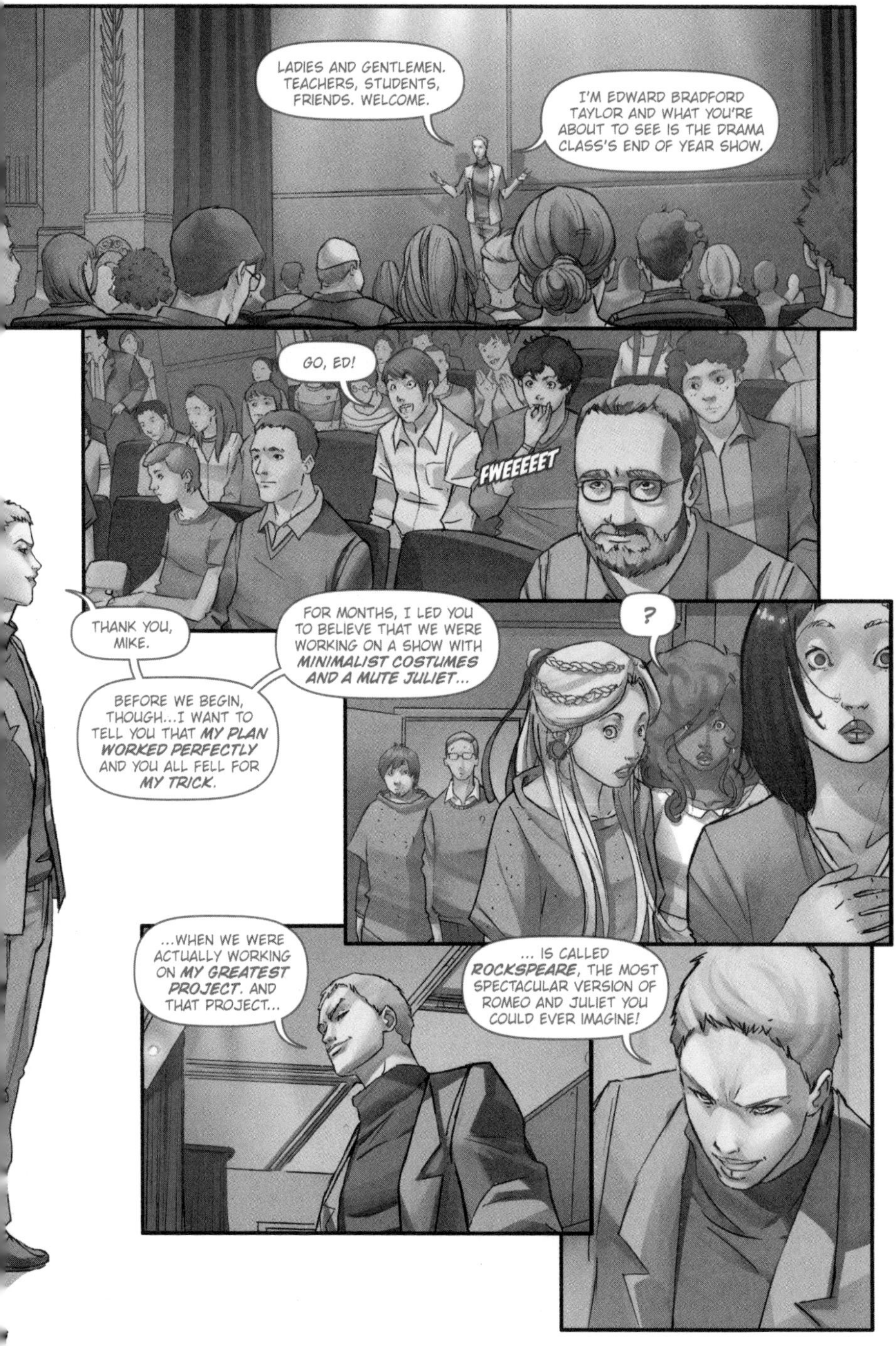
LADIES AND GENTLEMEN. TEACHERS, STUDENTS, FRIENDS. WELCOME.
I'M EDWARD BRADFORD TAYLOR AND WHAT YOU'RE ABOUT TO SEE IS THE DRAMA CLASS'S END OF YEAR SHOW.
GO, ED!
FWEEEEET
THANK YOU, MIKE.
BEFORE WE BEGIN, THOUGH...I WANT TO TELL YOU THAT MY PLAN WORKED PERFECTLY AND YOU ALL FELL FOR MY TRICK.
FOR MONTHS, I LED YOU TO BELIEVE THAT WE WERE WORKING ON A SHOW WITH MINIMALIST COSTUMES AND A MUTE JULIET...
?
...WHEN WE WERE ACTUALLY WORKING ON MY GREATEST PROJECT. AND THAT PROJECT...
... IS CALLED ROCKSPEARE, THE MOST SPECTACULAR VERSION OF ROMEO AND JULIET YOU COULD EVER IMAGINE!

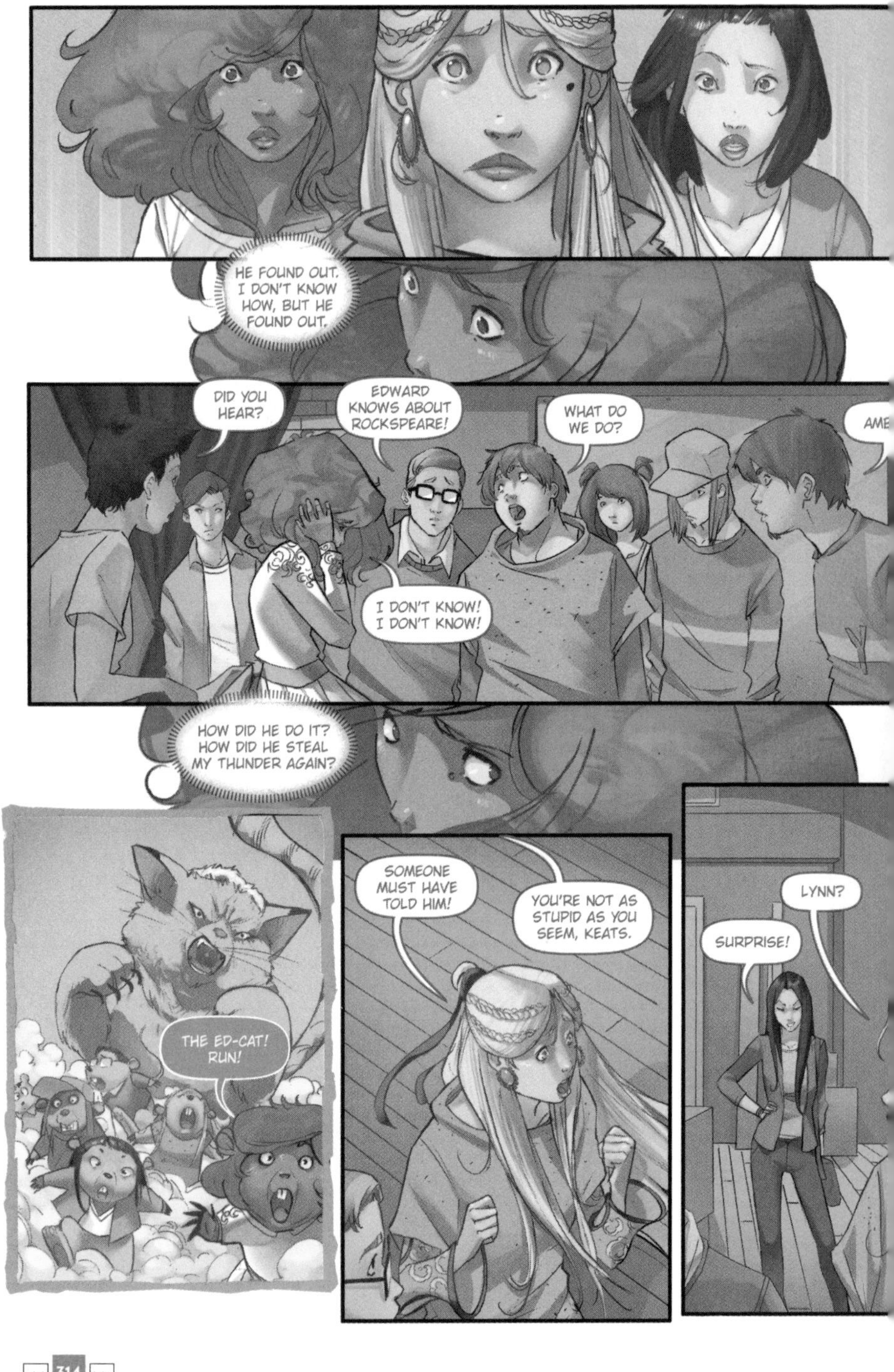
HE FOUND OUT. I DON'T KNOW HOW, BUT HE FOUND OUT.
DID YOU HEAR?
EDWARD KNOWS ABOUT ROCKSPEARE!
WHAT DO WE DO?
I DON'T KNOW! I DON'T KNOW!
HOW DID HE DO IT? HOW DID HE STEAL MY THUNDER AGAIN?
THE ED-CAT! RUN!
SOMEONE MUST HAVE TOLD HIM!
YOU'RE NOT AS STUPID AS YOU SEEM, KEATS.
LYNN?
SURPRISE!

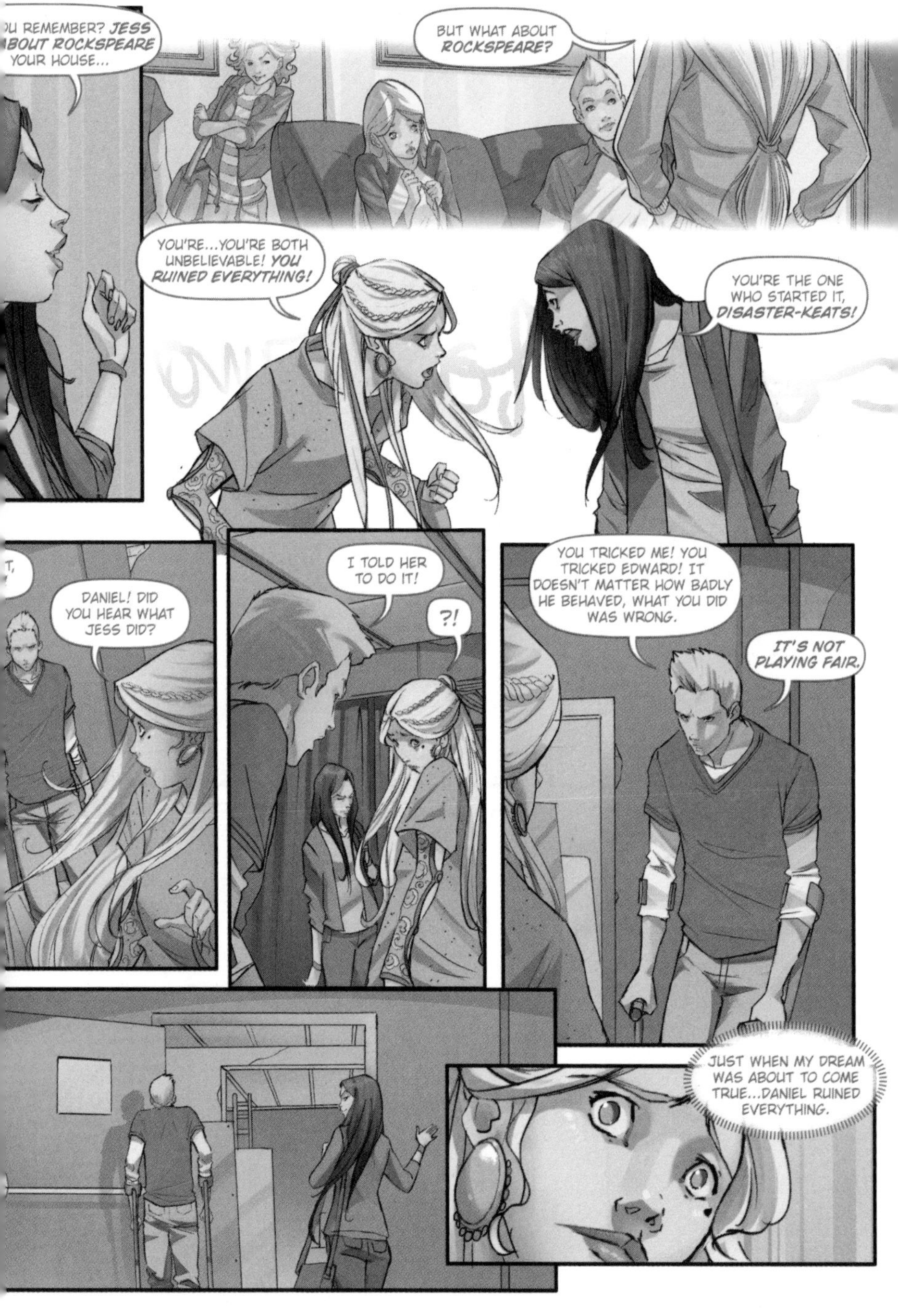

OU REMEMBER? JESS
BOUT ROCKSPEARE
YOUR HOUSE...
BUT WHAT ABOUT ROCKSPEARE?
YOU'RE...YOU'RE BOTH UNBELIEVABLE! YOU RUINED EVERYTHING!
YOU'RE THE ONE WHO STARTED IT, DISASTER-KEATS!
DANIEL! DID YOU HEAR WHAT JESS DID?
I TOLD HER TO DO IT!
?!
YOU TRICKED ME! YOU TRICKED EDWARD! IT DOESN'T MATTER HOW BADLY HE BEHAVED, WHAT YOU DID WAS WRONG.
IT'S NOT PLAYING FAIR.
JUST WHEN MY DREAM WAS ABOUT TO COME TRUE...DANIEL RUINED EVERYTHING.

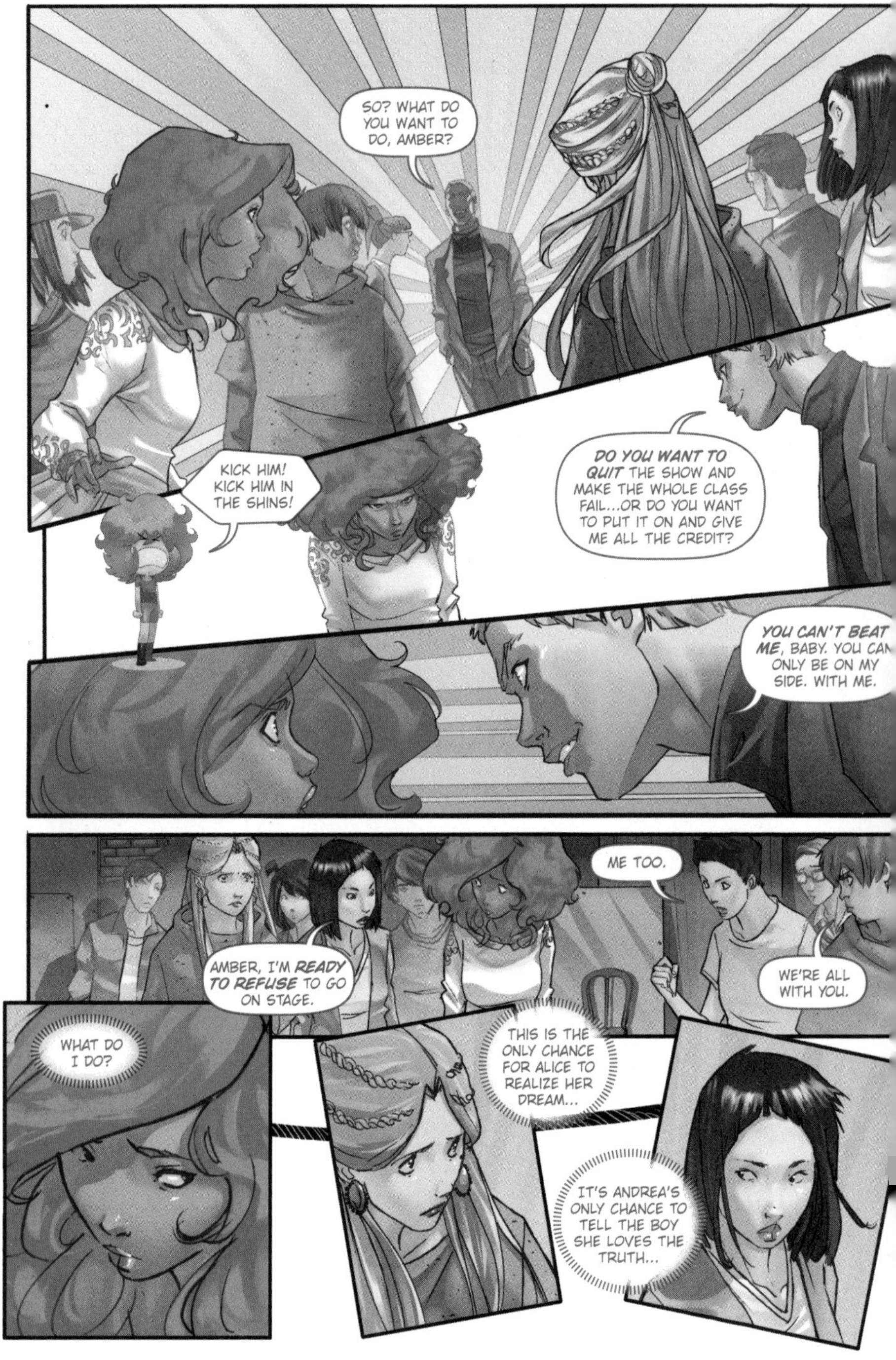
SO? WHAT DO YOU WANT TO DO, AMBER?
DO YOU WANT TO QUIT THE SHOW AND MAKE THE WHOLE CLASS FAIL...OR DO YOU WANT TO PUT IT ON AND GIVE ME ALL THE CREDIT?
KICK HIM! KICK HIM IN THE SHINS!
YOU CAN'T BEAT ME, BABY. YOU CAN ONLY BE ON MY SIDE. WITH ME.
AMBER, I'M READY TO REFUSE TO GO ON STAGE.
ME TOO.
WE'RE ALL WITH YOU.
WHAT DO I DO?
THIS IS THE ONLY CHANCE FOR ALICE TO REALIZE HER DREAM...
IT'S ANDREA'S ONLY CHANCE TO TELL THE BOY SHE LOVES THE TRUTH...

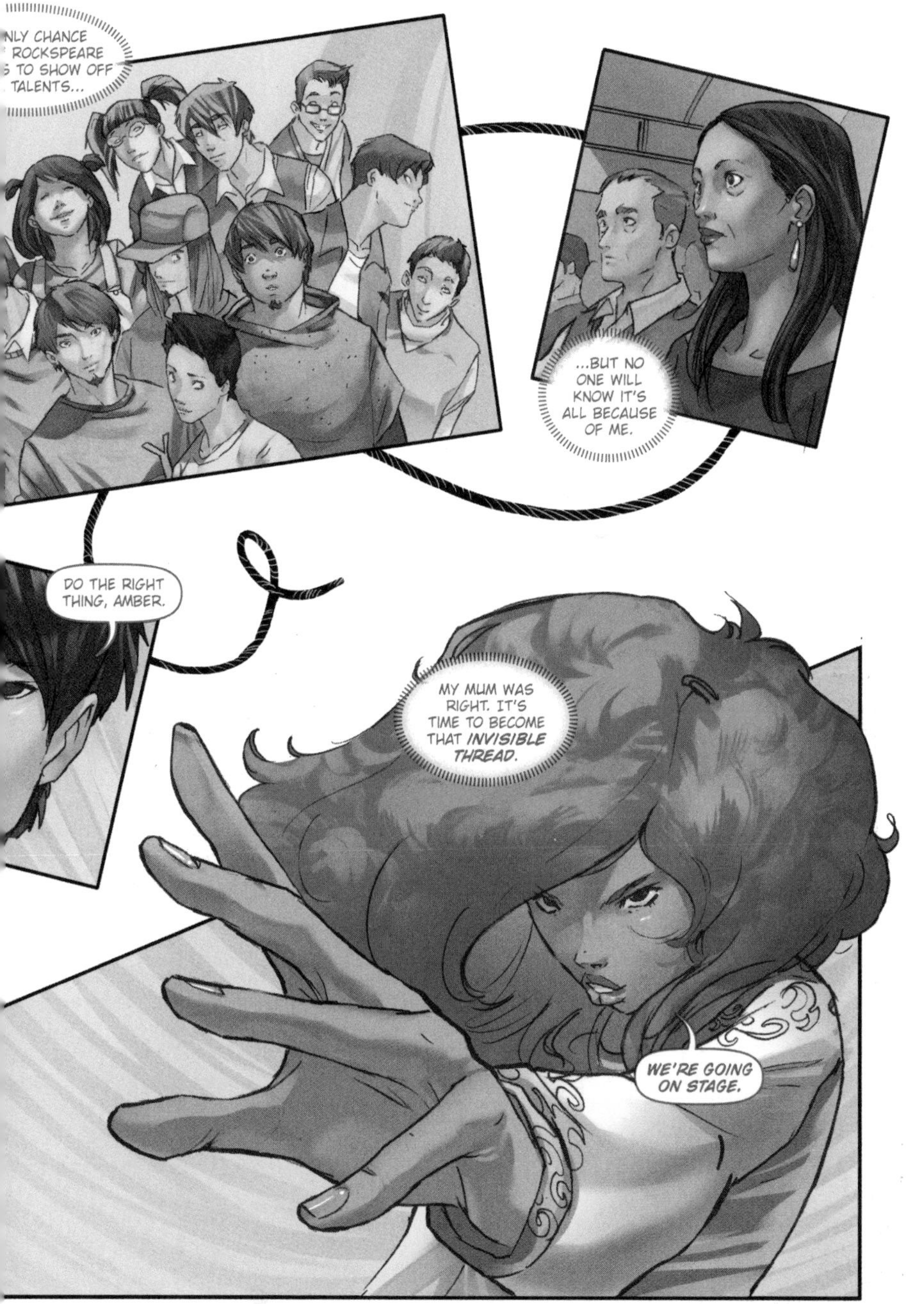
NLY CHANCE
ROCKSPEARE
TO SHOW OFF
TALENTS...
...BUT NO ONE WILL KNOW IT'S ALL BECAUSE OF ME.
DO THE RIGHT THING, AMBER.
MY MUM WAS RIGHT. IT'S TIME TO BECOME THAT *INVISIBLE THREAD.*
WE'RE GOING ON STAGE.

END OF CHAPTER 35

FOREVER FRIENDS

Brick Lane Theatre
07:10 PM

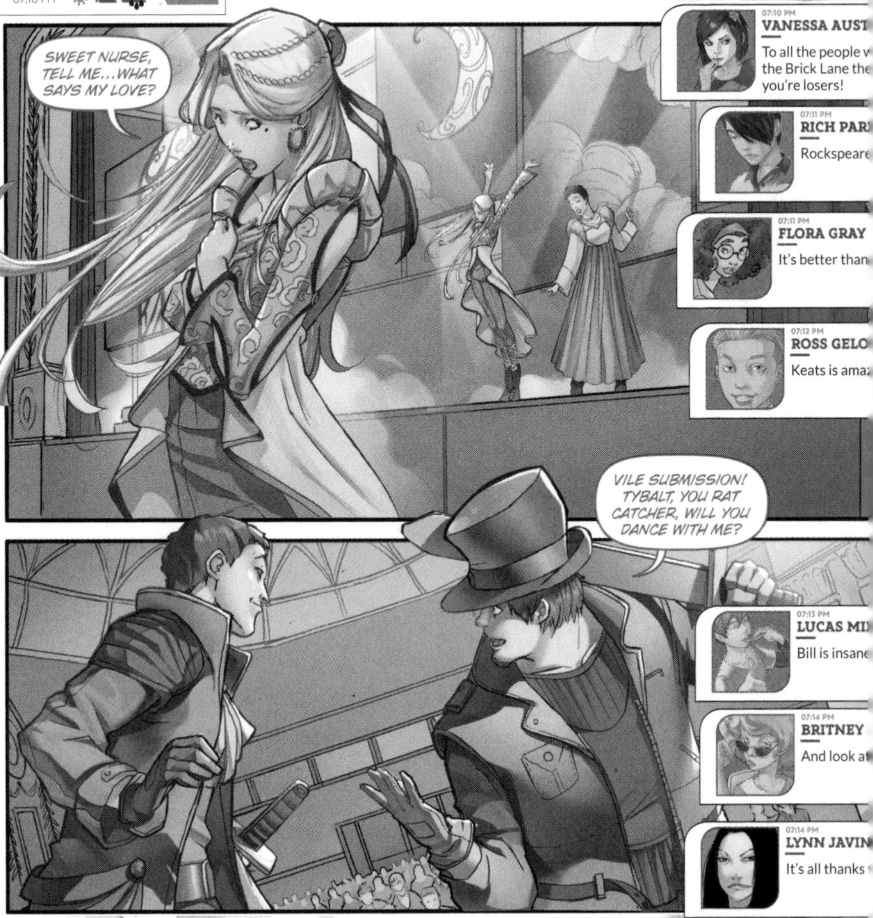
SWEET NURSE, TELL ME...WHAT SAYS MY LOVE?
07:10 PM
VANESSA AUST
To all the people v
the Brick Lane the
you're losers!
07:11 PM
RICH PAR
Rockspeare
07:11 PM
FLORA GRAY
It's better than
07:12 PM
ROSS GELO
Keats is ama
VILE SUBMISSION! TYBALT, YOU RAT CATCHER, WILL YOU DANCE WITH ME?
07:13 PM
LUCAS MI
Bill is insane
07:14 PM
BRITNEY
And look a
07:14 PM
LYNN JAVIN
It's all thanks

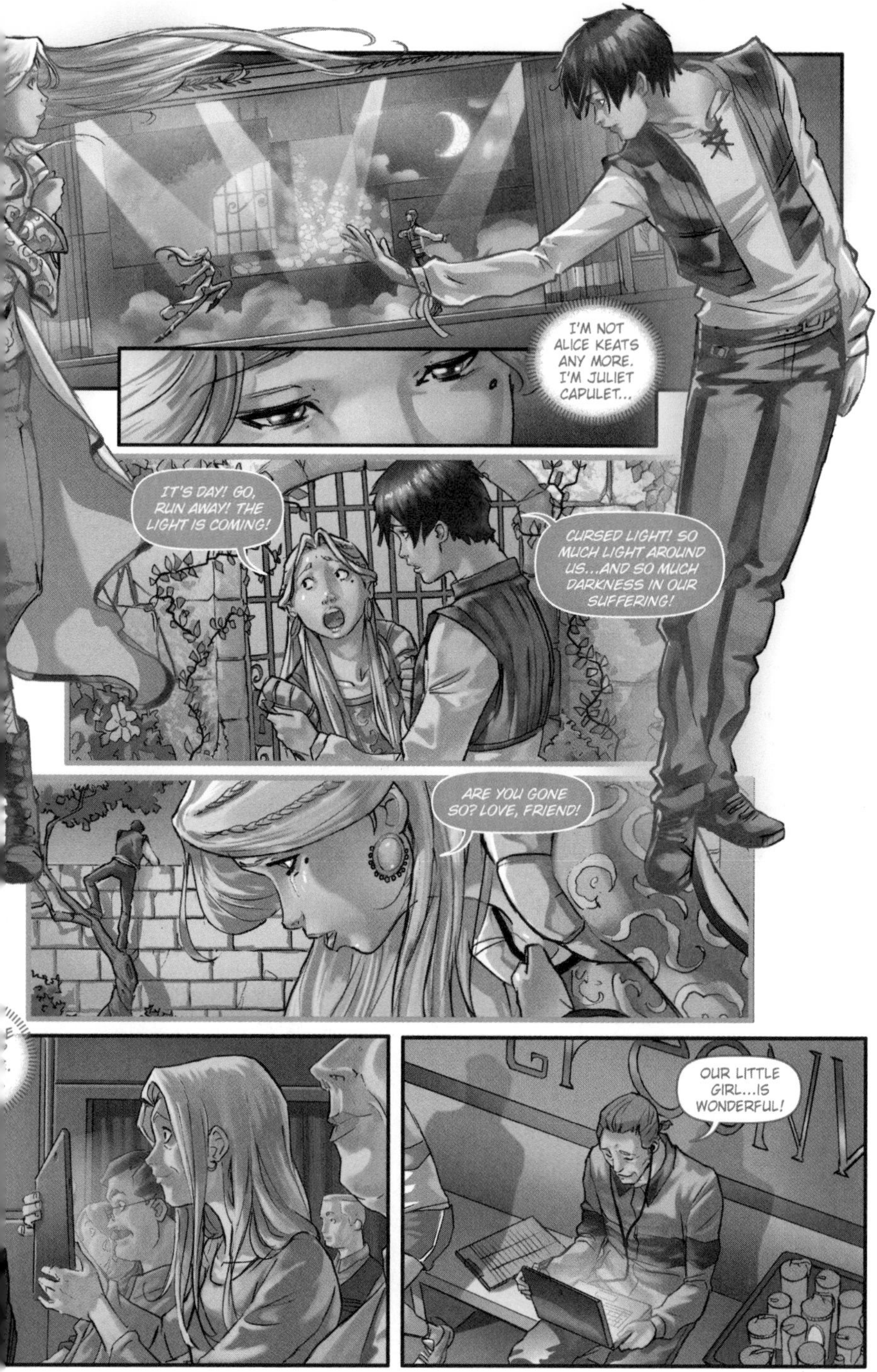
I'M NOT ALICE KEATS ANY MORE. I'M JULIET CAPULET...
IT'S DAY! GO, RUN AWAY! THE LIGHT IS COMING!
CURSED LIGHT! SO MUCH LIGHT AROUND US...AND SO MUCH DARKNESS IN OUR SUFFERING!
ARE YOU GONE SO? LOVE, FRIEND!
OUR LITTLE GIRL...IS WONDERFUL!

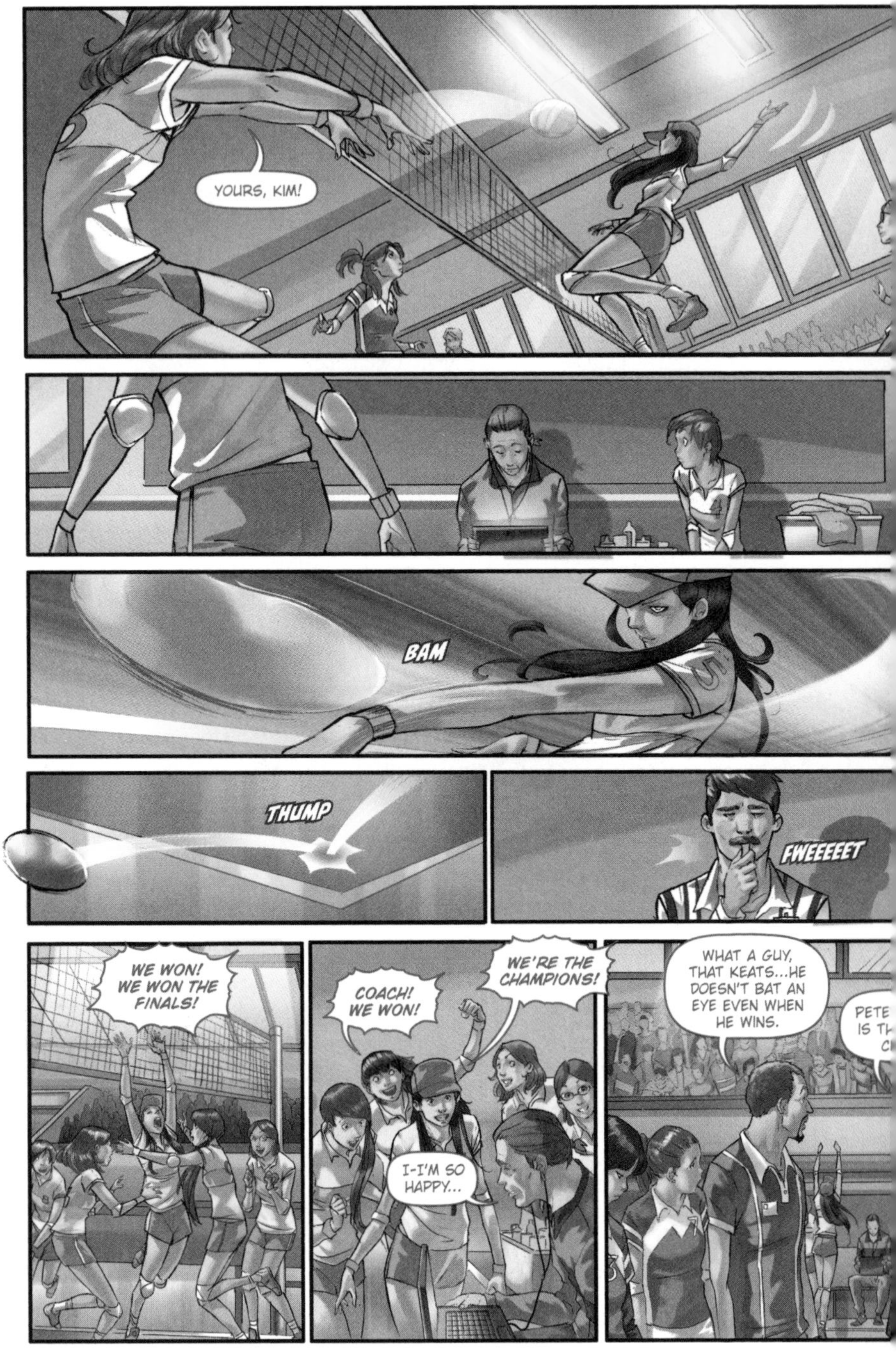
YOURS, KIM!
BAM
THUMP
FWEEEEET
WE WON! WE WON THE FINALS!
COACH! WE WON!
WE'RE THE CHAMPIONS!
I-I'M SO HAPPY...
WHAT A GUY, THAT KEATS...HE DOESN'T BAT AN EYE EVEN WHEN HE WINS.

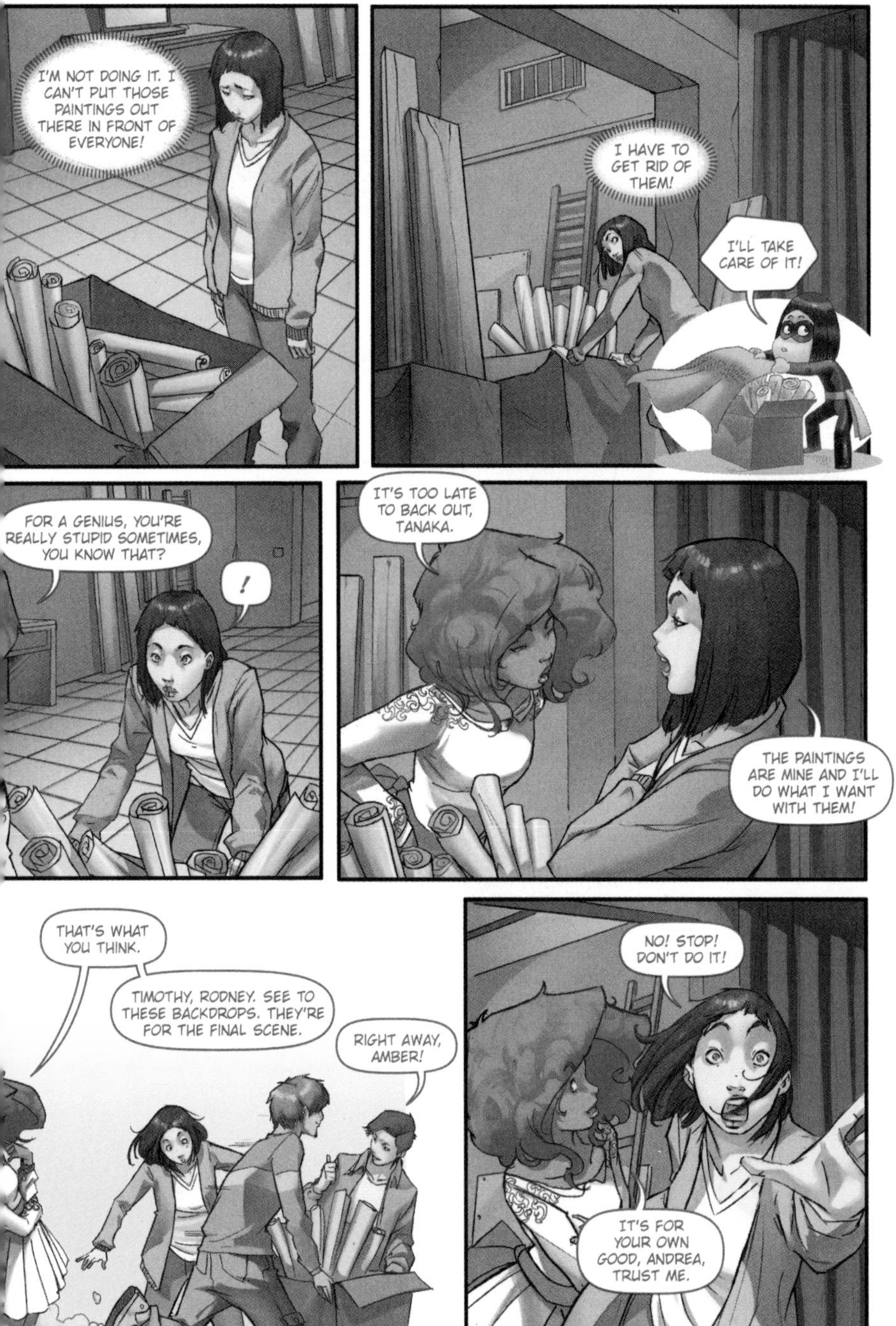
I'M NOT DOING IT. I CAN'T PUT THOSE PAINTINGS OUT THERE IN FRONT OF EVERYONE!
I HAVE TO GET RID OF THEM!
I'LL TAKE CARE OF IT!
FOR A GENIUS, YOU'RE REALLY STUPID SOMETIMES, YOU KNOW THAT?
!
IT'S TOO LATE TO BACK OUT, TANAKA.
THE PAINTINGS ARE MINE AND I'LL DO WHAT I WANT WITH THEM!
THAT'S WHAT YOU THINK.
TIMOTHY, RODNEY. SEE TO THESE BACKDROPS. THEY'RE FOR THE FINAL SCENE.
RIGHT AWAY, AMBER!
NO! STOP! DON'T DO IT!
IT'S FOR YOUR OWN GOOD, ANDREA, TRUST ME.

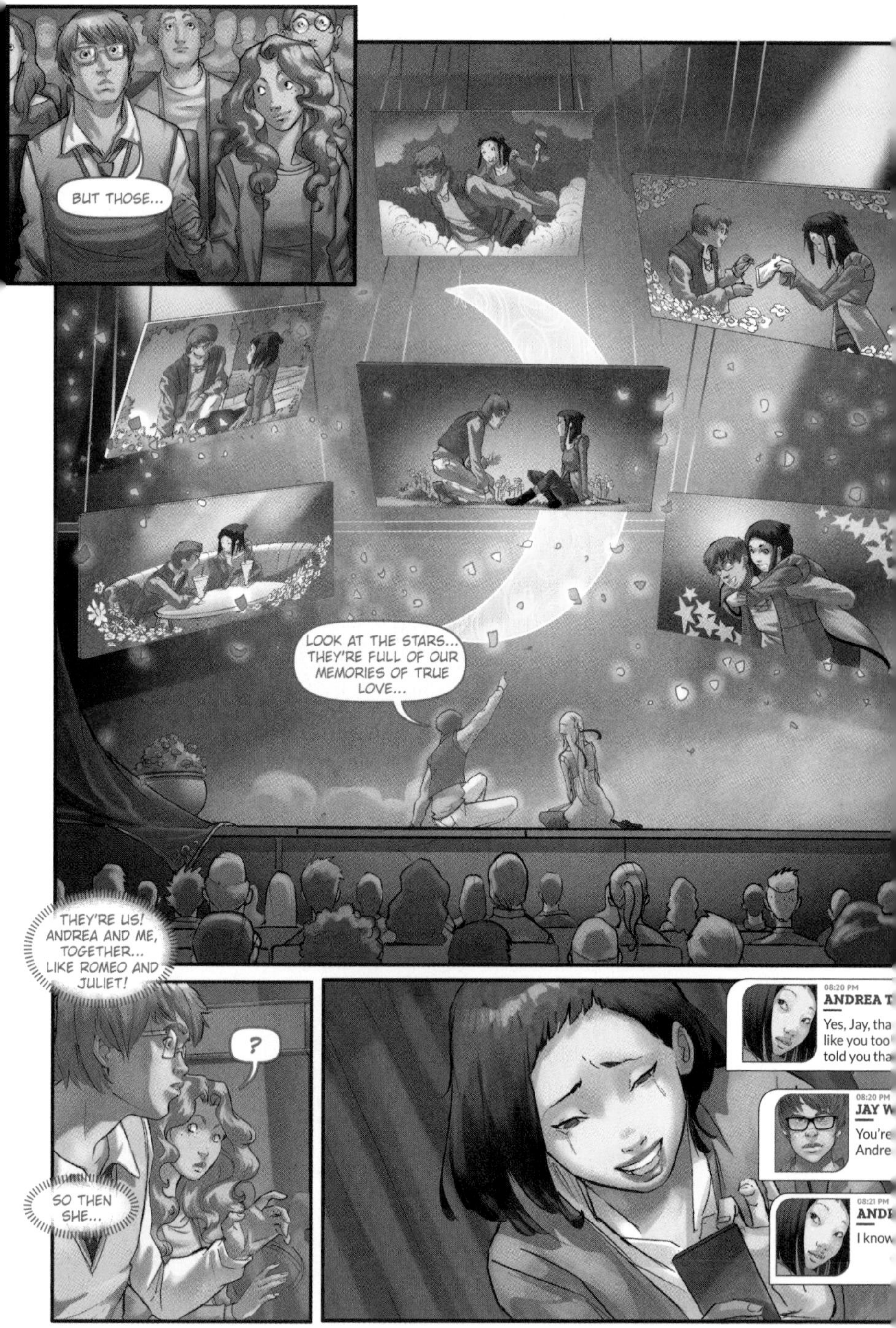
BUT THOSE...
LOOK AT THE STARS... THEY'RE FULL OF OUR MEMORIES OF TRUE LOVE...
THEY'RE US! ANDREA AND ME, TOGETHER... LIKE ROMEO AND JULIET!
?
SO THEN SHE...
08:20 PM
ANDREA T
Yes, Jay, tha
like you too
told you tha
08:20 PM
JAY W
You're
Andre
08:21 PM
ANDI
I know

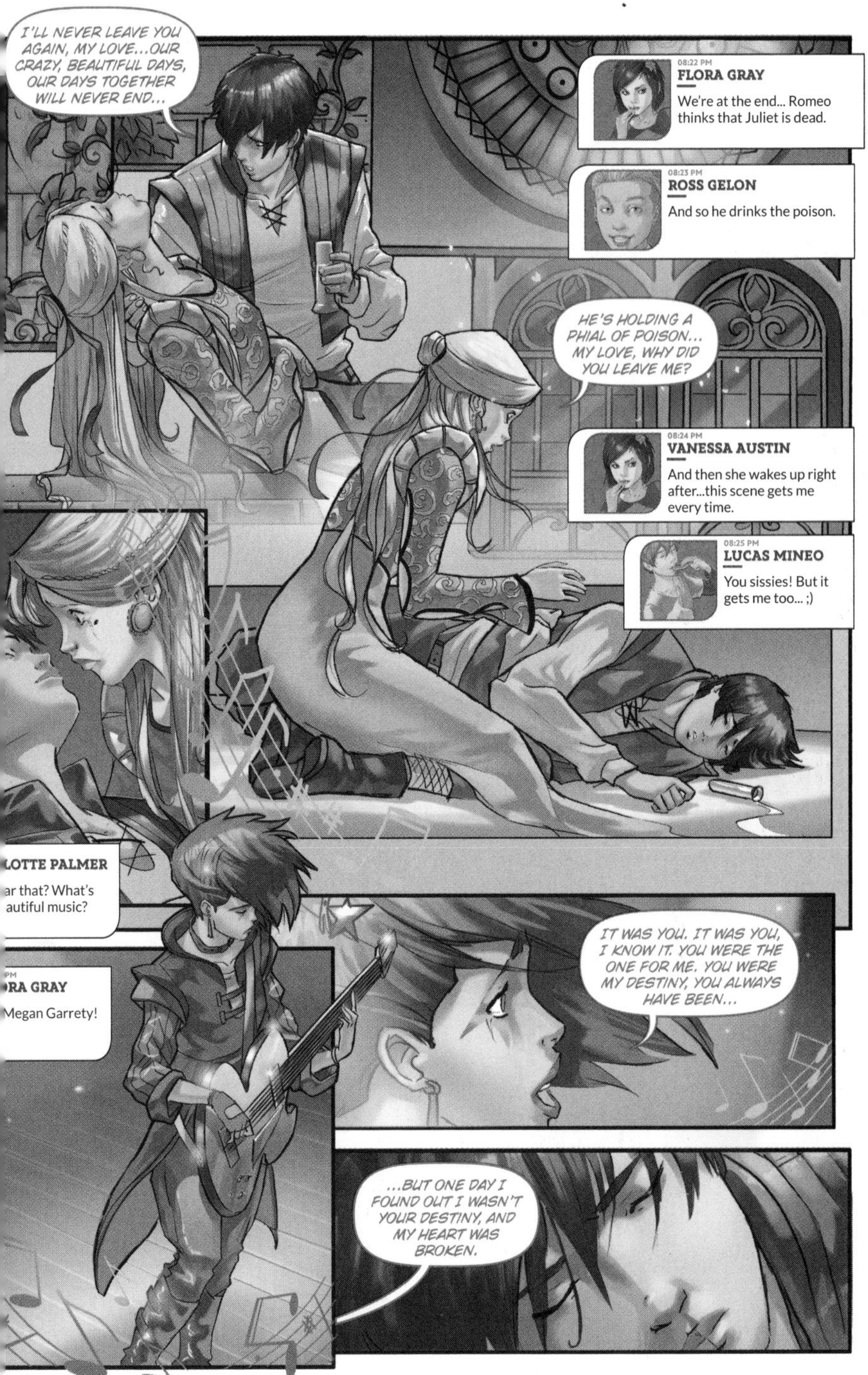
I'LL NEVER LEAVE YOU AGAIN, MY LOVE...OUR CRAZY, BEAUTIFUL DAYS, OUR DAYS TOGETHER WILL NEVER END...
08:22 PM
FLORA GRAY
We're at the end... Romeo thinks that Juliet is dead.
08:23 PM
ROSS GELON
And so he drinks the poison.
HE'S HOLDING A PHIAL OF POISON... MY LOVE, WHY DID YOU LEAVE ME?
08:24 PM
VANESSA AUSTIN
And then she wakes up right after...this scene gets me every time.
08:25 PM
LUCAS MINEO
You sissies! But it gets me too... ;)
LOTTE PALMER
ar that? What's autiful music?
PM
RA GRAY
Megan Garrety!
IT WAS YOU. IT WAS YOU, I KNOW IT. YOU WERE THE ONE FOR ME. YOU WERE MY DESTINY, YOU ALWAYS HAVE BEEN...
...BUT ONE DAY I FOUND OUT I WASN'T YOUR DESTINY, AND MY HEART WAS BROKEN.

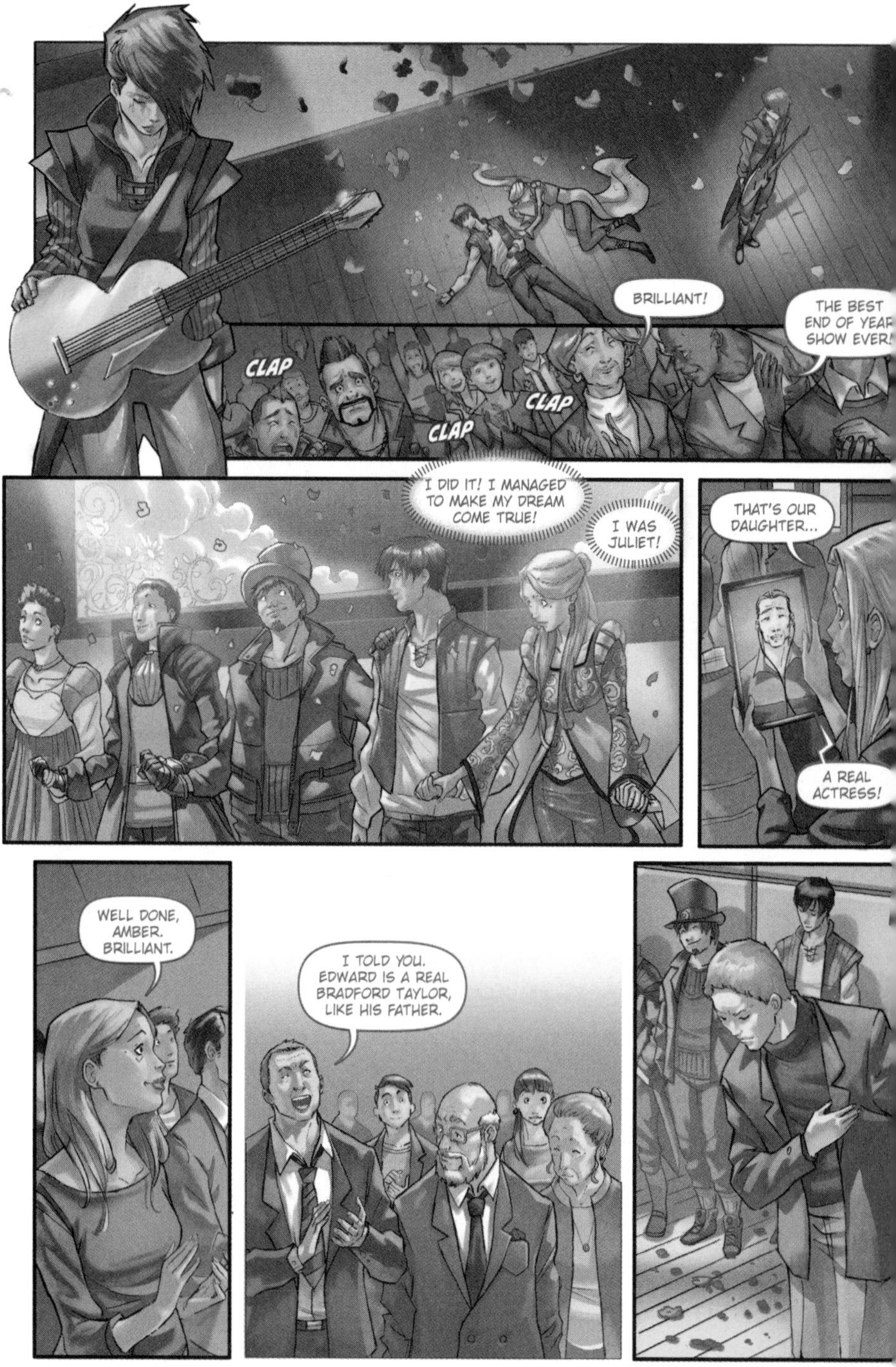

CLAP
CLAP
CLAP
BRILLIANT!
THE BEST END OF YEAR SHOW EVER!
I DID IT! I MANAGED TO MAKE MY DREAM COME TRUE!
I WAS JULIET!
THAT'S OUR DAUGHTER...
A REAL ACTRESS!
WELL DONE, AMBER. BRILLIANT.
I TOLD YOU. EDWARD IS A REAL BRADFORD TAYLOR, LIKE HIS FATHER.

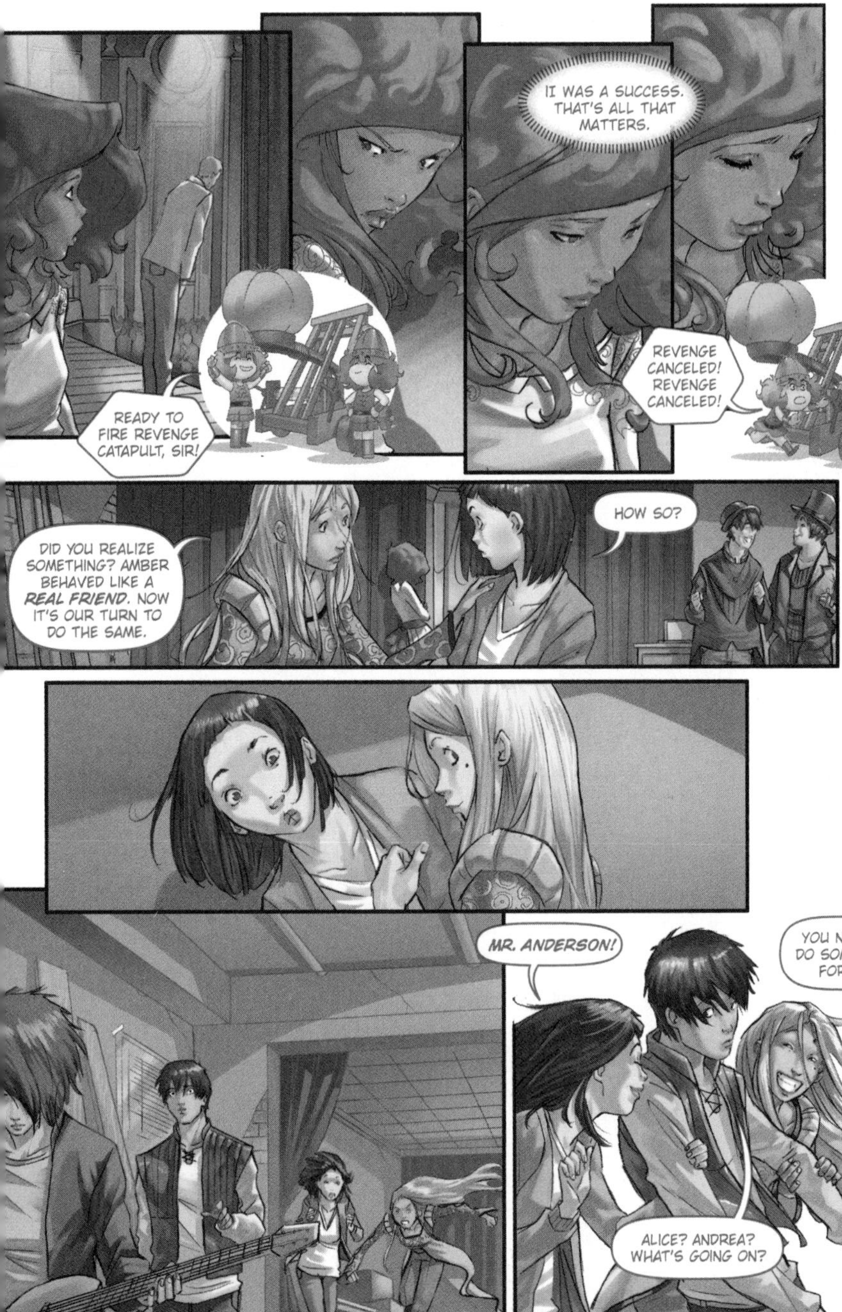
READY TO FIRE REVENGE CATAPULT, SIR!
IT WAS A SUCCESS. THAT'S ALL THAT MATTERS.
REVENGE CANCELED! REVENGE CANCELED!
DID YOU REALIZE SOMETHING? AMBER BEHAVED LIKE A **REAL FRIEND**. NOW IT'S OUR TURN TO DO THE SAME.
HOW SO?
MR. ANDERSON!
YOU NEED TO DO SOMETHING FOR US!
ALICE? ANDREA? WHAT'S GOING ON?

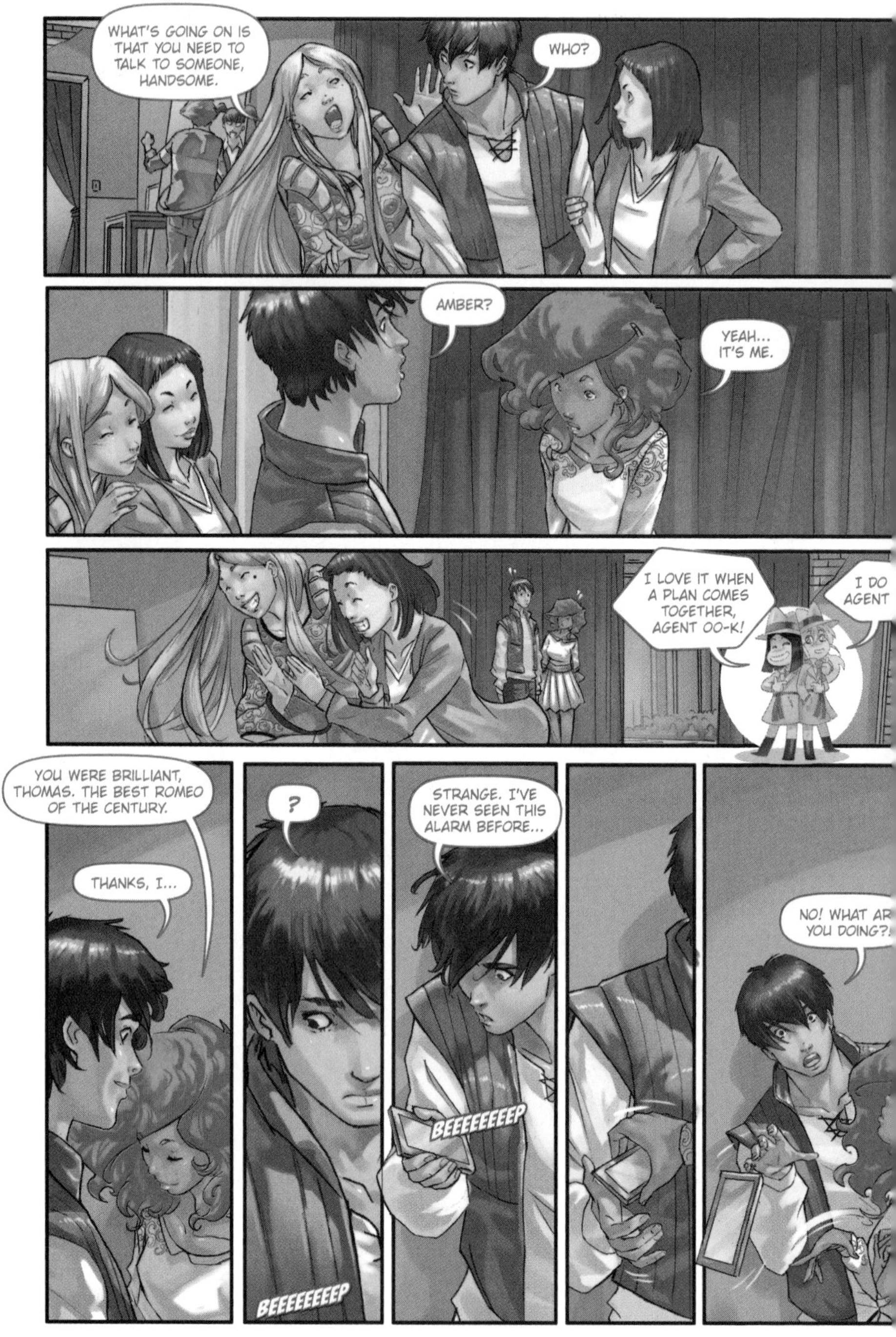
WHAT'S GOING ON IS THAT YOU NEED TO TALK TO SOMEONE, HANDSOME.
WHO?
AMBER?
YEAH... IT'S ME.
I LOVE IT WHEN A PLAN COMES TOGETHER, AGENT OO-K!
I DO AGENT
YOU WERE BRILLIANT, THOMAS. THE BEST ROMEO OF THE CENTURY.
THANKS, I...
?
BEEEEEEEEP
STRANGE. I'VE NEVER SEEN THIS ALARM BEFORE...
BEEEEEEEEP
NO! WHAT AR YOU DOING?!

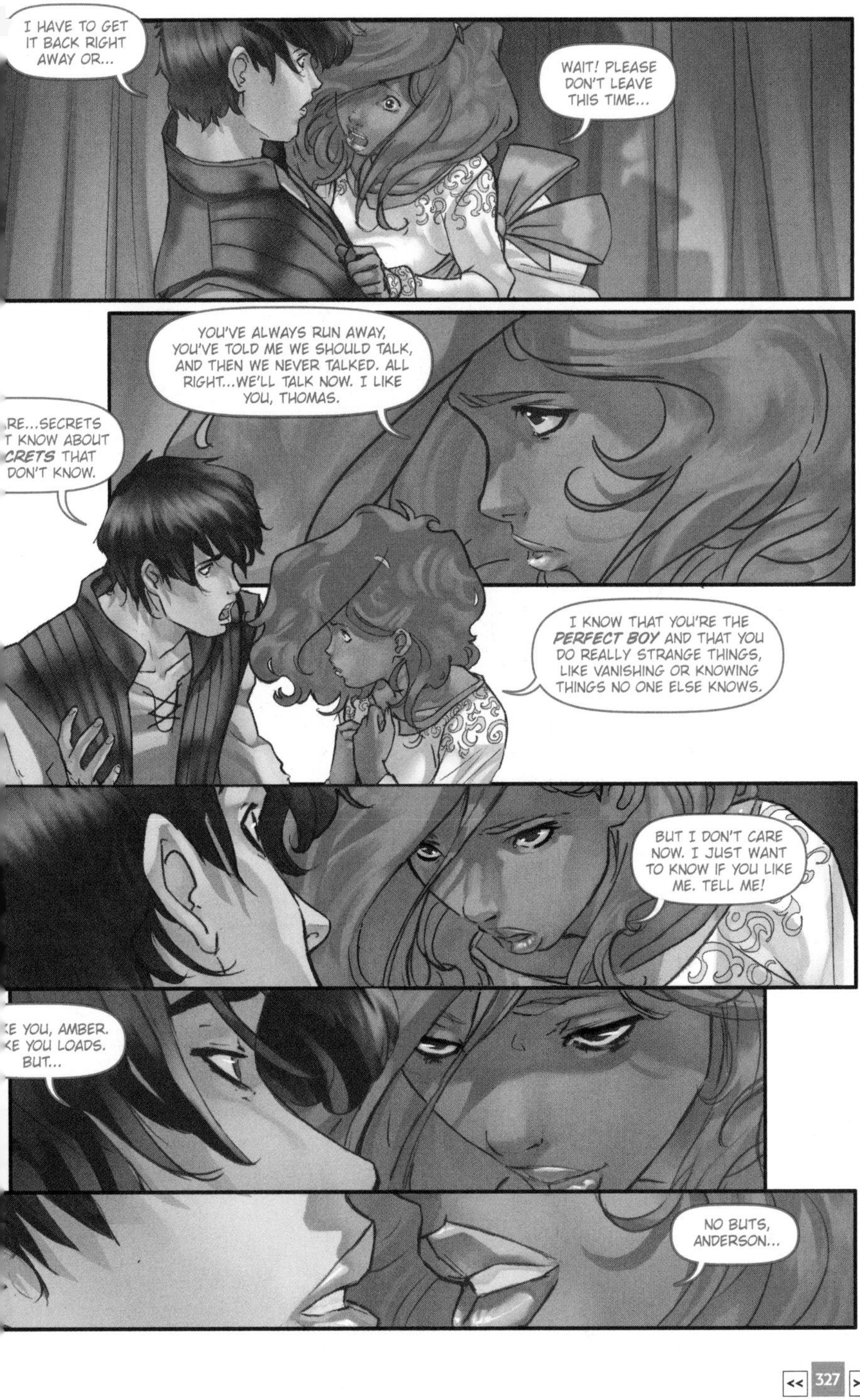

I HAVE TO GET IT BACK RIGHT AWAY OR...
WAIT! PLEASE DON'T LEAVE THIS TIME...
YOU'VE ALWAYS RUN AWAY, YOU'VE TOLD ME WE SHOULD TALK, AND THEN WE NEVER TALKED. ALL RIGHT...WE'LL TALK NOW. I LIKE YOU, THOMAS.
RE...SECRETS T KNOW ABOUT CRETS THAT DON'T KNOW.
I KNOW THAT YOU'RE THE PERFECT BOY AND THAT YOU DO REALLY STRANGE THINGS, LIKE VANISHING OR KNOWING THINGS NO ONE ELSE KNOWS.
BUT I DON'T CARE NOW. I JUST WANT TO KNOW IF YOU LIKE ME. TELL ME!
E YOU, AMBER. E YOU LOADS. BUT...
NO BUTS, ANDERSON...

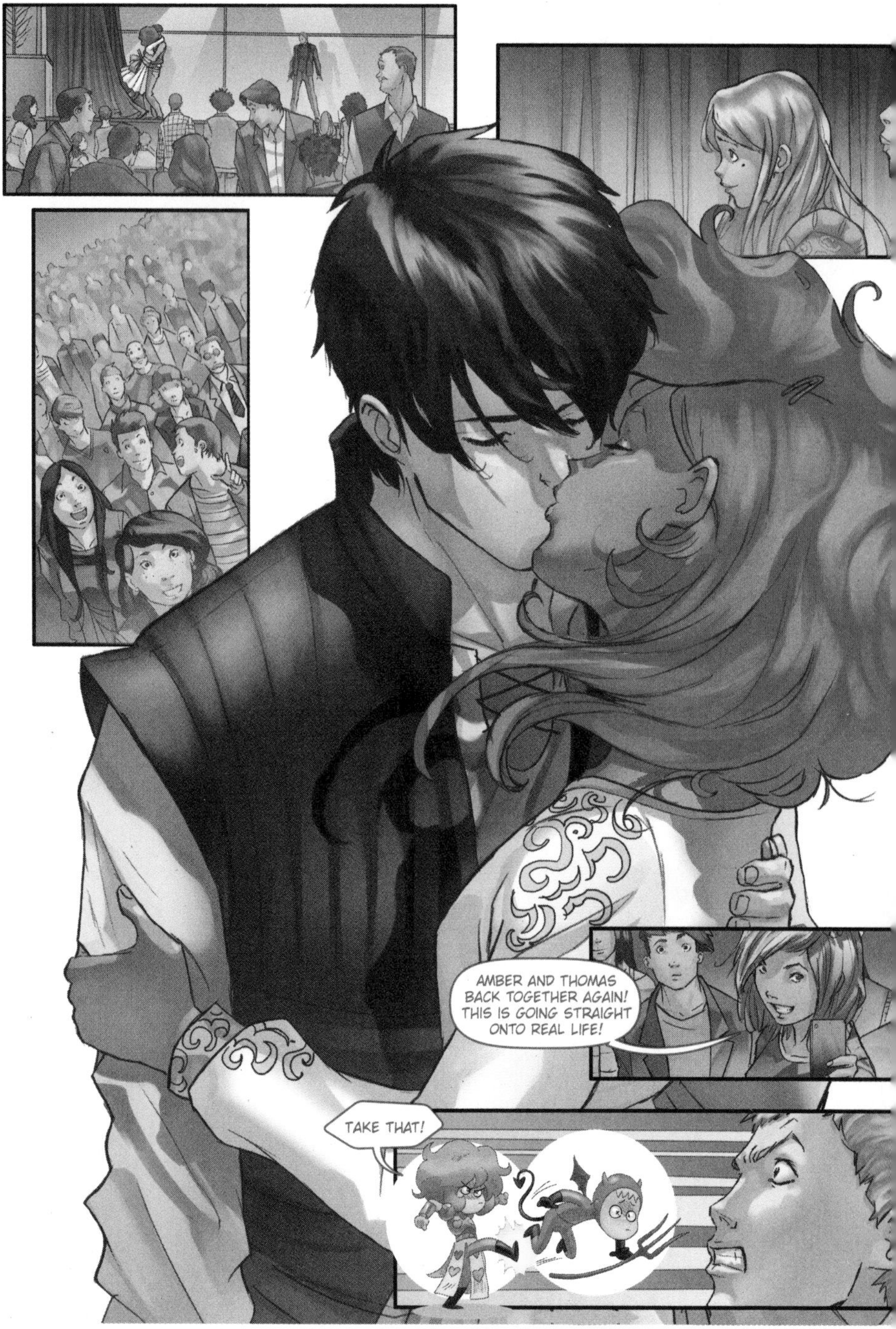
AMBER AND THOMAS BACK TOGETHER AGAIN! THIS IS GOING STRAIGHT ONTO REAL LIFE!
TAKE THAT!

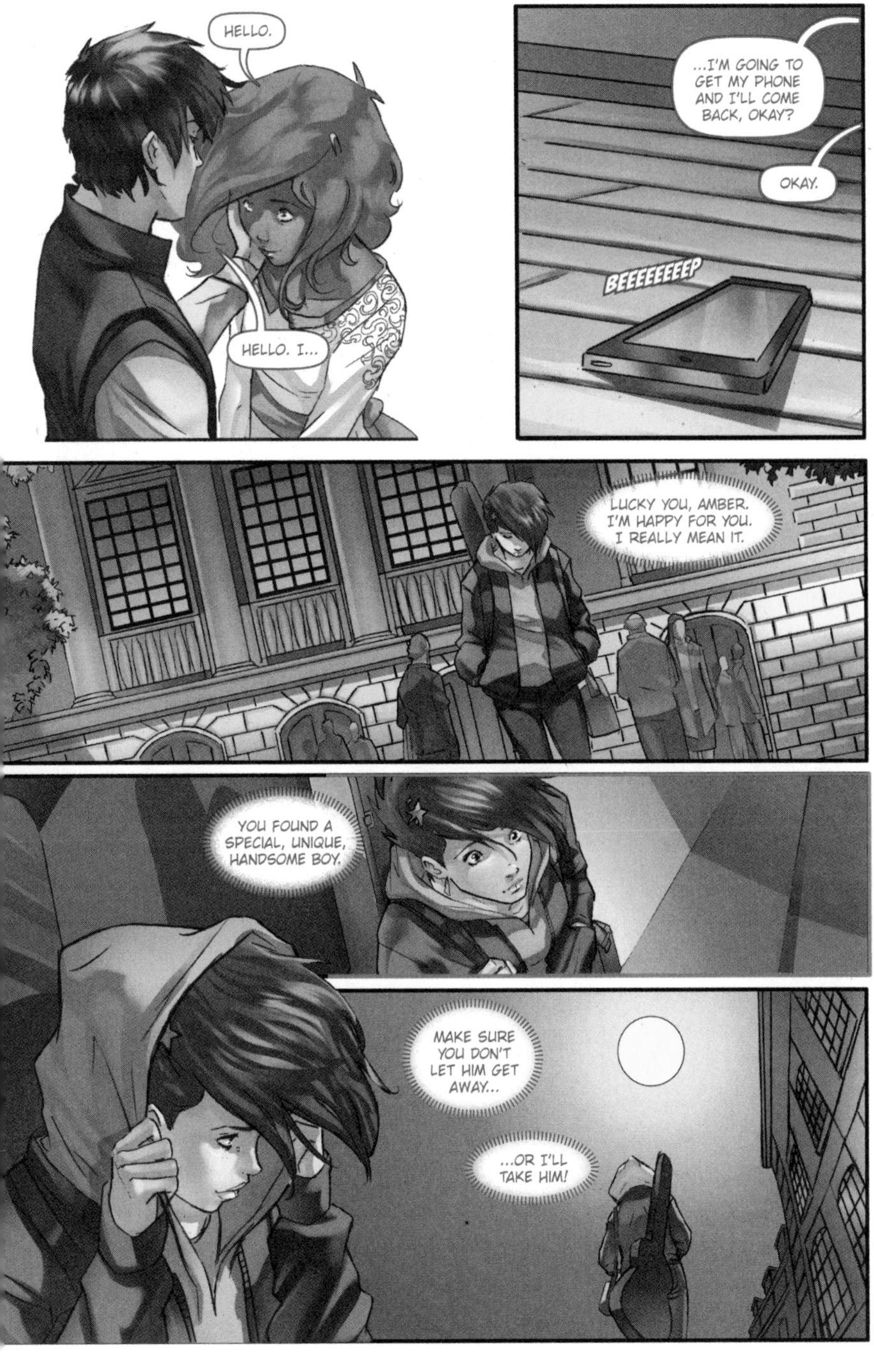
HELLO.
HELLO. I...
...I'M GOING TO GET MY PHONE AND I'LL COME BACK, OKAY?
OKAY.
BEEEEEEEEP
LUCKY YOU, AMBER. I'M HAPPY FOR YOU. I REALLY MEAN IT.
YOU FOUND A SPECIAL, UNIQUE, HANDSOME BOY.
MAKE SURE YOU DON'T LET HIM GET AWAY...
...OR I'LL TAKE HIM!

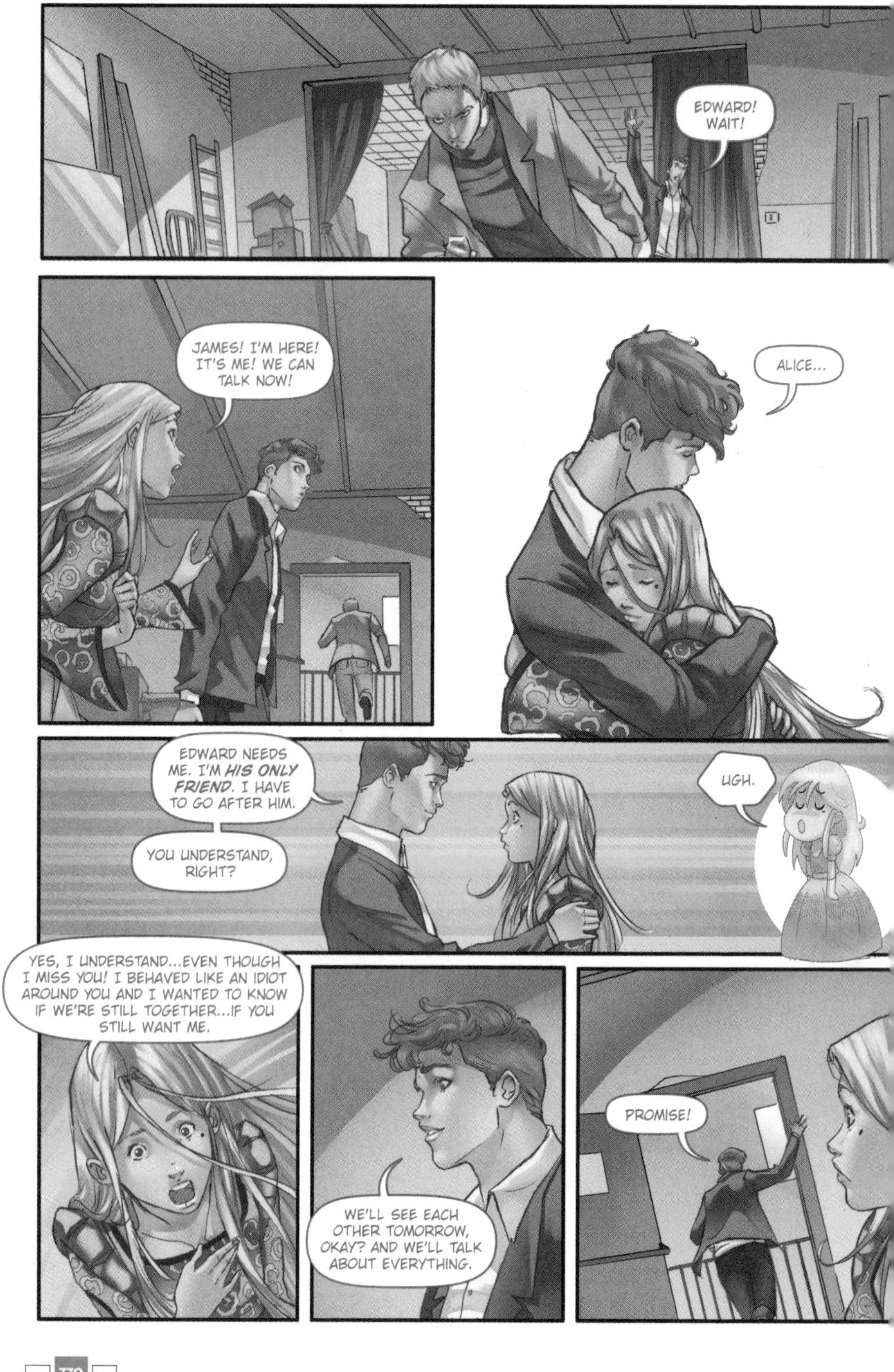
EDWARD! WAIT!
JAMES! I'M HERE! IT'S ME! WE CAN TALK NOW!
ALICE...
EDWARD NEEDS ME. I'M **HIS ONLY FRIEND**. I HAVE TO GO AFTER HIM.
YOU UNDERSTAND, RIGHT?
UGH.
YES, I UNDERSTAND...EVEN THOUGH I MISS YOU! I BEHAVED LIKE AN IDIOT AROUND YOU AND I WANTED TO KNOW IF WE'RE STILL TOGETHER...IF YOU STILL WANT ME.
WE'LL SEE EACH OTHER TOMORROW, OKAY? AND WE'LL TALK ABOUT EVERYTHING.
PROMISE!

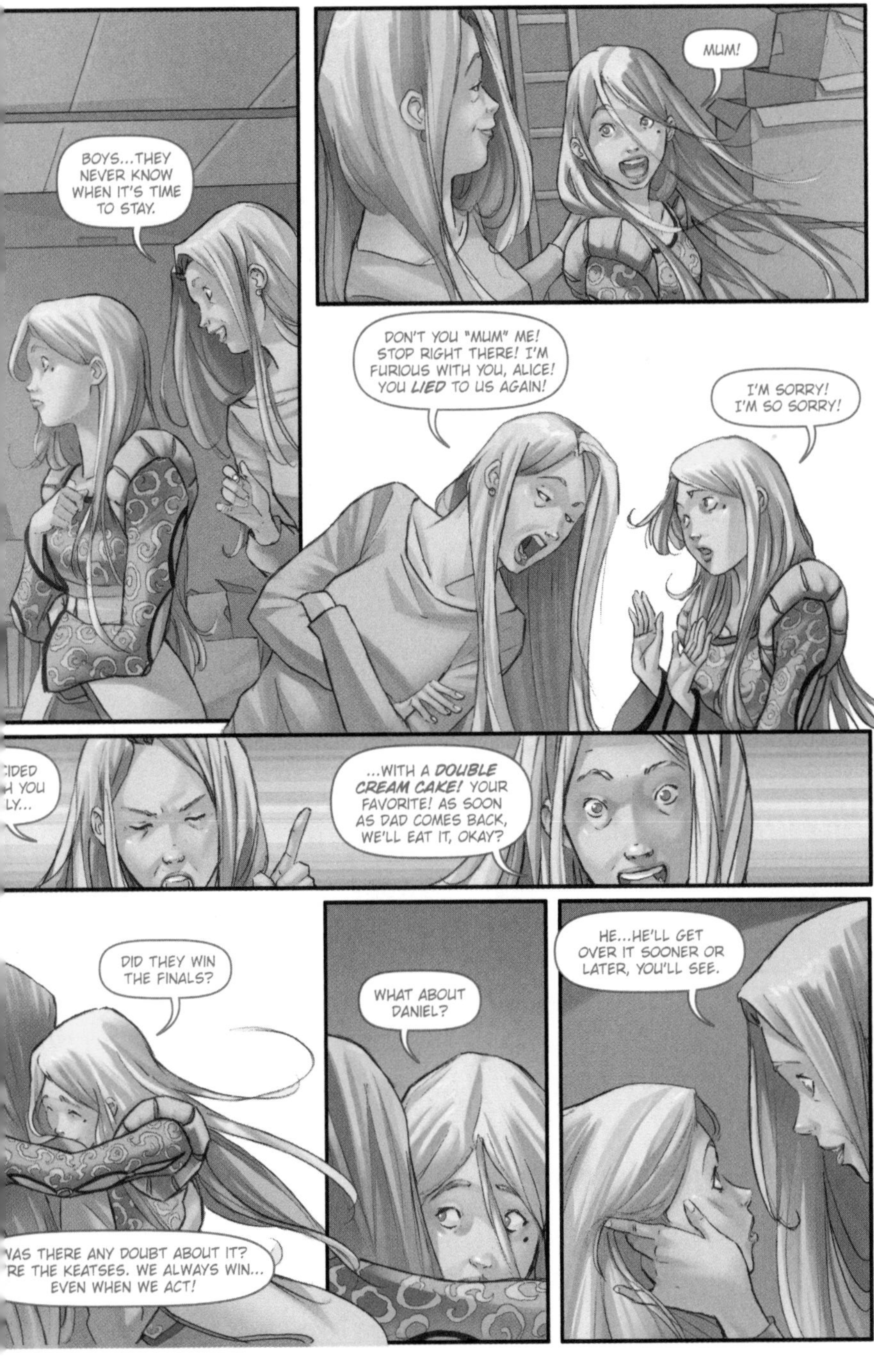

BOYS...THEY NEVER KNOW WHEN IT'S TIME TO STAY.
MUM!
DON'T YOU "MUM" ME! STOP RIGHT THERE! I'M FURIOUS WITH YOU, ALICE! YOU LIED TO US AGAIN!
I'M SORRY! I'M SO SORRY!
CIDED H YOU LY...
...WITH A DOUBLE CREAM CAKE! YOUR FAVORITE! AS SOON AS DAD COMES BACK, WE'LL EAT IT, OKAY?
DID THEY WIN THE FINALS?
VAS THERE ANY DOUBT ABOUT IT? RE THE KEATSES. WE ALWAYS WIN... EVEN WHEN WE ACT!
WHAT ABOUT DANIEL?
HE...HE'LL GET OVER IT SOONER OR LATER, YOU'LL SEE.

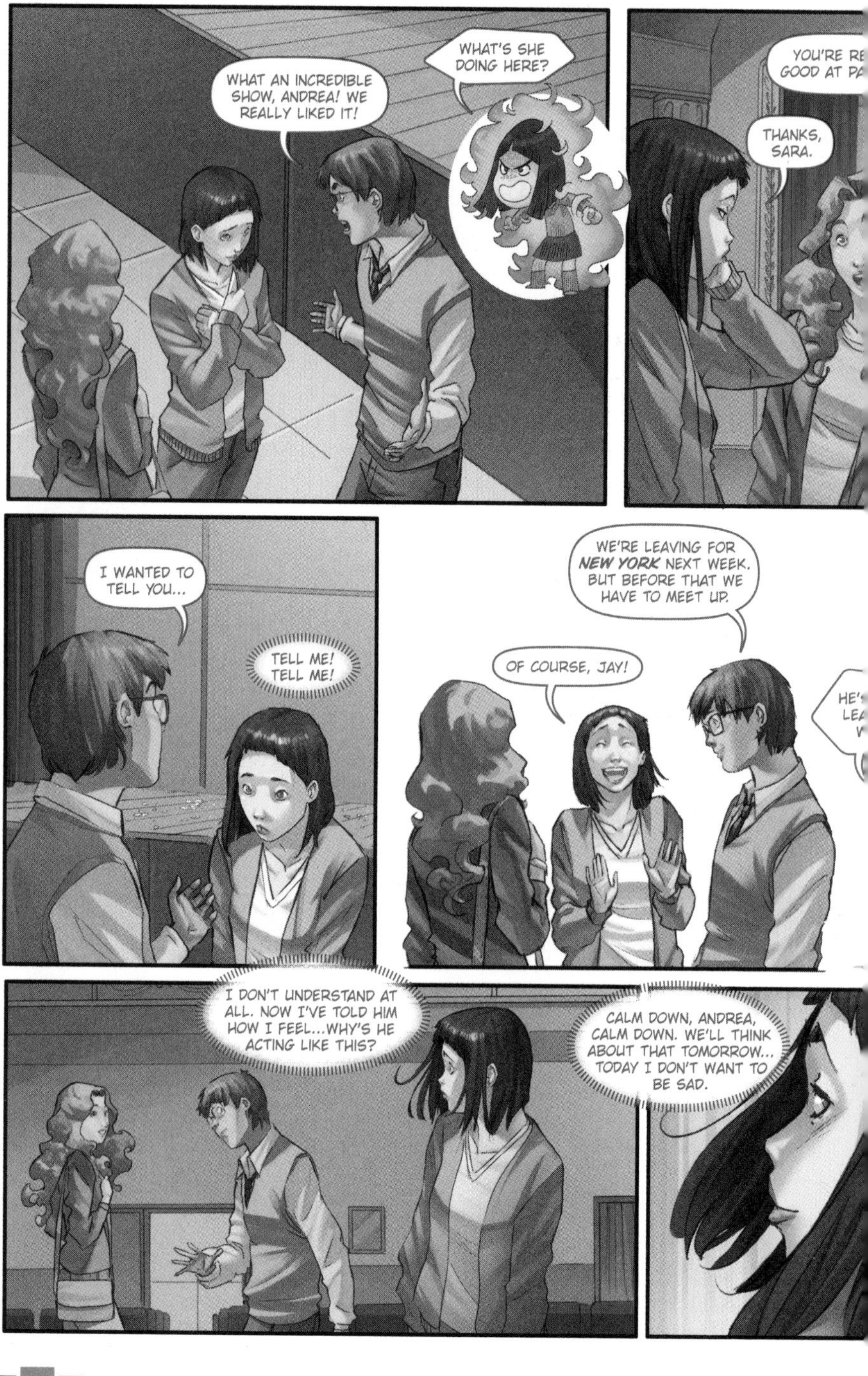

WHAT AN INCREDIBLE SHOW, ANDREA! WE REALLY LIKED IT!
WHAT'S SHE DOING HERE?
YOU'RE
GOOD AT
THANKS, SARA.
I WANTED TO TELL YOU...
TELL ME! TELL ME!
WE'RE LEAVING FOR NEW YORK NEXT WEEK. BUT BEFORE THAT WE HAVE TO MEET UP.
OF COURSE, JAY!
I DON'T UNDERSTAND AT ALL. NOW I'VE TOLD HIM HOW I FEEL...WHY'S HE ACTING LIKE THIS?
CALM DOWN, ANDREA, CALM DOWN. WE'LL THINK ABOUT THAT TOMORROW... TODAY I DON'T WANT TO BE SAD.

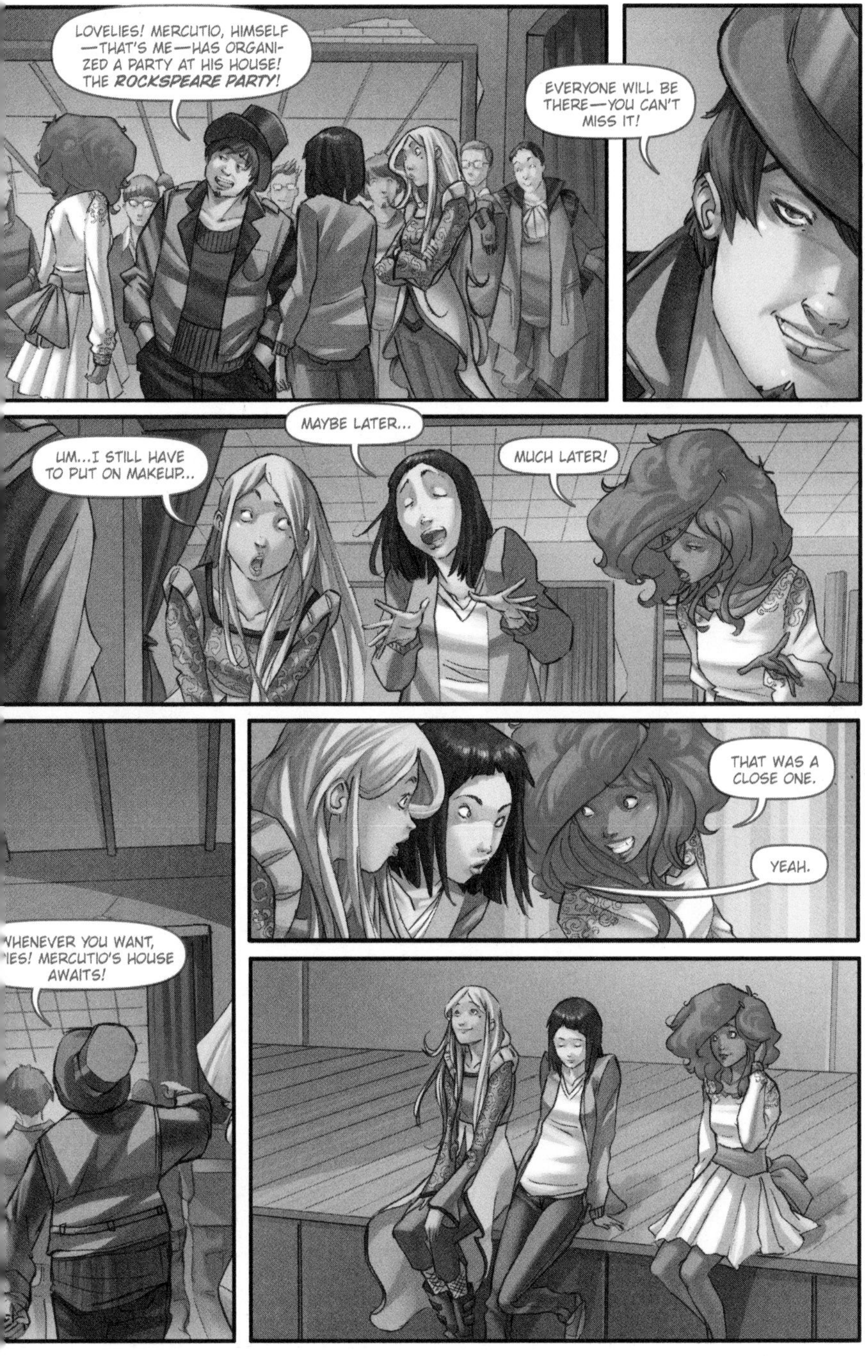
LOVELIES! MERCUTIO, HIMSELF —THAT'S ME—HAS ORGANIZED A PARTY AT HIS HOUSE! THE ROCKSPEARE PARTY!
EVERYONE WILL BE THERE—YOU CAN'T MISS IT!
UM...I STILL HAVE TO PUT ON MAKEUP...
MAYBE LATER...
MUCH LATER!
THAT WAS A CLOSE ONE.
YEAH.
WHENEVER YOU WANT, IES! MERCUTIO'S HOUSE AWAITS!

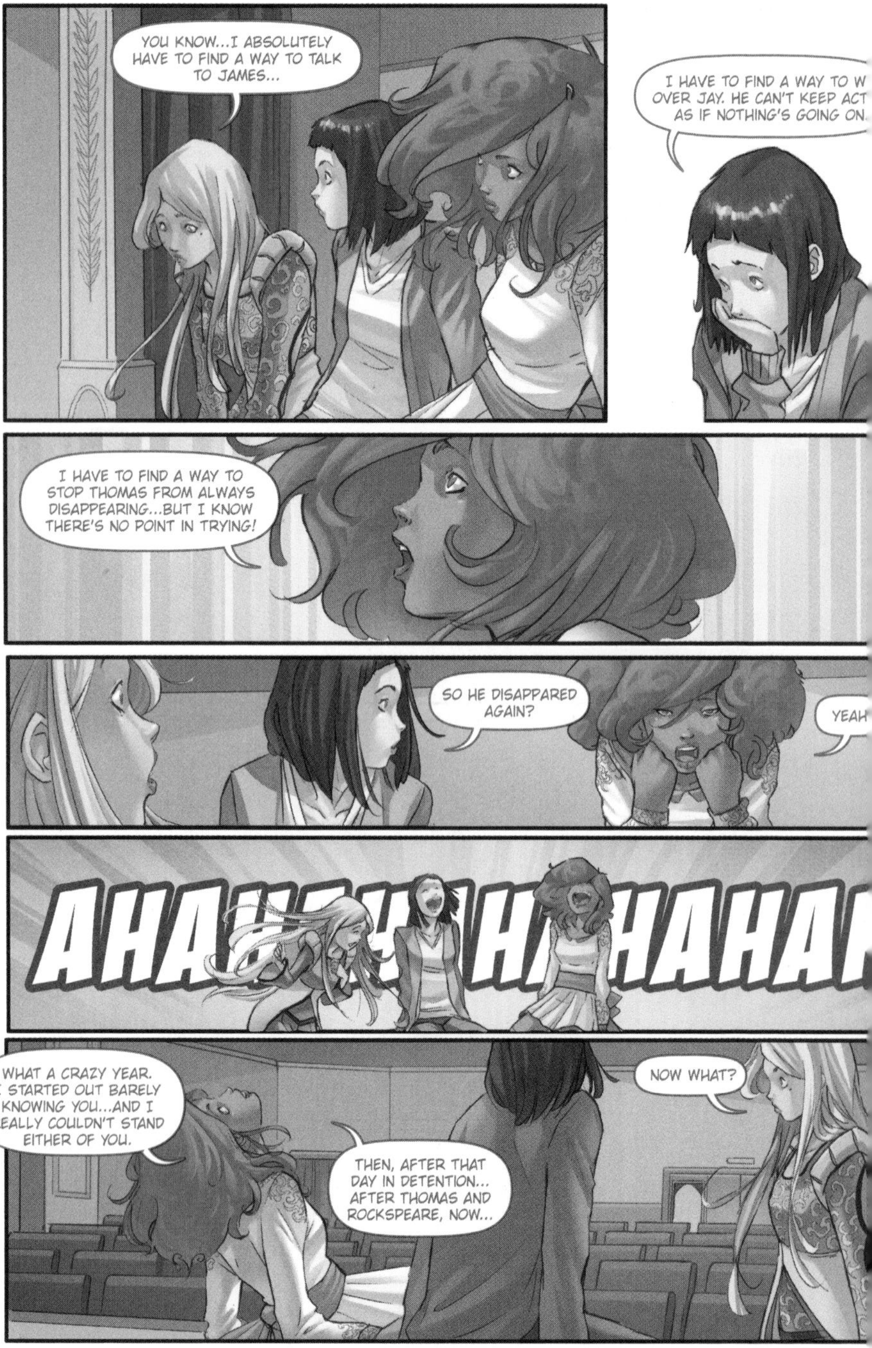
YOU KNOW...I ABSOLUTELY HAVE TO FIND A WAY TO TALK TO JAMES...
I HAVE TO FIND A WAY TO W OVER JAY. HE CAN'T KEEP ACT AS IF NOTHING'S GOING ON.
I HAVE TO FIND A WAY TO STOP THOMAS FROM ALWAYS DISAPPEARING...BUT I KNOW THERE'S NO POINT IN TRYING!
SO HE DISAPPARED AGAIN?
YEAH
AHAHAHAHAHAHAHAHA
WHAT A CRAZY YEAR. I STARTED OUT BARELY KNOWING YOU...AND I REALLY COULDN'T STAND EITHER OF YOU.
THEN, AFTER THAT DAY IN DETENTION... AFTER THOMAS AND ROCKSPEARE, NOW...
NOW WHAT?

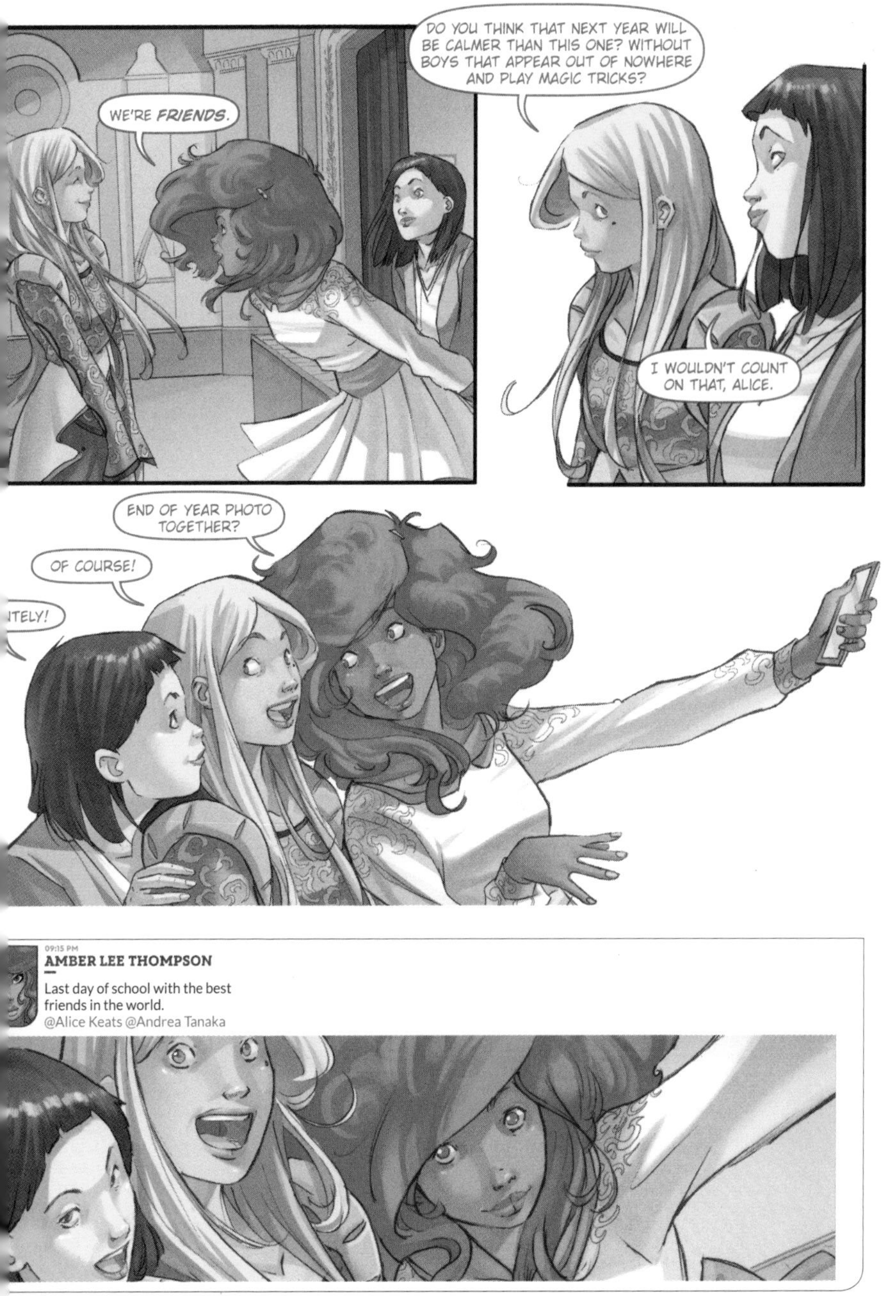
WE'RE FRIENDS.
DO YOU THINK THAT NEXT YEAR WILL BE CALMER THAN THIS ONE? WITHOUT BOYS THAT APPEAR OUT OF NOWHERE AND PLAY MAGIC TRICKS?
I WOULDN'T COUNT ON THAT, ALICE.
END OF YEAR PHOTO TOGETHER?
OF COURSE!
ITELY!
09:15 PM
AMBER LEE THOMPSON
Last day of school with the best friends in the world.
@Alice Keats @Andrea Tanaka

END OF CHAPTER 36

#HEARTS ONSTAGE
Script: Alessandro Ferrari
Layout and Cleanup: Alberto Zanon
Emotidolls: Andrea Scoppetta
Color: Massimo Rocca, Pierluigi Casolino, Andrea Scoppetta, Mario Perrotta, Slava Panarin, Giuseppe Fontana, Gianluca Barone, Cristina Toniolo, Barbara Bargiggia, Francesca Mengozzi, Giovanni Marcora, Mario Perrotta, Paco Desiato, Antonia Angrisani, MAD5 Factory
Watercolor backgrounds: Valeria Turati
Translation: Edizioni BD and Erin Brady
Lettering and Infographic: Edizioni BD

COVER
Layout and cleanup: Alberto Zanon
Color: Slava Panarin

CONTRIBUTORS
Tomatofarm

DISNEY PUBLISHING WORLDWIDE
Global Magazines, Comics and Partworks

Publisher
Lynn Waggoner

Editorial Team
Bianca Coletti (Director, Magazine)
Guido Frazzini (Director, Comics)
Carlotta Quattrocolo (Executive Editor, Franchise)
Stefano Ambrosio (Executive Editor, New IP)
Camilla Vedove (Senior Manager, Editorial Development)
Julie Dorris (Senior Editor)
Behnoosh Khalili (Senior Editor)
Jonathan Manning (Assistant Editor)
Mina Riazi (Assistant Editor)

Design
Enrico Soave (Senior Designer)

Art
Ken Shue (VP, Global Art), Roberto Santillo (Creative Director), Marco Ghiglione (Creative Manager), Manny Mederos (Senior Illustration Manager, Comics), Stefano Attardi (Computer Art Designer)

Portfolio Management
Olivia Ciancarelli (Director)

Business & Marketing
Camilla Vedove (Managing Editor), Mariantonietta Galla (Marketing Manager), Virpi Korhonen (Editorial Manager)

© 2018 Disney Enterprises, Inc.

LETTERING ASSISTANCE FOR YEN PRESS EDITION
Rachel J. Pierce

Real Life, Vol. 2 © 2018 by Disney Enterprises

English translation © 2018 by Disney Enterpris

YEN PRESS
1290 Avenue of the Americas
New York, NY 10104

VISIT US AT
yenpress.com
facebook.com/yenpress
twitter.com/yenpress
yenpress.tumblr.com
instagram.com/yenpress

First Yen Press Edition:
July 2018

Library of Congress Control Number: 20189

ISBNs:
978-0-316-47716-1 (paperback)
978-1-9753-2880-1 (ebook)

10 9 8 7 6 5 4 3 2 1

LSC-C

Printed in the United States of America